A QUESTION OF TRUST

"What is it? You look like you've just seen your own ghost."

A desperate ache lanced through Seregil as he looked down into Alec's dark blue eyes.

Damn you, Nysander!

"I can't tell you, *tali,* because I'd only have to lie," he said, suddenly dejected. "I'm going to do something now, and you're going to watch and say nothing."

Taking the final page of the manuscript, he twisted it into a tight squib and tossed it into the fire.

"But what about Nysander?" Alec asked. "What will you tell him?"

"Nothing, and neither will you."

"But—"

"We're not betraying him. You have my oath. I believe he already knows what we just learned, but he can't know that you know. Not until I tell you it's safe. Understand?"

"More secrets," Alec said, looking solemn and unhappy.

"Yes, more secrets. I need your trust in this, Alec. Can you give it?"

Also by Lynn Flewelling

Luck in the Shadows

Traitor's Moon

The Bone Doll's Twin

Hidden Warrior

The Oracle's Queen

Shadows Return

The White Road

Stalking Darkness

LYNN FLEWELLING

Bantam Books
New York Toronto London Sydney Auckland

STALKING DARKNESS
A Bantam Spectra Book/March 1997
All rights reserved.

SPECTRA and the portrayal of a boxed "s" are trade-
marks of Bantam Books, a division of
Random House, Inc.

ISBN 0-553-57543-0
Published simultaneously in the United States and Canada

Bantam Books are published by Bantam Books, a division
of Random House, Inc. Its trademark, consisting of the
words "Bantam Books" and the portrayal of a rooster, is
Registered in U.S. Patent and Trademark Office and in
other countries. Marca Registrada. Bantam Books, New
York, New York.

PRINTED IN THE UNITED STATES OF AMERICA

OPM 22 21 20 19 18 17 16

For my sons Matthew and Timothy, who laugh
at the same goofy things I do.
You're the best, guys.

Special thanks to Doug Flewelling, Darby Crouss, Laurie Hallman, Julie Friez, Scott Burgess, Anne Groell and the Bantam folks, and my agent Lucienne Diver for all their support, input, and wonderfully ruthless editing.

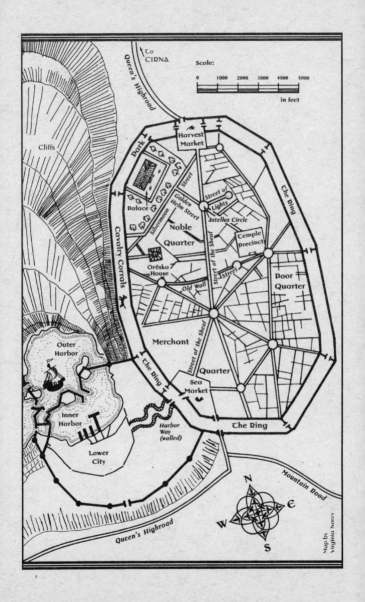

Scale:

0 1000 2000 3000 4000 5000

in feet

To CIRNA

Queen's Highroad

Cliffs

Park

Harvest Market

Street

Street of Lights

Golden Helm Street

Silvermoon Street

Astellus Circle

Palace

Noble Quarter

Temple Precinct

Oreska House

Street of the Sheaf

Street

Poor Quarter

Old Wall

Cavalry Corrals

The Ring

Merchant Quarter

Street of the Sheaf

Outer Harbor

The Ring

Sea Market

Inner Harbor

Harbor Way (walled)

Lower City

The Ring

Queen's Highroad

Mountain Road

Map by Virginia Norey

N
W E
S

PROLOGUE

The lean ship smashed through foaming crests, pounding southwest out of Keston toward Skala. By night she ran without lanterns; her crew, accomplished smugglers all, sailed with eyes lifted skyward to the stars. By day they kept constant watch, though there was little chance of meeting another ship. Only a Plenimaran captain would chance deepwater sailing so late in the year and this winter there would be none so far north. Not with a war brewing.

Ice sheathed the rigging. The sailors pulled the halyards with bleeding hands, chipped frozen water from the drinking casks, and huddled together off watch, muttering among themselves about the two gentlemen passengers and the grim pack of cutthroats who'd come aboard.

The second day out, the captain came above slobbering drunk. Gold was no use to dead men, he howled over the wind; foul weather was coming, they were turning back. Smiling, the dark nobleman led him below and that was the last anyone heard of the matter. The captain fell overboard sometime that same night. That was the story, at least; the fact was that he was nowhere to be found the next morning and their course remained unchanged.

The mate took over, tying himself to the wheel as they wallowed along. Blown off course, they missed Gull Island and sailed on without respite through lashing sleet and exhaustion. On the fourth day two more men were swept away as waves nearly swamped the ship. A mast snapped, dragging its sail like a broken wing. Miraculously, the ship held true while the remaining crew fought to cut away the tangled ropes.

Clinging among the frozen shrouds that night, the men muttered again, but cautiously. Their finely dressed passengers had brought ill fortune with them; no one wanted to chance attracting their eye. The ship plunged on as if helpful demons guided her keel.

Two days out from Cirna the gale lifted. A pale sun burst through the shredding clouds to guide the battered vessel westward, but foul luck still dogged her. A sudden fever struck among the crew. One by one, they sickened, throats swelling shut as black sores blossomed in the warmth of groins and armpits. Those untouched by the illness watched in horror as the gentlemen's men-at-arms laughingly tossed the bloated corpses overboard. None of the passengers sickened, but by the time they sighted the towering cliffs of the Skalan Isthmus the last of the crew could feel the weakness overtaking them.

They reached the mouth of Cirna harbor in darkness, guided by the leaping signal fires that flanked the mouth of the Canal. Still sagging at the wheel, the dying mate watched the passengers' men strike the sails, lower anchor, and heave the longboat over the side.

One of the gentlemen, the dark-haired one with a long scar under his eye, suddenly appeared at the mate's elbow. He was smiling, always smiling, though it never seemed to reach his eyes. Half-delirious, the mate staggered back, fearful of being devoured by those soulless eyes.

"You did well," the dark man said, reaching to tuck a heavy purse into the mate's pocket. "We'll see ourselves ashore."

"There's some of us still alive, sir!" croaked the mate, looking anxiously toward the signal fires, the warm lights of the town glimmering so close across the water. "We've got to get ashore for a healer!"

"A healer, you say?" The dark gentleman raised an eyebrow in concern. "Why, my companion here is a healer of sorts. You had only to ask."

Looking past him, the mate saw the other man, the weedy one with the face like a rat's, at work chalking something on the deck. As he straightened from his task the mate recognized the warning symbol for plague.

"Come, Vargûl Ashnazai, isn't there something you can do for this poor fellow?" the dark man called.

The mate shuddered as the other man glided toward him. Not once during the voyage had he heard this man speak. When he did now the words were unintelligible and seemed to collect in the mate's throat like stones. Gagging, he slumped to the deck. The one called Ashnazai laid a cold hand against his cheek and the world collapsed in a blaze of black light.

Mardus stepped clear of the bile spreading out from the dead sailor's mouth. "What about the others?"

The necromancer smiled, his fingers still tingling pleasantly from the mate's death. "Dying as we speak, my lord."

"Very good. Are the men ready?"

"Yes, my lord."

Mardus took a last satisfied look around the deck of the ravaged vessel, then climbed down to the waiting boat.

Cloaked in Ashnazai's magic, they passed the quay and custom house without challenge. Climbing a steep, icy street, they found rooms ready for them at the Half Moon tavern.

Mardus and Ashnazai were just settling down over a hot supper in Mardus' chamber when someone scratched softly at the door.

Captain Tildus entered with a grizzled man named Urvay, Mardus' chief spy in Rhíminee for the past three years. The man was invaluable, both for his skill and his discretion. Tonight he was dressed as a gentleman merchant and looked distinguished in velvet and silver.

Urvay saluted him gravely. "I'm glad to see you safe, my lord. It's nasty sailing this time of year."

Mardus dismissed Tildus, then waved the spy to a nearby chair. "What have you to report, my friend?"

"Bad news and good, my lord. Lady Kassarie is dead."

"That Leran woman?" asked Ashnazai.

"Yes. The Queen's spies attacked her keep about a week ago.

She died in the battle. Vicegerent Barien committed suicide over the matter and there are rumors that the Princess Royal was implicated somehow, though the Queen's taken no action against her. The rest of the faction has gone to ground or fled."

"A pity. They might have proved useful. But what about our business?"

"That's the good news, my lord. I have new people in place with several influential nobles."

"Which ones?"

"Lord General Zymanis, for one—word is he's about to be commissioned with overseeing the lower city fortifications. And one of my men just got himself betrothed to Lady Kora's second daughter and has the run of the villa. But of particular interest, my lord—" Urvay paused, leaning forward a little. "I'm in the process of establishing a contact inside the Orëska House."

Mardus raised an eyebrow. "Excellent! But how? We haven't been able to get a spy in there for years."

"Not a spy, my lord, but a turncoat. His name is Pelion í Eirsin. He's an actor, and highly thought of at the moment."

"What's he got to do with the Orëska?" demanded Vargûl Ashnazai.

"He's got a lover there," Urvay explained quickly, "a young sorceress said to be the mistress of one or two of the older wizards as well. Her name's Ylinestra, and she's got a bit of a reputation around the city; a fiery little catamount with an eye for handsome young men and powerful old ones. This man Pelion is evidently part of her collection. Through him we may be able to get to her and perhaps others. She's not a member of the Orëska herself, but she lives there and has rooms of her own."

"I hardly think we need the services of some slut to get into the place," the necromancer scoffed.

"Maybe not," Urvay interrupted, "but this slut numbers the wizard Nysander among her lovers."

"Nysander í Azusthra?" Mardus nodded approvingly. "Urvay, you've outdone yourself! But what have you told this actor of yours?"

"To him, I am Master Gorodin, a great admirer of his work. I also understand how important patronage is to a young actor on the rise, and to a certain playwright who's willing to create roles especially for him. In return, my new friend Pelion passes on whatever bit of gossip he picks up around town. He likes the deal, and knows better than to ask too many questions. As long as the gold flows, he's ours."

"Well done, Urvay. Spare no expense with him. We must infiltrate the Orëska before spring. You understand? It is imperative."

"I do, my lord. Shall I make arrangements for you in Rhíminee?"

"No. Nothing's to be arranged in advance. I'll contact you when I need you. For now, keep an eye on Pelion and his sorceress."

Urvay rose and bowed. "I will, my lord. Farewell."

When he was gone Mardus returned to his interrupted meal, but Vargûl Ashnazai found his appetite had fled.

The Orëska, he thought bitterly, fingering the ivory vial that hung from a chain around his thin neck. That's where *they'd* gone, the thieves who'd stolen the Eye from under his very nose.

Mardus had nearly killed him that night in Wolde. Worse yet, he'd threatened to banish him from their quest. If Mardus had entrusted *him* with the disks in the first place, of course, it would never have happened, but that was a point not worth arguing. Not if he cared to live longer than his next word.

His standing with Mardus had eroded steadily ever since. Even with the power of the Eye itself to aid him, he'd been unable to exercise sufficient power over the fugitives to stop them. The Aurënfaie had proven infuriatingly resistant to his magicks and when he'd finally succumbed to the *dra'gorgos* attack at the inn, the boy, that wretched *boy*, had outmaneuvered them, spiriting his partner away before Mardus and his men could reach the place.

Still holding the vial between his fingers, Vargûl Ashnazai pictured the precious blood-soaked slivers of wood inside, slivers he'd gouged from the floor of the Mycenian inn where his *dra'-gorgos* had overtaken them.

The talisman he'd made with their blood was a powerful guide, so powerful that he'd almost caught them at Keston. But then they'd slipped on ahead by sea and another's power was growing around them, occluding his own. He'd recognized the resonance of the magic at once. Orëska magic.

And so Mardus and his men had tracked them by methods thoroughly mundane, while he, a necromancer of the Sanctum, rode along like so much useless baggage.

Mardus had been sanguine. They already knew where the thieves were headed, result once again of Mardus' cold-blooded methods rather than his own. One of the river sailors captured after the destruction of the *Darter*—this, at least, was Vargûl's work—had screamed out with his last breath what they'd needed to know.

To be sitting here now, no more than two days ride from the stronghold of his enemies, was maddening.

So close! he thought, closing his fist around the vial.

Mardus saw, and guessed his thoughts. "Why not scry for them again?"

Vargûl Ashnazai shifted uncomfortably. "It's been the same for weeks now."

Mardus glanced over at him, much the way any man might look at another who's said something mildly surprising. But Mardus was not just any man. As his gaze met Ashnazai's, the necromancer felt a stab of fear. It was not madness he saw in his companion's eyes—never that—but something worse, an obdurate purposefulness steeped with the shadow of their god. Mardus might not have magic, but he had power. He was touched, chosen.

Held in that remorseless gaze, Ashnazai felt the blood slow in his veins. Clasping the vial more tightly, he placed his other hand over his eyes and summoned the image of the thieves.

For a moment he felt the reassuring pulse of his own considerable power. The inner blackness flowed through him to the vial and beyond, using the essence of the blood to seek its source. Ever since the thieves had reached Rhíminee, however, a veil had dropped over them. Someone had placed a protective spell over them, and the resistance to his magic was fierce and decisive.

This time was no different. The moment he focused his concentration on their location, he was blinded by a searing vision of fire and huge, leathery wings. The message was clear enough: *These people are under the protection of the Orëska. You cannot touch them.*

Gasping, Ashnazai let go of the vial and pressed both hands to his face.

"No change?"

Ashnazai could tell without looking up that the bastard was smiling.

"Then Urvay's actor is truly a blessing placed in our path. If these two are still under the protection of the Orëska wizards, where better to seek them?"

"I hope you're right, my lord. When I find them, I'll crush their beating hearts in my hands!"

"Vengeance is a dangerous emotion."

Looking up, Vargûl Ashnazai saw a familiar blankness pass across his companion's face, the touch of the god.

"You should be grateful to them for leading us to the completion of our quest," Mardus continued softly, staring into the depths of his cup. "This actor and his sorceress are the seal on that. Patience is the key now. Be patient. Our moment will come."

1
A Lousy Night For It

Sleet-laden winds lashed in off the winter sea, racketing through the dark streets of Rhíminee like a huge, angry child. Loose shingles and roof tiles tore free and clattered down into streets and gardens. Bare trees swayed and clashed their branches like dead bones in the night. In the harbor below the citadel, vessels were tossed from their moorings to founder against the moles. In upper and lower city alike, even the brothel keepers put up their shutters early.

Two cloak-wrapped figures slipped from a shadowed courtyard in Blue Fish Street and hurried east to Sheaf Street.

"I can't believe we're out in this to deliver a damn love token," Alec groused, shaking his wet, fair hair from his eyes.

"We've got the Rhíminee Cat's reputation to maintain," Seregil said, shivering beside the boy. The slender Aurënfaie envied Alec his northern-bred tolerance for the cold. "Lord Phyrien paid for the thing to be on the girl's pillow tonight. I've been wanting a peek into her father's dispatch box anyway. Word is he's maneuvering for the Vicegerent's post."

Seregil grinned to himself. For years, the mysterious thief known only as the Rhíminee Cat had assisted the city's upper class in their endless intrigues; all it took to summon him was gold and a discreet note left in the right hands. None had ever guessed that this faceless spy was virtually one of their own, or that the arrangement was as much to his benefit as theirs.

The wind buffeted at them from all sides as they pressed on toward the Noble Quarter. Reaching the fountain colonnade at the head of Golden Helm Street, Seregil ducked inside for a moment's shelter.

"Are you sure you're up to this? How's your back?" he asked as he stooped to drink from the spring at the center of the colonnade.

Less than two weeks had passed since Alec had pulled Princess Klia from the fiery room below the traitor Kassarie's keep. Valerius' malodorous drysian salves had worked their healing magic, but as they'd dressed tonight he'd noticed that the skin across the boy's shoulders was still tender-looking in places. Not that Alec would admit it and risk being sent back, of course.

"I'm fine," Alec insisted as expected. "It's your teeth I hear chattering, not mine." Shaking out his sodden cloak, he tossed one long end over his shoulder. "Come on. We'll be warmer if we keep moving."

Seregil looked with sudden longing toward the entrance to the Street of Lights across the way. "We'd be a hell of a lot warmer in there!"

It had been months since he'd visited any of the elegant pleasure houses. The thought of so many warm, perfumed beds and warm, perfumed bodies made him feel even colder.

Invisible in the shadows, Alec made no reply, but Seregil heard him shifting uncomfortably. The boy's solitary upbringing had left him uncommonly backward in certain matters, even for a Dalnan. Such reticence was unfathomable to Seregil, though out of respect for their friendship he did his best not to tease the boy.

The fashionable avenues of the Noble Quarter were deserted, the great houses and villas dark behind their high garden walls. Ornate street lanterns creaked unlit on their hooks, extinguished by the storm.

The house in Three Maidens Street was a large, sprawling villa surrounded by a high courtyard wall. Alec kept an eye out for bluecoat patrols while Seregil tossed the grapple up and secured the rope. The roar of the storm covered any noise as they scrambled up and over. Leaving the rope in a clump of bushes, Seregil led the way through the gardens.

After a brief search, Alec found a small shuttered window set high in a wall at the back of the house. Climbing onto a water butt, he pried back the shutter with a knife and peered inside.

"Smells like a storeroom," he whispered.

"Go on then. I'm right behind you."

Alec went in feet first and disappeared soundlessly inside.

Climbing up, Seregil sniffed the earthy scents of potatoes and apples. Squeezing through, he lowered himself in onto what felt like sacks of onions. He reached out, finding Alec's shoulder in the darkness, and together they felt their way to a door. Seregil eased the latch up and peeked out into the cavernous kitchen beyond.

The coals in the hearth gave off enough of a glow to make out two servants asleep on pallets there. Deep snores sounded from the shadows of a nearby corner. To the right was an open archway. Tapping Alec on the arm, Seregil headed for it on tiptoe.

The arch let onto a servant's passage. Climbing a narrow staircase, they crept down a succession of hallways in search of Lord Decian's private study. Not finding it, they moved up to the next floor and chanced shielded lightstones.

By this dim light they saw that these nobles left their shoes outside their bedroom door for a servant to collect and clean. Seregil nudged Alec and flipped him the sign for "lucky." The lord of the house had only one daughter; it was a simple matter to find the footgear appropriate for a maiden of fifteen.

A pair of dainty boots stood before a door at the far end of the corridor. A stout pair of shoes next to them warned that the young woman did not sleep alone.

Seregil stifled a grin. Alec was in for more than he'd bargained for, in more ways than one.

Alec lightly fingered the latch, found the door unbarred. The delivery was his task tonight, more training in the ways of the Cat. This sort of job, though hardly as significant as their recent work for Nysander, required a high level of finesse and he was anxious to prove himself.

Sliding his lightstone back into his tool roll, Alec took a deep breath and lifted the latch.

A night lamp burned on a stand beside the bed. The hangings were open and inside he could see a young girl with heavy braids asleep on the side nearest the door, her face turned to the light. Beside her, a larger form, her mother or nurse perhaps, stirred restlessly beneath the thick comforter.

Creeping to the side of the bed, he took out the token, a tiny scroll pushed through a man's golden ring. Left to his own devices, he'd simply have put it on the lamp stand and been done with it, but Lord Phyrien had been very exact in his instructions. The ring must be left on his sweetheart's pillow.

Bending over the girl, Alec placed the ring as specified. Too late he heard Seregil's sharp intake of breath. The heavy ring immediately rolled down the curve of the pillow and struck the girl on the cheek just beside her mouth.

Startled brown eyes flashed wide. Fortunately for Alec, she saw the ring before she could cry out. Her look of fear changed instantly to one of mute joy as she mistook his muffled form for that of her lover.

"Oh, Phyrien, you *are* bold!" she breathed, stealing a quick look at the sleeping woman beside her. Grasping Alec's hand, she drew it gently but insistently under the bedclothes.

Alec blushed furiously in the depths of his hood. Like most Skalans, she slept nude. He didn't dare resist, however. Any kind of struggle would not only seem suspicious, but probably shake the bed enough to awaken its other occupant.

"You're so cold!" she said with a hushed giggle, pulling his hand still lower. "Kiss me, my brave lover. I'll warm you."

Holding his hood in place with his free hand, Alec pressed his lips hastily to hers, then motioned warningly at the other woman. Pouting prettily, the girl released him and tucked the token away beneath her pillow.

With his heart hammering in his ears, Alec extinguished the lamp and hurried back out into the corridor.

"Seregil, I—" he began in a whisper, but his companion cut the apology short, grabbing him by the arm and hustling him off the way they'd come.

Damn, damn, damn! Alec berated himself. *A simple little delivery job and I cock it up.*

Braced every moment for an outcry, they hurried down to the kitchen and weaseled back out the storeroom window. Outside, Seregil was still implacably silent. Climbing over the wall, he set off at a run. Alec followed, grimly convinced he was in disgrace.

Three streets from the villa, Seregil suddenly stopped and

hauled him into an alleyway, then bent over, hands on knees, as if to catch his breath.

Braced for a scathing lecture, it took Alec a moment to realize that Seregil was laughing.

"Bilairy's Balls, Alec!" he burst out. "I'd give a hundred sesters to have seen the look on your face when that ring rolled away. And when she tried to pull you into bed—" He sagged against the aley wall, shaking with laughter.

"But it was so stupid," Alec groaned. "I should have seen it would slide off."

Seregil wiped his eyes, grinning. "Maybe so, but these things happen. I don't know how many times I've pulled a blunder like that. It's the recovery that counts and you did just fine. 'Learn and live,' I always say."

Relieved, Alec fell into step beside him as they headed for home. Before they'd gone another block, however, Seregil let out another snort of laughter. Leaning heavily on Alec's shoulder, he moaned in a lilting falsetto, "Kiss me, my brave lover. I'll warm you up!" then staggered away, cackling into the wind.

Perhaps, Alec thought in exasperation, he hadn't heard the last of the matter after all.

Back at Cockerel Inn, they nicked a late snack from Thryis' pantry and crept up the hidden staircase on the second floor. Warding glyphs glowed briefly as Seregil whispered the passwords. At the top of the stairs, they crossed the chilly attic storeroom to their own door.

The cluttered sitting room was still warm from the evening fire. Tossing his wet cloak over the mermaid statue by the door, Alec shucked off soaked clothing as he crossed to his bed in the corner by the hearth.

Seregil watched with a faint smile. The boy's considerable and, to his way of thinking, unnatural degree of modesty had lessened somewhat over the months of their acquaintance, but Alec still turned away as he stripped off his leather breeches and pulled on a long shirt. At sixteen he was very like Seregil in build: slim, lean, and fair-skinned. Seregil quickly busied himself sorting a pile of correspondence on the table as the boy turned around again.

"We don't have anything in particular planned for tomorrow,

do we?" Alec asked, taking a bite from one of the meat pies they'd purloined.

"Nothing pressing," said Seregil, yawning hugely as he went to his chamber door. "And I don't intend to be up before noon. Good night."

With the aid of a lightstone, he navigated past the stacks of books and boxes and other oddments to the broad, velvet-hung bed that dominated the back of the tiny room. Peeling off his wet garments, he slipped between the immaculate sheets with a groan of contentment. Ruetha appeared from some cluttered corner and leapt up with a throaty trill, demanding to be let under the covers.

It had been a busy year overall, he thought, stroking the cat absently. Especially the past few months. Just realizing how long it had been since he'd visited the Street of Lights underscored the general disruption of his life.

Oh well. Winter's here. There'll always be work enough to keep us occupied, but plenty of leisure too for the pleasures of the town. All in all, I'd say we've earned a bit of a respite.

Imagining quiet, snowy months stretching out before them, Seregil drifted contentedly off to sleep—

—only to lurch up sometime soon after from a nightmare of plummeting into darkness, Alec's terrified cry ringing in his ears as they fell down, down, past the walls of Kassarie's keep into the gorge below.

Opening his eyes with a gasp, Seregil was at once relieved and annoyed to find himself slumped naked in one of Nysander's sitting-room armchairs.

There was no need to ask how he'd gotten there; the green nausea of a translocation spell cramped his belly. Pushing his long, dark hair back from his face, he scowled wretchedly up at the wizard.

"Forgive me for bringing you here so abruptly, dear boy," said Nysander, handing him a robe and a steaming mug of tea.

"I assume there's a good reason for this," Seregil muttered, knowing very well that there must be for Nysander to subject him to magic so soon after the shape-changing incident.

"But of course. I tried to bring you earlier, but you two were busy burgling someone." Pouring himself a mug of tea, Nysander settled into his usual chair on the other side of the hearth. "I just looked in for a moment. Were you successful?"

"More or less." Nysander appeared in no hurry to elucidate, but it was obvious he'd been working on something. His short grey beard was smudged with ink near his mouth, and he wore one of the threadbare old robes he favored for his frequent all-night work sessions. Surrounded by the room's magnificent collection of books and oddities, he looked like some down-at-the-heels scholar who'd wandered in by mistake.

"Alec is looking better, I noticed," Nysander remarked.

"He's healing. It's his hair I'm concerned about. I've got to get him presentable in time for the Festival of Sakor."

"Be thankful he came away no worse off then he did. From what Klia and Micum told me, he's lucky to be alive at all. Ah, and before I forget, I have something for the two of you from Klia and the Queen." He handed Seregil two velvet pouches. "A public acknowledgment is impossible, of course, but they wished to express their gratitude nonetheless. That green one there is yours."

Seregil had received such rewards before. Expecting another trinket or bit of jewelry, he opened the little bag. What he found inside reduced him to stunned silence.

It was a ring, a very familiar ring. The great, smooth ruby glowed like wine in its heavy setting of Aurënfaie silver when he held it closer to the fire.

"Illior's Light, Nysander, this is one of the rings I took from Corruth í Glamien's corpse," he gasped, finding his voice at last.

Nysander leaned forward and clasped his hand. "He was your kinsman and Idrilain's, Seregil. She thought it a fitting reward for solving the mystery of his disappearance. She hopes you shall wear it with honor among your own people one day."

"Give her my thanks." Seregil tucked it reverently away in its bag. "But you didn't magick me out of bed just for this?"

Nysander sat back with a chuckle. "No. I have a task which may be of interest to you. However, there are conditions to be set forth before I explain. Agree to abide by them or I shall send you back now with all memory of this meeting expunged."

Seregil blinked in surprise. "It must be some job. Why didn't you bring Alec?"

"I shall come to that presently. I can say nothing until you agree to the conditions."

"Fine. I agree. What are they?"

"First, you may ask no question unbidden."

"Why not?"

"Starting now."

"Oh, all right. What else?"

"Second, you must work in absolute secrecy. No one is to know of this, particularly not Alec or Micum. Will you give me your oath on it?"

Seregil regarded him in silence for a moment; keeping secrets from Alec was no easy business these days. Still, how could something so shrouded in mystery fail to be interesting?

"All right. You have my word."

"Your oath," Nysander insisted somberly.

Shaking his head, Seregil held out his left hand, palm up, before him. "*Asurit betuth dös Aura Elustri kamar sösui Seregil í Korit Solun Meringil Bôkthersa.* And by my honor as a Watcher, I swear also. Is that sufficient?"

"You know I would never impose such conditions on you without good reason," the wizard chided.

"Still, it seems to be happening quite a lot these days," Seregil retorted sourly. "*Now* can I ask questions?"

"I will answer what I can."

"Why is it so crucial for Alec and Micum not to know?"

"Because if you let slip the slightest detail of what I am about to tell you, I shall have to kill all of you."

Though spoken calmly, Nysander's words jolted him like a kick in the throat; he'd known the wizard too long to mistake his absolute sincerity. For an instant, Seregil felt as if he were looking into the face of a stranger. Then suddenly, everything fell into place as neatly as a three-tumbler lock. He sat forward, slopping hot tea over his knees in his excitement.

"It's to do with this, isn't it?" he exclaimed, tapping his chest. There, beneath Nysander's obscuring magic, lay the branded imprint of the wooden disk he'd stolen from Duke Mardus at Wolde—the same strange, deceptively crude disk that had nearly taken his life. "You went white the night I told you about showing a drawing of it to the Illioran Oracle. I thought you were going to fall over."

"Perhaps now you understand my distress," Nysander replied grimly.

They'd never spoken of that conversation, but the dread Seregil had felt then returned now in full force. "Bilairy's *Balls*! You'd have done it, too."

Nysander sighed heavily. "I would never have forgiven myself, I assure you, but I would also have been furious with you for forcing me into such an act. Do you recall what I said to you then?"

"To pray I never found out what that disk really is?"

"Precisely. And to undertake this task, you must continue to accept that as my answer on the subject."

Seregil slouched glumly in his chair. "Same old answer, eh? And what if I say no to all this? That if you don't tell me the whole story I want no part of it?"

Nysander shrugged. "Then as I said before, I shall remove all memory of this conversation from your mind and send you home. There are certainly others who could aid me."

"Like Thero, I suppose?" Seregil snapped before he could stop himself.

"Oh, for—"

"Does *he* know the Great Secret?" The old jealousy gripped Seregil's heart. The last thing he wanted to hear was that the young assistant wizard knew more of this than he did.

"He knows less than you," Nysander replied, exasperated. "Now do you want the task or not?"

Seregil let out a frustrated growl. "All right, then. What's this all about?"

Nysander pulled a sheet of vellum from his sleeve and handed it to him. "To begin with, tell me what you make of this."

"Looks like a page from a book." The vellum was darkened with age or weather. Seregil rubbed a corner of it between his fingers and sniffed it, then examined the writing itself. "It's old, four or five centuries at least. Poorly kept at first, though later carefully preserved. And the vellum is human or Aurënfaie skin, rather than kid." He paused again, examining the stitching holes on the left edge. "These are still intact, showing that it was carefully removed from a book, rather than torn. It was already damaged by dampness, though. Judging by the color I'd say the page was steeped in poison after that, but that's obviously been neutralized or we wouldn't be handling it."

"Quite so."

Oblivious now to everything but the task at hand, Seregil tugged absently at a strand of hair.

"Let's see. The writing is Asuit Old Style and it's written in that language, which originated with the hill people north of Plenimar. From that we can infer that our author was either from that region or a scholar of languages."

"As you are, dear boy. I assume you can read it?"

"Hmm—yes. Looks like the ravings of a mad prophet. Very poetic, though. 'Watch with me, beloved, as demons strip the fruit from the vine.' Then something about horses—and 'The golden flame is married with darkness. The Beautiful One steps forth to caress the bones of·the house . . .' No, that's not right. It's 'the bones of the world.'"

Moving to the table, he pulled a lamp closer. "Yes. I thought it was just a few errors with the accent marks, but it isn't. There's a cipher here."

Nysander passed him a wax writing tablet and a stylus. "Care to try it?"

Scanning back through the document, Seregil found sixteen words with misplaced accents. Listing only the wrongly accented letters, he came up with twenty-nine.

Frowning, he tapped the stylus against his chin, "This is a bitch of a thing."

"More difficult than you know," said Nysander. "It took my master Arkoniel and myself over a year to discover the key. Mind you, we were working on other things at the time."

Seregil tossed aside the stylus with a groan. "You mean to tell me you've broken this already?"

"Oh, yes. That is not the task, you see. But I knew that you would prefer to work with the original and draw your own conclusions."

"So how does it work?"

Joining him at the table, Nysander turned the wax tablet over and began to write rapidly. "To begin with, the accented letters come out to nonsense, a fact it took a discouragingly long time to discover. The key is a combination of syllabification and case. As you know, Old Asuit is an inflected language with five cases. However, only three—the nominative, dative, and genitive—are used for the cipher. For instance, look at the words making up the phrase 'of the world.' "

Seregil nodded thoughtfully, muttering to himself, "Yes, it was that misplaced accent that threw me. It should be over the second vowel of the last syllable, not the first."

"Correct. As 'world' is in the genitive case and the misplaced accent appears in the antepenultimate syllable, you use the last letter of that word. If it occurs in the same case but on the second, or penultimate, syllable, then you use the first."

Seregil looked up and grinned. "I didn't know you were such an accomplished grammarian."

Nysander allowed himself a pleased wink. "One learns a thing or two over the centuries. It is truly an exquisite system, and one fairly secure from inadvertent detection. In the nominative case, an erroneous accent over the antepenult indicates that you take the last letter of the word immediately following the one wrongly accented, and so forth. In the dative case only the accents over the penult have any significance. The upshot of it all is that you come out with just fifteen letters. Properly arranged—keep your eyes on the writing now—properly arranged they spell out *'argucth chthon hrig.'* "

"Sounds like you're getting ready to spit—" Seregil began, but the words died in his throat as the writing on the page swirled into motion. After a few seconds it disappeared entirely, leaving in its place a circular design resembling an eight-pointed star that covered most of the page.

"A magical palimpsest!" he gasped.

"Precisely. But look more closely."

Tilting the vellum closer to the lamp, Seregil let out a low whistle; the entire design was made up of the finest calligraphic writing. "Our mad prophet must have written this with a hummingbird's quill."

"Can you read it?"

"I don't know. It's so cramped. The script is Konic, used by the court scribes in the time of the early Hierophants, but the language is different, as if the writer wanted to approximate the sounds of one language with the alphabet of another. Yes, that's exactly what he was doing, the clever old bastard. So, attacking it phonetically—"

Muttering under his breath, Seregil slowly worked his way through the tangled writing. Half an hour later he looked up with a triumphant grin. "Pure Dravnian! Nysander, it's got to be Dravnian."

"Dravnian?"

"The Dravnians are a tribal people scattered through the glacial valleys of the Ashek Range, north of Aurënen. I haven't been up there since I was a boy, but I've studied the language. Great ones for sagas and legends, those Dravnians. They have no writing themselves, but this captures the sound of it. This fellow was certainly a student of obscure tongues. Once you untangle all this mess, it's just the same few words written over and over again to form the design. Written in blood, too, by the way and probably his own if he was loony enough to create something like this."

"Perhaps," Nysander broke in. "But can you make out what it says?"

Seregil glanced up at him, then let out a crow of triumph. "Ah ha! So that's what this is all about. *You* can't read it!"

Nysander affected a pained look. "I would remind you of the oaths you have given—"

Seregil held up a hand, grinning smugly. "I know, I know. But after all your restrictions and secrecy, I think I've earned the right to gloat a little. All it says is, 'Stone within ice within stone within ice. Horns of crystal beneath horns of stone.' Or vice versa. There's no way of telling which is meant to be the first line. Why he would go to such extremes to hide anything as obscure as this is beyond me, though."

"Not at all, not at all!" Nysander clapped Seregil on the shoulder, then began pacing excitedly. "The palimpsest begins in Asuit Old Style, an archaic language of Plenimar, which predates the Hierophantic settlements. The seemingly meaningless hidden phrase *'argucth chthon hrig'* operates as the key word to the hidden writing. This, in turn, is composed in the alphabet of the Hierophantic court, based at that period on the island of Kouros, yet in the language of an obscure tribe of the southern mountains across the Osiat Sea near Aurënen. I had reason to suspect as much but you, dear boy, have provided the final clues. What an amazing document!"

Seregil, meanwhile, had been doing some further pondering of his own. "The Dravnian tribes keep to the highest valleys of the Ashek Range, building their villages along the edges of the ice fields. 'Stone within ice within stone within ice.' And the horns of stone part reminds me of a story the mountain traders used to tell, something about a place up there where demons dance across the snow to drink the blood of the living. It was called the Horned Valley."

Nysander halted in front of Seregil, grinning broadly. "You have a mind like a magpie's nest, dear boy! I never know what odd bit of treasure will tumble from it next."

"If the Horned Valley really exists, then all this"—Seregil tapped the stained vellum—"it's not just some convoluted riddle. It's a map."

"And perhaps not the only one," said Nysander. "According to recent intelligence from Plenimar, several expeditionary forces have been dispatched west toward the Strait of Bal. We could not imagine what they were up to, but the Ashek peninsula lies in that direction."

"At this time of year?" Seregil shook his head. Crossing the Bal meant making for the southern rim of the Osiat Sea, a place of dangerous shoals and forbidding coastlines in the best of weather. In the winter it would be worse than treacherous. "So whatever this 'stone within ice' thing is, the Plenimarans want it pretty badly. And I take it you don't mean for them to get it?"

"I hope that you will assist me in forestalling that event."

"Well, it would certainly help to know what I'm looking for. If it wouldn't mean revealing too many sacred mysteries, that is."

"It is rumored to be a crown or circlet of some sort," Nysander told him. "More importantly, it possesses powers similar to those of the coin, which you have already experienced."

Seregil grimaced at the memory. "Then I'll be certain not to wear it this time. But if your information is correct, haven't the Plenimarans stolen a march on us?"

"Perhaps not. The fact that they sent several expeditions suggests that they do not know the object's precise location. We, on the other hand, may have just determined that. And I am able to transport you there in a much swifter fashion."

Seregil blanched. "Oh, no! You can't—A translocation from here to the Asheks? Nysander, I'll be puking for hours."

"I am sorry, but this matter is too important to chance anything else. Which brings us to the matter of Alec. Will he be difficult about being left behind?"

Seregil raked a hand through his hair. "I'll manage something. When do I leave?"

"By midday if you can manage it."

"I think so. What will I need, besides the obvious?"

"How would you fancy playing an Aurënfaie wizard?"

Seregil gave him a wry look. "Sounds fun, so long as we aren't relying on my magical abilities."

"Oh my, no," Nysander said with a laugh. "I shall provide you with items necessary to give credence to the role, and those for the task itself." He paused and clasped the younger man by the shoulders. "I knew you would not fail me, Seregil."

Seregil raised an eyebrow wryly at the wizard. "Bet now you're glad you didn't kill me, eh? What's the hour?"

"Nearly sunup, I should think. Regrettably, I must send you back the same way you came."

"Twice in one night? Just be sure you drop me handy to a basin!"

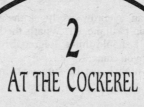

2
AT THE COCKEREL

Alec woke to the sound of sleet lashing across the roof. Ruetha had burrowed under the covers sometime in the night. He stroked the thick white ruff under her chin and the cat broke into a loud purr.

"What are you doing here?" he asked sleepily.

Sitting up, he saw Seregil's battered old pack sitting ready outside the bedroom door. Seregil's sword belt was draped over it, the newly mended quillon shining in the milky morning light.

Alec eyed the tidy pile with rising suspicion; Seregil had obviously been up for some time, making preparations for a journey. And he hadn't bothered to wake him.

"Seregil?" Poking his head around his friend's door, Alec found the normally cluttered little room utterly impassable.

"Morning!" Seregil called cheerily from somewhere beyond an overturned chest.

"What's going on? Have you been up all night?"

"Not all night." Seregil waded free of the mess with an armload of heavy sheepskin clothing and dumped it by the pack. "I found this," he said, handing Alec a dusty sack containing half a dozen complex locks. Some were still attached to splintered fragments of wood.

"Thought you might like to have a go at these, since you've mastered most of the others on the workbench. Be careful, though. Some of them bite."

Alec set the bag aside without comment and leaned against the door frame. Seregil was dressed for traveling and still hadn't told him to start packing.

"What's going on?" he asked, watching as Seregil wrestled a pair of long snowshoes out of a wardrobe. "Where are you going to find snow in this weather?"

"Give me a minute, will you?" said Seregil, checking the rawhide webbing. "I've got a few more things to find, then I'll explain what I can."

Alec let out a sigh and went to the window over the workbench. The panes rattled as a fresh gust of wind buffeted the inn. Outside he could see Thryis' son Diomis hurrying across the back court. Curtains of icy rain rippled past, obscuring all but the closest buildings. Behind him, he could hear Seregil still rummaging about.

Fighting down his rising impatience, he pulled on a pair of breeches and set about lighting the fire. The coals had died in the night. He heaped tinder and kindling on the ashes and shook out a firechip from the jar by the hearth. Flames leapt up and he stared into them, trying to marshal his racing thoughts.

"You know, from the back your head looks like a disheveled hedgehog," Seregil remarked, emerging at last. Ruffling Alec's ragged hair, he dropped into his favorite chair by the fire.

Alec was not amused. "You're going off alone, aren't you?"

"Just for a few days."

There was a guardedness in Seregil's tone that Alec didn't like. "On a job, you mean?"

"I can't say, actually."

Alec studied his friend's face. On closer inspection, he noticed that Seregil looked rather pale. "Is this because of last night? You said—"

"No, of course not. This is something I can't speak of to anyone."

"Why not?" the boy demanded, stubborn curiosity mingling with disappointment.

Seregil spread his hands apologetically. "It's nothing to do with you, believe me. And don't bother pressing."

"This is something for Nysander, isn't it?"

Seregil regarded him impassively. "I need your word you won't track me when I go."

Alec considered further objections, then nodded glumly. "When will you be back?"

"In a few days, I hope. You'll have to do that papers job for Baron Orante, and anything else coming in that looks like a one-man job. There's Mourning Night to think about, too, if I'm not back in time."

"Not back in time?" Alec sputtered. "That's only a week away, and you're holding a party at Wheel Street that night!"

"*We* are holding a party," Seregil corrected. "Don't worry. Runcer sees to all the arrangements, and Micum and his family will be here by then, too. You'll just have to play host. Remember Lady Kylith, the woman you danced with our first night there?"

"We're sitting with her at the Mourning Night ceremony."

"Right. She'll see to your etiquette."

"People are bound to ask about you, though."

"As far as anyone knows, Lord Seregil is still away recovering from the shock of his arrest. Tell anyone who asks that I was delayed. Cheer up, Alec. Chances are I'll be back in plenty of time."

"This secret job of yours—is it dangerous?"

Seregil shrugged. "What do we do that isn't? The truth is, I won't know much myself until I'm in the middle of it."

"When are you leaving?"

"As soon as I've had something to eat. Get dressed now and we'll have our breakfast downstairs."

Alec smelled freshly baked bread as they crossed the lading room to the kitchen.

The breakfast uproar was over. A scullery boy was scrubbing down the scarred worktables while Cilla bathed Luthas in a pan. Old Thryis sat peeling turnips by the hearth, a shawl draped over her shoulders against the damp.

"Well, there you are at last," the old woman greeted them, though she seldom saw Seregil before noon. "There's tea on the hob and new current buns under that cloth there. Cilla made them fresh this morning."

"And how's this lad today?" Seregil smiled, holding a fore-finger out to the baby. Luthas immediately grabbed it and pulled it into his mouth.

"Oh, he's feisty," replied Cilla, looking rather dark under the eyes. "He's got a tooth coming and it wakes us all night."

Alec shook his head. One minute Seregil was speaking of mys-terious journeys, the next here he was playing uncle to the baby like he hadn't a care in the world.

Not that his affection for Luthas wasn't genuine. He'd told Alec how Cilla had offered him the honor of fathering her child when she'd made up her mind to avoid conscription. Seregil had politely declined. While his interest in women seemed marginal at best, Alec suspected the real reason for Seregil's reticence was that it would have cost him his friendship with her grandmother. Thryis had been a sergeant in the Queen's Archers in her youth and despaired that neither her son nor granddaughter had followed a military career before settling down. Cilla had never revealed who the child's father was, but the man must have been dark. She was fair, while her son's eyes and hair were as brown as a mink's.

Going to the hearth, Alec leaned down next to Thryis and reached for the teapot warming by the fire.

"You're looking down in the mouth today," Thryis observed shrewdly. "Going off without you, is he?"

"He told you?"

The old woman gave a derisive snort. "He didn't have to," she scoffed, deftly quartering a turnip and pitching it into a kettle beside her. "There he is in his old rambling boots, chipper as a sparrow. And you here with the long face and still in your shirt-sleeves? Don't take no wizard to figure that one."

Alec shrugged. Thryis had run the Cockerel since Seregil secretly bought it twenty years before. She—together with her family and Rhiri, the mute ostler—was among the select few who knew anything of Seregil's double life.

"Now, don't go fretting yourself over it," she whispered. "Master Seregil thinks the world of you, and no mistake. There's none he speaks so well of 'cept Micum Cavish, and those two have been friends for years and years. Besides, it'll give you and me a chance to talk shooting again, eh? There's still a trick or two

I haven't shared and that fine black bow of yours shouldn't be gathering dust."

"I guess not." Alec gave her a quick peck on the cheek and went to sit across from Seregil at the breakfast table.

Studying his friend's face as Seregil joked with Cilla over breakfast, Alec felt certain he saw small lines of tension around his eyes. Whatever this secret job was, there was more to it than he was letting on.

There was no use asking further about it, though. Upstairs in their room again, Seregil finished with his scant collection of gear and clapped a battered hat on his head.

"Well, take care of yourself," he said, "especially on that job for the baron. I don't want to find you in the Red Tower when I return."

"You won't. Want help getting all that down?"

"No need." Shouldering his pack, Seregil clasped hands with him. "Luck in the shadows, Alec."

And with the flash of a crooked grin, he was gone.

Alec listened to his footsteps fading rapidly away. "And to you."

Seregil paused in the kitchen on his way out. Pulling up a stool beside Thryis, he slipped her a flat, sealed packet.

"I'm leaving this with you. I've got to go off for a few days. If I don't come back, this should take care of Alec and the rest of you."

Frowning, Thryis fingered the wax seals. "A will, is it? No wonder young Alec was looking so dark."

"He doesn't know, and I'd like to keep it that way."

"You've never left a will before."

"It's just in case I meet with an accident or something." Shouldering his pack, he headed for the door.

"Or something!" The old woman's mouth pursed into a skeptical line. "Mind that a 'something' don't jump up and bite you on the arse when you're not looking."

"I'll do my best to avoid it."

Outside, the sleet had turned to rain. Pulling the hood of his patched cloak up over his hat, he dashed across the slick cobbles to the stable where Rhiri had his new mare saddled and ready. Tossing the fellow a gold half sester, Seregil swung up into the saddle and set off at a gallop for the Orëska House.

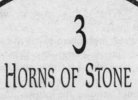

3
HORNS OF STONE

It was midafternoon before Nysander completed his preparations for the translocation.

"Are you ready, Seregil?" he asked at last, looking up from the elaborate pattern chalked on the casting-room floor.

"As ready as I'm likely to be," Seregil said, sweating in his heavy sheepskins. He carried his pack, snowshoes, and pole to the center of the design and piled them on the floor.

"These should establish your reputation as a wizard." Nysander held up a half-dozen short willow rods covered with painted symbols. "When broken, each will produce a different gift for your hosts. But you must be certain to keep this long one with the red band separate from the rest. It contains the translocation spell that will carry you back."

Seregil tucked the red wand carefully away in a belt pouch, then slipped the others inside the white Aurënfaie tunic he wore beneath his heavy coat.

"These are the most crucial items, however," the wizard continued, stepping to a nearby table. On it sat a wooden box two feet square and fitted with a leather shoulder strap and a strong catch. It was lined with sheets of silver engraved with magical symbols and contained two flasks wrapped in fleece.

Seregil frowned. "What if this crown or whatever it is that I'm after is too big to fit inside?"

"Do the best you can and return to me at once."

Seregil lifted the flasks. They were heavy, and the wax seals covering the corks were also inscribed with more symbols. "And these?"

"Pour the contents around the crown and inscribe the signs of the Four within the circle. It should weaken any wards protecting it."

A nasty twinge of uncertainty shot through Seregil's innards. "Should?"

Nysander wrapped the flasks carefully in the fleece and shut them in the box. "You survived the magic of the disk with no assistance. This should be sufficient."

"Ah, I see." Seregil glanced doubtfully at his old friend. "You believe the same inner flaw that kept me from becoming a wizard protects me from magic as well."

"It seems to be the case. I only wish it did not cause you such distress with translocations. Considering the distance involved in—"

"Let's just get it over with." Seregil gathered his gear in his arms as best he could. "The Asheks are far enough west that I should have a few hours of light left, but I'd rather not press my luck."

"Very well. I have done a sighting and should be able to send you to within a few miles of a village. It will be safest to drop you on the glacier itself, rather than risk hitting the rocky outcroppings along the edge."

"*That's* very comforting. Thanks so much!"

Ignoring the sarcasm, Nysander placed his fingertips together in front of his face and began the incantation. After a moment a particle of darkness winked into being within the cage of his fingers. Spreading his hands slowly, he coaxed it larger until it spun like a dark mirror in front of them.

Seregil stared into it for a moment, already queasy. Tightening his grip on his snowshoes, he took a resolute breath, closed his eyes, and stepped forward.

The whirling blast of vertigo was worse than he'd feared. For most people, a translocation was as simple as stepping from one room to another. To Seregil, however, it was like being sucked down in some vile black whirlpool.

It seemed to go on endlessly this time, buffeting him with darkness. Then, just as suddenly, he tumbled out into frigid brightness and sank up to his hips in drifted snow.

Stuck fast, he bent forward and spewed out his scant breakfast. When the spasms were over, he struggled free and crawled away from the steaming mess. Collapsing on his back, one arm over his eyes, he lay very still as the world spun sickeningly. The wind sighed over him, blowing fine ice crystals across his lips. Rolling onto his belly, he retched again, then cleaned his mouth with a handful of snow.

At least Nysander can aim, he thought, looking around.

The glacier hung in a steep valley. At its head a few miles away a pair of high peaks towered above the rest, marking a narrow pass and giving the valley the name Seregil had remembered. Slanting sunlight reflected back from the white expanse before him, bright enough to make his eyes water. Frozen waves, wind scoured out of the hardpack, thrust glistening up through the fresh powder to cast shadows as blue as the sky overhead.

Seregil's heavy outer garments kept the worst of the biting cold at bay, but his nose and cheekbones were already numb. His breath condensed with every exhalation, freezing in a glistening rime on the fur edging of his cap. Untangling the snowshoes, he checked them for damage and quickly strapped them to his boots. His thick gloves were cumbersome, but it would be courting frostbite to remove them even briefly.

With firmer footing on the snow now, he set out for a nearby rise to get his bearings. Anyone backtracking his trail would discover that he had more or less fallen from the sky, but that couldn't be helped; he was, after all, supposed to be a wizard.

From the top of the rise he spotted thin columns of smoke marking a village a few miles away on the western slope. Farther down the valley he could just make out a second village. The first was closer to the "horns of stone," so he headed west.

He was still nauseated and the thin, frigid air cut at his lungs, making dark spots dance in front of his eyes. Setting himself a steady pace, he marched along until he struck a trail leading toward the village. He was within half a mile of it when a pack of children and dogs appeared, running out to meet him.

Seregil paused, leaning on his snow pole with a grin of relief. Dravnian hospitality was legendary among those few who knew of it. Members of a neighboring village were greeted as family, which they often were. Anyone from beyond the limiting peaks was regarded as a veritable marvel. Goats were probably already being slaughtered in his honor.

"May I visit your village?" he asked in Dravnian as the children crowded excitedly around him.

Laughing, they shouldered his baggage and led him in. Dogs barked, goats and sheep bleated from their stone enclosures. Villagers hailed him like some returning hero.

The little settlement was made up of a collection of squat towers, round two-story affairs of piled stone topped with conical felt roofs. The main doors were set high in the upper level and reached by a ramp when the snow was not piled up to the doorsill. At the center of the village stood a tower broader than the rest. A sizable crowd had already collected outside, hoping for a look at the newcomer.

The Dravnians were a short, broad-set people with black, almond-shaped eyes and coarse, dark hair that they wore slicked back with liberal applications of oil. A few among them, however, had lighter hair or finer features that spoke of mixed blood—probably Aurënfaie, since few others found their way to these remote valleys.

The headman of the village was one of these half castes. As he stepped forward, smiling broadly, Seregil saw that the man's eyes were the same clear grey as his own.

"Welcome in this place, Fair One," the fellow greeted him in a patois of broken Aurënfaie and Dravnian. "I am Retak, son of Wigris and Akra, leader of this village."

"I am Meringil, son of Solun and Nycanthi," Seregil answered in Dravnian.

Grinning, Retak lapsed back into his native tongue. "We've not seen one of your tribe since my grandfather's time. You honor our village with your presence. Will you feast with us in the council house?"

"You honor me," Seregil replied, bowing as gracefully as his thick clothing allowed.

The upper level of the council house, used as a communal storehouse, was floored over except for the large central smoke hole. Rough stone steps led down to the lower chamber, where a huge fire of dried dung chips had already been kindled in a fire pit surrounded by thick carpets and bolsters. Women bustled excitedly around a cooking fire across the room, preparing the ritual meal.

Seated at the central fire with Retak and the other principal men of the village, Seregil closed his eyes for a moment as his belly did a slow, uneasy roll. The smell of slaughtered animals, mingled with the more immediate aromas of unwashed bodies and greased hair, was overpowering after the clear mountain wind.

Every available inch seemed to have been filled by curious villagers. People talked excitedly on all sides, leaning across their neighbors to shout to someone else or calling down from above for details. Children ringed the smoke hole overhead, chattering like swallows. The women labored with noisy cheer, wielding cleavers and clattering skewers and bowls.

Seregil felt all eyes on him as he stripped off his heavy outer garments. Posing as a traveler from his native Aurënen, Seregil had worn traditional garb. His long white tunic and close-fitting trousers were comfortable and unadorned except for thin bands of patterned weaving at the hem and neck. To complete the effect, he pulled a loosely woven head cloth from inside his tunic and wrapped its many folds about his head with practiced skill, leaving long ends hanging down his back. A small, ornate dagger hung at his belt, but he laid it and his sword aside as a gesture of good faith.

An excited hum went around the room as he reclined at last and accepted a bowl of *llaki* from Seune, the headman's wife. He sipped the fermented milk as sparingly as good manners allowed. His duty as guest was to repay hospitality with news and he slowly related such events from the south as might be of interest to them. Most of it was thirty years out-of-date, mixed in with snippets he'd picked up since his banishment, but it was all fresh to the Dravnians and very well received.

When he'd finished, the traditional storytelling commenced. Great lovers of tales that they were, the Dravnians had no system of writing. Each family had its own special stock of stories that only members of that clan could relate. Other tales were general property and were demanded of those who told them best. The children frequently chimed in with familiar lines and the women were called upon for the proper songs.

Seregil joined in with tales of his own and was quickly hailed as a *biruk*, "one who remembers many stories"—highest praise in such company. By the time a gigantic platter of roasted goat was set before them, he'd begun to enjoy himself.

Roasted shanks, haunches, and ribs lay arranged on the communal platter in a great ring surrounding cooked entrails, sweetbreads, and boiled goat's heads. When the guest and council had eaten their fill, the platter would pass on to the secondary guests, and after them the children and dogs. Seregil was served by Seune and her eldest daughters.

The two girls knelt on his right, holding out slabs of dark bread that their mother loaded with choice bits of meat. Nodding polite acceptance, Seregil picked up a chunk of meat and bit into it, signaling his hosts to begin.

The tough, savory meat settled the last of his queasiness and when the meal was over he made a great show of presenting gifts to Retak and his village.

Motioning for the others to clear a space in front of him, Seregil secretly palmed one of Nysander's painted wands from his sleeve and snapped it between his fingers while making elaborate motions with his other hand. Several bushels of fruit appeared instantly out of thin air before his delighted audience.

The baskets passed from hand to hand and up to the crowd overhead as the people exclaimed over their good fortune.

Smiling, Seregil drew another wand, which produced a casket of silver coins. The Dravnians had no use for currency, but were pleased by the glint of the metal and the fineness of the designs. Subsequent conjurings brought bolts of bright silk and linen, bronze needles, coils of rope, and bundles of healing herbs.

"You are a Fair One of great magic and generosity, Meringil, son of Solun and Nycanthi, and a true *biruk*," Retak proclaimed, clapping Seregil on the shoulder. "You shall be known as a member of my clan from this day. What can we offer you in return?"

"It is I who am honored by your excellent hospitality. My gifts are given in thanks for that alone," Seregil replied graciously. "Though there is a matter in which you may be able to assist me."

Retak motioned for the others to pay attention. "What has brought you so far to our valley?"

"I've come seeking a place of magic spoken of in certain legends. Do you know of such a place?"

The reaction was instantaneous. The elders exchanged hesitant looks. A woman dropped a spit with a clatter. Overhead the chil-

dren left off exclaiming over their new treasures and leaned farther
over the hole to listen.

Retak motioned with his staff and an ancient little man wearing
a coat decorated with sheep's teeth shuffled forward. In the firelight he looked like an ancient tortoise, with a tortoise's leathery,
slow-blinking gaze. Kneeling slowly before Seregil, he held up a
bone rattle in one tremulous hand and shook it in a wide circle
before speaking.

"I am Timan, son of Rogher and Borune," he said at last. "And
I tell you that there is such a place in this valley. It has been the
duty of my clan to watch over it since the time of the spirit's
anger. It is a spirit home, deep in the rock beneath the ice. How it
came there no man knows. Sometimes the door is there and sometimes it is not there, according to the will of the spirit."

"And this spirit has grown angry?" asked Seregil.

Timan nodded, shaking the rattle softly in time to his words. It
was more of a chant than a story, as if he'd told it many times
before, and in exactly the same words.

"The spirit made a chamber for men to dream in. Some had
visions. Some did not. Some heard the voice of the spirit. Some
did not. All was with the will of the spirit. When the spirit chose to
speak, those who heard were called blessed, bringers of great luck
to their clan. But many generations ago the spirit grew angry. Men
came out maddened. They did deeds of terrible evil. Others never
returned and no trace of them could be found. A man of my clan
was the first to go mad, and so it has been the burden of my clan to
guard the spirit home since that time."

He stopped, wrinkled mouth moving in silence, as if he'd run
out of sound.

"Why do you seek this place?" Retak asked.

Seregil stared into the fire for a moment, quickly weaving this
new information into a usable form. "I'd heard legends of this
place and was curious to see if they were true. You know that the
Aurënfaie are people of great magic. I have shown you my powers
already. If you will show me this sacred place, I will speak with
your spirit and find out why it's so angry. Perhaps I can even make
peace between you again."

A murmur of approbation went around the cramped room.

Old Timan laid his rattle at Seregil's feet. "This would be a
great feat indeed. Many times I have tried to placate the spirit, but

it has been silent to me, or driven me out with terrible noises in my head. Truly, can you do such a thing?"

"I'll try," Seregil replied. "Bring me to the spirit chamber at first light tomorrow and I'll speak to your spirit."

The murmur changed to a roar of acclaim.

"The guest sleeps in my house this night," Retak announced proudly, ending the feast. "The mountain nights are harsh for your kind, Meringil, but I have many healthy daughters to keep you warm."

Overhead the children shouted with delight as the older girls craned for a better look at Seregil.

Seregil blinked. "What?"

"To get a round belly from a guest gives a young woman highest status," Retak explained happily. "New blood brings new strength to the whole village. My own grandfather was a light-eyed Aurënfaie, as you can see. But not a great magician like you! Tomorrow Ekrid's clan will offer you hospitality, and then Ilgrid's and—"

"Ah, of course." Seregil looked around to find mothers reckoning on their fingers their place in the hierarchy. Clearly, there were a few Dravnian guesting customs he'd forgotten about.

Ah, Nysander, he groaned inwardly, scanning the gaggle of moonfaced maidens, reading clearly enough the greedy gleam behind their modest smiles. *This had damn well better be the right valley!*

Alec lowered himself from the villa window, then whirled in alarm as a menacing snarl erupted on his right. There'd been no sign of a dog when he'd first climbed into the baron's courtyard, but there was sure as hell one here now.

What he could see of it in the darkness was big, and the rising timbre of the growl was enough for him to imagine the beast closing in on him, ears laid back, teeth bared.

It was too far to the courtyard wall for a dash. Racking his memory for the thief's charm Seregil had shown him, he raised his left fist with index and little fingers extended. Snapping his hand to point the little finger down, he whispered hoarsely, "Peace, friend hound."

The growling ceased at once. A cold nose thrust briefly against his palm, then he heard the dog padding away.

It had never occurred to Alec to ask how long the charm lasted. Taking no chances, he ran for the wall. The top was studded with shards of glass and crockery set in mortar; in his haste he reached carelessly and caught his left hand on one of the jagged points, gashing the palm just above the wrist. Pain bloomed through his hand as a warm trickle oozed down into his sleeve. Hissing softly through his teeth, he slid down the far side and headed for home.

His route took him by Wheel Street and he halted a moment at the corner, holding his torn hand to his chest. It would only take a moment to duck in there, and he knew where Seregil kept bandages and salve—

The growing throb in his hand decided him.

Letting himself in the front door, he took out a lightstone and whistled softly to the dogs, making himself known. A huge white shape materialized at once. Marag padded out of the dining room, wagging a greeting as he sniffed Alec's hand. His mate would be on patrol in the back court. Accompanied by the hound, Alec walked through the main hall to the kitchen.

The supplies he wanted were on the shelf by the door. Carrying the rags and salve pot to the table, he set his lightstone by them and examined the gash. It was jagged and sore, but no major veins or tendons seemed to be damaged.

"This must be my unlucky hand," he muttered, rubbing his thumb over the shiny circular scar left by the cursed disk they'd stolen from Mardus. They'd both been branded by it—Seregil on his chest where it had hung, Alec on the palm of the hand as he'd grasped it during their strange struggle at the inn.

He bandaged the cut as best he could one-handed, then sat back and stroked Marag's silky head. The thought of his own bedchamber upstairs was tempting. He was cold and tired and suddenly Blue Fish Street felt very far away. But there was always the complication of appearances; Sir Alec and Lord Seregil were not expected to arrive for several more days and it wouldn't do to have untoward signs of occupation just yet. With a resigned shrug, he cleared away the evidence of his visit and set out through the dark, cold streets.

Within a block of Wheel Street he suddenly sensed pursuit. Stealth was difficult on the icy streets and whoever it was shadowing him was making a poor job of concealing their movements. When Alec slowed, they came on. When he increased his pace, so did they. It was too dark to see, but he could hear more than one set of feet. One of them had metal nails on the soles of his boots; in the silence of the street, Alec could hear them scraping against the cobbles.

There was no question of returning to the house. Even if he could get back past his pursuers, he couldn't risk leading them there.

Ahead of him, a street lantern burned at the intersection of Wheel and Golden Helm. A right turn would bring him to the Astellus Circle and the Street of the Sheaf. There was a chance of meeting with a Watch patrol there, but he couldn't be sure of it. A left turn would take him toward Silvermoon Street and the Palace.

At the corner he deliberately walked through the pool of light and swung sharply to the right. Once beyond it, he doubled quickly back toward Silvermoon. His pursuers caught the trick, however, and charged after him, their boots clattering on the paving stones.

There was nothing left to do but run. Abandoning any attempt at stealth, Alec pelted down the center of the broad boulevard, cloak flapping behind him. High garden walls presented an unbroken barrier on either side, blocking any hope of a quick side-step. The pounding of his feet and those closing in on him echoed like the clatter of dice in a cup.

Tearing his cloak strings loose, Alec let it fall away behind him. A muffled curse rang out an instant later, and the sound of a man falling heavily.

Dashing past another lantern, he glanced back to see two swordsmen no more than twenty yards behind.

He veered into Silvermoon Street and saw the wall surrounding the palace grounds looming on his right. As he'd hoped, a watch fire burned in front of one of the postern gates. He dashed toward it, lungs bursting.

A cluster of soldiers of the Queen's household guard were huddled around the brazier. At the sound of Alec's approach, four came forward with swords drawn.

"Help!" gasped Alec, praying they didn't attack as he barreled into their midst. "Footpads—chasing me—back there!"

Two men grasped him by the arms, half restraining, half supporting him as he skidded to a halt.

"Steady, lad, steady there," said one.

"I don't see anyone," growled another, squinting in the direction Alec had come from.

Looking back, Alec saw no sign of his mysterious pursuers.

The first guard ran a skeptical eye over his fine coat and sword. "Footpads, eh? More likely an angry father or husband at this hour. Been up to mischief, have you?"

"No, I swear," Alec panted. "I was coming home late from— from the Street of Lights." The others grinned knowingly at this.

"Just the place to get your purse lightened, one way or another, eh?" the sergeant said with a chuckle. "Well, it's late for the nighthawks to be out, but they might just lurk around for you. Do you live close by?"

"No, across the city."

"Then you're welcome to tuck up here with us round the fire 'till first light."

Alec gratefully accepted a spare cloak and a pull from a water skin, then settled down with his back to the wall, the warmth of the brazier warming his face and chest. All in all, he thought as he drifted off to sleep, it wasn't the worst end to an evening's work.

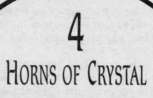

4

HORNS OF CRYSTAL

Retak's daughters bid Seregil a fond farewell as he and their father left to meet Timan at the council house early the next day. To Seregil's dismay, a crowd had already assembled and many had snowshoes and poles ready.

Timan presented a young man to him. "I am too old now to make the journey, but my grandson, Turik, knows the place. He can guide you. These others will carry your belongings and gift offerings for the spirit."

Seregil groaned inwardly. The last thing he wanted was an audience, but he was too close to his objective to risk offending the village. Amid much cheering and singing, they set off for the head of the valley.

The Dravnian youths marched along easily, talking and joking as they broke trail. Seregil toiled doggedly in their wake, struggling with the thin air and a poor night's rest. One of Retak's sons fell in beside him, grinning.

"You had good hospitality last night, eh? My sisters were happy this morning."

"Oh, yes," wheezed Seregil. "I was kept very warm, thank you."

They reached the base of the pass just after midday. Turik called a halt while an older man named Shradin went ahead to scout the snow.

Turik pointed up the pass. "The spirit home is there, but it's difficult going from here—fissures beneath the snow and avalanches. Shradin can read the snow better than anyone in the village."

Squatting on their snowshoes, the others watched as the guide explored the pass.

"Well, what do you think?" asked Seregil when Shradin returned.

The Dravnian shrugged. "It's only a little dangerous today. Still, it would be better if just a few go on from here. Turik knows the way and I know the snow. The rest of them better go home."

After some disgruntled grumbling, the others headed back to the village.

Shradin took the lead as they began their cautious ascent, Seregil and Turik following in single file. Seregil watched in silent admiration as the man probed ahead with his pole, leading them safely around deep fissures concealed just beneath the deceptively unbroken snow. Glad as he was of this, however, Seregil couldn't help glancing nervously up at the tons of snow and ice clinging precariously to the mountainsides above.

As they neared the top of the pass, Turik took the lead.

"We are almost there," he said at last, pausing for Seregil to catch his breath.

Struggling up a last, steep face, Turik halted again and began casting around where the lip of the glacier met the rock face. After frequent sightings up at the peaks and much prodding with his pole, the young Dravnian raised his hand and waved for the others.

Hung with icicles and half drifted over with snow, the opening of the passage resembled a fanged and sullen mouth. Digging with hands and snowshoes, they soon cleared the opening and peered down the steep black tunnel that descended into the ice.

Seregil felt a strange tingling in his hands and up his back as he leaned over it; strong magic lay below.

"The first part of the way is slick," Turik warned, pulling a sack of ashes from his bag. "We'll need to scatter these as we go, or it's nearly impossible to climb back out again."

"I have to go alone from here," Seregil told him. "My magic is strong, but I can't be distracted worrying about the two of you. Wait for me here. If I'm not back by the time the sun touches that peak, come down for me, but not before. If your spirit kills me, give all my things to Retak and say he is to divide them as he sees fit."

Turik's eyes widened a bit at this, but neither he nor Shradin argued.

Seregil took off his bulky hat and tied his long hair back with a thong. Taking the small lightwand from his tool roll, he grasped the handle in his teeth and shouldered an ash bag and the cumbersome box.

"Aura's luck be with you," Shradin said solemnly, using the Aurënfaie name for Illior.

Let's hope it is, Seregil thought nervously as he began his descent.

The steep tunnel was narrow and slick as glass in places. Scattering ash in front of him, he crawled down, dragging the box behind. By the time the ice gave way to a more level stone passage, he was smeared black from head to foot.

The magic permeating the place grew stronger as he went down. The uncanny tingle he'd first noticed increased swiftly. There was a low buzzing in his ears and he could feel an ache growing behind his eyes.

"Aura Elustri málrei," he whispered, speaking the invocation to Illior aloud to test the effect. The silence absorbed his words without an echo and the tingling in his limbs continued unabated.

The tunnel ended at a tiny natural chamber scarcely larger than the passage itself. The shards of a broken bowl lay against the far wall.

The ceaseless noise in his ears made concentration difficult as Seregil began a careful search of the place. It wasn't a steady tone, but rose and fell erratically. At times he seemed to catch a faint hint of voices beneath the rest, but put it down to imagination.

Satisfied at last that no other passages were concealed by any method he could detect, he tucked his chilled hands into his coat and hunkered down to review the few facts he possessed.

"Horns of crystal beneath horns of stone. Stone within ice within stone within ice," the palimpsest had said.

Seregil looked around, frowning. *Well, I'm certainly beneath horns of stone. And to get here I've gone through the ice first, and then stone.*

That left stone within ice still to go, but where? Though obscure in method, the palimpsest had been quite specific in giving the necessary directions. If there was some secret way beyond this point, then logic suggested that the final clues leading to it were also concealed in that same document.

Massaging his throbbing temples, he closed his eyes and recalled the details of the palimpsest's various inscriptions. Could he and Nysander have missed something in the rambling prophecies? Or perhaps Nysander had been wrong in his assertion that only one side of the document concealed a palimpsest.

Now there was an uncomfortable thought.

He was startled from his reverie by a blast of cold air. Opening his eyes, he found himself lying in the snow outside the tunnel entrance with Turik and Shradin kneeling over him with obvious concern. Over Shradin's shoulder he saw that the sun was already low behind the designated peak.

"What happened?" Seregil gasped, sitting up.

"We waited as long as we could," Turik apologized. "The time came and went for you to return. When we went down, we found you in a spirit dream."

"There's a storm coming," added Shradin, frowning up at the clouds. "They come on fast this time of year. We need to get back to the village while there's still light enough to go down safely. There's no shelter here, and nothing for a fire."

Seregil looked around in sudden alarm. "My sword! And the box—Where are they?"

"Here, beside you. We brought them out, too," Turik assured him. "But tell us, did you speak to the spirit? Do you know the reason for its anger?"

Still chagrined at having fallen so easily under the spell of the place, Seregil nodded slowly, buying time as he collected his thoughts.

"It's not your spirit who is angry, but another, an evil one," he told them. "This evil one keeps the other prisoner. It's a very strong spirit. I must rest and prepare myself to banish it."

Shradin looked up at the sky again. "You'll have time, I think."

Taking up their packs and poles, the Dravnian guides led Seregil back to the village for another night of exhausting hospitality.

As Shradin had predicted, a savage blizzard roared in through the teeth of the mountains during the night. People fought their way through the howling wind to drive their livestock up the ramps into their towers, then sealed their doors and settled down to wait out the storm.

It raged steadily for two days. One house lost its felt roof, forcing the inhabitants to flee to a neighboring tower. At another, a woman gave birth to twins. Otherwise, the time was given over to eating, storytelling, and general husbandry. The Dravnians were philosophical about such conditions; what was the use of complaining about something that happened every winter? The blizzards were even beneficial. They piled snow around the house and helped keep the drafts out.

One family in particular regarded this storm as a stroke of luck, for it kept the Aurënfaie guest in their house for two nights.

Seregil was less complaisant about the situation. Ekrid had nine children, six of them daughters. One girl was too young, another in the midst of her menses, but that still left four to contend with and he didn't much like the competitive gleam in their eyes as they welcomed him.

To further complicate matters, the lower level had been given over to Ekrid's herd of goats and sheep, and their bleating and odor lent little to the general atmosphere. For two days, Seregil had to choose between evading the amorous advances of the girls or trying to walk three feet without treading in shit. His success was limited on both counts and his concentration on the problem at hand suffered.

Stretched out with two of Ekrid's daughters still twined around him the second night, Seregil stared up at the rafters and decided he'd had enough of women to last him for some time. Shifting restlessly in their musky embrace, he caught a hint of answering movement across the way where Ekrid's sons slept. One of them *had* made long eyes at him the evening before— He gave the possibility a moment's consideration, but resolved dourly that there was little to be gained in that direction. The young man smelled as strongly of goat tallow and old hides as his sisters, and lacked a front tooth besides.

Lying back, he allowed himself a moment's longing for his own clean bed and a freshly bathed companion to share it. To his surprise, the anonymous figure swiftly transformed into Alec.

Father, brother, friend, and lover, the Oracle of Illior had told him that night in Rhíminee.

He supposed that, after a fashion, he had been father and brother to Alec, having more or less adopted him after their escape from Asengai's dungeon. Seregil smiled wryly to himself in the darkness; it'd been the least he could do, considering that Alec was one of dozens of innocents captured and tortured by Asengai's men during their hunt for Seregil himself.

In the months since then they'd certainly become friends, and perhaps something more than friends.

But lovers?

Seregil had kept this possibility resolutely at bay, telling himself the boy was too young, too Dalnan, and, above all, too valued a companion to risk losing over something as inconsequential as sex.

And yet, lying exhausted among Ekrid's daughters, he suffered a guilty pang of arousal as he thought of Alec's slender body, his dark blue eyes and ready smile, the rough silken texture of his hair.

Haven't you had enough hopeless infatuations in your life? he scowled to himself. Rolling onto his belly, he turned his thoughts to the palimpsest, running through its cryptic phrases once again.

Horns of crystal beneath horns of stone. Stone within ice within stone within ice.

Damn, but there seemed little enough to be wrung out of it at this point. Slowly he repeated the phrase in its original Dravnian, then translated it into Konic, Skalan, and Aurënfaie, just for good measure.

Nothing.

Start again, he thought. *You're overlooking something. Think!*

After this came the directions to the chamber. Before it were the prophetic ramblings: first the dancing animals, then the bones, and the strange words of the unscrambled cipher that unlocked the secret—

"Illior's Eyes!"

One of the girls stirred in her sleep, running a hand down his back. He forced himself to lie still, heart pounding excitedly.

The phrase! The phrase itself.

Those alien, throat-scraping words. If they were the key to the palimpsest, then why not to the magic of the chamber itself?

Assuming he was correct, however, this raised other considerations. If the words were simply a password spell, then he could probably use them without danger to himself or anyone else. But if they worked a deeper magic, what then?

He could go back to Nysander now with what he already knew. Still, the Plenimarans might be beating a trail up the valley at this very moment and Nysander would be too drained from the first translocation spell to send him or anyone else back immediately. Unless, of course, he enlisted the aid of someone more magically reliable rather than risk mishap—Magyana perhaps, or Thero.

To hell with that! I haven't come this far for someone else to see the mystery's end. First light tomorrow I'm going up that pass again, avalanches be damned.

As he drifted happily off to sleep, he realized that the wind had dropped at last.

Someone pounded on Ekrid's door just before dawn, waking the household.

"Come to the council house!" a voice shouted from outside. "Something terrible has happened. Come now!"

Extricating himself from a soft tangle of arms and thighs, Seregil threw on his clothes and ran for the council house with the others.

Faint, predawn light painted the snow blue, the towers black against it. Snowshoeing through the icy powder, Seregil found the village almost unrecognizable. The storm had buried the towers up to their doorsills, leaving the exposed upper story looking like an ordinary cottage drifted up with snow.

Shouldering his way through the crowd at the council house, he hurried downstairs to the meeting chamber.

The central fire had been lit and beside it crouched a woman he hadn't seen before. Surrounded by a silent, wide-eyed crowd, she clutched a small bundle against her breast, wailing hoarsely. Retak's wife knelt beside her and gently folded back the blanket. Inside lay a dead infant. The stranger clutched the baby fiercely, her hands mottled with frostbite.

"What happened?" Seregil asked, slipping in beside Retak.

He shook his head sadly. "I don't know. She staggered into the village a little while ago and no one has been able to get any sense out of her."

"That is Vara, my husband's cousin from Torgud's village," a woman cried, pushing her way through the crowd. "Vara, Vara! What's happened to you?"

The woman looked up, then threw herself into her kinswoman's arms. "Strangers!" she cried. "They came out of the storm. They refused the feast, killed the headman and his family. Others, many others, my husband, my children— My children!"

Throwing back her head, she let out a scream of anguish. People gasped and muttered, looking to Retak.

"But why?" Retak asked gently, bending over her. "Who were they? What did they want?"

Vara covered her eyes and cowered lower. Seregil knelt and placed a hand on her trembling shoulder.

"Were they looking for the spirit home?"

The woman nodded mutely.

"But they refused the feast," he went on softly, feeling a coldness growing in the pit of his stomach. "They affronted the village, and you would not deal with them."

"Yes," Vara whispered.

"And when the killing started, then did you tell them?"

Tears welled in Vara's eyes, rolling swiftly down her cheeks. "Partis told them, after they killed his wife," she sobbed weakly. "He told them of Timan and his clan. He thought the killing would stop. But it didn't. They laughed, some of them, as they killed us. I could see their teeth through their beards. They laughed, they laughed——"

Still clutching her dead child, she slumped over in a faint and several women carried her to a pallet by the wall.

"Who could do such things?" Retak asked in bewilderment.

"Plenimaran marines," Seregil growled, and every eye turned to him. "These men are enemies, both to me and to you. They seek the evil that lurks in your spirit home. When they find it, they'll worship it and sacrifice living people to it."

"What can we do?" a woman cried out.

"They'll come here," a man yelled angrily. "Partis as good as set them upon us!"

"Do you have any weapons?" Seregil asked over the rising din.

"Nothing but wolf spears and skinning knives. How can we fight such men with those?"

"You're a magician!" shouted Ekrid. "Can't you kill them with your magic?"

Caught in a circle of expectant faces, Seregil drew a deep breath. "You've all seen the nature of my magic. I have no spells for killing men."

He let disappointment ripple through the crowd for an instant, then added, "But I may have something just as effective."

"What is that?" the man demanded skeptically.

Seregil smiled slightly. "A plan."

• • •

Retak called a halt at the base of the pass as the first lip of sun showed over the eastern peaks. Shradin went ahead to assess the danger. The others—every man, woman, and child of Retak's village—waited quietly for word to move on. Mothers whispered again to their younger children why they must keep silent in the pass. The infants had been given *llaki* to make them sleep.

Seregil climbed an outcropping and shaded his eyes as he looked back across the snowfield. Blue shadow still lay deep in the valley, but he could make out a dark column of men closing in on the village. It wouldn't take long for them to see that their prey had fled, or what direction they'd gone.

"There they are," he whispered to Retak. "We have to move on quickly!"

Hardly daring to breathe, they continued up the pass.

It was a fearsome journey. The villagers moved as swiftly as they could, some bowed under loads of fuel and food, others carrying children on their backs or aged relatives on litters. Only the muffled creak of snowshoes and pack straps broke the silence. Old Timan trudged painfully along near the rear, supported by Turik and his brothers.

Mercifully, Vara had died and she and her child were hidden now in the drifts beyond the goat enclosures. But her death was not in vain; she'd given Retak's village time to prepare.

Shimmering veils of snow blew across the pass, dislodging small falls down the slopes. These gave out harmlessly in fine bits of crust, rolling down to leave mouse trails across their path. Ominous cracks and groans echoed between the cliffs overhead, but Shradin gave no warning sign and Retak silently motioned his people on.

Trudging along in their midst, Seregil was deeply moved by the mix of fear, trust, and determination that drove these people forward. They'd welcomed him—a stranger—given him the best of all they had. When Retak claimed him as a member of his clan, it was meant literally. In the eyes of the Dravnians he was now a blood member of the community for as long as he wished to claim kinship.

The Plenimaran marines pursuing them had been offered the same welcome.

Looking back as they neared the cave, he saw that the enemy had reached the village and was now turning toward the pass.

You bastards! he thought bitterly. *You'd carve these people up like sheep for whatever lies hidden at the end of that tunnel, just as you slaughtered Vara's village. But you were sloppy in your work, my friends, and that makes all the difference!*

Up ahead Retak conferred briefly with Shradin, then motioned for a halt. Seregil climbed up to join them.

"Do those men know how to read the snow?" Shradin whispered.

"Let's hope not. Retak, tell the others to move a bit higher and watch for your signal. Are the young men in place?"

"They're ready. But what if this plan of yours doesn't work?"

"Then we'll need another plan." Feeling much less assured than he sounded, Seregil went to take his own position.

The villagers nervously watched the Plenimarans approach. The sun was higher now, and glinted back from spear points and helmets below. What first appeared only as a long, dark movement against the snow soon resolved into individual men toiling toward them.

Whatever the Plenimarans think they're after here, they're not taking any chances, Seregil thought, counting over a hundred men. He glanced briefly up the slope, trying to make out the mouth of the spirit chamber tunnel and wondering again what could be worth all this.

The Plenimarans were close enough for Seregil to make out the insignia on their breastplates before Shradin finally waved up to Retak. The headman raised his staff overhead with both hands and let out a bloodcurdling yell. Every villager joined in, bellowing and screaming at the top of their lungs. At the same moment Seregil, Shradin, and the young men of the village shoved at their piles of loosened rock and ice chunks, sending them careening down the steep slope.

For an instant nothing happened.

Then the first rumblings sounded along the western face as tons of snow and ice sloughed off, plunging down on the Plenimaran column.

Seregil could see the pale ovals of upturned faces as the soldiers realized too late the trap they'd been drawn into. The neat column wavered and broke. Men foundered in the snow, throwing aside their arms as they sought some direction of escape from the implacable wave bearing down on them.

The avalanche overtook them in seconds, carrying men like

dead leaves in a flood, blotting them from sight. A great cheer went up from the Dravnians and the sound brought down a second deafening avalanche from the east wall. It crashed down the valley to lap over the first with a roar of finality that echoed for minutes between the stark, sun-gilded peaks.

Shradin pounded Seregil joyfully on the back. "Didn't I say it would fall just so?" he shouted. "No one could have survived that!"

Seregil took a last wondering look down at the massive slide, then waved for Turik. "It's time I completed my work. This evil must be removed from your valley so no others will come seeking it."

Amazingly, the tunnel opening was still clear, though drifts were piled thickly around the spot. With the women singing victory songs behind him, Seregil once again made his way down the slick, cramped passage. The noises in his head and the tingling in his skin were as bad as before, but this time he ignored them, knowing what he had to do.

"Here we are again," he whispered, reaching the chamber. Refusing to consider the various ramifications of being wrong about the nature of the magic, he hugged the box against his side and said loudly, *"Argucth chthon hrig."*

An eerie silence fell over the chamber. Then he heard a soft tinkling sound that reminded him of embers cooling on a hearth. Tiny flashes like miniature lightning flickered across the rock face at the far end of the chamber.

Seregil took a step back, then dove for the mouth of the tunnel as the stone exploded.

Jagged shards flew up the tunnel, hissing like arrows as they scored the back of his thick coat and trousers. Others ricocheted and spattered in a brief, deadly storm around the tiny chamber.

It was over in an instant. Seregil lay with his arms over his head a moment longer, then cautiously held up the lightstone and looked back.

An opening had been blasted in the far wall, revealing a dark space beyond.

Drawing his sword, Seregil approached and looked into the second chamber. It was roughly the size of his sitting room at the Cockerel, and at the back of it a glistening slab of ice caught the glow of his lightstone, reflecting it across a tangle of withered corpses that covered the floor.

The constant cold beneath the glacial ice had drawn the moisture from the bodies over uncounted years, leaving them dark and shrunken, lips withered into grimaces, eyes dried away like raisins, hands gnarled to talons.

Seregil sank to his knees, cold sweat running down his chest beneath his coat. Even in their mummified state, he could see that their chests had been split open, the ribs pulled wide. Only a few months earlier his friend and partner, Micum Cavish, had come upon a similar scene nearly a thousand miles away, in the Fens below Blackwater Lake. But there some of the bodies had been newly killed. These had been here for decades, perhaps centuries. Putting this together with Nysander's veiled threats and secrecy, Seregil felt a twinge of genuine fear.

The singing whine in his ears was much worse here. Kneeling there at the mouth of the chamber, Seregil suddenly envisioned what the victims' last moments must have been.

Waiting to be dragged into the killing chamber.

Listening to the screams.

The steam rising from torn bodies—

He could almost catch the sound of those tortured voices echoing back faintly over the years.

Shaking such fancies off uneasily, he climbed in to examine the mysterious slab.

The rough-hewn block of ice was half as long as he was tall, and nearly four feet thick. The aura of the place was worse here; a nasty prickling sensation played over his skin, like ants beneath his clothes. His head pounded. The ringing in his ears swelled like a chorus of voices wailing an octave beyond the scope of pain.

More disturbing still was the sudden flair of pain around the scar on his chest. It burned like a fresh wound, driving a deep spike of pain at his heart.

Working swiftly, Seregil took the two flasks from the box, unwrapped them, and poured out the dark contents of the first in a circle on top of the ice. With his dagger, he scratched the symbols of the Four inside the circle: a lemniscate for Dalna; Illior's simple crescent; the stylized ripple of a wave for Astellus; the flame triangle of Sakor. They formed the four points of a square when he had finished.

Unnatural flames licked up as the liquid ate into the ice and a soft, answering glow sprang up in the center of the slab, revealing the outline of a circular object embedded there.

A fresh blast of pain tightened Seregil's breath in his throat. He reached into his coat and felt wetness there. Tearing open the neck of his coat and shirt with bloodied fingers, he found that his skin had opened around the edges of the scar.

There were voices all around him now, whispering, sighing, keening. His hands shook as he quickly emptied the second vial onto the ice. More flames licked up, guttering in the faint, unnatural breeze rising around him. Invisible fingers brushed his face, plucked at his clothing, stroked his hair.

A first translucent point of crystal protruded from the shrinking ice, quickly followed by seven more in a slanting ring.

The singing, at once tortured and exultant, rose to fill the cramped chamber. Seregil pressed his hands to his ears as he crouched, waiting.

The magical liquid burned and boiled away until eight blade-like crystal spikes were revealed, set in a circlet of some sort.

Seregil bent to pull it free and a drop of blood fell from his chest onto the ice within the circlet. He paused, strangely fascinated, as another followed, and another. A stone shard had grazed the back of his hand and this, too, was oozing blood. A rivulet of it ran down between his fingers onto the point he was grasping, streaking it like ruby as it trickled to the little pool gathering in the center of the crown.

The singing was clearer now, suddenly sweet and soothing and somehow familiar. Seregil's throat strained to capture the impossible notes as the blood dripped down from his chest.

Not yet, the voices crooned. Unseen hands stroked him, supporting him as he stooped over the crown. *Watch! See the loveliness being wrought.*

The gathering blood sank into the ice as an answering rubescent blush spread slowly up through each crystal point.

Oh, yes! he thought. *How beautiful!*

Their sides were sharp. They cut into his palms as he gripped them. More blood trickled down and the crystal blushed a darker red.

But a new voice was intruding from a distance, rough and discordant.

Nothing, sang the voices. *It is nothing. There is only our music here. Join us, lovely one, join our song, the only song. For the Beautiful One, the Eater of Death—*

It was distracting, this ugly new tone. But as he bowed his head, straining against this raw new voice he found that it, too, was familiar.

He'd almost succeeded in blocking it out when all at once he recognized it—the sound of his own hoarse screams.

The beautiful illusions shattered as searing bolts of pain slammed up his arms, seeking his heart.

"Aura!" he cried out, wrenching the crown free with the last of his strength. *"Aura Elustri málrei!"*

Staggering through a haze of agony, he thrust the crown into the silver-lined box and drove the latch into place.

Silence fell like a blow. Collapsing among the corpses, he pressed his bloody hands to the front of his coat. *"Marös Aura Elustri chyptir,"* he murmured thankfully as he slipped into a half faint. *"Chyptir marös!"*

The Beautiful One, the voices had said. *The Eater of Death.*

Gradually he became aware of another presence in the chamber, and with it a pervasive sense of peace mingled with sadness.

This, he realized, must be the true spirit, the one that had created this place and inhabited it until the crown was hidden here. With an ironic grin, he recalled the tale of warring spirits he'd concocted for Turik and Shradin the first time he'd come out of the cave. It seemed he'd spoken the truth in spite of himself.

"Peace to you, spirit of this place," he rasped in Dravnian. "Your sanctuary will be properly cleansed."

The presence gathered around him for a moment, soothing away his pain and weariness. Then it was gone.

Shouldering the box, Seregil crawled slowly back up the tunnel. Turik and Timan were keeping watch at the opening when he stumbled out into the sunlight.

The old man clutched Seregil's arm wordlessly, tears of gratitude glittering in his rheumy eyes.

"He lives! The Aurënfaie's alive! Bring bandages," Turik called to the others, examining Seregil's hands with concern.

The cry passed from mouth to mouth and soon the whole village had gathered solemnly around them.

"Terrible sounds came out of the ground, then all was still," Retak told Seregil. "Timan said you had driven out the bad spirit, but he didn't know if you'd survived the ordeal. Tell us of your battle with the evil spirit!"

Seregil groaned inwardly. *Bilairy's Balls, they want another story!*

Climbing to his feet, he held up the box. "I've captured the evil spirit that troubled you. It's imprisoned here."

Round-eyed, the Dravnians regarded the battered wooden chest. Even the children did not venture to approach it. Filthy and exhausted, Seregil did his best to look like a victorious wizard as he mixed fact and fiction to best effect.

"In the time of Timan's ancestor, this evil thing came to your valley and invaded the spirit home, holding the true spirit prisoner and troubling those who entered the chamber. I found its secret lair and battled it there. It was a strong spirit and it fought mightily, as you can see."

The villagers' eyes grew rounder as they pressed around him to see what sort of marks a spirit left on a man.

"By my magic, and by the powers of sacred Aura and the true spirit of this place, I vanquished and captured it. Your spirit came to me, easing my wounds and asking that the sanctuary be cleansed so that your people may once again come to it in peace. There are bodies there now, victims of the evil one. You must not fear them. Take them away and burn them as is proper, so that their spirits can rest. This is no longer a place of evil."

The Dravnians cheered wildly as he paused to catch up with his own invention. By the time they'd settled down again, he was ready.

"If any man comes seeking the evil one, bring them to this place and tell them how Meringil, son of Solun and Nycanthi, mage of Aurënen, captured the evil spirit and took it away forever. Remember this day and tell the story to your children so that they will remember. Let no person among your clans forget that evil was cast out from here. And now I must go."

The villagers surged forward, imploring him to stay. Unvisited maidens wept with disappointment and one of Ekrid's daughters threw herself into his arms sobbing. Putting her gently aside, he gathered his gear and palmed the last of Nysander's painted wands from the pouch at his belt. He snapped it behind his back and the Dravnians shrank back in fear as the translocation vortex opened behind him. Waving a last farewell, he forced a smile as he stepped backward into emptiness.

• • •

Thero was on his way upstairs when a muffled crash halted him in his tracks. There was no doubt where the sound had come from; every door along the curved corridor—the bedchambers, the guest room—stood open except one.

The sitting-room door, with its magical wards and protections, was always kept shut unless Nysander was inside. Nonetheless, putting his ear to the door, Thero heard a low groan inside.

"Nysander!" he called, but his master was already hurrying down the tower stairs, robes flapping beneath his leather apron.

"There's someone in there," Thero exclaimed, gaunt face flushed with excitement.

Nysander opened the door and snapped his fingers at the nearest lamp. The wick flared up and by its light they saw Seregil sprawled in the middle of the room, his back arched awkwardly over the pack he wore, the strap of the battered wooden chest tangled around one leg. His eyes were closed, his face colorless beneath streaks of grime and blood.

"Get water, a basin, and linen. Hurry!" said Nysander, going to Seregil and pulling at the front of his coat.

Thero hurried off to fetch the required articles. When he returned a few moments later, Nysander was examining a raw wound on Seregil's chest. "How bad is it?" he asked.

"Not so bad as it looks," said Nysander, covering the wound with a cloth. "Give me a hand with these filthy clothes."

"What happened to him this time?" Thero asked, gingerly pulling off the unconscious man's boots. "He's got the same sort of preternatural stench he had when he came back—"

"Very similar. Fetch the things for a minor purification. And, Thero?"

Halfway out the door already, Thero paused, expecting some explanation.

"We shall not speak of this again."

"As you wish," Thero replied quietly.

Focused on Seregil, Nysander did not see the hot color that leapt into Thero's sallow cheeks beneath his thin beard, or the sudden angry set of his jaw.

Later, with Seregil asleep under Thero's watchful eye, Nysander paid his nightly visit to the lowest vault beneath the Orëska House. He was not the only one who wandered here late at night. Many of the older wizards preferred to pursue their research when the scholars and apprentices were out of the way. Proceeding on through the long passages and down stairways, he nodded to those he met, stopping now and then to chat. He'd never made any secret of his evening constitutionals. Had anyone over the years ever noticed that he seldom followed the same route twice? That there was always one point, one stretch of blank, innocent wall, which he never failed to pass?

And how many of these others, Nysander wondered as he went on, kept watch as he did over some secret charge?

Reaching the lowest level, he wended his way with more than even his usual caution through the maze of corridors to the place, though his carefully woven magicks kept all from perceiving the box he carried.

Satisfied that he was unobserved, he lowered his head, summoned a surge of power, and silently invoked the Spell of Passage. A sensation like a mountain wind passed through him, chilling him to the bone. Hugging the grimy box to his chest, he walked through the thick stonework of the wall and into the tiny chamber beyond.

5

ARRIVALS

Alec squinted as sunlight flashed off the polished festival gong under his arm. Shifting his grip, he struggled the rest of the way up the ladder braced against the front of the villa.

"Really, Sir Alec, this is not necessary. The servants always take care of these details!" Runcer dithered from the curb, clearly embarrassed by this display of labor but powerless to countermand it.

"I like to keep busy," Alec replied, undeterred.

He'd reluctantly resumed his public role at Wheel Street the day before. The Festival of Sakor began tonight and—Seregil or no Seregil—Sir Alec had to make an appearance. Runcer was stubbornly determined to defer to him as master of the house in Seregil's absence, a role he was acutely uncomfortable with. He detested being waited on, but every servant in the house seemed to take it as a personal affront every time he so much as fetched his own wash water or saddled a horse.

Grasping the wooden brace set into the wall, Alec slid the gong's leather hanging straps over it. They held and it swung gently in the morning breeze, a rectangular battle shield displaying the elaborate sunburst design of Sakor.

Runcer handed up a swath of black cloth and Alec draped it carefully over the shield face.

Similar gongs were being hung all across the city. Mourning Night, the longest of the year, began with solemn ceremonies at the Temple of Sakor. The symbolic passing of the old god would be enacted, and every fire in the city extinguished except for a single firepot guarded by the Queen and her family at the temple. At the first hint of dawn the following morning, the gongs would be uncovered and sounded to welcome the resurrected god as runners carried the new year's fire to every hearth. Similar versions of the ceremony would be carried out all over Skala.

He was halfway down the ladder when a rider clattered around a corner down the street. Recognizing Seregil's glossy Aurënfaie mare, Alec jumped down and ran to meet them.

Seregil reined Cynril to a walk and looked Alec over with a disapproving frown as he continued up the street. "Out in your shirtsleeves like a common laborer? What will the neighbors say?"

"I did remark upon it, my lord," Runcer commented blandly as they came up.

"I guess they'll say I'm more likely to do a lick of honest work than my fop of a guardian," Alec said with a laugh, too relieved to see Seregil safely home to care what anyone thought.

Wherever Seregil had been, he'd costumed himself carefully for the role of returning lord. His mud-spattered boots and gauntlets were of the finest chestnut-brown leather, his riding mantle lined with dark fur. Beneath it he wore a velvet surcoat, and tall pheasant feathers bobbed at a jaunty angle from the jeweled cockade of his cap.

"Ah well, we must forgive him his rough ways," Seregil said, throwing an arm around Alec's shoulders as they went inside. "These northern squire's sons are badly raised—too much honest labor in their youth. How's everything here?"

"Come see for yourself."

Inside, the main hall was still swarming with servants. The carpets were being rolled back in preparation for the night's dancing and fragrant garlands of plaited wheat and winter greenery festooned the walls. Rich aromas had been floating out from the kitchen since dawn. The feast after the ceremony would be cold, but well laid on.

"What about the lightwands?" asked Seregil as he sat to tug off his boots.

"They arrived from the Orëska House yesterday, my lord," Runcer informed him, hovering close at hand. "Nysander í Azusthra and Lady Magyana ä Rhioni have confirmed that they will contribute to the evening's entertainment again this year."

"Good. Any word from the Cavishes?"

"They are expected this afternoon, my lord. I prepared the upstairs guest chambers myself."

"We'll leave you to it, then. Come on, Alec, you can give me the news while I freshen up."

"Nysander's invited the Cavishes to sit with him," Alec told him as they went up the stairs to Seregil's room, adding wistfully, "I wish we could."

"I know, but Kylith's group is likely to be more informative. Besides, you need practice playing nobility."

Seregil's bedchamber overlooked the garden at the back of the villa. Unlike the other rooms, it was furnished in Aurënfaie style, with walls whitewashed rather than frescoed, and the furnishings were done in pale woods and simple lines. In contrast, the cushions, carpets, and hangings around the bed were vibrant with pattern and color.

The shutters had been opened and a fire crackled invitingly in the marble fireplace.

"Runcer's right, you know," he went on, tossing his cloak over a clothes chest and going to the fire. "It's not good for you to be seen out there in your shirtsleeves. When you're playing a role—"

Alec sighed. "You play it to the bone, I know, but—"

"No excuses. It's part of the game." Seregil leveled a gloved forefinger at him. "You know as well as I do that it doesn't matter at the Cockerel or half the time around here, but on a real job something like that could get you killed! When you play Sir Alec, you must *be* Sir Alec. Either live it from the heart, or stand outside yourself like a puppet master and direct every movement. You've seen me do it often enough."

Alec stared glumly out over the snow-dusted garden. "Yes, but I doubt I'll ever be as good at it as you."

Seregil let out an impatient snort. "Horseshit. That's what you said about swordplay, and look how you've come along. Besides, you're a natural actor when the role doesn't go against your stiff-necked, Dalnan yeoman's pride. Relax! Flow with the moment."

Seregil suddenly grabbed him by the arm and whirled him into an eccentric jig around the room. Alec hadn't even heard him approach. But he recovered swiftly and took the lead.

"But Sir Alec *is* a stiff-necked Dalnan yeoman," he said, laughing as he clomped through the steps of a country dance Beka and Elsbet had taught him.

"Wrong!" Grinning wickedly, Seregil yanked him into a formal pavan. "Sir Alec is stiff-necked Dalnan *gentry*. Besides, he should be picking up a few of Lord Seregil's airs along the way."

Alec leaned back in mock horror. "Maker's Mercy, anything but that!" Still gripping Seregil's gloved hand, his thumb found a ridge beneath the thin leather. Frowning, he felt at it. "What's this? A bandage?"

"It's nothing, just a few scrapes." Seregil stripped off the gloves and showed him thin strips of linen across each palm. "And what about you?" He turned Alec's left palm up and examined the scab there.

"I cut myself going over a wall the other night," Alec told him, letting Seregil's obvious evasion go without argument, knowing it would be futile to press him. "I got chased on the way home afterward, too, but I got away all right."

"Any idea who it was?"

"Footpads, probably. I didn't get much of a look at them."

"How many 'thems' were there?"

"Three, I think. I was too busy rabbiting to take count."

"Let's hear it."

Dropping into a chair by the fire, Alec launched into a well-rehearsed and somewhat embellished account of his escape down Silvermoon Street.

"That was quick thinking, using the palace guard for protection," said Seregil when he'd finished. "And speaking of the Palace, I've got something for you—a little thank you from the Queen and Klia, I think."

He took a small pouch from his coat and tossed it to Alec. Opening it, the boy found a heavy silver cloak brooch fashioned to look like a wreath of leafy branches surrounding a deep blue stone.

"Silver leaves." Alec smiled slightly as he admired it. "The first time I met Klia up in Cirna I was calling myself Aren Silverleaf."

"That's a good stone," Seregil remarked, looking at it over his shoulder. "You could get a fine horse for that, if you ever need to.

Just be sure not to let on where it came from, or why. We've got reputations to hide."

Illia Cavish burst into the hall like a small, happy hurricane just after midday. "Uncle Seregil! Alec! We're here!"

From the musicians' gallery, Seregil watched as she tackled Alec, who'd just come out of the dining room.

"I can stay up for the party this year because I'm six now," she announced, hugging Alec excitedly. "And I got new shoes and a real gown with a long skirt and two petticoats and— Where's Uncle Seregil?"

"I'm on my way," Seregil called. Going down the steep narrow stairs from the gallery, he strode across the hall and claimed a hug of his own. "Did you ride in from Watermead all by yourself, madame?"

Illia pulled a long face. "Mother's still being sick from the baby, so she had to ride in a cart with Arna and Eulis. Father and Elsbet and me all had to ride slow. But he let me come ahead when we got to your street. I'm the van soldier!"

"I think you mean vanguard," Alec corrected with a smile.

"That's what I said, silly. Do Elsbet and I get to sleep in the room next to yours, Uncle? The one with the dragon-shaped bed and the ladies painted on the walls?"

"Of course you do, so long as *you* don't pop out at the guests once you've been put to bed the way you did last year."

"Oh, I'm much too old for that now," she assured him, taking him and Alec by the hand and drawing them toward the door. "Come on, now. Father and Mother must be here by now."

Wheel Street was thick with traffic, but Seregil quickly spotted Micum's coppery head bobbing toward him through the press, followed by his second daughter and a covered cart driven by a pair of servant women. Old Arna spied him and waved.

"I see Illia found you," Micum said with a grin as they dismounted in front of the house.

Seregil embraced his old friend, and then Elsbet, dark and shy in her blue riding gown. "You're just in time. Alec's done all the work."

"We'd have been here sooner if I could have ridden," Kari complained, struggling from a nest of cushions and robes in the cart. Weeks of morning sickness had thinned her face, but the journey had put the challenging glint back in her dark eyes. Micum helped her down and she embraced Alec and Seregil happily.

Seregil eyed her rounding belly. "Breeding agrees with you, as usual."

"Don't tell her that before breakfast just yet," Micum warned.

Old Arna made a blessing sign in her mistress' direction. " 'The sicker the mother, the stronger the son.' "

Kari rolled her eyes behind the old woman's back. "We've heard that at least three times a day for the past month. Even if it's another girl, I expect the child will be born with a sword in her hand."

"Another Beka," Alec said, grinning.

"And what about you?" Seregil asked Elsbet. "Last I heard, you were going to stay on at the temple school."

"That's right. Thank you for recommending me. It's what I've always wanted to do."

"First Beka's commission with the Queen's Horse Guard, and now Elsbet a scholar." Kari slipped an arm about Elsbet's waist and gave Seregil a dark look. "Thanks to you, I'll be lucky to get any of my girls married off before they're old and grey."

"Scholars marry, Mama," Elsbet chided.

"I'll get married!" Illia chimed in, still clinging to Alec's hand. "I'm going to marry you, Alec, aren't I?"

The boy gave her a gallant bow. "If you still want me when you're grown up a beauty like your mother and sister."

Elsbet blushed noticeably at this. "How are you, Alec? Father told us you were hurt saving Klia."

"I'm pretty well healed, except for this," he replied, running a hand ruefully over his ragged hair. "Klia came out of it looking worse than I did."

"It was very—brave of you. To run into the fire like that, I mean," she stammered. Blushing more hotly than ever, she hurried after Arna into the house.

Alec turned to Kari with a perplexed look. "Is she all right?"

Kari slipped her arm through his with an enigmatic smile. "Oh, she's just turned fifteen, and you're a hero, that's all. Come along now, brave Sir Alec, and let's see what can be done about your hair. We don't want you looking like the tinker's boy in front of Lord Seregil's fine lady friends tonight."

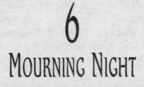

6
MOURNING NIGHT

Lady Kylith's tapestry-draped box commanded an excellent view into the Sakor Temple portico. Seregil and Alec reached the Temple Precinct an hour before sunset and found their hostess and six other guests already chatting over dainties and wine.

It was a frosty evening and everyone's breath puffed out in little clouds as they talked. All were warmly swathed in black cloaks or robes out of respect for the occasion, but gold and jewels caught the light on wrists and circlets.

"Ah, now our little party is complete!" Kylith rose smiling to kiss Seregil.

He returned the kiss with genuine affection. They'd been lovers for a time years ago, and friends ever since. Kylith must be nearing fifty now, he realized, but time had refined both her famous beauty and wit.

All of these were in full force as she turned to Alec, still hanging shyly back. "And you and I meet again under far more pleasant circumstances, Sir Alec. I trust no one will be arresting Lord Seregil tonight?"

Alec executed a perfect bow. "I believe he's rescheduled all arrests until tomorrow, my lady."

Well done, Sir Alec, Seregil thought to himself with a smile.

From the corner of his eye, he saw several of the others exchange discreet glances. Most of Rhíminee knew he'd been taken from his villa in chains only a few weeks before. Kylith had deftly removed any tension surrounding the incident by making light of it.

"Seregil, you'll sit there by Lord Admiral Nyreidian," she said, waving him to a seat beside a portly, black-bearded noble. "He's overseeing the outfitting of the Queen's privateer fleet and I know you'll want to hear all about it. Sir Alec, you sit here between us so that we may renew our acquaintance. But first you must be properly introduced—Lord Admiral Nyreidian í Gorthos, Lady Tytiana ë Reva and Lady Breena ë Ursil of the Queen's court, Sir Arius í Rafael, and my very dear friend Lady Yriel ë Nikiria."

Pausing, she placed her hand over that of a uniformed woman on her right. "And this is Captain Julena ë Isai of the White Hawk Infantry, the newest addition to our little salon."

Seregil eyed the captain with discreet interest; she was rumored to be Kylith's latest paramour.

"My friends, you all know Lord Seregil í Korit," she continued. "And this charming young man is Lord Seregil's protégé, Sir Alec í Gareth of Ivywell. His late father was a knight of Mycena, I believe."

Alec's spurious pedigree elicited the hoped-for lack of interest. Leaving him to stumble charmingly along through Kylith's courtly flirtations, Seregil turned his attention to the other guests, where more interesting game was afoot.

"I expect war will be a relief for Phoria," Lady Tytiana was saying. As Mistress of the Queen's Wardrobe, she was a valuable and generally reliable gossip. "She's still under a bit of a cloud, you know, after that horrible business with the Vicegerent's suicide— Oh, Lord Seregil, forgive me. I didn't mean to be indelicate."

"Not at all, dear lady." Seregil flicked a crease from his black mantle. "My name *was* cleared, so my honor is no more blemished than usual."

A ripple of laughter went round the little circle. He'd cultivated his reputation as a charmingly dissipated exile carefully over the years. While his distant relation to the royal family granted him access to most of the more fashionable salons, it was generally supposed that his foreign birth and dilettante ways kept him safely outside the complex intrigues of the city. As a result, he was taken lightly but told a great deal.

"As I was saying," Tytiana went on, "I shouldn't wonder that she'd be relieved to go off to war. Nothing like a few victories to improve one's popularity. And just between ourselves, Phoria could use some goodwill among the people, even without that other unpleasantness. An heir apparent with no offspring is always—awkward."

"She's a fine cavalry commander, though," said Captain Julena.

Admiral Nyreidian leaned back and laced his fingers over his considerable paunch, "True, but she'll be at a disadvantage unless the Plenimarans are foolish enough to attempt overrunning Mycena. Plenimar is a naval power, always has been. I've advised the Queen so and she agrees. The lower city defenses are being built up as we speak."

"Only yesterday I overheard Queen Idrilain ordering two hundred wagonloads of fine red clay from Piorus to slake the slopes below the citadel," Lady Breena chimed in. "That's not been done since her great-grandmother's day."

"Surely they wouldn't be so bold as to attack Rhíminee directly?" Seregil ventured over his wine.

Nyreidian cast a rather patronizing look his way. "They've done it before."

"So you are preparing to meet them on their own terms. It must be an enormous undertaking."

"I believe I've seen every sailor, fisherman, and pirate that ever sailed between here and the Strait of Bal!" the admiral replied. "The harbor's alive with them. And investors, too. Privateering is a lucrative venture. Have you considered backing a vessel, Lord Seregil?"

"Sounds like an interesting mix of patriotism and profit. Perhaps I should look into it."

"Vessels are getting scarce already, I must warn you. Every shipbuilder in Skala has all the work he can handle, refitting old ships and building new. But the real trick is to find a decent captain."

"And yet war has not been officially declared. How can the Queen send out privateers without giving provocation? Surely she doesn't mean to precipitate a conflict?"

Nyreidian stiffened perceptibly. "I'm sure our Queen does nothing without the best interests of Skala in mind."

"But of course," murmured Seregil. "The fact that the Queen has entrusted you with this undertaking is ample proof of the gravity of such measures."

Alec breathed a sigh of relief when Kylith turned her attention to her other guests. His repertoire of invented history was slim and he was out of his depth for small talk. Luckily, no one else seemed particularly interested in him.

Seregil was still busy with the fat admiral, so he leaned his elbows on the rail to watch the spectacle unfolding before him.

The tiers of viewing boxes where he sat stood at an angle on the south side of the square, just in front of the Dalnan temple grove. Across the square another set of tiers partially obscured the fountain courts and delicate, brightly colored archways of the Temple of Astellus. The Temple of Illior was hidden by the back wall of the box to the east.

Cordoned-off pathways between the four temples quartered the broad square. Black-robed festival goers were already packing the open areas and crowding into the courtyards and porticoes of the other temples. Gulls wheeled overhead, mingling with flights of brown doves from the Dalnan grove.

Before him, the black Temple of Sakor stood massive and stark against a riotous sunset. Broad bars of light spilled out between the square pillars of the portico, silhouetting the gongs that hung between them.

Inside stood an altar of polished black stone. A great fire burned on it, illuminating the huge golden shield that hung suspended just behind. This, Seregil had explained earlier, was called the Aegis of Sakor. It was twenty feet high and its sunburst device was set with hundreds of smooth-polished rubies that seemed to pulse with life in the flickering firelight.

An honor guard was massed in formation on the broad stairs in front of the temple; somewhere in those faceless ranks Beka Cavish was standing watch with her regiment. He envied her just a little. The soldier's life seemed an uncomplicated one to him; no pretending, no disguise—just honor, duty, and the bravery to stand by your comrades in battle.

"I suppose they do not celebrate the Sakor Festival with such display in Mycena?" Lady Kylith remarked, breaking in on his thoughts.

"No, my lady," Alec replied, raising his voice for Seregil's benefit. "Even the Harvest Home at the end of Rhythin isn't a patch on this."

"Lord Seregil will have explained to you, I am sure, about the extinguishing of the flames?"

"Yes. I imagine this will be an uncomfortable night."

"The soldier's vigil is very weary." Kylith cast a regretful glance in Julena's direction and Alec guessed the captain would be going back on duty soon. "But for the rest of us, it's a merry time. Moonlit parties, blind games, and chases. It's a fine night for lovers, as well. They say half the people born in Rhíminee can count back from their birth to this night."

Her perfume drifted over him as she leaned closer. "And who will be keeping you warm in the darkness, hm?"

A sudden fanfare from the temple spared him the necessity of a reply.

A hush fell over the crowd as a long procession of priests filed out from the interior of the temple. Chanting and playing reed flutes, sistrums, deep-throated horns, and timbrels, they formed themselves into two ranks flanking the Aegis. The skirling music had an ancient, mournful sound.

"The Song of Passing, sung in the original Konic tongue," Seregil whispered. "Most of this ceremony dates back at least a thousand years."

At the end of the chant, an ornately robed figure was carried forward on a litter, face covered by a golden sun mask, an unsheathed broadsword lying across his knees.

"That's the oldest of the Sakor priests, dressed to represent the dying god," Seregil went on. "He brings the great Sword of Gërilain."

"Was it really hers?" Alec whispered. Gërilain was the first of Skala's hereditary queens instituted by the prophecy of Illior six centuries before.

"Yes. The Queen's reinvested with it each year."

When Old Sakor had been positioned in front of the altar, a priest stepped forward and addressed him in the same ancient tongue.

"She's imploring Sakor not to abandon the people," Seregil interpreted. "This next part goes on and on, but the gist of it is that

Sakor appoints the Queen as their guardian and gives her the sacred firepot and sword."

As predicted, Sakor's reply took some time. The lower portion of the sun mask was constructed to amplify his voice, which was rather thin and creaky. When this dialogue was completed, horns sounded and the grand procession began.

Contingents of priests emerged from the other temples, each bearing a figure representing their patron deity on a litter.

The Dalnans came first, with Valerius playing Dalna. Seated beneath an arch of laurel and ivy, the irascible drysian was uncharacteristically resplendent in a green robe heavily embroidered with gold and carried a ceremonial staff wrought in ivory and gold. Someone had managed to tame his wild hair into some semblance of order beneath his circlet, but his beard bristled as aggressively as ever as he glared out over the crowd.

"I'm no Dalnan, of course, but I don't think Valerius presents a particularly comforting figure as the Maker," Seregil murmured, eliciting chuckles of assent from several of the other guests, including Alec.

Astellus would serve as Sakor's guide on his journey to the Isle of the Dawn. A plump blond priestess dressed in a simple blue and white tunic and broad-brimmed hat played this role, complete with wayfarer's staff and wallet. Grey-backed gulls, living emblems of the Traveler, rose up from the fountain courts of the temple and circled overhead as she was carried forth.

Illior was also being played by a woman. She sat stiffly in her flowing white gown and serene golden mask, right palm raised to display the elaborate circular emblem that covered her palm.

The three groups met at the center of the square to await the final contingent. Horns sounded again. A squadron of cavalry in ceremonial scarlet and black advanced from the entrance of the Temple Precinct, followed by the royal family.

"Is that her? Is that the Queen?" Alec whispered, craning for a better look.

"That's her."

Grey-haired and solemn, Idrilain sat her charger like the warrior she was. Her golden breastplate was emblazoned with an upraised sword and the crescent of Illior; an empty scabbard hung at her side.

With her rode the Consort Evenir, her second and much younger husband. Behind the royal couple came her sons and daughters. Among these rode Klia, resplendent in the dress uniform of the Queen's Horse.

Alec's hand rose to the silver brooch holding the ornamental cloak at his shoulder as he watched her in the distance. Until now he'd seen her only as another cheerful, mud-spattered soldier, someone who'd treated him like a comrade, never standing on ceremony. Watching her now—among her true kind and against the pageantry of the ceremony—was like seeing a stranger.

The procession advanced at a stately pace to the steps of the temple, where Idrilain dismounted and strode up to stand opposite Old Sakor and the other priests, her consort and children behind her. From this point, the ritual proceeded in the modern tongue.

Idrilain's voice was clear and steady as she spread her arms and performed a chant hailing Sakor as Protector of the Hearth and the Sword of Peace.

"Let not the darkness come upon us!" she cried at its conclusion.

The massed crowd took up the cry, repeating it in a great voice until Valerius stepped forward and raised his staff in both hands. When the crowd quieted again, he sang the Song of Dalna, his deep, resonant voice carrying well in the open air.

Alec knew this song well. When the crowd repeated the closing line, "The Maker has made all, and nothing can be lost in the hand of the Maker," he joined in gladly, ignoring the glances he attracted from Kylith's other guests.

Astellus and Illior helped Old Sakor to his feet and the assembled priests commenced a low keen.

"Who shall keep watch?" the priests of Sakor sang. "Who shall guard the Flame?"

Masked Illior answered, reciting the revelation of the Afran Oracle. "So long as a daughter of Thelátimos' line defends and rules, Skala shall never be subjugated."

The Queen stepped forward and was exhorted by Old Sakor to keep watch over her people through the long night and the new year to follow. Bowing solemnly, she pledged herself and her generations to the guardianship of Skala and was given the Sword of Gërilain and a large firepot. When she turned, holding both aloft, the crowd erupted into cheers of assent.

The last of the day's light was fading from the western sky as two priests led out a black bull. Handing the firepot to Phoria, Idrilain raised the sword in her right hand and placed her left on the animal's brow, pressing gently as she spoke the ritual greeting.

The bull snorted and twisted its neck, nicking the edge of her mantle with the tip of one horn.

A restless murmur rippled through the crowd like wind across a barley field; an unwilling victim was a poor omen.

The animal showed no further sign of resistance, however, as the priests pulled its head back and Idrilain slashed its throat. Dark blood spurted out, steaming in the cold air, and the animal collapsed without a struggle. Idrilain extended the blade to Old Sakor, who dipped a finger in the blood and anointed his forehead and hers.

"Speak to your people, O Sakor!" she intoned. "You who pass away from all living things and return renewed. What is your prophecy?"

"Let's see what they've come up with this year," someone murmured.

"You mean it's not real?" Alec whispered to Seregil, rather shocked.

Seregil gave him a hint of the crooked smile. "Yes and no. Divinations are gathered for months from all the major temples around Skala. They vary in form from year to year, but they're generally quite supportive of current policy."

Standing before the Aegis, Sakor faced the people and raised his hands.

But before he could speak, a sudden wind gusted through the square, billowing robes and snatching at cloaks and scouring dust and dead leaves up in little whirlwinds. Banners whipped loose from the fronts of boxes. Shield gongs swung on their long chains, clashing ominously against the pillars of the temple.

Startled from their evening roosts, gulls and doves burst into the air again in a flurry of wings, only to be met by scores of ravens. Swooping out of the surrounding gloom as mysteriously as the wind that bore them, the black birds attacked in a frenzy, stabbing with thick beaks, tearing with taloned feet.

The spectators below watched helplessly as black wings beat against white or brown; upturned faces were spattered with blood and sticky scraps of feathers. Then startled cries rang out as broken bodies plummeted down around them.

In the temple, Idrilain stood with sword drawn, fending off scores of ravens that dove at the sacrificial bull. Phoria and her brothers and sisters leapt to her aid, driving the carrion birds off.

Beside them, Valerius laid about with his staff. Even at this distance Seregil and Alec could see the crackling white nimbus that glowed dangerously around its ivory head. The Illioran priestess, still inscrutable behind her mask, raised her hand again and a brilliant, multihued flash blazed out, leaving inert mounds of black feathers scattered in its wake. Soldiers closest to the temple ran back up the steps to assist the Queen, while others tried to maintain order as thousands wailed and screamed and sought to flee.

A thick cloud of ravens circled the square now, diving and slashing like hawks. Others flocked boldly on railings and temple pediments. One large bird flapped down to perch on the edge of Kylith's box and seemed to regard Alec thoughtfully with one black, unblinking eye.

Seregil raised his hand in a warding sign and Alec saw his lips move, although it was impossible to make out the words over the chaos around them. The raven uttered a mocking croak and flapped away.

Then, as quickly as they'd come, the baneful black horde retreated, pursued by the surviving gulls. The doves had been no match for their attackers; soft brown bodies lay scattered around the precinct by the dozens.

As the noise of the birds subsided, a new and ominous sound boomed forth from the temple.

The Aegis of Sakor, untouched by any hand, rang with a low, shivering roar. In front of it, the flames of the alter fire flared from yellow to deep bloodred.

Four times the Aegis sounded, and then four times again.

"Hear me, my people!" cried Idrilain. "Sakor speaks, sounding a call on the Aegis itself. Attend to the prophecy!"

The multitude stood motionless as Old Sakor was helped forward again, swaying visibly as he raised a trembling hand.

"Hear, O people of Skala, the word of Sakor," he called in his reedy old man's voice. "Make strong your walls, and let every sword be whetted. Guard well the harvest and build strong ships. Look to the east, O people of Skala. From thence comes thine enemy—" He paused, and the trembling seemed to worsen. "From thence—"

He sagged heavily against Valerius for a moment, then straightened and took a step forward unaided. In a voice of startling clarity, he cried out, "Prepare you in the light, and in the shadow. From thence comes the Eater of Death!"

"The what—?" Alec looked to Seregil again, but found him white-faced and grim, one gloved hand clenching the side of the rail where the raven had perched.

"Seregil, what's wrong?"

His friend sat up abruptly, as if waking from an evil dream, and warned him off with a discreet but emphatic hand signal.

"We have heard your word, O Sakor!" said the Queen, speaking into the silence that still gripped the crowd. "We shall be prepared!"

Another roar of acclaim went up as Old Sakor was carried down the stairs of the temple to begin the long march to the waterfront in the lower city. There, accompanied by Astellus, he would set sail ostensibly for the Isle of the Dawn to be reborn and return on the morrow in the guise of a much younger priest.

The altar fire dwindled and went out and a hundred deep-throated horns sounded from the roof of the temple, signaling for every fire in the city to be extinguished.

The remaining priests joined the procession while the Queen took her place before the altar to begin the sacred vigil.

"What a remarkable performance!" said Lady Yriel with an uneasy laugh. "I think they rather overdid it this year, don't you?"

"Most impressive," Kylith agreed lightly as servants appeared at the door of the box with lightstones on long wands to assist their departure. "But I suspect Lord Seregil has something equally impressive planned for us at his gathering. Will you two share my coach?"

Seregil rose and bent over her hand. "Thank you, but I think we'll wait here until the crowd thins a bit, then ride back."

"Games in the dark, eh?" She brushed his cheek with her lips, then Alec's. "I'll meet you at Wheel Street."

Seregil sat motionless for some moments after the others had departed, resting his elbows on the rail.

"What's the 'Eater of Death'?" asked Alec uneasily. "It sounded like a threat, or a warning."

"I'm sure it was," Seregil muttered, gazing down into the square. It was full dark now, and the moon and stars shed pale brilliance over the city, casting the world into sharp contrasts of silvery light and inky shadow. Lightwands bobbed here and there in the hands of those wealthy enough to afford them, and faint laughter and cries of "Praise the Flame!" echoed up to them as people jostled each other in the darkness.

Something in his friend's face made Alec still more uneasy. "Any idea what the priest meant by it?" he asked.

Seregil pulled his hood up against the night's chill as he rose to go. Alec couldn't see his face as he replied, "I can't say that I do."

7

AN INFORMATIVE EVENING

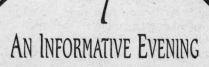

The Wheel Street house was already full of music by the time they returned. Alec handed his dark cloak to a servant at the entrance and followed Seregil into the hall.

A number of guests were already enjoying the wine and food. Each had been presented with a brightly ribboned lightwand upon arrival and these provided a cool, shifting light as people danced or strolled about the room.

A flurry of applause greeted them as Runcer gravely announced their arrival from his station by the door.

"Welcome to my home on this dark, cold night!" Seregil called out. "For those of you who've not yet met my companion, allow me to present Sir Alec í Gareth of Ivywell."

Alec made a graceful bow and quickly scanned the room for familiar faces. Kylith's party was there, but there was no sign yet of Nysander or the Cavishes. In a far corner, however, he spotted a knot of officers in the green and white of the Queen's Horse Guard. Klia's friend and fellow officer, Captain Myrhini, saluted him with her lightwand from their midst and Alec waved back, wondering if Beka was with her.

He was just heading over to find out when

Seregil slipped a hand under his arm and steered him off toward a group of nobles.

"Time to play the gracious hosts."

Together, they made a circuit of the room, moving smoothly from one conversation to another, most of which centered around the omens at the ceremony.

"I thought they rather overdid the thing this year," sniffed a young nobleman introduced as Lord Melwhit. "What doubt is there that war is coming? Preparations have been going on since summer."

A grave, blond woman turned from a conversation with Admiral Nyreidian and greeted Seregil in Aurënfaie.

"*Ysanti maril Elustri*, Melessandra ä Marana," Seregil returned warmly. "Allow me to present Sir Alec. Lady Melessandra and her uncle, Lord Torsin, are the Skalan envoys to Aurënen."

"*Ysanti bëk kir*, my lady," Alec said with a bow.

"*Ysanti maril Elustri*, Sir Alec," she returned. "Lord Seregil is instructing you in his native language, I see. There are so few nowadays who speak it well."

"And fewer still who speak it so well as you, dear lady," added Seregil.

"It's a pretty language, if one can manage it," Nyreidian rumbled. "I wouldn't dare attempt it in front of you, Lord Seregil. I'm told my pronunciation is grotesque."

"It is!" Melessandra agreed, laughing. "Forgive our interruption, Lord Seregil, but we were just debating whether the portents at the temple tonight were genuine. Would you care to venture the Aurënfaie view?"

Alec watched with interest as Seregil struck a thoughtful pose.

"Well, to question the omens' veracity would be tantamount to casting doubt on the Oracle itself, wouldn't you say?"

She gave the admiral a pointed look. "Many would not hesitate to do so."

Seregil tactfully changed the subject. "I understand your uncle accompanied the remains of Corruth í Glamien back to Virésse?"

"Yes, and allow me to offer my sympathies for the loss of your kinsman," said Melessandra. "It must have been a terrible shock in the midst of your own difficulties."

"Thank you. The reports given by the Queen's agents who found him were chilling, to say the least. Yet some good may come of it. Have you heard what the council's reaction was in Aurënen?"

Melessandra rolled her eyes. "Complete uproar. You know the old guard still contends that Skala is accountable for the actions of the Lerans. Yet there are those among the younger members who argue more and more for an end to isolationism. Adzriel ä Illia is one of the chief proponents for reconciliation."

"Illia?" asked Alec, pricking up his ears at the familiar name.

"Certainly," Seregil said, giving him a level look that warned discreetly against questions. "What else would it be? Unless you're confusing her with Adzriel ä Olien again?"

"Oh—yes. I suppose I must be," Alec managed, wondering what blunder he'd committed this time.

"Family names are so much simpler in Mycena," Seregil went on lightly. "Poor Alec is still struggling with all our lengthy patronymics and matronymics and lineages."

Melessandra appeared sympathetic. "It must be overwhelming if you're not born to it. But there's Lord Geron and I must speak with him at once. *Erísmai*."

She gave Alec a last, rather puzzled look, then strolled away accompanied by Nyreidian and the others.

"I said something wrong, didn't I?" Alec whispered hurriedly, before some other guest descended on them.

"My fault," Seregil replied with a slight smile. "If I'd been here this last week I'd have thought to prepare you better. Illia was my mother's name. My eldest sister, Adzriel ä Illia, was recently made a member of the Iia'sidra."

"Sister?"

Never, in all the time Alec had known him, had Seregil mentioned his family, or almost anything else about his past in Aurënen. Alec had come to assume that his friend was as much an orphan as himself.

"And *eldest*? How many do you have?"

"Four, actually. I was the only boy, and the youngest," Seregil replied somewhat tersely.

"Little brother Seregil?" Alec smothered a grin as his entire perception of his friend subtly shifted. He could sense the old barriers going up again, however, and prudently changed the subject. "It sounds like the Skalans want Aurënen as allies again, like they were in the Great War."

"They do, but bad blood over Corruth will get in the way. Our recent discovery may make things worse rather than better, at least for now."

"But it's been almost three hundred years since Corruth disappeared."

"Remember who we're talking about, Alec. Many of the most powerful people on the Iia'sidra were his friends and contemporaries. They haven't forgotten the reception he received from the Skalans when he married their queen, or his suspicious disappearance after her death. If Lera hadn't had the poor sense to leave her half sister Corruthesthera alive, there might have been war between the two nations then. As for a new alliance, I'm afraid that may depend more on the Plenimarans in the end. If they join with Zengat—"

"Oh, Lord Seregil! There you are!"

A gaggle of young nobles crowded noisily around them, wreathed in expectant grins.

"We thought you'd never come home," chided a young woman, wrapping her arm through Seregil's. "You missed my autumn revel this year, you know."

Seregil pressed a hand dramatically to his heart. "As I stood on a rolling deck under a full red moon that night, my thoughts were all of you. Can you forgive me?"

"It was a crescent moon; I recall it perfectly. But I'll grant you a conditional pardon if you'll introduce me to your new friend," she fluttered, looking boldly across at Alec, who'd been crowded to the edge of the circle.

Alec smiled his way through an onslaught of complex introductions, noting as he did so that his polite greetings were not always returned with the same grace. A number of them, in fact, were decidedly cool.

Seregil hesitated as he came to a handsome, auburn-haired dandy surrounded by an entourage of admirers. "Forgive me, sir, I don't believe I've had the pleasure?"

The man gave an elaborate bow. "Pelion í Eirsin Heileus Quirion of Rhíminee, dear sir."

"Not the acclaimed actor, who just played 'Ertis' at the Tirarie?" gasped Seregil.

The man puffed visibly. "The same, my lord. I pray you'll forgive my intrusion, but my companions insisted."

"On the contrary, I'm delighted! I hope you'll let me know when you next perform. By all reports, you're the next Kroseus."

"I've been fortunate, " Pelion demurred modestly.

"And well patronized," a man beside him announced. "Do you know that his current role was written specifically for him?"

"We knew you wouldn't mind," a sallow youth confided smugly to Seregil. "Poor Pelion is in love, you see, and his lady friend may turn up here tonight. It's all very tragic and impossible. But we've got another treat for you. Donaeus has composed the most cunningly subtle epos in twenty-three parts. It's a marvelous piece of art!"

Seregil turned to the poet in question, a petulant-looking giant in worn velvets. "Twenty-three parts? What a monumental undertaking."

"It's glorious," a girl effused. "It's all about the death of Arshelol and Boresthia, but done in the most original fashion. And of course, he'll need a patron. You really must hear it."

"Donaeus, read it for him at once!" cried the sallow one. "No one appreciates the new verse styles so well as Lord Seregil. I'm sure Sir Alec could spare him for a bit."

The slight was not lost on Alec. There were a few suppressed titters, but he maintained his composure.

"Go on, by all means." He smiled, locking gazes with his ostensible rival. "The significance of poetry has always eluded me. Honest ballads and sword fights are more to my taste."

"Well then, let's go up to the library," said Seregil, giving Alec an amused wink as he ushered them upstairs.

Turning, Alec nearly collided with Myrhini and Beka Cavish, who'd drifted over with their uniformed comrades.

"Arrogant little turds, aren't they?" Beka muttered, glowering after the poet's entourage. "I run into a bit of that myself now and then."

"What could they have against me?" Alec burst out, not knowing whether to be more amused or insulted.

"Nothing, except that you had the poor taste to be born north of the Cirna Canal."

"There are always a few like that." Myrhini shrugged, then skillfully snagged a tray of wine cups from a passing server. "Scattering a few teeth usually quiets 'em down. In your case though, it's more likely just whey-blooded jealousy. There's more than a few among that set who'd like to be in your boots."

She paused to run an eye over him. "You're looking fitter than last time I saw you. Klia's at the Vigil, and sends her regards. I go on duty in a few hours, but felt honor-bound to assess the new recruit here, seeing as how she's under my command. Rider Beka tells me you've crossed blades a time or two— But here's someone else we know!"

"Valerius of Colath, Drysian of the First Order and High Priest of the Temple of Dalna at Rhíminee," Runcer announced.

Valerius strode into the room still clad in his ceremonial robe and circlet, though he'd exchanged the ivory staff for his old wooden one.

"The blessing of Dalna be on this house and those within it," he intoned, thumping the floor.

Alec hurried forward to greet him. "Welcome. Seregil just went upstairs to hear a poet, but he should be back soon."

The drysian let out an inelegant snort. "That fool Donaeus, no doubt, spouting his doggerel in twenty-three fatuous farts? He must still be scratching around for a patron. He read bits of the mess at Lady Arbella's banquet last week. Fairly took away my appetite. If he corners Seregil with the whole of it, we're not likely to get him back before dawn."

"Maybe Alec should go rescue him," suggested Beka.

"No, leave him. Serves him right for encouraging that pack of pedantic buffoons. What knavery have you two been up to these days? Learning swordplay, I hear, Alec?" The drysian lowered his voice to a confidential rumble. "You'll need it, considering the company you've fallen into."

"And look at you!" he exclaimed, glowering at Beka. "Running off to join regiments instead of getting married like a good Dalnan girl? This young fellow here is about your age, isn't he?"

"Leave off, you," Myrhini cried, laughing as Beka shifted uncomfortably. "She's the best rider I've had this year and I don't want to lose her to the hearth."

"Valerius!" Seregil called as he came down the stairs, apparently having escaped from the poets on his own. "Did you get Old Sakor safely launched?"

Valerius chuckled. "There's considerable chop on the harbor tonight. Poor old Morantiel was as green as a squash before they left the mooring, but I suspect he'll survive."

"I thought he sounded rather unsteady during the prophecy," Seregil remarked casually, signaling for a wine server.

"After all these years of shamming, I imagine it was a bit of a shock when something mystical actually occurred."

"Then you believe it was genuine?"

Valerius raised a bristling eyebrow. "You know as well as I do it was. I don't know what that 'Eater of Death' business was all about, but I didn't like the feel of those ravens."

At the door, Runcer stepped forward again and announced, "Nysander í Azusthra Hypirius Meksandor Illandi, High Thaumaturgist of the Third Orëska, with the Lady Magyana ä Rhioni Methistabel Tinuva Ylani, High Thaumaturgist of the Third Orëska. And Sir Micum Cavish of Watermead, with Dame Kari and daughters Elsbet and Illia."

Nysander and Magyana, normally the least ostentatious wizards of the Orëska, had put on the rich ceremonial robes befitting their status in honor of the occasion. Behind them, the Cavishes were as splendidly rigged out as any lord in the room. Illia clung to her mother's hand, squirming with excitement in her new dress. Elsbet looked poised and solemn in burgundy velvet.

"Didn't you invite Thero?" Alec whispered teasingly to Seregil.

"I *always* invite Thero! But watch. We're in for a treat."

At his signal, the musicians stilled their instruments. The other guests stepped back as Nysander escorted Magyana to the center of the room. With a slight nod to their host, he waved a hand about in a swift, careless gesture and the painted walls sprang to life.

The high chamber was frescoed from floor to ceiling to imitate a forest glade. The branches of life-size oaks hung with flowering vines extended across the vaulted ceiling overhead. Between their grey trunks distant vistas of mountain and sea were visible. Even the stone gallery at the back of the room, where the musicians softly played, was carved and latticed to resemble a leafy bower.

At Nysander's command, golden light from some unseen sun glowed across the scene. A soft breeze stirred around the room, carrying with it the scent of flowers and warm earth overlaid with a hint of the distant painted sea. The painted trees stirred in the breeze, dappling shadows across the floor. Painted birds left their places and fluttered through the branches, filling the air with song.

A murmur of delight greeted the display, but the wizards were not finished. Magyana drew a crystal wand from her sleeve and wove the tip of it in the air, conjuring a perfect sphere of iridescent light the size of a pomegranate.

"Come, my lord." She smiled, motioning to Seregil. "As host, the honor belongs to you."

"An honor which I in turn bestow on Sir Alec on this, his first Mourning Night with us."

Amid a flurry of applause, Alec followed Magyana's whispered instructions and reached out a finger as if to burst a child's soap bubble.

At his touch the sphere burst in a brilliant scintilla of light. Seconds later the thud of hooves against turf sounded near the gallery as a herd of white deer materialized in the painted forest and galloped once around the room before settling to graze near the dining-room archway. Rainbow-winged serpents swooped up from a painted cavern, singing with beautiful voices. Winged sprites and willow branch maidens peeped shyly from tree trunks.

Laughing and clapping delightedly, the guests spun around to take in the spectacle. Illia pulled loose from Kari and ran to Beka, leaping into her sister's arms.

"It's magic, Beka! Real wizard magic! And you've got your uniform. You're a horse guard!"

Beka hugged her back, grinning. "That's just what I am."

"We must have proper music!" cried Seregil. "Fiddlers, give us 'The Shepherd's Idyll'!"

The musicians set to with a will and couples paired for the sprightly dance.

"Here you are!" Kari exclaimed, coming to embrace her eldest daughter.

"She was afraid we wouldn't see you before tomorrow," Micum explained. "She's been fretting about it all afternoon."

"Oh, I was not," snapped his wife. "Turn around, girl. Let me see all of you!"

"Thero was otherwise engaged, I see," Seregil remarked with a sly glance at Nysander.

"Ah, hello, Valerius," said Nysander, escorting Magyana over to them again. "You acquitted yourself bravely in the sanctuary this evening. Were the ravens saying anything intelligible?"

"We were just discussing that," the drysian replied. "Heavy-handed as the Sakorans are with their 'oracles,' they weren't responsible for the birds, or that business with the Aegis, if I'm any judge."

"It was unquestionably magic of some sort," mused Magyana. "It may be a portent from Sakor, but it bodes ill nonetheless."

"It certainly bears looking into," agreed Nysander, "but just now I cannot seem to resist the music. Do you think we have a dance or two left in us, my dear?"

"I think they'll have to chain your feet together to keep them still when they bury you," Magyana replied with a twinkle.

Valerius watched with gruff fondness as the pair danced away. "Ridiculous, that Orëskan celibacy of hers. Those two should have married centuries ago." Then something else appeared to catch his eye and a wry grin spread in the depths of his black beard. "Now *there's* someone I didn't expect to see here tonight. And just look who he's with!"

"Ylinestra ä Maranial Wisthra Ylinena Erind, Sorceress of Erind," announced Runcer. "And Thero í Procepios Bynardin Chylnir Rhíminee, Wizard of the Second Order, of the Third Orëska."

"Well, well!" murmured Seregil.

Thero did look uncharacteristically sanguine, standing at the head of the chamber with Ylinestra on his arm. The sorceress' silk gown glittered with jeweled beading and the bodice, fashionable in the extreme, showed pink half-crescent hints of nipple beneath the heavy necklace of pearl and jet she wore over her bared breasts. Her ebony hair was caught back in a similar jeweled web, exposing a graceful white neck.

Seregil propelled Alec forward with a gentle nudge. "Come on, Sir Alec. Let's greet our illustrious guests."

"Welcome to my home, lady," he said, stepping up to kiss her hand.

"Thank you, Lord Seregil," she replied with a cool nod. "And this must be your new companion I've been hearing so much about?"

"Alec of Ivywell," Alec told her, wondering with sudden discomfort whether she recalled their first brief, tempestuous meeting soon after his arrival at the Orëska House. If she did, however, she gave no sign of it. Extending her hand, she enveloped him with a heart-stopping smile. "Ah, a Mycenian. How delightful."

She clearly meant for him to kiss her hand and he bent dutifully over it. A faint perfume rose in his nostrils, subtle yet strangely compelling. Her hand, so warm and soft, lingered in his, and as he raised his head, his eyes swept across her breasts to her lovely violet eyes with a studied enjoyment he wouldn't have imagined himself capable of. Still she held him, and her low-pitched voice sent an unfamiliar tingle through his body when she spoke.

"Nysander speaks so warmly of you. I hope that we may know one another better."

"I'm honored, lady," Alec replied, his voice sounding distant in his ears. She withdrew her hand at last and the world returned to normal.

"Good evening," Thero said stiffly, looking somewhat less than pleased to be there.

"Forgive Thero's bad grace," Ylinestra murmured, once more wrapping Alec in the warm embrace of her eyes. "He is here only as a favor to me, I fear, and is being quite sulky. Come, Thero, perhaps wine will improve your disposition."

As he escorted her into the throng, the actor Pelion stepped into their path with an elaborate bow, which Thero evaded with a curt and proprietary nod. Pelion fell back a pace, then followed Ylinestra with lovesick eyes.

"Ah, so that's the actor's hopeless love," Seregil noted with a smirk. "He's certainly got some competition tonight. And if Thero gets any stiffer, he's likely to fall over and break."

"She was kind of abrupt with you, I thought," observed Alec.

"Well, I'm not exactly her type. Evidently you are."

Alec colored warmly. Her perfume still clung to his fingers. "I only greeted her."

The musicians struck up a reel and he turned to watch the dancers. Micum swirled by with Kari, laughing and smiling; Nysander and Magyana followed close behind. One of the poets had somehow captured Elsbet and she blushed happily as he swept her along. Across the room, Ylinestra was chatting with the actor while Thero hovered close at hand with badly concealed impatience.

"What's she doing with Thero?" Alec wondered aloud.

"Judging by the look of him, nothing he'd want Nysander to know about," Valerius remarked.

"Nysander knows," said Seregil. "I think he was getting bored with her, anyway, but I still say it was bad manners for her to grab Thero next."

"I doubt if she was the only one doing the grabbing," scoffed Valerius. "If he wants to stick his head in the dragon's mouth, let him. Just see that young Alec here keeps a safe distance."

"I just *greeted* her, for—" Alec sputtered, but was interrupted by Myrhini and Beka.

"I'm off for the Vigil," said Myrhini. "Hope to see you all at the investiture tomorrow."

As soon as the captain was gone, Beka turned to Alec with a knowing grin. "Ylinestra's very beautiful, wouldn't you say?"

Alec groaned. "What was I supposed to do, knock her down?"

"For a minute there I thought you were going to."

"Well, I'm sure I'm no danger to her, when she can obviously have her pick of any man in Rhíminee," he countered. "What about you, though? Can you dance in uniform?"

Beka looked down at her tabard and boots. "I think we can manage."

They made a passable business of the reel and went on dancing when the next song began. In truth, Beka was in such high spirits over her commission that Alec thought she could probably fly if the notion struck her. They soon caught each other's rhythm and went on dancing with scarcely a break until Micum cut in to say that Kari and the younger girls were retiring for the night.

"I didn't realize how late it had gotten," Beka said, letting go of Alec's hand with evident regret. "I'll go up and visit with Mother a while before I head back to the barracks. I've got to be up early for the ceremony."

Giving Alec a quick peck on the cheek, she added, "You and Seregil are coming, aren't you? There'll be hundreds of us, of course, so you probably won't even see me."

"With that hair?" Alec teased, tugging at the end of her coppery braid. "You'll stick out like a drunkard's nose!"

"I'll remember that remark the next time we work on your swordplay," Beka warned with a dire grin. "Until tomorrow, then."

Left to his own devices again, he looked for Seregil and spotted him on the far side of the crowded floor. No sooner had he worked his way through the crowd, however, when Seregil was waylaid by a noble complaining at length about some shipping venture he and Seregil were involved with. Alec listened politely for a time, but his attention soon wandered.

Looking around, he realized that the number of guests was dwindling. Off for more "games in the dark," as Kylith had teased. Nysander and Magyana were still there, moving with stately grace through the circle of a galliard. Thero was dancing as well, but not with Ylinestra.

"Where's she gotten to?" Alec wondered, looking around again.

In the garden.

The soft, caressing whisper came at his very ear, for him alone to hear.

Come into the garden.

There was no question this time; it was Ylinestra's voice.

The mysterious summons came again, and with it a delicious languor. A couple walked past, lightwands in hand, and he marveled at the rainbow corona surrounding each glowing stone. The whole room, in fact, had taken on a warmer tone. Perhaps Nysander and Magyana were tinkering with their creation? Skirting the dancers, he slipped unnoticed into the dining room and on out into the darkened garden.

Here. Come to me.

The voice guided him to a far corner of the garden screened by a small arbor.

He heard a faint sigh of silk and Ylinestra's pale face resolved from the darkness. Her hands found his and lifted them to rest just above her hips. She was slender and supple between his hands and he spread his fingers to better appreciate the sensation of her warmth beneath the cold fabric.

"My lady, I don't understand," he whispered, some small, distant part of him distinctly alarmed at his own actions. He'd never felt like this in his life.

"What is there to understand, lovely boy?"

How small she seemed, here in the darkness. Her lips brushed his chin as she spoke, her violet eyes pools of night just below his own.

"But Nysander— Thero? I thought—"

She laughed softly, and the sound drowned his own trepidation in another rush of voluptuous sensation. "I do as I please, Alec, and I take what I want. And just now, I want you."

Her hands found his again, holding his palms flat against her as she slid them upward. The roughness of embroidery met his touch, then the netted web of the necklace over her breasts.

"You're trembling. Does my little magic frighten you? Do *I* frighten you?"

Alec drew a ragged breath. "I—I don't know."

Part of him sensed a snare, a trap, yet his whole body was gripped by a yearning unlike anything he'd ever known. Her scent

filled his nostrils again as she slipped his fingertips beneath the
edge of her necklace to press the bare, yielding swell of a breast.

"You have only to ask, Alec. I'll release you if you ask. Shall I
free you?"

She slipped a hand to the back of his neck to rest where
Seregil's so often did. Then she kissed him again, her lips
parting, tongue gently seeking entrance and gaining it as her other
hand stroked his side. Pulling him closer, she kissed her way to
his neck.

"So young, so smooth," she murmured, the touch of her breath
sending a profound warmth to his loins. "So beautiful. Have you
known a woman? No? So much the better." She shifted slightly,
bringing a half-exposed nipple against his fingers. "Tell me, shall I
release you now?"

"Yes! No— I don't know—" Alec groaned softly, then
embraced her. Magic or not, newly awakened passions suffused
him and he found her lips again, returning kiss for kiss.

"Close your eyes, my darling," she whispered. "Shut them tight
and I'll show you another trick."

Alec obeyed, and was startled to feel himself falling, tumbling
onto something soft. When he opened his eyes again, the two of
them were lying in the heavily draped enclosure of a huge bed.
The forbidden glow of candlelight filtered through layers of colored silk, just bright enough for him to see that somewhere in the
transition, their clothing had been left behind.

"Something wrong, my dear?" asked Nysander, seeing
Magyana frowning over his shoulder as they danced.

"I was just watching Thero. He's looking dour again, and he
seemed to be having such a pleasant time. Has Seregil been
teasing him again?"

"Not that I observed."

Thero hovered grimly in a far corner, oblivious to the band
of nymphs dancing on the wall just behind him as he scanned
the room.

"I suspect Ylinestra has found more spirited companionship for
the evening," he guessed.

"Mmm. Well, that is a great deal less surprising than seeing
them together in the first place. What in the world does she want
with him?"

"He is not such a bad-looking lad," Nysander said. "And he *is* young."

"Yes, but he's also your assistant," sniffed Magyana. "I realize you don't mind, but it still seems rather tactless of them."

Nysander chuckled knowingly. "Passion is seldom governed by such niceties."

Just then, however, he caught sight of Seregil standing by the cider barrel. He was fiddling absently with a mug and looking rather perplexed.

"Come, my dear, you must be thirsty," said the wizard, steering her in Seregil's direction.

"You haven't seen Alec in the last few minutes?" Seregil asked as they joined him.

The gloves were gone, Nysander noted, but a spotless strip of linen still bound each hand. He wondered what sort of explanation he'd concocted for his guests.

"Why, no. Is he missing?" replied the wizard.

"I don't know. It's been almost an hour since I last saw him. I've just been all over the house and he's not here. It's not like him to wander off. Could you take a look?"

Nysander closed his eyes and sent a seeking through the house and surrounding neighborhood, then shook his head.

"You don't suppose—?" Magyana gestured discreetly in Thero's direction.

Reluctantly, Nyander sent another of the spells to Ylinestra's chamber, intending nothing more than a brief glimpse to ascertain the boy's presence.

As he'd feared, Alec was there, but the energies surrounding him were not sexual.

"What is it? Is something wrong?" Seregil asked beside him.

Nysander held up a warning hand without opening his eyes. "He is well. But I shall need a few moments—"

Intensifying the spell, he found Ylinestra crouched over Alec, who appeared to be asleep, sprawled on his back among the disheveled blankets with a blissful smile on his face. In contrast, Ylinestra's face was a hard mask of concentration as she wove an unfamiliar sigil in the air above him. As it took form, the peaceful expression drained from Alec's face. At first he simply looked blank, then his brow furrowed as he unconsciously turned his face away, a low sound of protest rattling in his throat. The sorceress leaned closer, enlarging the glowing symbol, then struck him sharply on the cheek in frustration.

"That will be quite enough, Ylinestra!"

She whirled in surprise. The sigil snapped out of existence.

"Nysander? How dare you spy into my chamber!" she hissed, eyes wide with outrage at his disembodied intrusion. "You have no right!"

"More right than you, to work magic on an unwilling subject," Nysander retorted sternly. "Send him back at once or I shall fetch him myself."

"Such a fuss," she purred, stroking a hand down Alec's belly, knowing he would see. "I assure you, I did him no harm."

"That remains to be seen."

A moment later Nysander felt a ripple of magic from upstairs. When had she mastered the translocation spell?

With Seregil and Magyana close behind, he went up and found Alec deeply asleep in his own chamber. Satisfied that the boy was unharmed, he placed a protective ward over the bed to curtail any further mischief and quietly closed the door.

"Well, I suspect I won't be teasing him about his virginity anymore," Seregil said, sounding a bit wistful. "He certainly fell in to the spirit of the evening in a hurry."

"I doubt it was entirely his own doing," Magyana said, wrinkling her nose in prim distaste. "If it turns out he was coerced, I want to know about it. There's no place for that sort of behavior in the Orëska."

"Certainly not," Nysander said, thinking more of the mysterious sigil she'd been using. "Still, if it was his choice to go off with her, we must not make a fuss. He is old enough to decide that sort of thing for himself."

Seregil let out an abrupt laugh. "I suppose he is, really. But it may cause a bit of a chill between him and Thero."

The roar of festival gongs woke Alec at dawn. Blinking, he gazed up in groggy confusion at the bed hangings, a pomegranate pattern worked with scarlet and gold.

He'd gone to sleep beneath layers of colored silk lit by candle glow. Ylinestra had been looking down at him, her eyes vague with pleasure. A delicious ache ran through him at the memory, but with it came a twinge of anxiety that he couldn't immediately explain.

Stretching himself fully awake, he sat up to find Seregil dozing in an armchair beside the bed. He was still wearing last night's breeches and shirt. Slouched to one side, arms crossed tightly across his chest, he looked profoundly uncomfortable.

Alec shook him gently by the elbow and he jerked awake, rubbing painfully at his neck.

"How'd I get here?" Alec asked.

"She sent you back, I guess." The beginnings of a dangerous grin played at the corners of his mouth. "Ylinestra, eh? And after all Valerius' warnings. Enjoy yourself?"

"Oh—yes. I mean, I did, I guess—"

"You *guess*?"

Alec fell back against the pillows with a

groan. "It's just that, well—I think she used some magic. At first, anyway."

"So that's what it takes." Chuckling, Seregil leaned forward and touched a finger to Alec's cheek. "And the kind that leaves marks, too. You all right?"

Alec brushed his hand away, feeling more awkward than ever. "Yes, of course I'm all right. It was great. Just sort of—strange." He hesitated. "Do you dream? Afterward, I mean?"

"I usually talk. Why, did you?"

"Yes. I remember thinking that I was falling asleep but not wanting to. And then I saw the spinning dagger."

Seregil raised a questioning eyebrow. "The what?"

"The spinning dagger that Nysander used when I swore the Watcher's oath. It was right in front of my face, just like before, and I was afraid to say anything for fear it would cut me. I could hear Nysander's voice, too, but like it was coming from far away. I couldn't understand what he was saying. There was something else, too." He squeezed his eyes shut, trying to seize the elusive fragment. "Something about an arrow."

Seregil shook his head. "You're whisked away and made love to by the most exotic woman in Rhíminee and it gives you night-mares? You're a strange creature, Alec, a very strange creature." He grinned. "I just hope you're not too worn out. This is the biggest celebration of the year. And we'd better get ready. The Cavishes are probably already at breakfast downstairs."

Alec lay in bed a moment longer after he left, trying to sort out his feelings about the previous night's unexpected climax. He knew better than to imagine that Ylinestra considered him any-thing more than a virginal conquest; he doubted she'd give him a second glance the next time they met.

At least he hoped not. Pleasurable as the physical act—or rather, acts—had been, the whole affair had left him feeling low and begrimed. Seregil's well-intentioned ribbing had only under-scored his own confusion.

The sorceress' scent rose from his skin as Alec threw back the covers and got up. Wrapping himself in a robe, he called for the chambermaid, asking her to prepare a bath and see to it that his bedding was changed.

The bath helped considerably and he headed downstairs in somewhat better spirits. His one remaining qualm was that Seregil had already blabbed his exploits to Micum or Kari. But no one gave signs of being any the wiser when he joined the cheerful group around the dining table, although Seregil did raise a questioning eyebrow at his damp hair.

Illia was too excited by the prospect of a day in the city to let anyone linger over their morning tea. As soon as the meal was finished the whole party set off for the Temple Precinct. Kari and the girls rode in a comfortable open carriage, with the men riding attendance on horseback.

In contrast to the austerity of Mourning Night, Sakor's Day was celebrated with wild abandon. Horns blared, ale flowed, bonfires blazed at all hours.

Looking around as they rode, it appeared to Alec that there was a performance of some kind—animal trainers, jugglers, troops of actors performing out of skene wagons, fire dancers, and the like—on virtually every street corner. Food sellers, gamblers, whores, and pickpockets mingled with the revelers, plying their trades.

"It's all so loud and exciting!" exclaimed Elsbet, riding along beside him.

"You'll get used to it," Alec replied.

The girl grinned. "Oh, I look forward to that."

The main event of the day was the annual investing of new troops at midday. Sakor was the patron god of soldiers and the recognition of new troops was at once a martial and religious occasion.

In the Temple Precinct, the tiers of seating had been cleared away to make room for the ranks of new soldiers formed up in front of the Sakor Temple.

The day was a cloudless, bitter one and even Alec was glad of the heavy, fur-lined cloak he wore over his velvet surcoat. Seregil chatted idly with other nobles, introducing Alec to this one or that as the fancy took him.

"I've never seen so many new recruits, have you?" Kari asked Seregil, shading her eyes with one hand as they stood together on the steps of the Temple of Illior.

He shook his head. "No, never."

"Where's Beka?" Illia demanded, bouncing excitedly on her father's shoulder.

"Over with those in green there." Micum pointed out the Queen's Horse, raising his voice to make himself heard.

Glancing at Kari, Alec thought she looked rather sad and

thoughtful. As if sensing his gaze, she looked over at him and held a hand out for his.

By the time the last ranks had marched in, the close-packed regimental groupings looked like colored tiles in a huge mosaic. The Queen's Horse was a block of green and white directly in front of the Temple of Sakor.

"Look, there's the Queen," said Micum. "They'll start now."

Looking solemn and proud despite her long vigil, Idrilain took her place between the pillars of the Sakor Temple. She wore flowing robes of state and an emerald diadem and carried the Sword of Gërilain upright on her shoulder like a scepter. The golden Aegis gleamed behind her as she stood motionless before the troops, the faint vapor of her breath visible on the cold air. The tableau was intentional; there was no doubt to whom the oath was to be given. The priests might be allowed their mysteries in the darkness, but here, in the light of day, stood the embodiment of Skalan power.

Placing the sword point downward in front of her, Idrilain grasped the hilt in both hands and began the ritual.

"Come you here to swear the Oath?" she cried, her voice carrying clear and harsh as if across a field of battle.

"Aye!" came the response from a thousand throats, thundering in the stone confines of the precinct. From the corner of his eye, Alec saw Micum and Seregil drop their hands to their sword hilts, as did many around them. Without a word, he did the same.

"To whom do you swear?"

"To the throne of Skala and the Queen who rules!" returned initiate soldiers.

"By what do you swear?"

"By the Four, by the Flame, by our honor, and our arms!"

"Swear then to uphold the honor of your land and Queen!"

"Aye!"

"Swear then to give no quarter to the adversary."

"Aye!"

"Swear then to spare the supplicant."

"Aye!"

"Foreswear all that brings dishonor upon your comrades."

"Aye!"

Idrilain paused, letting a moment pass in stillness. Then, in a voice that would have done credit to any sergeant, she barked out, "Display arms!"

With a ringing of steel, the various regiments brandished their weapons: swords and sabers glinted in the sunlight; small forests of lances sprang to attention; archers beat arrow shafts against longbows, producing a strange clacking sound; artillery soldiers held catapult stones aloft. Standards unfurled on cue to snap brightly over the throng.

"Then so are you all sworn together!" cried Idrilain, raising her sword overhead. "By the Four and the Flame, by land and Queen, by honor and arms. Warriors of Skala, sound your cries!"

A deafening roar filled the square as each regiment shouted its own battle cry, vying with the others to make their voices heard.

"The Queen's honor!"

"Sakor's Fire!"

"Honor and steel!"

"The Flame on the Sea!"

"True aim and well sped!"

"The White Hawk!"

Drummers and pipers stepped from behind the temple pillars, setting up a martial tattoo. Great horns as long as the men that sounded them blared and bellowed on the rooftops as the ranks turned and began to march out of the square.

"It all makes you want to join in with it, doesn't it?" Alec grinned, pulse quickening with the beat of the drums.

Laughing, Seregil threw an arm around Alec's shoulders and drew him away, shouting over the din, "That's the whole idea."

The clamor at dawn went unheard by Nysander. Seated cross-legged on the floor of the casting room, a long dead candle guttered out before him, he floated in the dim oblivion of meditation. Images came and went, yet nothing substantial came into his grasp.

After seeing Magyana to her tower door the previous night, he'd made his usual tour of the vaults beneath the Orëska, then found himself leaving first the House, then the sheltered gardens, to stalk alone through the windy streets.

Hands clasped behind his back, he walked aimlessly, as if trying to escape the anger that had been building slowly inside him from the moment he'd found Ylinestra hovering over Alec in her chamber.

Much of this anger was directed at himself. Ylinestra had meant no more to him than a voluptuous diversion possessed of a mind of uncommon ability. Yet he had allowed his carnal desires to blind him to the true depths of her cupidity. Her sudden dalliance with Thero had reawakened his lulled sense of prudence. What he'd witnessed this night strengthened his suspicions.

He let out an exasperated growl. The Black Time was coming, he knew, coming in the course of his own Guardianship. Was he prepared?

Hardly.

He had an assistant he could not completely trust and yet hardly dared release. A sorceress twenty decades his junior had him passion-blind. And Seregil!

Nysander clenched his hands, digging the nails into his palms. Seregil, whom he loved as a son and a friend, had very nearly condemned himself to death through his own obstinate inquisitiveness. Alec would prove no different in time—that much was already clear.

For the first time in years, he found himself wondering what his own master would have to say about all this. Arkoniel's craggy face came to him as readily as if he'd seen him only the day before.

He'd been old when Nysander had first met him and never seemed to change. How fervently the young Nysander—that desperate, quick-tempered urchin of the streets, plucked starving from the squalor of the lower city—had tried to emulate the old man's patience and wisdom.

But from Arkoniel he'd also inherited the burden of the Guardianship, that dark thread of knowledge that must be kept at once intact and concealed. A thread that the events of the past few months, beginning with Seregil's finding the cursed disk and culminating tonight with the omens at the ceremony, showed to be nearing its end.

Finding no answers in the night, he'd returned to his tower and prepared for a formal meditation. Dawn found him motionless and seemingly serene. He'd been dimly aware of Thero's arrival and respectful withdrawal.

As the last light of Sakor's Day faded above the tower dome, Nysander opened his eyes, no wiser than when he'd begun. Denied inspiration, he was left with facts. Seregil had stumbled across the disk, ostensibly by accident, then found his way to the

Oracle of Illior, who'd recited a fragment of a prophecy no one but Nysander himself had any business knowing about. Last night the same words—"Eater of Death"—had been spoken by the priest of Sakor following the strange omen of carrion birds.

Rising, he worked the stiffness from his joints and set off for the Temple Precinct again.

A cold sliver of moon was just sliding up from behind the white dome of the Temple of Illior when he arrived. Taking this as a favorable sign, he entered the temple and donned the ritual mask.

He'd sought the counsel of the Oracle only a few times before, and then more often in the spirit of curiosity. His devotion to Illior took a different form than that of the priests.

But now he hurried onward with a growing sense of anticipation. Snapping a light of his own into existence, he made his way down the twisting, treacherous stairway to the subterranean chamber of the Oracle. At the bottom he extinguished the light and strode on through the utter blackness of the corridor, more convinced with every step that the poor, mad creature at its end had answers to offer.

A lumpish, disheveled young man squatting on a pallet bed looked up as he entered. This was not the same Oracle Nysander recalled, of course, yet all the rest was as before: the profound silence, the dim, cold light, the attendants seated motionless on either side of the idiot vessel of the Immortal, featureless silver masks gleaming from the depths of their cowls.

"Greetings to you, Guardian!" he cried, vague eyes locking with Nysander's.

"You know me?"

"Who you are is nothing," the Oracle replied, rocking slowly from side to side. "*What* you are is everything. Everything. Prepare, O Guardian. The ordeal is close at hand. Have you preserved what was entrusted?"

"I have." Nysander suddenly felt weary beyond words. How many times had he walked through the dusty labyrinth beneath the Orëska House, feigning absent curiosity? How many years had it taken to cultivate his reputation as an eccentric, albeit powerful, dabbler? How much had he sacrificed to uphold the trust of generations?

"Stand ready, O Guardian, and be vigilant," the Oracle continued. "Your time approaches out of darkness and hidden places.

The minions of the Adversary ride forth in secret glory. Your portion shall be bitter as gall."

The silence closed over them again like the surface of a pool. Into that silence Nysander slowly recited words that, to his knowledge, had not been said aloud in nearly five centuries. It was a fragment of the "Dream of Hyradin," the one faint ray of hope he and all his predecessors had clung to down the long years of their vigil.

" 'And so came the Beautiful One, the Eater of Death, to strip the bones of the world. First clothed in Man's flesh, it came crowned with a helm of darkness and none could stand against this One but Four.

" 'First shall be the Guardian, a vessel of light in the darkness. Then the Shaft and the Vanguard, who shall fail and yet not fail if the Guide, the Unseen One, goes forth. And at last shall be again the Guardian, whose portion is bitter, as bitter as gall.' "

The Oracle said nothing to this, but gazed up at him with eyes that held no alternative.

After a moment, Nysander bowed slightly and went back the way he'd come, in darkness and alone.

9

AN UNEXPECTED ALLY

Alec had hoped that their stay at Wheel Street would be brief—a week perhaps, to satisfy appearances. But the week stretched into two, and then lengthened to a month. Seregil had "daylight business" to attend to, as he called his numerous legitimate interests around the city. They spent a great deal of time in the lower city, where he met with ship captains in warehouses smelling of tar and low tide, or haggled with traders at the customs houses. This meant that for the time being their comfortable rooms over the Cockerel were generally off-limits; they couldn't chance a connection being made between Lord Seregil and the inn.

The business transactions bored Alec, but he contented himself with observing how Seregil played the role. Despite his affectations, he had the common touch that invited confidence and respect. He also had a reputation for openhandedness in certain matters; tradesmen were happy enough to pass on whatever rumors were current and there was little going on, legal or otherwise, which Seregil didn't soon hear of.

Equally important were the evening salons. Once it was known that the elusive Lord Seregil was home at last, a veritable deluge of scented, wax-sealed invitations poured in.

Thrown together night after night with nobles of all degrees, Alec gradually learned the gentle art of conversational thrust and parry so necessary to navigate the intricate waters of Skalan politics.

"Intrigue!" Seregil laughed when Alec groaned over manners once too often. "That's our bread and butter, and the only intrigues that pay are those of the wealthy. Smile nicely, nod often, and keep your ears open."

Alec's presence excited a certain amount of comment at first, and rumors regarding his relationship with Seregil circulated hotly. The higher-minded accepted that he really was Seregil's ward, or perhaps his illegitimate son, though the majority of opinion tended toward less altruistic possibilities. Alec was mortified, but Seregil shrugged it off.

"Don't let it bother you," he counseled. "In these circles the only thing worse than being slandered is not being talked about at all. In a month or two they'll forget all about it and think you've been around for years."

To this end, they made a point of frequenting the better theaters and gambling houses. The Tirarie Theater in the Street of Lights was a favorite haunt of Seregil's, particularly when Pelion í Eirsin was on stage.

Alec was an instant aficionado of drama. Brought up on ballads and tavern tales, he was amazed to see stories played out by a full cast in costume. Whether he understood the story line or not—and he frequently didn't—the pageantry of it was enough to keep him enthralled through the entire performance.

And through it all, Alec's education continued—lock work and swordsmanship, etiquette and lineage, history and disguise, the picking of surcoats and the picking of pockets—together with a hundred other skills Seregil deemed indispensable for an aspiring spy.

One grey morning several weeks after the Festival Seregil handed Alec a sealed note from the pile of new correspondence at his elbow as they sat over a late breakfast.

Breaking the seal, he read a hastily scrawled note from Beka Cavish.

> Can get free a few hours this afternoon. Fancy a ride? If so, meet me at the Cirna Road gate at noon.
>
>   —B.C.

"You don't need me this afternoon, do you?" he asked hopefully, passing the note to Seregil. "I haven't seen her since the investiture."

Seregil nodded. "Go on. I think I can manage without you."

Arriving at the Harvest Market well before the appointed time, Alec found Beka already waiting for him by the city gate. The way she sat her horse, reins held casually in one hand, her other elbow cocked out at a jaunty angle beneath her green cloak, spoke volumes; she looked born to soldiering.

"Aren't you still the fine young dandy?" she called as he maneuvered Windrunner through the market crowd.

"Seregil's making a gentleman of me, after all." He struck a haughty pose. "Soon I'll be too good to hang about with the likes of you."

"Then we'd better get on with it while we still can. I need a good run," she said, grinning at him. Nudging Wyvern into a trot, she led the way through the gate.

As soon as they were past the curtain wall beyond, they kicked their mounts into a gallop and rode north along the cliffs. The frozen roadway rang like metal under their horses' hooves; the sea gave back a metallic sheen beneath the pale winter sky. To the east, the mountain peaks gleamed white against the lowering sky.

Side by side, cloaks streaming out behind them, Alec and Beka raced along the highroad for a mile or more, then veered off into a meadow overlooking the sea.

"That's quite a harness you've got on Wyvern," Alec remarked, noting the leather breastplate and frontlet.

"That's to accustom him to the feel of it," she explained. "For battle, the leather's replaced with felt pads and bronze plates."

"How do you like military life? And what do I call you now?"

"We all start as riders, although those of us with commissions are actually officers from the start. I'll be a lieutenant when we ride off to the war. Right now all the new riders are divided up into training decuria. I'm in the first turma under Captain Myrhini. Lieutenants lead three decuriae, but it's the captain more often than not who leads the drills—"

"Hold on!" Alec interjected, reining in. "You soldiers speak a different language. What's a turma?"

"I'm still getting it all straight myself," she admitted. "Let's see, now—ten riders make a decuria, which is led by a sergeant. Three decuriae to a turma, commanded by a lieutenant; three turmae to a troop and four troops to a squadron; two squadrons to the regiment. What with officers, sutlers and the like, there's about eight hundred of us altogether. Captain Myrhini has command of First Troop of the Lion Squadron under Commander Klia. Commander Perris commands the Wolf Squadron. And the Queen's oldest son, Prince Korathan, is the regimental commander."

"Sounds like a pretty exclusive bunch."

"The Horse Guard is an elite regiment; the officers are all nobles. The riders all have to provide their own mounts and prove themselves at riding and shooting, so most of them are from well-to-do families as well. I'd never have gotten a commission without Seregil's help. Still, elite or not, you should see some of the young blue bloods tumbling off their horses as they try to draw! I tell you, I've never appreciated Father's training so much as now. Sergeant Braknil thinks Captain Myrhini will want to keep me in her troop when I've finished training. I'll have thirty riders under me. But how about you? I suppose Seregil's keeping you pretty busy?"

"Oh, yes." Alec rolled his eyes. "I think I've gotten all of ten hours sleep this week. When we're not arguing with traders or going off to some fancy gathering, he's got me sitting up half the night memorizing royal lineages. I think he secretly means to make me into a scribe."

A little pause spread out and in it he felt the distance opening between them as they headed down their divergent paths. What he really wanted to tell her about were their nocturnal adventures, but Seregil was adamant about secrecy outside Watcher circles. At some point, he thought, Nysander ought to recruit Beka.

Looking up, he found her studying his face with a faint smile. It occurred to him that having grown up around Micum and Seregil, she probably had a fair idea of his unspoken life.

"Did I tell you Seregil's teaching me Aurënfaie?" he said, anxious to reestablish common ground.

"Nös eyír?"

He laughed. "You, too?"

"Oh, yes. Elsbet and I were always pestering him to teach us when he came to visit. She had a better head for it, naturally, but I know a little. I suppose you'll need it, too. It's all the fashion among the nobles."

"Seregil says most of them sound like they're talking through a mouthful of wet leather when they try. He's making certain I get it right. *Makir y'torus eyair.* How's that?"

"Korveu tak melilira. Afarya tös hara'beniel?" she replied, wheeling her horse and kicking it into a gallop.

Assuming it had either been an insult or an invitation to another race, Alec galloped after her.

Dusk was settling outside the windows of Seregil's bed-chamber when Alec strode in with flushed cheeks and new snow melting in his hair. The sweet tang of a cold ocean wind still clung to him.

"Tell me we don't have to dress up tonight!" he pleaded, drop-ping down on the hearth rug by Seregil's feet.

Seregil laid his book aside and stretched lazily. "You look like you've had quite an afternoon."

"We rode for miles! I should have taken my bow—we ended up in the hills and there were rabbits everywhere."

"I may have some other hunting for you." Seregil pulled a small scroll from his belt and brandished it between two long fin-gers. "This was left at the Black Feather for the Rhíminee Cat. It seems Lady Isara has lost some compromising letters and she wants them back. She thinks Baron Makrin's study is a good place to start looking."

"Tonight?" Alec asked, all weariness instantly forgotten.

"I think that's best. It's a pretty straightforward burglary, nothing fancy. Midnight's soon enough. We'll have to wait until the household's settled down, but I don't want to be out in the cold any longer than we have to."

The wind tugged at their cloaks as Seregil and Alec set off for the baron's villa on the west side of the Noble Quarter. They wore coarse workman's tunics, and old traveling cloaks covered the swords slung out of sight over their backs.

They'd gone only a few blocks when Seregil suddenly sensed someone on the street behind them. Touching Alec lightly on the arm, he turned a corner at random and caught a hint of motion in the shadows behind them.

"Just like that time I was chased into Silvermoon Street," Alec whispered, glancing back nervously.

"I had the same thought, though it's probably just someone out for a midnight stroll. Let's find out."

Leaving the baron for later, he turned right at the next corner, heading east into the heart of the city.

A slice of moon broke free from the clouds, giving just enough light for Seregil to make out a large, dark form trailing them from a discreet distance.

Not so innocent after all, he frowned to himself. Keeping up a steady pace, he strode on into the increasingly poorer streets of the southeast quarter. Their man still kept his distance, but matched them turn for turn.

"Do you hear that?" Alec asked softly.

"Hear what?"

"That little scraping sound, when he walks over a patch of bare cobbles. I heard it that other time, too."

"Well then, we'd better let him introduce himself."

Wending his way into a disreputable warren of darkened tenements and warehouses, Seregil spotted a familiar alleyway. Pretending to stumble, he reached out and grasped Alec's elbow and signed for him to follow.

Ducking into the alley, he quickly tore off his cloak and tossed it behind a pile of refuse, then pulled himself through a crumbling window frame overhead. Alec was up beside him in an instant. From this vantage point, they watched as their man hesitated, then drew a falchion and went slowly on into the shadows of the alley. From this angle, Seregil couldn't make out his face.

An amateur, but persistent, Seregil thought, watching as he went half the length of the alley before realizing that it was a dead end, and that his quarry was nowhere in sight.

As he turned, Seregil and Alec dropped lightly to the pavement and drew their swords.

"What do you want?" Seregil demanded.

Undaunted, their pursuer took a step forward, weapon at the ready. "If ever you called yourself Gwethelyn, Lady of Cador Ford, and Ciris, squire of the same, then we've a matter of restitution to discuss."

"Captain Rhal!" Alec examined.

"The same, boy."

"You're a long way from the *Darter*," said Seregil, hoping he didn't sound as shaken as he felt.

"And a good thing, too," Rhal retorted stiffly, "seeing that she lies rotting at the bottom of the Folcwine River."

"What's that to do with us?"

Rhal advanced another step, flinging his hat aside. "I've traveled a long way to ask *you* that. Two days below Torburn we put in for water at a little place called Gresher's Ferry. A pack of swordsmen were waiting for us there, and who do you suppose they wanted?"

Alec shifted uncomfortably beside him.

"I'm sure I have no idea," Seregil replied. "Who were they looking for?"

"Two men and a boy, they claimed, but it was you they meant, sure enough. If I hadn't caught you out of your woman's riggings I might not have tumbled, but it was you."

"You're mistaken, though I suppose you set them after us anyway?"

"By the Old Sailor, I did not!" Rhal retorted angrily. "I might have saved myself the loss of a fine ship if I had."

Certain disturbing questions had occurred to Seregil during this exchange, but before he could ask any the three of them were startled by a sudden commotion behind them at the mouth of the alley.

A gang of back alley toughs materialized out of the shadows armed with swords, cudgels, and daggers. Seregil saw in an instant that there were enough of them to be trouble.

To his surprise, he found Rhal at his side, sword leveled at the newcomers. Alec cast him one questioning look, then fell in beside the captain as the ambushers charged in at them.

Rhal took the center, striking right and left with workmanlike efficiency. Seregil had just time enough to pull the poniard free of his boot before he found himself fighting two-handed against a ruffian wielding a quarterstaff.

The alley made for close quarters fighting and the three of them were soon being forced back inch by inch toward the dead end at their backs.

"Trouble above!" Rhal bellowed as a hail of stones and roof tiles clattered down from overhead. "Press the bastards!"

A heavy tile struck his arm, jarring his sword from his hand. A tall footpad closed in, but Seregil whirled and buried his poniard between the man's ribs. Beside him, Alec struck another across the face. Rhal rolled hastily out from under their feet, scrambling through the dirty snow for his weapon.

More stones rained down but thanks to the darkness or someone's poor aim, most of this load landed among the attackers. In the resulting confusion, Seregil and the others broke free to the street, the gang hot on their heels.

Freed from the confines of the alley, he rounded on the man nearest him and ran him through, then blocked a swing from a quarterstaff. He'd lost sight of Alec, but a fierce yell just behind told him the boy was holding his own.

Seregil was just facing off with two of the footpads when the shrill alarm of a Watch trumpet rang out nearby. A moment later a Watch patrol galloped into sight down the street, weapons drawn. The footpads left off at once and melted away into the shadows like sea smoke before a freshening breeze.

"Come on!" Seregil hissed at Alec and Rhal, and bolted off in the opposite direction.

"What are we running for?" Rhal panted.

"So we don't spend the night inventing lies for some thick-headed bluecoat," Seregil snapped.

Dodging into the next side street, he spotted a sagging bulk-head at the base of a tenement just ahead. Hoping for the best, he yanked up one of the flat doors and tossed in a lightstone. Worn steps led down to a disused cellar.

"Down here!"

Alec and Rhal dove for cover and he followed, pulling the door shut overhead again.

Crouched tensely in the musty darkness, they listened as the Watch made a cursory search of the area and then moved on.

Seregil looked over at Rhal. "Now, you were saying—?"

For the space of a few heartbeats Rhal stared blankly back at him, then burst out laughing. "By the Mariner, I came here to stick a knife in you and now I'm indebted to you for my life. You two had no call to cover me as you did just then."

"You had no call to let us go that night on the *Darter*," Seregil replied, picking up the light and heading for the stairs. "But you did, and here we are. The boy and I have some business to attend to just now, but I'd like to continue our earlier discussion. Meet us at the inner room of the Bower in Silk Street, say in an hour's time?"

Rhal considered the invitation, then nodded. "All right then. An hour."

Seregil lifted the bulkhead door cautiously, then climbed out with Alec close behind.

"Are we really going to meet him?" Alec asked as they hurried away.

"He tracked us to Wheel Street. I think we'd better find out how he managed that, don't you?" Seregil scowled, making no effort to mask his concern. "And who it was that came to him looking for us, although I think I can guess."

The answering look of fear on Alec's face told Seregil that he could, too.

Their unanticipated run-in with Rhal had sapped every ounce of enjoyment from the night for Alec. He floundered through the job in a daze of apprehension. Seregil had said nothing more on the matter so far, but he couldn't shake the conviction that his own callow ignorance aboard the *Darter* had somehow led Rhal to them after all these months. And if he'd tracked them, then why not Mardus?

Luckily for him, the burglary was not a particularly challenging one. Evidently a smug, unimaginative fellow, Makrin had hidden the letters in a locked box behind a bit of loose woodwork in his study. Seregil spotted it while Alec was still sorting through the contents of the writing table. With Lady Isara's letters in hand, along with a few other items of interest, they stopped briefly at Wheel Street to deposit the goods, then set off on horseback for the Bower.

This was a discreetly respectable establishment Seregil often used for assignations. A yawning pot boy led them to a room at the back. Rhal was already there, but not alone; Alec immediately recognized the two men with him as the helmsman and first mate from the ill-fated *Darter*. They recognized him as well, and returned his greeting with guarded nods, weapons close at hand.

Rhal pushed a wine jug over to them as he and Seregil joined him at the table.

Seregil poured himself a cup, then said without preamble, "Tell me more about Gresher's Ferry."

Rhal eyed him knowingly. "As I said, a pack of armed men was laying for us there."

"A rough-lookin' crew," the helmsman, Skywake, added darkly. "They didn't have no uniforms, but they sat their horses like soldiers."

Alec's heart sank still lower, though Seregil's face remained a carefully neutral mask.

"They came asking after two men and a boy, said they'd stolen the mayor's gold up in Wolde," Rhal continued. "When I told 'em I hadn't carried any three such as they described, they pulled swords and swarmed all over my vessel, bold as you please. Then their leader—a big, black-bearded son of a whore with an accent thick as lentil porridge—he laid into me, calling me a liar and worse in front of my own crew. The more he went on, the less I liked it. By the time he stopped for breath, I'd sooner been drowned than give him satisfaction. So I kept mum and finally they rode off.

"We went on downriver and I thought that was the end of it, but that same night a fire started in the hold and burned so fierce we couldn't even get down to douse it. Everyone got off, but my ship lies burnt and broken against the mud bank below Hullout Bend. That's just a bit too much of a coincidence for my taste, especially since we were carrying silver and bales of vellum that voyage."

"Not the most flammable of cargoes." Seregil regarded Rhal impassively over the rim of his cup. "And so you came looking for us."

"You're not going to tell me you were traveling in disguise just to make a fool of me?" Rhal snorted.

"No."

Nettles slammed his fist down on the table. "Then it was you they was looking for!"

"I don't know anything about that," Seregil maintained. "What I'm interested in is how you found me."

"Not much trick to that," Skywake told him, jerking a thumb at Alec. "This boy of yours asked around amongst the crew how to get to Rhíminee just before you got off."

Idiot! Alec silently berated himself, his worst fears confirmed.

"Who did he talk to?" asked Seregil, not looking at him.

"There were a bunch of us on deck that day, as I recall," Nettles replied. "Skywake, you was there, and the cook's boy."

"That's right. And Applescaith. He was the one wanted him to go overland the whole way, remember?"

"Aye. Him, too. And Bosfast."

Alec sat staring down at his wine cup, mouth set in a grim line. How could he have been so green? He might just as well have drawn their pursuers a map.

Seregil took another sip of wine, considering all this. "And so, with nothing more than a few tenuous suspicions, you chuck everything and head off for Skala to stick a knife in me?" He shook his head in evident bemusement. "Rhíminee's a big place. How in the world did you expect to find us?"

Rhal scrubbed a hand over his thinning hair and gave a short chuckle. "If you aren't the damnedest creature for brass. All right then, I'll tell you straight. You're looking at a ruined man. All I came away with was my instruments and this."

Rhal held up his left hand, displaying a large garnet ring on his little finger. Alec recognized it as the one Seregil had worn while playing Lady Gwethelyn, but what was Rhal doing with it? Looking at Seregil for a reaction, he saw the hint of a smile tugging at the corner of his friend's mouth.

"With the *Darter* beyond fixing and winter coming on, I didn't see too many prospects for me in the north," Rhal went on. "I was a deepwater sailor in my youth. I took up the Folcwine passage when my uncle willed me his ship and the chance to be my own master. Now with the war brewing up for spring, I figured I maybe could sign on with the navy.

"To tell you the honest truth, I didn't really expect to find you. Then I caught sight of your boy back around the time you had all that trouble with the law. Since then, we've kept watch on that fancy house of yours, hoping to have a quiet chat, as it were. You're a hard pair to track down, though."

"It was you that chased me that night," said Alec.

"That was us." Rhal rubbed a knee with a rueful grin. "You're a tricky little bugger, and fast. I'd figured you two for soft gents and didn't think you'd give us much trouble. After seeing the way you handled yourselves in that alley, though, I believe I'm glad those footpads showed up when they did."

Seregil gave him the crooked grin. "It may be good fortune for all of us, meeting up again."

"How do you figure that?"

"You two"—Seregil turned to Skywake and Nettles—"do you fancy signing on as common sailors with a war coming?"

"We go where our captain goes," Skywake replied stoutly,

though it was clear neither he nor the former helmsman were enthusiastic about the prospect.

Seregil looked back to Rhal. "And you, Captain—I'd think it would be difficult to serve after having a vessel of your own."

Alec began to suspect where this conversation was headed.

"Of course, I'd be the last person to discourage anyone from fighting the Plenimarans," Seregil drawled, "but it seems to me there are more rewarding ways of going about it. Have you considered privateering?"

"I've considered it." Rhal shrugged, studying the other man's face with a sharp trader's crafty interest, "but that takes a strong, swift ship and more gold than I'm ever likely to see."

"What it takes," Seregil said, reaching into his belt pouch, "is the proper investors. Would this get you started?"

Opening his hand, Seregil showed them an emerald the size of a walnut glowing in the hollow of his palm. It was one of many such stones Seregil kept handy as a conveniently portable form of wealth.

"By the Sailor, Captain, did you ever see the like of that!" Nettles gasped.

Rhal glanced down at the stone, then back at Seregil. "Why?"

Seregil placed the stone in the center of the table. "Perhaps I appreciate a man with a sense of humor."

"Skywake, Nettles, wait outside," Rhal said quietly. As they left, Rhal made a questioning gesture in Alec's direction.

Seregil shook his head. "He stays. So, what do you think of my offer. It won't be repeated once we leave this room."

"Tell me why," Rhal repeated, picking up the gem. "You've heard my story and told me nothing, yet you offer me this. What's it really paying for?"

Seregil chuckled softly. "You're a clever man, away from the ladies. Let's understand one another. I've got secrets I prefer to keep, but there are surer ways than this to protect them, if you take my meaning. What I'm offering you, *all* I'm offering you, is a mutually beneficial business proposition. You find a ship, see to the crew, the provisioning, everything. I provide capital, in return for which I receive twenty percent of the take and passage wherever I say, whenever I require it, which will most likely be never. The rest of the profits are yours to be divided in whatever fashion you see fit."

"And?" Still skeptical, Rhal put the stone back on the table.

"Information. Any document confiscated, any rumors from

prisoners, any encounter that seems out of the ordinary—it all comes to me directly and not a word to anyone else."

Rhal nodded, satisfied. "So you're nosers, after all. Who for?"

"Let's just say we consider Skalan interests to be our own."

"I don't suppose you have any proof of that?"

"None whatsoever."

Rhal drummed his fingers lightly on the tabletop for a minute, calculating. "Ship's papers in my name alone, and I run my vessel as I see fit?"

"All right."

Rhal tapped the emerald. "This is a good start, but it won't pay for a ship, nor get one built before midsummer."

"As it happens, I know of a vessel being refitted at a boatyard in Macar. The principal backer's been having second thoughts." Seregil produced a stone identical to the first. "These should be ample evidence of good faith. I'll make arrangements to have all further funds paid out to you in gold."

"And what if I just slip the cable tonight with these?"

Seregil shrugged. "Then you'll be a relatively wealthy man. Are we to say done to it or not?"

Rhal shook his head, looking less than satisfied. "You're an odd one, and no mistake. I've one last condition of my own, or it's no deal."

"And that is?"

"If I'm to keep faith with you, then I want your names, your true names."

"If you've tracked me to Wheel Street, then you've already heard it; Seregil í Korit Solun Meringil Bôkthersa."

"That's a mouthful by half. And you, boy. You got a fancy long hook, too?"

Alec hesitated, and felt Seregil's foot nudge his own beneath the table. "You'll have heard mine, too. Alec, Alec of Ivywell."

"All right, then, I'm satisfied." Pocketing the gems, Rhal spit in his palm and extended his hand to Seregil. "I say done to it, Seregil whoever-you-are."

Seregil clasped hands. "Done it is, Captain."

Alec was very silent as they rode back to Wheel Street. Passing through the glow of a lone street lantern, Seregil saw that he was looking thoroughly miserable.

"It's not as bad as all that," he assured him. "Anyone looking for Lord Seregil knows where to find him."

"Sure, but what if it hadn't been Wheel Street he followed us to?" Alec shot back bitterly.

"We're much more careful about that. No one's ever tracked me there."

"Probably because you were never stupid enough to give them the damn directions!"

"Still, considering the circumstances—me too sick to think straight, you not knowing the country—I don't know what else you could have done, except maybe have waited until we were off the ship to ask the way. You didn't know any better then. You do now."

"A fat lot of comfort that'll be when some other old mistake of mine catches up with us," Alec persisted, looking only slightly less miserable. "What if the next one who shows up is Mardus?"

"Even if those were his men that boarded Rhal's ship—and I admit, it sure sounded like them—he didn't tell them anything."

"Then you think we're safe?"

Seregil grinned darkly. "We're never safe. But I do think if Mardus had tracked us down, we'd have heard from him by now. I mean, he'd have to be insane to hang about in Rhíminee for any length of time the way things are now."

10

THE BURDEN OF TRUTH

Sarisin wore into Dostin, tightening winter's embrace on the city. Snow gusted down out of the mountains, only to be followed by icy rain off the sea that reduced it all to thick, dirty slush and churned ice, treacherous underfoot. Smoke from thousands of chimneys mingled with the fog and hung in a grey haze over the rooftops for days at a stretch.

Preparations for war continued amid a constant stream of rumor and minor alarms. Skalan merchants were harassed in Mycenian towns, warehouses were rifled or burned. Plenimaran press gangs were reported on the prowl in ports as far west as Isil. Word circulated that more than a hundred keels had been laid down in Plenimaran shipyards.

No major host could be raised before spring, but the forces already billeted in Rhíminee were more visible than usual as they worked on the city's defenses and drilled outside the walls. Seregil and Alec often rode over to view the Queen's Horse at their maneuvers, but their friends there seldom had time for more than a brief hello.

At Macar, Rhal's ship was progressing rapidly under the captain's sharp eye. As Seregil had anticipated, once assured of the good faith between them, Rhal looked out for his silent backer's interests as if they were his own.

It would be another two months before the vessel could be launched, but he already had Skywake and Nettles combing seaports up and down the coast for sailors. The one subject he kept silent on was the vessel's name. When Alec asked, Rhal only winked, telling him it was bad luck to say before she was launched.

Though by no means oblivious to the import of the events unfolding around him, Alec moved through the grey midwinter days in a state of increasing contentment. He'd gradually settled into the role of Sir Alec and had lost most of his awkwardness around the nobles. He was happiest, though, honing his more illicit skills as he worked side by side with Seregil as the Rhíminee Cat or on Watcher business for Nysander.

He also came to appreciate the amenities of life at Wheel Street. In his former life, wandering the northlands with his father, winter had always meant hardship—slogging up and down trap lines, sheltering in brushwood huts, and the snowy solitude of the forest.

Here, fires burned at all hours against the ever-present damp and cold. Thick carpets covered the floors, food and wine were there for the asking, and warm baths—for which he had finally acquired a taste—could be had at any hour in a special room just down the hall. Some of his fondest memories of those days would be sitting by a snug fire on a stormy day, enjoying the sound of the rain lashing against the shutters.

As always, life with Seregil had a charmed quality; his enthusiasm and irreverent good humor buoyed Alec along as a seemingly endless progression of lessons were placed before him. The more Alec learned, the more he found he felt like a man who'd thirsted for years unknowing, only discovering his need when it finally began to be slaked. In return, Alec tried to teach Seregil archery and, despite all evidence to the contrary, stubbornly refused to give him up as a hopeless cause.

One stormy afternoon Seregil discovered Alec in the library, frowning pensively as he scanned the shelves.

"Looking for something in particular?"

"Histories," Alec replied, fingering the spine of a thick volume. "Last night at Lord Kallien's salon, someone was saying how this war may be as bad as the Great War. I got to wondering what that one was like. You've told me a bit about it, but I thought it would be interesting to do some reading on it. Do you have anything?"

"Nothing much, but the Orëska library does," Seregil replied, inwardly delighted at this show of scholarly initiative. Alec generally preferred more active pursuits. "We could ride over if you'd like, and see Nysander, too. It's been days since we've heard from him."

Sleet pelted wetly down on them as they galloped through the streets of the Noble Quarter to the Orëska House. As soon as they entered the enchanted gardens surrounding it the sleet turned to warm, gentle rain.

Turning his face up to it, Seregil wondered if any of the wizards ever got bored with the perpetual summer that surrounded the place.

Crossing the second-floor mezzanine on their way to Nysander's tower, Alec nudged Seregil and pointed to the walkway across the atrium.

"Look there," he murmured with a slight grin.

Following his nod, Seregil saw Thero and Ylinestra walking along arm and arm. As they watched, Thero threw his head back and let out a genuine laugh.

"Thero laughing?" Seregil whispered in amazement.

Alec watched as the pair disappeared down a corridor. "Do you think he's in love with her?"

"He probably is, the poor idiot. Or maybe she's magicked him."

He'd meant it as a joke on Thero, but Alec's sudden blush made him wish he'd kept it to himself. The boy never spoke of his own apparently cataclysmic tryst with the sorceress, or betrayed any sign of jealousy when speculating on her other attachments, but he was rather brittle about the circumstances.

Magyana answered their knock at the tower door. She had a few willow leaves caught in her silvery braid and a smudge of damp earth on her chin.

"Hello, you two!" She exclaimed, letting them in. "I just dug some lovely orris root in the garden and brought some up to

Nysander, but he's not here. Wethis says he's off visiting Leiteus í Marineus again."

Seregil raised a questioning eyebrow. "The astrologer?"

"Yes, he's been spending quite a lot of time with him these last few weeks. Evidently there's some sort of conjunction they're both interested in. I've got a potion on the boil back at my work-shop so I can't linger, but you can come in and wait for him."

"No, we've got other business while we're here. Maybe we'll catch up with him later."

"I see." She paused, studying his face for a moment in the most unsettling way. "You haven't seen him lately, have you?"

"Not for a week or more," Alec told her. "We've been pretty busy."

There was something hovering behind the old wizard's eyes that looked very much like concern, though she seemed to be masking it. "Is something wrong?" asked Seregil.

Magyana sighed. "I don't know. He just looks so worn-out all of a sudden. I haven't seen him look this tired in decades. He won't talk of it, of course. I wondered if he'd said anything to you?"

"No. As Alec said, we've hardly seen him since the Festival except over a few quick jobs. Maybe it's this business with Lei-teus. You know how he drives himself when he's working on something."

"No doubt," she said, though without much conviction. "Do look in on him when you can, though." She hesitated again. "You two aren't angry with one another, are you?"

A sudden image leapt in Seregil's mind; the night they'd unraveled the palimpsest together, and Nysander suddenly looking at him with a stranger's eyes as he warned—*if you let slip the slightest detail of what I am about to tell you, I shall have to kill all of you.*

He pushed the memory away before it could show in his face. "No, of course not. What would I be angry about?"

Leaving Nysander's chambers, Alec followed Seregil back down through the warren of stairways and corridors to the ground floor.

"The Orëska library is actually scattered all over the building," Seregil explained as they went. "Chambers, vaults, closets, forgotten cupboards, too, probably. Thalonia has been the librarian for a century and I doubt even she knows where everything is. Some books are available to anyone, others are locked away."

"Why, are they valuable?" asked Alec, thinking of the beautifully decorated scrolls Nysander had lent him.

"All books are valuable. Some are dangerous."

"Books of spells, you mean?"

Seregil grinned. "Those, too, but I was thinking more of ideas. Those can be far more dangerous than any magic."

Crossing the atrium court, Seregil swung open the heavy door to the museum. They hadn't been in here since Alec's first visit during Seregil's illness. As they passed the case containing the hands of the dyrmagnos, Tikárie Megraesh, Alec paused, unable to resist peering in at them in spite of his revulsion. Recalling the trick Seregil had played on him last time, he kept his friend carefully in sight.

The wizened fingers were motionless, but he could see freshly scored marks in the oak boards lining the bottom of the case beneath the cruel nails.

"They look quiet enough—" he began, but just then one of the hands clenched spasmodically.

"Bilairy's *Balls*, I hate those things!" He shuddered, backing hurriedly away. "Why do they move like that? Aren't they and all the other pieces of him supposed to be dying?"

"Yes." Seregil looked down at the hands with a puzzled frown. "Yes, they are."

Alec followed Seregil through a stout door at the back of the museum and down two sets of stairs to a series of corridors below the building.

"It's this one here," said Seregil, stopping before an unremarkable door halfway down the passage. "Stay here, I'll go find a custodian to let us in."

Alec leaned against the door and looked about. The walls and floors were made of stone slabs, laid smooth and tight together. Ornate lamps were fastened in brackets at intervals, giving enough light to see clearly from one end of the corridor to the other. He was just wondering whose job it was to keep all those lamps full when Seregil came back with a stooped old man in tow.

The custodian rattled the door open with a huge iron key and then handed Alec a leather sack. Inside were half a dozen large lightstones.

"No flames," the old man warned before creaking off again about his business. "Just leave them outside the door when you've finished."

The chamber was a large one, and filled with closely spaced shelves of books and scrolls.

Holding one of the stones aloft, Alec looked around and groaned. "It'll take us hours to find anything here!"

"It's all very logically arranged and docketed," Seregil assured him, pointing out little cards tacked to the shelves here and there. On each, a few words in faded script indicated general subject areas. "Histories of the Great War" took up several bookcases at the back of the room. Judging by the undisturbed layers of dust on most of them, there had been little interest of late in the subject.

Seregil clucked his tongue disapprovingly. "People ought to make more use of these. The past always sets the stage for the future; any Aurënfaie knows that."

Alec looked at the closely packed tiers in dismay. "Maker's Mercy, Seregil. I can't read all these!"

"Of course not," said Seregil, climbing a small ladder to inspect the contents of an upper shelf. "Half of them aren't even in your language and most of the others are ponderously boring. But there are one or two that are fairly readable, if I can just remember where to look. You browse around down there; stick to things less than two inches thick to begin with and see if you can read them."

If there was a system to the arrangement of the books, it eluded Alec. Books in Skalan stood check by jowl with those in Aurënfaie and half a dozen other languages he couldn't begin to guess at.

Seregil appeared to be right at home, though. Alec watched as his companion went busily to and fro with his ladder, muttering under his breath as he went, or exclaiming happily over old favorites.

Alec had already extracted half a dozen suitably slim volumes when the ornate binding of a thicker one caught his eye. Wondering if it had illustrations, he pulled it out. Unfortunately, this one served as a sort of keystone, for the ones on either side of it let go and most of the shelf cascaded to the floor at Alec's feet.

"Oh, well done!" Seregil snickered from somewhere beyond the next shelves.

Alec set his books aside with an exasperated sigh and began replacing the others. He hadn't been *all* that interested in the war in the first place; his simple query was turning out to be considerably more trouble than it was worth. As he slid a handful of books back into place, however, he noticed something sticking out from behind some others. Curious, he carefully pulled it free and found that it was a slim, plainly bound book held shut with a latched strap. Encouraged by its size more than anything else, he tried to open it, but the catch wouldn't give.

"How are you making out?" asked Seregil, wandering back with a book under his arm.

"I found this in back of some others. It must have fallen in behind." On closer inspection, he saw that it was actually a case of some sort. There was no writing anywhere on it to suggest what its contents might be. "I can't get it open."

Alec jiggled the catch a last time, then handed it to him.

Seregil glanced it over and passed it back. "There's no lock; the catch is just corroded good and tight. It can't have been opened for years. Oh, well, it probably wasn't anything very interesting anyway."

He gave Alec a challenging grin, one Alec had seen often enough before.

"What, here?" he whispered in surprise.

Seregil leaned against a bookcase and gave a careless shrug. "It's not much good to anyone that way, is it?"

After a quick, rather guilty look around to make sure the custodian hadn't returned, Alec drew the black-handled poniard from his boot and worked it under the strap. The deadly sharp blade cut easily through the leather. Sheathing it again, he gently opened the cover and found a loose sheaf of parchment leaves inside. They were badly stained and scorched along the bottom edge, some burned half away. Small, close-packed script covered each on both sides.

"Aura Elustri!" Grinning excitedly, Seregil lifted out the first sheet. "It's in Aurënfaie. It looks to be a journal of some sort—" He read a few lines. "And it's definitely about the war."

"It's so weathered I can hardly make it out," said Alec, taking up another page. "Not that my Aurënfaie's all that good to begin with."

"Anyone would have a hard time making this out." Seregil squinted down at the cramped text a moment longer, then closed it and tucked it under his arm with the other book he'd chosen. Sorting through the ones Alec had selected, he discarded all but

two and hurried Alec upstairs again, obviously eager to tackle the
journal.

Back at Wheel Street again, they retreated to Seregil's chamber
with a supply of wine and fruit. When the fire had been replen-
ished and the lamps lit against the early evening gloom, they
began sorting through the sheets on the hearth rug.

Taking up a page, Seregil studied it closely. "Do you know
what this is?" he exclaimed with a smile of pure delight. "These
are fragments of a field journal kept by an Aurënfaie soldier
during the war. Alec, it's an eyewitness account of events six centuries old! Just wait until we show Nysander. I'll bet no one even
knew this was there, or it would have been in a different vault."

The pages were badly shuffled in places and it took some doing
to sort them out. The translation from Aurënfaie to Skalan was
easy enough; deciphering the crabbed and often smeared writing
while searching through mismatched pages was another matter.
Seregil finally found what appeared to be the earliest entry and
settled back in a nest of cushions on the floor to read it aloud.

They soon pieced together that the author had been a young
archer, part of a regiment of well-to-do volunteers raised by a
local noble. He'd been a faithful diarist, but the entries dealt
mostly with skirmishes and fallen comrades. It was clear that the
Aurënfaie had hated their Plenimaran adversaries, who were con-
sistently depicted as harsh and brutal. There were several mercifully terse descriptions of their barbaric treatment of captured
soldiers and camp followers.

The first series of entries ended with a detailed description of
his first sight of Queen Gërilain of Skala. Referring to her as "a
plain girl in armor," he nonetheless praised her leadership. He
spoke only Aurënfaie, it seemed, but quoted several lines of a
powerful rallying speech she'd given before the Third Battle of
Wyvern Dug, which someone had translated for him. He described
the Skalan soldiers admiringly as "fierce and full of fire."

Stretched out on the carpet, watching the shadows playing
across the ceiling, Alec let the words paint scenes in his imagination. As Seregil read about Gërilain, the first warrior queen, he
found himself picturing Klia, although she was anything but plain.

The second fragment had been written in Mycena during the
battles of high summer, when the regiment had been joined by a

contingent of Aurënfaie wizards. This was followed by an intriguing line about "the necromancers of the enemy," but the rest of the page had been destroyed.

Muttering again, Seregil sorted through the few remaining pages. "Ah, here we are. Part of it's missing, but it begins, 'and our wizards have moved to the front, ahead of the cavalry. The Skalan captain met these forces only two days ago and cannot speak of them without paleness and trembling. Britiel í Kor translated for us, saying he tells of dead men rising from the field to fight the living.' "

"Just like in the legends," Alec murmured, forgetting for a moment that this was a factual account and not some bardic tale.

" 'We've heard this account too often now to call him mad,' " Seregil read on. " 'The Skalan captain claims Plenimar has a terrible war god. We have heard wounded enemies calling upon *Vatharna*. Now learn this is their word for god even they will not name. Nor will Skalans speak it, saying instead with great hatred, Eater of—' "

He faltered to a halt.

"Eater of Death!" Alec finished for him, scrambling up to his knees. "That's it, isn't it? Just like in the prophecy at the Sakor Temple. We've got to find Nysander. The Eater of Death must be that death god you told me about, the bad luck one, Seri—"

Seregil lunged forward, pages scattering as he clamped a hand over Alec's mouth.

"Don't!" he hissed, face white as chalk.

Alec froze, staring up at him in alarm.

Seregil let out a shaky breath and dropped his hand to Alec's shoulder, gripping it lightly. "I'm sorry. I didn't mean to scare you."

"What's the matter?"

"Be still a minute; I have to think."

Seregil felt as if a black chasm had suddenly opened beneath them.

Seriamaius.

—if you let slip the slightest detail of what I am about to tell you, I shall have to kill all of you

join our song, the only song. For the Beautiful One, the Eater of Death—

For an instant the only thing that made any sense was the solid feel of Alec's shoulder, the warm brush of the boy's hair as it fell across the back of his hand.

Memories crowded in on each other, treading dangerously on each other's heels as they threatened to coalesce into a pattern he didn't wish to see.

The palimpsest, telling of a "Beautiful One" and leading to a crown surrounded by the dead. Micum's grim discovery in the Fens. The ragged leather pouch that Nysander had burned. And the coin, that deceptively prosaic wooden disk that had nearly killed him with madness and dreams—dreams of a barren plain and a golden-skinned creature that embraced him, demanding a single blue eye that winked from a wound over his heart. Voices singing—over a barren plain, and deep in the depths of a mountain cavern as blood dripped down to pool on the ice. Nysander's threat—a warning?

"Seregil, that hurts."

Alec's soft, tense voice brought him back and he found himself clutching the boy's shoulder. He hurriedly released him and sat back.

Alec closed cold fingers over his own. "What is it? You look like you've just seen your own ghost."

A desperate ache lanced through Seregil as he looked down into those dark blue eyes.

if you let slip the slightest detail
Damn you, Nysander!

"I can't tell you, *tali*, because I'd only have to lie," he said, suddenly dejected. "I'm going to do something now, and you're going to watch and say nothing."

Taking the final page of the manuscript, he twisted it into a tight squib and tossed it into the fire.

Alec rocked back on his heels, watching in silent consternation as the parchment blossomed into flame. When it was consumed, Seregil knocked the ash to bits with the poker.

"But what about Nysander?" Alec asked. "What will you tell him?"

"Nothing, and neither will you."

"But—"

"We're not betraying him." Seregil took Alec by the shoulders, more gently this time, drawing their faces close together. "You have my oath on that. I believe he already knows what we just learned, but he can't know that you know. Not until I tell you it's safe. Understand?"

"More secrets," Alec said, looking solemn and unhappy.

"Yes, more secrets. I need your trust in this, Alec. Can you give it?"

Alec looked sidelong at the fire for a long moment, then locked eyes with him again and replied in halting Aurënfaie, *"Rei phöril tös tókun meh brithir, vrí sh'ruit'ya."*

Though you thrust your dagger at my eyes, I will not flinch. A solemn oath, and one Seregil had pledged him not so long ago.

Seregil let out a small, relieved laugh. "Thank you. If you don't mind, I think I'll take a rest. Why don't you go have a look through those books we found?"

Alec got up to go without a word. But he paused in the doorway, looking back at Seregil still sitting by the fire.

"What does *tali* mean? Is it Aurënfaie?"

"Tali?" A ghost of the old grin tugged at one corner of Seregil's mouth. "Yes, it's an Aurënfaie term of endearment, rather old-fashioned, like beloved. Where'd you pick that up?"

"I thought—" Alec regarded him quizzically, then shook his head. "I don't know, at one of the salons, probably. Sleep well, Seregil."

"You, too."

When Alec was gone, Seregil walked to the window and rested his forehead against one cold pane, staring out over the dark garden.

Stone within ice. Secrets within secrets. Silences inside of greater silences.

In all the time he'd known Nysander, he had never felt such distance between them. Or so alone.

Several days passed before Alec realized that they were not going to talk of the matter again. Despite his oath, it troubled him greatly. This silence toward the wizard seemed to create a small cold gap in a relationship that had been so seamlessly warm and safe. For the first time in months he found himself wondering about Seregil's loyalties.

Try as he might to banish such thoughts, they nagged at him until at last he came out with it as they were out walking in the Noble Quarter one evening.

He'd feared that Seregil would evade the question or be annoyed. Instead, he looked as if he'd been expecting this discussion.

"Loyalty, eh? That's a large question for a thinking person. If you're asking if I'm still loyal to Nysander, then the answer is yes, for as long as I have faith in his honor. The same goes for any of my friends."

"But do you still have faith in him?" Alec pressed.

"I do, though he hasn't made it easy lately. You're too smart not to have noticed that there are unspoken things between him and me. I'm trying hard to be patient about all that, and so must you.

"But maybe that's not the real issue here. Are you losing faith in me?"

"No!" Alec exclaimed hastily, knowing the words were true as he spoke them. "I'm just trying to understand."

"Well, like I said, loyalty is no simple thing. For instance, would you say that you, Nysander, and I are loyal to Queen Idrilain and want to act in the best interests of Skala?"

"I've always thought so."

"But what if the Queen ordered us, for the good of Skala, to do harm to Micum? Should I keep faith with her or with him?"

"With Micum," Alec replied without hesitation.

"But what if Micum, without our knowledge, had committed treason against Skala? What then?"

"That's ridiculous!" Alec snorted. "He'd never do anything like that."

"People can surprise you, Alec. And perhaps he did it out of loyalty to something else, say his family. He's kept faith with his family but broken faith with the Queen. Which outweighs the other?"

"His family," Alec maintained, although he was beginning to feel a bit confused.

"Certainly. Any man ought to hold his family above all else. But what if his justified act of treason cost hundreds of other families their lives? And what if some of those killed were also friends of ours—Myrhini, Cilla, Thero. Well, maybe not Thero—"

"I don't know!" Alec shrugged uncomfortably. "I can't say one way or the other without knowing the details. I guess I'd just have to have faith in him until I knew more. Maybe he didn't have any choice."

Seregil leveled a stern finger at him. "You always have a

choice. Don't ever imagine you don't. Whatever you do, it's a decision and you have to accept responsibility for it. That's when honor becomes more than empty words."

"Well, I still say I'd have to know why he did it," Alec retorted stubbornly.

"That's good. But suppose, despite all his kindness to you, you discovered he really had betrayed your trust. Would you hunt him down and kill him as the law required?"

"How could I?"

"It would be difficult. Past kindness counts for something. But say you knew for certain that someone else would catch him—the Queen's officers, for instance—and that they'd kill him slowly and horribly. Then wouldn't it be your duty, as a friend and a man of honor, to see to it that he was granted a quick, merciful death? Looked at from that angle, I suppose killing Micum Cavish might be the greatest expression of friendship."

Alec stared at Seregil, mouth slightly ajar. "How the hell did we come to me killing Micum?"

Seregil shrugged. "You asked about loyalty. I told you it wasn't easy."

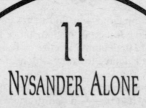

11

NYSANDER ALONE

The hands moved more often now.

As Nysander gazed down at them through the thick sheet of crystal that covered the case, a trick of the light superimposed his reflection over the splayed hands below, creating the illusion that his head lay within the case, gripped in the withered talons of the dead necromancer. The face he saw there was a very old one, etched with weariness. While he watched, the hands slowly curled into fists, clenching so tightly that the skin over one knuckle split, showing brown bone beneath.

Continuing grimly on through the deserted museum, Nysander half expected to hear the Voice from his nightmares, roaring its taunting challenge up through the floor from the depths below. Those dreams came more often now, since Seregil's return from the Asheks.

Summoning an orb of light, Nysander opened the door at the back of the museum chamber and began the long descent through the vaults.

He'd wooed Magyana here in the days of their youth. When she'd remained obdurate in her celibacy, they had continued to share long discussions as they wandered along these narrow stone corridors. Seregil had often come with them during his ill-starred apprenticeship, asking a thousand questions and poking into everything.

Thero came with him occasionally, though less often than he once had. Did Ylinestra bring him down here to make love, Nysander wondered, as she had him? By the Four, she'd warmed the very stones with her relentless passion!

He shook his head in bemusement as he imagined her with Thero; a sunbird embracing a crow.

He'd never completely trusted the sorceress. Talented as Ylinestra was at both magic and love, greed lurked just behind her smile. In that way she was not unlike Thero, but Thero was bound by Orëska law; she was not.

The fact that she had gone from his bed to Thero's troubled Nysander in a way that had nothing to do with former passions, though he had been unable to convince Thero of that. After two tense, unpleasant attempts, Nysander had dropped the subject.

Other wizards might have dismissed an assistant over such a matter, he knew, yet in spite of their growing differences, Nysander still felt a strong regard for Thero and refused to give up on him.

And mixed with that regard, he admitted once again in the silence of the vaults, was the fear that many of his fellows in the Orëska would be glad to take on Thero if he let him go. Many were critical of Nysander's handling of the talented young wizard, and thought Thero was wasted on the eccentric old man in the east tower. After all, he'd ruined one apprentice already, hadn't he? Small wonder Thero seemed discontent.

But Nysander knew the boy better than any of them and believed with every fiber of his being that given his head at this stage of training, the young wizard would ultimately ruin himself. Oh, he would earn his robes, of course, probably in half the time it would take most. That was part of the problem. Thero was so apt a pupil that most masters would joyously fill his head with all they knew, guiding him quickly through the levels to true power.

But more than a keen mind and flawless ability were needed to make so powerful a wizard as Thero would undoubtedly become. Ungoverned by wisdom, patience, and a compassionate heart, that same keen mind would be capable of unspeakable havoc.

So he kept Thero with him, hopeful to change him, fearful to let him go.

There were moments, such as the night he found him tending to

Seregil's injuries after the misadventure in the sewers, when Nysander caught a gleam of hope—signs that Thero might be coming to understand what it was that Nysander was asking of him beyond the mere learning of magic.

Reaching the door to the lowest vault, he shook off his reverie and hastened on.

Few had reason to go to this lowest vault, which for time out of mind had been the Orëska's repository for the forgotten, the useless, and the dangerous. Many of the storerooms were empty now, or cluttered with mouldering crates. Other doors had been walled up, their frames outlined with runic spells and warnings. But as he walked along, the sound of his footsteps muffled on the dank brick underfoot, he could hear the bowl and its high, faint resonance, audible only to those trained to listen for it. The sound was much stronger than it once had been.

The wooden disk had had little effect on it; its power was incomplete separated from the seven others Nysander knew existed somewhere in the world. The crystal crown was a different matter. As soon as he'd placed it here, the resonance of the bowl had grown increasingly stronger, and with it his nightmares.

And the movements of the necromancer's hands in the museum.

How Seregil had survived his exposure to the disk unprotected by anything but his own magical block was still a mystery. Equally mystifying was how little protection all Nysander's carefully prepared spells and charms had been for Seregil from the effects of the crown. In the first case he should have died, in the second he should have had absolute protection, yet in both cases he had sustained wounds but survived.

All this, taken together with the words the Oracle of Illior had spoken to Seregil, left Nysander with the uneasy conviction that much more than mere coincidence was at work.

Stopping, he faced the familiar stretch of wall yet again. With a final check to be certain no eyes, natural or otherwise, were upon him, he spoke a powerful key spell and cast a sighting through stone and magic to the small hidden room beyond.

Immured in the darkness of centuries, the bowl sat on the tiny chamber's single shelf. To the uninitiated, it was nothing more than a crude vessel of burnt clay, unremarkable in any way. Yet this homely object had dominated his entire adult life, and the lives of three wizards before him.

The Guardians.

To one side of the bowl lay the crystal box containing the disk; on the other, still smeared with the ash of Dravnian cook fires, was the flat wooden case holding the crown.

For no better reason than curiosity, he spoke the Spell of Passage and entered the chamber.

Magic crackled ominously around him in spite of the wards and containment spells. Taking a lightstone from his pocket, he held it up and regarded the bowl solemnly for a moment, thinking again of his predecessors. None of them, not even Arkoniel, had anticipated ever adding to the contents of this hidden and most guarded chamber. Now he had, not once but twice, and their combined song was a pulse of living energy.

His hands stole to the containers on either side of the bowl. *What would that song be if I opened these, brought even these three fragments together without the rest? What could be learned from such an experiment?*

His right thumb found the catch on the wooden box, rubbed tentatively at it—

Nysander jerked back, made a warding sign, and retreated the way he'd come. Alone in the corridor, he broke the Spell of Passage and slumped against the opposite wall, his heart pounding ominously in his chest.

If just three fragments of the whole could force such thoughts into his mind, then he must be all the more vigilant.

Forced those thoughts into your mind, old man, a niggling inner voice chided, *or revealed them there? How many times did Arkoniel warn you that temptation is nothing more than the dark mirror of the soul?*

Inevitably, regret followed hard on the heels of memory. Arkoniel had taught him well and early the responsibility of the Guardians, allowing him to share the weight of the secret they preserved. Whom did he share it with?

No one.

Seregil could have been trusted, but the magic had failed him. Thero had the magic, but lacked—what?

Humility, Nysander decided sadly. The humility to properly fear the power contained in this tiny, silver-lined chamber. The more apparent Thero's abilities became over the years of his apprenticeship, the more certain Nysander was that temptation would be his undoing. Temptation and pride.

Feeling suddenly far older than his two hundred and ninety-eight years, Nysander pressed a hand to the wall, bolstering the warding spells, changing and strengthening them to conceal what must remain concealed. It was a task he'd once thought he would pass along as his master had passed it to him. Now he felt no such certainty.

12
BEKA'S SEND-OFF

Seregil and Alec were lingering over a late lunch one bright afternoon toward the middle of Dostin, when Runcer entered the room with a ragged young girl in tow. Seregil looked up expectantly, recognizing her as the sort who made her living as a message carrier.

"Beka Cavish sends word that the Queen's Horse is riding out at dawn tomorrow," the girl recited stiffly.

"Thanks." Seregil handed her a sester and pushed a plate of sweets her way. Grinning, the child snatched a handful and hid them away in the folds of her ragged skirt.

"Take this message to Captain Myrhini, of the Queen's Horse," he told her. "As Beka Cavish's patron, I'm honor-bound to give her and her turma a proper send-off. The captain is asked to attend and keep order. She may bring anyone else she likes, so long as she gives Beka and her riders a night out. Got that?"

She proudly repeated it back word for word.

"Good girl. Off you go." Turning back to Alec, Seregil found his young friend frowning worriedly.

"I thought you said nothing would happen before spring?" Alec asked.

"The war? It won't," Seregil replied, somewhat surprised by the news himself. "The Queen must have some reason to think the Plenimarans mean to move in early spring, though, and wants troops near the border in case of trouble."

"This doesn't give us time enough to send for Micum and Kari."

"Damn! I didn't even think of that." Seregil drummed his fingers on the polished tabletop a moment. "Oh, well. We'll ride out tomorrow with the details. In the meantime, we've got a party to prepare for."

Word soon came back by the same messenger that Captain Myrhini would release Lieutenant Cavish and her riders for the evening, with the expectation that sufficient food and drink were included in the offer. Seregil had already turned his attention to the preparations with an efficiency that astonished Alec.

Within a few hours, extra servants had been engaged, a raucous group of musicians was installed in the gallery with their fiddles, pipes, and drums, and a steady stream of deliveries from the market had been whipped into a proper feast by the cook and her crew.

In the meantime, the salon was cleared of all breakables and three long trestle tables set up, together with hogsheads of ale and wine set on pitched braces at the head of the room.

Beka and her turma rode into Wheel Street at sunset. They were an impressive sight in their spotless white breeches and green tabards sewn with the regimental crest.

A little daunting even, thought Alec, standing next to Seregil at the front door to welcome them. He'd always envied Beka just a little, being part of such an elite group. The idea of riding into a pitched battle surrounded by comrades had a certain romantic appeal.

"Welcome!" Seregil called.

Beka dismounted and strode up the front steps, her eyes shining almost as brightly as the burnished lieutenant's gorget hanging at her throat.

"You do us a great honor, my lords," she said loudly, giving them a wink.

Seregil bowed slightly, then looked over the crowd of riders milling behind her. "That's a rough-looking bunch you brought. Think they can behave themselves?"

"Not a chance, my lord," Beka replied smartly.

Seregil grinned. "Well then, come on in, all of you!"

Alec's awe diminished somewhat as the men and women of Beka's command filed past into the painted salon. He'd only seen them at a distance on the practice field before—dashing figures clashing in mock battle. Now he saw that most of them were scarcely older than he. Some had the bearing of landless second sons and daughters or merchant's scions; others—those who stood gaping at the opulent room—came from humbler backgrounds and had earned their place by sheer prowess and the price of a horse and arms.

"I'd like to introduce my sergeants," Beka said. "Mercalle, Braknil, and Portus."

Shaking hands with the trio, Alec guessed that most of them had come up through the ranks. Sergeant Mercalle was tall and dark-complected. She was also missing the last two fingers of her right hand, a common wound among warriors. Next to her stood Braknil, a big, solemn-looking man with a bushy blond beard and weather-roughened skin. The third, Portus, was younger than his companions and carried himself like a noble. Alec wondered what his story was; according to Beka, it seemed unlikely that he would not be an officer of some rank.

Seregil shook hands with them. "I won't embarrass your lieutenant by telling you how long I've known her, but I will say that she's been trained by some of the best swordsmen I know."

"I can believe that, your lordship," Braknil replied. "That's why I asked to serve with her."

Beka grinned. "Sergeant Braknil's too tactful to say so, but he was one of the sergeants assigned to train the new commissions when I came in. I started out taking orders from him."

"A title may guarantee an officer's commission, but it doesn't guarantee the officer's quality," Mercalle put in rather sourly. "Especially if there hasn't been a real war to winnow out the chaff in a while. I've seen a good many sporting the steel gorget who won't see high summer."

"Mercalle's our optimist," Portus chuckled, and Alec heard the remnants of a lower city accent behind the man's smooth words.

"It's early for you to be sent north, isn't it?" he asked ingenuously.

"There are rumblings from Plenimar already," Beka told him. "Queen Idrilain and the Archons of Mycena all want troops in place near the west border of Plenimar before the roads thaw into mud holes next month. They're not making any secret of it, either. The Sakor Horse Regiment and a squadron of the Yrkani Horse have already headed up to Nanta. We'll be going farther east."

" 'First in, last out,' " Portus said proudly. "That's been our motto since Gërilain's day."

"The Queen's Horse Guard started as the token group of soldiers King Thelátimos gave his daughter after the Oracle said a woman was to lead the country," Seregil explained. "She surprised everyone when she led them successfully in battle."

Braknil nodded. "One of my ancestors was with Gërilain and there's been at least one of my family with the Guard ever since."

Stationed by the front door, Runcer announced gravely, "Captain Myrhini and Commander Perris, of the Queen's Horse, my lords."

Myrhini strode in, accompanied by a handsome uniformed man Alec had seen around the drilling field. Beka and her riders instantly snapped to attention.

Myrhini introduced her companion as Commander Perris, who led one of the other squadrons of the regiment, then looked around, scowling. "What, no one drunk yet? Lieutenant Beka, explain yourself."

"I'll see to it at once, Captain!" Beka replied, coloring a bit.

Seregil laid a hand on her arm. "I thought perhaps some of your soldiers might be a bit self-conscious dancing with each other, so I took the liberty of inviting a few other guests to liven things up."

At his gesture, the musicians struck up a sprightly tune and a score of richly dressed men and women entered from the dining room, streaming out to partner the soldiers.

"Who are they?" asked Beka, her eyes widening in surprise.

Seregil exchanged an amused look with Alec. "Oh, just a few friends of mine from the Street of Lights who think the Queen's best regiment deserves nothing less than the best."

Myrhini covered a smile as Beka's eyes went wider still as she recognized the significance of the colored tokens each elegant "guest" wore discreetly on their clothing or in their hair—white, green, rose, or amber.

Alec leaned closer to Beka. "From what I understand, you'll want to stick with amber."

"From what I understand, Sir Alec, I think I'll stick with you," Beka retorted, slipping her arm through his. "Come on and show a soldier a good time, eh?"

• • •

"You are a generous patron," Commander Perris noted with amusement. "Mind if I join in? I see a familiar face or two."

"By all means," Seregil said, smiling.

Myrhini followed Seregil to the table and accepted a cup of wine. "They can do with a bit of spoiling," she said, watching the milling throng with obvious affection. "It'll be cold camps and long riding for us between now and spring."

"And then?" asked Seregil.

Myrhini glanced at him over the rim of her cup, then sighed. "And then it will get worse. Most likely a lot worse."

"Will this lot be ready?"

"As ready as green soldiers can be. These ones here are some of the best, and so is Beka. I just hope they can stay alive long enough to get seasoned. Nothing but battle experience can do that for them."

By midnight Alec was drunker than he'd ever been in his life and not only knew all the riders and courtesans by name, but had danced with most of them.

He'd just staggered through a reel with a blue-eyed, tipsily amorous rider named Ariani when Corporal Kallas and his twin brother Aulos grabbed him and hoisted him onto one of the tables.

"Lieutenant says you're lucky," Kallas bawled, pulling off his tabard and handing it up to Alec. "So we're making you our mascot, young Alec my lad."

Alec pulled on the uniform and made the company an exaggerated bow. "I am honored!"

"You are drunk!" someone shouted back.

Alec considered this, then nodded solemnly. "I am that, but as the Maker teaches us, in the depths of the cup lies the back door to enlightenment—or something like that, anyway." Snatching up a half-full bottle of wine, he waved it in their general direction. "And the drunker I get, the braver and worthier you all look to me!"

"A visionary of the vine," Kallas exclaimed, spreading his arms in mock reverence. "Give me your blessing, O beardless sage!"

Alec obligingly slopped some wine on the man's upturned face. "Long life and a hollow leg, my son."

Laughing and cheering, the rest of the riders crowded around for his benediction. Quite a number were missing, he noted, and so were most of the courtesans.

He sprinkled the supplicants liberally, doing each in turn until he came to the last, Beka. Her freckled face was flushed with wine and dancing; her wild red hair had escaped her braid and floated in untidy wisps around it. She was as drunk as any of them, and as happy.

As she grinned expectantly up at him, however, Alec felt a brief, sobering chill. His friend, his almost sister, was going off to war.

"Come on, mascot, don't you have any luck left for me?" she demanded.

Grabbing up a fresh bottle, Alec upended it over her head. "Long life, and luck in the shadows and the light."

Beka sputtered and laughed and those around her cheered.

"Well done, mascot," Kallas said. "A blessing that wet's likely to make her immortal!"

"I hope so," Alec whispered, looking down at her. "I do hope so."

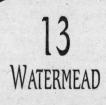

13
WATERMEAD

"Master Micum, there's riders coming up the hill," a servant shouted to him across the snowy pasture.

Standing atop the hayrack, Micum shaded his eyes against the late afternoon sun and quickly scanned the frozen river boundary. Two horsemen were riding up from the bridge a mile below.

He'd been leery of unannounced visitors since returning from the northlands that past autumn. Despite all Nysander's assurances to the contrary, he still didn't feel easy in his mind about Mardus and his gang.

So he studied the riders with a chary eye. Seeing that they kept to the main track, and rode at an unhurried canter with weapons sheathed, he ruled out enemy or messenger. They were still too far away to make out faces, but he soon recognized the horses.

Frowning, he pushed his way through the colts milling around the hayrack and set off for the house. More often than not, unexpected visits from Seregil meant a summons to Watcher business. Kari was three moons gone now and the sickness had passed, leaving in its wake the glowing bloom of mid term pregnancy. Nonetheless, she was older this time and he disliked the thought of leaving her.

A farm hand met him apologetically in the courtyard. "Illia run ahead with the dogs to meet 'em soon as she made out who it was, Master Micum. I didn't think it no harm."

"Not this time maybe, Ranil, but I don't like her getting in the habit of it," Micum retorted gruffly.

Seregil and Alec clattered into the court a few moments later, with Illia perched proudly on Alec's saddlebow. They were both looking a little pale, Micum noted, but they seemed in good spirits otherwise.

"So I might have to marry Alec when I'm grown," Illia was prattling across to Seregil. "I hope that won't hurt your feelings too much."

Seregil slapped a hand over his heart like a troubadour in a mural. "Ah, fair maiden, I shall slay a thousand evil dragons for you, and lay their steaming black livers at your dainty feet, if only you will restore me to your favor."

"Livers!" Illia buried her face against Alec's shoulder with an outraged giggle. "You wouldn't bring me livers, would you, Alec?"

"Of course not," Alec scoffed. "What a disgusting present. I'd bring you the eyeballs for a necklace, and all their scaly pointed tongues to tie your braids with."

Shrieking with delight, Illia slid off into her father's arms.

"Hey, little bird, what are you doing running off by yourself?" he asked sternly.

"It's just Uncle Seregil and Alec. And I wasn't alone," she added coyly, shawl askew as she spread her arms grandly over the pack of great shaggy hounds jostled around them, like a general over her troops. "Dash and all the others came with me."

"You know the rules, young miss," Micum remonstrated. "Run in now and tell your mother who's here."

"What brings you two up?" he asked, turning back to the others with a twinge of relief; they were dressed for visiting rather than traveling.

Seregil waded through the dogs to hand him a stitched packet of letters. "Beka asked us to bring this out to you. Her regiment left at dawn."

"What, today? We should have been there to see her off!"

"There wasn't time," Alec explained quickly, coming up beside Seregil. "The orders came yesterday. We gave her and her riders a proper send-off last night, though." He rubbed his head with a rueful grin. "I think I'm still a little drunk."

Seregil ruffled Alec's hair with playful impunity. "Runcer will be a couple of days clearing up the wreckage. Between that, and the complaints from the neighbors, we figured it might be a good time for Lord Seregil and Sir Alec to lay low for a few days. We thought we'd put up here, if that's agreeable."

"Yes, of course," Micum replied distractedly, fingering the packet of letters. "Where were they headed?"

"The western border of Mycena," Seregil told him. "Word is Idrilain wanted them in place before the Klesin thaws muck up the roads next month. The Queen's Horse was the first to go, but the city was swarming with soldiers by the time we rode out. Idrilain isn't taking any chances."

Micum shook his head, wondering how Kari was going to take this news. "Ranil, see to their horses. If you two will excuse me a minute, I want a look at these."

Seregil laid a hand on his arm as he turned to go. Casting a quick glance toward the door, he said in a low voice, "There's something else. Rhal tracked us down in Rhíminee about a month ago."

Micum tensed. "That river trader?"

Seregil nodded. "Some foreign-sounding swordsmen showed up looking for the three of us after Alec and I had gotten off. Rhal covered our tracks, and soon after the *Darter* went down under questionable circumstances. We've been careful since, and there's been no sign of trouble so far, but with spring coming on—you never know. That's another reason we want to move back to the inn."

"What's Nysander say to all this?"

Seregil shrugged. "He's keeping a wizard eye out for trouble. So far he hasn't spotted anything."

"They must have lost us in Mycena," Alec put in, sounding as if he and Seregil had had this discussion before. "Otherwise, we'd have been approached or attacked."

"So you'd think," Micum allowed. "Still, you're smart to be careful. Go see to your gear. I'll break the news to Kari."

"We won't hurry, then, eh?" Seregil said, giving him an understanding look.

• • •

Kari took the news of Beka's departure more calmly than Micum had feared. Reading over Beka's letter, and those from Elsbet, she merely nodded and then folded them carefully back into the wrapper.

Old Arna and the other household servants joined them by the central fire in the hall as Seregil described Beka's departure in glowing detail.

"They looked grand, riding out of the city by torchlight," he said. "Klia and the high officers rode at the fore in full uniform, helmets and all. And there was our Beka at the head of her turma with a steel lieutenant's gorget at her throat. The horses had bronze chest plates and cheek pieces that jingled like bells as they rode."

"She wrote that she's in Captain Myrhini's troop," noted Kari, stroking Illia's dark head as the little girl leaned against her knee.

"Myrhini's as good a captain as there is," Micum said, pulling her close. "The frontier will be quiet for a while yet, too. The Pleni-marans couldn't get that far west much before mid-Lithion at the earliest and probably not until early summer. She'll have time to find her feet before any trouble starts."

"I hope so," murmured Kari. "Will there be more letters?"

"Dispatch riders go back and forth as often as possible," Seregil assured her.

"That's good, then."

Micum exchanged uneasy glances with the others, but after a moment she simply tucked the letters away and rose with her usual briskness.

"Well, Arna, you and I had better go see to the supper. Micum, tell the men to set up the tables. You two chose a good night to come, Seregil; we've got venison pie and apples baked in cream."

The meal was the usual noisy communal affair and the guests were summoned to give news of the absent daughters between mouthfuls. Watermead was a country household, close-knit and loyal. The servants wouldn't be satisfied until they'd had descriptions of Beka's regiment twice over and a detailed account of Elsbet's studies at the temple school.

Later, when a loudly protesting Illia had been put to bed and the servants had spread their pallets in the warmth of the hall, Micum and Kari joined Seregil and Alec in the guest chamber.

"Tell me about your reunion with this fellow Rhal," Micum said when he'd poured hot spiced cider for everyone.

Sprawled crossways on the bed, Seregil launched into what sounded like a highly colored tale of their ambush of Rhal and the subsequent battle with a mob of alley toughs. Alec's prowess was featured in such flattering detail that the boy, who was sitting close beside Kari, flushed with surprise.

"Well done, Alec," Kari laughed, hugging him.

"This Captain Rhal of yours sounds like a man worth knowing," Micum said. "I've thought so ever since you told how he let you go that night."

"Micum told me something of your trip, but I'd like to hear your version of it," said Kari. "Did he really fancy Seregil, Alec?"

Alec grinned. "I half fancied him myself, when he was all prettied up. As it was, I had all I could do to keep the two of them at arm's length."

With frequent interruptions from Seregil, he went on to describe Rhal's attempts at seduction, and Micum noticed that both of them skillfully omitted any mention of the wooden disk, or the influence it had exerted over Seregil. In this account, Rhal had simply walked in on Seregil in an unfortunate state of undress. It all came out sounding a great deal more humorous than the original version Micum had heard in Nysander's tower.

"Ah, Seregil," Kari exclaimed, wiping her eyes with the corner of her apron. "I've never known anyone who could get himself into such messes, and then right back out again!"

"It would have been considerably more difficult if Alec hadn't been such a faithful defender of my virtue." Seregil gave Alec a courtly nod.

"My lady," Alec murmured, rising to give him a bow of such elaborate solemnity that they all burst out laughing again.

"I was watching Seregil's face tonight," Kari said as they lay together in the darkness that night. "He's in love with Alec, you know. He wasn't last time they were here, or even at the Festival, but he is now."

"Are you surprised?" Micum yawned, resting a hand lazily on the roundness of her belly, hoping to feel the new life fluttering there.

"Only that it took so long. I doubt he knows it yet himself. But what about Alec?"

"I don't think such a thing would occur to him, with his upbringing and all."

Kari let out a long sigh. "Poor Seregil. He has such rotten luck when it comes to love. Just once, I'd like to see him happy."

"Seems to me you had your chance about twenty years back," Micum teased, nuzzling her bare shoulder.

"When it was *you* he fancied, you mean?" She rolled quickly on top of him, pinning him playfully as she straddled his thighs. "And if I had relinquished my claim to you, sir?" she challenged. "What would you have done then, eh?"

"I can't say," he replied, pulling her mouth to his with one hand, finding the generous curve of her hip with the other. "Perhaps it would've been handy, having a bed mate who's good with a sword."

"It's true I don't bring anything sharp into bed with me."

"Mmmmm—I can feel that," Micum rumbled contentedly. "Perhaps it's just as well things worked out the way they did."

Kari moved over him like a blessing, her lips hot against his brow. "I like to think so."

Seregil hadn't shared a bed with Alec since their last visit to Watermead. He'd thought nothing of it then; such arrangements were common, especially in old country houses.

But this time was different.

He wasn't certain just when his feelings had gotten away from him, or why. Months of close living and shared dangers, perhaps, together with the genuine affection Seregil knew had existed between them almost from the start.

It figures, he thought dourly as they undressed for bed. He never could seem to love anyone who could return the favor.

Not that Alec didn't care for him in his own honest, Dalnan way—Seregil had no doubt of that. But he did doubt that Alec's heart skipped a dizzy beat at the mere thought of sliding in between shared sheets.

Out of deference to Alec's modesty—or so he told himself—he kept his long shirt on and pulled up the coverlet.

The old bedstead, built for company, was a wide one and Alec kept to his side of it as he climbed in. "You're quiet all of a sudden," he remarked, oblivious to Seregil's inner turmoil.

"All that wine last night left me tired." Seregil mustered a yawn. He could go sleep in the hall, he supposed, but that would take some explaining later on. Better to stay here and hope he didn't talk in his sleep.

Alec settled against the bolsters with a sigh of contentment. "Me, too. At least we can get some rest while we're out here. So quiet. No jobs or midnight summons. No worries—" His eyes drifted shut and his voice trailed off into deep, even breathing.

No worries.

Seregil sat up to extinguish the lamp, but paused, caught by the sight of Alec's thick, honey-gold hair fanned out across the pillow. His expression was peaceful, guileless. His lips curved in a faint smile as if good dreams had already come to him.

For an instant Seregil wondered what it would feel like to have that golden head against his shoulder, the warmth of Alec's body against his own.

If it had been simple lust Seregil felt, he could easily have driven it off. But what he felt for Alec at that moment went far beyond that.

Seregil loved him.

Little more than the length of a tailor's yard separated them, but it might just as well have been the breadth of the Osiat Sea. Allowing himself nothing more than a deep, silent sigh, he blew out the lamp and lay back, praying for sleep.

Rising early the next morning, Micum found Alec stacking wood in the kitchen. The boy had changed his city clothes for plain garb and was sharing some joke with Arna and young Jalis. Watching a moment from the doorway, Micum was struck again by how easily Alec seemed to fit into the rhythm of the household.

Or anywhere else, come to that, he amended, thinking of all the roles and identities Alec had played in the time he'd been with Seregil. They were like water, those two, always shifting shape.

"It's a fine day for hunting," he announced. "The deer have been thick up on the ridge this year. His lordship up yet?"

Alec brushed dirt and bark fragments from his tunic. "He was still buried somewhere under the covers last time I looked. I don't think he slept well last night."

"Is that so?" Micum went to the kitchen door and reached outside for a handful of loose snow. "Well then, he wants waking up,
doesn't he? I'm sure he'd hate to miss such a beautiful morning."

Mirroring his grin, Alec got himself a handful and followed
Micum to the bedroom.

The shutters were still closed, but there was enough light for
them to make out the long form beneath the quilts on Seregil's
side of the bed.

Together, Micum signed to Alec.

Stalking in silently, they threw back the quilts and launched
their assault, only to find they'd ambushed a bolster.

The shutters banged open behind them and two familiar voices
shouted, "Good morning!"

Startled, Micum and Alec looked up just in time to catch
a faceful of snow from Seregil and Illia, laughing victoriously
outside.

"Sneak up on me, will you?" Seregil jeered as he and the
girl fled.

"After them!" cried Micum, scrambling out through the window.

An ungainly chase ensued. Illia wisely dodged into the kitchen
and was granted asylum by Arna, who brandished a copper ladle
at all would-be abductors.

Seregil wasn't so lucky. Never at his best in a daylight fight, he
stumbled over one of the excited dogs who'd joined in the hunt
and was tackled by Alec. Micum caught up and together they
heaved Seregil into a drift and sat on him.

"Traitor!" he sputtered as Alec thrust a handful of snow down
the back of his shirt.

Micum cut him short with another handful in the face. "I
believe I owed you that," he chortled, "and here's another with
interest."

By the time they let him up, Seregil looked like a poorly carved
sculpture done in white sugar.

"What do you say to a hunt?" Micum asked, attempting to
brush him off a bit.

"Actually, I had more of a quiet day by the fire in mind,"
Seregil gasped, shaking snow from his hair.

Grabbing him, Micum tossed him easily over one broad
shoulder. "Find me a fresh drift, Alec."

"There's a good one right there."

"I'll go, I'll go, damn you!" howled Seregil, struggling like a cat.

"What did I tell you?" laughed Micum, setting him on his feet. "I knew he'd want to."

With dry clothes and a quick breakfast, the three of them set off into the hills above Watermead with bows and hounds.

The dogs struck the trail of a boar first, but Micum called them off that, since they hadn't brought spears.

For the rest of the morning they found nothing but birds and rabbits. At Alec's insistence, Seregil had brought a bow and no one was more surprised than he when he managed to hit a roosting grouse.

They were just thinking of stopping for a midday meal when the dogs flushed a bull elk from a stand of fir. They chased it for nearly half an hour before Alec put a broadhead shaft into the great beast's heart, dropping it in midleap.

"One shot, by the Maker!" Micum exclaimed, swinging out of the saddle to inspect the kill.

"Quick and clean," said Alec, kneeling to inspect the shot. "That way they don't suffer."

Alec had dropped armed men with the same merciful economy, thought Micum, inspecting the red-fletched shaft protruding from the animal's side.

They built a fire and began dressing out the carcass. It was messy work; the snow around them was soon stained a steaming scarlet. Opening the belly, Micum tossed the entrails to the dogs and presented the heart and liver to Alec, his due for the killing shot.

"We'll need more water before we're done," Micum remarked as they set about the skinning.

Alec wiped his bloodied hands in the snow. "We passed a stream a ways back. I'll go refill the water skins."

Seregil paused in his work, following Alec with his eyes until the boy had ridden out of sight between the trees. Beside him, Micum smiled to himself, thinking of what Kari had said.

"He's grown up a lot, hasn't he?" he ventured presently.

Seregil shrugged, going back to his skinning. "He's had to, ramming around with the likes of us."

"You've come to think quite a lot of him, I'd say."

Seregil saw through his flimsy words in an instant and his smile faded to hard, flat denial. "If you think I—"

"I'd never think ill of you for the world. I just think that heart of yours leads you down some hard trails, that's all. You haven't said anything to him, have you?"

Seregil's face was a careful mask of indifference, but his shoulders sagged visibly. "No, and I'm not going to. It wouldn't be— honorable. I have too much influence over him."

"Well, he loves you well in his own fashion," Micum said, unable to think of anything more optimistic.

The silence spun out between them again, less comfortable this time. Loosening the last bit of hide, Micum set his knife aside.

"Do you have any idea what Nysander is up to? I haven't heard a thing from him since the Festival."

This time there was no mistaking the troubled look in his friend's eyes.

"Secrets, Micum. Still secrets. He's driven me half-mad with them," Seregil admitted, warming himself at the fire.

"Have you found anything out on your own?"

Seregil stirred the embers with a branch, sending up a little flock of sparks. "Not much. And I'm oath-bound not to talk about it. I'm sorry."

"Don't apologize. We both know how the game works. How's Alec handling it, though? He's smart enough to put things together and I'd say he's about as easy to put off a scent as you are."

"True." Seregil gave a humorless laugh. "I'm worried, Micum. Something really bad is coming down the road and I can't tell who's in the way."

Micum hunkered down beside him. "If anyone can look out for him, it's you. But there are some other things you could be telling him. He has a right to know."

Seregil shot to his feet and waved at Alec as he rode out of the trees toward them.

"Not yet," he said, his voice too soft for Micum to tell if the words were a command or a plea.

14
THE STREET OF LIGHTS

After three days at Watermead, Alec and Seregil returned to the city under cover of night and made their way quietly back to the Cockerel. Runcer would keep up appearances at Wheel Street; Lord Seregil was in town, but not always available.

Thryis and the others had gone to bed when they arrived, but the aromas still lingering in the darkened kitchen—new bread, dried fruit, garlic, wine, and ashy coals banked on the hearth—were enough welcome for Alec.

Ruetha appeared from somewhere and followed them up to the second floor. Alec scooped her up and held her until Seregil had disarmed the succession of warding glyphs that protected the hidden stairway leading to their rooms. Alec grinned to himself as Seregil whispered the passwords that had once sounded so exotically magical.

The command for the glyph at the base of the stairs was *Etuis miära koriatüan cyris.* "Your grandmother insults the chickens."

Halfway up: *Clarin magril.* "Raspberries, saddle."

For the hidden door at the top of the stairs the word was *Nodense*: "Almost."

The nonsense was intentional, making it virtually impossible for anyone to guess the secret words. Only the final command, the one for the door into the sitting room, had any meaning. *Bôkthersa* was the name of Seregil's birthplace.

Seregil crossed the room with the aid of a lightstone and lit the fire. As the flames leapt up, he surveyed the room in surprise. "Illior's Hands, don't tell me you cleaned the place up before you left for Wheel Street?"

"Just enough so I could walk across the room safely," Alec replied, going to his neat, narrow bed in the corner near the hearth. He didn't particularly mind Seregil's chaotic living habits, but he did dislike stepping on sharp objects barefoot, or having heavy things fall on him from shelves. Hanging his sword and bow case on their nails above the bed, he stretched out with a contented sigh.

Seregil collapsed on the sofa in front of the fire. "You know, it strikes me that this is all a bit of a comedown for you. After having your own chamber, I mean. Perhaps we should think about expanding our accommodations here. There are empty rooms on either side of us."

"Don't bother on my account." Yawning, Alec crossed his arms behind his head. "I like things just as they are."

Seregil smiled up at the shadow of a dusty cobweb wavering overhead. "So do I, now that you mention it."

Their pleasure at returning to the inn was marred by a sudden scarcity of jobs. The few that had come in during their absence were petty matters, and over the next week new ones were slow to follow. For the first time in their acquaintance, Alec saw Seregil grow bored.

To make matters worse, late winter was the dreariest season in Rhíminee despite the lengthening days. The icy rains brought thicker fog in off the sea, and a grey dampness seemed to get into everything. Alec found himself sleeping well past dawn, and then nodding off over whatever he was doing in the evening with the sound of the rain lulling him like a heartbeat. Seregil, on the other hand, became increasingly restless.

Returning from a visit with Nysander one dank afternoon near the end of Dostin, Alec found Seregil working at the writing desk. The parchment in front of him was half-covered with musical notations, but he appeared to have lost interest in the project. Chin on hand, he was staring glumly out at the fog slinking by like a jilted lover.

"Did you check with Rhiri on your way up?" he asked without turning his head.

"Nothing new," Alec replied, unwrapping the books the wizard had lent him.

"Damn. And I've already checked everywhere else. If people keep behaving themselves like this we'll be out of a job."

"How about a game of bakshi?" Alec offered. "I could use some practice on those cheats you showed me yesterday."

"Maybe later. I don't seem to be in the mood." With an apologetic shrug, Seregil returned to his composition.

Suit yourself, thought Alec. Clearing a space on the room's central table, he settled down to study the compendium of rare beasts Nysander had given him. The text was somewhat beyond his ability, but he stubbornly puzzled it out, relying on the illustrations for clues when the gist of a passage eluded him. With cold mists swirling against the windowpanes, a fire crackling on the hearth, and a cup of tea at his elbow, it was not an unpleasant way to occupy an afternoon.

It did require considerable concentration, however, which quickly proved difficult as Seregil abandoned the desk and began wandering around the room. First he toyed with an unusual lock he'd picked up somewhere, grinding noisily away at the wards with a succession of picks. A few moments later he tossed it onto a shelf with the others and disappeared into his chamber, where Alec could hear him rummaging through the chests and trunks piled there and muttering aloud, either to himself or the ever faithful Ruetha.

Presently he reappeared with an armload of scrolls. Kicking the scattered cushions into a pile in front of the fire, he settled himself to read. But this pursuit was equally short-lived. After a brief perusal involving considerable rustling of parchments and muttered asides, each document was relegated in rapid succession into the fire or onto a dusty pile beneath the couch. With this task completed, he lay back among the cushions and began to whistle softly between his teeth, keeping time to his tune by tapping the toe of one boot against the ash shovel.

Not even Nysander's excellent bestiary could withstand such distraction. Realizing he'd just read the same sentence for the third time, Alec carefully closed the book.

"We could do some shooting in the back court," he suggested, trying not to let his exasperation show.

Seregil looked up in surprise. "Oh, sorry. Am I disturbing you?"

"Well—"

He stood up again with a sigh. "I'm not fit to be around today, I'm afraid. I'll get out of your way." With this he returned to his room, emerging a few moments later wearing his best cloak. He'd changed his rumpled tunic for a proper surcoat and breeches, too, Alec saw.

"Where are you off to?"

"I think I'll just walk awhile, get some air," Seregil said, avoiding eye contact as he hurried to the door.

"Wait a minute, and I'll go with you."

"No, no, you go on with your reading," Seregil insisted hurriedly. "And tell Thryis not to wait supper for me. I could be late."

The door closed after him and Alec found himself in sole possession of their rooms.

"Well, at least he didn't take his pack this time," he grumbled to Ruetha, who'd stationed herself on a stack of books beside him. Tucking herself into a neat loaf, the cat merely blinked at him.

Alec opened his book again, but found he couldn't concentrate at all now.

Giving up, he made another pot of tea and looked into Seregil's bedroom while it steeped; no clue was immediately apparent in that chaotic jumble.

What's he up to, dashing off like that?

Except for that one mysterious journey, Seregil had included him in every job since the Festival. But he hadn't acted like he was going out on a job just now.

The parchment was still on the desk. Bending over it, Alec saw that it was the beginnings of a song. The words were badly smudged in places, and whole lines had been struck through or scribbled over. What remained read:

Shelter awhile this poor tattered heart.
Cool my brow with your kiss.
Tell me, my love, you'll lie with me only.
Lie to me all night like this.

Sweet is the night, but bitter the waking
When the sun harries me home.

Others there'll be, who drink at your fountain
While I toss cold and alone.

Yellow as gold, the hair on your pillow,
Green as cold emeralds, your eyes.
Dear as the moon, the cost of your favors,

Below this half a dozen lines had been struck out with what appeared to be increasing frustration.

The margins of the sheet were filled with half-completed sketches and designs—Illior's crescent, a perfectly drawn eye, circles, spirals, arrows, the profile of a handsome young man. In the lower left corner was a quick but unmistakable sketch of Alec scowling comically over his books, which Seregil must have drawn from his reflection in the windowpane.

As he set the sheet aside, a familiar binding caught his eye among the books stacked on the workbench next to the desk. It was the Aurënfaie journal case they'd discovered in the Orëska library. He'd assumed Seregil had returned it with the others; he certainly hadn't said anything more about it, or about their discovery of the reference to the mysterious "Eater of Death."

Opening it, Alec gently turned the fragile pages over. Though he couldn't read them, they all looked just as he remembered them.

He replaced the case as he'd found it, and for the first time wondered if Seregil's restlessness lately was due to something more than just bad weather and boredom. Come to think of it, he'd been restless at Watermead, as well. Those nights they'd shared the guest chamber bed, his friend had often tossed and muttered in his sleep. He hadn't done that before. What secrets was he wrestling with?

"Or maybe he's just pining for his green-eyed mistress?" Alec speculated aloud, scanning the parchment again with an amused chuckle. Ruetha appeared to have no opinion on the matter, however, and he found himself pacing as he rehearsed various nonchalant comments he could use to broach the subject when Seregil returned.

Whenever that turned out to be.

Lost in the quiet of the murky afternoon, he went back to his book and read until the light failed. When he got up for a fresh candle, he saw that the rain had stopped. Beyond the courtyard wall, the street lanterns glowed enticingly through the mist.

Suddenly the room seemed close and stale. There was really no reason he shouldn't go out. Why hadn't he thought of it sooner? Throwing on a surcoat and cloak, he headed downstairs.

The door between the kitchen and lading room was open. Through it he could see Cilla serenely nursing Luthas in the middle of the dinnertime bustle, sorting through a basket of apples with her free hand as she did so. The baby sucked greedily, tugging at the lacings of her open bodice. Her exposed breast throbbed gently with the rhythm of his demand.

Alec's experience with Ylinestra had considerably altered his reaction to such sights. He colored guiltily when she looked up and caught him hovering in the doorway.

"I thought you'd gone out already," she said.

"Ah—no. I was just, that is— It's stopped raining, you see, and I'm just going out for a walk." He gestured vaguely toward the door behind him.

"Could you hold the baby a minute before you go?" she asked, pulling Luthas off the nipple and holding him up. "My arm'll break if I don't shift over."

Taking the child, Alec held him while Cilla moved her baskets and uncovered her other breast. It was swollen with milk; a thin stream jetted from the nipple as she moved. Alec was close enough to see the pearly drops that fell across the deep red skins of the apples. He looked away, feeling a little dizzy. Luthas let out a sleepy burp and nuzzled at the front of Alec's cloak.

"The way he eats, you'd think I'd not have a drop to spare, but just look at me!" Cilla exclaimed merrily, taking the child back and putting him to breast on the other side. "Maker's Mercy, I've got more milk than Grandmother's goat."

Unable to think of a suitable reply to this, Alec nodded a hasty farewell and turned to go.

"Hey, Alec. Take this for your troubles," she said, tossing him an apple.

Feeling wetness beneath his fingers, he tucked it into a pocket and retreated to the back courtyard.

There, with the fog cool on his face, he allowed himself a moment's guilty pleasure replaying the scene in his mind. Cilla had never treated him as anything but a friend and until just now it had never occurred to him to think otherwise of her. Of course, the fact that she was at least six years older than he made it unlikely that her opinion would change.

Settling his sword belt against his hip, he pulled his hood well
up and set off through the back gate with no particular destination
in mind. The fog carried the smell of smoke and the sea. He tossed
a corner of his cloak over one shoulder, enjoying the feel of the
cold night air.

Skirting the Harvest Market, he strolled through Knife Maker's
Lane to Golden Helm and followed it, watching the evening traffic
bustle past. As he reached the Astellus Circle, he was suddenly
struck by a new and unexpected inspiration.

Across the busy circle, beyond the pale, templelike fountain
colonnade, stood the gracious arch that marked the entrance to the
Street of Lights. He'd been down this street many times on the
way to the theater and gambling houses there, and Seregil had
often jested about stopping in at a brothel afterward, but somehow
it had never happened. He'd never imagined it would.

Until now.

The colored lanterns—rose, amber, green, and white—
glowed softly through the mist, each color signifying what sort
of companionship was available within. Rose meant women for
men, he knew, and white was women for women; amber meant a
house for women, too, but the prostitutes there were male. Most
enigmatic of all, however, was the green lantern, signifying male
companions for male patrons. Worse yet, some houses showed
several colors at once.

There's no reason to be nervous, he thought as he crossed to
the arch. After all, his clothes were presentable, his purse was
heavy, and thanks to Ylinestra, he wasn't completely inexperienced. As his friends never seemed to tire of pointing out, he *was*
of age for such diversions. There was no harm in just having a
look around, anyway. Nothing wrong with being curious.

As usual, the street was busy. Riders on glossy horses and car-
riages displaying the blazons of noble houses and wealthy merchants clattered past as he strolled along, looking with new eyes at
the establishments showing the pink lantern. Groups of rich young
revelers seemed to be everywhere, their boisterous laughter
echoing in the darkness.

A woman wearing the uniform of the Queen's Household
Guard was bidding a lingering good-bye to a half-dressed man in a
doorway beneath an amber lamp as he passed. Next door, a well-
heeled sea captain and several of his men burst from one house
showing the rose light and, after a moment's consultation, stormed

off across the street to one with a green. Lights glowed in nearly every window; muffled laughter and strains of music drifted everywhere, adding to the festive feel of the place.

It occurred to him as he walked along that the color of a lantern was not a lot to go on for such a decision. No doubt Seregil could have suggested a few likely places, but that wasn't much good to him now. At last, he settled on a house near the middle of the street for no better reason than that he liked the carvings on the door. Just as he was about to go in, however, a door swung open across the street and a group of young men spilled out in a flood of light and music. A man was singing inside, and the voice stopped Alec in his tracks. The clear, lilting tenor was unmistakably Seregil's.

> *"Yellow as gold, the hair on your pillow,*
> *Green as cold emeralds, your eyes.*
> *Dear as the moon, the cost of your favors,*
> *But priceless, the sound of your sighs."*

Well, well! So here you are, thought Alec. *And you figured out that last line, too.*

Wondering what role his friend was playing tonight, he crossed the street and hurried up the stairs and into the spacious vestibule beyond. In his haste, he collided with a tall, handsomely dressed man just inside the door.

"Good evening," he exclaimed, catching Alec lightly by the shoulders to steady himself. His hair was streaked with silver, but his long, handsome face was youthful as he smiled down on Alec.

"Excuse me, I wasn't looking where I was going," Alec apologized.

"No harm done. I'm always glad to meet anyone so anxious to enter my house. You've not been my guest before, I think. I'm Azarin."

The man's blue eyes swept over him in what Alec sensed was well-practiced appraisal. He'd given no patronymics and Alec's name was not asked for.

Evidently he'd passed muster, for Azarin slipped his arm through Alec's and drew him with gentle insistence toward a curtained archway nearby.

"Come, my young friend," he said warmly, drawing aside the curtain. "I believe you'll find the company most congenial."

"Actually, I was just—"

Taking the room in at a glance, Alec froze, all thought of Seregil momentarily forgotten.

Beyond the curtain, a broad staircase led down into an opulent salon. The air in the softly lit room was heavy with incense. The walls were painted in Skalan fashion with superb murals and, while erotic themes were not uncommon, these were unlike any Alec had encountered before.

Green, he thought numbly, heart tripping a beat as he gazed around.

The murals were divided into panels, and each presented handsome male nudes intertwined in passionately carnal acts. The sheer variety was astonishing. Many of the feats depicted appeared to require considerable athletic ability and several, thought Alec, must have been pure fantasy on the part of the artist.

Dragging his gaze from the paintings, he swiftly took in the occupants of the astonishing chamber. Men of all ages reclined on couches arranged around the room, some embracing casually as they gave their attention to a young lute player by the hearth, others laughing and talking over gaming tables scattered here and there. Couples and small groups came and went up a sweeping staircase at the back of the room. There was no unseemly behavior, but many of them wore little more than long dressing gowns.

The patrons seemed to be mostly noblemen of various degrees, but Alec also recognized uniforms of the Queen's Archers, the City Watch, several naval tunics, and a red tabard of the Orëska Guard. He even recognized a few faces, including the poet Rhytien, who was currently holding forth to a rapt audience from the embrasure of a window.

The courtesans, if that was what one would call them, were not at all what he'd expected; some were slight and pretty, but most of them looked more like athletes or soldiers, and not all of them were young.

He hadn't heard Seregil's voice again since he'd entered, but he saw him now lounging on a couch near the hearth. He had one arm around a handsome, golden-haired young man and they were laughing together over something. As the courtesan turned his head, Alec recognized him—it was the same face Seregil had sketched on the margin of the song. Even from this distance, Alec could see the fellow had green eyes.

His heart did another slow, painful roll as he finally allowed himself to focus on Seregil.

His friend wore only breeches beneath his open robe and his dark hair hung disheveled over his shoulders. Slender, lithe, and completely at ease, he could easily have been mistaken for one of the men of the house. In fact, Alec silently admitted, he outshone them all.

He was beautiful.

Still rooted where he stood, Alec suddenly felt a strange division within himself. The old Alec, northern-bred and callow, wanted to bolt from this strange, exotic place and the sight of his friend stroking that golden head as absently as he'd petted the cat a few hours earlier.

But the new Alec, Alec of Rhíminee, stood fast, caught by the elegant decadence of the place as his ever-present curiosity slowly rekindled. Seregil hadn't noticed him yet; to see him like this in such a place made Alec feel as if he were spying on a stranger.

Seregil's strange, virile beauty, at first unappreciated, then taken for granted as their familiarity grew through months of close living, seemed to leap out at him now against the muted backdrop of the crowd: the large grey eyes beneath the expressive brows, the fine bones of his face, the mouth, so often tilted in a caustic grin, was relaxed now in sensuous repose. As Alec watched, Seregil leaned his head back and his robe fell open to expose the smooth column of his throat and the lean planes of his chest and belly. Fascinated and confused, Alec felt the first hesitant stirring of feelings he was not prepared to associate with his friend and teacher.

Still hovering at his elbow, Azarin somewhat misinterpreted his bedazzled expression. "If I may be so bold, perhaps you lack experience in such matters?" he asked. "Don't let that trouble you. There are many hours in the night, take your time." He swept a graceful hand at the murals. "Perhaps you'll find inspiration there. Or have you a particular sort of companion in mind?"

"No!" Startled out of his daze, Alec took a step backward. "No, I didn't really— I mean, I thought I saw a friend come in here. I was just looking for him."

Azarin nodded and said, ever gracious, "I understand. But now that you are here, why not join us for a while? The musician is new, just in from Cirna. I'll send for wine."

At Azarin's discreet summons, a young man detached himself
from a knot of conversation nearby and came up to join them.

"Tirien will attend you in my absence," said Azarin. Giving the
two of them a final, approving look, he disappeared back into the
vestibule.

"Well met, young sir," Tirien greeted him. Thick black hair,
glossy as a crow's wing, framed his face and a soft growth of new
beard edged the hollows of his cheeks. His smile seemed genuinely friendly. He was dressed in breeches, boots, and a loose
shirt of fine linen; for a moment Alec mistook him for a noble. The
illusion was shattered, however, when Tirien stepped closer and
said, "There's a couch free near the fire, if you like. Or would you
prefer to go up at once?"

For one awful moment Alec was speechless; what in Illior's
name was he to do? Glancing past Tirien's shoulder, his eyes happened to fall on one of the panels. The young prostitute turned to
follow his gaze, then smiled.

"Oh, yes, I'm quite good at that. As you can see, though, we'll
need a third man."

Seregil's eyes widened in genuine amazement at he caught
sight of Alec framed in the salon entrance, amazement followed
at once by a bittersweet pang of something deeper than mere
surprise.

The boy had obviously stumbled into Azarin's house by mistake—the tense lines around his mouth and faint, betraying color
in his cheeks attested as much.

I'd better go rescue him, he thought, yet he remained where he
was, letting the scene play on a bit longer.

A quick glance around the room confirmed that Alec was
attracting the notice of other patrons, as well. And no wonder,
Seregil thought with a stab of something dangerously close to possessiveness. For a moment he allowed himself to see Alec through
the eyes of the others: a slim, somberly dressed youth whose
heavy, honey-dark hair framed a finely featured face and the
bluest eyes this side of a summer evening sky. He stood like a
half-wild thing, poised for flight, yet his manner toward the young
prostitute was almost courtly.

Tirien leaned closer to Alec and the boy's mask of composure

slipped a bit, betraying—what? Alarm, certainly, but hadn't there
been just a hint of indecision?

This time Seregil couldn't deny the hot flash of jealousy that
shot through him. Thoroughly annoyed with himself, he began
disentangling himself from Wythrin.

"Do you want to go back up now?" the young man asked hopefully, sliding a warm hand up his thigh.

This gave him pause. Seregil touched the back of one hand
to Wythrin's cheek, savoring the faint roughness of it. This one,
a favorite for some time now, had charms of his own, and
talents that spared Seregil's heart even as they satisfied his need.
Wythrin, and others like him, offered safe, guiltless passion, free
of obligation.

"In a moment. There's someone I need to talk to first."

He'd get Alec out of whatever jam he'd stumbled into, whether
that sent him upstairs with Tirien or not, Seregil told himself
sternly, then lose himself once more in Wythrin's deep bed. It was
as simple as that.

Alec quickly realized that Tirien had no intention of being put
off. His own increasingly embarrassed protestations that he had no
experience in such matters only seemed to whet the courtesan's
interest. It wasn't the first time Alec had run into this attitude;
country virgins seemed to be a rare and much sought-after novelty
in Rhíminee.

For a fleeting instant it occurred to him that Tirien was attrac-
tive, but he dismissed the treacherous thought at once; that sort of
thinking was not going to get him out of this mess.

To his relief, he saw Seregil coming his way. Clearly amused,
he gave Alec a discreet *need help?* sign. Alec answered with a
quick nod.

At that, Seregil strode up to them and slipped an arm around
Alec's waist. "There you are at last! Forgive me for intruding,
Tirien. My friend and I have some business. Will you excuse us
for a moment?"

"Of course." The young courtesan withdrew with a graceful
bow, betraying only the faintest hint of disappointment.

Alec braced for the inevitable ragging as they withdrew to the
vestibule, but Seregil simply said, "I didn't expect to see you
here."

"I heard you singing. I mean, I thought it sounded like you and—well, I just came in." Aside from the fact that he was stammering like an idiot, Alec was suddenly all too aware of the fact that Seregil's arm was still around him. Strange, enticing scents clung to his friend's skin and hair, unlike his usual clean smell. The troublesome new feelings stirred again, closer to the surface this time, but just as confusing. "I didn't think to check the lantern. I just came in."

Seregil chuckled softly. "Curious as usual, eh? Well, now that you're in, are you going to stay? Tirien's an excellent choice. Azarin knows his business."

"No." Alec glanced at the young prostitute, still waiting hopefully nearby, then hastily back to Seregil. There was no hint of challenge in his friend's face, just bemusement. Why then, held in the calm gaze of those grey eyes, did his own agitation increase? The situation was well past his ability to explain.

"No, I was just looking for you. I'd better go. This place makes me feel strange."

"There's more than incense burning in those bowls. But I assume if you were just passing by, then you're here on business of your own? Let's see now, how long has it been?"

"I was thinking of it," Alec admitted. He could feel the warmth of Seregil's skin through the thick silk of the robe now. "I don't know—I might just go on home."

"Don't be silly," Seregil said, releasing him at last. "I was planning to go back upstairs, but that can wait." The grin flashed again, and Alec abandoned all hope of escape. "There's a place just down the street that's probably more to your liking. And long overdue, too. I'll be right back."

Returning to the main room, he said something to Tirien. The man gave Alec a last wistful look, then drifted away.

Leaning in the shadow of the arch, Alec watched Seregil take leave of his companion, who was clearly dismayed by his departure. After a brief, animated exchange, Seregil pressed him back on the couch with a deep, lingering kiss, then disappeared up the stairs.

He came down again a few moments later fully dressed, sword belt slung over one shoulder.

"Come along," he said jauntily, leading the way to a villa down the block.

Well, at least there's a pink lantern here, Alec thought, nervous again as Seregil urged him up the stairs.

Seregil appeared to be well known here. A number of women greeted him enthusiastically as he led Alec into the salon. This establishment was quite similar to Azarin's. Erotic tapestries and statuary adorned this room and lovely women in various states of dishabille entertained their patrons, brilliant and lovely as rare birds.

As they handed their cloaks and swords to a page, a richly dressed woman left a knot of conversation and rushed to embrace Seregil. Her skin, generously exposed by the blue silk gown she wore, had a golden olive tone Alec had never seen before. Thick black ringlets hung in a shining cascade to her waist.

"Where have you been keeping yourself, you rogue," she cried with obvious delight.

"A million places, Eirual, my love, but none so pleasant as here," Seregil replied, kissing her throat lasciviously.

She laughed, then pushed him away, dark eyes widening in mock reproach. "I know that scent. You've been to Azarin's already. How cruel you are, coming to me with your fires already spent."

"Spent? My fires?" Seregil caught her close again. "And when, my lovely one, have you ever known *that* to be the case?"

"I'd like to put you to the test—upstairs."

"I accept your challenge gladly, madame, but first we have to find companionship for my young friend."

Alec had been gazing around the room during this exchange, his heart pounding in a manner even his old, Dalnan-bred self could find no argument with.

"I think he's found someone already," Eirual said with an amused smile.

Alec nodded shyly at a slender, blue-eyed brunette in burgundy silk. "She's very pretty."

"Myrhichia?" Eirual shot Seregil an arch look as she summoned the woman. "He has excellent taste, this friend of yours."

"He hasn't disappointed me yet," Seregil replied, giving Alec a wink.

Myrhichia glided over, wrapped in perfume and mystery. She was older than Alec had supposed, older than he, but that didn't matter—there was something familiar about her, something that made him wave aside the offer of wine and let her lead him up the stairs to her room.

It wasn't until she turned to speak to him over her shoulder that he realized how much she resembled Seregil, or rather Seregil as he'd looked playing Lady Gwethelyn aboard the *Darter*. It was an unsettling revelation and he did his best to put it out of his mind as they entered her chamber. Looking around, Alec felt the last of his trepidation giving way to sensuous anticipation.

A fire cracked invitingly on the hearth, its flames softly illuminating the small, elegant room. The bed was high and draped with patterned hangings. Huge cushions were piled near the hearth, together with a few oddly shaped stools. An elaborate washstand was half-visible behind a painted screen in a shadowy corner.

Myrhichia stood demurely at the center of the room, offering him the choice of where to begin. "Does it please you?" she asked, cocking her head prettily.

"Yes," he whispered. Closing the door, he went to her and loosened the jeweled pin holding her hair. It tumbled free over her shoulders in dark, sandalwood-scented waves.

Where his experience with Ylinestra had been out of his control from the first, this woman seemed content to let him direct things. He touched her face, her hair, then hesitantly brought his lips to hers. Her hands found his face, his shoulders, then slid slowly lower.

The fastenings of her gown were no challenge for Alec's expertly trained fingers; her clothes and his were soon in a pile at their feet.

"Shall I light a lamp?" she whispered as he took her hungrily in his arms.

He shook his head, pressing his body against the yielding roundness of breasts, belly, and thighs, letting the feel of her envelop him. "The fire's enough."

Still holding her, he sank down onto the cushions by the hearth. The warring sensations of the long, confusing evening seemed to coalesce and clarify as he at last abandoned himself to the powerful simplicity of desire.

Eirual was half Zengati, Aurënen's traditional enemy. It was that, together with the dark beauty of her race, that had first attracted Seregil. Though hardly more than a girl at the time of their first meeting, she'd been a fiery lover and he'd entertained notions of taking her away for himself. She'd been the one who'd dashed that plan; she liked her work, she'd told him firmly. What's more, she planned to own a brothel of her own one day, just as her mother and grandmother had before her. Although his pride had been somewhat jarred, Seregil had respected her wishes and over the years they'd become friends.

She'd achieved her dreams. She was now the owner of one of the city's finest and most nobly patronized pleasure houses. This often brought interesting bits of information her way and, though she was no gossiping whore, she was aware of Seregil's supposed connections to Rhíminee's mysterious "Cat" and had often found it lucrative to pass on certain facts and rumors.

Their reunion this night had been spirited in spite of Seregil's earlier activities. Afterward, they lay tangled together in the damp, disheveled sheets and laughed together over little things.

Presently she sighed, then said, "You know, I saw something rather odd a few weeks ago."

"And what was that?" he murmured, contentedly admiring the contrast of his skin against hers as he stroked her thigh.

"I entertained a new visitor last week, a stranger. He was well turned out and behaved himself, but I could tell from his way of speaking and the state of his hands he wasn't upper class, just a common fellow who'd come into gold and meant to treat himself. You know the sort."

"But he was handsome and broad-shouldered and smelled of honest labor," Seregil teased. "Sounds delightful. Let's have him in."

"As if I'd share you! But I admit I was intrigued at first, though he turned out very ordinary in the end. No, I think you'd be more interested in what fell out of his coat than what fell out of his breeches."

"Oh?" Seregil raised a questioning eyebrow, knowing better than to hurry her. She always enjoyed spinning out a tale.

"He'd thrown his clothes every which way, so when he was snoring afterward—which was all too soon, I might add—I decided to tidy up a bit. A letter fell from his coat when I picked it up. The ribbon had come loose and I took a quick peek. He stirred a moment later and I had to put it away, but I had time to recognize the handwriting, and the seal at the bottom."

"Did you, you clever girl? Whose was it?"

"Lord General Zymanis'."

"Really?" Zymanis had recently been appointed to oversee the defenses of the lower city. "How do you know it wasn't a forgery?"

Eirual traced a playful finger around his navel. "Zymanis is a very dear friend of mine, as you well know. Two months ago he knocked his ring against that bedpost there behind you and chipped the stone seal. It was a tiny piece, really, but he made such a fuss over it! Quite spoiled the mood. This chip makes a tiny flaw in the impression, so tiny that most people wouldn't even notice it. But I knew what to look for and it was his, all right. What do you think of that?"

Seregil cupped her full breast in his hand like a goblet and kissed it reverently. "I think, in your place, I'd have found some way of inquiring where this lover of yours could be found again."

Eirual pressed closer with a luxuriant sigh. "Sailmaker Street in the lower city. A tenement with a red and white lintel. His name is Rythel, a big, blond fellow with a lovely soft beard, very handsome."

"And you don't think this visitor of yours ought to have such a letter?"

Eirual shook her head. "For starters, it was addressed to Lord Admiral Nyreidian. I've never met the admiral, but I'd bet a month's gold he doesn't have fresh calluses on his hands and stained fingernails."

"Or a yellow beard," mused Seregil, thinking of the man he'd met at the Mourning Night ceremony. Nyreidian had spoken of his own commission from the Queen, too, overseeing privateering ships.

"Zymanis wouldn't let a fellow like this step on his shadow, much less write letters to him." She gave him a sly sidelong glance. "I thought maybe your friend the Cat might be interested?"

"He just might."

"I could tell him myself," she wheedled, not for the first time. Over the years the unseen Rhíminee Cat had taken on a glow of romance for many, who envied Seregil his apparently favored status.

Seregil kissed his way slowly across her chest. "I've told you before, love, he's not what you think. He's a nasty, weedy little man who spends half his time wading through the sewers."

"Last time you said he was a hunchback," she corrected, stroking his head.

"That, too. That's why he keeps out of sight, you see, because he's so hideous. Why, his boils alone are enough—"

"No more!" Eirual laughed, admitting defeat. "Sometimes I think *you're* the Cat, and you just make all the rest up to hide it."

"Me? Wading through sewers and running errands for bored nobles?" He pinned her down, feigning outrage. "Fancy me mincing across the roof slates!"

"Oh, yes," Eirual gasped, giggling helplessly at the thought. "You're the terror of the town."

"You've pegged me wrong, my girl. There's only one thing I put that kind of effort into."

"And what's that, may I ask?"

Seregil leered down at her. "I'll show you."

The candle had burned to a stub when he slipped from her bed. Eirual stirred drowsily. "Stay, love. I'll be cold without you."

He drew the comforter up under her chin and kissed her. "I can't tonight. I'll send a nice present tomorrow."

"All right, then." She smiled, already half asleep again. "Something with rubies and I might forgive you."

"Rubies it is."

He dressed quickly and blew out the candle. Closing her door quietly behind him, he headed for Myrhichia's room down the corridor.

He had to knock several times to get a response. She opened the door a few inches at last, peering out with a resentful pout.

"He's sleeping," she informed him, pulling her dressing gown closed.

"How inconsiderate." Pushing past her, Seregil strode into the bedchamber. Alec lay sprawled on his back in the bed, his sleeping face the picture of weary bliss.

Looks like he managed to enjoy himself after all, he thought with a mix of pride and wistfulness, glancing around at the disordered room.

Ignoring the courtesan's simmering displeasure, Seregil leaned down and shook him by the shoulder. Alec stirred drowsily, murmuring something amorous as he reached to pull Seregil into bed.

When his fingers encountered wool rather than whatever he'd been dreaming of, however, he snapped fully awake.

"What are *you* doing here?" he gasped, sitting up.

"Sorry." Seregil crossed his arms, grinning. "Terrible timing, I know, but something's come up and I may need your help."

Alec glanced quickly from him to the girl. "A job? *Now?*"

"I'll wait for you downstairs. Don't be long."

Alec let out an exasperated sigh. Before he could get up, however, Myrhichia dropped her robe and slipped back into bed beside him.

"Does he always barge in like that?"

"I hope not," muttered Alec.

"Are you going to leave me now?" She nibbled teasingly down the side of his neck as her hand slipped up his thigh to more sensitive regions.

He could picture Seregil pacing impatiently downstairs, waiting for him, but Myrhichia was putting up a persuasive argument under the covers.

"Well," he sighed, letting her push him back against the bolsters, "maybe not right this second."

Seregil had the bones of a workable plan in mind by the time he got downstairs. Strolling into the cloak room, he found it conveniently unattended.

He soon had what he wanted; he returned to the salon with an officer's mantle and a wineskin concealed beneath his own cloak, Alec's sword belt and cloak over his arm.

To his surprise, Alec had still not come down. Rather annoyed, he settled in a chair near the door to wait.

It was late now. A few girls remained in the salon, playing bakshi to pass the time while they waited for whatever late-coming patrons might show up. Having seen Seregil come down, they paid little attention to him.

Minutes passed and still no Alec.

Seregil was just about to leave without him when the boy came down the staircase. His loose shirt flapped around his legs as he struggled with his coat, one sleeve of which appeared to be inside out. Getting himself more or less sorted out at last, he hurried to join Seregil.

"Delayed, were you?" Seregil inquired with a smirk, tossing him his cloak and sword.

"Myrhichia isn't very happy with you," Alec grumbled, flushed and out of breath. He wrapped his sword belt around his hips and fastened the buckle. "I'm not so sure I am, either. If this is just another silly lover's token—"

Seregil tugged Alec's collar straight, still grinning. "You think I'd ruin your fun for that? Come on, I'll tell you about it on the way."

Outside, he glanced around quickly, then whispered, "I think Eirual may have put us onto a spy."

Alec brightened up at once. "That's worth getting out of bed for."

"Did you ride?"

"No."

"Good, we'll hire horses and abandon them if we have to. I'll explain as we go."

Leaving the warm glow of the lanterns behind, they hurried into the embracing darkness.

15
THE HUNT COMMENCES

"Where are we going?" Alec asked as Seregil headed west through the dark streets. The quickest way to the lower city was down the Harbor Way.

"I need a very special horse for this one," Seregil explained. "There's an ostler over by the Harvest Gate who's likely to have what I want, and still be hiring out at this hour."

Pausing, he opened the wineskin and took a sip, then sprinkled a more liberal libation down the front of his surcoat. Evidently satisfied with the effect, he passed it to Alec.

Grinning, he did the same. "Drunk, are we?"

"Oh, yes, and I'll be worse off than you. You'll be playing the sensible friend."

"Don't I always?" Alec took another fortifying sip and capped the skin.

A lantern was still burning in front of the ostler's stable. Seregil fell into a loose, unsteady walk as they stepped into the circle of light.

"Ostler!" he called, striking an arrogant pose, fists on his hips. "Two gentlemen need mounts. Show yourself, man."

"Here, sirs," a man replied, opening a side door a crack for a wary look at the late customers.

Seregil shook his purse at him. The ring of

coins had the desired effect; the ostler swung the stable doors wide and held the lantern while they inspected the half-dozen horses inside.

Alec quickly found a decent mare and the man saddled her for him.

Seregil was longer at it. After much pacing and muttering, he finally settled on a rawboned grey.

"I'm not one to tell a lord his business, but he's made a poor choice with that one," the worried ostler whispered to Alec. "Old Cloudy there has been off his feed for days and has a cough. If you'd speak to your friend for me, I'll see to it he has the best of my stable."

Alec gave him a reassuring wink and counted out a generous stack of silver. "Don't concern yourself. We're going to play a joke on a friend and your grey is just what we need. We'll take good care of him, and have them both back before dawn."

They set off at a trot, but before they'd gone a quarter of a mile Seregil's cob stumbled to a halt, nearly throwing him over its head. Jerking its head down, it let out a hollow, braying cough.

"Poor old fellow." Seregil patted the animal's neck. "You're better than I could have hoped for. We'll have to send a drysian to look at him."

"What do you think this spy of yours is up to?" Alec asked as they continued at a walk.

Seregil shrugged. "Hard to say yet. Eirual thinks this fellow Rythel has some documents that he shouldn't. I want to see if she's right."

"Do you think he's a Plenimaran?"

"Too soon to say. At times like this it's best to keep an open mind until you have hard facts. Otherwise, you just run around trying to prove your own theory and overlooking important details that may turn up in the process. It could be there's nothing to it at all, but it's more interesting than anything else we've seen in the last few weeks."

Well-dressed, slightly intoxicated lords heading down to the lower city for a roister were of little concern to the guards at the Sea Gate. The sergeant-at-arms waved them through with a bored look and returned to the watch fire.

At the bottom of the Harbor Way they rode east along the waterfront past the custom houses and quays into a moderately respectable street lined with tenements.

A few lights showed behind shuttered windows, but most of the neighborhood was asleep. A dog howled mournfully somewhere nearby, the sound carrying eerily through the streets. Seregil's horse twitched its ears nervously, then let out another rattling cough in a jingle of harness.

"Here's Sailmaker Street," said Seregil, reining in at the mouth of an unmarked lane. Unclasping his mantle, he threw it to Alec and shook out the mantle he'd brought from Eirual's. It belonged to a captain of the White Hawk Infantry and bore a large, distinctive device.

"Who'd you steal that from?" Alec asked, watching him put it on.

"Borrowed, dear boy, borrowed," Seregil corrected primly.

Alec peered up and down the poorly lit street. "That must be the house there," he said, pointing to one at the end of the lane. "It's the only one with a striped lintel."

"Yes. You hang back and be ready for trouble. If it comes to any sort of a chase, I'd better ride double with you. I don't think poor old Cloudy has much run left in him."

Seregil emptied the last of the wine over his mount's withers, bunched the mantle awkwardly over one shoulder, and pulled one foot loose from the stirrup. Settling into a loose, drunken slouch, he nudged the horse into a walk. Riding up to the door, he kicked loudly at it.

"You! In the house!" he bawled, swaying precariously in the saddle. "I want the leech, damn him. By Sakor, send out the bastard son of a pig!"

A shutter slammed back just above his head and an old woman popped her head out, glaring down indignantly.

"Leave off with that or I'll have the Watch down on you," she screeched, swinging a stick at his head. "This is an honest house."

"I'll leave off when I've got his throat in my hand," Seregil yelled, kicking the door again.

"You're drunk. I can smell you from here!" the old woman said scornfully. "Who is it you're after?"

Just then, the grey jerked its head down in another racking cough.

"There, you hear that?" Seregil roared. "How in the name of Bilairy am I supposed to explain this to my commander, eh? Your leech has ruined the beast. Gave him a dose of salts and half killed him. I'll run my sword up his arse, that pus-faced clod of shit! You send out the leech Rythel or I'll come in after him."

"You whoreson drunken mullet!" The old woman took another swing at him with her cudgel. "It's Rythel the *smith* that rooms here, not Rythel the leech."

"Smith?" Seregil goggled up at her. "What in the name of Sakor's Fire is he doing dosing my horse if he's a smith?"

Lurking in the shadows at the mouth of the street, Alec shook with silent laughter. It was as good a performance as any he'd seen at the theater.

"Half the men on the coast are called Rythel, you fool. You've got the wrong man," the old landlady sputtered. "Smith Rythel is an honest man, which is more than can be said for you, I'm sure."

"Honest man, my ass!"

"He is. He works for Master Quarin in the upper city."

She disappeared and Seregil, no doubt with knowledge born of long experience, reined his horse out of the way just as she emptied a chamber pot over the sill at him.

Seregil made her an ungainly bow from the saddle. "My humblest apologies for disturbing your rest, old mother."

"You'd best sleep on your belly tonight," the old woman cackled after him as he rode unsteadily away.

"That wasn't exactly subtle," Alec observed, still laughing as they headed back to the Harbor Way.

"A drunken soldier making a ruckus at the wrong house in the middle of the night on Sailmaker Street?" Seregil asked, looking pleased with himself. "What could be subtler than that? And successful, too. Now we know that this Rythel is a journeyman smith of some sort. Which leaves us still asking what he's doing with gold enough for the Street of Lights and a lord's papers in his pocket."

"And why he had that much gold on him with the papers *still* in his pocket."

"Exactly. And what does that suggest?"

"That he's been up to whatever he's doing for a while already," replied Alec, looking back toward the waterfront. "We'll have to get into his rooms, and we'd better find out who Master Quarin is."

"We'll start tomorrow. Hold up a minute."

Seregil's grey was wheezing dejectedly now. Reining in by a lantern at the foot of the Harbor Way, he dismounted and took the animal's head between his hands. "I'd better ride double with you, Alec. This poor old fellow's at the end of his strength. I'd better change cloaks, too."

Alec kicked a foot out of the stirrup and held his hand down. Grasping it, Seregil climbed up behind him and wrapped an arm around his waist.

Alec felt another unexpected twinge of sensuality at his touch, faint as a bat's whisper, but unmistakable. There was certainly nothing seductive in the way Seregil gripped a handful of his tunic to keep his balance, yet suddenly he had an image of that same hand stroking the head of the young man at Azarin's brothel, and later embracing dark-eyed Eirual.

Seregil had touched him before, but never with anything more than brotherly affection. Alec had seen tonight what sort of companions his friend chose—Wythrin and Eirual, both of them exotic, beautiful, and undoubtedly skilled beyond anything Alec could conceive of.

What's happening to me? he wondered dejectedly. Maker's Mercy, he could still smell Myrhichia's lush scent rising from his skin. From some neglected corner of his heart, a small voice seemed to answer silently, *You're waking up at last.*

"Anything wrong?" asked Seregil.

"Thought I heard something." Alec nudged the horse into a walk.

Seregil bunched the stolen cloak out of sight beneath his own. "I suppose we really should return this. I don't want any of Eirual's women getting into trouble on my account. I don't suppose you'd mind going back there twice in one night?"

Alec couldn't see his friend's face, but he could tell by his voice that he was grinning.

"Me? Where will you be?" asked Alec.

"Oh, not too far away."

Alec shifted uncomfortably in the saddle. "You're going back to Azarin's."

He heard a throaty chuckle behind him. "Fowl never tastes as savory when you're hungry for venison."

At least you know what you want, Alec thought grudgingly.

16
Smiths and Beggars

Cilla was just stirring up the fire when Seregil returned to the Cockerel the next morning.

"Is Alec back?" he asked.

"I haven't seen him since yesterday afternoon. You haven't gone and lost him, have you?"

"Let's hope not." Grabbing a few apples from a basket, he headed for the back stairway.

"Hang on, I've got something for you," Cilla called after him. She pulled a small, sealed packet from behind the salt box on the mantel and gave it to him. "Runcer sent this over from Wheel Street. A regimental courier from the Queen's Horse delivered it there."

Pocketing the apples, he examined the packet as he continued upstairs. The folded parchment was sealed with candle drippings and covered in smudged finger marks. Directions to Lord Seregil's house were written across the front in Beka Cavish's impatient, upright hand.

Opening it, he read the brief letter inside.

Dear S. & A.
27 Dostin—Have reached Isil. Tomorrow we move into Mycenian territory. One of the other turmae lost a rider at bridge over

the Canal at Cirna when his horse bolted and threw him over the edge. Horrible.

The weather is foul. It's still very much winter up here. The worst enemy we've faced so far is boredom. Capt. Myrhini and some of the other officers break the monotony with their war stories. Some of the best come from the sergeants, however.

Billeted tonight in stables of Baron of Isil's estate. The glory of a soldier's life, eh, Seregil?

—B. Cavish

Reaching their rooms, he found Alec asleep on his narrow cot, clothes dropped in a careless heap on the floor. Seregil sat down on the clothes chest at the end of the bed and tapped him on the foot.

"Good morning. We've got news from Beka."

Alec growled something into the pillow, then rolled over. He blinked sleepily at the morning light streaming in at the windows, then at Seregil. "You just getting in?"

Seregil tossed him an apple. "Yes. Tirien asked after you, by the way, and sends his regards."

Alec shrugged noncommittally and bit into his apple. "What's Beka say?"

Seregil read him the letter.

"Maker's Mercy!" Alec muttered, hearing of the man lost off the Canal bridge. He disliked heights and Seregil had to coax him across the bridge the first time he'd traveled over it.

"Let's see," said Seregil when he'd finished, "if they were in Wyvern Dug two weeks ago and headed southeast from there, they could be across the Folcwine River by now."

"Sounds like she's doing well with it all."

"I wouldn't expect anything else of her. Beka's as good with people as she is with horses and swordplay. I'll bet you a sester she's wearing a captain's gorget the next time we see her."

If we see her again, skittered at the back of his mind as he said this, but he pushed the doubt away. He thought he saw a shadow of the same thought cross Alec's face, and the same quick denial.

"Where do we start today?" Alec asked, pushing a handful of tousled hair back from his eyes.

Seregil went to the hearth and stirred up the remains of last night's fire. "I'd like to find this Master Smith Quarin first.

Unfortunately we don't know what kind of a smith he is, do we? Goldsmith, silversmith, swordsmith, blacksmith—"

Alec chewed thoughtfully, watching him. After a moment he said, "How about an ironsmith?"

Seregil glanced down at the poker in his hand, then saw that Alec was looking at it, too.

"You said Lord Zymanis is in charge of the lower city defenses, so he's more likely to need an ironsmith than a goldsmith, right? And Eirual said he had rough hands."

"You've got a clearer head than I do this morning," Seregil said, chagrined not to have thought of it himself.

"I imagine I got more sleep."

Seregil glanced over at him in surprise, fancying he heard an edge of disapproval in Alec's tone. After last night's evident success with Myrhichia, he'd assumed the boy was cured of any undue scruples. Evidently he still retained his Dalnan attitude toward establishments like Azarin's. *Well, that's just too damned bad for him.*

"There are ironsmiths scattered all around the city but they all belong to the same guild," he said aloud, letting the moment pass. "I'll have Thryis send one of the scullions over to ask after Quarin. In the meantime, I think I'll have a bit of a rest."

By midday they'd learned that Master Quarin's shop lay in Ironmonger Row near the Sea Market Gate. They set off soon after, dressed as ragged cripples.

Alec's face was half-obscured by a dirty bandage. Seregil wore an old wreck of a hat tied on with a scarf so that the brim curved down to his chin on either side. Their disguises had the desired effect. As they crossed the back court Rhiri saw them and shook a rake threateningly in their direction.

"Ah, the ubiquitous beggar," Seregil chuckled when they'd scuttled out the gate. "No one is ever surprised or glad to see you anywhere in the city."

Begging bowls in hand, they set off for Sheaf Street, the broad avenue that ran through the city between the Harvest and Sea Market gates.

As expected, they attracted little attention as they made their way through the crowded streets. Carts and wagons rumbled past endlessly. Tinkers and knife grinders chanted their availability in singsong voices. Dirty children dodged through the crowds, chasing dogs or pigs or each other. Soldiers were everywhere, along with malodorously genuine beggars and a few early whores importuning passersby.

Watching for their chance, they stole a ride on the back of a hay wagon and clung to the tail posts as it jolted over the cobbles.

"Look there," said Seregil, pointing behind them.

Alec looked and winced inwardly. Half a block back, five heads swayed on pikes set upright in the back of a rough wooden cart surrounded by a grim formation of the City Watch. He'd seen such displays before; this was the fate of traitors and spies in Rhíminee. Their decapitated bodies would be lying in the cart below, on their way to the city pit.

"Maker's Mercy, that's getting to be a common sight," he muttered. "If we're right about our man—"

"—then he'll come to the same end." Seregil eyed the heads impassively. "I wouldn't dwell on that, if I were you. I don't."

Especially since you came within spitting distance of ending up that way yourself, Alec thought grimly. He still had nightmares about that sometimes, and what would have happened if he and Micum had failed to clear Seregil's name from the Leran's carefully contrived treason charges. He wondered if Seregil did, too.

As soon as the brightly colored awnings of the Sea Market came into sight, Seregil jumped down from the cart and led the way into Ironmonger Row, a twisting side street of open-sided workshops and smoke-stained buildings. Playing his role, he doubled over into a crabbed, sidelong limp and grasped Alec's arm.

In spite of the name, metal workers of all sorts plied their trade here, taking advantage of the proximity to both the port and the marketplace.

Acrid fumes stung Alec's eyes as they made their way through the din. Inside the workshops he could see half-naked men silhouetted against the red glare of the forges, looking like vengeful demons as their hammers struck sparks from glowing metal. Apprentices ran here and there with tools and hods of coal; others sweated over the bellows, pumping until the forges glowed yellow-white. Pots, swords, tools, and bits of armor hung over doorways advertising the wares being crafted within.

Pausing at the first they came to, Seregil limped up to an apprentice and asked after Quarin.

"Master Quarin?" The boy pointed farther down the narrow lane. "His place is way down near the wall, biggest on the block. You can't miss it."

"Many thanks, friend," croaked Seregil, taking Alec's arm again. "Come along, son, we're nearly there."

For a single, disorienting instant Alec stared down at him. They hadn't discussed their roles in detail—hearing himself unexpectedly called "son" so many months after his father's death sent a sickening chill through him. Guilt followed hard on the heels of it; he hadn't thought of his father in weeks, perhaps longer.

Seregil peered up at him from under his hat, one sharp grey eye visible. "You all right?"

Alec stared straight ahead, surprised at the stinging behind his eyelids. "I'm fine. It's just the smoke."

Dodging heavy wagons and wrathful shouts, they finally located Quarin's shop. It was a huge establishment, much larger than the rest, and housed in a converted warehouse.

Seregil hung back a moment, sizing the place up through the open door. "Two forges that I can see from here," he whispered. "See those fellows with the metal studs across the top of their aprons? They're all master craftsmen. Master Quarin must be well established to have a crew like that under him. Let's go see what he knows of our friend Rythel."

Just inside the door, they found a woman in a studded apron putting the final touches on an elaborately decorated gate. Catching sight of them, she paused, resting her hammer on one knee.

"You want something here?" she called.

Seregil lowered his voice to a windy growl. "Is this Master Quarin's shop?"

"That's the master, there at the back." Hefting her hammer again, she pointed out a bluff, white-haired old man standing behind a worktable with several other smiths, metal stylus in hand.

"It's a Master Rythel we was sent to find," Alec told her. "We've a message to deliver and we was told he works here."

The woman sniffed scornfully. "Oh, him! He and his crew are down at the western sewer tunnel in the lower city."

"Friend of yours, dearie?" Seregil wheedled, giving her a wink beneath the cracked brim of his hat.

"He's nobody's friend here. Upstart nephew of the master, is all. That sort always nabs the plums, and damn all to the rest of us. Be off with you, and I hope you charge him double for the message. The bastard can well enough afford it."

Alec gave her a respectful bob of the head. "Thanks and Maker's Mercy to you. Come on, Grandfather, we've got a long walk ahead of us."

"Grandfather, eh?" Seregil eyed him wryly as they continued on toward the Sea Market.

"You could be anything under there. That smith didn't seem to care much for Rythel, did she?"

"I noticed that," said Seregil, straightening up and stretching his back. "The guild smiths are a proud, stiff-necked lot and seniority is everything to them. Sounds like Quarin put some noses out of joint giving the job to a relative."

"Why would anyone begrudge him working in the sewers?"

"If they're in the sewers, then they must be replacing the iron grates that guard the channels coming down from the citadel. Who do you suppose ordered that job?"

"Lord General Zymanis."

"By way of whatever underlings handle the details, anyway, which would make it a particularly lucrative contract, with extra pay for the smith in charge of the repairs and his crew. She said he'd 'nabbed the plums,' remember?"

"That still doesn't explain why Rythel would have papers with Lord Zymanis' seal."

"No, but it does establish the beginnings of a plausible connection. The letter he had was addressed to Admiral Nyreidian. We met him at Kylith's gathering at the Mourning Night ceremony, if you recall."

"The lord who'd just been commissioned to oversee the privateers!" Alec exclaimed. "That has to do with the war, too."

"Which means we're probably right about Rythel being a noser of some sort."

They walked on in silence to the Harbor Way. Presently Seregil looked up again and said, "If we're right, then I may need to play with this Rythel a bit, see what I can get out of him. When we get down there, I'd better stay out of sight and let you play messenger. If he is a fellow professional, then I don't want to chance him recognizing my voice later on."

At the harbor they made their way west beyond the last quays and warehouses to a stretch of rocky land that hugged the base of the cliffs. A freshly rutted wagon track led on out of sight among the twisted jack pines and hummocks. Following it for a quarter of a mile or so, Alec and Seregil found Rythel's crew at the head of a steep, malodorous gully.

From where Alec and Seregil stood, the entrance to the sewer channel was about five hundred feet up the cut. The opening was the same size and shape as an arched doorway, tall enough for a man to walk through without ducking his head. A noisome grey torrent flowed out over its threshold and on down through a stone sluiceway to the sea beyond. A foul odor hung over the rocky cleft and Alec noted that the workmen wore wet rags over their noses and mouths. Vinegar cloths, he guessed, to protect them from the evil humours of the place.

A forge had been set up near the opening and the black smoke from it collected sullenly on the damp air. A small wagon stood nearby and half a dozen armed bluecoats were lounging against it.

"What are they doing there?" Alec asked as they looked out from behind the cover of a boulder.

"Watching for gaterunners and spies. The sewers go everywhere under the city."

"What are gaterunners?"

"Thieves, mostly, who know how to get past all the gates and grates and travel the tunnels. They know more about where those channels lead than anyone, even the Scavenger Guild. You'd better go have a look."

Leaving Seregil behind the rock, Alec hugged his rags about himself and followed the stony track up toward the forge.

"What do you want here?" a soldier demanded, looking more bored than suspicious.

"I've got a message for one of the smiths," Alec replied. "Man named Rythel."

"Go on then, but be quick about it," the guard said, waving him on.

At the forge two apprentices were doggedly pumping the bellows, while another held an iron rod in the coals with heavy tongs. Behind them, a smith was shaping a glowing spike of iron on the anvil. Short and dark-haired, he didn't match the description Eirual had given Seregil.

Alec waited until the man paused in his hammering, then stepped up and touched his brow respectfully.

The smith eyed his rags suspiciously. "What do you want?"

"Begging your pardon, master, but I've got a message sent for Master Rythel," Alec replied with a beggar's unctuous civility.

"Tell it quick and be off with you. The guards don't like anyone hanging about."

"That I can't, sir," Alec told him plaintively, twisting the hem of his tunic in his hands. "Begging your pardon, but I was given good silver to deliver it to nobody but Rythel his self. It'd be worth me livelihood if word got around I passed on private messages to anyone as demands to know 'em."

The smith was less than sympathetic. "Bugger your livelihood. Rythel would have my hammer if I let you go wandering around in there."

This exchange appeared to be a welcome diversion for the sentries. "Aw, he looks harmless enough," one called over, taking Alec's side. "Let him wait out here, why don't you? The message is for Rythel, after all."

"Aye, and one he'd be none too happy to miss, if you take my meaning." Grinning, Alec made a lewd two-fingered sign.

"All right, then, but it's on your heads," the smith growled, finding opinion against him. "Sit on the end of that cart, you, and don't stir."

Alec's champions lost interest in him as soon as they'd had their victory. Perched on the back of the open cart, he swung his feet idly and hunted imaginary lice among his rags.

The cart was loaded with iron grates. These were simple, sturdy affairs of upright bars and crosspieces. Apparently they were made at the shop in the upper city, then carried down for final fittings here. At the forge, the smith and his helpers were putting the last touches on one, trimming the crosspieces to fit caliper measurements and fashioning hot iron from the forge into the final bars. When they'd finished with that, heavy metal flanges were fastened to the outermost uprights, top and bottom. The lower flanges had heavy pins protruding down from them; the upper did not.

Presently several workmen came out of the tunnel. Their faces were covered with the vinegar cloths, but one was noticeably taller than the rest, and bushy blond hair showed beneath the rim of his leather cap.

"Ordo, we'll want those rivets when we go back in," he called to the smith at the forge. "Are they hot yet?"

"Whenever you're ready for 'em, Master Rythel. And this

young fellow's been waiting for you." The smith hooked a thumb in Alec's direction, adding pointedly, "Sergeant Durnin said it was all right."

Rythel pulled off his face cloth and scrubbed a hand over the thick, well-trimmed beard beneath it. "What do you want?"

Alec jumped down and bobbed an anxious bow. "I've a message for you, master, from a woman."

The man's scowl lessened appreciatively. Waving for Alec to follow him, he moved away from the others.

"What woman and what message?" he asked.

"A dark-haired bawd in the Street of Lights, master. She says she prays you remember her fondly, and that you'll come back to her soon as ever you're able."

"Did she give her name?" Rythel asked, looking pleased.

"No," Alec told him with a worried frown, then, as if suddenly remembering, added, "but she's in the House of the Swans."

"I know the one," Rythel said, recognizing the name of Eirual's establishment. "Anything else?"

"That's the whole of it, just as she sent. And if I may say, master, I was lucky to find you—"

"Yes, yes!" Reaching into a wallet at his belt, Rythel dropped a few coins into Alec's outstretched palm. "Tell your lady I'll see to her when I can. Now off with you."

"Maker's Mercy to you," said Alec, hurrying away. As he passed the soldiers he looked at the coins Rythel had paid. They were all coppers. Showing them to the grinning soldiers, he spat sideways and muttered, "Stingy son of a bitch. Let him carry his own messages."

Their laughter followed him up the gully.

At the boulder Seregil fell into step beside him and Alec told him all he'd seen as they walked back along the track.

Seregil rubbed his hands together with satisfaction. "Well, now we know what our noser looks like."

"We still don't know much about him, though."

"But if that woman at the shop is anyone to go by, I think we can find those willing to gossip. You carried that off well, as usual. I think maybe we'll use you for the jilt again tonight."

Alec grinned happily at the praise. "What will I be this time?"

"A doughty, fresh-faced country lad, looking for an apprenticeship and a few friends."

Alec's grin widened. "That has a familiar ring to it."

Standing at the end of Ironmonger Row, the Hammer and
Tongs was a traditional gathering place for the smiths in that part
of town. Most outsiders were actively discouraged by that close-
knit fraternity, who considered the alehouse their personal sanctuary and unofficial guildhall, but no one objected to the little
wayfaring minstrel who came in out of the storm that evening.
Such musicians, hardly more than beggars, were common enough
in the city, playing for pennies in taverns and market squares. His
cloak, stitched all over with scraps of colored cloths and cheap
beads, and the flutes protruding from various pockets granted him
entrance and a place near the fire.

Selecting a long wooden flute, Seregil piped out a simple tune
and then sang the verse in a voice that would have made Rolan
Silverleaf cringe. Fortunately, his present audience was less dis-
criminating and a small crowd had soon gathered at his end of the
room. Rythel was not among the company, but he soon found
Alec, looking the perfect bumpkin with his homespun tunic and
scrubbed, beardless face. The boy gave a slight nod, signaling that
all was well.

From his seat by the fireside, Seregil could see that Alec had
been adopted by a group of drinkers, and that the woman they'd
spoken with at Quarin's shop was among them. Judging by how
they included him in their jests, he had obviously made a favorable impression.

Seregil piped on, keeping an ear open for useful tidbits of conversation around him until Alec left. He played a few short ditties,
collected his coppers, and followed.

Alec was waiting for him at the public stable where they'd left
horses. Stripping off their disguises in the shadow of an alley, they
put on plain clothes and rode to a dram house near the north wall
of the Ring.

"I didn't have much luck, unless you want to know the current
price of pig iron," Seregil said as they sat down at a corner table.
"How did you make out?"

"You were right about noses being out of joint among Quarin's
people," Alec told him. "Maruli and some of the other smiths gave
me a real earful. Not only is Rythel Quarin's nephew, but he
hasn't been with him that long. He had a shop of his own down in

Kedra, but it burned four months ago. That's when he showed up here."

"Is Quarin fond of his nephew?"

"Not anymore. Old Alman Blackhand told me things were friendly at first, but that there've been hard words. Quarin's hardly spoken to him since he handed him the sewer job. And some think it's strange that Rythel lodges apart from his uncle."

"Interesting. Were any of those you spoke with part of Rythel's crew?"

"A few, and they don't much like him either. He has a sharp tongue and treats them like first-month apprentices, always looking over their shoulder. Early on in the job he found fault with the way the grates were being secured. Now he does most of the final fitting himself."

Seregil raised an appraising eyebrow. "I'll just bet he does."

"They've been at it for a little over three weeks. All the old grates had to be pulled out and the masonry knees repaired. That's why the guards are there. They're putting in the new grates now. Alman is in charge of measuring the part of the sewer tunnel where the grate will be, so that the flange pins and holes will set in properly, but Rythel does the final seating and pinning. And the grates are fixed, not gated. That's about it, except that I've been told to see Quarin about an apprenticeship."

"Hopefully it won't come to that."

Alec leaned closer, lowering his voice. "Do you think Rythel could be tampering with the grates?"

"Judging by his behavior, we can't afford to overlook the possibility. The question is how, and whether any of the other workmen are in on it. And who's backing this whole thing, of course."

"It's got to be the Plenimarans."

"I mean specifically who, and whether or not Rythel knows who's running the show. We've got to move very carefully, Alec. We don't want another cock-up like the raid at Kassarie's. We got the big snake there, but all the little ones slithered safely away. We'd better go talk to Nysander. This looks to be Watcher business."

He must still be keeping company with Ylinestra, Alec thought wryly as Thero let them into Nysander's tower. Several long scratches were visible on the young wizard's neck just above the collar of his robe. She'd left similar marks on Alec during their single encounter.

He's welcome to her, Alec decided.

Having let them in, Thero returned to a worktable spread with open books. "Nysander's downstairs," he told them.

"You'd better come down with us," said Seregil as he started down the stairs.

Thero shot Alec a look of surprise.

"Watcher business, maybe."

Alec was pleased to see the hint of an expectant smile cross Thero's face as he hurried to join him. He was a cold fish, and no mistake, but in the months since he'd helped secure Seregil's release from prison, albeit grudgingly, Alec had come to feel a certain sympathy for the stiff young wizard, and respect. He was talented, and his arrogance seemed a shield for his own inner loneliness. As for the rivalry between him and Seregil, Alec had quickly learned that this was as much Seregil's fault as Thero's.

They found Nysander in his favorite sitting-room armchair, the floor around him covered in charts of some sort.

"Well, there you two are," he exclaimed, looking up with a pleased smile. "How long has it been? Two weeks?"

"Closer to four," Seregil said. "Business has been slow lately, but we may have run across something interesting."

With Alec's help, he quickly sketched out what they'd learned over the past two days. Thero sat a little apart, arms crossed, nodding silently to himself as he listened.

"Dear me, that does sound suspicious," Nysander said when he'd heard their report. "I seem to recall hearing that one of Lord Zymanis' valets disappeared not too long ago. I had not heard of any stolen documents, though. Most curious. I assume you mean to make a closer investigation?"

Seregil nodded. "Tonight, but we'll have to be careful. So far Rythel is the only fish in our net. I don't want to get the wind up him before we find out who's behind all this."

"Have you looked into his lodgings?" asked Thero.

"Not yet. Tenements are terrible for housebreaking—every room occupied and half the time no corridors, just a series of rooms letting one onto another. I thought we'd have a look at the sewer tunnel first, then proceed from there."

"Yes, that seems to be the logical course," said Nysander.

"How do you propose to get in with the tunnel so carefully guarded?"

"The lower end is, where they're still working," said Alec. "But it shouldn't be at the upper end, where they started. There's no need, since the grates are fixed and they started at the top and worked down toward the lower city end. Seregil figures there must be at least five or six between the city wall and the sea."

"Anyone planning to bugger about with any of the grates later on would have to do them all," Seregil added. "I know of an access passage near the south wall that should lead down to the head of the channel. If we can get to it from this end, we should be able to find out what they've been up to."

"When will you go?" asked Nysander.

"Tonight seems as good a time as any," replied Seregil, standing to go. "I'll let you know if we need any help."

"Luck in the shadows," said Thero as he passed.

Seregil raised an eyebrow in mild surprise, then touched a finger lightly to one of the scratches on Thero's neck. "And to you."

Tamír the Great's builders had laid down the sewers of Rhíminee before a single building was constructed, thereby sparing the new capital the unpleasant and often unhealthy filth common to most large cities. So extensive was it, and so often modified and enlarged to accommodate the growth of the city over five centuries, that now only the Scavenger Guild knew the full extent of it. Even among the Scavengers, most knew only the section that they maintained, and they guarded their knowledge jealously.

Alec and Seregil waited until the second watch of the night before making their way to the southern ward of the city. Though armed, they went cautiously, fading silently into alleys or doorways whenever a Watch patrol happened by.

The entrance they'd targeted was located in a small square behind a block of tenements by the south wall of the city. Half-covered by an unkempt clump of mulberry bushes, the low, iron-strapped door was set into the wall itself. The small grate near the top of it reminded Alec uncomfortably of a prison door, but he kept this to himself as they set down the torches and pry bars they'd brought with them.

He stood behind Seregil and held his cloak

out with both hands to hide the light of his companion's light-wand. Kneeling in front of the door, Seregil probed the keyhole with a hooked pick, soon producing a succession of grating clicks. The door swung in on blackness. Gathering their gear again, they slipped inside.

Alec tacked a square of heavy felt over the grate, then looked around the little entrance chamber. In front of them, stone steps led downward through an arched passage and out of sight. The faint stench already permeating the air left no doubt they were in the right place.

"Here, we'd better put these on now." Seregil pulled vinegar-soaked face rags from a leather pouch and handed one to Alec. Leaving their cumbersome cloaks, they lit their torches with a firechip and started down, Seregil in the lead.

"Why did they build it so big?" Alec whispered; the arched passage was nearly ten feet high.

"For safety. The poisonous humours that can collect down here rise. The theory is that this design lets them collect overhead, with good air below. Keep an eye on the torches, though; if they burn blue or gutter, the air's bad."

The stairway led down to a tunnel below. Narrow walkways bordered a central channel, full to the brim now with a swift, evil-smelling stream.

Turning to the right, they followed the tunnel for several hundred feet. The recent rains had swelled the flow, and it had overflowed whole sections of the raised walkway, forcing them to wade ankle deep in the foul, frigid waters.

Suddenly they heard high-pitched growling and squeaking coming from the darkness ahead. Seregil edged forward, torch held high, until they came to an iron grate fixed across the width of the tunnel.

The lower ends of the vertical bars extended down into the channel and the body of a small dog was caught against them, held there by the pressure of the stream as it flowed through. Dozens of fat, snarling rats swarmed over the carcass, tearing at it and each other. Others paddled down the channel toward the feast or perched on the crosspieces of the grate. They paid little attention to the human interlopers as they fed, beady eyes glaring red in the torchlight.

"This one is gated," whispered Seregil, driving off the closest rats with the burning torch. "It's locked up, but it's nothing we can't manage. Want to do the honors?"

"Go ahead," Alec rasped, not wanting to have to squeeze past his companion in such a narrow place.

Jiggering the lock, Seregil swung back a narrow section of grate on protesting hinges and stepped through, Alec close on his heels.

There were more rats beyond, rats everywhere. The chuckle of the flowing water and the sounds of the rats echoed in the silence as they paused at a sort of crossroads where another channel flowed into the one they were following. Leaping the four feet to the other side, they continued on to a second hinged grate. Beyond this the way began to slope downhill noticeably.

No other tunnels intersected theirs and finally they came to a fixed grate. The ironwork was new and of the same design Alec had seen at the work site. The broad flanges set at the four corners of the grate rested against stone knees jutting from the walls of the tunnel and were held in place by thick iron pins set in holes drilled into the stone.

"Here we are," Seregil whispered, setting down his bundle. "Light your torch from mine and go check that side."

"What are we looking for, exactly?"

"I don't know, so be thorough. It could be some fault in the iron or the stone."

Alec jumped across the channel and began his examination of the ironwork, looking first for something as obvious as bars sawn through. They seemed sound enough, however. The sockets for the pins had been sealed with rivets hammered in hot and the lower flanges, which bore the weight of the grate, rested solidly against the stone knees.

"Let's try moving it," said Seregil.

Grasping two crosspieces, they braced their shoulders against the bars and lifted. The grate lifted an inch or two.

"Push!" Seregil grunted, shaking his side of it.

But the grate was solidly held in place by the pins. Giving up, they let it fall back into place with a dull clank.

"I thought maybe he'd sawn off the lower pins," Seregil panted, flexing his arms. "I guess not."

"It did move, though." Alec squinted up at the flanges overhead. It was impossible to see anything from this angle, so he climbed the crossbars for a closer inspection, torch in hand.

• • •

Across the channel, Seregil was about to do the same, but his torch was burning low. Pulling a fresh one from his belt, he paused to light it from the old one. "See anything?"

"There's nearly three inches of pin exposed up here," Alec replied, clinging one-handed to the top of the bars.

"I'm no expert, but that seems like a lot. How does it look?"

"Like a metal pin." Alec held his torch closer. "No marks or cuts. Hold on. Hey, it's melting like wax and there's—"

"Be careful!"

Searing white sparks erupted inches from Alec's face with an angry spitting sound. With a startled cry, he dropped his torch and threw an arm across his face.

"Alec! Alec, get down," Seregil yelled.

Alec crouched awkwardly, one leg jammed between the bars. Overhead, sparks still rained down from the sizzling corona of light.

Dark spots danced in front of Seregil's eyes as he launched himself across the channel. Grabbing Alec, he dragged him to the floor and tried to roll him onto his belly to smother the smoldering patches on his tunic.

"My eyes!" Alec gasped, struggling away in pain and confusion.

"Hold still," Seregil began, but Alec's foot found sudden purchase against the wall and, with a final lurch, he toppled Seregil backward into the icy channel.

Fortunately, Seregil had the presence of mind to clamp his mouth shut as he went under. For a horrifying second he tumbled helplessly against the side of the channel, unable to find the bottom with his feet. Fetching up against the grate, he righted himself and used the crossbars to pull himself back onto the walkway.

Sputtering and retching, he grasped Alec by the back of the tunic and hauled him out of range of the sparks, then held him forcibly still while the white light faded slowly to a small orange glow. One torch still burned, and by it he could see the thin pall of smoke curling lazily near the roof.

Alec groaned again, hands pressed over his face. Fearing the worst, Seregil dug the lightwand from his sodden tool roll and pulled the boy's hands away to inspect the damage.

Alec's hair and the vinegar mask had protected most of his face from the sparks, but half a dozen tiny blisters were already bubbling up on the backs of his hands. Tears streamed down his cheeks as he turned his head from the light.

"Can you see anything?" Seregil asked anxiously.

"I'm beginning to." Alec pressed one sleeve across his eyes, then blinked. "Why are you wet?" A look of shocked realization slowly spread across his face. "Oh, no. Oh, Seregil, I'm sorry!"

Seregil managed a tight grin, trying hard not to think about the water dripping down his face toward his mouth.

"What was that light?" Alec asked.

"I don't know." Going back to the grate, he climbed up to inspect the damage. "The pin is burned completely away, stonework cracked from the heat, top of the flange warped. And whatever it was, it must work on the other side, too, or you still couldn't move the grate."

Jumping the channel, he gripped the handle of the lightwand between his teeth and climbed up to inspect the upper corner.

"Tell me again what you saw."

Still blinking, Alec came across and picked up the torch. "I held the flame close to the pin, trying to see if it had been cut. It must have been the heat, because the surface of the pin began to melt and run like wax. I think I saw something white underneath, just before it flared up the way it did."

Craning his neck cautiously, Seregil found several inches of exposed pin between the flange and the stonework above. Using the tip of his dagger, he scraped gently at the surface of the pin. Curls of some black, waxy substance shaved off easily, revealing a white layer below.

"You were right. A band of silvery white metal has been set into the pin."

The white substance cut easily as lead. Extracting a tiny sliver, he handed it down to Alec on the tip of his blade. "Put it on the floor and light it."

Alec set the sliver gingerly on the floor and, standing well back, held the torch to it. It burst at once into a brief, sputtering blaze of light that left black burns on the stone.

Alec let out a low whistle. "Bilairy's Balls, I think we found what we're looking for."

"There must be enough iron in the center of the pin to strengthen it, but this stuff burns right through it."

"Is it magic?"

Seregil cut away another small sample of the white substance.

"Maybe. I've never seen anything like it, but Nysander might know."

Seregil placed the shavings carefully in the little ceramic jar he'd carried the firechip in, then handed it down to Alec.

"I sure made a mess of that corner," Alec said, casting a worried look at the blackened stonework.

"True." Seregil climbed down to join him. "Our saboteurs are bound to come checking sooner or later and even if they don't, there are the Scavengers to consider. We'd better get Nysander down here, or Thero."

Alec's sight slowly returned to normal as they cleaned up the site as best they could and started back.

"What about the locks?" he asked, reaching the first of the gated barriers.

"Best leave 'em as we found 'em," Seregil replied. "I'll scout ahead to the next one. You catch up."

The lock was rusty; swearing softly under his breath, Alec ground a pick against the wards until something dropped into place.

Seregil was out of sight beyond a bend in the tunnel by then. Anxious to leave the rats and echoing dampness behind, Alec hurried after him.

He'd just caught sight of him ahead near the intersection of channels when Seregil suddenly collapsed sideways into the water with a startled grunt. The torch he'd been carrying hung precariously over the edge and by its light Alec saw two ragged, hooded figures jump out from the side tunnel, cudgels raised as they reached for Seregil's floating form.

Without stopping to think, Alec let out a yell, drew his sword, and charged.

The gaterunners were caught by surprise, but the one closest to Alec got a long club up in time to block the first downward slash. Alec jumped back a pace and braced, ready to fight.

The narrowness of the walkway kept the fight to a one against one affair, but it also severely restricted the range of Alec's swings. His opponents were more accustomed to such conditions. The second quickly jumped across the channel to outflank him from behind. Alec did the same, keeping his face toward them. He couldn't see Seregil anywhere.

The current must have swept him back the way we came, he thought, and for a sickening instant he pictured the dog's carcass and its attendant rats trapped against the lower bars of a grate. The gaterunners didn't allow him time to dwell on the image, however. The one on his side of the channel was advancing, cudgel at the ready. From the corner of his eye, Alec saw the other reaching into his tattered tunic for something, presumably a knife or dart. Suddenly, however, the runner slumped against the wall with a high-pitched wail, clutching at a throwing knife protruding from his shoulder.

"Hammil!" the one facing Alec cried out, and he realized it was a woman.

"Let's not anyone be stupid," said a familiar voice from the shadows downstream.

Alec and the woman both turned in time to see Seregil step into sight on the far side. He was wetter than ever but held a second dagger at the ready as he walked slowly toward the wounded runner. The boy scuttled weakly back, still clutching his arm.

"We don't mean any harm here," Seregil said calmly, motioning for Alec to back slowly away.

The woman pushed her hood back, showing a harsh, deeply lined face. "Get away from my boy," she growled, shaking her club threateningly in Alec's direction.

"You started this. What do you want?" asked Seregil, stopping a few paces from the boy, dagger in hand.

"Nothin'," the woman replied. "You's just strangers is all, and strangers is getting to be a hazard down here. We've lost friends to strangers down here lately."

Seregil sheathed his knife. Bending over the fallen boy, he examined the wound, then pulled the small throwing blade out. "It's not too bad a cut," he told the woman over his shoulder. "You're lucky my aim was off."

"I'm alright, Ma," the young gaterunner gasped, cringing away from Seregil. By the dying light of the torch, Alec saw that he was younger than himself. He could also make out a thin ribbon of blood running down Seregil's right cheek.

"You all right?" Seregil called over.

"Yes. Are you?"

Seregil nodded, then stepped over the wounded boy and addressed his mother again. "I'll leave yours if you'll leave mine," he told her, holding his hands out palm up.

Without a word, she sprang across, grabbed the boy up, and hurried him away into the shadows.

Alec crossed over and reached to inspect the cut on Seregil's scalp. "That's quite a lump she raised."

"Serves me right," he muttered through chattering teeth. "Illior's Fingers! Jumped by a pair of gaterunners. If the cold water hadn't brought me around I'd have drowned."

"I'm glad you didn't kill him. He couldn't have been more than twelve."

Seregil braced one arm against the wall and let out a long sigh. "Me, too. It's strange for them to have attacked in the first place. Runners are usually a pretty elusive lot. They steal and spy, but they generally avoid a fight."

Frowning, Alec pulled off his face rag and pressed it to the cut on Seregil's head. "Are you sure you're all right? You're looking kind of shaky."

Seregil closed his eyes for a moment, resting one hand on Alec's shoulder. Then, taking the cloth from him, he held it himself and continued on down the tunnel. "Come on, let's get out of here. I've had all the swimming I care for tonight."

They reached the upper entrance behind the mulberry bushes without incident, but the combined effects of cold and the blow were beginning to take their toll on Seregil.

"You go for Nysander," he said, shivering even with his dry cloak pulled tightly around him. "I'd better stay and make sure no one tumbles to our little adventure in the meantime."

To his surprise, Alec balked.

"No, you go," he stated flatly. "Your head is still bleeding and I can hear your teeth chattering from here."

"I'll survive," Seregil retorted. "I don't want you here alone. What if someone does show up?"

"All the more reason for you to hurry," Alec said stubbornly. "I'll stay out of sight—they'll never know I'm here. You're the one needs looking after. Go on!"

Seregil could tell by the set of Alec's jaw that his mind was made up. Cutting a small strip from the hem of his cloak, he handed it to Alec. "Hang on to this. Nysander can use it to find you. And keep out of sight no matter what, understand? No heroics."

"No heroics."

Seregil let out a defeated sigh. "If I'm not back soon, you get back to the Orëska, understand?"

"All right, yes! Will you just go? I don't want to be here all night." Pulling up his hood, Alec melted back into the shadows.

The pounding in Seregil's head worsened as he dashed through the darkened streets toward the Orëska, but he managed to ignore the pain by worrying about Alec instead. Despite his faith in the boy's quick wits, he couldn't seem to shake off visions of Alec being caught unawares by the Watch or stealthy spies returning to check their handiwork.

Arriving at the Orëska filthy, wet, and bloody, he argued his way past the watchman and hurried up the twisting stairs to Nysander's tower.

Thero opened the door and recoiled, covering his nose with one full sleeve. "By the Four!" he gagged, blocking the doorway. "You smell like you just crawled out of the sewers."

"Very observant of you. Get out of my way."

"You're not coming in here like that. Go down to the baths first."

"I don't have time for this, Thero. Now move or I'll move you."

The two glared at each other, years of mutual dislike laid open between them without the gloss of banter or social nicety. Either could have done the other considerable harm if it came to open confrontation, and they both knew it.

"Alec's alone out there, and we need Nysander's help," hissed Seregil.

With a last disgusted look, Thero stepped aside and let him through to the workroom. "He's not here."

"Where is he?"

"Out for his nightly walk, I imagine," Thero replied stiffly. "Or perhaps you've forgotten about those?"

"Then summon him!" Seregil paused, took a deep breath, and said through clenched teeth, "If you *please*."

Thero conjured a message sphere with a casual wave of his hand. Balancing the tiny light over his palm, he said to it, "Nysander, Seregil needs you right away. He's in the workroom." The light shot away through the floor. He waved Seregil to a wooden bench near one of the tables, but remained standing himself.

The young wizard was immaculate as ever, Seregil noted sourly, his robe spotless beneath his leather apron, his curly black hair and beard neatly trimmed, blunt-fingered hands unsullied. The thought that he'd inhabited that angular frame himself, if briefly, still made him cringe inwardly. That Thero had had the use of his body didn't bear thinking about.

"You're bleeding," Thero said at last, stepping reluctantly toward him. "I'd better have a look."

Seregil drew back from his touch. "It's just a scratch."

"You have a lump the size of an egg over your ear and fresh blood on your cheek," Thero snapped. "What do you think Nysander would say if I let you sit there like that?"

Wethis, the young servant, brought clean water and dressings and Thero set about cleaning the wound.

Nysander returned just as he was finishing.

"What an unprecedented tableau," the wizard exclaimed, hurrying in between the stacks of manuscripts. He was dressed in a threadbare surcoat and trousers. Seregil noted with a twinge of pride how kind and unwizardly his old friend looked in comparison to his stiff assistant.

"By the Light, Seregil, what an appalling stench! When you have finished there, Thero, please go and find him a clean robe."

Folding the bloodied towel next to the basin, Thero disappeared down the back stairway to their quarters.

Nysander smiled, examining his assistant's handiwork. "He does surprise me sometimes. But where is Alec?"

"Take this." Seregil pulled out another scrap of cloth he'd cut from his cloak and pressed it into Nysander's hand. "We found what we were looking for, sabotage in the tunnels, but made one hell of a mess doing it. I need you to fix it up for us. Alec's waiting by the entrance, so we'd better hurry."

Nysander shook his head. "Yes, of course, but I see no reason to drag you out again. You are still chilled to the bone, and a translocation would not be the best thing for you after such a knock on the head."

Seregil rose to protest and was very surprised to feel the floor lurch beneath his feet in a decidedly unpleasant manner.

"There now, you see?" Nysander chided, pressing him back

down on the bench. "You go downstairs and sit by the fire. Alec can show me whatever it is I need to see."

"I can't just sit here," Seregil insisted again, though his head was still spinning. "We ran into one pair of gaterunners down there already tonight. There could be others, or worse."

Nysander raised a shaggy eyebrow at him. "Are you suggesting that Alec would not be safe in my company?"

Seregil sank his head in his hands as Thero reappeared with clean garments over his arm.

"I leave Seregil in your able care," Nysander told him. "I suggest a cup of hot wine and, by all or any means necessary, a bath." Clasping the scrap of woolen cloth Seregil had given him, he traced a series of designs on the air and disappeared into the wide black aperture that opened briefly beside him.

When Nysander opened his eyes again, he was in a small deserted square.

"There you are," whispered Alec, crawling out from behind a clump of leafless bushes. "Is Seregil all right?"

"Yes, just a bit dizzy. He says you have something to show me."

"Something we need fixed," the boy replied with a familiar grin. "Follow me."

This was the first time he'd actually seen Alec at work, and he was impressed with his quickness and efficiency.

"My, but Seregil has been busy with you!" Nysander remarked as Alec let him through the second gate.

"Ruint me for honest work, he 'as," Alec replied, making a passable stab at a dockman's accent. "It's not far now."

Reaching the damaged grate, Nysander climbed up to inspect the damaged stone and ironwork, then moved across to see the intact corner.

"I see," he murmured to himself, peering closely at the remaining pin. "Most ingenious. And ingenious of you to have discovered it. Yes, I am quite satisfied. Well done."

"Can you fix it?"

"Can I fix it?" Nysander snorted, climbing down again. Grasping the bars with both hands, he closed his eyes and listened to the voice of the cold iron. Letting his own energy pass into it through his hands, he visualized the metal, felt it stir under his hands.

• • •

Standing beside him, Alec felt a powerful ripple pass through the rank air. There were no flashes of light or magical signs, just the brief scrape and whine of metal. For a moment it seemed to Alec that the metal came alive, like a plant, growing and moving as it healed.

Looking up, he saw that the damaged corner now looked as it had before. "Illior's Light!" he gasped, hardly able to believe his eyes.

Nysander laughed. "I hope you did not expect me to come down here with a hammer and anvil." Opening his hand, he showed Alec a long iron pin. It was scored along its length where it had been driven through the flange and blackened from forging, except where the white metallic substance showed through near one end.

Without a word Alec scaled the left side of the grate to find a solid pin in its place.

"That's amazing," he exclaimed, tapping the iron with his knife blade.

Nysander shrugged. "It is only magic."

Seregil grudgingly accepted the willow bark infusion Thero prepared, then went down to the baths. As soon as he was clean and dressed, however, he returned to the workroom and refused to be moved, despite Thero's obvious desire that he wait elsewhere.

Anxious and impatient, Seregil prowled the crowded room, fiddling with bits of delicate apparatus.

"Give me that!" Thero snapped, snatching away a cluster of fluid-filled glass spheres. "Drop that and we'll be up to our eyes in swamp sprites. If you won't go downstairs then for Illior's sake, sit down."

"I know what it is." Scowling, Seregil climbed the stairway to the catwalk overhead and stared out through the thick glass panes of the dome, watching the movement of lights below.

By the time Nysander and Alec materialized neatly in the center of the room, it would have been difficult to say which of the two looked more relieved.

"There you are!" Seregil exclaimed, bounding down. "Any trouble?"

"No, everything looks as good as new," Alec told him, grinning.

"Shall I fetch fresh clothing?" Thero inquired, wrinkling his nose again.

"Yes, in a moment," said Nysander. "First, however, I must congratulate our two able spies on a most valuable find." He shook the iron pin from his sleeve. "I will keep this for now. Seregil, Alec tells me you took a sample of this curious white material?"

Seregil held up the small container. "Right here. Want to see it work?"

"Yes, but not here, I think. Too many flammable items." Taking a crucible from a nearby shelf, he ushered them into the casting room.

Placing a few of the white shavings in the crucible, Nysander set it on the floor and touched a candle flame to its contents. A small fountain of white sparks flew up and scattered across the floor.

"Incredible!" murmured Thero, nudging the remaining shavings about with a small glass wand.

Seregil watched him surreptitiously, recognizing the sudden light of enthusiasm in those pale eyes. At such moments he could almost see what maintained Nysander's hopes for the young man—the keen and wondering mind that underlay Thero's cold facade.

"Have you ever seen anything like this before?" Thero asked, turning to Nysander.

The older wizard lit another fragment, then sniffed at the smoke left behind. "It's a sort of incendiary metal, I believe. It's called Sakor's Bite or Sakor's Fire for obvious reasons. Very, very rare but"—Nysander paused to raise one bushy eyebrow at Seregil—"found in greater quantities in certain regions of Plenimar."

Seregil exchanged knowing grins with Alec. "Looks like we've got ourselves a decent bit of work at last."

18
ON THE SCENT

Over the next few days Alec and Seregil shadowed their man closely, but learned little more than that Rythel was annoyingly regular in his habits. He rose early, gathered his crew, and worked the day through without leaving the site. At night he took supper at his lodgings and turned in early.

Lounging across the street from the Sailmaker Street tenement the fourth evening, they saw a broad, ruddy young man step out into the street.

"That's the landlady's grandson," Seregil whispered to Alec. "He's been down to that tavern on the corner every night so far."

True to form, the fellow set off for the corner tavern, stopping to chat with neighbors along the way.

Seregil stood up and stretched, still following the young man with his eyes. "He looks like a talker to me. I think I'll nip in for a pint and try to strike up a conversation."

It was a clear, windless night, but cold. Moving restlessly from one cold doorway to another, Alec watched the house, and the half moon sailing slowly over it. It had gained the chimney by the time Seregil reappeared, chuckling to himself and smelling warmly of beer.

"You look pleased with yourself," Alec muttered, shifting his frigid feet.

"I am." Seregil threw his cloak back and presented him with a wooden cup of the Dog and Bell's best lager. "Let's go home. Rythel's unlikely to stir out for another couple of nights yet."

Alec took a grateful swallow of the watery beer as they headed back to the court where they'd left their horses. "Then you did get something out of the grandson?"

"Our smith appears to be equally disliked by almost everyone who knows him, with the exception of his landlady, who judges her tenants solely by how punctual they are with their rent. Her grandson, young Parin, has had a few run-ins with him around the house. Apparently harsh words were exchanged when Parin entered the smith's rooms unexpectedly one day. 'Mind you' "—grinning, Seregil mimicked Parin's somewhat slurred complaints—"'he was only messin' about with some drawerings. Not like he was tupping nobody or nothin'. Just drawerings, for the love a' hell! He's a queer one, and a miser, for all his high and mighty ways.'

"A shrewd judge of character, our Parin," Seregil said with a chuckle. "He wasn't much help about the nature of the 'drawerings,' but he did tell me that Rythel always keeps to his rooms on work nights, but come end of the week he goes on a regular spree."

Alec's hunter instincts stirred. "Tomorrow night."

"That's right. According to Parin, he appears downstairs in gentlemen's clothes, sends Parin next door to hire a horse, tips like the miser he is, and rides off not to be seen again until dawn or the next night."

"That explains how he came to be in the Street of Lights."

"And I'm willing to bet he makes a few other stops along the way. I think it's time Lord Seregil put in an appearance."

Alec shot him a sharp look. "Just him? What about me?"

Seregil threw an arm around his shoulders and playfully ruffled his hair. "Well now, if Master Rythel is out gambling and whoring all night, what better time for a bit of housebreaking?"

•   •   •

The following evening Rythel rode out from Sailmaker Street just as expected. The streets were busy, making it an easy matter for Seregil to follow him up to the main city. A heavy cloak masked the fine surcoat and breeches he'd put on for the evening's role.

The smith rode easily, apparently enjoying the evening air, and ended up at the Heron, a stylish gambling house on the eastern fringe of the Merchant's Quarter.

That's a lucky turn. Seregil grinned to himself, watching from a distance as Rythel disappeared inside. Lord Seregil was well known at the Heron from the days when he'd made his living in such dens. And gaming-house friendships were easy enough to manage.

Leaving Cynril with a groom, he strode inside. The elderly doorkeeper took his cloak with a bow.

"Good evening, my lord," the old man said. "It's been some time since we last saw you. Will anyone be joining you?"

"No. A canceled engagement has left me at loose ends." Pausing, he slipped a discreet coin to the man, murmuring, "Any new blood tonight, Starky?"

Stark palmed the bribe and leaned closer. "A few, my lord, a few. Young Lady Lachia has become quite addicted to bakshi since her marriage, but her husband's with her tonight and he may know you rather too well from times past. There's a country knight, Sir Nynius, with plenty of gold and a passion for eran stones who plays badly as a rule. And there's a third, a newcomer. Not noble, but well turned out. Calls himself Rythel of Porunta."

"How will I know him?"

"He's tall and fair, with quite an impressive beard. I expect you'll find him in the card room. A bold player, as I hear it, though not always clever. He's become a regular over the past month or so and takes both wins and losses philosophically."

Seregil slipped him a second coin and a wink.

"Illior's luck to you, my lord."

The Heron was a modestly opulent establishment divided into a number of large rooms. Those near the front featured various sorts of games open to all comers; smaller rooms at the back were reserved for private affairs.

Seregil found Rythel in one of the latter, settled down to a round of Rook's Gambit with several rich merchants and a few officers of the Queen's Archers. A number of them knew Seregil and invited him to join in. He took the empty chair nearest Rythel and set his purse on the table.

"Good evening, Lord Seregil," Vinia the wool merchant greeted him, gathering up the brightly painted cards for a new deal. "The hazard is three gold sesters, the limit eight. As the new player, you begin the bid."

Keeping one eye on Rythel's style, Seregil played conservatively for the first few rounds, managing to collect a modest pile of winnings. He chatted with the others as they played, spicing the light banter with investment advice and allusions to recent successful ventures, including an interest in the privateer fleet being overseen by Nyreidian.

Rythel listened with polite interest, saying little until the deal came around to him again.

"I suggest a change of game," he said, gathering the pack. "Sword and Coin? There are enough of us to partner two games."

The other players were agreeable and when the chairs and tables had been shifted, Seregil was not surprised to find himself sitting across from Rythel. With a silent nod to Illior, he settled down to make his partner a richer man.

The less circumspect players were soon winnowed out as Seregil, no stranger to creative card shuffling, gently tipped the scales in his and Rythel's favor. Rythel, too, showed signs of certain talents; in an hour's time the two of them had exhausted the resources of the other players.

Seregil gave him a slight bow as they rose to divide their winnings and extended his hand. "Well played. I'm Lord Seregil, as you may have gathered. And you?"

"Rythel of Porunta, my lord." His hand was hard in Seregil's, but not as stained and roughened as he'd expected. The man had obviously taken pains to hide his current occupation.

"Porunta? That's down near Stoneport, isn't it? What brings you so far north this time of year?"

"I'm in commerce there, my lord, in a modest way." Rythel paused, giving Seregil a disarmingly open smile. "I must confess, some of the ventures you've mentioned tonight interest me."

"A man of vision, eh?" Seregil said with a knowing wink. "I'm a great admirer of ambition, and our brief partnership tonight didn't do my purse any harm. Perhaps you'd like to discuss things further over a bit of supper?"

"I'd be honored, my lord," Rythel replied, just a hint too eager.

"Anyplace in particular?"

Rythel shrugged. "No, my lord. I've no plans for the night."

Damn, thought Seregil. *Looks like we'll spend the evening plying each other with drink and fishing for secrets.*

A harsh, clear dawn was breaking when Seregil returned to the Cockerel. Alec was asleep on the couch, legs stretched out toward the ruins of a fire. He awoke with a start when Seregil flopped wearily down beside him.

"Well, how did it go?"

Seregil shrugged, running both hands back through his hair. "He's not the greatest spy in the world, but he knows how to keep his mouth shut. We spent most of the night drinking at the Rose, then he decided he wanted a woman. I hoped maybe he needed to meet someone at a brothel, but instead he was ready to take up with the first pair of clapmongers we passed in the street. I finally managed to steer him into the Black Feather."

"The Feather? That's quite a comedown from Eirual's."

"The same thought occurred to me. Either he was putting on an act for my benefit, or his fortunes fluctuate considerably from week to week. It's something to keep an eye on. At any rate, we parted company there a few hours ago and I followed him down to Sailmaker Street. He didn't go out again."

"Sounds like a wasted evening."

"As far as this sewer business goes it was. Still, you can't spend a whole evening drinking and whoring with a person and not learn something. He's passing himself off as some well-heeled merchant and, to tell you the truth, he carries it off so well that I wonder if some of it isn't true. I'd say he's Skalan born, and has done a bit of this kind of work before—a small-time noser. The Plenimarans know how to find that type and use them."

Alec gave him a wry grin. "So do you."

"It's too soon to tell with this one, though." Seregil stretched wearily. His night at the Feather had left him feeling gritty and in need of a bath. "Although Lord Seregil clearly made quite an impression on him. I let a few details slip about privateers and suddenly he was my boon companion. I passed on a few rumors; it'll be interesting to see where they pop up later. How'd you do?"

Alec pulled a flattened roll of parchment from inside his tunic and waggled it triumphantly. Carrying it to the table, he pinned the corners down with books. As he reached to secure an upper corner, Seregil saw a ragged tear in his left sleeve that appeared to be stained with blood.

"What happened to you?"

Alec shrugged, avoiding his eye. "It's nothing."

"Nothing?" Grasping his friend's hand, he pushed the torn sleeve back. A rough bandage was tied around the boy's forearm and stained through with a circle of dried blood the size of a two-sester piece. "Nothing doesn't usually bleed like that."

"It's just a scratch," Alec insisted.

Ignoring Alec's objections, Seregil drew his dagger and cut away the dressing. A shallow, jagged cut began at a puncture just below his elbow and ended dangerously close to the delicate tendons just above Alec's wrist.

"Illior's Fingers, you could get blood poisoning with a cut like that!" he gasped, fetching brandy to clean the wound. "What happened?"

"I just slipped going over the roof to his window," Alec admitted with a grudging sigh. "I figured that would be the safest route in, but it was a little steeper than I thought, and the slates were really slick—"

"Ever heard of rope?"

"By the time I realized I needed one, I was already up there. Anyway, my sleeve caught a nail sticking out of the gutter—"

"The gutter?" Seregil sputtered, feeling his stomach give a little lurch. "You went over the *edge*? It's a forty-foot drop to stone paving! What in the name of Bilairy's—"

"Actually, there's a shed right under his window," Alec corrected. "It would've broken the fall—"

"Oh, so you had it all carefully planned, then?" Seregil said with heavy sarcasm.

Alec shrugged again. "Learn and live, right?"

Illior's Light, that must be the same look I give Micum or Nysander when they're berating me for surviving some stupid escapade! Shaking his head, Seregil turned to inspect Alec's work, a crude, gridlike drawing done in charcoal and smudged here and there with blood.

"This is a copy of a map I found in a hollowed-out post of Rythel's bed," explained Alec, frowning down at it. "It's not very good, I know, but I knew I'd never remember any of it unless I marked it out somehow."

"You didn't steal this parchment from his room?"

"Of course not! I remembered what Parin said about drawings in his room and thought I might need to copy something. I took all the materials with me."

"Except a rope."

At first glance Alec's map, done in a feverish haste by an unpracticed hand, seemed little more than a meaningless scrawl of lines.

"I think it's a map of the sewers," said Alec. "There wasn't any writing on it, just marks here and there, but it looked a lot like those plans we found at Kassarie's, remember?" He pointed to a circle near the bottom of the sheet. "I'd say this represents the outlet where they're working, and this is probably the top of the channel, where we found the sabotaged grate."

Seregil nodded slowly, then tapped a spot just beyond where a number of lines radiated out from a single terminus. "Several large channels come together here. One goes west, toward the Noble Quarter; this one here probably leads under the middle of the city— Is this exactly what you saw, line for line?"

"I think so, but I didn't get all of it. It was really complicated and I was jumping at every noise. Finally I did hear someone coming, so I just grabbed what I had and rabbited. Sorry."

"No, no, you did well," Seregil mused, still puzzling over the layout. "This is solid grounds for arresting him, but how in hell did he get this much information?"

"Could the Plenimarans use it to attack the city through the sewers?"

"Not a full-scale attack, but they could cause plenty of other mischief—enemy sappers opening gates from inside, assassins popping out of the royal privies, or anywhere else in the city, for that matter." Straightening up, he thumped Alec proudly on the shoulder. "Good work. This is more than I came up with."

Alec colored, grinning. "The smiths I talked to from his crew expect to be done in a couple of weeks. That means that Rythel has to complete whatever work he has left on this by then." He paused. "What I want to know is how he learned all this if he never goes out at night and never leaves the work site?"

"That's the real question, isn't it? Exploring and mapping out all these tunnels would take weeks, months even. But what if you find someone who knows already?"

"Like a Scavenger!"

"Or a gaterunner. What did that one who jumped me say?"

"Something about strangers in the sewers, someone she was afraid of."

"Right." Seregil looked down at the smudged parchment, tapping his chin thoughtfully. "I wonder what Tym's up to these days?"

"Tym?"

"You must remember him, the thief who cut your purse for me that time?"

Alec grimaced. "I remember him, all right. He's not a gaterunner, is he?"

"No, but he has connections there, and just about everywhere else among the poor and the criminal. That's what makes him so useful to us."

"I didn't think it was his charm," Alec remarked sourly.

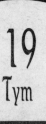

19
Tym

"How do you know he'll come?" Alec asked as they climbed to the empty room over the nameless lower city slophouse the following evening.

"He'll come." Seregil eyed the greasy table with distaste, then sat down on one of the stools next to it. "He's probably already around somewhere."

He hadn't been hard to contact. An informal network permeated the lowest classes of the city like the roots of a tree; a coin and discreet word with the right party was usually sufficient.

Almost before Seregil had finished speaking, they heard a light step on the stairs behind them. Tym paused in the doorway, scanning the room suspiciously. With a deferential nod to Seregil, he sauntered in.

Alec eyed the thief with carefully guarded dislike. The last time Alec had seen him was outside the city that day with Micum and Beka. Cocky with his new skills, Alec had surprised him in a crowd, hoping to pay him back for cutting his purse. Instead, Tym had nearly knifed him.

He was still thin and dirty as ever, and still cloaked in an air of hungry arrogance. Slinging one leg over the bench opposite Seregil, he favored Alec with a long, appraising sneer.

"Still with 'im, eh? Must be gettin' something you like."

Alec returned the look impassively.

Tym snorted a brief, humorless laugh and turned his attention to Seregil. "You asked after me?"

Seregil rested one fist on the table and slowly opened it to display a thick silver half sester.

"Any queer customers about?" he asked, using the common slang for spy.

Tym snorted again, a harsh, ugly sound. "What do you think?"

Seregil snapped his hand closed over the coin, opened it again. A second coin glittered in the hollow of his palm. "Are you working for any of them?"

Tym eyed the coins, an almost thoughtful look smoothing his narrow face for an instant. "Think I'd tell if I was?"

Seregil's hand closed, opened. Four coins.

Alec studied Tym's face. The aloof mask stayed firmly in place.

"Could be," Tym replied cautiously.

Close. Open. No coins.

That got a reaction. Tym sat forward, looking like a man who'd just overplayed his game.

"Bugger! No, I ain't working for nobody, but there's them that might be."

Seregil opened his hand again. Five coins.

"Rat Tom come by a stash real suddenlike, wouldn't say where from," Tym confided, all crafty compliance now.

"Where's Rat Tom now?"

Tym shrugged. "Turned up dead in an alley not two weeks ago, throat cut."

"Who else?"

"Fast Mickle claims he did a papers job in Helm Street."

"What house?"

"Don't know."

"Where could I find Fast Mickle?"

Tym shrugged again. "Ain't seen him for a while."

Seregil snatched the coins away with a disgusted sigh and rose, motioning for Alec to follow. "Let's go. There's nothing to be learned here."

"There's talk," Tym added hastily.

Halfway to the door already, Seregil turned with an exasperated frown. "What talk?"

"It's the gaterunners mostly. Some turn up flush all of a sudden, then they turn up dead or not at all."

Alec exchanged a quick look with Seregil, thinking of what the woman had told them in the sewers.

"Madrin, Dinstil, Slim Lily, Wanderin' Ki, all of 'em dead one way or another just in the last month," Tym continued. "Tarl's been lookin' for Farin the Fish for a week now."

"I thought Farin was a breaker?" Seregil returned to the table. Alec remained standing just behind him.

"He is, but still it's funny he's gone. Him and Tarl been together for years."

"Any others?"

"Virella maybe, she's another runner, but you don't never know with her. And that young breaker, Shady—they found her floating in the harbor out past the moles. Some are even wondering about the Rhíminee Cat, but he's another you don't never know about."

Seregil jingled the coins in his fist. "Who's supposed to be doing all this killing?"

For the first time Tym looked uneasy. "Don't know. Don't *nobody* know, and that is strange. The snuffers claim ain't none of them doing it. Folks is gettin' nervous. You don't hardly know whether to take a job or not."

"I have a job, if you're interested," Seregil told him, sliding the silver enticingly closer.

Tym looked hungrily at the stack of coins. "This wouldn't be a running job would it?"

"No, just a snoop. There's a house near here I want watched. If you see anyone you know go in—breaker, runner, keek, anything—I want to know about it. Or anyone you think doesn't fit with the neighborhood. Is that clear?"

"Breakers and runners?" Tym's eyes narrowed again. "This got to do with the killings?"

"Maybe he's scared," Alec suggested quietly, speaking for the first time.

Tym lurched up, gripping the hilt of his knife. "Maybe I ought to fix that pretty face of yours!"

"Sit down!" barked Seregil.

Alec stiffened, but remained where he was. Tym sullenly obeyed.

"Now," Seregil resumed calmly, "do you want the job or not?"

"Yeah, I want it," Tym growled. "But it'll cost you."

"Name your price."

"Two sesters a week."

"Done." Seregil spat in his palm and clasped hands with the thief. As Tym tried to withdraw his, Seregil gripped it tight.

"You've never turned on me yet. This would be a poor time to start." Seregil smiled, but that only made the threat implicit in his tone more ominous. The force of it drove the cocky sneer from Tym's face. "If anyone tumbles and offers you more to turn to them, you smile and you take their money, then you come straight back to me."

"I will, sure I will!" Tym stammered, wincing. "I ain't never turned on you. I ain't going to."

"Of course you aren't." Seregil relinquished his hold at last, but the imprint of his long fingers glowed for a moment in white, bloodless stripes across the back of the thief's hand. "The house is the tenement in Sailmaker Street with the red and white striped lintel. You know the one?"

Tym nodded curtly, flexing his hand. "Yeah, I know it."

"You can start now. Report to me in the usual way."

Alec shook his head incredulously as Tym disappeared down the stairs. "You actually trust him?"

"After a fashion. He just needs the occasional reminder." Seregil drummed his fingers lightly on the table. "In his own way, Tym trusts me. He trusts that I'll pay. He trusts that I won't double-cross him, and he trusts that I'll hunt him to the ends of the earth and slit his throat if he turns on me. You'd do well to watch your step with him, though. That was no idle threat just now."

"I was just trying to push him along," Alec began, but Seregil held up a hand.

"I know what you were doing, and it worked. But you don't understand people like him. He respects me because he fears me. I nearly killed him once and he's the sort that takes to you afterward because of it. But he'd slice you open in a minute and worry about my reaction later. Insulting him the way you did is enough to make him your enemy for life."

"I'll keep that in mind," Alec said. He'd never quite gotten around to telling Seregil of his last confrontation with Tym. Now didn't seem to be the right time, either, but he stored away the advice.

20

MUCKING ABOUT

Through the next week the dreary Klesin rains rolled in off the sea in earnest, melting away the last of the filthy snow still lingering in the shelter of alleyways and corners, and insuring that Seregil and his company were perpetually damp.

Tym kept watch over the Sailmaker Street house, but reported nothing beyond Rythel's expected movements between there and the sewer site.

Work for the Rhíminee Cat—a papers job—came in at midweek. This fell to Alec, who spent the next few days scouting the household of a certain lord whose estranged wife wanted certain papers stolen. During the evenings, however, he became a welcome regular at the Hammer and Tongs. Whether Rythel would remain in his uncle's shop once the work was completed seemed to be a matter of speculation, though it was unclear whether this was grounded in some hint from Rythel or mere wishful thinking on the part of the other smiths.

Meanwhile, Seregil set to work on the connection between the smith and Lord General Zymanis, but his discreet inquiries yielded little beyond what Nysander had already told them.

A young valet had disappeared four months before, but there was no evidence that he'd stolen anything.

At week's end the winds changed, shredding the clouds into tatters of vermilion and gold against the late afternoon sky.

"Rythel will be going out soon. What's the plan for tonight?" asked Alec, gazing out the window beside the workbench.

Seregil looked up from a pick he'd been repairing and smiled. The slanting sunlight bathed Alec's profile as he leaned against the window frame, striking fiery glints in his hair and casting his cheekbones and the folds of his clothing into fine relief. *A painter should capture him like that, all light and eagerness.*

"What are we going to do?" Alec asked again, turning to look at him.

"Since we don't have any new information, I think I'll shadow him this time," Seregil replied, sliding the pick back into Alec's tool roll and handing it to him. "Why don't you go ahead with that papers job for Lady Hylia?"

Alec grinned. "On my own?"

"You've done all the legwork. You're sure Lord Estmar will be away until tomorrow?"

"That's what his cook says. It looks like an easy job, too. Lady Hylia's instructions to the Cat said the papers she wants are hidden in the wine cellar. The door leading down to it is in the second pantry, which has a decent-sized window."

"All the same, take your time and be careful," Seregil cautioned. "The cook knows your face. You can't afford to get caught."

"I know, I know," Alec muttered happily, only half listening as he checked his tools and tucked the roll away in his coat. "I expect I'll be done by midnight, in case you need me later on."

"I'll look for you here if I do."

Either he's following some plan, or he's the most dismally predictable spy in Rhíminee, Seregil thought, watching from a discreet distance as Rhythel went into the Heron.

A few coins to the doorkeeper, Stark, bought Seregil hourly reports on the goings-on inside. Rythel asked after Lord Seregil and expressed regret at not finding him among the company. He soon consoled himself by falling in with another young noble, the son of Lady Tytiana, Mistress of the Queen's Wardrobe. They parted company early, however, and Seregil shadowed him to the Maiden's Laugh, a moderately respectable tavern and brothel near the center of the city. Settling in with the tavern crowd downstairs, Seregil soon charmed a weary tap girl into confiding which girl Rythel had gone up with, which room was hers, and that he'd paid for the entire night.

After giving the pair time to settle in, Seregil slipped through the boisterous crowd and made his way unnoticed up the stairs to a dim third-floor corridor. Waiting until he was alone in the passage, he went to the door at the end of it and peered through the keyhole.

Inside, Rythel and his woman were attending earnestly to business. The tiny room had no window or other exit that Seregil could see.

Paid for the whole night, did you? Seregil thought, stealing back the way he'd come.

Outside, he unhobbled his mare and glanced up at the moon; just past midnight. Alec was probably back by now, waiting for word from him. Gathering the reins, he headed for the Cockerel.

Alec was home. Seregil found him pacing morosely in front of the fire. He was still wearing his cloak, and there were twigs and dead leaves tangled in his hair.

"Problem with the job?"

Alec paused, scowling. "Lord Estmar is out for the night, but his new lady friend isn't. Seems she decided to have a few hundred friends in while he's gone. The whole damn place was lit up bright as noon. I skulked around the garden for hours, thinking things might die down. I gave up when fresh musicians showed up just before midnight. Anything new with Rythel?"

"Only his choice of whores," Seregil replied. "Come on. I've had enough of trailing around after this bastard. Show me this map of his."

"All right." Alec arched an eyebrow knowingly, then went to his bed and pulled a coil of rope from beneath it. "And this time, I'm prepared."

• • •

Galloping through the darkened city under a wan, lopsided moon, Alec felt a hunter's thrill of anticipation. The seemingly fruitless days of stalking Rythel wouldn't be wasted if they could use him and his map to bring down larger game. And for once, he was the one to lead. He was rather proud of himself for finding the hollowed bedpost on his own and was looking forward to showing Seregil.

Just as they came within sight of the Sea Market, however, one of Nysander's tiny message spheres materialized suddenly in front of Seregil. Although Alec could not hear it, he knew by the way his friend reined sharply to a halt that there was about to be a change in plans.

"What did he say?" he asked when the little light had winked out.

Seregil pushed his hood back and Alec saw that he was frowning. "He wants us at the Queen's Palace immediately. He didn't say why, just that I should come right away, and bring you if you're with me."

"Damn! Look, you could go back and I'll meet you—"

"He asked for both of us."

"But what about the map? And what if Rythel *does* come back and then heads out somewhere else?"

"I know, I know—" Seregil shrugged. "But Watchers can't ignore a summons to the Palace. Besides, Rythel's out for the night and Tym's clever enough to keep an eye on things until we get back. Come on now. Back we go!"

But Rythel did return to Sailmaker Street, and not long after Seregil and Alec turned back toward the Palace.

What the bloody hell are you doing home on this fine night? Tym thought. More surprising yet was the fact that the smith was not alone. A lantern still burned over the door and by its light Tym caught a glimpse of the two men with him. They had their hoods pulled forward, but the gleam of their fine boots in the lamplight told him they were not denizens of the area. Reaching behind him, he gave a rough shake to the small ragged boy dozing against the alley wall just behind him.

"Skut, wake up, damn you!"

The child jerked up, instantly tense and alert. "Yeah, Tym?"

"You ever see any gentleman types go in there?"

"Naw, nothing like that."

Watching a house was child's work, and it hadn't taken Tym long to find a child to help him do it. Having survived to the lucky old age of nine, scrawny, gap-toothed little Skut knew all the Folk as well as he did himself and feared Tym's wrath enough to be dependable. It was Skut, in fact, who'd spotted a gaterunner called Pry the Beetle late that same afternoon while Tym was off to his supper. The Beetle had shown up soon after the smith returned from work that evening and, by Skut's estimation, stayed long enough for a decent conversation.

Learning this, Tym had gone off again to track the Beetle down and soon found him already half-drunk in one of the filthy water-front stews the runner frequented. A little silver loosened the man's tongue and Tym judged the resulting information well worth the price. It seemed a certain tenant on the top floor of the Sailmaker Street house was buying information about the sewers, information only a Scavenger or runner was privy to, so to speak. Tym allowed himself a wolfish grin; that was just the sort of infor-mation Lord Seregil might loosen his purse strings for.

Returning to Sailmaker Street, he'd settled in for another uneventful evening, but here was something else unexpected. And lucrative, no doubt.

He waited until light showed through a chink in the shutters of the smith's room, then turned to Skut again.

"I'm going up for a listen. You keep your eyes open down here and give the signal if anyone comes along that might see me," he whispered, punctuating his instructions to the boy with a light cuff over the ear. "You doze off while I'm up there and I'll strangle you with your own guts, you hear?"

"I ain't never dozed on nobody," Skut hissed back resentfully.

Unwittingly following the same route Alec had taken several days before, Tym clambered up the rickety wooden stairs at the back of the house and crept over the slates to the edge of the roof just over Rythel's window. Stretched out on his belly, he peered carefully over for an upside-down view of the window below. A crack at the top of the left shutter showed only a thin slice of the room, but he could just make out scraps of the conversation going on inside.

"Three more days." That was the smith; Tym had heard him speak in the street.

"Well done," said another man. "You'll be well rewarded."

"I have another letter, as well."

"Are you certain no one—" a third man broke in, and this voice carried a strong Plenimaran accent.

Tym heard movement inside and the voices dropped too low for him to make out. Cursing silently, he kept still, hoping they'd move closer to the window.

He was just wondering if he should chance opening the shutter a bit more for a peek when some inner alarm sent an uncomfortable prickle down his spine. Gripping the lead gutter with one hand, his knife in the other, he twisted sharply around, scanning back up the steep pitch of the roof.

There, just to the left of a chimney pot, the black outline of a head was visible above the roof peak.

More of the figure rose up, moving with uncanny silence.

There's something wrong about him, was Tym's first thought.

The other stood in full view now, a long black stain against the starry sky. He looked unusually tall, and he didn't move right, either. There was none of the ungainliness of a cripple—and what in hell would a cripple be doing up here?—but a queer set to the shoulders of the silhouette, the crooked thrust of the torso over the legs—

The other suddenly jerked his head in Tym's direction. The thief could still make out no more than the stranger's outline, but he knew instinctively that he'd been spotted.

The figure stooped, bent down as if making Tym a ridiculously low bow. But that was not the end of it, and Tym's mouth suddenly went dry.

The other somehow curled himself downward, arms still at his sides, until his hooded head touched the roof slates below his feet. Down he went, and down, sinuous as an eel—chest, belly, legs, all bent at angles chillingly wrong. And like some huge and loathsome eel, the long black shape began slithering down toward him.

A coldness that had nothing to do with the weather reached Tym, driving a numbing ache into his bones that left his hands as stiff and useless as an old man's. Still, it wasn't until the stench hit him that he began to suspect the sort of nightmare that was bearing down on him.

For the first time in his hard, rough life, Tym screamed, but the ignominious sound came out of his throat as a faint, futile squeak.

The thing came to a halt scant inches away from where he crouched and coiled upright again.

Instinct overrode terror. Still clutching his knife, though he could scarcely feel it in his fist, Tym lunged up and slashed at the apparition and felt his hand pass through a vacant coldness where the thing's chest should have been. The attack overbalanced him on the slick slates and he crouched again, wobbling for balance.

The black thing hovered motionless for a moment, radiating its icy stench. Then it laughed, a thick, bubbling laugh that made Tym think of rotting, bloated corpses floating in foul water.

The hideous thing raised long, wrong-jointed arms and he braced for a blow.

But it didn't strike at him.

It pushed.

Standing faithful watch in the shadow of the alley, Skut saw a dark form topple from the roof. Plummeting down, headfirst, the falling man struck the cobbled pavement of the yard with a dull thud.

Skut froze, waiting for an outcry. When none came, he crept out to the body, squinting down at it in the waning moonlight.

Tym was unmistakably dead. His head had been smashed into a terrible lopsided shape. His chest was caved in like a broken basket.

Skut stared down in shocked disbelief for an instant, then burst into tears of frustration. The bastard hadn't paid him yet!

Tym carried no purse, no valuables. Even his long knife was missing from its sheath.

Wiping his nose on his arm, Skut gave the body a final, furious kick and disappeared into the night.

21
BLOOD TELLS

Vargûl Ashnazai moved restlessly around Rythel's tiny room while the smith was making his report to Mardus. So far the man's spying attempts had turned up little of any significance, for all his self-important airs. But his sabotage of the sewer channels had been brilliantly carried off and, more importantly still, his compilation of the map of sewer channels beneath the western ward of the city. Mardus had it before him now, making a final painstaking check before paying the smith for its delivery.

Ashnazai's job was to maintain a cloaking glamour about the two of them; through Rythel's eyes, they were fair, heavyset men with Mycenian accents. He also had a *dra'-gorgos* on watch, ranging the courtyard out-side—not an especially taxing task for a necromancer of his degree, but a necessary one, as it turned out. Soon after their arrival, he suddenly felt a silent call from the *dra'gorgos*. Closing his eyes, he sent a sighting through his dark creation and discovered the intruder on the roof overhead, a rough-looking young fellow with a knife.

Vermin, he thought. *A common thief.* With a barely perceptible smile, he mouthed a silent command. A moment later he felt the stalker lunge and heard a satisfying thud from the yard below. Mardus glanced up from the document the smith was showing him.

"It's nothing," Ashnazai assured him, going to the window and pushing back one of the warped shutters. As he looked down at the body sprawled below, a small figure darted over to it from the deep shadows across the street. Ashnazai sent a quick stab into this one's mind: a child thief, too grief-stricken at the loss of his compatriot to notice the ripple of blackness flowing down the side of the building toward him.

The *dra'gorgos* gave a hungry, questioning call. Ashnazai was about to release it for another kill when his hand brushed something on the windowsill, something that sent an unpleasantly familiar tingle through his skin. Incredulous, he forgot the child completely as he bent to scrutinize the sill.

There, so faint no one but a necromancer would ever have noticed, was a thin smear of blood. And not just any blood! Pulling out the ivory vial, he compared the emanations of its contents to these.

One of them. *Yes, the boy! Known here as Alec of Ivywell, minion of the Aurënfaie spy, Lord Seregil.*

That much they'd learned since their arrival in Rhíminee. Urvay had tracked the troublesome thieves as far as a villa in Wheel Street, where they acted the fine gentlemen as they consorted with nobles and royalty.

Ashnazai had seen them several times since then, could easily have had them at any point, but the two were still under Orëska protection; any move against them would alert the real enemies in the Orëska House. So he had stayed his hand and soon after the Aurënfaie and his accomplice had dropped maddeningly from sight yet again.

Vargûl Ashnazai clenched a hand around the vial for a moment, using its power to detect other traces of Alec's blood around the room: droplets on the shutter, a smudge on the table by Mardus' elbow, a tiny brownish circle dried on the floor near the hollow bedpost that Rythel thought such a clever hiding place, and none of it more than a day or two old.

Standing there, surrounded by the essence of the hated boy, Ashnazai experienced a brief twinge of the fear a hunter feels realizing that the prey he's been stalking has circled to stalk him. In the midst of his silent fury, he was startled to hear Rythel speak the Aurënfaie's name.

Seated at ease across the table from the smith, Mardus was regarding his spy with polite attention.

"Lord Seregil, you say?" Mardus inclined his head slightly as if greatly interested, but Ashnazi saw through the pose; at such moments Mardus reminded him of a huge serpent, chill and remorseless as it advanced unblinking upon its prey.

"A lucky meeting, my lord," the smith told him proudly. "I happened across him in a gambling house one night last week. He has quite an interest in the privateering fleet and likes to brag about it. A puffed-up dandy, full of himself. You know the sort."

Mardus smiled coldly. "Indeed I do. You must tell me everything."

Ashnazai bided his time impatiently as the smith described how he'd courted the supposed cully, and the information he'd had from him. He made no mention of the boy.

Standing behind the smith, Ashnazai caught Mardus' attention, pointed to the window, and held up the vial with a meaningful look. The other gave a slight nod, betraying no reaction.

"You've surpassed all expectations," Mardus told Rythel, passing him a heavy purse in return for the sewer map, together with a packet of the sabotaged grate pins. "You've done an excellent job with the map, and I believe I can arrange an additional reward once you've completed your work in the tunnels."

"Another week and it'll be done," the smith assured him, eyes alight with greedy anticipation. "If there's anything else I can do for you, you just say the word."

"Oh, I shall, I assure you," Mardus replied with a smile.

Unseen and unheard under the cover of Ashnazai's magic, he and the necromancer made their way down through the crowded rooms and stairways of the tenement to the yard.

The thief's body lay where it had fallen, twisted like a child's discarded doll.

Mardus turned the corpse's head with the toe of one boot. "The face is damaged, but it clearly isn't one of them."

"No, my lord, just a common footpad who blundered into the *dra'gorgos* by chance. But the boy has certainly been here within the past day or two. His blood is all over the room. He must have been wounded."

"But not by Rythel, I think. There was nothing in his demeanor to suggest he was hiding anything of the sort."

The necromancer closed his eyes for a moment, his pinched face narrowing still more as he concentrated. "There's blood on the eaves above the window. He must have cut himself breaking in."

Mardus looked down at the dead man again. "Two thieves in as many days? Rather a lot, don't you think, even for this part of the city." He watched with satisfaction as a fish hook of anxiety tugged in the necromancer's cheek. "A pity we weren't here the night our young friend made his visit," he continued. "Then it could have been him lying here dead and unable to be questioned, instead of this useless piece of meat. Get rid of it before it attracts any attention."

Vargûl Ashnazai muttered a summons through clenched teeth and the darkness beside them convulsed. A second *dra'gorgos* materialized, a wavering, faceless presence that hung like smoke for an instant before streaming down into the dead man's mouth and nose. The body gave a convulsive jerk, then lumbered clumsily to its feet. There was no semblance of life in the face; the dead glazed eyes remained fixed, the one on the ruined side of the head bulging grotesquely from its smashed socket.

Mardus regarded the thing with detached interest. "How long can you maintain it in this state?"

"Until it decomposes, my lord, but I fear it would be of little use. So much of the magic is consumed simply to animate it that it lacks the *dra'gorgos'* strength. That, of course, will not be the case once our purpose has been accomplished."

"Indeed not." Mardus touched a gloved hand briefly to the corpse's chest, feeling the black emptiness of death within—such power in that void, and so nearly in his grasp.

The necromancer spoke another command and the corpse loped away in the direction of the nearby harbor.

Still cloaked by the necromaner's spell, they rode up to the main city. The few folk they passed in the streets at that hour were aware of little more than a momentary chill, a fleeting bit of movement caught from the corner of the eye.

"It's of little consequence really, even if they do discover Rythel's work in the sewers," Ashnazai ventured nervously as they rode down Sheaf Street toward their lodgings near the Harvest Market. "The map is the important thing, and we have that.

Still, it's unsettling, having the two of them both nosing around Rythel."

"On the contrary, I see the hand of Seriamaius at work in it," said Mardus. "It seems our journey has been a long spiral path, one narrowing quickly now to tighten around our quarry. You may have been correct after all about these thieves being of some importance, Vargûl Ashnazai. They wouldn't be crossing our trail so often unless there is some greater purpose in it. We have only to bide our time until the others arrive. Meanwhile, I think it's time to deal with Master Rythel. Arrange something unremarkable, would you?"

Nearing the market, Mardus reined in. "I'm to meet with our new friend, Ylinestra. I shouldn't be long."

"Very good, my lord. I'll check on Tildus and the others at the inn."

Parting ways with the necromancer, Mardus turned his mount down a side lane. Halfway down it, he glanced at the fine pair of brass cockerels decorating the entrance to an inn of the same name. He'd passed through Blue Fish Street several times since arriving in Rhíminee and the figures, each holding a lantern suspended from an upraised claw, often caught his eye.

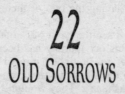

22

Old Sorrows

A Watcher password got them by the guards at the same postern gate Alec had used as a refuge a few months before. Riding through the palace grounds, they dismounted at a tradesman's door near the Ring wall of the Palace.

"I feared you would not come," Nysander said, hurrying them inside. As he reached to close the door behind them, Alec noticed the hem of a finely embroidered robe beneath the wizard's plain mantle.

"You caught us in the middle of a job," Seregil told him.

"I suspected as much, but I had no choice. Come, there is little time."

Nysander inscribed a faint sigil in the air over their heads, then led the way silently down a servant's passage. They hadn't gone far when a serving woman came around a corner ahead of them carrying an armload of linen. She looked directly at Alec as she passed, but gave no sign that she'd seen him.

Magic? Alec signed.

Seregil motioned him onward with an impatient nod.

I hope I don't have to find my own way out of here, Alec thought as Nysander hurried them up stairways and through more corridors and increasingly lavish public rooms. Climbing a final, curving stairway, they reached a closed door. Nysander took a key from his sleeve and let them into a long, dimly lit gallery.

An ornate balustrade screened by panels of wooden fretwork ran the length of the right side of the room. Light streamed up through the openings, casting netted patterns on the ceiling overhead.

Nysander raised a finger to his lips, then drew them to one of the panels. Putting his face close to the fretwork, Alec found himself looking down into a brightly lit audience chamber.

He'd seen Queen Idrilain only once before, but he recognized her at once among the small knot of people gathered around a wine table at the center of the room. Phoria sat at her left with several other people in Skalan court dress. To Idrilain's right sat a man and two women dressed in a fashion he'd never seen before.

All three wore tunics of soft white wool accented only by the polished jewels glowing on their belts, torques, and broad silver wristbands. Two of them, the man and the younger woman, wore their long dark hair loose over their shoulders beneath elaborately wrapped head cloths. The older woman's hair was silvery white, and on her brow was a silver circlet set with a single large ruby in a fan of blade-shaped gold leaves.

Intrigued, Alec turned to Seregil but found his friend pressed rigidly to the screen, his face a mask of anguish washed with stippled light.

What's he seeing? Alec wondered in alarm, looking down at the strangers again. Just then, however, the younger woman turned her head his way and Alec felt his breath catch in his throat as he recognized the fine features, dark shining hair, and large, light eyes—

Aurënfaie.

Still staring down, he reached for his friend's shoulder, felt the slight trembling there before Seregil shrugged him away.

The conference below continued for some time. At last the Queen rose and led the others out of the chamber. Seregil remained where he was for a moment, forehead resting against the screen as a single tear inched down his cheek. Wiping it quickly away, he turned to face Nysander, who'd stood silently behind them all the while.

"Why are they here?" Seregil asked, his voice husky with emotion.

"The Plenimaran Overlord died today," the wizard replied. "The Aurënfaie had the news before we did and translocated a delegation here tonight. There is still no official alliance between Plenimar and Zengat, but both Aurënfaie intelligence and our own suggests that secret agreements have in fact been made."

"What's that got to do with us?" Seregil's face was stony now, the naked sorrow too thoroughly erased.

"Nothing, as yet," said Nysander. "I summoned you here because the Iia'sidra has granted permission for you to speak with her briefly. There is a small antechamber just through that door behind you."

Still rigidly expressionless, Seregil stalked away into the next room.

As soon as he was gone, Alec let out a pent-up gasp. "Illior's Hands, Nysander—Aurënfaie!"

"I thought you should see them, too," Nysander said with a rather sad smile.

"Who's he meeting?"

"That is for Seregil to tell you. And with any luck, before you wear a trench in this excellent carpet."

Seregil paced the small, well-appointed sitting room, one eye on the side door. And as he paced, he fought to maintain some semblance of inner calm. There was a looking glass on the wall and he paused in front of it, ruefully inspecting his reflection. His hair was tangled and windblown, and a week of puzzling over Rythel had left dark circles under his eyes. The old surcoat he'd thrown on that evening was frayed at the cuffs and one shoulder was torn.

Don't I look the ragged outcast? he thought, giving the glass a humorless smile as he combed his fingers through his hair.

Behind him the side door opened and for a moment another face was reflected next to his, the two images so similar, yet worlds apart. When had his eyes grown so wary, the lines around his mouth so harsh?

"Seregil, my brother." Her pure, unaccented Aurënfaie washed through him like cool water.

"Adzriel," he whispered, embracing her. The scent of wandril blossoms rose from her hair and skin, blinding him with memories. She had been both sister and mother and suddenly he remembered what it had been to be a child, smelling her special scent as she comforted him or carried him home from some moonlit festival. Now she felt small in his arms and for a long moment he could do nothing but cling to her, his throat tightening painfully as he blinked back four decades of unshed tears.

Adzriel stepped back at last, still holding him by the shoulders as if afraid he'd disappear if she didn't.

"All these years I've carried the image of that unhappy boy looking down at me from the deck that awful day," she gasped, her own tears flowing freely. "O Aura, I missed seeing you grow into a man! Now look at you; wild as any Tírfaie and wearing a weapon in the presence of your kin."

Seregil quickly unbuckled his sword belt and hung it over a nearby chair. "I meant no offense. It's like another limb to me here. Come, sit down and I'll try to remember how civilized people act."

Adzriel stroked a hand through his unkempt hair. "And when were you ever civilized?"

Sitting down next to him on a divan, she drew a small bundle of scrolls from her tunic. "I have letters for you from our sisters and your old friends. They haven't forgotten you."

More memories held at bay pressed in, and with them a pang of long suppressed hope. Swallowing hard, he examined the heavy silver bracelet of rank on her wrist. "So you're a member of the Iia'sidra now. And an envoy, too. Not bad for someone who hasn't seen her hundred and a half birthday yet."

Adzriel shrugged, though she looked pleased. "Our family's tie to Skala may be useful in the coming years. Idrilain welcomed me as a kinswoman when we arrived, and spoke highly of you. From what little your friend Nysander í Azusthra had time to tell me, I gather you've been of some service to her?"

Seregil studied her face, wondering how much Nysander had said about their work. Little enough, evidently.

"Now and then," he told her. "What did your companions make of that, I wonder, Seregil the Traitor praised by the Skalan Queen? I remember old Máhalie ä Solunesthra, but who's the other?"

"Ruen í Uri, of Datsia Clan. And you needn't worry about either of them; they're both moderates, and good friends of mine."

"And you're here because of Plenimar?"

"Yes. All recent reports indicate an alliance being attempted with Zengat and there can only be one reason for that."

"To keep Aurënen too busy defending her western borders to ally with Skala. But if the Plenimarans had just left things alone, wouldn't the Edict of Separation have done their work for them?"

"There's been considerable progress against the Edict since you left. The recent discovery of our kinsman Corruth's body—well, you can imagine the effect that has had in the Iia'sidra."

Seregil watched her again; no, she didn't know the part he'd played in that, and his oath as a Watcher prevented him from telling her.

"Total uproar, I hope," he said with a smirk. "All those years of accusing every Skalan in sight of foul play. Old Rhazien's faction must be choking on their own isolationist rhetoric."

Adzriel chuckled. "Nothing so dramatic, but it has tipped the scales a bit for those of us who want to renew the old alliances. With Petasárian gone and his successor, young Estmar, already rumored to be the puppet of his own generals and necromancers, I don't think we can afford to stand alone any longer."

"Adzriel?" He hesitated, knowing what he must ask next, but dreading the answer. "Does this have anything to do with why you've been allowed to see me?"

"The lifting of your banishment, you mean?" Adzriel smoothed a thumb over one of the jewels in her bracelet. "Not officially. The time isn't right. Not yet."

Seregil jumped to his feet, clenching one hand against his side where his sword usually hung. "Bilairy's Guts, I was a *child*! Willful, misguided, guilty as hell, but still a child. If only you knew what I've done since then."

We found their precious Lord Corruth, Alec and I! The words burned his throat. "I know the Skalans, their culture and politics, their language, better than any envoy."

"Yes, but whose interests would you be representing?"

Adzriel's level gaze stopped him in his tracks. "So I'm to sit idle here while the Zengati boil out of the hills and descend on Bôkthersa once again?"

Adzriel sighed. "I hardly think you'll be idle, not when the might of Plenimar is pounding against your shores and their armies roll across Mycena to batter at your northern borders. And mark my words, it will come to that before it's over. I understand your pain, my love, but you've spent more than half your life here." She paused. "I sometimes wonder if things haven't worked out for the best, somehow."

"My being exiled, you mean?" Seregil stared at her. "How can you say that?"

"I'm not saying I'm glad you were taken from us, but in spite of all the loneliness and pain you must have known, I wonder if life among the Tírfaie doesn't suit you better? Truly now, could you ever be content to sit under the lime trees at home, telling tales to the children, or debating with the elders of the Bôkthersa Council whether the lintel of the temple should be painted white or silver? Think back, Seregil. You were always restless, always demanding to find out what lay over the next hill. Perhaps there's some purpose in it."

Rising, she took his hands in hers. "I know you've paid for your mistakes. Believe me, I want your exile lifted, but you must be patient. Changes are coming for Aurënen, great ones. Make your stand here for now, in this dangerous, wonderful land of yours. What say you, my brother?"

Still frowning, Seregil muttered, "Silver."

"What?" asked Adzriel.

"Silver," Seregil repeated, looking up with the crooked grin that had always won her over. "Tell the elders of the Council I said the lintel should be silver."

Adzriel laughed, a wonderful, radiant sound. "By Aura, Father was right! I should have beaten you more. Now where is this Alec í Amasa Nysander told me of? He interests me greatly."

"You know about Alec?" Seregil said, surprised.

"More than he does himself, it would seem," Adzriel chided.

Seregil gave her a chagrined look. It seemed Nysander had packed a great deal into a short conversation.

If Nysander hadn't been with him in the gallery, Alec would have been hard-pressed not to eavesdrop. As it was, he could hear a steady murmur of voices from beyond the door where Seregil had gone.

After what felt like an interminable length of time, the door opened and Seregil came back into the gallery, accompanied by the young Aurënfaie woman. His air of anguish was gone, erased by an almost sheepish grin.

Alec knew before his friend spoke who she must be. Her lips were fuller and had none of the hard set of Seregil's, but the beautiful grey eyes were the same, with the same expression of appraising intelligence.

"This is my eldest sister, Adzriel ä Illia Myril Seri Bôkthersa," said Seregil. "Adzriel, this is Alec."

What little Aurënfaie Alec knew deserted him. "My lady," he stammered, making a passable bow.

The woman smiled, holding out her hands for his. "My people seldom use such titles," she said in heavily accented Skalan. "You must call me Adzriel, as my brother does."

"Adzriel," Alec amended, savoring the sound of it, and the feel of her cool hands in his. Rubies and moonstones glowed in the rings she wore on nearly every finger.

"Nysander tells me you are my brother's valued companion, a person of great honor," she said, gazing earnestly into his face.

Alec felt his cheeks go warm. "I hope so. He's been a good friend to me."

"I am glad to hear such things said of him." Bowing gracefully to him and the wizard, she stepped back toward the door. "I hope one day soon I may greet you all in my own land. Until then, *Aura Elustri málron.*"

"So soon?" Seregil asked, his voice hoarse with emotion.

Alec looked away in embarrassment as the two embraced, speaking softly to each other in their own language.

"Aura Elustri málron, Adzriel tali," Seregil said, releasing her reluctantly. *"Phroni soutúa neh noliea."*

Adzriel nodded, wiping her eyes. Nysander went to her side and offered his arm. *"Aura Elustri málron,* dear lady. I shall accompany you back to the others."

"Thank you again, Nysander í Azusthra, for all your assistance in this matter." As she turned to go, however, she spoke once more to her brother in their own language, glancing at Alec as she did so.

"Quite right," Nysander said. "It is the boy's right to know; he should hear it from you."

With that, he escorted Adzriel back the way she'd come.

Turning to Seregil, Alec found his friend looking pale and uncomfortable again. "What did they mean?"

Seregil pushed a hand back through his hair and sighed. "I'll explain everything, but not here."

23
Revelations

The unexpected reunion with his sister had shaken Seregil to the core of his soul. A fierce sorrow seemed to emanate from him as they left the Palace, and the weight of it left Alec feeling mute and helpless. What could he say, what could he offer in the face of this? And what was it Nysander had meant, that Seregil had something to tell *him*?

He trailed anxiously in his friend's wake, the sound of their horses' hooves echoing from the ornate walls of villa gardens as the misshapen moon sank slowly toward the western rooftops. Alec couldn't forget the sight of that single tear rolling slowly down Seregil's face. He'd never imagined him capable of weeping.

Seregil paused long enough to steal two flasks of sweet red wine from a vintner's shop, then rode on until they reached the wooded park behind the Street of Lights. Dismounting, they led their horses along a path to an open glade beyond.

A small fountain stood at the center of the little clearing, its stone basin filled now with rain and dead leaves. Sitting down on the rim of it, Seregil handed Alec a flask, then uncorked his own and took a drink.

"Go on," he told Alec with a sigh. "You'll need it."

Alec found his hands were shaking. He took a long swig of the sweet, heavy wine, felt the heat curl down into his belly. "Just tell me, will you? Whatever it is."

Seregil was quiet for a moment, his face lost in shadow, then he gestured up at the moon. "When I was a child, I used to sneak out at night just to walk in the moonlight. My favorite times were in the summer, when people would come from all over Aurënen to the foot of Mount Barok. For days they'd gather, waiting for the full moon. When it rose over the peak, we'd sing, thousands of voices raised together, singing to the dragons. And they'd fly for us across the face of the moon, around the peak, singing their answering songs and breathing their red fire.

"I've tried to sing that song once or twice since I've been here, but do you know, it just won't come? Without all those other voices, I can't sing the Song of Dragons at all. As things stand now, I may never sing it again."

Alec could almost see the scene Seregil had described, a thousand handsome, grey-eyed folk in white tunics and shining jewels, massed beneath the round moon, voices raised as one. Standing here in this winter-ruined garden, he felt the crushing weight of distance that separated Seregil from that communion.

"You hoped your sister was going to say you could go home, didn't you?"

Seregil shook his head. "Not really. And she didn't."

Alec sat down beside him on the rim of the fountain. "Why were you sent away?"

"Sent away? I was outlawed, Alec. Outlawed for treason and a murder I helped commit when I was younger than you."

"You?" Alec gasped. "I—I can't believe it. What happened?"

Seregil shrugged. "I was stupid. Blinded by my first passion, I allowed what I thought was love to cut me off from Adzriel and all the others who tried to save me. I didn't know how my lover was using me, or what his intent really was, but a man died all the same, and the fault was rightly mine. The details don't really matter—I've never told anyone else this much, Alec, and I'm not going to say more now. Maybe someday— At any rate, two of us were exiled. Everyone else was executed, except my lover. He escaped."

"Another Aurënfaie came to Skala with you?"

"Zhahir í Aringil didn't make it. He threw himself overboard

with a ballast stone tied around his neck as soon as we lost sight of
the coastline. I very nearly did the same, then and many times later
on. Most exiles end up suicides sooner or later. But not me. Not
yet, anyway."

The few inches between them felt like cold miles. Clasping his
flask, Alec asked, "Why are you telling me this now? Does it have
something to do with what Nysander meant?"

"In a way. It's something I don't want secret between us anymore, not after tonight." He took another drink and rubbed his
eyelids. "Nysander's been after me since he met you to tell you
that—" Seregil turned to him and put a hand on his shoulder.
"Alec, you're 'faie."

There was a gravid pause.

Alec heard the words, but for an instant he couldn't seem to
take them in and make sense of them. He'd rehearsed a dozen dark
possibilities during their walk from the Palace, but this had not
been one of them. He felt the flask slip from his fingers, felt it
bounce on the damp, dead grass between his feet. "That can't be!"
he gasped, his voice unsteady. "My father, he wasn't—"

But suddenly it all fell into place—Seregil's questions about
his parents, veiled remarks Nysander had made, all the rumors that
he and Seregil were somehow related. The impact of this sudden
revelation made him sway where he sat. Seregil's grip on his
shoulder tightened, but he could scarcely feel it.

"My mother."

"The Hâzadriëlfaie," Seregil said gently, "from beyond
Ravensfell Pass near where you were born."

"But how can you know that?" Alec whispered. It felt like the
entire earth was spinning out from beneath his feet, leaving him
stranded in a place he couldn't comprehend. At the same time, it
all made terrible sense: his father's silence regarding his mother,
his distrust of strangers, his coldness. "Could she still be there?"

"Do you recall how I told you the Hâzadriëlfaie left Aurënen a
long, long time ago? That their ways are different than ours? They
don't tolerate any outsiders, especially humans, and they kill any
half-breeds that are born, along with the parents. Somehow your
mother must have broken away long enough to meet your father
and have you, but her own people must have hunted her down in
the end. Even if she'd gone back of her own accord, the penalty
would still have been death. It's a miracle your father and you
escaped. He must have been a remarkable man."

"I never thought so." Alec's pulse was pounding in his ears. This was too much, too much. "I don't understand. How can you know any of this?"

"I don't, for certain, but it fits the facts we do know. Alec, there's no getting around the fact that you *are* 'faie. I saw the signs that first morning in the mountains, but I didn't want to believe it then."

"Why not?"

Seregil hesitated, then shook his head. "I was afraid I was wrong, just seeing what I wanted to see. But I wasn't wrong— your features, your build, the way you move. Micum saw it right away, and the centaurs and Nysander and the others at the Orëska. Then, that first night we came back to the Cockerel, I went out again, remember? I went to the Oracle of Illior about another matter and during the divinations, he spoke of you, called you a 'child of earth and light'—Dalna and Illior, human and 'faie— there was no question what he meant. Nysander wanted me to tell you from the start but—"

At that, a wave of anger burst up through Alec's shocked numbness. Lurching to his feet, he rounded on Seregil, crying out, "Why didn't you? All these months and you never said *anything*? It's like that Wheel Street trick all over again!"

Seregil's face was half black, half bone pale in the moonlight, but both eyes glittered. "It's nothing like Wheel Street!"

"Oh, no?" Alec shouted. "Then what, damn it! Why? *Why didn't you tell me?*"

Seregil seemed to sag. Lowering his face, he rested both hands on his knees. After a moment he let out a ragged breath. "There's no single answer to that. At first, because I wasn't certain." He shook his head. "No, that's not true. In my heart I *was* certain, but I didn't dare believe it."

"Why not?"

"Because if I was wrong—" Seregil spread his hands helplessly. "It doesn't matter. I'd been alone for a long time and I thought I liked it that way. I knew if I was right, and if I told you then, *if* you'd even believed me, then it might create a bond, a tie. I wasn't willing to risk that either, not until I figured out who you were. Illior's Hands, Alec, you don't know, you *can't* know, what it was like—"

"Enlighten me!" Alec growled.

"All right." Seregil let out another unsteady sigh. "I'd been exiled from my own kind for more years than you've been alive. Any Aurënfaie who came to Skala knew who and what I was, and was under prohibition to shun me. Meanwhile, all my human companions age and die before my eyes."

"Except Nysander, and Magyana."

"Oh, yes." Now it was Seregil who sounded bitter. "You know all about my apprenticeship with him, don't you? Another failure, another place I didn't belong. Then, from out of nowhere, comes you, and you were—are—"

Alec looked down at the bowed figure before him and felt his anger slipping away as quickly as it had come. "I still don't understand why you didn't want to say anything."

Seregil looked up at him again. "Cowardice, I guess. I didn't want to see the look that's on your face right now."

Alec sat down next to him again and sank his face in his hands. "I don't know what I am," he groaned. "It's like everything I ever knew about myself has been taken away." He felt Seregil's arm go around his shoulders, but made no move to push him away.

"Ah, *tali*, you're what you've always been," Seregil sighed, patting his arm. "You just know it now, that's all."

"So I'll see Beka get old, and Luthas, and Illia and—"

"That's right." Seregil's arm tightened around him. "And that wouldn't be any less true if you were Tírfaie. It's not a curse."

"You always talk like it is."

"Loneliness is a curse, Alec, and being an outsider. I don't have a clue why the two of us ended up in the same dungeon cell that night, but I've thanked Illior every day since that we did. The greatest fear I've had is losing you. The second greatest is that when I finally did tell you the truth, you'd think it was the only reason I'd taken you on in the first place. That isn't so, you know. It never was, not even in the beginning."

The last of the shock and anger drained away, leaving Alec exhausted beyond measure. Reaching down, he retrieved the wine flask and drained what was left in it. "It's a lot to take in, you know? It changes so much."

For the first time in hours Seregil chuckled, a warm, healing sound in the darkness. "You should talk to Nysander, or Thero. Wizards must go through these same feelings when they learn they have magic in them."

"What does it mean, though, with me being only half?" asked

Alec as a hundred questions and comparisons flooded in. "How long will I live? How old am I, really?"

One arm still around Alec, Seregil found his own flask again and took a sip. "Well, when the 'faie blood comes from the mother it's generally stronger. I don't know why that is, but it's always the case and all those I know of lived as long as the rest of us, four centuries or so. They mature a bit faster, so you're about as old as you thought. There's also a good chance you'd inherit any magic she had, although it seems like that would have shown itself—" He trailed off suddenly, and Alec felt him shiver. "Damn it, I'm sorry I didn't say anything sooner. The longer I waited, the harder it got."

Without giving himself time to evaluate the impulse, Alec turned and put both arms around Seregil, hugging him tightly. "It's all right, *talí,*" he whispered hoarsely. "It's all right now."

Taken by surprise, Seregil hesitated a moment, then returned the embrace, heart beating strong and fast against Alec's. A weary peacefulness came over Alec at the feel of it, and with it a whisper of pleasure at their closeness. From where they sat, Alec could see the glimmer of a few lanterns shining through the bare trees from the Street of Lights beyond. Seregil's fingers were twined in his hair at the nape of his neck, he realized with a guilty start, the same way he'd touched the young man at Azarin's a few short weeks ago.

First that strange, perception-altering night, he thought wearily, and now this. Illior's Hands, if things kept up in this manner, he'd end up not knowing who he was at all!

Releasing him at last, Seregil looked up at the moon, half-hidden in the tangled treetops.

"I don't know about you, but I've had about all the excitement I can deal with for one night," he said with a hint of his crooked smile.

"What about Rythel?"

"I guess Tym can keep an eye on things one more night. We'll track him down in the morning."

As they mounted for the ride home, it was Alec's turn to chuckle.

"What's so funny?"

"It could have been worse, I guess," Alec told him. "In the old ballads, orphans turn out to be the long-lost heir to some kingdom, which means they end up either cooped up in the family castle learning royal manners, or get sent off to slay some monster for a bunch of total strangers. At least I get to keep my old job."

"I don't think anyone will get much of a ballad out of that."

Alec swung up into the saddle and grinned over at him. "That's fine by me!"

24
BEKA

"Where are we?" Zir shouted over the jingle of harness.

"We're in Mycena!" someone else called back.

Beka grinned in spite of herself. They'd worn the joke threadbare weeks ago, but every once in a while someone trotted it out again just to break the monotony.

Sergeant Mercalle's riders were in high spirits this morning. Beka had received orders to take a decuria and ride to a nearby market town to buy supplies for the troop. Mercalle had won the toss.

For weeks they'd ridden through rolling, snow-covered hills, oak forest, and empty fields; past thatch-roof steadings and small country towns where soldiers of any sort were regarded with guarded resentment. Mycena was a country of farmers and tradesmen. Wars interrupted commerce.

It had taken the regiment nearly a month to reach the port city of Keston—a month of cold camps and thrown-together billets in garrisons and courtyards, and slow-march riding over frozen roads. At night, the green new officers sat around the fire and listened to the veterans' war tales, hoping to pick up some of the things they hadn't had time to learn during their brief six weeks of training.

The more Beka listened, the more she realized that despite all their drilling and individual prowess with horse, sword, and bow, it would take a battle or two to sort out how well the turma worked together and trusted one another.

And how much they trusted her.

She'd noticed that many of her riders still looked more often to her sergeants for guidance than to her. That stung a bit, but then, they were the turma's only seasoned veterans. To their credit, they all showed the strictest respect for her rank, even Braknil, who was old enough to be her father.

In return, Beka was mindful of the fact that without Seregil's patronage and the commission it had won her, sergeant would have been the highest rank she could've hoped for in such a regiment. Some of the other squadrons' new lieutenants—the sons and daughters of Rhíminee lords—seemed to keep this in mind, too, and let her know with the occasional sneer or condescending remark. Fortunately, her brother officers in Myrhini's troop were not among these.

At Keston the regimental commander, Prince Korathan, had taken Commander Perris' Wolf Squadron and split off to follow the coastline. Commander Klia's squadron headed inland toward the Folcwine Valley. The Folcwine River was the southern leg of the great trade route that ran north all the way to the Ironheart range in the distant northlands. The river was the first prize the Plenimarans were expected to reach for.

That had been two weeks ago; it would be another two before they came to the river.

Turning in the saddle, Beka looked back at the column snaking darkly over the hills behind her: nearly four hundred horsemen and officers of Lion Squadron, the sledges of the sutlers and armorers, provision wains, livestock and drivers. It was like traveling with a small town in tow. Scouting trips, vanguard duty, even mundane provision runs like this offered a welcome break.

Catching Mercalle's eye, Beka said, "Sergeant, I think the horses could do with a run."

"You're right, Lieutenant," Mercalle answered with the hint of a smile; they both knew it was the restless young riders who needed it more.

Beka scanned the rolling terrain ahead of them and spied a dark

line of trees a mile or so off. "Pass the word, Sergeant. At my
signal, race for the trees. The first one who gets there has first
chance at the taverns."

Mercalle's riders fanned out smoothly, catcalling back and
forth to each other. At Beka's signal, they spurred their mounts
forward, galloping for the trees.

Beka's Wyvern could easily have outdistanced most of the
other horses, but she held back, letting Kaylah and Zir end the race
in a tie.

"I hear they always finish together," Marten grumbled as the
rest of the riders reined in around the winners. A few of the others
smirked at this. Sexual relations in the ranks were frowned on, and
a careless pregnancy got both parties cashiered, but it happened,
nonetheless. Still celibate herself, Beka chose to turn a blind eye to
who was sharing blankets with who. A number of her riders had
come into the regiment already paired, including Kaylah and Zir.
Others, like Mirn and Steb, had formed bonds during the march.

"Don't worry about it," Braknil had advised after she'd noticed
certain blankets moving late at night. "So long as it's honorable,
it'll just make them fight the enemy all the harder. No one wants to
look a coward to their lover."

Kaylah and Zir already seemed proof of this; during training
they'd competed fiercely against each other and everyone else.
Kaylah was a pretty blonde who looked almost too fragile for a
warrior's life, but she was like a centaur on horseback, and could
match anyone in the turma with a bow. Zir, a young, black-
bearded bear of a man, had Sakor's own sword arm mounted or
afoot.

The trees turned out to be a thick pine forest. Skirting along its
edge, they struck a well-packed road that led through in the direction of the town. Just before noon they came out on the far side
into a valley overlooking the town. It was a prosperous-looking
place, with a palisade for protection and a busy market square.

Their dark green field tunics attracted less attention than their
dress tabards might have, but the townspeople still looked askance
at their swords, bows, and chain mail.

Better us than the Plenimaran marines, Beka thought, pulling
her gorget from the neck of her tunic to show her rank.

Their Skalan gold was welcome enough, however. In less than
an hour's time they'd found all the supplies they'd been sent for—
parchment, flints, wax, honey, meal and flour, dried fruit and

beans, salt, smoked meats, ale, four fat sheep and a pig, oats and winter fodder for the horses—and hired three carters to haul the goods back to the column under escort.

Her riders had also found time to purchase items for themselves and those left behind with the rest of the turma: tobacco, playing cards, sweetmeats, fruit, and writing materials were always in demand. Some even had chickens and geese slung from their saddlebows. Mercalle shopped for the other sergeants; Portus was partial to nuts and raisins, Braknil to Mycenian cider brandy.

Mercalle glanced up at the sun as the carters secured the last of their load on their sledges and hitched up their oxen teams. "The column should have just about caught up by now. It'll make a shorter return trip for the carters."

"Everyone back?" asked Beka, counting faces.

"All accounted for, Lieutenant."

"Good. You, Tobin, and Arna take the point. The rest of us will ride escort with the sledges. We'll switch off point riders now and then, just to keep them from getting bored."

Mercalle saluted, and galloped off with the two riders. Beka and the rest fell in around the sledges.

No one seemed to mind the slower pace; it was pleasant to saunter along with the sun on their backs and a cold breeze in their faces. Leaving town by the same road they'd entered, they wended their way back up into the pines.

"Do you travel this road often?" Beka asked, striking up a conversation with the lead driver.

The man twitched the reins across his team's broad backs and nodded. "Often enough spring to autumn," he replied, his accent thick as oat porridge. "My brothers and me drive goods up to Torburn-on-the-River. Boats take it on to the coast."

"That must be a long trip at this pace."

He shrugged. "Three weeks up, three back."

"Have you heard much news here about a war coming?"

The carter spared her a sour glance. "I should think we have. Seeing as how we're like to get trampled once again when you lot and the Plenimarans go at each other. There's some say we ought to just trade land with one or t'other of ye, so's ye can fight without bothering us."

Beka bristled a bit at this. "We're on our way east to keep that from happening. Otherwise, your armies will be left on their own when Plenimar comes after your land and the river."

"They ain't took it yet. And you lot ain't never stopped 'em from wading in to try it."

Beka bit back a retort and eased her mount away from the sledge. There was no sense arguing the point. "Marten and Barius, you go take point. Tell Sergeant Mercalle I'll be up to relieve her as soon as the others get back."

"Right, Lieutenant!" Barius said, grinning through his new beard. He and Marten set off at a gallop, cloaks streaming behind them as they raced each other out of sight around a bend in the road.

The sound of their hoofbeats had just faded out of earshot when the scream of a horse raised the hair on the back of Beka's neck. Wheeling Wyvern, she saw Syrtas' mount buck him off behind the third sledge. The horse screamed again, then bolted for the trees.

Rethus reined in beside the fallen man, then slung himself from the saddle.

"Ambush!" they shouted, dashing for cover behind the sledge.

An arrow sang past Beka's horse and struck the side of the lead sledge. A glance told her that this was no military attack. The arrow was double fletched, rather than the military triple vane style, and the fletching was done clumsily, with one white vane and one a ragged brown.

"Bloody bandits!" the carter growled, pulling a short sword from under his seat and jumping over the side.

"Take cover!" Beka yelled, although the others were already doing just that. She slid off Wyvern with her bow in hand and whacked the horse on the haunches, hoping he'd get clear of the archers.

Heart pounding in her ears, Beka dove for the scant cover at the front of the sledge. Crouched there beside the carter, she tried to size up the situation.

The point riders weren't back yet; that left Zir, Kaylah, Corbin, Rethus, Mikal, and Syrtas—assuming none of them were already killed—and the three drivers.

Judging by the hail of arrows whining at them from the cover of the trees, however, her group was considerably outnumbered. Worse yet, they were being fired on from both sides of the road.

"You said nothing about bandits when we set out," she hissed to the driver.

"Ain't seen any most of the winter," he replied grudgingly.

"This crew's come north early. They must of laid for us until they saw you send off them other two."

Beka moved to the opposite side of the sledge just in time to spot three swordsmen running at them from the woods. Almost without thinking, she fitted an arrow to her bowstring and shot one of them; the other two fell to someone else's shafts.

Arrows snarled and hissed over her head as Beka dashed back to the next sledge, where she found Mikal, Zir, and Kaylah shooting wildly into the trees to either side.

"Stop shooting!" Beka ordered. "We can't afford to waste the arrows."

"What *do* we do?" Mikal demanded.

"Wait for a clear shot. And grab any spent arrow you can reach without getting hit."

Ducking low, she made it to the last sledge. Rethus and Corbin were unscathed. Their carter lay panting beneath the sledge, an arrow shaft protruding from his hip.

That first enemy arrow had cut Syrtas just above the knee before striking his horse. The wound was bleeding freely, but it didn't seem to be slowing him down much as he and the others shot into the trees.

Beka repeated the order, and then nocked another arrow on her bowstring, waiting for one of their attackers to show himself.

The bandits mistook their actions as a sign of surrender; in a moment the arrow storm stopped and swordsmen burst from the trees, yelling wildly as they charged the sledges on foot.

"Now hit them, both sides!" Beka shouted, scrambling to her feet. Heedless of any archers who might still be lurking in the trees, she sent shaft after shaft at the swordsmen running at her, downing three of them. For the first time since the skirmish began, it occurred to her that she was taking human lives, but the thought carried no emotion. The thrum of bowstrings and the cries and shouts of battle filled her mind, leaving room for nothing else. Beside her, Rethus fired with the same silent determination.

An arrow nicked the shoulder of her tunic and pinned her cloak to the side of the sledge behind her. Yanking the brooch pin loose, she dropped to one knee and continued to shoot.

A dozen or more bandits fell to their arrows, but an equal number were closing in around them.

"Swords!" Beka shouted. Drawing her blade, she strode out to meet a bearded man in scarred leather brigandine and ragged leggings. Ducking his wild swing with a broadsword, she whirled and struck at the back of his neck. She'd practiced the move a thousand times against her father and others; this time she drew blood.

There were plenty more with him, though, and she drew a long dagger in her left hand, using it to fend off thrusts to her open side.

Syrtas was to her right, Kaylah to the left. Covering each other as best they could, they waded into the knot of bandits.

The attackers outnumbered her side at least three to one, but Beka quickly realized that most of them relied more on brawn than skill. With almost disappointing ease, she ducked another swing and ran a man through, then pulled her blade free in time to strike another on the arm as he attacked Kaylah. The girl flashed her a grin, then lunged at a tall, scrawny youth who turned tail and fled.

Looking around, Beka realized that there were mounted fighters at work, too. Mercalle and the others had come back at some point and were charging into the fray, their helmets flashing in the sunlight as they scattered ambushers and struck down the stragglers with their swords.

The bandits were already beginning to fall back when more riders of the Horse Guard thundered down the road from the direction of the column. Tobin was at their head, with Portus and Braknil beside him.

The enemy broke for cover and the horsemen followed, driving them into the trees and dismounting to give chase.

"Come on!" cried Beka, rallying her blood-streaked comrades. "Let's not let them steal all the fun!"

When the rout was over, more than twenty ambushers lay dead in the snow. Beka's riders had sustained nothing worse than a few sword cuts and arrow wounds.

"By the Flame, that was a fair-sized gang," Mercalle exclaimed.

The lead carter crawled from under his sledge. "Looks like old Garon's crew. They been harrying the traders up and down the valley for nigh onto three years now. The sheriffs couldn't never catch 'em."

"They chose the wrong prey this time," Sergeant Braknil remarked, grinning as he strode over to join them. "Looks to me like you had things pretty well in hand by the time we got here, Lieutenant."

"I wasn't so sure," Beka said, noticing for the first time how shaky her legs felt. "What are you doing here, anyway? Not that I'm not glad to see you."

"When Barius and Marten showed up, I sent Tobin and Arna back," Mercalle explained. "But all of a sudden they came belting back with word that you were under attack. They didn't know how big the force was or who, so I sent Arna back to the column for help and came on with the others. As it turns out, Braknil had talked the captain into letting the rest of the turma come meet you. He and Portus were less than a mile away when Arna met them."

The rest of the turma had drifted over to listen. "Any losses?" she asked.

"Not a one, Lieutenant!" Corporal Nikides reported proudly. "Not bad for our first battle, eh?"

"I don't know that I'd claim routing bandits as a battle, but we acquitted ourselves well enough," Beka said, grinning around at the others. "You did well, all of you."

Braknil exchanged a look with Mercalle and cleared his throat. "With all due respect, Lieutenant, there's a custom some of the riders should observe. For their first kill, that is."

"Drinking the blood of the first man you kill to keep off the ghosts, you mean?"

"That's the one, Lieutenant. Some call it superstition nowadays, but I say the old ways are sound."

"I agree," said Beka. She'd heard of the custom from her father, and from Alec, who'd done the same after his first fight. "How many of you made your first kill today?"

Everyone in Mercalle's decuria stepped forward, and several more from the others. "All right, then. All of you archers, find your first killing shaft. Come back here when you find it. The rest of you bring your swords."

Beka walked to the body of the first swordsman she'd killed, a middle-aged brigand with a braided beard. He lay on his back, a look of mild surprise on his unremarkable face. She stared down at him a moment, making herself remember the murder in his eyes as he charged at her. She was glad to be alive, but not to have killed him. It was an odd mix of feelings. Shaking her head, she pulled the arrow from his chest and joined the others standing in a rough half circle beside the road. When everyone else had come back, she looked around and felt the weight of the moment settle upon her.

"Sergeants, I'm as new to this as the rest of them. Are there any special words to be spoken?"

"Whatever you want to say," Braknil replied with a shrug.

Beka raised the arrow in front of her. "May we all fight together with honor, mercy, and strength."

With that, she touched the arrowhead to her tongue and the coppery tang of the blood flooded her mouth. She wanted to grimace and spit, but she kept her face calm as she cleaned the arrowhead in the snow and dropped it back into her quiver.

"Honor, mercy, and strength!" echoed the others, doing the same with arrows and sword blades.

"I guess that's it. Now we've got supplies to deliver," she told them. "Anyone seen my horse?"

That evening Captain Myrhini's troop feasted on the first fresh meat they'd had in weeks and drank the health of Beka and her turma several times over.

When they'd finished and were settling in their tents for another cold night, Captain Myrhini drew Beka aside.

"I've been talking with some of Mercalle's riders," she said as they walked together past the campfires of the various turmae. "Sounds to me like you kept your head and took care of your people."

Beka shrugged. She'd been doing some thinking of her own. "It's a good thing. I made a mistake sending out two riders when three were already up on point. I don't think it was any accident that those ambushers jumped us when they did."

"Oh?" Myrhini raised an eyebrow. "What could you have done differently?"

"I was going to relieve Mercalle anyway. I should've ridden up alone and sent the other two back for their replacements."

"But that would have left your riders without an officer or sergeant."

"Well, yes—"

"And the way I hear it, it was you who kept those green fighters from wasting all their arrows on the bushes, which the raiders were probably counting on. The fact is, it was me who made a mistake today."

Beka looked at her in surprise, but Myrhini motioned for her not to interrupt. "I assumed that because we were in neutral territory, it was safe to send a decuria out on its own. If you'd had the turma with you, those brigands would never have attacked. Of course, you were far too tactful and inexperienced to bring this to my attention when I gave you that order, weren't you?"

Beka couldn't quite read the officer's cryptic smile. "No, Captain, it just never occurred to me that we'd need any more people than that for a supply run."

"Then we were both in error," Myrhini said. "But learn and live, as a certain friend of ours always says. You did well, Lieutenant. Sergeant Mercalle thinks you've got the makings of a good fighter, by the way."

"Oh?" Beka asked, caught between pleasure at the veteran's appraisal and a certain pique that the sergeant had evidently not had the same confidence in her abilities before now. "What made her say that?"

"I think it was the way you were grinning as you fought," Myrhini answered. "At least, that's what she hears from those fighting beside you. Tell me, were you scared?"

Beka thought about that a moment. "Not really. Not during the fight, anyway."

"Sakor touched!" the captain exclaimed, shaking her head. But Beka thought she sounded pleased.

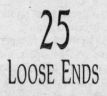

25
LOOSE ENDS

Clutching the stolen loaf beneath his shirt, Skut sprinted through the late afternoon crowd filling the marketplace. Behind him he could hear the furious bread seller shouting, "Stop him, stop thief!" A few people made halfhearted grabs at him, but the sympathy of the waterfront crowd was obviously with him. Reluctant to leave his wares open to further depredations, the bread seller quickly gave up and returned to his handcart.

Hunger knotted Skut's empty belly; Tym's death had thrown him off his game for three days now, and he'd had almost nothing to eat. Grabbing the loaf had been a desperate move, but he couldn't stand the gnawing ache in his gut any longer.

Keeping one eye out for trouble, he threaded his way through filthy alleys to a ruined warehouse on the western fringes of the lower city, his current home. One wall had burned and fallen in and the whole place reeked of old smoke, but an attic loft was still sound. Picking his way over the rubble, he climbed the makeshift ladder leading up to it.

Sunset light spilled across the floor below but the back of the loft was already lost in shadow. The grey doves roosting overhead shifted suspiciously as he peered over the edge of the platform.

"Kaber, you here?"

There was no answer.

That was a relief. He hadn't seen Kaber in a week and good riddance. The older boy had provided a certain amount of protection, but he was lazy and had lately taken to punching Skut when he didn't bring home enough for them to eat.

He went to the rusty brazier at the center of the loft and felt for the fire makings. His hand had just closed around the tinder bowl when suddenly he sensed movement behind him.

Skut was a quick lad, but not quick enough this time. Before he could stand up someone had thrown a heavy cloak over his head and pinioned his arms.

Snuffers! Skut thought desperately.

He squirmed wildly, struggling for his life, and felt his foot hit something with satisfying force. There was a soft grunt of pain, but strong arms caught his flailing legs. His captors lifted him off the floor, holding him so tightly he could scarcely wiggle.

"We're not here to harm you," said the one holding his arms. It was a man's voice, and soft. "I want to know about Tym."

"Don't know nothin'!" Skut whimpered, bucking helplessly.

"Oh, let's not go down that route, shall we? Word is you're the one who saw it happen. I only want to talk to you about it. Settle down now and I'll make it worth your while."

Skut resisted a moment longer, his thin body taut as a bowstring, then gave in. Whoever had a hold of him clearly wasn't about to let go.

"All right then, I'll tell you. Only let me down."

"Put him down."

Skut felt his legs released, though the one behind him maintained a strong hold around his chest and arms.

"Are you going to behave yourself?"

"Said I would, didn't I?" Skut mumbled, heart hammering in his throat.

"Sit down where you are."

Skut obeyed, then cried out in fear as something heavy settled on his thigh. Looking out from under the edge of the cloak, he saw that it was a rough sack.

"Go on, open it," the man urged, still behind him. He could see the boots of another just in front of him, the one who hadn't spoken yet.

With trembling hands, Skut opened the bag and was amazed to discover a small sausage, a wedge of cheese, and half a dozen boiled eggs. The toothsome aroma was unbearably good, but he was still suspicious. The one doing all the talking had a highborn sound to him. What'd he want with Tym?

"It's all right," said the second one, speaking for the first time. Another man. "Go ahead and eat. You look like you could use it."

The smoky garlic scent of the sausage was too much. Praying it wasn't poisoned, Skut took a cautious nibble, then another.

"What happened to Tym?" asked the first one.

"Fell off a roof, that's all," Skut replied around a mouthful.

"Tym *fell*?"

Skut shrugged, peeling one of the eggs with dirty fingers. "Saw him go over. He didn't yell or nothin', just toppled down."

"No one's found his body. Are you certain he was dead?"

"Course!" Skut snorted. "Think I wouldn't make sure? The bastard hadn't paid me yet. His head was all stove in and broken. He didn't have so much as a groat on him, neither, not even his knife."

His unseen interrogator seemed to consider this for a moment. "What were you doing there? What was it he was going to pay you for?"

"Well—" Skut hesitated. "I guess I could say, since he's dead and all. I was watching a house for him, the one he fell off of."

"What house?"

"Tenement house in Sailmaker Street. Tym said I was to keep an eye out for any shady sorts, especially breakers and gate-runners. And Scavengers, too."

"How long did you watch?"

"Most of a week." The sausage was good, best he'd ever tasted. On the strength of this, he added helpfully, "I seen one, too. Pry the Beetle come by day before Tym fell."

"Did Tym say why he wanted you to watch for these fellows?"

"No, and I didn't ask. When Tym wanted something done, you done it, that's all," Skut told him, adding somewhat pointedly, "Would've paid me, too, if he hadn't gotten his self killed."

The man chuckled in a friendly way. "A true man of honor, our Tym. Did you see anyone on the roof, or hear anything strange before Tym fell?"

Skut absently cracked a louse on his sleeve as he thought hard. "No, nothin'."

"What was he doing up on the roof in the first place?"

"Said he was going to have a listen on the feller he was watching, lived up on the top floor. That's where he went over, right at that window. You ain't going to kill me or nothing, are you?"

"No, but I'll give you a word of advice. Keep low and stop blabbing. You don't know who else might take an interest in you. Now I want you to sit tight awhile, until you know we're gone. I wouldn't want to have to hurt you after you've been so helpful."

"I won't twitch!"

A strong hand clamped menacingly down on Skut's shoulder. "And not a word to anyone about this little visit, right?"

"Right! You wasn't never here," he whispered, suddenly fearful again.

The hand withdrew. Skut heard a shuffle of boots, the creak of the ladder, then silence. He made himself count to a hundred twice before he dared pull the cloak off his head. When nothing stirred, he scrambled to kindle a light and found a sturdy dagger and a small cloth purse lying on the brazier grill. The bag held at least a sester's worth of pennies.

Highborn or not, those gents knew a thing or two, Skut thought wonderingly. Showing gold or silver around these parts could get you killed right quick, especially a skinny brat like himself. But a few coppers here and there were safe enough and a stash like this could keep him going a month or more. He turned the knife over with something like reverence, testing its wicked edge against his thumb. Just let Kaber try knocking him around again! Gathering what few belongings he owned, together with anything of Kaber's that struck him as useful, he set off in search of new lodgings.

"Sounds like an accident," Alec said as soon as they were well away from the ruined warehouse. "He must have slipped coming down those slates, just like I did."

Seregil looked doubtful. "It's hard to believe Tym could fall. He's been over those roofs all his life. And the missing knife, that bothers me. Tym only drew his blade when he meant to use it. If it was in its sheath when he fell, Skut would have taken it. He said himself it wasn't there. Besides, if Tym had gone clattering over the slates, the boy would have heard it."

"And what happened to the body?" mused Alec. They'd already made the rounds of the charnel houses. "From the sound of it, he didn't just get up and walk away."

Seregil shrugged. "There are plenty strange characters in Rhíminee who'd pay for a corpse."

Alec grimaced. "Like who?"

"Oh, the mad and the curious, mostly. There was one man, a lord, no less, who wanted to determine which organ contained the soul. Artists have been known to use them, too, sculptors in particular. I recall a woman was executed after it was discovered that she'd used human skeletons as armatures for statues she was casting for the Dalnan retreat house. According to the story, a priest stopped by her shop to see how the work was coming along and inadvertently knocked over one of the life-size clay models. The head struck the floor at his feet and split open to reveal an all too lifelike mouthful of teeth."

"You're joking!"

"It's the Maker's truth. Valerius has told that story a hundred times. 'Burn 'em or leave 'em alone!' was generally the moral of the tale. As for Tym, though, it could be necrophiles or just some poor starving sod—"

"Enough, I get the idea," Alec growled. He had no idea what a necrophile was and didn't think he wanted to know; the thought of cannibalism was nauseating enough all by itself.

"What? Oh, sorry. All that aside, I think it's more likely that Rythel or some of his associates caught Tym spying and wisely disposed of the body. We'd better have a look up there ourselves."

They waited until it was full dark, then rode down to Sailmaker Street. The inhabitants of the house were still awake and at their suppers; their own clatter would cover any noise Seregil might make going over the slates.

With Alec on watch below, he climbed the rickety stairs at the back of the house and pulled himself onto the roof. Looping a rope around a chimney pot, he crept cautiously down to the eaves just over Rythel's window.

He spotted the knife at once, its naked blade gleaming cleanly in the gutter.

Stretched out on his belly, face just inches from the knife, Seregil regarded it for a moment, wondering how Tym—quick, clever, deadly Tym—could have been caught out on the edge of a bare roof and not drawn a drop of blood before he died.

You were good, Tym, but it looks like we all meet our match sooner or later, he mused, reaching for the dead thief's knife. The thought sent a brief chill up his spine as he grasped the scarred hilt. Hurrying on its heels, however, came the still more chilling memory of sending Alec to burgle the room by himself. Was it any more than Illior's luck that whoever Tym had run afoul of had not been on hand for Alec's visit?

Tucking the knife into his belt with a silent prayer of thanks, he worked his way back the way he'd come and found Alec waiting across the street.

"I checked the yard," he told Seregil. "All I found was this." He held up a small, fancy button of carved bone. "Anytime I saw him, his clothes were pretty fancy under the dirt."

Seregil nodded. "True enough. What about bloodstains?"

"Too much rain and foot traffic. Did you have any luck?"

Alec's eyes widened a bit at the sight of the knife. "I'll be— But where does that leave us?"

"Nose deep in the shit heap, I suspect," Seregil sighed. "I expect that map is long gone, and it's two more days before we can check. Rythel will be done with his good work in the sewers by then and we still don't have a clue who's behind him on this. Now the bastard's cost me a good thief to boot."

Alec looked up at the place Tym had fallen. "If Nysander hadn't called us away that night—"

Seregil shook his head. "Then we'd be wiser or dead, too. It's useless to speculate. It's time to grab our man, but we've got to do it quick and proper. And for that, we'll need a wizard's help."

He touched Tym's dagger again. "Maybe Nysander can get something out of this, while we're at it. Let's see if he's home."

Galloping up the Harbor Way, they rode at full tilt through the streets toward the Orëska House. Catching sight of its high spires looming ahead of them at last, they were relieved to see a light burning in the east tower.

They found Nysander and Thero at work over a malodorous collection of bubbling limbics and crucibles. At one end of the worktable a handful of unpolished broad arrow points lay in a little heap on a leather pad.

Seregil saw Alec's eye stray toward these, but they had more pressing matters at hand.

"Can you get any sort of a sighting off this?" he asked, showing Nysander Tym's dagger.

Wiping his hands on a stained rag, Nysander took it and turned it over in his hands for a moment, then grasped it and closed his eyes.

After a moment, however, he shook his head and handed it to Thero. "There is a faint trace of magic about it, but I cannot say what sort or how long it had been there."

"Objects seldom retain much," Thero observed. "His body would have told us more."

"Obviously someone else knew that," Seregil muttered, dropping onto the nearest bench with a disgusted grunt. "We're getting nowhere! Let's just reel Rythel in. Week's end is the night after tomorrow. I say we keep a close eye on him, and hit him then."

"That would appear to be the next logical step," Nysander agreed. "What will you need?"

"A translocation key. Make it something small I can hand him without raising suspicion. A rolled document should do the trick. As Lord Seregil, I can talk it up to be a salable item. I think we can count on our man's greed."

"Excellent. And I shall make arrangements with the warder at Red Tower Prison. We will pop him into a cell before he can wiggle loose."

Seregil turned to Alec, hovering expectantly beside him. "You'll nip in and toss his room as soon as he leaves for his weekly whoring. Even if the map's gone, there may be something else incriminating lying around. We don't want to give anyone else time to clean up after him once we've got him. As soon as you're done there, meet us at the prison."

Alec grinned, ready for the hunt. "This shouldn't take too long."

Seregil grinned back, glad to see an end to this particular job. "Hell, we'll probably be able to catch the second performance at the Tirarie Theater!"

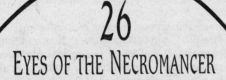

Vargûl Ashnazai looked resignedly around his latest lodging. The deserted house smelled of damp and mice, but the roof was sound and the hearth was usable.

He'd lost count of the inns and taverns they'd stayed at since their arrival in Skala three months before. Winter was harsher here than in his native Benshâl, but not so harsh as those they'd endured for three years as he helped Mardus scout the northlands for the Eyes and the Veil.

No, in Skala the necromancer's greatest hardship so far had been boredom. The Orëska's reach was long; no matter if they were in Rhíminee tracking Urvay's various spies and dupes, or sequestered at a deserted steading such as the one they now occupied, he could not afford to practice his art without first weaving a tight barrier of shielding spells. Such magicks had worked admirably with the avaricious young sorceress Urvay had netted for them. Ylinestra was altogether too sure of her powers; never once had she divined who, or what, Mardus truly was.

Throwing back the warped shutters, Ashnazai blinked out at the cove below the house. Great slabs of sea ice lay piled at the tide line, but beyond the shingle open water rippled grey-green in the morning light.

Yet another impediment nicely cleared away, he thought, smiling to himself. Urvay's actor dupe, Pelion, had leapt with predictable glee at the offer of a series of special engagement performances in the southern city of Iolus. He would have his triumphs there, no doubt, never knowing his life's thread had been measured to its final length, to be cut two weeks hence by an assassin already paid in full. And the beautiful Ylinestra, too, was living on ransomed time, along with all the others.

The months of waiting were nothing now, compared to the coming triumph. Ashnazai's revenge hung before him like a heavy, promise-filled fruit, almost ripe and soon to be within his grasp, a fruit that would ooze with the sweet liquor of blood when pressed. Two short nights, and all would be in place.

She would be here.

The stars stood out like glittering eyes against the midnight vault of the sky.

Standing beside Mardus on the beach, Ashnazai could hear Tildus' men moving through the trees that fringed the little cove, and the nicker of the horses that were tethered, ready for the night's ride. Other men patrolled the woods beyond the gully where an unlucky peddler lay face down in a brackish pool of water. There would be no witnesses.

They hadn't been waiting long when a black presence suddenly coalesced out of the darkness in front of them.

Ashnazai bowed gravely to the *dra'gorgos*.

"We will be with you presently," it announced in its hollow, wind-filled voice.

"All is prepared," Mardus replied. "We await you here."

Soon the light splash of oars came to them from across the water. Tildus and his men tensed, weapons drawn, as the black outline of a longboat came into view. Two sailors pulled the oars, while their two passengers sat motionless in the bow.

Reaching shore, one of the oarsmen jumped out and pulled the prow up onto the beach so that his passengers could disembark dry shod. The first to climb out was the gaunt, grey-beaded necromancer, Harid Yordun.

"Welcome, my brother," Ashnazai said, clasping hands with him, "and to Irtuk Beshar, our most esteemed lady."

Yordun gave a terse nod, then lifted his companion out onto the shore. Silent and invisible behind her thick veils, Irtuk Beshar extended a leathery, blackened hand in benediction.

27
RYTHEL'S END

At week's end Seregil and Alec lurked for the last time in the evening shadows across from the smith's tenement.

"You don't think he'll change his pattern, now that the job's finished, do you?" Alec asked for the third time that day. His new cronies at the Hammer and Tongs had passed on the news that the sewer contract had been fulfilled. So far, there was no word of Master Quarin awarding his nephew more work, or of Rythel requesting it.

Seregil stifled an impatient remark. "Wait another few minutes and we'll know. Hold on, there he is, and dressed fit for a ball, too!"

As Rythel paused by the lantern over his door, they saw the glint of gold embroidery on the coat beneath his fur-trimmed mantle.

"Looks like we guessed right," Seregil whispered. Under his black cloak he wore one of his finest claret-colored coats, white doeskin breeches, and a weighty purse.

A boy brought Rythel his mount and the man headed off in the usual direction.

"Luck in the shadows," Seregil whispered, quickly clasping hands with Alec. "See you at the prison."

Flashing him a happy grin, Alec ghosted off toward the tenement's back stairs.

Seregil let Rythel round the corner down the street, then mounted Cynril and set out to arrange a chance meeting with his quarry.

Tonight Rythel bypassed his usual haunts and made straight for the Street of Lights.

They must have given you a nice bonus today, Seregil thought, shadowing him to a gambling house called the Golden Bowl. *Perhaps you're even thinking of setting up in a new line of work with the proceeds. I wouldn't make too many plans just yet, my dear fellow.*

Reestablishing contact proved an easy enough matter. Seregil had hardly stepped inside the card room where Rythel was playing before the man was hailing him like an old comrade.

"Sir Rythel, how good to see you again!" Seregil greeted him, shaking hands warmly as he joined him at the table.

This was clearly a triumph of sorts for Rythel; Seregil could see him scanning the other nobles at the table, gauging their reaction to his reception by one of their own.

"Well met, Lord Seregil," Rythel exclaimed, taking up his cards again. "We'll be getting up a game of Coin and Sword next. Perhaps you'd partner me?"

With the subtlest of winks Seregil nodded, bidding his time.

As before, Seregil talked a great deal during the game, interspersing his gossipy chatter with casual references to various business ventures. He could see Rythel rising to the bait; another few rounds and he'd suggest they retire for a quiet drink somewhere. A private room here would do nicely.

Seregil had just broached the suggestion when a ragged lad appeared with a message for Rythel.

Laying his cards aside, Rythel scanned the scrap of parchment and then tucked it carefully away inside his coat.

"You must excuse me," he said, sweeping his winnings into his purse. "I have a small matter to attend to, but I shouldn't be long. Could we meet here in, say, an hour or two?"

"I expect I'll be here most of the night," Seregil replied, nodding cordially. Then, to set the hook, he gave him a rakish wink and added, "There's a small matter I would appreciate your assistance with. Small but quite possibly lucrative. We can discuss it when you return."

"I'm at your service, my lord." Giving Seregil and the others a bow, he hurried out.

"And since my partner has deserted me, I think I'll take a

moment to freshen up." Leaving the table, Seregil retrieved his cloak and hurried outside.

To his surprise, he saw Rythel strolling away on foot. Keeping well back, Seregil followed.

It was a warmish night. The last grimy remnants of snow steamed in the damp night air, mingling with the light fog rolling up from the harbor. Early spring was fast coming to Skala; the dank, rotted smell of it was on the air.

Rythel whistled softly through his teeth as he left the Street of Lights and skirted the Astellus Circle to Torch Street. This soon led them to the narrower streets of the nearby merchants district.

Where in Bilairy's name is he headed to? Seregil wondered.

Ahead of him, Rythel passed out of sight around a corner. Seregil was hurrying to catch up when the quiet of the evening was shattered by the screams of maddened horses. Running to the corner, he saw Rythel some thirty feet away, standing frozen in the middle of the lane as a team of draft horses charged out of the mists at him, the heavy wagon they pulled fishtailing wildly behind them. The lane was desperately narrow; even if Rythel managed to dodge the horses, he would almost surely be crushed by the cart.

With a nightmarish feeling of impotence, Seregil could not even shout as Rythel just stood there, hands raised as if he meant to halt the beasts.

The lead horse struck him full on, cutting short his ragged scream and trampling him beneath its huge hooves. Then the cart jolted sideways and a leg spun out from beneath it, severed by one iron-rimmed wheel.

Seregil leapt back to the safety of the corner and watched the wagon thunder by. Foam hung from the horses' mouths; their eyes rolled in panic. There was no driver on the bench. One long rein whipped uselessly across their backs.

As the wagon hurtled past, he saw several large hogsheads lashed in the back.

A brewer's wagon, out on the nightly rounds?

Like a nightmare vision, it vanished again into the fog with a thunder of hooves and jangling harness.

Crouched in the shadows, sword drawn, Seregil waited until the clamor had died away, watching to see if anyone would come. When no one did, he ran to where Rythel lay crushed against the wet cobbles.

Bile stirred bitterly at the back of his throat. It was as bad a mess as he'd ever seen made of a man. The torso was smashed. Pressing the back of one hand over his mouth, he recognized a familiar sourness amid the horrid stench that rose from the mangled flesh.

I bought you that wine, Seregil thought, averting his eyes from the contents revealed in the ruins of the ruptured stomach.

Lips pressed in a thin line of anger and disgust, he dragged the severed leg back and laid it over the corpse, then took out Nysander's magicked scroll, the one he'd meant to hand Rythel only moments before. Grasping it in one hand, Rythel's sound right arm in the other, he pried the wax seal loose with his thumb. An instant later, the street was empty.

"NYSANDER!"

Seregil's furious shout echoed up the prison corridor, jarring Nysander, Alec, and Thero from their patient vigil. Nysander was the first to recover. Rushing to the cell door, he cast a light spell and peered in through the grate. Inside, Seregil crouched over what appeared to be a tangled mass of clothing. The stink that hit the wizard's nostrils told another story. The door swung open at his command and he stepped in.

"By the Four! What happened?"

"He was run down in the street," Seregil hissed between clenched teeth. "I was practically within arm's reach of him— He just stood there like a rabbit while a runaway brewer's wagon rolled over him and I couldn't do a thing to save him."

Nysander heard a gagging sound behind him and looked up in time to see Thero staggering blindly out, one hand clapped across his mouth. Grim-faced and pale, Alec remained at the open doorway, watching as Seregil stripped back the dead man's blood-soaked garments with savage thoroughness, his fine clothing already smeared with foul-smelling muck.

Seregil was pale as milk, too, but his eyes blazed with fury. Kneeling on the other side of the body, Nysander held his hands a few inches above Rythel's ruined head.

"Again, I sense nothing," he sighed. "You must tell me everything. Was it an accident?"

"I'm getting very leery of 'accidents,' " growled Seregil.

He turned the body over and a bloody purse fell into the straw with a sodden chink of coins. He turned out the purse, inspected the remains of the coat, and then flung the whole lot across the cell.

"Damn it to hell!" he raged. "Damn it to hell! There *was* a note. Someone summoned him to that place, someone he knew. He sauntered off to his death whistling like a bridegroom! Alec, get the boot off that leg and check it."

Alec dutifully tugged at the boot on the severed leg. It was snugly fit and he had to brace his foot on the remains of the thigh to get it off. Pulling it free, he felt inside and shook his head. "Nothing here either."

"Or here." Seregil tossed the other boot aside and yanked off the remains of the dead man's trousers. After another careful inspection, he leapt up with a guttural cry and slammed one blood-stained hand against the cell wall.

Just then Thero reappeared at the doorway. "Forgive my weakness, Nysander," he mumbled, still looking green. "Is there anything I can do?"

"Look well," Nysander replied somberly. "Someday your vocation will take you from the shelter of the Orëska House; you must be strong enough to face such ugliness. This may have been an accident—"

"An accident!" Seregil burst out, glaring down at the body. "Bilairy's Balls, Nysander, the man was murdered, and so was Tym."

"Probably so. And we still do not know who was masterminding this man's work."

"But the map—?" Seregil turned to Alec.

"It wasn't there," Alec replied dully, staring at Rythel. "*Nothing* was there. Clothes, papers, chests, everything—gone. The room had been turned out. I don't think he was planning to go back there again. The old woman who owns the house said everything had been taken away by cart this afternoon."

Nysander closed his eyes a moment, then sighed. "Thero and I will retrace your paths tonight using our own methods. Should we uncover anything, I shall inform you at once."

Slipping a hand beneath Alec's arm, Nysander drew the boy from the cell. But Seregil remained, crouching gloomily over the body.

"You clever son of a whore," he whispered at it, barely loud enough for Nysander to overhear. "You were better than I thought."

28
A GLIMPSE OF PROPHECY

"**F**ather! Father, where are you?"

Gripping a handful of Valerius' magical herbs, Alec ran headlong down the bare passageway. There were no doors, no windows, just endless walls of stone as he turned corner after corner, following the splashes of dark blood on the floor and the wracking sound of his father's labored breathing. But no matter how fast he ran, Alec couldn't catch up with him.

"Father, wait," he pleaded, blinded by tears of frustration. "I found a drysian. Let me help you. Why are you running away?"

The hoarse wheezing changed as his father tried to speak, then fell deathly silent.

In the awful stillness, Alec heard a new and ominous sound, the soft tread of footsteps behind him, echoing his pace. When he stopped the sound disappeared; when he went on, they dogged him.

"Father?" he whispered, hesitating again.

The sound of footsteps continued this time, and suddenly he was mortally afraid. Over his shoulder he saw only empty passageway behind him, stretching away until another bend cut off the line of vision. And still the footsteps came on, closer and louder.

The flesh between Alec's shoulder blades

tightened as he fled, expecting any moment to be grabbed from behind. The sound of pursuit grew nearer, closed in behind him.

Wresting his sword clumsily from its sheath, Alec whirled to fight. Instead of his sword, however, he found himself grasping a blunt arrow shaft.

And facing a wall of darkness.

Alec lurched up in bed and hugged his knees to his chest, shivering. His nightshirt was soaked with icy sweat and his cheeks were wet with tears. Outside, a storm had blown up. The wind made a lonely moaning in the chimney and lashed rain against the windows.

His chest hurt as if he really had been running. Taking a few deep breaths to calm himself, he focused on the red glow of the hearth and tried to exorcise the nightmare's bitter imagery. His heart had almost slowed to normal when he heard a floorboard creak across the room.

"That's the third time this week, isn't it?" Seregil asked, stepping into the glow of the hearth. His cloak looked sodden, and water dripped from his tangled hair.

"Damn, you startled me!" Alec gasped, hastily wiping his eyes on a corner of the blanket. "I didn't expect to see you back tonight."

It had been nearly a week since Rythel's death and none of them, not even Nysander, had been able to find evidence tying the smith to anything other than the sewer sabotage and a few indiscretions at various gambling houses. Everyone had given up by now except Seregil, who'd grown increasingly short-tempered as he pursued one false scent after another. Lately Alec had found it wiser to keep out of his way when they weren't working. He'd taken it as a hopeful sign this evening when Seregil slouched off to the Street of Lights in search of consolation; his untimely reappearance now didn't bode well.

But Alec saw nothing but genuine concern in his friend's expression as Seregil fetched cups and the decanter of Zengati brandy from the mantel shelf. Sitting down on the foot of Alec's bed, he poured out liberal doses for them both.

"Bad dreams again, eh?" he asked.

"You knew?"

"You've been thrashing in your sleep all week. Drink up. You're as pale as old ashes."

The brandy warmed Alec's belly, but his nightshirt was clammy against his back. Tugging a blanket around his shoulders, he sipped in silence and listened to the wind sobbing under the eaves.

"Want to talk about it?"

Alec stared down into the shadows in his cup. "It's just a dream I keep having."

"The same one?"

He nodded. "Four or five times this week."

"You should have said something."

"You haven't exactly been approachable lately," Alec replied quietly.

"Ah, well—" Seregil pushed his fingers back through his hair. "I never was very gracious in defeat."

"I'm sorry about the map." The thought of it had plagued Alec through the long, unhappy week. "I should have taken it when I had the chance."

"No, you did the right thing at the time," Seregil assured him. "We just seemed to have a lot of bad timing with this business. If I'd gone after Rythel sooner, or if he'd held off getting killed another half an hour, we'd have had him. There's no changing what happened, though. Now tell me about this dream."

Alec took another sip of brandy, then set the half-finished cup aside and recounted all the details he could remember.

"It doesn't sound so bad, just telling it," he said when he'd finished. "Especially that last part. But in the dream, it always feels like the worst part. Even worse than my father—"

He broke off, surprised at the tightness in his throat. He sat staring down at his hands, hoping his hair veiled his face for the moment.

After a while Seregil said gently, "You've had a lot to contend with lately, what with finding out the truth about your birth and then this. Seeing Rythel all mangled in that cell must have dredged up some unpleasant memories. Maybe this is your way of finally allowing yourself to mourn your father's death."

Alec looked up sharply. "I've mourned him."

"Perhaps, *tali*, but in all the time we've been together you scarcely ever mention him or weep for him."

Alec rolled the edge of blanket between his fingers, surprised at the sudden bitterness he felt. "What's the use? Crying doesn't change anything."

"Maybe not, but—"

"It wouldn't change the fact that I couldn't do anything for my own father but sit there watching him shrink like a burnt moth, listening to him drown in his own blood—" He swallowed hard. "Besides, that's not even what the dream was about, really."

"No? What, then?"

Alec shook his head miserably. "I don't know, but it wasn't that."

Seregil gave him a rough pat on the shin and stood up. "What do you say we scrounge breakfast with Nysander tomorrow? He's good with dreams, and while we're there, you could talk to him and Thero about this life span business. With all the uproar over Tym and Rythel, you haven't had much time to absorb it all."

"It's been easier, not thinking about it," Alec said with a sigh. "But I guess I would like to talk to them."

In the darkness of his own bed, Seregil lay listening to Alec's breathing soften back into sleep in the next room.

"No more dreams, my friend," he whispered in Aurënfaie, and it was more than a simple well-wishing. He could almost hear the Oracle's mad whispering in the shadows, echoing over the weeks and months with increasing insistence and clarity. *The Eater of Death gives birth to monsters. Guard you well the Guardian! Guard well the Vanguard and the Shaft!*

The shaft. An arrow shaft, like the one Alec clutched in his dreams night after night—useless, impotent, without its broadhead point.

It could mean a thousand different things, that image, he told himself, struggling angrily against his own instant certainty that another fateful die had been irrevocably cast in a game he could not yet comprehend.

The storm blew itself back out to sea before dawn. The soaring white walls, domes, and towers of the Orëska House sparkled against a flawless morning sky ahead of them as Seregil and Alec rode toward it. Inside the sheltering walls of the grounds, the scent

of new herbs and growing things enveloped them in the promise of
a spring not far behind in the outside world.

Nysander and Thero had other guests breakfasting with them.
The centaurs, Hwerlu and his mate Feeya, had somehow navigated
the maze of stairways and corridors, not to mention doorways not
designed to admit creatures the size of large draft horses. Magyana
was there as well, sitting on the corner of the table with her feet
propped on a chair next to Feeya.

"What a pleasant surprise," Nysander exclaimed, pushing
another bench up to the impromptu breakfast spread out on a
worktable. Most of the regular victuals were laid out—butter and
cheese, honey, oat cakes, tea—together with a huge platter of fruit.
The usual breakfast meats had evidently been banned for the occasion, in deference to the centaurs. Giving Seregil a meaningful
stare from under his beetling brows, he added, "I do hope this is a
social call."

"More or less," Seregil said, piling a plate with bannocks and
fruit. "Alec's feeling a bit lost about living for a few extra centuries. I thought you wizards could give him some helpful guidance, since it takes your sort by surprise, too."

"So he finally told you," said Magyana, giving Alec a hug.
"And high time, too."

Hwerlu let out a snort of surprise. "Not until now does he
know?" He said something to Feeya in their whistling language
and she shook her head.

Turning to Alec, Hwerlu smiled. "We saw it that first day you
came here, but Seregil says not to tell you. Why?"

"I guess he wanted me to get used to him first," Alec said,
shooting Seregil a wry look.

"I suppose that would take a long while," Thero threw in.

"Yet, as things have turned out, I now believe Seregil may have
been wise to wait," said Nysander. "It is more than a sense of obligation or fear which keeps you with him, is it not, Alec?"

"Of course. But the idea that I could be sitting here three or
four hundred years from now—" He stared down at his plate,
shaking his head. "I can't imagine it."

"I sometimes still feel that way," said Thero.

Seregil looked at the younger wizard in surprise. In all the time
he'd known him, he'd never heard Thero reveal a personal feeling.

"I'd guessed it when I was a boy," Thero continued. "But
it was nonetheless overwhelming to have it confirmed when the

wizards examined me. Yet, think of what we'll experience in our lifetimes—the years of learning, the discoveries."

He's almost human today, Seregil thought, studying his rival's countenance with new interest.

"I made a poor job of telling you," he admitted to Alec. "I was feeling a bit shaky that night myself, after seeing Adzriel and all, but what Thero says is true. It's what has kept me sane after I left Aurënen. Long life is a gift for those with a sense of wonder and curiosity. And I don't think you'll ever have any shortage of those qualities."

Nysander chuckled. "Indeed not. You know, Alec, that for over two centuries I have studied and learned and walked in the world, and yet I still have the satisfaction of knowing that should I live another two hundred years there shall still be new things to delight me. Magyana and I have gone out into the world more than many wizards and so, like Seregil here, we have seen many friends age and die. It would not be truthful to tell you that it is not painful, yet each of those friendships, no matter how brief, was a gift none of us would sacrifice."

"It might sound hard-hearted, but once you have survived a generation or two, it becomes easier to detach yourself from such feelings," added Magyana. "It isn't that you love them any less, you just learn to respect the cycles of life. All the same, I thank Illior the two of you found each other the way you did."

"So do I," Alec replied with surprising feeling. He colored slightly, perhaps embarrassed by his own admission. "I just wish I could have talked to my father about it, about my mother. Seregil's spun out a good theory about what must have gone on between the two of them, but now I'll never know the real story."

"Perhaps not," said Nysander. "But you can honor them by respecting the life they gave you."

"Speaking of your parents, Alec, tell Nysander about that nightmare you've been having since Rythel got killed," Seregil interjected, sensing the opening he'd been hoping for.

"Indeed?" Nysander cocked an inquiring eyebrow at the boy.

"Can you describe it?" asked Magyana. "Dreams are wondrous tools sometimes, and those that come to you more than once are almost always important."

Seregil kept a surreptitious eye on Nysander while Alec went through the details of the nightmare; he knew the old wizard too well not to see a definite spark of interest behind Nysander's facade of thoughtful attentiveness.

"And that's always the last of it, and the worst," Alec finished. Even with the morning sun streaming down through the glass dome overhead, he shifted uneasily as he described the final image.

Magyana nodded slowly. "Violent events can summon up other painful memories, I suppose. Though your father died of the wasting sickness rather than violence, it must have been a time of terrible fear and pain for you."

Alec merely nodded, but Seregil read the pain behind his stoic expression.

"Yes, and coupled with the shock of learning your true parentage, it could create such images in the mind," Nysander concurred, although the look he gave Seregil showed that he had other ideas on the matter. "I would not worry too much about them, dear boy. I am certain they will pass in time."

"I hope so," sighed Alec. "It's getting so I hate to go to sleep."

"Nysander, do you still have that book of meditations by Reli ä Noliena?" asked Seregil. "Her philosophy might be of some use to Alec just now. I seem to recall seeing it on the sitting-room bookshelves somewhere."

"I believe it is," replied Nysander. "Come along and help me look, would you?"

Nysander said nothing as they descended the tower stairs. As soon as the sitting-room door was firmly shut behind them, however, he fixed Seregil with an expectant look.

"I assume there is some matter you wish to discuss privately?"

"Was it that obvious?"

"Really now. Reli ä Noliena?" Taking his accustomed seat by the hearth, Nysander regarded Seregil wryly. "I seem to recall that you have on numerous occasions referred to her writings as utter tripe."

Seregil shrugged, running a finger along the painted band of the mural that guarded the room. "First thing that popped into my head. What do you make of this dream of Alec's, and the headless arrow shaft? I have a feeling it's tied in with"—Seregil paused, acknowledging Nysander's warning look—"with that particular matter about which I am not allowed to speak."

"It does seem a rather obvious correlation. No doubt you are thinking of the words of the Oracle?"

" 'The Guardian, the Vanguard, and the *Shaft*.' "

"It is certainly possible that there is a connection, although why it should suddenly surface now, I do not know. Then again, it could conceivably be nothing more than it appears. Alec is an archer. What stronger image of helplessness could there be for him than a useless arrow?"

"I've tried to tell myself that, too. We both know who this Eater of Death is; I've been touched twice by the dark power and was damn lucky both times to get away with life and sanity intact. So I want to believe that Alec isn't getting pulled into this web, but I think he is, that that's exactly what that dream means. You believe that, too, don't you?"

"And what would you have me do?" Nysander asked with a trace of bitterness. "If we are dealing with true prophecy, then whatever must happen will happen, whether we accept it or not."

"True prophecy, eh? Fate, you mean." Seregil scowled. "So why dream? What's the use of being warned about something if you can't do anything to avoid it?"

"Avoiding something is seldom the best way to resolve it."

"Neither is sitting around with your head up your ass until the sky falls in on you!"

"Hardly, but forewarned is forearmed, is it not?"

"Forearmed against what, then?" Seregil asked with rising irritation as an all-too-familiar guarded look came over the wizard's face. "All right then, you're still guarding some dire secret, but it seems to me that the gods themselves are giving hints. If *you're* the Guardian, which you've admitted already, and *if* Alec, our archer, is the Shaft, then am I the Vanguard?" He paused, mentally trying the title on for size. But the bone-deep feeling of certainty he'd had about Alec eluded him. "Vanguard, those who go before the battle, one who goes in front— No, that doesn't resonate somehow for me. Besides, the Oracle wouldn't tell me to guard myself. So why would he tell me anything at all unless—"

"Seregil, please—"

"Unless there's a fourth figure to the prophecy!" Seregil exclaimed, striding excitedly back and forth between the hearth and the door as the myriad possibilities took shape in his mind. "Of course. Four is the sacred number of the Immortals who stand against the Eater of Death, so—" The inner certainty was there now. No matter what answer Nysander gave, he knew instinctively that he was on the right track now. "Illior's Light,

Nysander! The Oracle wouldn't have spoken to me as he did if there wasn't a reason, some role for me to play."

Nysander stared down at his clasped hands for a moment, communing with an inner voice. Taking a deep breath, he said quietly, "You are the Guide, the Unseen One. I did not tell you before for two reasons."

"Those being?"

"First, because I still hoped—continue to hope, in fact—that it will not matter. And secondly, because I know nothing more than that. None of the Guardians ever has."

"What about the Vanguard?"

"Micum, most likely, since he has also been touched by these events. For the love of Illior, Seregil, do stop that pacing and sit down."

Seregil came to a halt by the bookshelves. "What do you mean, you hope it won't matter?"

Closing his eyes, Nysander massaged the bridge of his nose with thumb and forefinger. "Just as there have been other Guardians, so have there been other Shafts, other Guides. It is as if they always exist from generation to generation, kept in readiness in case—"

"In case what?"

"I cannot say. I confess I still cling to the hope that this terrible evil may yet be forestalled. For now, I must guard my secret as I have done. What I can tell you, seeing that you have guessed so much, is that the four figures of the prophecy have always been known to the Guardians, but what their functions are has never been revealed. But if you are the Unseen One, Seregil, if Alec is the Shaft and Micum the Vanguard, then there is nothing any friend or foe can do to alter that."

Seregil let out an exasperated growl. "In other words, all we can do is wait for this terrible Something to happen. Or *not* happen, in which case we spend the rest of our lives waiting because we won't know that it isn't going to happen after all?"

"That is, no doubt, one of the reasons that the Guardians keep such knowledge from the others. It serves little purpose for you to know, and will only make you uneasy. On the other hand"—he paused, looking up at Seregil with a mix of concern and pity—"I suspect that my hope to pass my burden on to a new Guardian will prove a vain one. Mardus had the wooden disks; other Plenimarans came to the Asheks on your very heels, seeking the crown.

There are other objects—magical ones—some in Plenimar, others thankfully scattered to lost corners of the world. It was only by chance that my master, Arkoniel, came into possession of the palimpsest that led you to the crown. Clearly the Plenimarans are making a more deliberate effort to recover them. It bodes ill, dear boy, most ill.

"As for your dilemma"—Nysander gave him a weary smile—"may I remind you that if you were not such a intolerable meddler you would not be in this quandary."

"What about the others?"

Nysander spread his hands. "I do not forbid you to tell them what you know, but reflect a moment on what you have just said. Even knowing, there is nothing yet to be done; our fates rest on the knees of the immortals."

"And a damned uncomfortable seat that is," Seregil grumbled.

"I agree. And perhaps a dangerous one now. We must all live cautiously for a time."

"I can keep an eye on Alec, if that's the way you want it, but what about Micum?"

"I placed a number of protective spells around the three of you as soon as you came back from the north. Since then someone has tried to break through those surrounding you and Alec a few times, but—"

"What?" An icy stab of fear lanced through Seregil's chest. "You never—"

"I was not surprised by such attempts," Nysander told him calmly, "and they have failed, of course. The spells surrounding all of you are intact, making it impossible for you to be seen magically. Thus far, there have been no disturbances in the spells surrounding Micum or his family."

"Bilairy's Balls! Do you know who was doing this?"

"Unfortunately, the seekers are equally well shielded. Their magic is very strong and they know how to protect themselves."

"I don't like this. I don't like this at all," muttered Seregil. "There are more ways than magic to find someone. Hell, Rhal showed up, didn't he? Who's to say Mardus or his dogs haven't, too? Poor Alec had no idea how to cover his tracks."

"Whatever happens, you must not blame the boy," cautioned Nysander.

"Who said anything about blame?" Seregil ran his fingers back through his hair in frustration. "He did a damn fine job, given the circumstances. He saved my life. Now it's up to me to protect him. And Micum; knowing what I do, I'm honor-bound to give him any warning I can."

Seregil braced for further argument, but instead, Nysander sighed and nodded. "Very well, but only as much as is absolutely necessary."

"Fair enough. Damn, they'll be wondering where we are by now." Seregil rose to go back upstairs, but Nysander remained where he sat.

"Seregil?"

He turned back to find Nysander regarding him sadly.

"I hope, dear boy, that no matter what the coming days bring, you will believe I never foresaw this time coming during my Guardianship, or that its advent would enmesh any of you."

Seregil gave him a grudging grin. "You know, I've spent most of my life listening to legends or telling them. It should be interesting being part of one. I only hope the bards who tell it years from now will be able to end with 'And the Band of Four all lived with great honor for many years thereafter.' "

"As do I, dear boy. As do I. Make some excuse for me, would you? I would like to sit here for a while."

Silence closed in around Nysander after Seregil had gone. With his hands resting on his knees before him, he allowed himself to go limp in the chair, listening to the sound of his breathing and his heart until he was aware of nothing else. Then, slowly, he opened himself to the invisible currents of foreseeing, using the faces of his three chosen comrades to call in the energies he sought. Grey images stirred sluggishly before his mind's eye, the tangled flux of *Shall/Might/Should* and *Imagine*. How to pluck crumbs of truth from a future as yet unfixed—

—*the hands of Tikárie Megraesh, the icon of his dreams and visions, opened before him. Voices came faintly through the murk, shouting, raging, weeping. He could hear the clash of weapons, men shouting—*

Then, harsh as a blow, came the vision of a black disk surrounded by a thin white nimbus of fire. It seemed to glare at him, like an accusing eye.

• • •

A familiar perfume wafted out to Seregil as he neared the workroom door. Opening it, he found Ylinestra sitting next to Magyana. A quick glance revealed an interesting tableau around the breakfast table. As usual, Ylinestra looked intentionally stunning as she chatted with Magyana, with her shining black hair braided loosely over one shoulder of her loose-flowing gown. Magyana appeared to be a willing conversationalist, but Seregil thought he detected faint lines of distaste around her eyes.

Feeya was not so subtle. She'd moved to the other end of the table and stood eyeing the sorceress with evident dislike.

Thero seemed torn between embarrassment and lust. Alec stood at what might be considered a safe distance from his former seducer, carrying on some earnest conversation with Hwerlu.

All eyes turned Seregil's way as he entered.

"Ah, here they are," said Magyana. "But where is Nysander?"

"Oh, he got distracted by something down in his study," Seregil replied.

"How unfortunate," sighed Ylinestra. "I was hoping I could lure him out to the gardens for a while."

"You know how he is. He's likely to be a while."

"I'll tell him you were looking for him," Thero offered a trifle stiffly. "In the meantime, perhaps I—"

"Ah well, another time," Ylinestra said breezily, gliding to the door.

When she was gone Feeya whistled something to Hwerlu, who laughed.

"She says the smell of the woman makes her belly hurt," he translated.

"Mine, as well," Magyana agreed with a mischievous smile. "Although I daresay most men find the scent alluring enough. She must be missing Nysander. That's the third time this week she's come looking for him. Isn't that right, Thero?"

"I don't keep track," the young wizard said with a shrug. "If you'll all excuse me, I've got work of my own I'd better get started on."

Alec chuckled as he and Seregil set off for the Cockerel again. "I'll bet you a sester he waits until everyone else clears out, then goes after her."

"That's a loser's bet," Seregil said with a crooked grin. "I've never seen it fail; when a cold fish like Thero finally does fall in love, it makes a total fool of him."

"You know, I think you're too hard on him."

"Is that so?"

Alec shrugged. "I didn't care much for him at first, either, but now he doesn't seem so bad. He helped save our lives during that raid on Kassarie's keep, and he was useful during that whole business with Rythel, too. Since then, he's been almost—friendly. Nysander may be right about him, after all. As arrogant and cold as he can seem, underneath I don't think he's so bad."

Seregil gave Alec a skeptical grin. "You've a charitable nature. We've got more important things to worry about than Thero right now, though. I'll explain it once we get home."

They both rode with hoods pulled forward, but Alec guessed even without seeing his friend's face that something of note had come up during Seregil's separate conversation with Nysander.

"What is it?" he asked, unable to guess from Seregil's guarded tone whether the matter was likely to be a job or a problem.

Seregil shook his head. "Not here."

They spoke little the rest of the way back to the inn, but Alec noted that the route they took to approach it was more cautiously circuitous than usual.

Thryis hailed them as they passed the kitchen door. "I didn't hear you go out," she said, sharpening knives by the fireside. "Rhiri brought in a message for you last night, but it wasn't sent for the Rhíminee Cat. It's there on the mantelpiece behind the salt box."

Seregil found it, a coarse square of paper tied with greasy twine and sealed with candle drippings.

"Anything else?" asked Seregil, bending down to tickle Luthas, who sat playing with a wooden spoon at his great-grandmother's feet.

"No, nothing."

"How many are there in the inn today?"

"I think this wind's blown all our custom away," the old woman grumbled, testing the edge of a cleaver against her thumbnail. "There were those six draymen in the big room, but they left first thing this morning. All we've got left now is a horse trader and his son in the room at the front and a cloth merchant in for the spring trade. I've never seen it so slack this time of year. I sent Cilla and Diomis out to see what's what down at the market."

Suddenly Luthas startled them all with an angry squall.

"By the Flame, he's been restless all morning," Thryis sighed. "Must be another tooth coming."

"I'll get him." Alec scooped up the child, bouncing him gently in his arms, but the child howled on.

"You're wanting your mother, aren't you, dear one?" Thryis smiled, offering him his spoon. But Luthas knocked it away and cried louder, squirming like an eel.

"Find me that rag of his," Alec called to Seregil over the uproar.

Rummaging in the nearby cradle, Seregil found a colorful kerchief with a knot tied in the middle and held that within reach. Luthas grabbed it and stuffed the knot in his mouth, chewing at it with a decidedly disgruntled air. After a moment he relaxed drowsily against Alec's shoulder.

"You're quite the nursemaid these days," whispered Seregil.

"Oh, they're great friends, these two," Thryis said fondly.

Alec was just attempting to lay the child in his cradle when Rhiri stamped in, slamming the door behind him. Luthas jerked awake, crying ferociously.

The mute ostler gave Alec an apologetic nod, then pulled a small scroll tube from his jerkin and handed it to Seregil.

"Come on!" groaned Seregil, motioning for Alec to follow.

Back in their disordered sitting room again, Seregil flopped down on the couch and opened the scroll tube, which contained a jeweled ring and the usual request for the Cat's services. Setting these aside with an impatient sniff, he cut the string on the folded paper and smoothed it out on his knee.

"Well now, here's a bit of good news," he exclaimed happily. "Listen to this. 'In Rhíminee Harbor, awaiting your pleasure. Ask for Welken at the Griffin.' It's signed 'Master Rhal, captain of the *Green Lady*,' and dated yesterday."

"Yesterday? We'd better get down there."

"Another hour won't matter." His smile faded as he waved Alec to a chair. "We've got something else to deal with first."

Alec sat down, studying Seregil's face uneasily; he didn't look happy.

"First, you have to swear secrecy under your oath as a Watcher," Seregil began with uncharacteristic gravity.

A thrill of anticipation went through Alec as he nodded. "I swear. What's going on?"

"Those dreams of yours, with the headless arrow shaft? They meant something to Nysander. To me, too, really, the moment you told me about it last night, but I had to have Nysander hear it to be certain."

"Of what?" Alec asked uneasily.

"There's so much to tell you, it's hard to know where to begin." Seregil studied his clasped hands for a moment. "That first night we came here, I went out again."

"To the Temple of Illior."

"That's right, but I never told you why I went there, did I?"

"No, never."

"I went hoping the Oracle could tell me something about that wooden disk we brought back from Wolde." Seregil touched a hand to his breast where the hidden brand lay.

Alec stared at him in disbelief. "Does Nysander know?"

"He does now, but that's not the point. The Oracle didn't tell me anything specific about the disk, but he did say something that I know now was a piece of a prophecy. He spoke of the Eater of Death—"

"Just like in the journal we found, and at the Mourning Night ceremony."

"Yes, and then he told me I was to guard three people he called the Guardian, the Vanguard, and the Shaft. And there's a fourth, the Unseen One or Guide. That's me, it seems, and Nysander's the Guardian. After hearing about your dream, we think you might be—"

"The Shaft," Alec said softly, remembering the headless arrow and the feeling of helplessness he always felt at the sight of it.

"Apparently Nysander has had some presentiment that Micum is the Vanguard."

"But the Eater of Death is Seriamaius." He saw Seregil flinch as he said the name aloud. "This Shaft and Guardian business, it's connected somehow. Oh, wait a minute—" Alec's belly twisted into a queasy knot. "That disk, that damned wooden disk that made you so sick and crazy. That's what you went to the Oracle to ask about, so it must have something to do with the prophecy."

"It does," said Seregil. "But what, I don't know. Nysander won't say, except that the disk is part of something bigger, something the Plenimarans are willing to go to any lengths to get. When I went away just before the Festival of Sakor, it was to get another object before the Plenimarans did, a sort of crown. It had the same sort of evil magic about it, only worse." His face darkened as some memory surfaced. "Much worse, and much more dangerous. But I got it."

"There were other disks just like the one we stole," Alec recalled, his mind racing. "Maybe they had to be all together to have their full effect."

"That's right. Which means if we'd been greedy and taken them all, you and I probably wouldn't have made it as far as Boersby. I've wanted to tell you all this before, but Nysander swore me to silence. I wouldn't be telling you now, except that you seem to be part of it, too."

"Of what?" demanded Alec. "What does the Shaft do? If Nysander has the disk and the crown, then the Plenimarans aren't going to get them and whatever they're part of can't happen, right?"

"I guess that's the idea. But why would you be having these dreams now, if that's all there is to it, eh?"

"Do you think Mardus could still be after us? Bilairy's Balls, Seregil, if Rhal could find us, then why not him?"

Seregil shrugged. "It's not impossible. He didn't strike me as the sort who gives up easily. But why hasn't he shown up yet? It's been months now, and if he had any idea that we have the crown as well, then he or somebody like him will be certain to come after it sooner or later. There's something else, too. You remember Micum's description of the ritual sacrifice he found up in the Fens?"

"All those bodies cut open," Alec said with a small shudder.

"I found the same sort of thing with the crown. All the bodies were ancient there, but the mutilations were the same, breastbone split, ribs pulled back like wings. Now Nysander claims that all this may come to nothing, that there have always been Guardians and Shafts and so forth chosen just in case. But he didn't sound all that confident. That's why I'm telling you this, and why we've got to warn Micum. I want you to ride out there tomorrow and tell him just what I've told you."

"What about you?"

Seregil smiled darkly. "There are a few old mates of Tym's I'd like to have a chat with. If Plenimarans are getting into Rhíminee, then someone has got to know about it."

"They covered their tracks pretty well with that business in the sewers," Alec reminded him.

"Except for Rythel. There's almost always a Rythel in any plot. When you get to Watermead, what I've told you is for Micum's ears alone. Do whatever you can to get him alone but try not to raise suspicion. Kari usually knows when something's up. And ask him about his dreams while you're at it, although I expect he'll scoff.

"It's a lot to take in, I know. Like I said, Nysander claims this may all come to nothing, but I don't think he really believes it. I know I don't."

Half-realized images whirled through Alec's mind, too chaotic to grasp. Yet bits and pieces seemed to stand forth from the general maelstrom, like branches in an eddy. "So Nysander has at least two pieces of whatever this thing is: the disk and the crown. But there must be something else, right?"

"What do you mean?"

"Well, if he's been the Guardian all these years, then what's he guarding?"

Seregil's eyes widened in surprised realization. "That's a good question. But somehow I doubt we'll ever know."

Resuming their roles of Lord Seregil and Sir Alec for the day, they emerged from the Wheel Street villa at midday and rode down to the lower city to inspect a certain privateering vessel anchored just beyond the quays. They found Rhal's man still waiting at the Griffin. A day and night spent in a tavern notwithstanding, he was still sober enough to row them out to the ship.

"That's 'er," he said proudly, nodding over one shoulder as he rowed them toward a sleek, twin-masted raider. The *Green Lady* sported fighting platforms fore and aft. Even to Alec's untutored eye there was no mistaking her prime purpose.

"Bilairy's Balls, what's *that* supposed to be?" Seregil asked as they crossed beneath her prow. Fitted under the bowsprit was the painted statue of a woman.

"Figurehead," Welken replied. "Lots of the new ships has 'em. Said to bring luck. Captain Rhal got the best carver in Iolos to do our lady there; she's even got a real golden ring on her finger with a great red stone winking in it. Captain says her round belly'll bring us a full hold."

Dark hair streamed over the woman's shoulders and the carved skirts of her emerald-green gown flowed back from a rounded, pregnant belly. One outstretched hand pointed ahead; the other lay modestly over her heart.

Alec broke into a broad grin as he squinted up at the painted wooden face; it was not fine work, but the resemblance to Seregil was obvious to anyone who'd seen him playing a Mycenian gentlewoman aboard the *Darter*.

Still staring up, Seregil swore pungently under his breath.

Alec stifled a snort of laughter and asked innocently, "Does she have a name?"

"Oh, aye. Captain calls her Lady Gwethelyn."

"It suits her," Alec observed, still fighting to keep a straight face.

"Charming," muttered Seregil.

Climbing a rope ladder, they found Rhal waiting for them on deck. After a brief tour, he ushered them belowdecks to his aft cabin. Though by no means luxurious, it was a far cry from the cramped quarters he'd entertained them in aboard the *Darter*.

"I hope that figurehead of yours brings you luck," Seregil remarked dryly, taking a chair.

"Aye, and I don't doubt we'll be needing it soon," Rhal said, pouring wine for them. "The weather is settling out early this year. With the old Overlord dead, there isn't much to hold the Plenimarans back now. Of course, his son Estmar isn't Overlord yet. According to Plenimaran custom, there's a month of official mourning before he can be crowned. That should give us another few weeks."

Seregil shook his head, frowning. "I wouldn't count on it. There have been rumors of Plenimaran scouts sighted as far west as the Folcwine River."

This had come as troubling news, Alec reflected. The swift-moving units of the Queen's Horse Guard were scouting there, too, but there'd been no word from Beka in weeks.

"Well, whatever happens, the *Lady* and her crew are ready," Rhal assured them stoutly. "She sailed easy as a swan coming up from Macar and as you saw, we're fitted out with grapples, catapults, and fire baskets. When we set off raiding I'll have twenty archers among my crew and ten more hired on special."

"Impressive. When do you sail?"

Rhal stroked his dark beard. "Soon as we get the Queen's Mark."

"The only thing that separates privateers from pirates," Seregil interjected for Alec's benefit.

"That, and the percentage of the take appropriated for the royal treasury," Rhal added. "I figure we'll do coasting trade until the war breaks out in earnest; goods loads, transporting soldiers, that sort of thing. The crew needs a proper sea run. Word is there's already plenty of activity down around the Inner Sea and the Strait, lots of fat Plenimaran merchant ships carrying supplies and gold up toward Nanta. And of course, I stand ready to honor our bargain, though I don't see how you'll find me if you need me."

"We thought of that," Alec said, flipping him a silver medallion. "It's magicked. Just hang it up in here somewhere and a wizard friend of ours can sight off it wherever you are."

Rhal studied the emblem of Illior stamped into the face of the disk. "This has a lucky feel to it, too, and we can use all of that we can get."

"Then the best of it to you," said Seregil, rising to go. "I hope your ship's belly is as full as your figurehead's before long."

Rhal scratched his head sheepishly. "Oh, you noticed that, did you? She was a fine-looking woman, that Gwethelyn. Thinking back to that night I caught you out, I don't know if I was more angry or disappointed. But in the end I'd say meeting you brought me luck, so there she is. The *Green Lady*'s a fine ship and she'll do us all proud."

Since they were already dressed for the part, Alec and Seregil put in a suppertime appearance at Wheel Street, then slipped back to the Cockerel after dark. Once there, Seregil went straight to his room and rummaged out his tattered beggar's rags.

"Are you going out tonight?" asked Alec, leaning in the doorway as Seregil changed clothes.

"There are some thieves and nightrunners I want to speak with. I'm not likely to find them in daylight. I probably won't be back before you go, so get some rest and leave early. Before I go, though, let's hear what you're going to tell Micum. Things happened pretty fast today. I want to be sure you've got everything straight."

Alec recited as best he could what Seregil had told him about the prophecy and dreams. Seregil made one or two corrections, then nodded approval.

"Just right. I don't know what Micum will make of all this but at least he'll know what's in the wind." Clapping on his old felt hat, he stepped past Alec and began dusting himself with ashes from the hearth.

"I'll come back as soon as I've talked to him," said Alec, "I could be back by nightfall."

"There's no need. Stay the night and come back in daylight."

Alec opened his mouth to protest further, but Seregil forestalled him with an upraised hand. "I mean it, Alec. If we are in danger, then the more care we take the better. I don't want you getting caught out in some lonely place after dark."

Still slouching unhappily in the doorway, Alec frowned down at his boots. The truth was, he suddenly didn't like the thought of leaving Seregil alone here, either, though he knew better than to say so.

Seregil seemed to guess his thoughts just the same. Adjusting a greasy patch over one eye, he came over and grasped Alec by the shoulders. "I'll be all right. And I'm not shutting you out of anything, either."

Despite the patch, tangled hair, and ridiculous old hat that partially obscured his friend's features, Alec heard the warm earnestness in his voice clearly enough.

"I know," he sighed. "You missed a spot." Reaching over, Alec smeared ashes over a bit of clean skin just under Seregil's right cheekbone. His friend's one visible eye widened noticeably. Strange feelings stirred again, and Alec felt himself blush.

Seregil held his gaze a moment, then cleared his throat gruffly. "Thanks. We don't want any telltale signs of cleanliness giving me away, do we? I'll take a run through the stable dung heap before I go, just to make sure I've got the right odor about me. Take care."

"You, too." Alec felt another twinge of unease as Seregil headed out the door. "Luck in the shadows, Seregil," he called after him.

Seregil looked back with a crooked grin. "And to you."

Left to himself, Alec set about packing the small bundle for his journey. But he soon found himself repeatedly packing and unpacking the same few items as his thoughts wandered over the harried events of the day, and his strange unease over Seregil's departure.

• • •

That night Alec's nightmare returned, but this time there was more to it.

In the end, when he turned to look for his pursuer, blocks of stone slid out of the wall beside him, tumbling to the floor with a hollow crash. Gripping the headless arrow, he forced himself to go to the opening in the wall and look through. He could see nothing but darkness beyond, but he could hear a new sound, one that was at once as ordinary and as inexplicably terrifying as the sight of the simple arrow shaft.

It was the booming grumble of the sea battering a rocky shore.

29
HARBINGERS

Alec opened his eyes well before dawn. Too anxious to sleep, he dressed quickly and went down to the stable to saddle Patch.

A damp grey mist hung over the city, presaging a foul day, but in the Harvest Market the first traders and stall keepers were already preparing for the day's business. Alec paused to buy a bit of breakfast, then headed for the gate. To his surprise, pikemen of the City Watch stepped out to block his way.

"State your name and business," one of them said, stifling a yawn.

"What's this?"

"Queen's orders. Anyone going in or out of the city gets recorded. State your name and business."

Just a spy riding out to warn an old friend that the Immortals may have designs on his future, Alec thought wryly.

"Wilim í Micum of Rhíminee," he said aloud. "I'm heading up to Tovus village to see a man about a horse."

A guard seated at a rough table by the gate busily recorded this information in a day book.

"When do you expect to return?" asked the first guard.

"With luck, late tonight." As he said it, Alec realized that sometime between last night and now, he'd made up his mind to return that day, no matter what Seregil said. There was no good reason he couldn't make the trip in a day if the weather didn't turn too bad.

Riding north along the highroad, he watched a cheerless grey dawn crawl slowly up from the eastern horizon. The first crocus and snowdrops were blossoming in the ditches, but the pallid light seemed to rob both them and Alec's spirits of any color.

His dreams had left him feeling gritty-eyed and dour. The farther he rode from Rhíminee, the more heavily the weight of a formless dread seemed to weigh on his heart.

It was midmorning when Alec crossed the bridge and started up the hill toward Watermead. Micum's hounds came pelting out to meet him, but there was no sign of any other welcome.

Wondering where Illia could be, he entered the courtyard to find a farm hand waiting for him.

"Good morning, Sir Alec. If you're looking for the master, he ain't here. He and the family up and headed over to Lord Warnik í Thorgol's estate in the next valley day before yesterday. Folks are gathering there from all over the district to talk about defenses for the war."

Alec slapped his gloves against his thigh in exasperation. "When do you expect them back?"

"Not until tomorrow, maybe longer."

"Is that Master Alec?" Kari's old woman servant, Arna, called out the front door. "Come on in, love. This house is always open to you. You can put up here until they return. Is Master Seregil behind you on the road?"

"No, I'm alone." Still mounted, Alec considered the offer. "How long would it take for me to get to Warnik's?"

Arna considered this a moment. "Well, you'd have to go down to the highroad and then north to the next valley. What would you say, Ranil, he could be there in two hours or so, couldn't he?"

"Two hours, eh?" Two there, two back here, and another two back to the city, plus however long it took to explain things to Micum. Alec frowned to himself. With this weather, he would be riding home in the dark.

"Oh, aye," said Ranil. "And you'd be wanting a fresh horse to give young Patch here a spell. Course, if you're in a particular hurry, you might want to try the old hill track."

"He doesn't want to go riding up the hills today," scoffed Arna, pulling her shawl closer about her skinny shoulders. "That trail will be nothing but a ribbon of mire with all the thaw and rain."

"How long does that way take?" Alec pressed, trying hard not to let his impatience show.

"I dunno." Ranil scratched his head as he considered the question. "Perhaps no more than an hour, if you rode hard and didn't lose yourself. Myn's the one who'd know best. He comes from over in that valley."

"There now, so he does," said Arna, sounding as if the next valley were some exotic distant land. "Myn's the one could tell you, Master Alec. Perhaps he could guide you."

"Where is he?" Alec asked.

"Myn? Now let's see, Ranil, where's Myn today?"

"Gone over to Greywall with the reeve," Ranil replied. "That's five miles or so east of here."

Another costly detour. "Ranil, is this hill track of yours far from here?" asked Alec.

"No, you know the one, sir. Ride back down to the stream at the bottom of the hill and you'll strike it running to your right along the near bank."

"You mean that trail that leads up to the pool where the otters live?" Alec exclaimed in relief. He'd ridden there with Beka.

"Aye, that's the one," said Arna. "It's a rough track beyond, though, or so I hear."

"I'm used to that," said Alec, dismounting. "I will borrow a horse, though, and leave my pack here. I'll be back for Patch before dark."

He was underwater. Looking up, he could see the surface shimmering just above him, a shifting silver mirror that reflected nothing. Just beyond the surface something dark moved, like a man standing against the sky—

Seregil uncurled with a startled grunt as something prodded him roughly between the shoulder blades.

"Told you he was alive!" he heard a woman say.

Two bluecoats were looking down at him from horseback, early morning light glinting from their helmets. A third stood over him holding a truncheon in both hands.

"Come on, you. On your feet," the one with the truncheon

growled, looking like he'd just as soon give a beggar another good jab for good measure.

"Maker's mercy and blessings on you," Seregil whined.

"Keep your blessings, you Dalnan mudlark."

Seregil pulled his dirty rags closer about him and got stiffly to his feet, wondering how in hell he'd let himself doze off in the middle of the east end stews.

He'd been watching a nearby slophouse, hoping to snag a certain informant who often drank there. The dingy establishment was shuttered now, his man long gone.

Grabbing Seregil roughly by the arm, the bluecoat marched him past the horses to a high-sided cart. "Get up there and be quick about it."

Scrambling over the tailboard, Seregil found half a dozen sullen beggars and whores already huddled inside.

Disgusted with himself, Seregil clung to the hard bench as the cart lurched on. Something nagged at the back of his mind, some dream he'd been having when the bluecoats had woken him. But it was gone. Time now to deal with the present situation.

"I ain't done nothing," he protested querulously, tucking his chin down against his chest. "I've done nothing a'tal. What are they at, taking a poor cripple up like this?"

"Haven't you heard?" a ragged girl asked tearfully. "Word come that war's started. It's the Beggar Law for us!"

Seregil stared at her mutely as the irony of the situation struck home. Ancient and time-honored, the Beggar Law stated that in time of war all vagrants, beggars, and criminals were to be either pressed into military service or cast out of the cities to fend for themselves. In the event of a siege, no precious stores would be wasted on societal parasites.

Looking around at his fellow unfortunates—the tearful whore, a pair of vaguely familiar thieves, a one-armed drunken giant covered in sour vomit, a half-starved boy—Seregil had all he could do not to laugh at his own unwitting miscalculation in choosing a disguise.

Stay with this lot and I'll find myself facing down a Plenimaran cavalry charge with nothing but a pike in my hands, he thought grimly. *I might just as well have taken a pleasant ride out to Watermead with Alec for all the use I've been so far.*

• • •

Alec didn't see the otters as he rode past their pool, although there were footprints and slide marks enough to show that they were still in residence there.

Beyond the pool, the trail grew steeper, winding steadily uphill around thick fir trunks and boulders bigger than his borrowed mare. Crusts of snow still lingered under roots and rocky overhangs, but the air was sweet with the scents of tender new growth and moist earth. Despite the rain already pattering down through the boughs, it felt good to be in the woods. After a winter spent mostly in the confines of Rhíminee's intricate streets, the simple task of following a disused woods trail held a comfortable familiarity.

Spring runoff and fallen needles had obscured long stretches of the trail. In other places, it crossed open expanses of bare ledge with nothing but the tumbled remains of a few small cairns to show the way.

The forest grew thicker as he went along. Thick stands of hemlock and fir laced their branches overhead, shutting out what little light the day had to offer. Winter storms had felled trees across the trail, forcing him to dismount frequently and lead his horse around or over.

After an hour of struggling along, he still hadn't seen any sign that he'd reached the pass Ranil had spoken of. The wind picked up suddenly, lashing a torrent of icy rain down through the trees. Cursing, Alec pulled his cloak around him and tucked it under his thighs to keep out the wet as long as he could.

At last he reached the crest of the pass. From here the trail seemed to open up a bit, but before he could make up any lost time he rounded a bend and found himself faced with the worst deadfall so far.

The ground was steep here, and the path hugged a small cliff face to the left. A thick hemlock had fallen across against the rock face, its thick branches forming a dark green palisade higher than Alec's head.

He could have wormed his way through, but the horse was another matter. Cursing Ranil again, and himself for listening, he dismounted again to look for a way around.

Trees groaned in the wind around them as Alec led his horse off the trail, following the trunk to its base. A tangled network of roots twenty feet across lay exposed there, torn from the thin, stony soil in some past storm.

His horse shied as they went around it, spooked perhaps by the gnarled fists of the roots or the roar of the storm. Gripping the reins in one hand, he pulled the animal's head down and threw his cloak over its eyes. By the time he'd climbed the bank back up to the trail he was soaked to the skin and covered in mud.

He had one foot in the stirrup to mount when the mare shied again. Alec staggered awkwardly, pulling his foot free in case she bolted.

The move probably saved his life. He'd just gotten both feet on the ground when he caught a hint of motion out of the corner of one eye and instinctively flinched.

Something struck his left shoulder hard before he could turn, hard enough to knock him sideways. Scrabbling backward, he tugged his sword free and got it up in time to make his attacker pause.

The ragged bandit held a club in both hands, grinning wolfishly as he circled for another strike. He was gaunt but sinewy, with a long reach behind the long club he wielded. Alec suspected he was overmatched, but that his sword had surprised the man, judging by the wary way he watched it, still not pressing the attack.

"What do you want?" Alec demanded as the first shock of the attack passed.

The bandit gave him a nasty, gap-toothed grin. "What else you got?" he sneered, jerking a thumb down the trail. "We already got yer 'orse."

Alec glanced quickly in that direction and saw a harsh-faced woman leading his horse away.

"I have gold," Alec told him, ignoring the dull pain that ran down his left arm as he pulled his purse from his belt and shook it so the coins inside jingled. "You're welcome to it, but I need that horse."

"Did you hear the fine young gentleman's offer, me love?" the bandit exclaimed gleefully. "He wants to buy back his 'orse!"

The woman gave a listless shrug and said nothing.

"Give us the bag, then, and we'll shake on the bargain," the bandit offered, sidling closer.

Alec lowered his sword and held out the purse, as if he'd been gulled into the bargain. As he'd expected, the bandit immediately struck at him. Jumping back, he blocked the blow and swung a slashing stroke that opened the front of the man's jerkin and some of the skin below.

"Bilairy's Collops, the little bastard cut me!" the bandit snarled in surprise. "Got teeth, have you, you whelp? I'll soon blunt 'em!" Gripping his club in both hands, he flew at Alec and swung another blow at his head.

The bandit was strong; blocking the swing with a two-handed parry, Alec felt a nasty jolt down both arms. Pushing him away, he fell back, letting the man push him toward the deadfall. Rain ran down into his eyes as he blocked blow after blow, hoping to make his attacker think he was a novice swordsman.

Still moving backward, he felt branch tips graze his neck. It was time to hazard his one gambit.

He lowered his sword and turned slightly, as if he meant to run for it. As Alec had hoped, his opponent struck at him, and hit the springy branches of the hemlock instead. Overbalanced by the force of his own swing, he stumbled.

Alec whirled and struck him a savage blow to the shoulder. The blade glanced off bone, flaying the muscle from shoulder to elbow in a great bloody flap.

Alec had expected the blow to stop the man in his tracks, but it didn't. With a howl of pain, the bandit dropped his club and grappled Alec, locking his good arm around the boy's neck and dragging him to the ground as he choked him.

Raw, severed flesh slapped against Alec's face, and the hot blood pulsing from the wound spurted into his mouth and eyes. His sword was useless at such close quarters. Dropping it, he tore at the arm around his throat, but the man held on, pinning him down as he locked his hand around Alec's windpipe.

Blood loss alone should be weakening him, Alec thought grimly as his vision began to darken. Through a red haze he saw mindless determination still burning in the haggard, white face above his, felt it in the hard hand crushing his throat; the man might just live long enough to kill him first.

Letting go of the man's arm, Alec felt for the slender, black-handled dagger in his right boot. His fingers found the rounded pommel and closed over it, pulling it free. Gripping it, he drove it with the last of his strength into the bandit's neck. More blood spurted out, steaming hotly against his face as the world went dim around him.

The sound of fading hoofbeats brought him around again a moment later. From the sound of them, the woman had decided the horse was booty enough and taken off with it as soon as her man went down. Alec pushed the dead man off and sat up, but it was too late. She was already out of sight.

Wet, bruised, and muddier than ever, Alec got to his feet only to find that his legs were not ready to support him just yet. Staggering away from the body, he braced himself against the tree trunk and waited for the world to stop spinning around him. He tasted blood in his mouth and spat repeatedly, trying to get rid of the revolting metallic taste.

He supposed he should be grateful for the woman's cowardice. She'd taken the horse, but had left his purse, his weapons, and his life, for that matter. She'd had ample opportunity to knife him.

Hoping he'd already covered at least half the distance to Warnik's valley, he set off on foot again.

The trail was no better on this side of the pass but the downhill grade made for easier walking. Coming to a stream, he waded in to wash off some of the filth. His clothes were ruined, but it was a relief to cleanse away more of the blood. He could still taste it at the back of his mouth and retched suddenly, remembering the feel of it spurting down on him.

A more immediate worry, however, was whether or not the bandit's woman would decide to circle back for another try, drawn by a delayed desire for revenge or his purse. Wading out of the stream, Alec scanned the surrounding forest with renewed wariness. Thick underbrush pressed close on both sides of the trail, the potential for ambush unlimited. The storm blew on, hastening the afternoon darkness already thickening into mist beneath the tangled forest roof.

Seregil was obliged to delay his escape. Soon after they picked him up, the Watch patrol entered the East Ring to begin a sweep of the shanties there. Even if he got away now, there was nowhere to run.

Other bluecoats were already at work there, pulling down the shacks and piling the scrap wood onto carts, clearing the Ring to serve its wartime purpose as a killing zone between the inner and outer walls of the city. The marketplaces and circles all around the city would be cleared as well for similar reasons. Despite its size and grandeur, Rhíminee had been designed first and foremost to be a defensible citadel.

Most of the shantytown denizens had cleared out already,

warned by the vagrant's sixth sense that trouble was brewing. Those that had remained were rounded up and sorted out. Cripples and mothers with young children were allowed to stay in the city, as well as any able-bodied person willing to work for their keep or fight. Unpatriotic ne'er-do-wells would have to fend for themselves in the countryside.

The cart was full by midday and the patrol headed back through the east ward. Seregil stood at the rear of the cart, maintaining his air of sullen bewilderment until a familiar street corner came into view.

Taking the three bluecoats riding behind the cart by surprise, Seregil vaulted over the side, dodged between their horses, and tore off down the street. Behind him, his fellow prisoners cheered him on with delighted jeers and catcalls.

Two of the guards wheeled in pursuit, but Seregil had chosen his moment carefully. Running back to the familiar street, he bolted around the corner.

It was more of an alley than a street. There were no side ways leading off it and the far end was blocked by a high wooden barrier. Without slowing, Seregil launched himself at it, found purchase with hands and feet, and clambered over the top just as the furious guards thundered up.

On the far side, another alley angled off toward a larger street. The bluecoats knew this section of the city nearly as well as he did himself; he could hear the approaching clatter of hooves ahead of him as he ran. Dodging down a side lane before they caught sight of him, he slipped into the narrow space between two sagging tenements and came out in a tiny, weed-choked courtyard.

Here he bounded up a rickety exterior stairway to a disused attic. The cache of spare clothing and knives he'd hidden there months ago was still under the warped floorboards, no worse for wear except for a few beetles and some mouse turds. Whistling softly through his teeth as he shook them out, he changed clothes and settled down at the garret window to outwait his pursuers' patience. It was only a filthy beggar they'd lost. They wouldn't waste much time hunting for him.

Hungry, wet, and footsore, Alec finally reached the edge of the woods by late afternoon. Through the trees ahead he could see a rolling valley stretching out before him.

A small log house stood near the trail, with a low byre and a goat pen beside it. Too tired to care what he must look like, he headed for it, hoping to beg a little food and some directions.

As he approached the place, a huge mongrel charged out of the byre, baying as it charged toward him.

"Soora thasáli," Alec said quickly, making the left-handed charm sign Seregil had taught him. It worked to a degree; the dog halted a few feet away, but remained on guard, growling every time he moved.

"Who's that?" a man called out, emerging from the byre with an ax gripped in both hands.

"Sir Alec of Ivywell," Alec replied, holding his hands out, palm up. "I had some bad luck up the trail. Bandits stole my horse. Could you—"

"That so?" The man stepped nearer, squinting for a better look at him.

Alec had managed to wash off most of the blood, but his bedraggled clothing and sword appeared to inspire little confidence.

"Lots of bandits about just now," the man went on, still wary. "Stole two of my milch goats just the other day. Could be you're one of 'em come back to rob me again. Tugger!"

The dog crouched, baring its fangs.

"No, please! *Soora thasáli.*" Alec fell back a pace, making the sign again. "Listen, I'm only trying to get down to—"

"Here now, what're you up to with my dog?" the man demanded. "Tugger, on him!"

"No—*soora thasáli*—if you'd just listen—"

"Damn you, Tugger, at him!"

"*Soora th*—Shit!" Alec took to his heels with Tugger snapping at the ends of his cloak close behind.

The dog chased him until they were well out of sight of the cottage, then stood its ground in the center of the trail, snarling every time Alec chanced a backward look.

Winded and irate, Alec ran on until he was certain the dog had given up, then collapsed on a rock to get his breath. Evidently Seregil's dog magic worked best without the cur's master on hand to countermand it.

Less than half a mile farther on he struck the main road and soon met a string of heavy oxcarts heading for Warnik's estate. At the sight of Alec's gold the lead carter and his wife agreed to let him ride with them.

Climbing into the cart, Alec stretched out gratefully among the bales and baskets.

"Maker's Mercy, lad! You've had rough traveling, ain't you?" the woman asked, turning to look him over.

"I had a little trouble coming over the hill trail," Alec told her.

"The hill trail," snorted the carter. "What in the world made you go that route when it's faster on the highroad?"

"Faster?" Alec groaned. "I thought the hill track was a shortcut."

"What looby told you that? It's my livelihood, driving these roads, so I guess I know a thing or two. It don't take more than two hours by cart from this valley around to the next one, less on a good horse. The hill track this time of year? By Dalna, you're lucky you got over at all."

The late afternoon light was already beginning to fail when they arrived at Lord Warnik's fortified keep. A gate in the curtain wall swung wide for the carts and they rumbled to a halt in the bailey yard.

"We've got someone looking for one of his lordship's guests," the carter told the reeve who came out to take charge of their stores.

"I'm looking for Micum Cavish of Watermead," Alec explained. "I need to speak with him at once."

The reeve gave him an appraising once over, then motioned to a stable boy loitering nearby. "Portus, go and find Sir Micum. Tell him there's a messenger boy waiting his pleasure in the bailey."

Alec stifled a smile, then bid the carter and his wife farewell. A large brazier had been set up in the yard and he drifted over to join the knot of guards and servants who'd gathered around it. Sitting in the cart in wet clothes had chilled him through. Leaning close to the fire, he ignored the curious glances his sword and filthy clothes attracted.

A few minutes later he saw Micum stride into the bailey. He was dressed in a fine coat and furs, and looked rather harried.

"Someone looking for me?" he called out.

"Me, sir," Alec said, reluctantly leaving the brazier.

"What is it then?" Micum asked impatiently. He stopped, recognizing Alec as he came closer. "By the Flame—!"

"Greetings, Sir Micum," Alec said, covering a discreet warning gesture with a bow. "Is there someplace we could speak privately?"

Taking Alec by the arm, Micum drew him into the stable. Grabbing a horse blanket from a nearby stall, he handed it to Alec.

"What happened to you?" he whispered. "And what are you doing here of all places?"

Alec pulled the smelly blanket around him gratefully and sat down on an upended bucket with his back against a post. "It's a long story," he sighed. "I ran into a bandit on the hill track—"

"The hill track. What possessed you to come that way this time of year?"

Alec cut him short with a weary gesture. "Believe me, I won't do it again."

"And you were attacked by bandits. Were you on foot?"

"As a matter of fact, no. I borrowed a fresh mount at Watermead, and they took it. That is, she took it, his woman. I killed the man— Anyway, I'll pay you for the horse and I'll need another to get home from here. But that's not what I came to tell you. Seregil and Nysander think the four of us—them, you and I—may be mixed up in some sort of prophecy having to do with the Eater of Death and that wooden coin we found up in Wolde."

Micum looked less surprised than Alec had expected. "After what I saw up in the Fens, that makes some sense. But what have we got to do with it?"

Alec told him what Nysander had revealed, his own dreams, and the possible connections between the coin and the Plenimarans.

Micum listened without comment. When Alec finished, he shook his head slowly. "These Illiorans and their dreams. You mean to tell me that he sent you clear up here by yourself in this weather just to tell me that something bad might happen and that he's not even certain what it is?"

"Well, yes. But Seregil says he thinks Nysander's not telling us everything yet, and that he seems genuinely worried."

"If Nysander's worried, then we'd do well to pay heed. But first we need to get you into some dry clothes. I'll wager you haven't eaten all day, either. Come on in."

"I'd better not," Alec said. "Seregil didn't want Kari or anyone to see me up here like this."

"All right, then. You wait here and I'll bring things out. Stay put."

Micum returned quickly with a bundle of clothes and a mug of steaming soup, a hunk of fresh bread balanced on top.

"Strip off those wet things," he ordered.

Alec pulled off his coat and shirt, anxious to get into warm clothes. As he was about to pull on the thick tunic Micum had brought him, the man let out a low whistle and touched a finger to a long purple bruise darkening across Alec's left shoulder.

"Fetched you a good one, didn't he?"

"I was lucky; he was aiming for my head. My arm's fine, though." Pulling on the tunic and breeches, he wrapped his hands around the hot mug and took a sip of the thick, steamy broth. "Maker's Mercy, that's good! So, about that horse? I mean to go back tonight."

Micum's heavy red brows drew together ominously. "Now look here, Alec. You're hurt, tired, and chilled through and it's already starting to get dark. Stay here tonight and get an early start in the morning."

"I know I should, but I can't. Seregil's trying to track down some Plenimaran spies, and he may need my help." *Whether he knows it or not,* he added mentally. It wasn't exactly lying to Micum. Not exactly.

Micum looked like he was about to argue the point, but then he just shook his head and said gruffly, "All right then. I can't force you. I've got a horse you can take if you promise to stick to the road and not go gallivanting around through the woods with it in the dark!"

Alec grinned as he clasped his friend's hand. "You have my word on it."

Alec saddled Micum's Aurënfaie black quickly, not wanting to give him time to reconsider.

"I should be home before midnight," he said as he mounted and settled his sword against his thigh under his borrowed cloak.

"Maybe," said Micum, still looking dubious. "Don't gallop yourself into a ditch for the sake of an hour, you hear?"

"I hear."

Micum reached up and clasped Alec's hand tightly again, a shadow of worry crossing his face as he looked up. "Safe journey to you, Alec, and luck in the shadows."

Alec returned the grip, then walked the black toward the gate. He was just about to ride out, however, when he realized he'd forgotten something. Turning, he rode back to where Micum stood watching by the stable door.

"By the way, Seregil wanted me to ask if you've had any strange dreams lately."

Micum shrugged, grinning. "Not a one. Tell him I leave that sort of thing to you. I do my best fighting when I'm awake."

Thryis and the others sat pushing their suppers around their plates in silence that night. The announcement of war had come at midmorning and the news of Plenimar's attack on Mycena the previous day had thrown the city into an uproar.

Bluecoat patrols were out in force, rounding up beggars and keeping the peace. Down in the harbor, fighting ships that had rocked at anchor like winter ducks hoisted their colors and sailed out through the moles to join others from ports up and down the coast. At the Harvest Market vendors' stalls were being moved aside to make way for ballistas and catapults.

Diomis had spent the afternoon in the streets, trying to sort some sense out of the ebb and flow of rumors flying freely around the city: the Plenimaran fleet had been spotted off the southern tip of Skala; the fighting was centered around the island of Kouros; it was a land attack—the enemy had crossed the Folcwine and was marching west toward Skala; Plenimaran marines were at the Cirna Canal.

A Queen's herald had arrived at the market at last with solid news; the Plenimarans had made a surprise attack against Skalan troops somewhere in Mycena.

"It makes my old fingers itch for a bowstring even now," Thryis commented wistfully as her family and Rhiri gathered in the kitchen for the evening. "I still remember that battle we fought above Ero. A clear summer morning, not a breath of wind to spoil the shot, and a hundred of us lined up behind the infantry with our longbows. When we let fly, the Plenimarans fell like a swath of wheat before a scythe."

"They'll be fighting in mud and rain, starting in this early. I wonder how Micum Cavish's girl is making out—" Diomis broke off in surprise as a tear trickled down his daughter's cheek. "Why, Cilla, you're crying. What's the matter, love?"

Cilla wiped her cheek and hugged the baby to her, saying nothing.

"Luthas' dad is a soldier, isn't he, dear?" her grandmother asked gently, patting the girl's shoulder.

Cilla nodded mutely, then hurried up the back stairs with Luthas in her arms.

Diomis rose to follow, but Thryis stopped him. "Let her go, son. She's never talked of the man before; I don't suppose she'll say anything now until she's a mind to."

"What do you know about that?" he said, scratching under his beard in bemusement. "You'd think if she cared for whoever this fellow is enough to weep for him now, she'd have said more about him to us. Why do you suppose she keeps it such a damned secret?"

"Who knows? I always thought maybe he'd broken promises to her, but she wouldn't cry for him if he had. Ah well, Cilla's always had her own way of doing things."

They sat quietly a moment, listening to the crackle of the fire. Then Rhiri tapped the table with his spoon and made a hand sign.

"No, I have had no word of them since yesterday," Thryis told him. "Alec's Patch was gone this morning, but both of Seregil's horses are still in their stalls, aren't they?"

Rhiri nodded.

"I wouldn't worry about those two," said Diomis. "You go on up to bed now, Mother. Me and Rhiri will see to things down here."

"Make certain the doors are barred," Thryis warned as he helped her to her feet. "Rhiri, don't you forget to put oil in the lanterns out front. With all the excitement today some folks may get up to mischief. I want the court well lit."

"Aye, we will, Mother," sighed Diomis. "Haven't we seen to

the closing up these last twenty years? Rhiri, you go on out and check the stable. I'll take care of the front room."

Rhiri gave a quick salute and went out through the lading-room door to the back court.

In the front room Diomis checked the bar on the door and extinguished the lamp. The hearth fire was out; with only two guests in the inn, he hadn't bothered to keep it burning when they'd turned in early. He was just checking the shutter hooks when he heard the familiar rattle of the front door latch.

Diomis peered through the crack of the shutter but saw no horses in the courtyard.

"Who's that?" he called.

There was no answer except a crisp rap on the door.

Diomis had no patience for games tonight. "We're closed up! Try the Rowan Tree, two streets over."

The unseen visitor knocked again, more insistently this time.

"Now look here—" Diomis began, but was cut short by the crash of the kitchen door slamming back on its hinges.

31
THE FIRST BLOW

Topping the crest of a hill just north of Watermead, Alec was surprised to see a long line of torches in the distance. As they came closer, he saw it was a column of cavalry under the red and gold insignia of the Red Serpent Regiment. Reining in, he hailed the first of the outriders as he came abreast of him.

"What's going on?" Alec called out.

The soldier slowed his horse. "War, son. It's war at last. Pass it on to all you meet."

"This early in the year?" Alec exclaimed.

"Looks like the bastards were spoiling for a fight," the man replied grimly. "A Plenimaran raiding party ambushed some of our cavalry up in the Mycenian hill country. We're headed north to join with the Queen's Horse Guard. Word is they took the brunt of it, as usual."

"The Queen's Horse? I know someone in that regiment. Could you take a message for me?"

"No time, son," the man said, spurring away as the column caught up.

The hundred or more riders wore red and gold tabards over their chain, and their huge black horses rang with harness and breastplates. Then, like an apparition in the deepening dusk, they disappeared over the crest of the hill.

"Maker's Mercy, here you are at last!" Arna exclaimed, coming out into the courtyard to meet him. "Did you have trouble on the way?"

Alec was in too much of a hurry to properly address that. "Just tell that fellow Ranil not to send anyone else that way," he said, leading Micum's black to the stable. "I had news on the road, though. The war's started."

Arna's hands flew to her wrinkled cheeks. "Oh, my poor Beka! She's up on the border already. Do you think she's in it yet?"

Alec didn't have the heart to lie. Turning, he took the old servant by the shoulders. "The soldier who gave me the news said the Queen's Horse was in it, yes. Micum didn't know any of this; word hadn't reached Warnik's yet. I imagine they'll hear it there before long, but in case they haven't, you tell Micum first, then let him break it to Kari, all right?"

"I will, love, I will," Arna sighed, dabbing her eyes with a corner of her shawl. "Wouldn't you just know it? Nothing will do for her but to enlist, then doesn't she land smack in the middle of things. And her not even twenty yet."

"Well, she's a good soldier," said Alec, as much for his own comfort as hers. "With Micum and Seregil for teachers all those years, and then Myrhini—that's as good training as anyone could have."

Arna gave his arm a squeeze. "Maker love you, sir, I hope you're right. I'll go get you something to eat as you ride. Don't you go off without it, hear?"

By the time he'd shifted his borrowed saddle onto Patch's back, she was back with a bundle of food tied up in a napkin and several torches. Mounting he lit one from the courtyard lantern and set off on the final stretch to Rhíminee under a clouded, moonless sky. He met more columns of riders and foot soldiers along the way, but didn't stop for news.

He came in sight of the city just before midnight. The highroad followed the top of the cliffs above the sea and from here he could see down to the harbor where lines of watch fires outlined the moles, shining brightly across the dark expanse of water. More signal fires burned on the islands at the mouth of the harbor, and torches had been lit along the city walls above.

The north gate was open under heavy guard to allow for the passage of troops. Inside, the Harvest Market looked as if a war had already been fought there. Piles of scrap wood and tangled shreds of colored canvas were all that appeared to be left of the booths and stalls he'd ridden past that same morning. Despite the lateness of the hour, soldiers were at work everywhere, setting up ballistas and hauling off refuse. From now on, it appeared, merchants would have to carry on their business under the open sky or from the backs of carts.

Steering Patch through the chaos of the market square, Alec rode on into the maze of side streets beyond to Blue Fish Street. Light still showed around the front shutters, although in the excitement Rhiri had let the lanterns hanging at the Cockerel's front gate go out.

Thryis will be after him for that, Alec thought, riding around to the back courtyard.

He stopped at the stable long enough to unsaddle Patch and throw a rug over her steaming back. Leaving her with water and feed, he let himself through the lading-room door and hurried up the back stairway. With all the uproar around town, perhaps Seregil would overlook the fact that Alec had ignored his admonition to spend the night at Watermead.

He knew the way upstairs well enough not to bother with a light. On the second floor he gave the corridor a cursory glance, then headed up the hidden stairs to their rooms. The keying words for the glyphs had become habit to him by now, and he spoke them with absent haste as he went up. In his eagerness to find Seregil, he failed to notice that the warding symbols did not make their usual brief appearance as he passed.

No final dream or vision prepared him.

Nysander was dozing over an astrological compendium by his bedroom fire when the magical warning jolted him to his feet; the Orëska defenses had been breached. The alarm was followed by a storm of message spheres, swarming like bees through the House as every wizard in the place called out for information.

Or in fear.

Invaders in the atrium! Golaria's voice rang out in a red flash.

A dying cry from Ermintal's young apprentice stabbed at Nysander's mind like a shard of glass, and then that of Ermintal himself—*The vaults!*—cut short by another burst of blackness.

Through the onslaught of voices Nysander called out to Thero. There was no response.

Steeling himself for the battle he'd hoped never to fight, Nysander cast a translocation and stepped through the aperture into the corridor of the lowest vault just beyond the secret chamber. Shadowy figures waited for him there. He took a step toward them and stumbled. Looking down, he saw what was left of Ermintal and his apprentice, recognizing them by the shredded remains of their robes. Other bodies lay heaped beyond them.

"Welcome, old man." It was the voice from Nysander's visions. Magic crackled and he barely managed to throw up a defense before it struck him in a roar of flame. The corpses sizzled and smoked as it passed.

Regaining his balance, Nysander retaliated with lightning, but the smaller of the two invaders merely lifted a hand and brushed it aside to explode against the wall. By its light, Nysander saw it was a dyrmagnos. Beside it stood a figure so cloaked in a shifting veil of shadows that Nysander could not be certain at first if it was human or supernatural.

"Greetings, old man," the dyrmagnos hissed. "How weary you must be after your long vigil."

Not Tikárie Megraesh, but a woman, Nysander thought as he took a step toward her. She was a tiny, wizened husk of a creature, blackened with years, desiccated by the evil that animated her. This was the ultimate achievement of the necromancer—the embodiment of life in death wearing the sumptuous robes of a queen.

Raising gnarled hands, she held up two human hearts and squeezed them until blood oozed out in long clots, spattering to the floor around her feet.

"The feast has begun, Guardian," the figure beside her said, and Nysander again recognized the voice of the golden-skinned demon of his visions. But it was an illusion. Through the veils of darkness, he saw a man—Mardus—speaking with the voice of the Eater of Death.

Just behind them, several other robed figures came into view. Nysander could smell the stench of necromancy coming from them and with it something heartbreakingly familiar—the unmistakable sweetness of Ylinestra's special perfume.

"After all these years of anticipation, you have no reply?" the dyrmagnos sneered.

"There has never been any reply for you but this." Raising his hands, Nysander launched the orbs of power that burned against his palms.

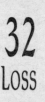

32
LOSS

The moon had passed its zenith by the time Seregil came back to Blue Fish Street. It had been a pointless day overall. With the Beggar Law in force, most of his more valuable contacts had fled or gone to ground. Those that he had managed to track down had no fresh information on Plenimaran movements in the city. If the enemy was in town, he was keeping a low profile.

Weary as Seregil was, however, the sight of the unlit lanterns in front of the inn brought him up short. A tingle of presentiment prickled the hairs on his neck and arms. Ducking quickly into a shadowed doorway across the street, he scrutinized the courtyard for a moment, then drew his sword and crept cautiously across to the front door.

It was slightly ajar.

Leaving it untouched, he crept around to discover the back door open as well. He pushed it wide with the tip of his blade, tensed for attack, but there was no sound from inside.

An unlucky door filled his nostrils as he entered the kitchen; the stale, flat smells of a cold hearth and lamps left to gutter out on their own. Taking out a lightstone, he saw nothing out of place, except for Rhiri's pallet, which was missing from its place near the hearth.

On the second floor the signs were more ominous. Thryis and her family were not in their rooms and only Cilla's bed appeared to have been slept in; the linens were thrown hastily back, and the coverlet hung awry over the side. Next to the bed, an overturned chair lay in the shattered remains of a washbasin.

A grim heaviness settled in the pit of Seregil's stomach as he moved on to the guest rooms at the front of the inn. Only one had been occupied. The unlucky carter and his son lay dead in their beds, smothered with the bolsters.

The hidden panel leading to the stairs up to his rooms appeared untampered with from the outside but opening it, he found that the warding glyph at the base of the stairs had been tripped. There were spots of blood on the lower steps, and several were smeared where more than one person had stepped in them before they'd dried. The glyphs farther up were simply gone. Still gripping his sword in his right hand, he drew his poniard with his left hand and mounted the stairs.

The doors at the top of the stairs stood open, showing darkness beyond. If there was anyone lurking in the disused storage room, it was best to find out now while there was still a chance of easy retreat. Fishing a lightstone from a pouch at his belt, he tossed it into the room. The stone skittered noisily across the floor, illuminating the few crates and boxes scattered there. No one jumped out to attack, but the floor told a tale it didn't take Micum Cavish to read; people had been in and out of his rooms, quite a number of them. Some had been dragged and some had been bleeding.

The final warding glymph on the door to the sitting room was gone, too. Taking a deep breath, Seregil flattened himself against the wall next to the door frame and slowly turned the handle.

A band of eerie, shifting light spilled across the floor at his feet, and with it came a horrendous slaughterhouse stench. Weapons clutched at the ready, he stepped inside. Even with all the warning he'd had, his first glimpse of what lay beyond struck like a blow.

Several lamps had been left burning, and pale, unnatural flames danced on the empty hearth. Someone had turned the couch to face the door, and on it four headless bodies sat as if waiting for him to return.

He knew who they were even before he looked past them to the heads lined up on the cluttered mantelpiece. The strange light cast their features into tortured relief: Thryis, Diomis, Cilla, and Rhiri seemed to look with dull incomprehension toward their own corpses, which some monstrous wit had arranged in attitudes of repose. Diomis leaned against his mother, one arm draped over her bloody shoulders. Cilla sat next to him, slumped against the remains of Rhiri.

There was blood everywhere. It hung in congealed ribbons from the mantelpiece and pooled on the hearthstones below. It had dried in scabrous crusts on the pitiful bodies. There were great sticky smears and handprints on walls.

There had been a struggle. The dining table had been knocked sideways, spilling a sheaf of parchment onto an already blood-soaked carpet. The writing desk was overturned in a litter of quills and parchment, and the shelves to the left of it had been pulled down. As he stooped to inspect the mess more closely, something in the shadows beneath the workbench caught his eye, stopping his breath in his throat.

Alec's sword.

He dragged it out and examined it closely. Dark stains along its edge showed that Alec had put up a fight before losing it. Gripping it by the hilt, Seregil was surprised by a brief, irrational burst of anger.

I told him to stay at Watermead!

The door to his bedroom was shut, but bloody footprints led inside. Taking a jar of lightstones from a nearby shelf, he kicked the door open and tossed them in.

An unearthly yowl burst out from inside and Seregil raised his sword in alarm. It came again, ending in a drawn-out snarl. Following the sound, he saw Ruetha crouched on top of a wardrobe, eyes glowing like swamp fire. She hissed at him, then leapt down and scuttled away toward the front door.

Nothing appeared to have been disturbed here except the green velvet curtains of his bed. He never used them, but someone had pulled them shut all around the bed. Someone who'd left the bloody foot marks on the carpet.

Seregil's breath sounded loud in his ears as he forced himself across the room, knowing already whose body he'd find when he pulled the hanging aside.

"No," he said hoarsely, unaware that he was speaking aloud. *"No no no please no—"*

Gritting his teeth, he flung the curtain aside.

There was nothing on the bed but a dagger—a dagger with a hank of long yellow hair knotted around the hilt. Seregil picked it up with shaking hands, recognizing the black horn grip inlaid with silver; it was the knife he'd given Alec in Wolde.

For one blinding second he seemed to feel Alec's thumb on his face again, reaching to smudge over the clean spot on his cheek.

"Where is he?" Seregil hissed. Grabbing up his sword, he rushed out into the sitting room again. "You bastards! What have you done with him?"

An evil chuckle erupted beside him and Seregil froze, scanning the room. The laugh came again, lifting the hair in the back of his neck. He knew that voice.

It was the voice of the apparition that had dogged him through the Mycenian countryside; the one he'd fought through a fever dream the night Alec had torn the wooden disk from his neck.

But this time there was no black, misshapen specter. The voice issued from the writhing lips of Cilla's severed head.

"Seregil of Rhíminee and Aurënen!" Her glazed eyes rolled in their sockets, seeking him. "We found you at last, thief."

Diomis' jaws gaped with the same terrible voice. "Did you think we would allow you to escape? You have desecrated the sanctuary of Seriamaius, and defiled his relics."

"The Eye and the Crown." It was Rhiri now, who'd never had a voice in life.

"Thief! Defiler!" Thryis spat out, her withered lips curling back in a leer.

"Defiler! Thief!" the other heads cried in moaning, joyless chorus.

"Aura Elustri málrei," gasped Seregil, watching the grotesque performance with a mixture of outrage and revulsion. "What have you done with Alec? Where is he?"

They made no answer, but Rhiri's head tumbled to the floor and rolled at him, snapping its jaws and laughing, followed by the others.

"Forgive me, all of you." Feeling as if he were trapped in the worst of nightmares, Seregil raised his sword and hacked at the heads until only a scattered mass of hair and brains remained. In the midst of it he found four small charms, charred human finger bones wrapped with nightshade vine.

Choking back a wave of nausea, he cast a suspicious eye over the bodies, still slumped together on the couch.

"You deserved better than this," he whispered thickly. "Somehow—somehow I'll make this right."

Going back to his bedchamber, he pulled out his old leather pack and thrust in a few essentials. Then he wrapped Alec's dagger carefully in a large scarf and slipped it inside his tunic.

In the sitting room he took Alec's bow and quiver down from their hook over the bed and put them by the door, not allowing himself to wonder whether they would ever be needed again. The sword he slipped into his own sheath; he had no plans for sheathing his own until he was well away from here.

Skirting the mess on the hearth, he pulled the box of loose jewels on the mantelpiece free from a puddle of congealed blood and upended it into his pack. The spoils of years of casual pilfering tumbled out, glittering in the unnatural light of the fire. Alec had sorted them recently during a lesson on gem appraisal. A layer of bright rubies slid into the pack to fill the spaces between clothes and pouches, then emeralds, opals, amethyst, a handful of gold and diamond buttons they'd used for gaming stones.

His hands were beginning to shake. A lord's ransom spilled over the lip of the pack but he left the stones where they fell. Cinching the pack shut, he carried it to the door, then turned for a last look at the home he'd inhabited for nearly thirty years. He'd been happy here, perhaps happier than anywhere else in his life. Now all of it—the books, weapons, tapestries and statues, the shelves of accumulated relics and curiosities—all of it was nothing more than stage dressing for the mocking tableau centered around the mutilated corpses gathered here at his hearth.

Taking a large lamp from the table, Seregil whispered a quick prayer and emptied the oil over the bodies. Then he gathered every other lamp within reach, flung them against the walls, and scattered a jar of firechips over the spilled oil. Flames sprang up, quickly spreading out into sheets of hungry, purifying fire.

Shouldering the packs and weapons, Seregil fled down the stairs, leaving the doors open behind him.

As he hurried past Cilla's room on his way to the kitchen stairs, however, a muffled cry brought him to a halt. Dropping everything but his sword, he dashed into the room and flung the overturned chair aside. There, tightly wrapped in thick blankets to keep him still, Luthas lay squalling in his small trundle bed.

Cilla had heard her attackers coming. In what little time she must have had, she'd hidden her child, overturning the chair and pulling the blankets down over the edge of the bed to cover him from view.

He must have been asleep when I was in here before, Seregil thought, gathering up the furious child. *And if he hadn't cried—*

As Seregil turned to go, he caught sight of himself in Cilla's mirror. The image reflected there, white-faced, eyes black with rage, might have been his own vengeful ghost.

Smoke poured down through the ceiling boards as he hefted the pack and weapons again and carried Luthas downstairs. In the first, thin light of dawn, the familiar back courtyard had an unreal look, like a familiar place seen in a dream just before it transforms into something sinister. The weight of pack, swords, and child pulled at him, sapping his strength.

"Thank the Lightbearer, there you are!" a familiar voice called.

Turning in confusion, Seregil saw Nysander's young servant Wethis coming around the corner of the inn on a sorrel horse.

"I saw the smoke from up the street," Wethis told him, reining in. His clothing was torn and he had a bandage wound around one hand, Seregil noted with a fresh pang of dread. "When no one answered out front—"

"Everyone's dead," Seregil told him, his voice coming out thin and strained. "What happened to you? What are you doing here?"

"The Orëska was attacked last night," Wethis answered, his voice cracking with emotion. "It was terrible. Nysander— They found him in the lowest vault—"

"Is he dead?" barked Seregil.

Wethis flinched. "I don't know. Valerius and Hwerlu were with him when I left. They sent me after you. You have to go at once!"

Seregil dropped his gear and thrust Luthas up at the boy. "Take him, and have the rest of this brought to the Orëska. And see that the rest of the horses get out of the stable before the whole damn place goes up."

Leaving the boy to fend as well as he could, Seregil dashed into the stable and bridled Cynril.

Patch nickered at him from the next stall. Alec had taken the time last night to feed and cover her before going up, never suspecting what lay in wait.

Mounted bareback, Seregil rode out past Wethis and away from the burning inn without a backward glance.

The world seemed strangely muted as he galloped toward the Orëska. The streets, the pale morning sky, the sound of Cynril's hooves—all had a vague, muffled air, as if he were observing the scene from a distance through one of Nysander's magnifying lenses. But somewhere behind the protective barrier of shock, the anguish was building.

Not yet. Not yet. So much to do.

He pelted on through the streets, through the Orëska gate and the scented gardens, not slowing his horse until he reached the House itself. Reining in, he leapt from the saddle and took the steps two at a time.

The atrium reeked of smoke and magic. The mosaic floor was scorched and cracked, the dragon design nearly obliterated. Where the arched doors leading to the museum had been, there was now a gaping hole partially blocked by rubble.

Afterward, Seregil could not recall how he got upstairs, or who had let him into the tower, but when he finally stopped running, he was at Nysander's bedroom door and Valerius was blocking his way.

"Is he alive?" Seregil panted, heart hammering in his chest.

The drysian nodded, frowning. "Yes, for the moment at least."

"Then let me pass. I've got to talk to him!" Seregil tried to shoulder past but Valerius grabbed his arm, holding him back with considerable insistence.

"Gently, Seregil. Gently," he warned. "By all the medicine I know, he shouldn't have survived such an attack. A good many others weren't so fortunate. But all the same, he won't let any of us ease his pain as much as we should until he's spoken with you. Be quick and don't tax his strength. He's got none to spare."

Stepping aside, Valerius opened the door and followed Seregil in.

Nysander lay on his side beneath a clean white sheet. His eyes were shut, his face slack. Hwerlu knelt at the end of the bed, tears streaming from his strange horse eyes as he played a song of healing. Two unfamiliar drysians, a woman and a boy, stood chanting softly nearby.

Valerius exchanged a brief word with them and they withdrew.

Seregil went to the bed and knelt beside Nysander. The wizard's breathing was so shallow Seregil could scarcely hear it.

"What happened?" he whispered, gently touching the old man's cheek. It was as cold and moist as clay.

"There was a great noise in the night, like thunder and battle," Hwerlu told him, still playing as he spoke. "The sound of it woke us in our grove. As I ran to the House, I saw a dark shape rise above it, very large. It disappeared against the darkness of the sky.

I ran on, and inside I found a scene of such carnage—" The centaur's fingers faltered briefly on the harp strings. "The intruders
had brought swordsmen as well as wizards. So many dead!"

"But how?" Seregil asked in disbelief. "How did they get so
many in? Illior's Hands, this is the Orëska House!"

"Through the front gate, and the sewers, it appears," Valerius
said behind him.

"The sewers? But I thought that had all been taken care of after
Alec and I found out about Rhythel."

"As it turns out, the authorities concentrated only on those
routes that might lead toward the Palace. It's also possible
someone was paid to turn a blind eye here and there. Whatever the
case, just after the alarm went up, another group, mostly
swordsmen, burst through the garden. How they got in unnoticed
is another mystery, but the main attack seems to have come up
through the vaults."

Seregil sank his head into his hands. "All those dead gaterunners this winter. By the Four, if I'd gotten to Rythel sooner, we
might have been able to stop this!"

Nysander's eyelids fluttered slightly.

"Mardus," he whispered, the word scarcely audible. "It was
Mardus, I saw him, a dyrmagnos, more—"

His voice failed, but his lips kept moving. Seregil leaned down,
placing his ear close to Nysander's lips to catch the faint words.

"Eater of Death." It was hardly more than a breath, but unmistakable. Nysander shuddered and closed his eyes, fighting a wave
of pain. Yet he struggled on, forcing the words out breath by
breath. "Where—Alec?"

"They took him, left me this." Seregil pulled out the dagger and
held it up for Nysander to see.

The wizard gazed at the lock of hair, then squeezed his eyes
shut as another spasm wrenched through him.

"It's not your fault." The words felt like ashes in Seregil's
mouth. His emotional defenses were beginning to erode, laying
bare the first jagged shards of rage and grief lying just beneath the
surface.

"It has begun," Nysander gasped out, his agitation clear. It took
every ounce of will he possessed to go on shaping the words. "One
place and one time—in Plenimar, beneath the pillar of the sky—
The temple— temple—"

"A temple in Plenimar. Where, Nysander? Damnation, you have to tell me where!"

"Synodical—" Nysander murmured regretfully as blackness surged over him again.

"What? Nysander, what does that mean?" Seregil turned to Valerius. "Isn't there anything ·you can do? Alec's life may depend on it!"

Taking Seregil by the arm, Valerius drew him away from the bed. "Give him a little time. He must rest or he may never recover. You look like you could use some attention yourself. I'll call for Darbia."

"I don't need anything," Seregil hissed through clenched teeth, straining to see over the drysian's shoulder as the larger man urged him toward the door. "I've got to know what he meant! It may be too late already."

"If he doesn't rest now he'll never be able to tell you anything again. A few hours, perhaps less. Don't leave the tower, I'll come to you as soon as I've finished here. Now get out!" With a final none-too-gentle shove, Valerius thrust Seregil out into the corridor and shut the door in his face.

Seregil stood there, alone in the corridor, Alec's dagger clutched in one fist. Smoothing the lock of hair between his fingers, he spoke half aloud the words he'd bitten back in the sickroom.

"Tell me, Nysander, can your magic protect him now?"

M icum felt the roundness of Kari's belly between them as they embraced. Magyana's message sphere hovered nearby, gleaming greenly in the corner of their guest chamber at Lord Warnik's keep.

"I'm sorry, love, but something's happened and Magyana's waiting." Micum gently stroked a tear from her cheek. How many times had there been someone waiting, calling him away? How many times had he sent him on his way with that small, tight-lipped smile?

"Go on then," she said brusquely, folding her arms. "Sakor guide you safely back."

Shouldering his traveling bundle, Micum turned to the sphere. "I'm ready."

A large oval of darkness yawned where the sphere had been. With a final wave, he stepped through. An instant later he found himself standing in Nysander's casting room. A few feet away the wizard sat on a low stool, looking utterly exhausted. Her brocade robe was dirty and bloodstained, her long silver hair in disarray over her shoulders.

"What's happened?" Micum asked in alarm. Sinking down on one knee in front of her, he took her hands in his and found them icy cold.

"The Orëska House was attacked last night," she told him, her voice trembling.

"Nysander was hurt terribly, and many others are dead. I'd have brought you in sooner, but I had to rest a bit first. Oh, Micum, it was terrible, so terrible."

"Then they were right, after all," he groaned, gathering the old woman in his arms. "It was the Plenimarans?"

"Led by Duke Mardus himself. He had necromancers, and a dyrmagnos."

"Where's Seregil? And Alec?"

Magyana shook her head. "Wethis was sent to fetch them. They may be here already. Come, I must be with Nysander."

Downstairs they met a drysian woman coming out of Nysander's chamber with a basin and stained clothes.

"How is he?" asked Magyana.

"No worse," the woman replied gently.

Valerius was applying compresses to Nysander's chest and side as they entered. He pulled the sheet back over him as Micum approached, but not before he'd seen the terrible burns there. Nysander appeared to be asleep or unconscious, his face white as carved marble. Magyana drew a chair to the head of the bed and placed her hand on Nysander's brow.

"He's got a dragon's own constitution," Valerius said quietly, stroking his unruly black beard thoughtfully as he gazed down at Nysander. "How he fights! He'll heal if I can keep the infection from him. Have you seen Seregil yet?"

"No, I only just arrived. But they're here? They're all right?"

The drysian laid a hand on his arm and Micum's heart sank. "Seregil burst in about half an hour ago. He hasn't spoken to anyone except Nysander, but Alec's not with him. Wethis says he set fire to the Cockerel. As far as I know, only the baby—"

"Damnation!" Micum spun for the door. "Where is he?"

"The sitting room. If you—"

Micum didn't wait to hear more. Dashing the short distance down the corridor, he found the door open. Seregil stood leaning against the mantel, dressed in what appeared to be borrowed breeches and shirt. A great drift of maps and scrolls lay spread out around one of the armchairs, as if he'd been sitting there going through them earlier. There was a wine cup on the floor beside it, but as he looked up, Micum knew his friend was far from drunk. His pale face was nearly expressionless, except for his eyes. What Micum saw there sent a black stab of dread through him.

"Did Alec tell you about all this?" Seregil asked, far too calm for Micum's liking.

"The prophecy? Yes." Micum approached him slowly, the way he would a maddened horse. "Where is he? What happened at the Cockerel?"

Seregil held up something he'd been holding all along, a dagger with a long lock of blond hair knotted around it.

"Is he—?"

"I don't know."

Micum sank into a chair with a stricken groan. "He was in such a lather to get back. He was worried about you, I think, but I should've stopped him from going back."

"Perhaps I can help," Valerius said from the open doorway. Going to Seregil, he took the dagger and held it to his brow, murmuring a prayer or a spell.

"He's alive," he said, handing it back. "That's all I can tell from this, but he is alive."

"But for how long, eh?" Thin lines of tension around Seregil's eyes and mouth showed darkly in the firelight as he took the dagger back, clutching it against his heart. "We know what these bastards are capable of. It *was* Mardus after all, you know. Nysander saw him during the attack. And I think it's safe to assume that those were his men who came to the Cockerel, too."

"They found you."

Seregil's lips quirked into a parody of his old grin that sent another chill through Micum. "In a manner of speaking," he said, his voice nearly toneless now as he stared into the fire. "Alec walked into an ambush. I didn't show up until it was all over." His hands were trembling visibly now as he leaned against the mantel.

Giving Micum a compassionate nod, Valerius slipped quietly out.

"They killed— They killed everyone," Seregil whispered. "In my rooms. Except Luthas. Wethis has him. It's burning now, the whole place. Everything."

Micum shook his head as the horror of it sank in. "But Cilla, Thryis?"

"All of them."

Seregil's face seemed to crumple in on itself like a parchment thrown on a fire. "I did this, Micum," he gasped raggedly, clutching his head in both hands. "I brought this down on them, led the bastards to them. They were—"

Micum said nothing, simply put his arms around his friend and held him tight as Seregil shook helplessly with harsh, strangled sobs. In all the time Micum had known him, he'd seldom seen Seregil weep, and never as violently as this. Whatever he'd seen at the inn, whatever had been done there, it had wrenched something from his very soul.

"You couldn't have known," he said at last.

"Of course I should have!" Seregil shouted. Jerking away, he stared at Micum with wild, desolate eyes. "All the years they protected me, kept my secrets. Slaughtered! *Slaughtered*, as if they were animals, Micum! Then the shit-eating carrion scum— They cut off—"

He sank to his knees, burying his face in his hands as another fit of weeping rocked him.

Micum knelt, one hand on Seregil's shoulder, and listened with mounting horror and outrage as he choked out the details of what he'd found, what had been done to the bodies of those good people.

When he'd finished, Micum gathered him in again, unresisting now, and held him until Seregil had cried himself limp and silent. He remained there, leaning against Micum, for a moment longer, then sat back on his heels and wiped his face on his shirttail. His eyes were red, but he looked calmer now.

Micum's knees ached from kneeling. Sitting down among the strewn papers, he stretched one leg, then the other. "Tell me more about Alec."

Seregil held up the black and silver dagger, which he'd been clutching through the whole outburst. "It's his. They left it for me so I'd be sure to know they had him. From the looks of the room, they killed the others, and then waited for some length of time, hoping we'd show up. I found his sword under a table. He gave them a fight before they brought him down; there was blood on the edge of the blade." He took a deep breath, fighting for control. "I showed this to Nysander when I got here this morning. I think he knows where they're headed. He was trying to tell me when he fainted, but I think I may have figured it out."

Seregil retrieved a map from the scattered pile by the chair. As he spread it on the floor between them, Micum recognized the outline of the Plenimaran peninsula, but the spidery writing that covered it was unintelligible.

"What is that? I can't read any of it."

"Nysander's own writing system," Seregil explained. "I learned it back in my apprentice days. Before he passed out, Nysander spoke of a temple in Plenimar, saying it was under 'the pillar of the sky.' At first I thought it must be a monument of some sort and didn't have much hope of finding it. But look here." He pointed to a place on the northwestern coastline just above the isthmus. "See that small cross there? It marks the position of Mount Kythes, only here it's labeled 'Yôthgash-horagh.' "

Seregil looked up at Micum, the old intensity rekindling. "In the ancient tongue of Plenimar, that means Sky Pillar Mountain."

"Under the pillar of the sky." Micum looked at the map again. "You do realize, of course, that this place is well behind enemy lines now?"

"Yes, but if I understood what Nysander was trying to tell me, it's imperative that the four of us be there at some specific time. 'One place, one time,' he said, and 'synodical.' "

"What's that?"

Seregil shook his head, frowning. "I don't know yet, but it's important."

"It's all to do with that damn prophecy of yours, isn't it?" Micum scowled. "But what in hell did the Plenimarans attack the Orëska for?"

"They were after that wooden coin I stole from Mardus back in Wolde. Nysander had it and at least one other item of interest to them. He'd hidden them down in the lowest of the vaults. That's where the worst of the wizard battle took place."

Getting to his feet, Seregil straightened his ill-fitting clothes and headed for the door. "Come on, I want to see if Nysander's conscious yet. Then I'll need a look at the damage down below."

Micum followed, thinking of Mardus, and the fact that he'd taken Alec instead of killing him on the spot. This was tied in with what he'd found up in the Fens, he knew, but it was best not to think of that just now.

Valerius met them outside the bedroom door.

"Well, you're certainly looking better," he observed, looking Seregil over with gruff approval. "Red eyes, flushed cheeks. A good cry's just what you needed. Damn shame about the inn. That baby's fine, by the way. I've sent him to the temple for the time being. I suppose you'll tell me about the others when you're ready."

Seregil nodded. "Can I see Nysander now?"

"Still sleeping. Magyana and Darbia are watching him. They'll send for us as soon as there's any change."

"How soon do you think he'll wake up?" asked Micum.

"It's difficult to say. These old wizards are strange creatures; he has his own way of fighting for life." Valerius cocked an eyebrow in Seregil's direction. "I gather you haven't heard about Thero?"

"What about Thero?" Seregil asked sharply.

"He's gone," snorted the drysian. "They've searched high and low. He's not among the dead, nor anywhere in the House or the city. My guess is, he's with whoever it was attacked here last night."

"That traitorous bastard!" Seregil snarled. "He knew Nysander's ways, his habits, not to mention something of the Orëska defenses. There's more than iron grates guarding the sewer channels under this place. He let them in! Bilairy's Guts, he let them *in*!"

"We don't know that," Micum warned but Seregil wasn't listening.

"He knew whenever I was around, and where I lived!" White with anger, Seregil slammed a fist against the wall. "*Agrai methíri dös prakra,* he betrayed all of us. I'll feed him his own balls when I find him. *Lasöt arma kriúnti—!*"

Micum took the news more calmly. "If he was in on it, then so was Ylinestra. I suppose she's gone, too?"

Valerius shook his head. "Her body was in the vaults, among the enemy's dead."

Seregil loosed another sizzling volley of Aurënfaie curses. "How many of the Orëska House were killed?"

"Eight wizards, seventeen apprentices, twenty-three guards and servants, last I heard. And there are plenty of others who may not survive their wounds."

"And the enemy?"

"Twenty-seven dead."

Seregil gave the drysian a questioning look. "And the others? Wounded, prisoners?"

"Not a one," Valerius replied darkly. "That dyrmagnos creature saw to that herself. According to those who witnessed the fight, as soon as Mardus and his creature had disappeared from the vaults, and I do mean 'disappeared' in a thaumaturgic sense, every one of the surviving Plenimaran swordsmen there and up in the atrium just fell down dead where they stood. I've seen the corpses; there's not a mortal wound on them."

"I'll need to see them," said Seregil.

"I rather suspected you would. They've been laid out in the west garden."

"Good. But first I want to see the vault."

Tiles and rubble grated beneath their boots as Seregil and Micum crossed the atrium to the museum chamber. Whatever magic had blasted the doors from their hinges had carried through and smashed half the cases in the chamber. The case holding the hands of the necromancer was among these; the hands lay palm up among the splinters and shards like huge brown insects.

There were people everywhere in the vaults now. As they made their way down one level after another they met servants and apprentices carrying up rescued artifacts, and wizards weeping or wandering past in stunned silence.

A doorkeeper at the final door let them through without question. Torches and wizard's lights lit the maze of brick-paved passageways. By their light Seregil followed the traces of battle: a bloodied dagger abandoned at the turning of a hallway, dark smears and spatters on the pale stone walls, shattered pieces of an ivory rod, a corselet buckle, the charred remains of a wizard's robe.

Micum nudged a broken sword with his foot, then spread his arms to find that he could nearly touch both walls at once. "Sakor's Flame, it must have been a slaughter."

The sound of voices guided them the last of the way to Nysander's long-hidden cache hole behind an unremarkable expanse of wall halfway down one of the innermost corridors. A blacked hole a few feet above the floor led into darkness. Beside it stood a young assistant wizard Seregil vaguely recognized, together with several servants.

"You're Nysander's friend, aren't you?" she said. "Magyana told me you might come."

"This is it, then?" he said, peering into the hole.

"Yes, it's a room of containment, masterfully done. I don't suppose anyone but Nysander knew it was here all these years."

"Obviously, someone else guessed," Seregil retorted humorlessly. "Where did the attack come from?"

The girl colored indignantly as she pointed farther down the corridor. "There's a breach in the wall at the far end of this passage where a sewer channel runs within a few yards of the wall. As you say, they seemed to know just where to look."

She and the others retreated, leaving Seregil and Micum to their investigation.

"Thero could have known," Micum admitted, watching Seregil take out his tool roll and select a lightwand. "He might have guessed. Perhaps Nysander even told him."

"No. He didn't." Stooping, Seregil inspected the jagged opening. "Illior's Fingers, the stonework is three feet thick here, but there's no debris. I see something shiny on the far edge, though."

The opening was large enough for Seregil to wiggle through. Reaching in, he ran his fingertips cautiously over what felt like metallic nodules beading a section of broken stonework. "It feels like— Of course, it's silver. And something melted it; it ran like wax before it cooled. I'm going in for a look."

Micum frowned as he peered doubtfully into the dark, cramped space. "Do you think it's safe? Nysander must have had one hell of a lot of magic protecting whatever he had hidden in there."

"Any safeguards that existed must surely have been destroyed," the wizard said, placing his palms against the stone above the hole. "I sense only the residue."

Holding the lightstone in one hand, Seregil squeezed in headfirst. It was a tight fit. Jagged stone scraped at his hands and belly as he crawled through to the small chamber beyond.

"I'm in," he called back to the others. "It is a room of sorts, but too small to stand up in."

"What's in there?" asked Micum, peering in at him.

"Nothing. It's empty. But every surface from floor to ceiling is all black, and covered with magical symbols."

Seregil touched his palm to the wall beside him and recognized the soft, almost velvety texture of the surface at once; rubbing at a small section of it with his sleeve, he uncovered gleaming metal.

"It's silver, the whole room is sheathed with it." He was not surprised; taking all the details into consideration, he knew it to be nothing more than a larger version of the silver-lined box Nysander had given him to carry the crystal crown. "And here at the back there's a shelf running the width of the wall."

Examining this, he found three areas of bright metal on the

shelf, as if whatever had sat there had kept it from tarnishing. The central mark was roughly circular and about the size of his palm. To the left was a smaller but more perfectly round circle. To the right was a large square of silver, not so bright as the other two. Seregil recognized the last two outlines as those of the boxes holding the coin and crown, but what had the central object been? Judging by the relative lack of tarnish, it had been there the longest of the three, proving Alec's supposition that Nysander had been guarding something long before they had brought him the disk.

Bending over the mark with his light, he touched the outline, tracing it with his finger—

—his vision dissolved into a brief curtain of sizzling sparks, then darkness.

A single clear, attenuated note broke the silence surrounding him and for as long as it lasted he knew nothing else. It pierced him, bathed him, dancing along on the threshold dividing pleasure from pain. Gradually other notes joined the first and they had form, long heavy forms that gradually wrapped together like the strands of a great rope.

And he was one of those strands, twisted tight and drawn along with the rest toward some destination. It was not fear that shot through him now, but an horrific elation.

Other sounds gradually filtered in from beyond the umbilicus, and these were different.

Removed.

Not of the flow.

Countless black-feathered throats raising a deafening collective cry that swelled to a roar of diseased laughter, then faded away as the flow passed on.

Human screams, voices crying out in every language of the world.

The clash of battle.

Impossible explosions.

He burrowed deeper into the umbilical bundle but the intrusive sounds followed, rising to an awful crescendo before they faded as quickly as they had come.

Silence, gravid with a sense of immediacy.

At last another sound crept in between the strands; Seregil knew this sound and it inexplicably filled him with a greater dread than all the rest.

It was the heavy rumble of ocean surf—
"Seregil?"

The sound of Micum's worried voice broke through the vision, yanking him back to the cramped chamber.

"You all right in there?" Micum called again.

"Yes, yes, of course," Seregil replied thickly, although suddenly he didn't feel all right. He felt pissed as a newt.

Rising slowly, he staggered back to the opening and pulled himself through. Micum helped him to his feet, but his legs didn't seem to want to support him just yet. Sliding down with his back to the wall, he rested his elbows on his knees.

"What happened in there?" Micum demanded, studying him with apparent concern. "You don't look right."

"I don't know." There had been something, a fleeting glimpse of—what? Gone, nothing.

Seregil scrubbed his fingers back through his hair to clear his head. "Must have been some residual effect of Nysander's magic, or a pocket of bad air maybe. I just went a little light-headed. I feel better now."

"You were saying something about a shelf in there," said Micum. "Did you find something?"

"Just the marks. From the coin and the crown and the bowl."

"What bowl?"

Seregil blinked up at Micum. "I don't know. I just—know."

For the first time since he'd learned of Nysander's prophecy Seregil felt the faint, chill brush of fear, but it was tempered with a sudden burst of grim anticipation.

34
LIGHTNING FROM A CLEAR SKY

The blare of battle horns brought Beka up out of sleep just after dawn. Grabbing her sword, she ran from the tent.

"To arms! To arms!" a messenger shouted, riding through the encampment. "An attack from the eastern hills. To arms!"

Shading her eyes, Beka looked across the small plain that lay between the camp and a line of hills a mile to the east. Even with the sun in her eyes she could see dark ranks of horsemen and foot soldiers in the distance, perhaps as much as a regiment. The Queen's Horse was still at half strength; Wolf Squadron was patrolling the supply route that stretched back to the Mycenian coast twenty miles to the south.

Sergeant Braknil rushed up fully armed, his blond beard bristling. "What is it, Lieutenant?"

"Look there," said Beka, pointing.

"Damn! The scouts from Eagle troop said those hills were clear yesterday." The edge of Plenimaran territory lay more than twenty miles to the east.

The rest of the turma scrambled from their tents in various stages of readiness.

"Full armor," shouted Beka, dashing back to finish dressing. Outside, she could hear Portus,

Braknil, and Mercalle barking at their riders. "Lances and swords! Come on now, this is it!"

Minutes later all thirty riders were mounted and ready. Their chain mail, and the white horse and sword insignia on the fronts of their green tabards, showed bravely in the early morning light. Beka gave them a satisfied once-over, then led the way to where Captain Myrhini and the troop's standard-bearer were waiting. Lieutenant Koris' Second Turma galloped up to join them.

Myrhini sat her white charger and barked out orders in a voice that carried over the general outcry of the camp.

"Commander Klia wants our troop to hold this far right end of the battle line. Commander Perris' squadron will be to our left. Lieutenant Beka, I want your turma on our right. Koris, you've got the left. We'll show these sneaky bastards that you have to get up earlier than this to catch the Queen's Horse in bed on such a fine morning. Form up!"

Beka turned to her riders. "Sergeant Mercalle, you've got the center of our section. Sergeant Braknil, take right; Portus, the left."

The three decuriae fell into formation, lances waving like the spines on a sea urchin. Watching their faces, Beka saw in them a mix of fierceness and elation.

And fear.

They were a young group, among the youngest in the regiment and, despite all their hard training, they hadn't seen any worse action than their skirmish with bandits weeks ago. This was just as unexpected as that had been, but a hundred times more daunting. Thirty-three faces turned to Beka as she buckled on her white-crested helm. She knew as she looked at them that no matter how brave they were or how well they fought, there were bound to be some who wouldn't live to see the sun set.

"We'll show 'em today, right, Lieutenant?" called Corporal Kallas, giving her a nervous, cocky grin.

She grinned back. "Damn right we will! Honor, strength, and mercy, First Turma."

Waving bows and lances, they returned the cry.

The trumpet signal "canter advance" came down the line. Unsheathing her sword, Beka brandished it and yelled out, "Blood and Steel, First Turma!"

"Blood and Steel!" they roared back at her, shaking their lances.

The rumble of hooves and harness rang out on the morning air as the line advanced to meet the enemy cavalry. The trumpets sounded again, and the line sprang forward at a gallop across the plain. Spring was creeping slowly up into Mycena and their horses kicked up clods of half-frozen mud as they ran.

As the two forces hurtled at each other, closing the distance to seconds, Beka felt only a deadly stillness as she marked an oncoming Plenimaran officer. Both sides set up a blood-chilling battle cry as the two forces collided—cries quickly swelled by the screams of horses and soldiers.

Myrhini's troop was in the thick of it from the outset. By midmorning they had battled their way behind the enemy's flank. Regrouping, they wheeled back to attack the rear guard, only to have the Plenimaran cavalry fade away like smoke before wind at their advance, leaving a line of archers and pikemen in their wake to meet the Skalan charge.

Bloodied to the elbows, Beka and her remaining riders heard the trumpets sound the advance again and rode down on the enemy line through a hail of arrows. As she rode, Beka glimpsed soldiers falling and riderless horses veering wildly across the field. Sergeant Portus went down under his own horse, but there was no time to stop for him.

Plowing into the ranks of infantry, Beka's turma fanned out, striking left and right with swords as they pressed their mounted advantage.

Hewing her way through the chaos, Beka caught a welcome glimpse of regimental standards on the far side of the melee.

"Look there," she shouted to the others. "Second Turma's with us. Close the gap!"

She was wheeling her horse for a renewed charge when an enemy soldier struck at her with a javelin, catching her a glancing blow across the front of her left thigh just below the edge of her mail shirt.

He struck at her again, aiming for her throat. Beka rocked back in the saddle and grabbed for the shaft, using the man's own forward momentum to pull him off balance. As he staggered forward she struck him over the head with her sword. He fell back and disappeared under the crush of fighters surging around them.

Looking up, she saw Second Turma's standard tilt drunkenly in the distance, then disappear.

Cursing, Beka called out new orders and spurred forward to aide Corporal Nikides, who was about to be skewered from behind.

The battle raged on into early afternoon as the two forces battered each other in repeated charge and melee. There was no quarter given to the dead or dying; those who weren't carried from the field were trampled into the cold, reeking mud. Combatants on both sides were so filthy that it was difficult to tell friend from foe.

Though outnumbered, the Skalans refused to break and finally the Plenimarans gave way, disappearing back into the hills as quickly and mysteriously as they'd come.

Beka gritted her teeth and tried to concentrate on other things while the troop surgeon tugged the last stitches tight, closing the gash in her leg.

The hospital tent was crowded, the air rank with the stench of the wounded. Moans and cries came from all sides as the more seriously hurt begged for help, water, or death. A few feet away, a man screamed as an arrow was pulled from his chest. Dark blood bubbled out ominously from the wound. When he cried out again, more weakly this time, air from his punctured lung whistled through the hole.

The gash on Beka's thigh was a deep one and it hurt like hell now, though she'd hardly noticed it during the battle. No one had been more surprised than she when she'd fainted across her horse's neck when the fighting was over.

"There now, that should heal nicely if it doesn't fester," Tholes assured her, laying his needle aside and pouring a bit of sour wine over the wound. "Vinia will bind it up so you can ride."

There was a stir at the door of the hospital tent as Commander Klia entered, flanked by her three remaining captains, Myrhini, Perris, and Ustes. All four officers were covered with the filth of battle and Beka noted that Myrhini was limping on a bandaged foot. Captain Ustes, a tall, black-bearded noble, wore his sword arm in a sling and Perris had a stained bandage around his brow. Klia alone appeared to have come off without a scratch, although word was she'd been in the thick of it the whole time.

Magic, Beka wondered, *or just charmed skill?* Klia was a

skillful tactician, to be sure, but it was her preference for leading from the front that made her so popular with her squadron. After exchanging a word with one of the surgeons, she moved off among the wounded, praising and encouraging them, and asking for details of the battle as the fighters had seen it.

Myrhini spotted Beka and hobbled over. "First Turma distinguished itself again today. I saw you break through the line. How's the leg?"

Beka grimaced as Tholes' assistant finished bandaging her thigh. Hauling her torn breeches up, she flexed her leg. "Not so bad, Captain. I can ride."

"Good. Klia wants reconnaissance patrols out before dawn tomorrow. What state is your turma in?"

"Last I knew for certain, four dead including Sergeant Portus, and thirteen still unaccounted for. As soon as I get out of here I'll round up the rest and let you know." The truth was, she dreaded the final count. Lying here, she'd been unable to block the memory of young Rethus' broken body trampled in the mud. He'd been the first to stand with her during their first fight with the bandits.

Myrhini shook her head grimly. "Well, you may be better off than some. Captain Ormonus was killed in the first charge, along with most of his second turma. All told, we've lost nearly a third of the squadron."

Klia came over and squatted down beside Myrhini. Beka made her commander an awkward salute from where she lay. Klia looked older than her twenty-five years today. Tired lines had sunk in around her eyes and mouth and creased the smooth brow below her dark widow's peak.

"A force that large—" Klia growled under her breath, tugging absently at the end of her long brown braid. "A full regiment of Plenimaran cavalry and foot soldiers boiling down out of hills we've been patrolling for a week!"

She pinned Beka with an appraising look. "How do you suppose they managed that, Lieutenant?"

Beka looked out the tent flap to the distant hills visible beyond. "There are hundreds of little valleys up there. Anyone who knew the area could sneak small groups into them, keep quiet, no fires. When the time came, they'd send out runners with orders to mass at some central point."

Klia nodded. "That seems to be the general opinion. Myrhini

tells me you're a good tracker. If you learned any of it from your father and Seregil, then I know you're better than most. I want your turma to go up into those hills tomorrow, see what you can find."

"Yes, Commander!" Beka sat up and saluted again.

"Good. I can give you a few more riders if you think you'll need them."

Beka considered the offer, then shook her head. "No, we can move faster and quieter if there aren't too many of us."

Klia clapped her on the shoulder. "All right, then. This is like finding adders in the haymow, I know. Find what you can and send back word. Don't engage unless you're cornered. Myrhini, who else are you sending?"

"Lieutenant Koris is taking a decuria north into the steeper country. The rest of his turma will go up the central pass with me."

"I've sent word to Phoria that we need reinforcements here," Klia told them, rising to go. "With any luck the rest of the regiment will come up from the coast in a day or so. Good luck to you both."

"Take care of yourself, Commander." Myrhini grinned, thumping the toe of Klia's boot with her fist. "Don't go getting yourself gallantly killed while I'm gone."

"I'll wait until you get back," Klia shot back wryly. "I wouldn't want you to miss it."

"Sakor touched!" Myrhini muttered, watching her friend stride away. "Good luck to you, Beka, and take care."

"Thanks. I will," Beka said.

When Myrhini was gone, she got up and looked around for familiar faces among the wounded. She soon found some—too many, in fact. Ariani, a rider in Braknil's decuria, beckoned to her from a back corner of the tent.

She was wounded but looked able to ride. Some of those with her hadn't been so lucky. Mikal had taken a spear in the belly, and Thela had a shattered leg. Next to her, Steb sat slumped against his friend Mirn, one hand pressed to a bloody dressing over his left eye. That wasn't the worst of it, though.

The little group was gathered around the body of another comrade. It was Aulos, Kallas' twin. A Plenimaran foot soldier had unhorsed him just before the retreat, then hacked his lower belly open. His brother had carried him off the field and now sat cradling Aulos' head on his lap.

Beka felt her stomach go into a slow lurch. The surgeon had cut the remains of Aulos' uniform and chain mail away, only to find that there was not enough of his abdomen left to stitch back together. White and panting, the young man lay staring mutely up at his brother, their faces mirrors of agony. They'd always been inseparable, Beka recalled sadly, equally quick to sing or fight.

"They gave him a draught, but he still feels it," Kallas said softly as she knelt down beside him. Tears were coursing down his cheeks, but he remained motionless, patient as stone. "Tholes says there's nothing to do but to let him go. But he won't! He hangs on." Kallas paused, closing his eyes. "As his kinsman, Lieutenant, I ask permission—to spur him on."

Beka looked down into the wounded man's face, wondering if he understood what was going on. Aulos locked eyes with her and nodded slightly, mouthing *Please*.

"Find someone, Mirn. Quickly!" Beka ordered.

Mirn hurried off, returning a moment later with an orderly who quickly opened an artery in Aulos' leg. The wounded man's labored breathing slowed almost at once. With a last long sigh, he turned his face to his brother's chest and died.

"Astellus carry you soft, and Sakor light your way home," Beka said, speaking the soldier's brief prayer for the dead. The others echoed it in a ragged chorus.

"Those of you who can ride, help Kallas bury him, then find the rest of the turma. The rest of you stay here and wait for transport to the coast. You fought bravely, all of you. Captain Myrhini's proud of you. So am I."

Accepting the murmured thanks of the others, she limped outside as quickly as her leg allowed, only to be met by the sight of scores of bodies lined up on the ground like bundles of harvested grain. Syrtas was there, and Arna, Lineus, and Sergeant Portus. They lay looking up at the blue sky with empty eyes, like dirty, broken dolls discarded once and for all.

"Astellus carry you soft, and Sakor light—"

Beka's voice failed her. How many more times would she have to say that parting blessing today? Wiping a hand roughly across her eyes, she whispered the rest.

"Lieutenant Beka?" It was Zir, calling to her from the next hospital tent. He appeared to be unhurt, but his face was deathly pale. "It's Sergeant Mercalle— She's in here."

Squaring her shoulders, Beka followed him back into the stinking dimness.

The surgeons must have given Mercalle something for pain, for she smiled sleepily up at Beka. Both arms were splinted, and one of her legs. There were bandages wrapped tightly around her chest and rib cage, as well, and blood had seeped through these below her right breast and on her left side.

Beka knelt and rested a hand lightly on the sergeant's shoulder. "By the Flame, what happened to you?"

"Damned horse—" Mercalle rasped, shaking her head slightly. "When I heal up, I'm joining the infantry."

"She got thrown and trampled," Zir whispered. "Corbin was carrying her off the field when they both got hit with arrows. He was killed. I got her on my horse and brought her in. Tholes expects she'll live."

"Thank the Maker for that. Where are Kaylah and the others?" Beka asked.

"She's out looking for the missing ones, Lieutenant. You saw—" Zir nodded in the direction of the bodies outside, and she saw tears glistening in his eyes. "We'd just fought our way into the open, and thought we'd have a moment to collect ourselves. But there were Plenimaran bowmen there, too. By the Flame, Lieutenant, they hit us hard! Arna, Syrtas, and the others—they were in the lead and didn't have time to turn their horses."

Beka clasped his hand. "Go on. Find Kaylah and the rest. I'll be along soon."

"Lieutenant?" Mercalle's eyes were bleary, but she fixed Beka with a direct look. "You were fine on the field, Lieutenant. Real fine. And you're fine with them off the field, too. But you can't care too much, you know? You've got to care for them, but not too much. It's a hard thing to learn, but you won't last if you don't."

"I know." Beka sat a moment longer with her, realizing how much she was going to miss the older woman's presence in the turma. "When you get back to Skala—if you need anything—my father is Micum Cavish, of Watermead near Rhíminee."

Mercalle smiled. "I thank you for that, Lieutenant, but I've got a couple daughters back home. I'll try and get word to your folks, though."

There didn't seem to be much left to say after that. With a final word of thanks, Beka left the tent and limped past the corpses in search of the living.

• • •

The Plenimarans had mown through the encampment, destroying tents, wagons, and anything else in their path. Soldiers were at work everywhere now, trying to salvage what they could from the tangled wreckage.

Beka was just wondering which direction to try first when she heard her name called again and saw Corporal Rhylin waving to her from atop an overturned sutler's wagon.

"Praise the Flame!" he exclaimed, jumping down. He was taller than she by nearly a head and had an awkward, storklike quality when on foot that belied his prowess as a horseman.

"We didn't know what to think when you disappeared at the end," he told her. "There's been all sorts of rumors. Someone claimed Captain Myrhini went down."

"She's fine and so am I," Beka assured him, though the stitches felt like burning claws in her skin. "Where is everybody?"

"Just over that way." Rhylin waved a hand back beyond the line of hospital tents, adding glumly, "What's left of us, anyway. You'd better take my horse."

"We'll ride double. I want everyone together."

Rhylin swung up into the saddle and extended a hand. Gritting her teeth as another hot rope of pain pulled taut across her thigh, Beka climbed up behind him and gripped his belt.

"What can you tell me?" she asked as they set off.

"There are about a dozen of us accounted for who aren't too badly wounded. Sergeant Braknil's in charge of them. Mercalle's hurt badly and Sergeant Portus—"

"I saw him go down," said Beka, hearing the sudden strain in the man's voice. Rhylin had been Portus' corporal.

"Anyway, Sergeant Braknil sent some of us out looking for you. The others are scouting up food and gear," he told her.

Thank the Flame for that at least, Beka thought gratefully, imagining the stocky, blunt-spoken sergeant striding through the wreckage to whip things into order again.

"That's good. Mirn, Kallas, and Ariani will be back later. Steb and Thela are out of it for the time being—"

"Aulos?" Rhylin asked, and Beka felt him tense again. He'd come into the regiment with the twin brothers. They were from the same town.

"Dead," she told him. There was no use glossing it over, she thought, feeling weary for the first time that day. Like Mercalle had warned, death was something they'd all better get used to, and quickly.

As expected, Braknil had things well in hand. Food had been salvaged from somewhere, a few tents were up and, best of all, a dozen or more horses were hobbled nearby, a good many of them sporting Plenimaran tack.

A cheer went up as the others caught sight of them riding up.

"What's the word, Lieutenant?" Braknil asked as the others gathered anxiously around. He had a bloody rag wrapped around one forearm, but it didn't seem to be slowing him down.

Beka counted fourteen in all, plus the sergeant.

"The word is we got caught with our britches down," she replied wryly. "Commander Klia isn't too happy about that, but she thinks that First Turma can help make it right. What do you say?"

Another cheer went up, mingled with angry shouts of "Let's raid the bastards!", "Blood and Steel!", and "Lead on like you did today, Lieutenant, we'll follow!"

Beka eased herself down on a crate and motioned for silence. "It looks like two decuriae will have to do for now. Rhylin, I'm making you sergeant of Second Decuria. Who do you have left?"

Rhylin looked around. "Nikides, Syra, Kursin, Tealah, Jareel, and Tare."

"Braknil, what about First Decuria?"

The sergeant waved at the two exhausted young men beside him. "Just Arbelus and Gilly, so far."

"And us," called Steb, who'd just arrived with Kallas, Ariani, and Mirn.

"You're missing an eye!" Braknil said gruffly.

"I've still got one left," Steb replied, though it was clear he was in pain. "Come on, Sergeant. There aren't enough of us left to spare me. I can fight."

"All right, then," the sergeant said with a shrug. "Corporal Kallas, you're still sound?"

Still deeply shaken by the death of his brother, Kallas nodded grimly.

"So that makes seven in each decuria so far," Beka observed, counting them up. "All of you who were with Sergeant Mercalle, step forward. Tobin, Barius, you go into Braknil's decuria. Marten, Kaylah, and Zir, you're with Rhylin. As soon as we've got horses and gear sorted out, we have orders to head up into those hills as scouts."

"We couldn't make a worse job of it than Eagle troop," Kaylah muttered. Others growled angry agreement.

"Never mind that. The Plenimarans pulled a good trick this morning, it's true. It's up to us to make sure they don't do it again. We're going to poke our nose down every gully and snake hole until we find out where they're hiding. They can't conceal that many men and horses for long now that we know what they're up to. Sergeants, see that everyone scrounges up a decent horse, patrol gear, and a week's rations. Stow your tabards again, too. Maybe we can pull a few surprises of our own, eh? We ride out at dusk."

Beka sat where she was for a moment, watching the remains of her command bustle about. Most were sporting minor wounds. It was probably a mistake to take Steb, but as he'd pointed out, they couldn't afford to spare anyone who could still ride.

Twelve riders and two sergeants lost in a single day's fighting, she thought, *and half of those dead.*

It was a lucky thing they had a mission to take up their thoughts tonight.

A white linen pavilion had been erected for the Orëska dead. As Seregil and Micum passed by it the next morning, they heard soft chants and the weeping of those preparing the bodies for pyre or grave.

Farther on, the enemy corpses lay under the open sky. Judged by their clothing, they could have been laborers or thieves, but most of them had the build and scars of soldiers. A Scavenger cart stood ready nearby. Untended and unmourned, they would be hauled away and burnt without ceremony.

"Valerius said that after the attack was over, any of Mardus' men who weren't already dead just dropped in their tracks," Micum mused as he and Seregil walked around the bodies, seeking faces they'd seen with Mardus in Wolde all those months ago. "You figure the dyrmagnos did that?"

"Probably," Seregil said. He was still wearing his baggy borrowed clothes and looked as if he hadn't slept in a week. Micum knew for a fact that he'd sat awake with Nysander all night. They both had.

"But I doubt they killed all of their own people," Seregil went on, taking a closer look at a ragged, one-handed beggar. "Have you noticed that no one remembers seeing Mardus and the necromancers leave? Except Hwerlu, maybe. He said something about a huge dark shape rising over the House as he ran toward it. He didn't get there until it was over, so that may have been Mardus' exit. A dyrmagnos could have that kind of power."

Micum felt an unlucky chill go up his back. "Let's hope we can stay clear of the thing, then. Anything that can lay Nysander low and then fly off like a bat is nothing I want to face down."

A swarthy man with a scar through his bottom lip caught his eye. "I know him. He's one of Captain Tildus' men," Micum said, pointing him out to Seregil. "I drank with him a few times at the Pony in Wolde. He's one of them who gave Alec a hard time."

"I see an old friend, too." Seregil stood looking down at a lanky, rawboned man dressed in a soiled leather jerkin. "Farin the Fish, a gaterunner who came up missing a month ago. Tym mentioned him to me just before he disappeared himself. I don't recognize any of the others. Probably all Plenimaran soldiers and spies brought in for the job." He tapped his chin with one long forefinger as he frowned down at the dead. "You remember I ran into a Juggler up in Asengai's dungeon, that night Alec and I first met?"

"The Plenimaran assassins guild, you mean?"

"Yes." Seregil jerked a thumb at the corpses. "What would you bet there's a guild mark on one or two of these fellows?"

Micum grimaced in distaste. "Guess there's only one way to find out. What's it look like?"

"Three small blue dots tattooed to form a triangle. They're usually in the armpit," Seregil told him, adding with a wry grin, "At least this is better than going to the charnel houses."

Even in the scented coolness of the Orëska garden, however, it was not pleasant work.

Pulling at clothing and cold, stiff limbs, Micum found no tattoos, but two men did have suspicious scars about the size of a sester coin under their arms. The healed tissue was still pink and new.

"I think this might be something," he said.

Seregil came over for a look and nodded. "There are three more just like it over there. That scar isn't a burn or a puncture; the skin was sliced away on purpose. If it wasn't a Juggler's mark they cut out, then I'll wager it was something similar."

"That Mardus is a cagey bastard," Micum said with grudging admiration. "He wasn't taking any chances. Not that we can prove it now, though."

Seregil examined the scar. "You know, I've heard that these skin marks go deep. What do you think?"

Micum sighed. "It's worth a try, so long as no drysians catch us at it."

Slipping a tiny, razorlike blade from the seam of his belt, Seregil held the skin on either side of the mark taut with two fingers and sliced away the surface of the scar. When he'd pulled back the flap of skin, he and Micum inspected the livid flesh beneath.

"See anything?" asked Micum.

"No, they must've cut deep on this one. Let's try another."

Their second attempt was more successful. Scraping gently this time, Seregil uncovered the faint triangular imprint of the Juggler's guild mark still visible in the flesh.

Seregil rocked back on his heels with grim satisfaction. "That's proof enough for me."

"Maker's Mercy! What do you think you're doing?" It was Darbia, the dark-haired drysian who'd been helping tend Nysander. Bristling with indignation, she strode up and made a quick blessing sign over the corpse.

"Enemy or not, I cannot condone such barbarous behavior," she snapped.

"It's not desecration," Micum assured her, getting to his feet. "This man and several others wear the mark of Plenimaran spies. The Queen should be informed before any of these bodies are taken away."

The drysian crossed her arms, still scowling. "Very well then, I'll see to it."

"Did Valerius send you after us?" asked Seregil.

"Yes, Nysander is stirring a bit."

Without waiting to hear more, Seregil and Micum ran for the tower.

Magyana was still in the armchair by Nysander's bedside where she'd spent the night, one hand still on his brow.

Seeing her like that, Micum could almost feel her willing her own energy into her old love, trying to heal and sustain him with her own life force.

To Micum, Nysander looked worse than ever. His face was a dull, chalky grey, his eyes sunken deep in their sockets beneath the unruly white brows. His breathing scarcely lifted the sheet covering him but Micum could hear it, rasping faintly as dry leaves across stone.

The sight of him must have struck Seregil hard as well. He read a hint of despair in Seregil's face as he approached Nysander, and knew it was born of the conflict between Seregil's great love for Nysander and his desperate need to learn whatever he could to save Alec. Seregil paused long enough to cleanse his hands at the washstand, then knelt beside the bed and took Nysander's hand between his own. Micum moved around behind Magyana's chair in time to see Nysander's eyes slowly open.

"I found your map," Seregil told him, not wasting any precious time.

"Yes," Nysander mouthed, nodding slightly against the pillow. "Good."

"The Pillar of the Sky, Yôthgash-horagh. It's Mount Kythes, isn't it?"

Again, a slight nod.

"This temple you spoke of, it's on the mountain?"

"No," Nysander told them.

"Beneath it, underground?"

No response.

Seregil watched the wounded man's face for any movement, then asked as calmly as he could manage, "At the foot of it?"

Nysander's throat worked painfully as he struggled to speak. Seregil bent close, but after a few desperate efforts, the wizard's eyes closed.

Seregil rested his forehead against his clenched fists for a moment. Micum couldn't see Magyana's face from where he stood, but her hand was trembling as she reached to clasp Seregil's shoulder. "He's gone deep within himself again. I know how desperately you need to speak with him, but he's just too weak."

"Could you make anything out of that last bit?" Micum asked, refusing to give up hope.

Still kneeling by the bed, Seregil shook his head doubtfully. "He was trying to tell me something. It sounded like 'late us' or 'lead us,' but it was so faint I can't be certain."

Magyana leaned forward, gripping his shoulder more forcefully this time as she turned him to face her. "Leiteus? Could it have been the name Leiteus?"

Seregil looked up at her in surprise. "Yes! Yes, it could have been. And I've heard that name somewhere—"

Magyana clasped her hands together over her heart. "Leiteus í Marineus is an astrologer, and a friend of Nysander's! They've been consulting with each other about some comet for over a year now."

Seregil jumped to his feet and began searching the floor around Nysander's hearth. At last he bent and pulled a book from beneath an armchair.

"I noticed this lying open by his chair yesterday," he said, handing it to her.

She opened it and Micum saw that it was full of tables and strange symbols.

"Yes," she said, "this is one of Leiteus' books."

"Have you ever heard the word 'synodical'?" Seregil asked her with growing excitement.

"I believe it refers to the movements of the stars and planets."

Micum looked to Magyana in surprise. "You mean Nysander really was trying to send us to this astrologer fellow?"

"So it would seem."

" 'One place and one time.' That's what he said yesterday," Seregil reminded them. "A synodical event, like the advent of this comet. It must have some bearing on whatever Mardus is up to."

He bent to lay a hand against Nysander's pale cheek. "I don't know if you can hear any of this," he said softly, "but if you can, I'm going to Leiteus. Do you understand, Nysander? I'm going to speak with Leiteus."

Nysander gave no sign of consciousness. Seregil sadly stroked a lock of grizzled grey hair back from the old man's brow. "That's all right. I'm the Guide. You just leave it to me for now."

Outside the Orëska walls an early spring wind had blown up, clearing the sky and whipping corner whirlwinds out of the dead year's dust and leaves.

Galloping north out of the Harvest Gate, they left the highroad for a smaller one that wound along the sea cliffs.

The astrologer's modest walled villa sat perched on a headland overlooking the sea. Above it, gulls wheeled gracefully against the morning sky.

The courtyard gate was shut tight, but a servant soon answered Micum's relentless knock.

"My master is not accustomed to receiving visitors at this early hour," the man informed them stiffly, eyeing Seregil's unkempt appearance and ill-fitting coat with undisguised skepticism.

"We're here on a matter of the utmost interest to your master," Seregil replied, affecting his most arrogant tone. "Tell him that Lord Seregil í Korit Solun Meringil Bôkthersa and Sir Micum of Cavish, Knight of Watermead, require his attendance at once in a matter pertaining to his friend Nysander, High Thaumaturgist of the Orëska House."

Duly intimidated by the onslaught of titles, the man relented enough to escort them to a small sitting room overlooking the sea, while he went to speak with his master.

"Prophecies and astrologers," Micum grumbled, pacing around the tiny room. "Alec's carried off by crazy butchering bastards and we're weaving sails out of smoke!"

"It's more solid than that. I can feel it." Seregil sat down on a bench under the window and rested one elbow on the sill as he gazed out.

Having a thread to follow, even as tenuous a one as this, appeared to have restored the inner calm Seregil needed to function. After all the horror of the previous day, however, Micum wondered if he wasn't just a bit too calm.

And what if this astrologer doesn't have all the answers?

"How did Kari take you going off like this?"

Micum shrugged. "She's nearly four months gone with child, Beka's off in the middle of a war, and I charge off again with you. I swore to her I'd be there when her time comes."

Still looking out the window, Seregil said quietly, "You don't have to come, you know. Prophecy or not, the decision is yours."

"Don't talk like an idiot. Of course I'm coming," Micum retorted gruffly.

"I've made my choice and I'll stick by it," he went on, sitting down next to Seregil. "Though I'll admit I don't like it. Nysander talks of a band of four and here we sit, knocked down to two before we even begin."

"We're still four, Micum."

Micum stared down at the mosaic under his feet for a moment, then laid a hand on Seregil's thin shoulder. "I know what Valerius said yesterday. I want to believe it as much as you, but—"

"No!" Seregil glared at Micum. "Until I hold his body in my hands, Alec is alive, do you hear?"

Micum understood the anguish behind Seregil's anger all too well. If Alec was alive, Seregil would fight through fire and death to save him. If Alec was dead, then he'd do the same to track down his killers. Either road, he blamed himself.

"You know I love the boy as much as you do," he said gently, "but it won't do him a damn bit of good for us to let that cloud our thinking. If we're going to come up with any sort of plan we have to at least take into consideration that he might be dead. If this 'Shaft' person of yours is really meant to be an archer, then we'd better—"

Seregil stared out the window, his mouth set in a stubborn line. "No."

They were interrupted by the arrival of a short, well-fed man in an enormous dressing gown.

"I beg pardon, gentlemen," he apologized, yawning as he ushered them into a spacious consultation room. "As you've no doubt surmised, the nature of my studies requires that I work at night. I'm seldom awake at this hour. I've sent for strong tea, so perhaps you would—"

"Forgive me, but I assume you're unaware of the attack on the Orëska House last night," Seregil broke in, "or that Nysander í Azusthra has been seriously wounded."

"Nysander!" Leiteus gasped, his robe billowing around him as he sank into a chair. "By the Light, why would anyone want to harm that decent old fellow?"

"I can't say," answered Seregil, his manner now betraying none of the emotion of a moment before. "He sent us to you, though he was too weak to tell us why. Magyana says he'd consulted you on some astrological matter recently. It could have some bearing."

"Do you think so?" Leiteus fetched a pile of charts from a nearby shelf and shuffled quickly through them. "If only he'd allowed me to do that divination for him. He was gracious about it, of course, but so— Ah, here it is!"

He spread a large chart out on a polished table and peered down at it. "He was interested in the movements of Rendel's Spear, you see."

"A comet?" asked Seregil.

"Yes." The astrologer pointed to a series of tiny symbols arcing across the chart. "It has a synodical cycle of fifty-seven years. This is the year of its return. He helped me calculate the date of its appearance."

Seregil leaned forward eagerly. "And you have it?"

The astrologer referred to his parchments again. "Let me see, going by the observations recorded in Yrindai's Ephemeris, as well as our own calculations, I believe Rendel's Spear should be visible on the fifteenth night of Lithion."

"That gives us just over two weeks, then," Micum murmured.

"Of course, it will remain in the sky for nearly a week," Leiteus added. "It's one of the largest comets, a most impressive display. Of particular interest both to Nysander and myself, however, is the fact that this cycle of the comet coincides with a solar eclipse."

Seregil shot Micum a meaningful glance, then asked, "Would that also be considered a synodical event?"

"Certainly, and one of the rarer variety," replied the astrologer. "I assumed that's why Nysander was so curious about it."

"Eclipses are unlucky things," Micum noted. "I once knew a man who went blind afterward."

"It'll be a doubly unlucky day with the comet in the sky," Seregil added, though to Micum's ear he sounded more pleased than alarmed. " 'Plague stars,' I've heard these comets of yours called, bringers of ill fortune, war, disease."

"That's true, Lord Seregil," Leiteus concurred. "The College of Divination has already sent word to the Queen, advising the suspension of all trade on that day. People should keep to their homes until the evil influence passes. Such a conjunction has not occurred in centuries."

"And do you have a date for that?" asked Seregil.

"On the twentieth."

"Was there any other sort of information Nysander seemed interested in?"

The astrologer stroked his chin. "Well, he did ask me to calculate if such a conjunction had occurred before."

"And did you?"

Leiteus smiled. "I didn't have to, actually. As every Skalan astrologer knows, it was that very same conjunction that heralded the beginning of the Great War six hundred eighty-four years ago. So you see, Lord Seregil, your talk of unlucky 'plague stars' does have some basis."

• • •

Leaving the astrologer with assurances to send word of Nysander, Micum and Seregil headed back to the city.

"I admit, it makes some sense if you accept that Nysander's right about Mardus aiming for that conjunction," Micum said as they rode.

"He is right, I'm sure of it. Think about it, Micum. There haven't been any major incidents between Skala and Plenimar for twenty years, yet all of a sudden Plenimar decides to launch another war of aggression, just as they did in the Great War. And the old Overlord, who opposed such a war, conveniently dies just in time for his hawkish son to take the throne? And there's the same conjunction? And the attack on the Orëska? And if that whole business does all revolve around some rite or ceremony having to do with their Eater of Death, then what more propitious time could there be than during the conjunction?"

"But what is it all for?" Micum growled. "Those odds and ends that Nysander was guarding, what does Mardus want with them? If the Plenimarans need them that badly, and now, just as war is breaking out again—"

"That's just it, though. Nysander said he wasn't the first Guardian. His mentor, Arkoniel, was before him, and the wizard before him. Who knows how long Orëska wizards have been watching that same hidey-hole in the vaults? Those things could date all the way back to the Great War. You've heard the legends of necromancers and walking dead from that time, and everyone knows it was the wizards who finally turned the tide."

"You mean to say that the Plenimarans are going to use those things to summon the power of this god?"

"Something like that."

They both rode in silence for a long moment.

"Well, we'd better get moving," Micum said at last. "If you and Nysander are right, then we've only got two weeks to find this mysterious temple, if it exists, and a long way to go to get there. We'll have to hire a ship."

"I had Magyana send out word to Rhal this morning. We should be able to set sail by tomorrow or the next day."

He kicked his mount into a gallop toward the city gate. Micum spurred grimly on behind him.

• • •

Returning to the Orëska, they found Magyana and Valerius in Nysander's workroom. Seregil quickly outlined what they'd learned from Leiteus.

"So you see," he added, "it's imperative that we all be at this place together, at the given time."

"Haul Nysander off in a ship over spring seas? Are you both mad?" Valerius burst out, glaring at him and Micum. "It's absolutely out of the question. I forbid it!"

Clenching his fists behind his back, Seregil fought to remain calm as he looked to Magyana for support. "There must be some way we could make him comfortable."

But Magyana shook her head firmly. "I'm sorry, Seregil, but Valerius is quite right. Nysander must have solitude and peace to heal. Such a voyage in his present state would certainly kill him."

"Not to mention the fact that you're sailing off into the very teeth of a war," the drysian sputtered. "Even if he could stand being moved—which he can't—what if you're boarded or sunk? Bilairy's Balls, man, he's scarcely conscious more than a few minutes at a time!"

Seregil ran a hand back though his hair in exasperation. "Micum, you talk to them."

"Calm down," said Micum. "If Valerius says Nysander can't survive the voyage, then that's the end of that. But what about a translocation?"

Magyana shook her head again. "He's too weak to survive it, and even if he could, it would not be possible. Since the attack there are only three wizards left, including myself, who possess the skill to perform that spell. And it will be some time before any of us are strong enough to attempt it."

Seregil let out a frustrated growl, but Micum was still thinking. "Well, assuming that these Illiorans are on the right track with their prophecies and comets and all, then we wouldn't necessarily have to move him for almost—"

"Two weeks," cried Seregil. "Praise the Flame for hardheaded Sakoran common sense! You may have just saved us all, Micum. What do you say to that, Valerius? Would he be strong enough in two weeks?"

"With his will, it's possible," the drysian admitted grudgingly. "As for the state of his powers, though, only he could say."

Seregil gave the wizard a hopeful look. "Magyana?"

She contemplated her folded hands for a long moment, then said softly, "By then, yes, I should be able to assist him with a translocation of that distance. But the decision must be his."

Micum slapped a hand on the table and stood up. "Then it's settled. We'll sail without him and he can catch us up when the time is right."

Reaching into his purse, Seregil took out a small silver amulet, the twin of the one he'd given to Rhal.

"This will guide you to our ship, the *Green Lady*," he told Magyana, giving it to her. "There's no guarantee we'll still be with her then, but Rhal may be able to tell you where we've gone. Wait, there's another way, too."

He took a clean rag from a pile near the worktable. Pricking his thumb with his dagger, he dabbed a few spots of blood onto the cloth and knotted it tightly

"You won't miss me with that," he said. "Micum should do one, too, just to be safe. If you'll excuse me now, I want a moment with Nysander."

Magyana looked down at the stained cloth in distaste when Seregil had disappeared downstairs.

"I abhor blood magic," she said. "So does Nysander. Oh, Micum, do you really believe all this is what Nysander intended? Seregil has had so many terrible shocks."

"I don't know," Micum said quietly, pricking his own finger and staining another bit of cloth for her. "But I do know that nothing short of death is going to stop him from going on with it. If he's right, then maybe there's a chance of getting Alec back, and perhaps even stop whatever it is that the Plenimarans are up to. If he's wrong—" Micum gave a resigned shrug. "I can't just let him dash off by himself, can I?"

"And what of your own family?" asked Valerius as Micum stood to go.

For the first time that day Micum managed a wry smile. "Kari won't budge from Watermead unless the enemy's in sight. Warnik's given me his word to watch over her until I return."

The drysian smiled through his unruly beard. "A strong-minded woman, your wife. The eldest, Beka, is no different."

"By the Flame, Beka!" groaned Micum. "I promised Kari I'd ask Nysander to look for her."

"Rest yourself, Magyana," Valerius said as the wizard moved to rise. "Give me your hand, Micum, and think of your eldest daughter."

Clasping his staff in one hand, Valerius took Micum's in his other and closed his eyes. After several minutes he announced, "She is well. I see her riding with good companions."

"And Alec?" Micum asked, still gripping the drysian's hand. "Can you see anything of him?"

Valerius concentrated, frowning. "Only that he is not among the dead, nothing more. I'm sorry."

36
DARK DAYS FOR ALEC

Alec's teeth rotted and fell loose in his mouth. Hot bile rose in the back of his throat, made doubly foul by the feel of the snakes squirming in his belly. He wanted desperately to curl up, writhe away from the interminable agony, but the iron spikes driven through his hands and feet held him spread-eagled. Blind and helpless, he lay waiting for release back into the dark dreams where there was only the sighing of wind and water—

Occasionally faces would intrude on his darkness, swimming out of the murk only long enough to leer, fading back out of sight before he could put names to them.

Fevers rose, flaming across his skin to burn out every memory until nothing remained but the rush of the sea—

Alec felt the chill of a salt-laden breeze against his bare skin, but no pain. His limbs felt heavy, too heavy to move just yet, but he ran his tongue over his teeth and found them sound. How could a nightmare feel so real, he wondered, or leave him so drained and confused?

The cold breeze helped clear his mind, but the world was still rolling under him in a vaguely familiar fashion. Opening his eyes, he blinked up at broad, square-rigged sails bellied out against a noonday sky.

And two Plenimaran marines.

Scrambling up to his knees, Alec reached instinctively for his dagger, but someone had stripped him to his breechclout, leaving him helpless. The marines laughed, and he recognized them as two of the men who'd pushed him around in Wolde.

"Don't be frightened, Alec."

Alec rose slowly to his feet, too stunned to speak. Less than ten feet away, Duke Mardus leaned at his ease against the ship's rail. He'd been seated the one time Alec had seen him. He hadn't guessed how tall Mardus was. But the man's handsome, aesthetic face, closely trimmed black beard, and scarred left cheek—Alec remembered those well enough. And the smile that never quite reached his eyes.

"I trust you slept well." Impeccably dressed in leather and velvet, Mardus regarded him with all the solicitude of an attentive host.

How did I get here? Alec wondered, still at a loss for words. A few details trickled back to him: the frantic ride to Watermead, a snarling dog, unlit lanterns, hoping to find Seregil home. Beyond that, however, there was only a blank greyness tinged with dread.

"But you're cold," Mardus observed, unpinning the gold broach that secured the neck of his cloak. He motioned to the guards, who pulled Alec roughly forward and held him while Mardus swung the heavy folds around his bare shoulders.

Holding the brooch in place with one gloved hand, Mardus slid the long pin through one of the holes until its blunt point pressed against Alec's windpipe.

Terrified, Alec fixed his gaze in the buttons of Mardus' velvet surcoat and waited. The pin pressed harder against his throat, but not quite hard enough to break the skin.

"Look at me, Alec of Kerry. Come now, you mustn't be shy."

Mardus' voice was disarmingly gentle. Without wanting to, Alec found himself looking up into the man's black eyes.

"That's better." Still smiling, Mardus fixed the brooch in place. "You must not fear me. You're quite safe under my care. In fact, I shall guard you like a lion."

Alec felt someone come up behind him.

"Perhaps he does not understand his situation well enough to be properly grateful," a heavily accented voice hissed near his ear.

The speaker moved to stand by Mardus, and Alec recognized him as the silent "diplomat" who'd been with Mardus at Wolde.

"Perhaps not," Mardus said agreeably. "You must understand, Alec, that Vargûl Ashnazai was all for gutting you like a fish the moment he laid hands on you. Not an unjustified reaction, considering the trouble you and your friend have put us to over the past few months. It was I who prevented him from doing so. 'Why, he's nothing but an impressionable boy,' I said many times as we stalked the two of you through the streets of Rhíminee."

"Many times," the necromancer said with a poisonous smile. "Sometimes I fear that the softness of my Lord Mardus' heart will lead him into harm."

"And yet how else am I to feel when I see such an intelligent and enterprising young man fallen in with such company." Mardus shook his head sadly. "A renegade Aurënfaie spy, outcast from his own people to whore for the queen of a decadent land, and a wizard admitted even by his own kind to be a mad fool? 'No, Vargûl Ashnazai,' I said, 'we must first see if this poor lad can be saved.' "

Mardus grasped Alec by the shoulders, slowly pulling him close enough for Alec to feel the man's breath on his face. His eyes seemed to go an impossible shade darker as he asked, "What do you think, Alec? Can you be saved?"

Trapped in the intensity of Mardus' gaze, Alec kept silent. Despite the implicit threat behind those honeyed words, there was something dangerously compelling in the man's manner, a force of personality that left Alec feeling powerless.

"This one has a stubborn nature," the one called Vargûl Ash-nazai muttered. "I fear he will disappoint you."

"Let's not be hasty in our opinion," said Mardus. "This Seregil of Rhíminee may have some claim upon his loyalty. You did say, after all, that you believe young Alec here has Aurënfaie blood in his veins."

"I am certain of it, my lord."

"Perhaps that's the impediment. There were so many conflicting rumors around the city. Tell me, Alec, is he by chance your father? Or a half brother? Age is so difficult to gauge with these Aurënfaie and they are by nature deceitful."

"No," Alec managed at last, his voice sounding faint and childish in his ears.

Mardus raised an eyebrow. "No? But friend, certainly. He may have called you his apprentice during that unfortunate masquerade in Wolde, but your circumstances in Rhíminee belie it. So then, friend. Perhaps even lover?"

Alec felt his face go hot as the soldiers snickered.

"I recognize loyalty when I see it," Mardus said. "I admit I am impressed to find it in one so young, even if it is blind loyalty to a man who abandoned you."

"He didn't!" Alec snarled.

Mardus gestured around them at the ship, the empty sea stretching away on all sides. "Didn't he? Ah, well. I suppose it's of little consequence to me what you choose to believe. Still, you might wonder why this trusted friend of yours chose to leave you to your fate when he might have saved you."

"You lie!" Alec was trembling now. He still couldn't remember anything that had happened after his arrival at the Cockerel.

"Are you so certain?" Mardus' smile was tinged with pity. "Well, we'll speak again when you're less overwrought. Vargûl Ashnazai, would you be so kind as to assist Alec with some calming meditations?"

"Of course, my lord."

Alec tried to flinch away, but the guards held him still as the other man pressed cold, dry fingers against his cheekbone and jaw. For an instant Alec was overwhelmed by a thick, rotten odor, then a terrible blackness engulfed him, plunging him back into a morass of illness and pain where he couldn't escape the mocking echo of Seregil's long-forgotten warning, *Fall behind and I'll leave you, leave you, leave you—*

Alec awoke in the dim confines of a tiny cabin. Still panting from the residual terror of the necromancer's trance, he sat up in the narrow bunk and tried to make out his surroundings. There was no lantern, but the weak light filtering in through a grate in the cabin door was enough to illuminate the foot of another bunk against the opposite wall. Above the rush of water against the hull, he heard the distant, muffled sound of someone weeping loudly. The smell of rich broth wafted in from somewhere nearby, and he realized that he was hungry in spite of the lingering effects of the necromancer's magic.

Throwing off the thin blanket, he climbed out of the bunk, then froze. Now that his eyes had adjusted to the dim light, he could see that the other bunk was occupied. A figure lay stretched there under a blanket, face hidden in the shadows. Clearing his throat nervously, Alec reached out to touch the person's shoulder.

"Hello. Are you—"

A hand shot from beneath the blanket, grasping his wrist in a ferocious, ice-cold grip. Alec lunged back, but the other man hung on, lurching up as Alec tried to pull free.

"By the Light," Alec gasped. "Thero!"

The young wizard was as naked as Alec, and a set of branks had been fastened around his head. Iron bands encircling the lower part of his face held an iron gag piece in his mouth, while another passed tightly over the top of his head between his eyes to join the first in the back. An opening for his nose had been left in the vertical band and the whole thing was secured under his chin by a chain. When Thero tried to speak around the gag his voice was hardly intelligible. Saliva dripped from the corners of his mouth to collect in his sparse beard and Alec guessed from the look in his eyes that he was either insane or terrified.

"Ah'ek?" Thero managed, still gripping his wrist with one hand as he brought the other up to touch Alec's face. Wide iron bands inscribed with symbols encircled his wrists.

"What are you doing here?" Alec whispered in disbelief.

Thero gabbled thickly for a moment, his desperation clear. Then, releasing Alec, he beat his fists against his head until Alec had to restrain him.

"No, Thero. Stop it. Stop!" Alec shook him roughly by the shoulders. Thero's pale, bony chest heaved with emotion as he shook his head violently and tried to pull away.

"You've got to calm down and talk to me," Alec hissed, caught somewhere between anger and terror himself. "We're in one hell of a mess and we're going to need each other to get out of it. Now let me try and get this contraption off."

But the branks were locked securely in back and he had no tools to open it. He searched the cabin with the scant hope of finding something—a nail, perhaps, or a splinter of wood—to use as a makeshift pick. He found nothing except a bowl of broth by the door. Hungry as he was, he left it untouched in case it was drugged or poisoned. *Perhaps that's what's wrong with Thero,* he told himself as his stomach rumbled. The drooling creature cowering on the bunk bore little resemblance to Nysander's reserved assistant.

Giving up at last, he sat down beside Thero on the bunk. "There's nothing here. You've got to tell me what you know. Go slow so I can understand you."

Still wild-eyed, Thero nodded and said slowly around the gag, " 'Eye'ander's 'ead."

"What?" Alec gasped, praying he'd misunderstood.

" 'ysander dead. Dead!" Thero wailed, rocking violently back and forth in misery. "My fault!"

"Stop that," Alec ordered, shaking him by the shoulders. "Thero, you talk to me. What happened to Nysander? Did you see him killed or did Mardus just tell you it happened?"

"Carried me 'own, 'lack creatures—through walls, floors—!" Thero hugged himself, shuddering. " 'tacked 'rëska—'sander on the floor, they made me look. My fault, mine!"

"Why is it your fault?" Alec demanded, shaking him again. "Thero, what did you do?"

With a low moan, Thero wrenched away and curled deeper into the corner. There were long, curved scratches on his back and sides, and little crescent-shaped bruises along the tops of his shoulders.

"It was Ylinestra, wasn't it?" Alec asked, a vague, half-formed memory shifting uneasily at the back of his mind. "She did something, or you told her something?"

Thero nodded mutely, refusing to look at him.

Alec stared at him a moment longer, then rage exploded like a blazing sun in his chest. Grasping the iron band at the back of Thero's head, he yanked the young wizard out of his corner and shook him like a rat.

"You listen to me, Thero, and you listen well. If it does turn out that you betrayed us and got Nysander killed, then by all the Four I'll kill you myself and that's a promise! But I'm not sure about anything yet and I don't think you are, either. They've done something to your mind and you've got to fight it. Fight their magic and tell me what it was you said or did. What she did!"

" 'on't know," Thero whispered hopelessly, spittle running from the corners of his mouth. "She kep' me with her 'at night.

When black 'uns came, she 'eld me with 'agic. 'en she thanked me and she laughed—She *laughed*!"

Releasing Thero in disgust, Alec pressed his fists against his eyes until fiery stars danced behind his closed lids.

"Thero, what did they do to you? Why can't you use your magic?"

Thero held out one arm, showing him the strange iron band.

"These keep you from using your magic?" Alec reached out and felt the unnatural coldness of the burnished metal. Running his hands over them, he could find no sign of any seam, joint, or hinge.

"Think so—" Thero shifted uneasily, wiping at his damp beard. "Not 'ertain. So much confused, nightmares, voices! 'don't dare, A'ek, I don't dare!"

"You mean you haven't even tried?" Alec grasped Thero's arms, bringing the bands in front of his face. "You've got to try something, anything. For all we know these may just be a trick, something to cloud your mind."

Thero shrank back, shaking his head desperately.

"You have to," Alec insisted, feeling his own desperation creeping back. "We've got to get away from Mardus. There's a lot you don't know, but believe me, Nysander would want you to help me. If you want to make things right, then you've got to at least try!"

" 'ander?" Thero's chest heaved as he looked distractedly around the cabin, as if he expected to find Nysander there. " 'ander?"

Sensing a chink in whatever madness held Thero, Alec nodded encouragingly. "Yes, Thero, Nysander. Concentrate on him, his kindness, Thero, all the years you spent with him in the east tower. For the sake of the faith he placed in you, you've got to at least try. Please."

Thero twisted the edge of the blanket in his fists as tears rolled from his mad eyes. "P'rhaps," he whispered faintly, "p'rhaps—"

"Just something very small," Alec urged. "One of those little spells. What are they called?"

Thero nodded slowly, still twisting the blanket. " 'an'rips."

"That's right. Cantrips! Just a simple one, a tiny little cantrip."

Trembling visibly, Thero half closed his eyes in preparation for the spell but suddenly looked up again.

"You 'aid there's some'ing I 'on't know," he asked with a

sudden flash of his customary sharpness. "What? I's his 'sistant; why didn't he tell me?"

"I don't know," Alec confessed, getting the gist of Thero's question. "He told us—told me so little I'm not even sure what it's all about. But he swore me to secrecy. I shouldn't have said anything at all, I guess. Maybe later, when we're out of this—"

Alec trailed off, suddenly wary. Thero was watching him intently, hanging on every word. "We'll talk about it later, all right? Please, try the spell now."

" 'ell me first! Could 'elp!" Thero insisted, and this time there was no mistaking the feral intelligence in his eyes.

"No," Alec said, slowly moving away, though there was nowhere to go. "I can't tell you."

He tensed for some attack, but instead Thero slumped over sideways on the bunk like a discarded puppet.

The cabin door opened behind him and Alec felt a wave of terrible coldness roll into the room. Whirling in alarm, he confronted a walking horror.

It took a moment to see that the wizened husk had once been a woman. Lively blue eyes regarded him slyly from the masklike ruin of her face.

"That is most ungrateful of you, boy," she rasped, the cracked remnants of her lips curling back to reveal uneven yellow teeth, "but I think that you will tell *me*."

37
BEHIND THE LINES

Stretched prone on the crest of the hill, Beka and Sergeant Braknil shielded their eyes from the drizzle and surveyed the little village below. There were large granaries and warehouses there, the walls of which still had the pale gleam of new wood. Empty wagons of all descriptions stood near a sizable corral. All this, coupled with the cavalry troop billeted just outside the wooden palisade, added up to one thing: a supply depot.

"Looks like you were right, Lieutenant!" Braknil whispered, grinning wolfishly through his beard.

Satisfied with their reconnaissance, they made their way cautiously back to the oak grove where the rest of the turma was waiting.

"What's the word?" asked Rhylin.

"We found Commander Klia's adders," Braknil told him.

"A good nest of them, too," said Beka. "But only one nest, and it took us four days to do it. From the looks of it, I'd say it's just one link in a supply chain."

"You think we should look farther before we go back?" asked Corporal Kallas. He was still mourning his brother and had the look of a man who'd welcome a fight.

Beka looked around at their dirty, hopeful

faces. The depot was an important emplacement, enough of a find
to go back with now that their food was running low and the
weather had turned foul.

Her leg ached dully as she shifted her weight. The gash in her
thigh had festered just enough to kindle a fever. Though it broke
her sleep at night with confused dreams, it seemed to sharpen her
wits during the day, as fevers sometimes did.

"We'll circle wide and see if we can learn where the wagons
are coming from," she said at last.

For two days they followed the supply route as it wound south
into the steeper country above the head of the Plenimaran isthmus.
Beka kept her riders well up in the wooded hills, sending scouts
ahead and behind as they went. They spotted two separate wagon
trains heading west, but both were too heavily guarded to attack.

Their seventh day out dawned cold and foggy. Reining her
horse to the side of the steep track, Beka watched as the remains
of her turma rode past; the fog made it difficult to see more
than thirty feet in any direction and she couldn't afford to lose any
stragglers. The uncertain light and muffling effect of the mist lent
the riders a ghostly, insubstantial look.

They all rode with growling bellies. Their food was nearly
gone and game was scarce. With the rain and the plentiful mountain springs they had water enough, but hunger soon took the edge
off a soldier's strength. It would probably be wisest to turn back
today.

Just as she was about to call a halt, however, Braknil materialized out of the fog and cantered over to her.

"The scouts found a way station ahead, Lieutenant. They report
four big wagons unhitched there and only a handful of guards," he
informed Beka quietly, then added with a knowing wink, "Quite a
manageable gathering, I'd say. Especially in this weather, if you
take my meaning."

"I believe I do, Sergeant."

Leaving Rhylin in command, she followed Braknil to a stone
outcropping where Mirn was waiting with several horses.

"You can see it from just around the next bend in the trail," he
told them, his face flushed and eager beneath his shock of pale
hair. Mirn had always reminded Beka a bit of Alec, though a
taller, more muscular version.

Proceeding on foot, they found Steb keeping watch.

"You can see better now," he told them, pointing down a gap. "This breeze that's coming up should clear it off before long."

From where they stood, Beka could see a road winding through the narrow cleft of a pass. There was a way station there, an old tumble-down log building, but the stable and large corral next to it were sturdy and new. Rocky slopes rose steeply on both sides of the road, making it the only passable route of attack or escape.

"I've been watching the place," Steb told them. "I'd say there's no more than two dozen soldiers and a few wagoneers down there. Nobody's ridden in or out since we found the place an hour ago."

Judging by the activity in the yard, Beka guessed the wagoneers were getting ready to move out, though neither they nor their military escort seemed in any particular hurry. Many still lounged around the station door with trenchers and mugs. The breeze coming up the pass carried the tantalizing aroma of breakfast fires.

She studied the fog still shrouding the road leading up to the station. "If we move fast, we might get within two hundred yards of the enemy before they catch a good look at us."

"And if we circle by this trail and come in on the road from the east, chances are they'll think we're friendly forces anyway," whispered Braknil.

"Good idea. The Plenimaran cavalry columns travel at a canter in ranks of four. We'll line up in the same formation. Put anyone who's riding with Plenimaran tack in front in case they recognize the jingle of the harness."

Sergeant Braknil raised an eyebrow, looking impressed. "Who taught you to be such a sly thinker, Lieutenant?"

Beka gave him a wink. "A friend of the family."

Their ruse paid off. The Plenimarans scarcely looked up from their breakfasts as the turma came cantering toward them out of the mist. By the time they drew swords and broke into a gallop, it was already too late.

They thundered up to the station, whooping and screaming at the top of their lungs. A few of the Plenimaran soldiers stood their ground. Most broke and ran for cover in the station and outbuildings.

Galloping at full speed, the Skalans rode down the men who

stood against them. The Plenimarans put up a brief, determined fight but were no match for the flashing swords and iron-shod hooves that mowed them down. With the station's one line of defense destroyed, Beka shouted an order and the riders split into decuriae.

Braknil spotted men running for the cover of the stable and chose that as his target. Wheeling toward the low-roofed building, he and his riders drove the would-be escapees into the stable, then tossed the Plenimarans' own night lanterns into the straw piled outside the back door. Within seconds, screams rang out from the panicked horses stabled inside. Choking and cursing, those who'd taken refuge there came stumbling out again and were herded at sword point into the corral.

Rhylin and his decuria attacked the station building. Dashing up to the door, the ungainly sergeant leapt from his horse and threw himself against the door, knocking it open just as the men inside were trying to thrust the bar into place. His assault was successful, but he was nearly trampled for his efforts as the rest of his decuria, led by Kallas and Ariani, stormed in to his aid. The soldiers and wagoneers inside surrendered immediately.

Beka and a handful of riders rode off in pursuit of the Plenimarans who had fled at the first sign of attack. Most of those on foot were easily overtaken, but several who'd gotten onto horses broke away down the east road. Beka and her group took off in pursuit, but their quarry had the advantage of fresh horses and a knowledge of the country. Cursing under her breath, she turned back.

The remaining Plenimarans had been gathered in the station building.

"I took count, Lieutenant," Braknil informed her as she dismounted. "Nineteen enemy dead and fifteen taken, counting the wagoneers and stationmaster. Sergeant Rhylin's got the prisoners under guard."

Beka surveyed the bodies scattered between the buildings and the road. "Any losses for us?"

"Not a scratch," the sergeant replied happily. "Those little tricks of yours worked!"

"Good." Beka hoped her relief wasn't too obvious. "We don't want to make the same mistake as our friends in there, so post lookouts on the road. Corporal Nikides!"

"Here, Lieutenant." The young man rode over to where she stood.

"Get someone to help you check the wagons. Let's hope we haven't gone to all this trouble for a load of horseshoes and slop pails."

"Yes, Lieutenant!" Grinning, he snapped a salute and rode off again.

Inside the station, the Plenimarans sat packed together at the far end of the building's single narrow room under the watchful eyes of Rhylin's guards. Six of the captives were wagoneers; the rest wore black military tunics displaying a white castle emblem.

Rhylin snapped Beka a smart salute as she entered. "We've searched the prisoners and the buildings, Lieutenant. Nothing of note found. It looks like a routine supply train."

"Very good, Sergeant."

Beka's long red braid fell free over her shoulder as she removed her helmet. The prisoners exchanged glances and low murmurs among themselves at the sight of it. Several stared at her boldly and one spat sideways onto the floor.

Gilly moved to avenge the insult, but Beka stayed him with a glance.

"Who's the ranking officer here?" she demanded, not bothering to sheath her sword. The prisoners simply stared back at her, silent and insolent.

"Do any of you speak Skalan?"

Again the blank silence. The Plenimarans' disdain for female soldiers was legend, but this was her first exposure to it. A trickle of sweat inched down her back as all eyes turned to her.

Rider Tare, a young, red-haired squire's son with the solid build of a wrestler, stepped forward with a respectful salute. "By your leave, Lieutenant, I speak a little Plenimaran."

"Go on, then."

Tare turned and addressed the prisoners haltingly. A few snickered. None replied.

Well, I've got the badger by the hind leg, as the saying goes. Now what the hell do I do with it? Beka thought, racking her brain. The thought of Seregil's sly, lopsided grin brought her inspiration.

With a careless shrug, she said aloud, "Well, they had their chance. Sergeant Rhylin, see that they're securely bound. Sergeant Braknil, your decuria is in charge of burning the place."

A few of her own people exchanged worried looks, but the sergeants obeyed without question.

One of the wagoneers whispered excitedly to a grizzled soldier next to him. The man went an angry red, then hissed something back. Rising on one knee, the wagoneer bowed awkwardly to Beka.

"A moment, Lieutenant, I speak your language," he said in passable Skalan. "Captain Teratos says he will parley with your commanding officer as soon as he arrives."

Beka favored the Plenimaran captain with an icy look. "Wagoneer, first tell this man that I *am* the commanding officer here until the rest of our troop arrives. When my captain arrives, *she* will have less patience with him than I do. Then inform him that Skalan officers do not parley with those they have defeated. I will ask questions. He will answer them."

The wagoneer quickly interpreted Beka's words for the captain. The man stared at her for a moment, then spat wetly between his feet. This time Beka made no move to stop Gilly as he brought the flat of his sword down on the man's head.

"My men don't approve of his discourtesy, wagoneer," Beka went on calmly. "Tell him that we're hungry, and that the roasted flesh of our enemy is more succulent than pork. Sergeant Braknil, fetch the torches." Turning on her heel, she strode outside.

Braknil followed her out. "You don't really mean to burn those men?"

"Of course not, but we don't want them to know that, do we? Let's give them a few minutes to consider their situation."

Syra ran over to her just then, clutching a strip of salted fish and a cup of beer. "Lieutenant, Corporal Nikides sends you breakfast with his compliments," she said, handing them to Beka. "There's barley meal, too, but he said to tell you 'no slop jars.' "

Beka took a swallow of warm beer. "That's a relief. Spread the word; each rider is to take as much fish and meal as they can carry. We'll have to leave the beer. As soon as everyone has what they need, burn the rest. Sergeant Braknil, see that Rhylin's riders are relieved as soon as yours are supplied—"

She was interrupted by the sound of a horse coming in from the west. It was Mirn, who'd been sent out as a lookout.

"Enemy riders headed this way!" he shouted to her. "Cavalry column, two score riders at least."

"Damn!" Motioning the others to silence, she listened intently for a few seconds; no sound of the approaching riders yet. The mist was still with them, but the smell of the burning stable would carry for a mile. "Spread the word, Mirn. Everyone grabs an extra horse and food and heads east. If anyone gets separated, they're to circle back and head for the regiment with word of what we found. Go!"

Rhylin came running out of the station with his people. "What about the prisoners?"

"Leave them. Get out of here!" The staccato rumble of the approaching column was audible now.

Leaping onto her horse, Beka galloped to the wagon and yanked out the first sack her hand fell on. An arrow sang over her head as she slung the bag over her saddlebow. Another shaft thudded into the side of the wagon as she wheeled her mount, galloping down the eastern road just as the first of the Plenimaran outriders burst out of the thinning mist.

Hoping the fire at the station would halt at least some of the enemy, Beka led her riders deeper into Plenimaran territory.

38

THE GREEN LADY

It was silent and dark under the water. Seregil could see the bright silver surface wavering above him as he struggled, but something in the depths below gripped his ankle, holding him just out of reach.

A tall, dark figure loomed over him, distorted by the surface refraction. It saw Seregil floating helplessly below and beckoned to him.

With a final, frantic kick, he managed to get his face above water just long enough to fill his bursting lungs. As he did so, he looked up into the face of the man standing over him. The lips moved as he told Seregil what he must do.

He couldn't understand the words, but they filled him with such horror all the same that he cried out and water poured into his mouth as the unseen force below pulled him under again—

"Seregil! Seregil, wake up, damn it."

Gasping for air, Seregil focused on Micum's worn, freckled face, the ship, the open sea around them.

The ship. The open sea.

"Oh, shit, not again," Seregil groaned, pressing his fingers against his throbbing temples. Over his friend's broad shoulder, he saw a few sailors gathered nervously nearby, craning their necks for a glimpse of him.

"Did I—?"

Micum nodded. "They heard you clear back to the stern this time. This is the third time."

"Fourth." In the week since they'd set sail, the dream—whatever it was, since he couldn't recall it when he woke—had come more often. Worse yet, he was beginning to nod off at odd times during the day to have it, this time in broad daylight right here at the foot of the bow platform.

"Any man with time on his hands can report to me for extra duty," barked Captain Rhal, scattering the knot of gawkers as he stumped up the deck.

Reaching Micum and Seregil, he lowered his voice to a growl. "You said you'd keep to your cabin after the last time. The men are beginning to talk. What am I supposed to tell them?"

"Whatever you can," Micum replied, helping Seregil to his feet.

"Those two who were with you on the *Darter*, can they still be trusted?" Seregil asked.

"I've told them to keep their mouths shut about that and they will." Rhal paused, still frowning. "But Skywake's muttering about you being a jinx, a stormcrow. He knows better than to say it outright but the others are starting to sense it."

Seregil nodded resignedly. "I'll keep out of sight."

Micum followed as he headed for the companionway. "By the Flame, you'll get us pitched over the side for certain if you don't mind yourself," he muttered. "These sailors are worse than soldiers when it comes to anything that looks like an omen."

Seregil ran a hand back through his lank hair. "What did I say this time?"

"Same as before, just 'No, I can't' over and over until I got to you. I suppose I shouldn't have left you when I saw that you'd dozed off." Entering their cabin, Micum dropped onto his bunk. "Did you remember any of it this time?"

"No more than before," Seregil sighed, stretching out on his own bunk with a flask of ale. "I'm drowning, and I see someone looking down at me through the water. That's all I can ever recall, but it scares the hell out of me. The closer we get to Plenimar, the worse it feels."

"I'm not so happy about it myself," Micum said with a wry grin.

Since rounding the southern tip of Skala two days before,

they'd spotted half a dozen enemy vessels in the distance, and outrun two of these. This was another point of contention with the crew; there would be no bounty to divide up if they didn't engage.

"You don't suppose Nysander could be trying to reach you this way?" Micum asked without much hope.

"I wish it was, but I think I'd feel it if it was that." He took a sip of ale and stared disconsolately up at the cabin ceiling. "Illior's Light, Micum, what I *do* feel is a wrongness in him not being here. And Alec."

Seregil reached inside his coat, felt the dagger hilt there, and the soft lock of hair. If they were too late, if Alec died, was dead already—

"You never said anything to him, did you?" asked Micum. "About your feelings for him, that is?"

"No, I never did."

His friend shook his head slowly. "That's a pity."

Aura Elustri málreis, Seregil prayed silently, clenching the hilt until his knuckles ached. *Aura Elustri watch over him and keep him until I can plunge this same knife into the hearts of his enemies.*

The pounding of feet on deck overhead woke them just after dawn the next morning.

"Enemy sail off the port bow!" a lookout shouted.

Snatching up their swords, Seregil and Micum ran above.

Standing at the helm, Rhal pointed toward the northeastern horizon, where a black and white striped sail was just visible. "The bastards must've sighted us last night and trailed us."

"Can we outrun them?" asked Micum, shading his eyes. At this distance he could already make out the vessel itself, running low and fast over the waves.

"From the cut of their sails, I'd say not. Looks like we'll have to fight this time," Rhal replied with a certain grim satisfaction. "I know your feelings on this, Seregil, but it'd be best if we take the offensive."

Seregil said nothing for a moment, but appeared to be studying the oncoming vessel.

"The sails on that vessel aren't so different from ours, are they?" he asked.

"No, we're rigged out about the same."

"So you could sail this ship with those sails?"

Rhal grinned, catching his drift. "In the proper navy they'd call that a dishonorable trick."

"Which is why I stick with privateers," Seregil replied, grinning back. "The closer we get to Plenimar, the less attention we'd attract, at least from a distance."

"By the Old Sailor, Lord Seregil, you've the makings of a great pirate in you. Trouble is, if you want the sails off her, we can't use our fire baskets."

"Keep it as a last resort and throw everything else you've got at her."

"All hands, prepare for battle," Rhal sang out, and the call was passed down the deck.

The crew of the *Lady* sprang to action with a will. The pilot hove the ship around to meet the Plenimaran challenger. Hatches were dragged back, the catapults fitted into their bracing sockets along the deck and on the battle platforms fore and aft, and baskets of stones, chain, and lead balls hauled up from the hold. Rhal's archers took their places and the edge of every sword and cutlass was given a final touch of the thumb.

"She's showing the battle flag, Captain," the lookout shouted as they bore down on the enemy ship.

"Run up the same!" answered Rhal.

Micum lost sight of Seregil in the general confusion, but his friend reappeared moments later with Alec's bow.

"Here," he said, handing it to Micum without meeting his eye. "You're better with this than I am."

Before Micum could think of a reply, Seregil hurried off to join one of the catapult crews.

The Plenimaran ship swooped toward them across the waves like an osprey, closing the distance rapidly.

"A warship, Captain, and they got fire baskets lit!" the sharp-eyed lookout called down.

"How are they set?" Rhal bellowed back.

"Two catapults to a side, fore and aft! Fire baskets to the fore."

"Keep at her bow, helmsman!"

As the ships closed within a few hundred yards of each other, archers on both sides took aim. Standing with Rhal's bowmen along the port rail, Micum listened to the bowstring song of Alec's Black Radly as he loosed shaft after shaft at the enemy. The song was quickly answered. Plenimaran arrows whined and buzzed across the water at him like angry dragonflies. Welken, the faithful lookout, crashed to the deck with a shaft through his chest. Nettles was hit in the leg but kept on shooting. Others fell and the shouting and screams on both sides echoed over the water between the vessels.

No shortage of arrows, Micum thought, pulling enemy shafts from the deck and rail and sending them back the way they'd come.

The heavy thud of the catapults sounded fore and aft as catapults on both sides let fly. Flaming balls of a pitchy concoction known as Sakor's Fire sailed across the *Lady*'s bow, narrowly missing her forward sail. The *Lady* responded with double loads of chain that clawed through the enemy's rigging, collapsing one of her mainsails like a broken wing. Panicked shouts rang out on the enemy ship as she slowed.

"Hard about and give her another!" Rhal ordered. Skywake fought the rudder to port and the *Lady* leaned dangerously into the waves as they wheeled to press their advantage. A groaning volley from the port catapults smashed the Plenimarans' forward mast and the enemy ship yawed, wallowing in the swells.

Like a wounded dragon, the Plenimarans released a second volley of Sakor's Fire as the *Lady* passed. This one found its mark, striking the forward platform. An oily sheet of flame engulfed a catapult and its crew. Burning men fell writhing to the deck or leapt overboard. Sailors tore the covers from sand barrels lashed against the rails, smothering the flames before they could spread.

Choking on the smell of burning flesh, Seregil dropped his load of chain and ran up the platform ladder to help drag the wounded away from the flames.

"What now?" he called, spotting Rhal on the deck below.

"Hard around, strike sails and board 'em," Rhal yelled. "Makewell, Coryis, tell your group to stand ready with the grapples."

A final volley of stones from a Plenimaran catapult shattered the *Lady*'s main mast as she bore down on them. Dodging the fallen spars, the grappling crew tossed their hooks across and hauled the two ships together before the Plenimarans could cut the ropes. As soon as the bulwarks were close enough to leap, Rhal's fighters boarded the other ship and waded into the black-uniformed marines massed to repel them.

From his vantage point on the platform, Seregil scanned the fray for Micum's red mane. As expected, his companion was already across in the thickest of the fight.

The gods chose you well for the Vanguard, Seregil thought, shinnying down the ladder and elbowing his way to the rail. Reaching it, he did his best to ignore the foaming chasm that opened and closed beneath him as the two disabled vessels wallowed in the swells. He made his jump, drew his sword, and was immediately confronted by a Plenimaran sailor armed with a cutlass.

The battle soon spread to both ships. Somehow in the confusion, Micum and Seregil found each other and fought shoulder to shoulder, back to back, as the precariously balanced fight raged on.

For a time it seemed that it would go on indefinitely, but in the midst of the melee one of Rhal's seamen killed the captain of the Plenimaran ship. At almost the same moment, Micum struck down the commander of the marines. Confusion spread among the remaining enemy and they finally surrendered.

A cheer went up from the *Lady* as the surviving enemy sailors and soldiers threw down their weapons in surly submission. Whooping and howling their triumph, Rhal's men surged forward to loot the vanquished ship.

Exhausted, Seregil and Micum left them to it and jumped back aboard the *Lady.*

"By the Flame, that was a proper fight," Micum gasped, nudging a severed hand out of the way with his foot before collapsing on a bulkhead.

Looking his friend over, Seregil saw that Micum had come out with no more than a cut over one eye. He'd taken a shallow cut across the shoulder himself. Stripping off his tunic and shirt, he glanced at it, then held a wad of cloth against it to stanch the bleeding.

"Too close quarters for my taste," he said, collapsing on the deck with his back to the bulkhead.

Rhal appeared from out of the surrounding confusion and strode over to where they sat. "Well, we caught your ship for you but there's still better than twenty of her crew left standing," he informed Seregil. "I know we don't want to be weighed down with prisoners, but I'll tell you straight that I won't be a party to the execution of beaten men."

"Neither would I," Seregil told him wearily. "I say strip whatever we need off her, take the sails, and set the crew adrift on her with food and water. How long will repairs to the *Lady* take?"

Rhal rubbed his jaw, looking around at the damage. "We'll have to step a new mast and rig the new sails. No sooner than sunup tomorrow."

"How many days to Plenimar?"

Rhal eyed the sky. "Barring foul weather, I'd say three days, maybe four. Running with Plenimaran sails could save us a fight or two."

Seregil looked to Micum, but the big man merely shrugged.

"Do it, then," Seregil told the captain. "And put the Plenimarans to work, too."

39
TORMENT

ands. Hands on him, touching, seeking, tormenting.

Alec wrapped his arms around his knees, curling tightly in the darkness of the tiny cabin as he fought to block out the memory of being touched and wishing he still had Thero for company. He'd seen no sign of the young wizard since that first night on board the *Kormados*.

Mardus and his people were subtle in their methods; in all the terrible time since his capture they hadn't once broken the skin, or drawn so much as a drop of blood. But inside he hurt.

Oh, yes. He hurt very much.

The dyrmagnos Irtuk Beshar, a walking nightmare, had straddled him with her withered hams, flaking fingers scrabbling over him in a grotesque parody of lust as she ripped her way into his mind, raping the memories from him. She'd kissed him afterward, thrusting a tongue like a ragged strip of moldy leather against his clenched teeth.

The necromancer, Vargûl Ashnazai, assisted her in these interrogations and Alec soon came to fear him on a deeper level than he did the dyrmagnos or Mardus.

The former carried out her hallucinatory tortures with zest, but as soon as she'd finished,

Alec seemed to cease to exist in her mind. Mardus was more difficult to read. It was he who directed the tortures and put the questions to Alec, his eyes flat and soulless, his voice as gentle as a
father's as he named the next obscenity to be carried out. Otherwise, however, he treated Alec with a peculiar mix of distance and
solicitude that bordered on courtliness. In the worst moments of
torment, Alec sometimes caught himself inexplicably looking to
Mardus for rescue.

Ashnazai was different. In the presence of others, the necromancer maintained an impassive demeanor. Left alone with Alec,
the searing hatred spilled out like acid.

"You and your vile companion cost me great status that night
in Wolde," he'd hissed in Alec's ear as the boy lay trembling in
the darkness after one of the dyrmagnos' assaults. "At first I
thought only of killing you, but now, you see, I am given by the
Beautiful One to relish my revenge."

And relish it he did, until Alec came to dread the sight of him
more than any of the others. Ashnazai's attacks left no marks,
drew no blood. Instead, he salted his spells with lurid descriptions
of the murders he'd helped carry out at the Cockerel.

"It's a pity you didn't arrive earlier that night," he told Alec.
"The old woman never said a word, but how that foolish son
begged. And the girl! She stayed proud right up until they hacked
off the old bitch's head, then she screamed, those great breasts of
hers heaving. The men wanted to take her right there on the
bloody floor—"

Held silent and immobile by the magic, Alec could only
shudder as Ashnazai passed a clammy hand over his chest, then
traced a hard line down his breastbone. "Did you ever take her on
that floor, boy? No? Ah, well, I suppose other things happened
there, eh? But then, *snik, snik, snik,* like so we had the heads off
for the mantel decoration. I must say, your reaction was all that I'd
have hoped for. I nearly added your head to the collection, but
then I thought of a more—how would you say?"

The necromancer traced the line down Alec's chest a second
time with a look of almost dreamy pleasure. "A more *satisfying*
revenge. You shall pay for the difficulties you made, and be of
great use."

The implication was clear enough. Thinking of the bodies
Micum and Seregil had seen, with their chests split open, ribs

pulled back on either side like wings, Alec wished they had killed
him that first night.

The rounds of torture continued for several days and when
they'd finished with him, Alec finally understood why Nysander
had told Seregil and him so little. They wrung everything from
him, though it was nothing more than the fragment of the
prophecy.

"There now. Well done, Alec," Mardus said, smiling down at
him when the dyrmagnos had finished. "But your Guardian is
dead, this mysterious band of four he spoke of sundered, broken.
Poor Seregil. Even if he did desert you in the end, he must be
feeling a bit guilty at having brought such destruction down on so
many of his friends."

Torn loose from any shred of hope or pride, Alec could only
turn his face away and weep.

After the torture ceased, the soldiers became Alec's chief
source of daily misery. Among them were Mardus' captain,
Tildus, and the men-at-arms who'd bullied him in Wolde. With
Seregil's training to guide him, he looked for a weak link among
them, a man with some fatal streak of sympathy, but Mardus had
chosen his personal guard with care.

A harsh, brutal lot, they'd crowded to the grate to listen when
he was tortured. Now they were the ones who dragged him above
for the daily airings on deck that Mardus insisted upon. They
stood over him at meals, sniggered when he begged for a pail to
relieve himself. Few of them spoke any Skalan, but they managed
to get their crude jests and insults across. A few of them made free
with their hands, too, and laughed when he lashed out at them.

The worst among them was a hairy, muscular brute called
Gossol. During the brief struggle at the Cockerel the night of his
capture, Alec had smashed him in the mouth with the hilt of
his sword and broken off the man's front teeth. Gossol held a
grudge over it and made a special effort to torment him at every
opportunity.

On the morning of Alec's sixth day aboard, Gossol showed up
alone to escort him above. One look was enough to make Alec
brace for trouble.

"Come you, man child," Gossol ordered in broken Skalan. The stumps of his broken front teeth showed as he leered slyly and held up a cloak, the only garment Alec was allowed except for his clout.

Alec understood. He'd have to go get it.

"Come quick, not *seshka* Mardus keep wait," Gossol chided.

"Toss it here," Alec said, holding out his hand.

Gossol's grin widened dangerously. Leaning against the door frame, he gave the cloak a taunting shake. "No. You come, man child. Now."

Getting to his feet, Alec cautiously reached for the cloak. Gossol snatched it away and laughed as Alec jumped back.

"What? You afraid of Gossol, little man child?" He offered the cloak, pulled it back again with a sneer, then advanced on Alec, backing him into the narrow space between the bunk and the wall. "You be afraid, good. You break mouth of Gossol. Think whores like this mouth now? Eh? You know whore, I think." Gossol made a lewd gesture. "Whores don't like this broken mouth. Maybe you like, eh?"

Shoving Alec back against the wall hard enough to knock the breath out of him, he pinned him there with the weight of his body and kissed him savagely on the mouth. Alec struggled furiously, but Gossol held him fast with one hand and ran the other up Alec's belly to his nipple and gave it a vicious twist.

With a snarl, Alec gave up trying to push the heavy man off and instead bit him on the lip.

Gossol pulled away and drew back his fist, but Alec beat him to the punch. The moment his arms were free, he drove his fist into the startled guard's face and felt the satisfying crunch of bone as Gossol's nose splintered.

Maddened, he grappled with Alec again, throwing him back onto the hard bunk and locking a hand around his windpipe. As Alec fought for breath he heard someone else storm in, cursing in Plenimaran.

Tildus dragged the enraged soldier off and struck him hard across the jaw before pushing him into the arms of the other soldiers waiting at the door.

"Hell damn little bastard fool!" Tildus shouted, seeing blood on Alec's face and chest. He barked an order to another soldier in the companionway, then rounded on Alec again. "If any of this is yours, you dead as Gossol. No good if damaged. Mardus slice you up like an eel, eat your *rezhari* for dinner!"

Someone fetched a bucket of water and a rag and Tildus set about sponging the blood off Alec and looking for wounds.

As the guards pulled him this way and that, Alec considered what the captain had just let slip; Mardus wanted him with a whole skin, no blood spilled. That explained why they'd tortured him in the manner they had, but not why it was necessary.

When Tildus had finished, he pushed Alec back onto the bunk and threw him the cloak. "You lucky bastard today. No cuts."

"Very lucky indeed."

Looking past Tildus and the guards, Alec saw Mardus standing in the doorway with Vargûl Ashnazai.

"There has been some unpleasantness, I understand," Mardus continued, giving Tildus an ominous look.

The captain rattled off a terse reckoning in his own tongue. Mardus answered curtly in the same, and motioned to the necromancer.

Smiling thinly, Vargûl Ashnazai made his own inspection of Alec. "The boy remains unblemished, my lord."

"I'm glad to hear it. It would have been a great pity to have him come so close to our destination and then go to waste. Come, Alec, walk with me. There's something I think you'll enjoy."

Alec doubted it, but there was no choice but to obey. Under close guard, he followed Mardus above.

It was an achingly beautiful day. The sky arched over the rolling sea like a deep blue bowl. The ship cut through the white-capped waves, her striped sails filled by a sweet following wind that sang through the yards and seemed to cleanse some of the stench of captivity from his skin.

A large square of white canvas had been nailed to the deck just below the forward battle platform. Irtuk Beshar knelt at the center of it in an attitude of meditation, her hideous hands curled on her knees.

For the first time, Alec saw how most of the sailors and marines gave her a wide berth. Those who had to pass her kept their distance and averted their eyes.

This was also the first time he'd been able to observe her with any detachment. As usual, she wore rich, elaborate robes that contrasted hideously with her scabrous head and hands. A few wisps of long dark hair still clung to her scalp, and over it she wore a sort of veil fashioned from tiny gold chains and beads. Kneeling there in the bright sunshine, she looked as fragile as the dried carapace of a locust, but Alec knew better all too well. In the Orëska museum he'd seen the hands of another dyrmagnos, who'd been hacked to pieces and scattered. Even after a century, those hands still moved. Looking down at the small figure still meditating in front of him, Alec shuddered, wondering what the true extent of her power was.

Captain Tildus shouted something in Plenimaran and a contingent of marines lined up in two ranks flanking the square of canvas. A few sailors drifted over, but not many. Mardus nodded to Alec's guards and they moved him in front of the soldiers to the left.

Vargûl Ashnazai went below through a different hatchway. While he was gone, guards brought up another prisoner and stood with him opposite Alec.

It was Thero.

Alec's relief at seeing him was short-lived, however. The young wizard's face was as vacant as before beneath the iron bands of the branks, and there was the gleam of madness in his wide, staring eyes. A grizzled man in nondescript robes stood just behind him; another necromancer, he guessed.

Ashnazai returned, followed by two marines carrying a large chest on carrying poles. The box and poles were both covered with gold and unfamiliar symbols. This was set down in front of the dyrmagnos. As the others began chanting, Ashnazai opened the chest and lifted out a crystal diadem that glittered in the sunlight.

"Behold the Crown," he intoned reverently, placing it on the canvas before Irtuk Beshar.

The sight of it wrenched at Alec's heart. This was the mysterious object Seregil had risked his life to find for Nysander.

Ashnazai next lifted out a bowl made of crudely fired clay and placed it inside the circlet. "Behold the Cup!"

Last came a loop of golden wire on which had been strung a number of wooden disks. "Behold the Eyes of Seriamaius!"

Alec let out an involuntary gasp as the dyrmagnos began placing them, one by one, inside the cup.

Mardus turned to Alec. "You recognize those, I'm sure. Just think, if the two of you hadn't stolen one, you and poor Thero would not be standing here now. All those lives lost, all that destruction, Alec, because of that one impetuous act. Ah, but I'm forgetting that it was *Seregil* who committed the actual theft. That's what you told Irtuk Beshar, that you simply helped. But it all comes out the same in the end, doesn't it. Here you are with me, and there he is, safely back in Rhíminee, no doubt thinking himself very lucky. Can you still be loyal to this faithless friend of yours?"

"Yes." Alec met Mardus' gaze levelly in a show of bravado he didn't feel. Past Mardus, past the ship's rail and out over the wide sea he could see the tiny dot of an island on the horizon, too far away to be of any use.

Just like Seregil.

A wave of longing rolled over Alec, bringing the sting of tears to his eyes. All those days with Seregil taken for granted—the memory of them made him ache as he stood stranded among these enemies.

The dyrmagnos placed her withered hands over the crown for a moment, then called out harshly in her own tongue. There was a scuffling sound from belowdecks, followed by a terrified cry. A moment later Gossol was hauled on deck by several soldiers. Bootless and stripped to the waist, he looked around wildly at the gathering before him. When he saw the dyrmagnos, however, he went ashen, his great barrel chest heaving in voiceless terror.

"We were debating the choice of victim, but you have spared us the tiresome inconvenience of a lottery," Mardus informed Alec pleasantly. "This is only a preliminary sacrifice, of course. The blood of this ignorant lump has neither the power nor purity of, say, a half Aurënfaie boy or an Orëska wizard, but it's sufficient for our purposes today."

"That's why I'm still alive?" Alec managed, his voice scarcely more than a dry croak.

"Certainly," Mardus assured him, as if promising him some gift. "You and Thero are being reserved for the supreme moment. The power of your blood, Alec! The long years sacrificed. Yours will be deaths of highest honor. You should pay careful attention to this ceremony. Yours will be very much the same."

Gossol was thrown down on his back and held by four marines marked apart from their fellows by white headbands. A fifth man knelt holding a gag across the condemned man's mouth.

In the midst of his fear, Gossol suddenly locked eyes with Alec and shot him a look of pure hatred. The power of it tightened

Alec's throat and he quickly averted his eyes, hating the guilt washing through him.

As the incomprehensible chanting went on, he looked instead at Thero, trying to guess what was going on in the wizard's addled mind. Thero stood motionless, locked mute by whatever magicks the necromancers had placed over him. Only the spasmodic twitching of his fingers clutching the front of his cloak suggested that he comprehended anything around him.

Irtuk spoke again and the second necromancer lifted something from where she sat. As he passed it to Ashnazai, Alec saw it was a strange axlike weapon. The heavy, curving head had been chipped out of black obsidian and bound onto an iron haft. Despite its obvious weight, Vargûl Ashnazai raised it above his head with practiced ease. With no other paean than Gossol's strangled scream, he struck and the black blade cleaved open the doomed man's breastbone as neatly as a wood cutter would split an oak stave.

Alec turned his head quickly, squeezing his eyes shut until his head throbbed. But he could not escape the sounds that followed. Gossol's screams rose to a squeal before they choked off to a gurgle. There was the dry-stick sounds of bones breaking, and the wet suck of a carcass being opened. Eyes still closed, Alec remembered the feel of Vargûl Ashnazai's cold finger tracing a line down his bare chest.

He suddenly felt very light. Opening his eyes, he saw the sanded planks of the deck rushing up to meet him.

40

URGAZHI

Beka's scouts spotted the convoy of horse-
drawn wagons that morning and trailed it
as it wended south through the coastal foot-
hills. There were only ten of them, Gilly
reported, and only one decuria of cavalry to
guard them, a fact that confirmed Beka's
assumption that they were deep in the Plenimarans' northern territory now.

The country they'd come into was steep and
well wooded. Beka let the scouts keep the
wagons in sight, biding her time until they
stopped for the night.

The wagoneers made camp in a little forest
hollow by a stream just before sundown.
Leaving her main group of riders a quarter of a
mile down the road, Beka chose her fastest runners, Zir, Tobin, and Jareel, to accompany her,
and left Rhylin with orders to disrupt the camp
as soon as she had accomplished her mission.

Darkness fell, and the wagoneers lit cook
fires for the evening meal. Their escort posted a
few guards up and down the road.

Beka and her raiders stole through the darkness toward the supply wagons, each of them
armed with jars of firestones they'd captured in
a similar raid two days before. Reaching the
wagons, Beka looked underneath the nearest

and saw unsuspecting wagoneers cooking their evening meal less than twenty feet away.

With Zir keeping watch, Beka and the others split up and scattered firestones over the crates and bales in the wagon beds. Ribbons of smoke curled up quickly, but the wind was in their favor, blowing it away from the camp.

Rhylin had been watching for it as his signal, however. Beka's group had hardly finished their work before a frantic whinnying came from the Plenimaran horses picketed nearby.

Whooping and waving torches, Rhylin and his decuria drove the draft animals into the camp, scattering startled soldiers and drivers. Flames shot up in the wagons, adding to the confusion.

Before the Plenimaran guards had time to act, Braknil's decuria charged in with bows and loosed a hail of arrows to cover the retreat of the others. Beka and her group skirted the camp to meet Tealah, who was holding horses for them down the road.

An enemy shaft nicked Zir in the shoulder as he swung up into the saddle. Tobin took an arrow through the heart before he'd reached his horse.

Beka saw him fall but there was nothing she could do but look after the living.

"Retreat! Come on, before they get their horses back," she yelled. A Plenimaran swordsman charged at her, only to fall with a Skalan arrow in his back.

Leaving the camp in flames behind them, her riders thundered back down the dark road with victorious whoops and catcalls. Among the last to leave, Beka listened to the Plenimaran's angry outcry with satisfaction.

"Do you know what they called us?" Tare called out with a wild laugh as they rode away. "*Urgazhi!* Wolf demons."

An eerie chorus of yells and wolfish howls erupted from the others.

"Well done, *Urgazhi* Turma!" Beka laughed, as elated as the others.

"I say we've earned the honor," Sergeant Braknil added.

They were like wolves now—traveling by night, employing stealth and speed to attack any target weak enough to be taken, then fading back into the darkness before the enemy could get a clear look at how few of them there actually were.

Over the past two weeks they'd made nine raids, harrying

small convoys, burning barns and way stations, and fouling wells as they worked their way south through the hills toward the sea.

Their plan was to strike the coast and follow it north again in the hope of meeting a friendly force.

What Beka wasn't certain of was just how far south their raiding had driven them, or where the Skalan line currently was. Whatever the case, they'd have to fight like true *urgazhi* to get back.

"It's only me, Lieutenant!"

Beka opened her eyes to find Rhylin's long, homely face just inches above hers.

"It's almost sundown. You said to wake you," he said, hunkering down beside her.

Beka sat up and rubbed a hand over her face. "Thanks. I wasn't sleeping so well anyway."

Rhylin handed her his drinking skin, then ran a hand over the brown scruff of beard covering his jaw. "The fever hasn't come back on you, has it?"

"No, the leg's fine." Beka took a drink and handed it back.

They'd made camp in a beech grove. Buds were just breaking out on the branches overhead and through them she could see the first golden streaks of sunset.

"But you've still got the dreams, eh?" he asked, then shrugged when Beka glanced up sharply. "You've been thrashing and muttering some in your sleep."

"Well, I wish you'd tell me what I'm saying," Beka replied, hoping it was dark enough not to betray the color that rose in her cheeks. "I don't remember a damn thing when I wake up. Any word from Mirn or Gilly yet?"

"That's what I came to report. Kallas and Ariani just got back from tracking them. It looks like they've been captured."

"Damn." From what they'd seen so far, the Plenimarans weren't keeping prisoners alive, and her *urgazhi* had suffered losses enough already.

Getting to her feet, she glanced around the clearing. In Braknil's decuria only Kallas, Ariani, Arbelus, and one-eyed Steb were left. Rhylin had Nikides, Syra, Tealah, Jareel, Tare, Marten, Kaylah, and Zir. Of those, Tealah had suffered a sword cut during the third raid and couldn't use her left arm. Zir and Jareel had festering wounds, and Steb, still recovering from the loss of an eye, had a bad case of the scours.

Now Mirn and Gilly were gone.

"Who's out now?" she asked.

"Syra has the watch. Arbelus and Steb went scouting about an hour ago."

"Go wake the others and tell them to eat quickly. We ride as soon as it's full dark."

Rhylin gave a quick salute and started around the camp. Beka let out a slow, exasperated breath. She'd hoped the others hadn't noticed her nightly struggles. At least it had been Rhylin who'd brought it to her attention. Despite his ungainly appearance, he'd proven a good choice for sergeant. He had a calm steadiness about him that only seemed to increase under adversity.

Still, the last thing any of them needed right now was an officer who had bad dreams behind lines; yelling in your sleep was a good way to bring the enemy down on your neck. Rubbing her eyes again, she tried to remember what the dream had been, but nothing would come except a vague feeling of anxiety.

Giving up, she turned her thoughts to more practical matters. Reaching for her tucker sack, she dipped out a cupful of soaked meal and hastily downed it. Coarse and full of grit, the barley meal they'd captured in the last raid was hard on both teeth and stomach. Most of the time they couldn't chance a fire to boil it into porridge. Instead, they threw it into a leather bag with some water and fragments of dried fish for a few hours until it swelled into a gluey mass Nikides had dubbed "broken tooth pudding."

They were just saddling up for the night's ride when Steb came riding back.

"We found Mirn and Gilly, Lieutenant!" he informed Beka.

"Praise Sakor! Where?" Beka demanded as the others crowded around in uneasy silence.

"There's a Plenimaran column ahead about two miles. They've just stopped to make camp for the night. It's big, Lieutenant, fifty soldiers at least. And maybe twice that in prisoners marching afoot in chains."

"Prisoners?" Rhylin raised an eyebrow. "That's the first we've heard of that. And you're sure you saw Gilly and Mirn?"

Steb nodded, his good eye blazing with grief and anger. "The whoreson bastards planked them."

Braknil cursed, then spat angrily over his left shoulder.

"What do you mean, planked?" Beka demanded.

"It's an old Plenimaran soldier's trick, Lieutenant," the sergeant scowled. "You take a man, tie a plank across his shoulders, and then nail his hands to it."

Beka stood silent for a moment, feeling a black void opening in her heart. They'd been lucky so far, facing no more than a decuria or two of fighters and panicked wagoneers. And so far, they'd left no one behind but the dead. This was different.

She gripped her sword hilt and growled, "Let's go have a look."

Taking Braknil and Kallas, Beka followed Steb. *What must this be like for him?* she wondered, stealing a look at Steb's drawn face; the bond between him and Mirn was strong. The two were always together, whether it was around the fire at night, or fighting side by side like twin avenging furies. They usually took scout duty together, too. What had happened today?

The young rider remained grim and silent as he led them to the little hillside gully where Arbelus was keeping watch. Less than a mile below, the scattered campfires of the Plenimaran column winked in the darkness. Beyond the camp, the black expanse of the Inner Sea glimmered with the light of the first stars. The wind was coming off the water tonight and Beka caught a faint, unsettling sound on the air. After a moment she realized it was only the distant crash of surf growling like a hound in its sleep against the rocky cliffs.

"There's an old road that runs along above the shore," Arbelus told her. "They set up camp on the landward side of it."

"You're certain our men are still alive?" Beka asked, squinting down at the pattern of campfires.

"They were at sundown. I saw the guards prodding them in with the other prisoners for the night."

Beka chewed at her lip, still glowering at the enemy encampment. At last she turned to Braknil. "It's the first real force we've encountered so far. What do you think? Any chance of grabbing them out tonight?"

Braknil scratched under his bearded chin a moment, looking down at the fires. "I'd say not much, Lieutenant. They'll have the perimeter sewed tighter than a virgin's bodice. Even if we did manage to slip in, we'd never fight our way out if they tumbled to us."

Beka let out an exasperated sigh. "Sakor's Fist, first they aren't taking prisoners, then they've got a couple hundred. And where in hell did they get that many this far inside their own borders?"

Braknil shrugged. "That's a good question."

Arbelus looked up in surprise. "I never thought of that. But I'll tell you something even stranger."

"What's that?"

"Before they settled down for the night, they were marching north."

"North!" Beka exclaimed softly. "The Mycenian border can't be more than fifty miles from here, and not a single Plenimaran city in between. If they're going to all the trouble to take that many prisoners, why on earth aren't they taking them south where they could use them?"

She rested a hand on Steb's rigid shoulder. "Still, it makes our task easier. We planned to turn north along the coast anyway. We'll trail them, *haunt* them, by the gods, and watch for a chance to grab Mirn and Gilly!"

41
PECULIAR HOSPITALITY

The guards handled Alec with superstitious care after Gossol's sacrifice, but they clearly blamed him for the death of their "soldier brother."

Ashnazai came less often, too, although he still paid occasional visits in the middle of the night. Starting up out of some nightmare, Alec would smell the man's unclean odor in the darkness, feel the touch of cold fingers on his skin as Ashnazai plunged him into another punishing miasma of torment.

Locked alone in his tiny dark cabin, Alec grew increasingly despondent. He'd searched in vain for some means of escape, even if it meant throwing himself overboard, but there was none. Left with nothing to do, he slept a great deal, but his dreams were full of violence and omens. The dream of the headless arrow came far more often now, sometimes twice in one day.

Under such desperate conditions, he grew to look forward to his daily walk on deck with Mardus. Despite his chilling revelation at the ceremony, Mardus continued to treat him with a strange sort of solicitude, as if he enjoyed Alec's company.

At midmorning each day Alec was given a cloak and escorted above under guard. Fair weather or foul, Mardus would be waiting for him, ready to hold forth on whatever subject had taken his fancy that day. To Alec's considerable surprise, Mardus was a remarkably intelligent, well-spoken man, with interests as broad and varied as Seregil's. He was as likely to launch into a discussion of Plenimaran war tactics or a detailed comparison of Plenimaran and Skalan musical conventions, although his discourses often took a darker turn.

"Torture is an undervalued art form," he remarked as they strolled up and down with Vargûl Ashnazai one brisk morning. "Most people assume that if you cause enough pain you will achieve your end. While this may be true in some cases, I've always found that outright brutality is often counterproductive. Consider your own recent experience, Alec. Without drawing so much as a drop of blood, we were able to extract every scrap of information from you."

"Necromancy is a subtle art," Ashnazai interjected smugly.

"It can be," Mardus amended dryly, "although 'subtle' is hardly how I'd describe many of the necromantic procedures I have witnessed. But to return to the subject at hand, I assure you that had it not been for the prohibition against shedding blood, I could have accomplished the same result without such an extraordinary expenditure of magic."

Giving Alec a poisonous smile, Ashnazai asked, "I am curious, my lord, as to what your method would have been?"

Mardus clasped his hands behind him, considering the question as coolly as if Ashnazai had asked what he thought the price of grain would be this year. "I often begin with the genitals. While the blood loss is negligible, the pain and emotional anguish are exquisite. Once that level of pain is established, the prisoner is usually quite easy to manipulate. In Alec's case, I could leave him still fit for the slave markets. Only a fool would destroy such a pretty creature unnecessarily."

Trapped at sea in such company, Alec nearly succumbed to despair. By day he was the toy of his executioners. By night the muffled cries that sometimes came up from the hold below increased his sense of helplessness. The few times he dreamed of better days with Seregil or his father only made things worse when he woke up. Lying in the darkness, he would try to recall the smell of their rooms at the Cockerel or the color of Beka's eyes. Mostly,

however, he thought of Seregil and cursed Mardus for the seeds of
doubt he'd planted.

"He didn't abandon me. He didn't!" he whispered into the
darkness one night when his spirits were at their lowest. He forced
himself to recall his friend's grin when Alec had mastered a new
skill, the delight Seregil took in tormenting Thero, the grip of
Seregil's hand when he'd pulled him back from the edge of the
cliff after the ambush below Cirna.

And the way he'd looked that night at the Street of Lights. Alec
suddenly remembered the guilty pleasure he'd felt that evening,
and later at the casual touch of Seregil's hand resting on his
shoulder or the back of his neck—

His cheeks went warm now at the memory of that touch. It was
too painful to think of, now that he'd never feel it again—

"Stop it!" he hissed aloud. "He could come. He could be following right now!"

But not even Micum could track a ship across water.

Foundering in his own misery, Alec pulled the thin blanket
around himself and tried to recall fragments of conversation he
and Seregil had shared, just to imagine a friendly voice. He
dreamed of him that night, although he couldn't recall any particu-
lars when he awoke. But something had come back to him,
nonetheless. Seated on the bunk that morning, he chewed his
breakfast thoughtfully, summoning various lessons Seregil had
instilled in him over the long months of their acquaintance.

Everyone on board considered him powerless, a prisoner of
little consequence beyond whatever fate Mardus had in store for
him. It was time to put aside fear and begin to pay attention, real
attention, to what was going on around him, and then to ask questions—small, inconsequential ones at first—as he tested the water.
After all, he wouldn't die any faster for at least trying.

Learn and live, Seregil's voice whispered approvingly at the
back of his mind.

The soldiers' newfound wariness of him made it slightly easier
to talk to them, though Alec quickly discovered that all that mattered to them was their unswerving loyalty to Mardus, a fact
which made any overtures to them pointless. But he did learn that
they were making for some point on the northwestern coast of
Plenimar.

Later that same morning he made more of an effort at conversation with Mardus during their daily walk, allowing himself to be drawn into a discussion of archery. The next day they spoke of wines and poisons. Mardus seemed pleasantly surprised and began sending for him more frequently.

On the fifth day following Gossol's sacrifice, Tildus came for him at sunset. The bearded captain said nothing, but Alec didn't like the smug, secret smile Tildus gave him as they went above.

On deck Alec saw with alarm that the ritual space had been prepared again. A line of soldiers held torches to illuminate the freshly laid square of canvas where Irtuk Beshar was already bent over the bowl and crown. Beside her, Vargûl Ashnazai stood ready with the stone ax.

Thero was there, too, standing next to Mardus as slack-jawed as ever. All eyes seemed to turn to Alec as he approached.

"O Illior," he whispered hoarsely, feeling his knees go weak. Mardus had had some change of heart, his god had sent different instructions, Alec's questioning had led him into some fatal misstep—

Tildus gripped his arm more tightly and muttered, "Easy, man child. Not your time yet!"

"Good evening, Alec!" Mardus said, smiling as he swept a hand toward the eastern horizon. "Look there, can you make out the coastline in the distance?"

"Yes," Alec replied, a fresh coil of apprehension running up his back at the sight.

"That is Plenimar, our destination. Seriamaius has been kind, guiding us so smoothly along our course. And now it is time for the second act of preparation."

As Alec watched with mounting dread, ten men and women were dragged up on deck by the black-clad marines. This was the source of the weeping he heard in the night. This had all been planned in advance, the sacrificial victims packed away in the hold as carefully as the wine and oil and flour.

They were not soldiers, but thin, pale, ordinary-looking souls who blinked and wept as they were herded together near the rail. Most were ragged or dressed as laborers, just innocent victims, he guessed, plucked from the darkened streets of whatever ports the ship had put into before Rhíminee.

"O Illior," Alec whispered as Mardus came to stand beside him, hardly knowing that he spoke aloud. "No, please. Not this."

Mardus slipped an arm around his shoulders and closed his hand over the back of Alec's neck. Giving him a playful shake, he purred, "Ah, but you should savor it. Don't you understand yet how great a part you played in bringing this about?"

Faint with revulsion, Alec made the mistake of looking up at Mardus. For the first time he saw the depths of naked cruelty in his eyes, and in that awful moment he knew as certainly as he'd ever known anything that Mardus had purposefully allowed him to see behind the mask, was delighting in his fear and confusion, savoring it the way another man might savor the first caress of a long-desired lover. And perhaps worse even than this was the conviction that Mardus was nonetheless sane.

Some of the prisoners were staring at Alec, mistaking him for one of their murderers.

He couldn't watch this again. Tildus had moved away when his master had come over, and the rest of the soldiers were watching the ceremony. Jerking out of Mardus' grip, Alec dashed to the rail behind him with some instinctive, half-formed notion of throwing himself overboard, swimming as far as he could toward the shore, giving up if he had to—

He'd gone no more than two paces when a deadly coldness engulfed him, locking his joints, forcing him painfully to his knees. Some unseen power forced his head around to see Vargûl Ashnazai holding up a small vial of some sort that hung around his scrawny neck on a chain.

"Nicely done, Vargûl Ashnazai," said Mardus. "Move him a bit closer so that he can see."

Unable to turn his head or blink, Alec had no choice but to watch as the ten victims were dragged down onto the deck at Ashnazai's feet. Ten times the blade rose and fell with deadly efficiency and each heart was taken by the dyrmagnos and drained into the reeking cup.

Thero stood just beyond her and through his own helpless tears of rage and impotence, Alec saw tears coursing slowly down Thero's cheeks. It was an eerie sight, like watching a statue weep, but it gave him a sudden thrill of hope in the midst of the nightmare being acted out before him.

The white canvas was scarlet by the time the necromancer had finished. He and the dyrmagnos were smeared to the elbows, their robes sodden, hair matted with it. Blood had soaked across the deck to where Alec knelt, staining his bare knees.

Leaving the soldiers to pitch the bodies overboard, Mardus took Thero below again.

Vargûl Ashnazai walked over to Alec and laid one bloody hand on his head, breaking the spell.

Alec doubled over retching. Ashnazai snatched the hem of his blood-soaked gown out of the way with a grunt of disgust, then gave Alec a shove with one foot that sent him sprawling in sticky blood and vomit.

"I look forward to cutting you open," he sneered.

Scrambling back to his hands and knees, Alec glared defiantly back at him. The necromancer took an involuntary step back, raising his hand. Alec braced for some new agony, but Ashnazai merely turned on his heel and stalked away, snarling something to Captain Tildus as he passed.

Dread returned as a pair of soldiers stripped Alec and washed him down with buckets of cold seawater. When he was clean, they thrust him into a soft robe and turned him back to Tildus, who led him below to a spacious cabin in the stern.

To his amazement, he found Mardus, Ashnazai, Thero, Irtuk Beshar, and the silent, grey-bearded necromancer, Harid, reclining on cushions around a low table. A young serving boy placed another cup on the table, motioning for Alec to be seated.

"Come, Alec, join us," Mardus said, patting an empty cushion between himself and the dyrmagnos. He and the others had also changed clothes and cleansed away all traces of the murders he'd just witnessed.

It's as if none of that happened, he thought numbly, too shocked to protest as Tildus steered him to his place and pushed him down.

Thero sat on Irtuk Beshar's left. At her nod, he raised his cup mechanically to his lips. Wine dribbled down through his beard as he drank, his eyes locked on some distant point.

The sight filled Alec with a strange guilt, as if he'd spied on something unseemly. Looking away, he fixed his attention on his cup as the servant filled it with pale yellow wine.

"Come now, dear boy, why so shy?" Mardus coaxed, the mask of gentlemanly solicitude in place once more. "It's an excellent wine. Perhaps it will put some color back in those wan cheeks of yours."

"Strong emotion does so spoil a young man's beauty," Irtuk Beshar added, her coquettish tone as incongruous with her cracked, blackened face as her robes and veil.

The entire situation had such a surreal quality that Alec found himself replying, "I don't care for any, thank you," as if he were Sir Alec of Ivywell dissembling at some noble's banquet with Seregil.

"Such pretty manners, too," Ashnazai noted. "I am beginning to see your point, my lord. It will be a pity to kill him. He would ornament any gentleman's household."

Alec's sense of dreamlike detachment increased as the grisly conversation flowed around him in polite salon tones. If this was the onset of madness, then he welcomed it as a gift of Illior. Whatever the case, he suddenly felt a giddy lightness coming over him. He'd experienced this before, though never so intensely. When death was your only option, it made you feel very free indeed.

"My lord," he began. "What is this all about? The wooden disk, the crown? I know you're going to kill me as part of it, so I'd just like to understand."

Mardus smiled expansively. "I would expect no less of a person of your intelligence. As I have said, you and all your misguided friends have been instrumental in a grand and sacred quest. At first even I didn't perceive the significance of it, but Seriamaius has revealed how you were all simply instruments of his divine will."

Mardus raised his cup to Alec in a mocking salute. "You can't imagine the trouble you saved us, bringing so many parts of the Helm together for us to reclaim with a single brief stroke. Not to mention the damage we were able to inflict upon the Orëska in the process. Why, in one night we managed to accomplish what might otherwise have taken months, even years. And we do not have years, or even weeks, now."

"A helm?" Alec asked, seizing on this new reference.

Mardus turned to his companions, shaking his head. "Imagine! This Nysander, great and compassionate wizard that he is, had his closest friends carry out his thievery without the least hint of what they were being embroiled in. Why, he regarded Seregil and poor young Alec and Thero here almost as sons.

"Yes, Alec, the Helm. The Great Helm of Seriamaius. The coin, as you so amusingly refer to it, the cup, and the crown are all elements of a greater design. When brought together with the other fragments at the proper time, they will rejoin to form the Helm revealed to our ancestors by Seriamaius more than six centuries ago."

"It is the ultimate artifact of necromantic power," Irtuk Beshar told him. "He who wears it becomes the *Vatharna*, the living embodiment of Seriamaius."

"The legends from the Great War. Armies of walking dead," Alec said softly, thinking of the ancient journal he and Seregil had discovered in the Orëska library.

"Perhaps we have underestimated this child," the dyrmagnos observed, cocking her head to regard Alec more closely. "There may be depths within him still to be sounded."

Alec shuddered inwardly under the greediness of her scrutiny.

"Yet these tales of yours said nothing of the Helm?" Mardus continued. "I am not surprised. At the end of that war we were betrayed. Aided by traitors, fawning Aurënfaie wizards, and a pack of ragged drysians, the wizards of the Second Orëska managed to capture and dismantle the Helm before its full power could be invoked. Fortunately, they could not destroy the individual pieces. Our necromancers managed to recapture a few of them; the rest were carried off and hidden. For six centuries my predecessors have hunted for them, and one by one, they have been recovered."

"That's what you were doing in Wolde," Alec said slowly. "You'd been to the Fens, that village Mi—"

"Micum Cavish?" Ashnazai smiled as he broke off suddenly. "Don't trouble yourself. You screamed that name out to us already, just as you did all the rest of it."

Mardus paused as the serving boy brought in platters of roasted doves and vegetables.

"Do try to eat something," he said, serving Alec himself.

Surprised at his own hunger, Alec obliged.

"Now, where was I?" Mardus asked, spearing a dove for himself. "Ah yes. The three fragments guarded by Nysander were the last, and of those, the bowl was the most gratifying discovery. We knew of the others, you see, both stolen from under our very noses by your friend Seregil, as it turns out. But all trace of the bowl had been lost until the two of you led us to it with the theft of the Eye. And only just in time, too. As it is, we've only just enough time to complete the ritual preparations."

"The—sacrifices, you mean?" asked Alec.

"Yes." Mardus sat forward as the servant brought in a course of roasted pork. "Each soul taken, each libation of heart's blood, brings us closer to Seriamaius, to his great power. No man could be a vessel for such power, but through the Helm we may partake of some small portion of it. By 'small portion' you must understand I am speaking in relative terms. Once restored, the Helm will increase in power as more lives are fed to it until a single thought by the wearer can level whole cities, control thousands. And you, Alec, you and Thero, I am holding in reserve for the final sacrifice of the reconstruction ceremony. A hundred people will have perished before you, allowing you the privilege of watching every death until your own turns come, two last, perfect sacrifices. The blood is to a great extent merely symbolic of the life force given up to the god. The younger the victim, the more years taken, the richer the sacrifice."

Irtuk Beshar patted Alec and Thero on the shoulders. "A young Orëska wizard and a half 'faie boy—the youth of our greatest enemies! What could be more pleasing to our god than that?"

Alec regarded them a moment in stunned silence, trying to take it all in.

No, he thought numbly. *No, I will not be a part of that.*

"Thank you," he said finally. "I think I'm beginning to understand."

There were no guards in the room now. No spells or chains held him. Forcing himself to give no leading hint of his intentions, Alec suddenly lashed out across the table and snatched up a carving knife lying next to the platter of fowl. Clutching it in both hands, he drove the blade at his own ribs, praying for a quick kill.

To his horror and astonishment, however, he twisted around instead and plunged the blade into the chest of the young servant. The boy let out a single startled cry and collapsed.

"Really, Alec, where are your manners tonight?" Mardus exclaimed regretfully. "I've owned him since he was a child."

Alec stared down at the body, horror-struck at what he had done.

"Did you think us so lacking in imagination that we would not anticipate such a noble action on your part?" Irtuk chided. "You forget how intimately I know you, Alec. One of the first wards I placed upon you was one to guard against such ridiculous heroics. Anytime you try to hurt yourself, you shall only end up hurting another, like this poor innocent."

"O Illior!" Alec groaned, covering his face with his hands.

"Perhaps I am somewhat to blame," Mardus sighed. "My explanation may have given the boy the impression that he and Thero are necessary for the final realization of our plans."

Mardus' hands closed over Alec's, squeezing painfully as he pulled them aside to fix Alec with a look of sardonic pleasure.

"Understand this. The presence or absence of either one of you will not make the slightest difference to the god. It merely pleases me, and Vargûl Ashnazai as well, I am certain, that the two of you should be the final victims. Just imagine, dear Alec—watching all those others die, and you quite helpless to save them. And then, as your chest is split and your heart pulled free, your final thought will be that after all your meddling, all that extraordinary effort, it is *your* life bringing the Helm back into being! I'm only sorry that your friends will not be there to share in your reward. Now do try to eat something more. You're looking quite pale again."

42
LANDFALL

Seregil woke drenched in sweat, still caught in the nightmare's grip. Squeezing his eyes shut, he tried to hang on to the images of the dream, but as usual could recall nothing but the vague memory of a tall figure towering over him and the terrible sensation of drowning.

Micum had already gone above. Seregil lay a moment longer, half dozing as the first faint light of dawn brightened the cabin's single window. Was Alec awake, seeing that same light? he wondered, as he'd wondered every morning of the voyage. Was Alec alive at all? Would he be when the sun set?

He rubbed at his eyelids and felt the wetness seeping through his lashes. Early morning was the worst. During the day he could keep busy, bury his fear in the semblance of doing something useful. At night he simply closed his eyes and escaped into dreams and nightmares.

But here, in the half world of dawn, he had no defenses, no diversion. The longing for Alec's presence, the guilt and remorse at having brought him to this, the shame at never having told the boy how much he cared for him—it was all as raw as a wound that refused to heal.

And there was nothing to do but go on to

the end. Rolling out of the bunk, he threw on a surcoat over his shirt and went above without bothering to fasten it up.

On deck he turned his face to the wind and spread his arms. The cold salt breeze lifted his hair from his neck and blew his coat open, whipping his shirt against his ribs. Tilting his head back, he inhaled deeply, trying to cleanse away the sense of oppression. As he did so, he noticed a new scent on the wind, the smell of land.

Going to the starboard rail, he saw a dark, uneven line of mountains looming through the morning mist like a promise just out of reach. His sail-changing ploy had worked. They'd sailed within sight of Plenimar's northwestern coastline without challenge.

Rhal called out sharply somewhere to stern and Skywake barked an order. Looking around the deck for Micum, Seregil spotted him sitting on the forward bulkhead. He had a small mirror propped on one knee and was shaving his chin with the aid of a knife and a cup of water.

Micum looked up as he approached, then frowned. "Another bad night, eh?"

"Worst yet." Seregil combed his fingers back through his wind-blown hair. "It feels like someone's trying to tell me the most important thing in the world in a language I can't understand."

"Maybe Nysander can make something of it when he gets here."

"*If* he gets here," Seregil replied listlessly. He felt as if they'd been on this ship for years instead of weeks; Rhíminee, Nysander, Alec, the deaths they'd left behind, perhaps it was just all part of the same bad dream.

Micum gestured with his knife at a lonely peak to the north. "Rhal says that's Mount Kythes there. He thinks we can put ashore tonight. There's a—Bilairy's Balls, you're bleeding!"

Setting his knife and cup aside, he stood and tugged at the loose ties of Seregil's shirt.

"Damnation, it's that scar. It's opened up again," he whispered, touching a finger to Seregil's chest and showing him the blood.

Using Micum's shaving mirror, Seregil inspected the small trickle of blood oozing from the raised outline of the scar. He could even make out the faint whorls left by the disk, and the small square mark of the hole at its center. He also caught a glimpse of his own face, looking sallow and hollow-eyed in the early light. Pulling his coat shut, he fastened the top buttons.

"What does it mean?" Micum asked.

"Don't you remember what the date is today?" Seregil replied grimly.

Micum's jaw dropped. "By the Flame, I'd lost track being on a ship so long."

"The fifteenth of Lithion," Seregil said, nodding. "If Leiteus and Nysander were right in their calculations, Rendel's Spear should be in the sky tonight."

Seregil saw awe and concern mingle in his friend's eyes as Micum took a last look at the blood on his fingers before wiping them on his coat.

"You know I came along on this trip mostly to look out for you, don't you?" Micum said quietly.

"Yes."

"Well, I just want you to know that as of now, I'm beginning to be a believer. Whatever it was that left its mark on you there, it's working on us now. I just hope Nysander is right about Illior being the immortal who's leading us around."

Seregil grasped his friend's shoulder. "After all these years, maybe I'll finally make an Illioran out of you."

"Not if it means waking up looking like you do this morning," Micum countered.

"Still no dreams?" Seregil asked, still puzzled by the fact that of the four of them, Micum was the only one who hadn't had a premonition of some sort.

Micum shrugged. "Not one. Like I've always told you, I do my fighting when I'm awake."

The mountain loomed steadily larger ahead of them as they followed the coast north through the day. From a distance it seemed to rise directly up from the sea itself, its summit lost in a mantle of cloud.

"Pillar of the Sky, eh?" Rhal remarked, standing with Seregil and Micum at the rail that afternoon. "Well, they sure named it rightly. How in hell are you going to find this temple of yours on something that big?"

"It's somewhere along the water," Seregil replied softly, rubbing unconsciously at the front of his coat; Micum had tied a wadded bit of linen over the raw circle of skin. Oddly enough, the wound hardly hurt at all.

"Well, it'll take some doing to put you ashore." Rhal shaded his eyes, peering landward. The weather had remained clear through the day but a wind was blowing up out of the west, piling up the waves and lashing the foam from their white crests. "I see breakers against the rocks all up and down there. Most of it's cliff and ledge. You'll just have to coast along until you see a likely landing place."

"Is the boat ready?" asked Seregil.

Rhal nodded, his gaze still on the distant coastline. "Water, food, all that you asked for. I saw to it myself. We can cast you off as soon as you've packed in your gear."

"We'd best get at it then," Micum said. "It's been a while since either of us has sailed. I don't want to try this sea without some daylight ahead of us."

When the final pack and cask had been lashed into the *Lady*'s starboard longboat, Seregil and Micum took leave of Rhal.

"Good luck to you," the captain said solemnly, clasping hands with them. "Whatever it is the two of you are up to over there, give those Plenimaran bastards merry hell for me."

"Nothing will make me any happier," Micum assured him.

"Lay off the coast as long as you can," said Seregil. "If we're not back in four or five days, or if you get run off yourself, head north and put in at the first friendly port you find."

Rhal gripped Seregil's hand a moment longer. "By the Old Sailor, when this whole thing is over, I'd like to hear the tale of it. You look out for yourselves, and find that boy of yours."

"We will," Seregil promised, climbing into the boat. Crouching down beside Micum, he wrapped his hands around one of the ropes securing the boat's small mast.

"Hold tight!" Rhal called as his men set to work lowering it over the side. "Wait until we're well away before you put up your sail. Good luck, friends!"

The little boat swung precariously from the halyards as it was lowered down the side of the pitching ship. Waves slapped at it as they neared the water, then rolled in over the side. Clinging on as best they could, Seregil and Micum waited until they'd cleared the *Lady,* then unfurled the triangular sail.

The little boat yawed sharply, catching another wave over the side. Micum took the tiller and turned her into the wind while

Seregil hauled on the spar rope. As soon as they got her headed properly into the waves, he looped the spar rope over a cleat and set about bailing the craft out.

"You're the Guide," Micum said, shrugging out of his sodden cloak and settling himself more comfortably at the tiller. "What do we do now?"

Seregil gazed toward the distant shore. "Like Rhal said, get in close and coast along until we spot a landing place."

"There's a lot of coast there, Seregil. We could end up miles from wherever this temple of yours is."

Seregil went back to his bailing. "If I am the Guide of Nysander's prophecy, maybe I'll know the right place when I see it."

The words sounded weak and half-convinced even to him, but he didn't know what else to say. This certainly didn't seem like the proper moment to confess that except for a few fragmentary dreams and the bleeding scar on his chest, he was painfully unaware of any feelings of divine guidance.

As Rhal had observed, much of the coastline was ledge or cliff. The boom of the surf echoed back at them across the water and they could see the spume thrown up by the breakers. Great blocks of reddish granite shot through with bands of black basalt lay in tumbled disorder between the water and the trees above.

As far as the eye could see the land looked desolate and uninhabited. Dark forest blanketed the hills. Higher up, the stark, stony peak of the mountain rose forbiddingly against the evening sky. The setting sun behind them cast a thick golden light over the scene, enhancing briefly the color of water, sky, and stone. Great flocks of sea ducks and geese floated on the swells just beyond the pull of the breakers. Overhead, gulls uttered their whistling calls as they circled and dove.

"I never thought I'd be setting foot on Plenimaran soil," Micum remarked, steering them closer in. "I've got to admit, it's nice-looking country."

The sun sank lower. Kneeling in the bow, Seregil squinted intently at the harsh shoreline.

"I think we may be spending the night out here," Micum said, steering them past a rocky point.

"You may be— Wait!"

The forest was thick here, but he caught the distinct yellow flicker of firelight in the shadow of a cove. "Do you see that?"

"Could be a campfire. What do you say?"

"Let's have a look."

Steering into the cove, they discovered a tiny, sheltered beach at its head. Above the tide line, a large fire crackled invitingly, illuminating the thick tangle of evergreens that edged the shingle.

"It looks more like a signal fire," whispered Micum, tacking just off shore. "Could be fishermen or pirates."

"Only one way to find out. You stay with the boat."

Slipping over the side into the hip-deep water, Seregil drew his sword and waded ashore.

The beach lay at the head of a deep cleft in the surrounding ledge, making an oblique approach impossible, and the slanting evening light lit it like a stage. The shingle was made up of small, wave-polished stones that crunched and rattled under his boots as he continued up toward the fire.

I might just as well tie a bell around my neck, he thought uneasily, picturing archers tracking him from the ledges and swordsmen in the thickets.

But the cove was peaceful. Standing still, he listened carefully. Over the sigh of the wind, he heard the mournful music of doves and white throats in the woods, the clacking croak of a heron stalking the shallows somewhere nearby. No one was disturbing them.

Encouraged but wary, he crunched up the shingle to the fire. There was no sign of habitation, no packs or refuse. As he came nearer, he realized with a nasty start that the flames were giving off no heat. It was an illusion.

A branch snapped in the forest and he crouched, bracing for ambush. A tall, spare figure stepped from the trees.

"Here you are at last, dear boy," a familiar voice greeted him in Skalan.

"Nysander?" Still wary, Seregil remained where he was as the wizard pushed back his hood. Dressed for traveling, Nysander wore an old surcoat and loose breeches, and his faded cloak was held at the throat with the worn bronze brooch he always used.

As he came forward into the light, Seregil let out a startled gasp. Even in the ruddy light of sunset, Nysander looked ghostly. His face was the color of bone and more deeply lined than ever. Worse yet, he looked shrunken in on himself, diminished, like the gnarled caricature of an old man carved in fresh ivory. Only his bright eyes and the familiar warmth in his voice seemed to have come back to him intact.

The surprise of their unexpected meeting left Seregil wary of illusion, however. Quelling the impulse to embrace his old friend, Seregil kept his distance and asked, "How did you find us?"

Nysander made a sour face. "That blood charm you left with Magyana, of course. It took some managing and magic, but here I am."

Sheathing his sword, Seregil gave the old man a joyous hug. "I knew you'd do it, but by the Light, you look awful!"

"As do you, dear boy," Nysander chuckled.

Micum hauled the boat in and ran up the shingle to join them.

"You mean to say you were here waiting for us?" he cried, looking Nysander over in wonder. "How did you know? And why didn't you send us a message by magic?"

"All in good time," the old wizard sighed, sinking down on a driftwood log and waving the illusory fire out of existence. "I must admit, I am equally relieved to see you. I feared I might have missed you after all."

"Do you know anything about Alec?" Seregil asked hopefully, sitting down beside him.

"No, but you must not despair," Nysander told him, patting his shoulder kindly. "If he were dead, I would know it. The force of the prophecy is binding us closer with every passing day."

Micum kicked together a pile of driftwood sticks and fished a firechip from a pouch at his belt. "Well, I haven't had any great visions or dreams, but the more I see of this business, the more I believe it. By the Flame, Nysander, look at you. How can you have gotten here at all?"

"Look at me, indeed," Nysander replied rather ruefully. "One does not return from such a journey as the dyrmagnos sent me on without showing a bit of wear. But there was some value to it. While my body healed, my mind floated free among dreams and visions. I believe I know how to find the temple we seek. It is marked by a large white stone surrounded by black ones. And it is near the sea."

Disappointment settled in Seregil's belly like a bad dinner. "That's it? You're telling me in all the hundreds of square miles around that mountain we have to find *one* rock?"

"That's not much to go on," Micum noted, echoing his skepticism.

Yet Nysander appeared perfectly complaisant. "We will find it," he assured them. "It does not guarantee our success, but we will find it."

"I've been having dreams of my own," Seregil told him.

"You've done more than that," Micum snorted. "Show him your chest."

Seregil peeled off the bandage and showed Nysander the crusted yellow scab that had formed around the scar. "It must be some kind of sign. Leiteus claimed this was the night the comet would appear."

"Undoubtedly," Nysander agreed. "Whether it is an omen of good or ill remains to be seen. What was your dream?"

Seregil picked up a knife-shaped stone and rubbed it between his hands. "I can never remember much of it, just the image of a figure with a misshapen head looking down at me through water while I drown. Isn't there something you could do to sort of pull more of it out of me?"

Nysander shook his head. "I must conserve both my strength and my magic. What little I have was hard-won and will be needed for what lies before us now. Even the fire I used to signal you was from a spell Magyana made for me. As for the dream, it must be some sort of preparation for the task ahead."

Micum ran his hands back through his thick red hair and sighed. "Do you think you could be a bit more specific?"

Nysander nodded. "Before the attack on the Orëska I hoped I would never have to tell you. Afterward, I was unable to.

"As Seregil has told you, there is a prophecy which names four persons, the Guardian, the Shaft, the Vanguard, and the Guide. I am the Guardian, and have been since the days of my apprenticeship with Arkoniel. What we have guarded, there below the Orëska House, was a fragment of a necromantic object called the Helm of Seriamaius."

"The bowl," Seregil interjected.

Nysander glanced at him in surprise. "How on earth did you learn that?"

"More visions," said Micum, tossing wood on the fire. The sun was disappearing into the western sea, leaving the stars spread like a diamond veil above them.

"Yes, it was a bowl," Nysander went on. "And then Seregil and Alec brought me the wooden disk. Just before the Festival of Sakor, I sent Seregil after a third object, a crown which had been hidden deep in the Ashek mountains. He knew at once, both by the condition of the bodies of sacrificial victims he found there and the evil magic that surrounded it, that it was related to the disk. However, I told him nothing and swore him to secrecy. Not even Alec knew."

"I still don't see how you'd get any sort of helmet out of those odds and ends," said Micum.

"Their appearance hides their true form. A powerful protective glamour was placed on them by the necromancers who created them. Who would guess, even having all the pieces in hand, that a lopsided clay bowl, a crystal crown, and a handful of wooden disks could be parts of a common whole?"

"What does it do, when it's all put together?"

"It was created to channel the power of the dark god. No one knows how long it took to forge the different elements, or what magicks were used. It first appeared near the end of the Great War, when it was assembled and placed on a man they called the *Vatharna*, or chosen one. Fortunately, the wizards of Skala and Aurënen overcame the first *Vatharna* before he had the opportunity to fully manifest the magic of the Helm."

"You mean to say that this *Vatharna* of theirs would eventually have all the powers of their death god?" asked Micum.

"No one knows what the extent of its abilities might have been, but there is evidence that even in the short time it existed, the Helm granted its wearer terrible necromantic power. If it had not been dismantled when it was, I doubt anyone could have overcome it."

Seregil shook his head slowly. "Then those old tales of walking dead, armies of them, were true?"

"It is likely there is at least a kernel of truth in them."

"You said dismantled, not destroyed," Micum noted.

"So it was, to the great sorrow of subsequent generations. The wizards managed to reduce it to its component parts, but before they could learn how to destroy them, Plenimaran forces attacked to reclaim them. When it was clear that the Skalan position would be overrun, six wizards were chosen to flee with the pieces and hide them. Only one was ever seen alive again."

"The one who took the bowl," said Seregil.

"Reynes í Maril Syrmanis Dormon Alen Wyvernus. It was he who eventually created that chamber in the lowest vault of the Orëska, and he who passed the onus of Guardianship down to his successor, Hyradin, who passed it to Arkoniel, who passed it to me. Neither the Queen nor the Orëskan Council ever knew of its existence there. Any who tried to learn their secret were killed."

"These Guardians didn't even trust the other wizards?" said Micum.

"Who could be trusted with such knowledge? The Empty God understands nothing better than the dark corners of a mortal heart. Fear, pity, remorse, greed, the lust for power—these are the Eater of Death's most potent weapons."

"Did Thero know?" asked Seregil.

"No, he was not ready for such knowledge." Nysander rested a hand on Seregil's shoulder. "Part of my grief in losing you as an apprentice was the knowledge that you would have been such a worthy successor. From the day I took you on, I knew in my heart that you were capable of assuming the burden. When you could not learn the magic, I was devastated. But now I see that I was not mistaken about your worthiness, only about the role which you were destined to play. What you learned after leaving me, the life you went on to, it all prepared you to be the Unseen One."

Seregil scowled. "You think the gods made me a thief and a spy, just so I could steal the disk from Mardus? You think my whole life means nothing more than this one task? I refuse to believe that!"

"No, not entirely," Nysander said. "You recall me telling you that there is always a Guide somewhere, and all the others of the prophecy? Perhaps your life would have been no different if the Helm never existed, but being what you are, you are the Guide. I have speculated on it many times over the years, but it was only after you brought me the disk that I truly began to believe. When you were also able to snatch the crown away from the Pleni-marans, I prayed that it was simply good fortune, that by being vigilant I could keep all the fragments out of Mardus' hands and prevent the restoration."

"Then you knew about Mardus already?"

"Only that he was a bastard relation of the old Overlord, a noble of tremendous ability and ambition, and one of Plenimar's most formidable spies. Now I suspect he means to make himself *Vatharna*."

"He sounds like the right man for the job," Micum said, scowling. "But you still haven't told us where this prophecy of yours came from, or what it says."

"No one but the Guardians have ever heard it, or were ever meant to," Nysander replied solemnly. "While still a young man, the second Guardian had a dream vision which has been passed down from one Guardian to another ever since as our greatest source of hope. 'The Dream of Hyradin' is this: 'And so came the Beautiful One, the Eater of Death, to strip the bones of the world. First clothed in Man's flesh it came, crowned with a dread helm of great darkness. And none could stand against this One but a company of sacred number.

" 'First shall be the Guardian, a vessel of light in the darkness. Then the Shaft and the Vanguard, who shall fail and yet not fail if the Guide, the Unseen One, goes forth.' This same prophecy names the Pillar of the Sky, and speaks of a temple there."

"That gives us about as much to go on as your rock dream," Micum grumbled.

But Seregil felt a sickening chill pass through him, recalling the visions he had experienced when in contact with those pieces—the scenes of death and choruses of agony. "Then everything Mardus has done since Alec and I ran into him up in Wolde—the disk, Rythel and the sewer plot, the attack on you— it's all leading to him bringing all the pieces together again?"

"Of course, and bringing them together at the correct time and place. The time is during a solar eclipse five days from now."

"We'd guessed that already, after talking to your astrologer friend," said Seregil.

"Well done. Now that the three of us are together again, we must find the temple and see where the gods lead us from there. This time the Helm *must* be destroyed completely, and to accomplish that we must allow it to be reassembled—"

"What?" Seregil sputtered.

"It is the only way we can be certain that every fragment is accounted for," Nysander went on. "Arkoniel himself believed it was the only possible course of action and I believe he was right. If the knowledge passed down from Reynes í Maril is correct, then it takes a certain amount of time for the power of the Helm to gather itself, and more time for it to increase to its full potential. Therefore, once it has been reassembled we will have some brief moment of opportunity to strike. As the Guardian, I charge you both by your life and honor to strike whatever blow necessary to destroy the power of the Helm. Will you swear to that?"

"You have my oath on it." Micum extended his hand. Nysander took it and they looked to Seregil.

He hesitated, still toying with the beach stone, as an inexplicable ripple of misgiving went through him.

"Seregil?" Nysander raised an eyebrow at him.

Shrugging off his apprehension, Seregil tossed the stone aside and covered their hands with his own. "You have my word—"

As soon as his hands touched theirs, a sharp stab of pain lanced through his chest like an arrow shaft. Gasping, he pressed a hand over the scar.

Pushing Seregil's hand aside, Micum opened his coat and gently pulled the bandage off. "You're bleeding again," he said, showing Seregil and Nysander fresh blood on the linen dressing.

"It's nothing," Seregil rasped. "It must have broken open when I moved."

"Look there!" Nysander exclaimed, pointing up at the night sky.

A distant streak of red fire had appeared against the white band of stars to the east.

"Rendel's Spear!" Micum exclaimed.

They gazed up at the comet for a moment in silence, then Nysander said softly, "The necromancers call it by a different name."

"Oh? What?"

"Met'ar Seriami," the wizard replied. "The Arm of Seriamaius."

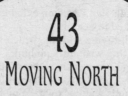

43
MOVING NORTH

"*M*et'ar Seriami!*"

Framed against the last light of sunset as he stood on the forward battle platform, Mardus swept a hand toward the fiery scintilla just visible above the eastern horizon. A victorious cheer went up from his men.

The throng assembled on the nearby shore echoed the cry, waving torches and shooting flaming arrows into the air over the cove. Drums throbbed out in the darkness.

Even before being brought on deck, Alec was uneasily aware of changes in the ship's routine. First, Mardus had foregone their walk that morning. Then the guards had brought Alec a long tunic, the first clothing he'd had since his capture. As the interminable day wore on, he felt the motion of the ship change and guessed that they were nearing the Plenimaran coast. He was proven correct that evening. When he and Thero were finally brought on deck, the *Kormados* was riding at anchor off a desolate shore. Desolate, but not uninhabited. There was an encampment of some sort, and he could see black uniformed men hailing the ship excitedly.

On board, Alec sensed an air of expectation. Everyone seemed to be watching the eastern horizon as the sun set. Finally, the comet appeared with the stars, a red point of light clearly visible below the waxing moon, and the great shout went up.

Standing under guard on deck, Alec leaned closer to Thero and whispered, "Look there. A plague star! Do you see it?"

"Plague star for you, maybe!" Captain Tildus scoffed disdainfully. "For us great sign. Lord Mardus and *voron* had say there should be such sign tonight."

"What did Mardus say just now—'Mederseri'?" Alec asked.

"Met'ar Seriami." Tildus searched for the words in Skalan to explain. "It is 'The Arm of Seriami.' A very great sign, I tell you before."

"Seriami? What I call Seriamaius?" A vague sense of dread gripped Alec as Tildus nodded. *"Aura Elustri mal—"*

"Shut that," Tildus growled, seizing Alec roughly by the arm. "Your madness gods don't be here. Seriami eat hearts of the false ones."

No other prisoners remained. Alec and Thero had been given proper clothing before being brought on deck, and their hands were bound securely behind their backs.

Thero moved like a sleepwalker, obeying simple commands, moving when ordered. Otherwise he remained motionless, his expression betraying nothing of what thoughts, if any, were going on within. The seamless iron bands on his wrists glinted softly in the torchlight as he moved, the unreadable characters incised into their burnished surfaces lined black with shadow.

That's the secret, Alec thought, convinced that these, rather than the branks, were the source of their enemies' control over Thero. If he could get those off somehow—

There was considerable activity on deck. Irtuk Beshar and the other necromancers stood together at the base of the platform, talking quietly among themselves as their traveling trunks were brought up from below and stacked by the rail.

Captain Tildus and a few of his men went ashore in a longboat, returning quickly with some news. Although Alec couldn't understand what they were saying, it was clear that Mardus was pleased with Tildus' report. When they'd finished, the captain shouted out a command and the sailors hurried to ready the rest of the ship's longboats for departure.

Mardus crossed the deck to where Alec and Thero still stood with their guards. "We'll be continuing our journey by land from here," he told Alec. "Thero is suitably restrained and I expect no difficulty from him. You, however, are another matter." He paused, and the scar beneath his left eye deepened as he smiled. "You've already proved yourself a slippery customer and once ashore you will no doubt be tempted to escape. I promise you, it would be a futile effort, and the consequences would be extremely unpleasant, but not fatal."

"More unpleasant than having my chest hacked open with an ax?" Alec muttered, glaring up at him.

"Immeasurably so." Mardus' eyes were depthless as the night sky, and as enigmatic. Turning on his heel, he strode away to oversee his men.

Shivering in spite of his warm clothing, Alec looked back at the comet glimmering on the lip of the world. This might not be the night for the final ceremony, but it couldn't be far off now. Whatever schedule Mardus was following, this comet was clearly a significant indicator.

Somewhere on that dark shore lay their destination, and his death.

It was only a short dash to the rail, he thought. If he moved quickly he could dodge the guards, take them by surprise, leap over.

And then what? Alec could almost see Seregil frowning impatiently at him from the shadows. *Assuming that you could swim with your hands tied, there are probably only about two hundred soldiers over there, not to mention at least one necromancer. Or were you just planning to take a nice deep breath down there in the blackness?*

And where, by the way, would any of that leave Thero?

Alec clenched his fists as desperation threatened to overwhelm him again. He wasn't ready to die, and he knew he couldn't abandon Thero. He had no idea how much of this whole business, if any, was actually the young wizard's fault; Thero's garbled confession had been too enmeshed in Irtuk's manipulations for Alec to give it full credence, though the doubt in his own mind was real enough. But guilty or not, he wouldn't leave him behind.

"You go now," one of his guards ordered, prodding him toward the last longboat.

It was too late to do anything but obey. *Illior and Dalna, gods of my parents, I beg your aid,* he prayed silently, moving forward.

As he neared the rail, he caught sight of something lying half hidden in the shadow of a bulkhead in his path, something he'd long since given up all hope of finding.

A nail.

Two inches long, square forged and slightly bent with use, it lay in plain view less than five feet from where he stood.

For one awful moment Alec was certain the guards had seen it, too, that someone was sure to snatch it away if he so much as glanced back at it. Perhaps Mardus himself had dropped it there, as a last cruel test.

There was only one way to find out.

The guard pushed him again, less gently this time. Alec pretended to stumble, then fell flat on his face.

He landed hard, but when he opened his eyes the nail was within an inch of his nose. Shifting as if he were struggling to get up, he quickly rolled over the nail, caught it with his lips and teeth, and had it safely stowed in his cheek by the time the guards pulled him to his feet.

It was as simple as that.

"What's all the fuss about down there?" Beka asked, joining the scouts on the crest of the hill overlooking the Plenimaran camp.

The Plenimaran column had headed steadily north since Beka and her riders began shadowing them. After three days they'd stopped on this lonely stretch of plain overlooking the Inner Sea. Beka and her people kept their distance, using their Plenimaran-shod horses for closer scouting so as to leave no enemy hoofprints to betray their presence.

For the past two days the Plenimarans had remained there with no apparent purpose. Just before sundown, however, a Plenimaran warship had sailed in from the west and dropped anchor.

"Looks like someone from the ship is putting ashore," Rhylin said, squinting into the last glare of sunset. "I don't know what all the hoorah is, though. They're all yelling and waving torches back and forth."

"Maybe that's it," Kallas whispered suddenly, pointing to the sky.

Looking up, the others saw a fiery streak of light moving slowly up the sky from the eastern horizon.

"Maker's Mercy, a plague star!" Jareel muttered, making a warding sign.

"I'd take that for an omen if ever there was one," Rhylin said, making a sign of his own. "If that's what they're cheering about down there, then I don't like it."

Beka had never seen a comet, yet the sight of this one brought with it a strange feeling of recognition similar to the one she'd experienced when she'd first heard the sound of the surf a few nights before. This time it was stronger, more unsettling. There was also a vague impression of—rightness.

"Lieutenant?"

Beka turned to find the others regarding her solemnly in the failing light.

"Could you make out any insignia on the ship?" she asked.

"She was running without colors," Rhylin replied. "We didn't see any cargo come off her, either, just people. What do we do now?"

"We could go down for a closer look once it gets dark," Steb suggested hopefully.

"*Urgazhi* style, quick in, quick out," urged Rhylin, taking his part.

Beka considered their limited options carefully before answering. She shared their frustration, knew how badly they wanted to make a move. More than once in the days since they'd been dogging the column they'd caught glimpses of Gilly and Mirn among the crowd of prisoners, staggering along under the weight of the planks nailed across their shoulders. In the end, however, it still boiled down to the fact that they were just fourteen against a hundred or more.

She shook her head slowly. "Not yet. If they don't move out tomorrow I'll reconsider, but I can't afford to lose any more of you. For now we wait and if they move north again tomorrow, we'll follow."

Steb turned away angrily, and several others groaned.

"I guess nobody'll be going by ship!" exclaimed Rhylin, gesturing toward the sea again.

The anchored vessel was on fire. As they watched in amazement, the rigging caught fire and sheets of flame spread to the sails.

"Bilairy's Balls, they scuttled her!" Jareel gasped. "A fire couldn't spread that quickly unless someone meant for it to. What the hell are they up to?"

Beka settled cross-legged on the grass, watching the reflection of the flames dancing across the water. "I guess we'll just have to stick with them until we find out."

The following morning Alec's guards woke him at dawn and led him to an iron cage mounted in the back of a small cart, the sort strolling players used to transport their trained animals. A thick mattress covered the floor of it, and there was a canvas awning over the top, but it still stank faintly of its former occupants.

Thero was already inside, seated cross-legged in the far corner. Like Alec, his hands were no longer tied, and he'd been allowed to keep his tunic and cloak.

"What a mangy pair of bear cubs," Ashnazai sneered, coming up to the bars behind Alec.

Alec moved away from him, although there wasn't really anywhere to go; the cage was only ten feet on a side.

"Lord Mardus is very busy now that we have landed, so I will be looking after you now," the necromancer went on.

He wrapped his hands around two of the bars, and Alec saw blue sparks dance over the iron, as if the cage had been struck by lightning. He jumped in alarm, and Ashnazai smiled his thin, unpleasant smile. In the clear light of the morning sun, his skin had a damp, unhealthy look, like the flesh of a toadstool.

"Don't you fear, dear Alec. My magic won't hurt you. Not unless you try to get out. And of course, you are far too intelligent to do anything so foolish."

Still smiling, he walked away. He looked like a winter scarecrow as the wind off the sea tugged at his dusty brown robe.

Hatred boiled in Alec's veins. Never in his life had he wanted so badly to kill a man. When Ashnazai disappeared beyond a row of tents, Alec turned his attention to the camp around him.

The back of the cart afforded a good view. From up here he could see the ranks of small white tents belonging to the soldiers and the herd of horses staked out beyond. The column that had met them on shore had at least fifty riders, as well as a crowd of people who were not in uniform and had the look of prisoners, although he was too far away to be certain. They had slept in the open under the watchful eye of swordsmen and archers. Mardus had brought at least a score of men of his own, making it a formidable force, all in the black uniforms of the marines. Going to the other side of the cage, he could see the smoking remains of the *Kormados* lying in the shallows like the skeleton of some wretched leviathan. *What happened to her crew?* he wondered. They'd even burned the longboats.

He didn't recognize the pair of soldiers who brought him breakfast a short time later. He spoke to them in the hope that they spoke some Skalan. If they did, they didn't let on. Giving him a scornfully direct look, they passed some remark between them, spat on the ground, and walked off a few paces to join the other guards assigned to watch him.

Alec hadn't really expected better from them. Sitting down beside Thero, he put a bit of bread in the young wizard's hand. When Thero did nothing, Alec said, "Eat."

Thero raised the bread to his mouth and took a bite. Crumbs fell into his beard as he slowly chewed and swallowed. Alec brushed them off and gave him a cup of water.

"Drink," he ordered wearily.

The column formed up at midday and set off north along the coast. The northwest coast of Plenimar was wild, rugged country. The track they followed wound in and out of swamps, meadows, and forests of pine and oak, always with the shadow of mountains on their right and the sea in sight on their left. The farther north they moved, the more forbidding the coastline became. Rocky shingle gave way to red granite ledges and cliffs. A cold, constant wind sighed through the trees, stirring the twisted branches of the jack pines and bringing Alec the sweet scents of the forest. It was colder here than in Skala, but he guessed that it must be sometime in mid-Lithion by now.

The nail was his talisman, his one remaining secret and symbol of hope. It was too large to keep in his mouth without attracting notice, but he didn't dare let it out of his possession, even to hide it in the mattress tick. Instead, he pierced it securely into the folds of his clothing. Recalling the incident on the ship, he was careful to keep it hidden from Thero, in case the necromancers or dyrmagnos decided to use the wizard to spy on him again.

So, keeping it hidden as best he could, Alec bided his time, waiting for some opportunity to present itself. Guards surrounded the cart day and night, but even without their presence he'd have

hesitated to attempt picking the lock; Ashnazai's little warning
demonstration with the bars suggested that such an effort would be
futile and probably dangerous. It was a frustrating situation. He
recognized the type of lock securing the door and knew the nail
would have been more than adequate for the job.

It was clear from the first that Vargûl Ashnazai was relishing
his new commission. He had none of Mardus' deceptive smooth-
ness, but contented himself with riding along beside the cart like a
dour specter.

Alec did his best to ignore him as the bear cart rolled and
jounced northward along the rutted coastal trail. Nonetheless, he
was often aware of the necromancer's gloating gaze.

Their first night on the road the column camped in the shelter
of an ancient pine grove. The sound of surf was loud. Looking
west past the huge, straight trunks, Alec could see the white spume
of the waves as they thundered against the ledges. It reminded
him of the sea sounds of his dreams, but it was not quite the same.

As darkness fell, another cheer went up and he guessed that the
comet must be visible again, although he couldn't see up through
the branches. Much later, he heard agonized screams in the darkness and knew that the sacrificial ritual was being carried out again
somewhere nearby. Even the guards around the cart shifted
uneasily and several made warding signs.

The cries went on longer this time. Feeling cold and sick, Alec
moved closer to Thero's sleeping form and covered his head with
his cloak.

Less than a year before, a younger, more innocent Alec had
lain awake all night in Asengai's dungeon, trembling and weeping
at every fresh cry that echoed from the torturer's room.

Weeks of death and torture in Mardus' company had almost
emptied him of such emotion. Pressing his hands over his ears, he
drifted into a restless doze with the survivor's uneasy prayer of
relief: *This time, at least, it wasn't me.*

*In his nightmare there was no invisible pursuer this time, only
the hoarse screams leading him on, faster and faster. With tears of
frustration coursing down his cheeks, he gripped the useless*

arrow shaft and ran until his chest ached. Rounding a corner, he staggered to a halt, his way blocked by a section of collapsed wall.

A thrill of hope shot through him at the sight of the ray of sunlight streaming in through a jagged break high in the stonework. From outside came the familiar rush and rumble of surf.

Clambering up the pile of broken stone, he squeezed out through the hole—

—and found himself standing alone on a granite ledge surrounded by thick fog that shrouded the view on all sides. Overhead, the faint disk of the noonday sun burned through the mist.

The crash of the surf was loud now, so loud that he couldn't tell which direction it was coming from. If he moved too far, went the wrong direction in the mist, he'd surely fall off the ledge. Crouching low, he moved slowly along on all fours until his hands touched water. The waves surged around him suddenly, flipping him on his back and tumbling him across the rocks. When the foaming waters receded again, the ledges were covered for as far as he could see with corpses of drowned men and women, their blue-white skin gleaming in the shadowless light.

The sea sound was fainter now, and over it Alec could hear harsh grunts and heavy, wet tearing sounds coming toward him in the fog. Terrified, naked, unarmed, he crouched among the corpses. Even the headless arrow was gone, carried off by the sea.

Soon he caught sight of weird, humped forms moving among the dead. The grunting and snuffling grew louder, closer.

Suddenly something grabbed him from behind in an icy grip, pulling him to his feet. Alec couldn't turn his head far enough to see what it was, but the putrid stench that rolled off it made him gag.

"Join the feast, boy," a gloating, clotted voice whispered close to his ear.

Struggling out of that loathsome grasp, Alec whirled to see what the creature was, but there was nothing there.

"Join the feast!" the same voice said again, still behind him no matter how fast he turned.

Stumbling backward, he fell into a heap of bloated corpses. No matter how he struggled he couldn't get up; every move enmeshed him more in a tangle of flaccid limbs.

"Aura Elustri málrei!" he screamed, flailing wildly.

"Join the feast!" the voice howled triumphantly.

Then the sun went black.

Alec jerked awake, still smelling the terrible death stench of the dream. A plump slice of moon visible through the branches told him it was still far from morning. Hugging his knees miserably, Alec took a deep breath, but the air smelled fouler every moment.

"Oh, Alec, I'm so frightened!"

Looking up in amazement, Alec saw Cilla crouched a few feet away. Illuminated by some ghostly inner light, she looked imploringly at him. Ghost or not, he was too relieved to see her whole again to be frightened.

"What are you doing here?" he asked softly, praying she wouldn't disappear as suddenly as she'd come.

"I don't know." A tear slid slowly down her cheek. "I've been lost for so long! I can't find Father or Grandmother anywhere. What's happened, Alec? Where are we?"

She looked so real that he took off his cloak and placed it around her shoulders. She pulled it around herself gratefully and leaned against him, feeling very solid and real. For a moment he simply knelt next to her, trying hard not to question her presence. At last, however, he pulled back a little and looked down at the top of her head resting against his chest.

"Why did you come?" he asked again.

"I had to," she whispered sadly. "I had to tell you—"

"Tell me what?"

"How much I hate you."

Her voice was so soft, so gentle, that it took a moment for the import of her words to sink in.

As his heart turned to lead in his chest, she said, "I hate you, Alec. It was your fault, even more than Seregil's. They saw you, followed you. You led them to us. I'm glad you're going to die."

"No! Oh, no, no, no, *no*!" Scrambling away, Alec flung himself into the farthest corner. "That's not true!" he cried. "It can't be true."

Cilla raised her head slowly, her eyes black hollows in the dim light of the moon. She smiled, and the fetid stench rolled through the cage again. Her smile widened to a grimace, a snarl, a silent scream, then a black arm shot from her mouth, lengthening impossibly as it reached for Alec. Locking black talons around his arm, it dragged him over Thero's limp body and back to her. For a moment his face was inches from hers, her wild eyes boring into his, mouth stretched obscenely around the arm protruding from it. Then her whole body swelled into a black, man-shaped form.

"Are you so certain?" the thing asked in the voice from Alec's nightmare. "Are you so very certain?"

Releasing him, it wavered, then flowed out through the bars like smoke.

"Damn you!" Alec screamed, knowing Vargûl Ashnazai was close by, watching. "Damn you, you blood-swilling son of a whore! You lie! *You lie!*"

A single harsh, mocking laugh answered him from the darkness beneath the trees.

44

WHITE STONE AND BLACK

The wind whipped Seregil's cloak around his knees and pulled at the bow case and quiver strapped to his old pack as he stopped to wait for Micum and Nysander. Looking back along the ledges to the north, he could just make them out, Nysander leaning on Micum and a stout staff as they picked their way over an expanse of tumbled stone. Over them loomed Mount Kythes, its jagged peak thrusting above the tree line like an elbow from a worn green sleeve.

Seregil shook his head in wonder. Despite Nysander's fragile appearance, the wizard had managed to keep up a steady pace over the past two days. Seregil and Micum took turns supporting him while the other scouted ahead. They were at the foot of the great mountain now, toiling south along the edge of the forest that flanked the coastline for as far as they could see. The area was rough and uninhabited, but there was the faint line of an overgrown road through the woods that followed the ledges.

Looking ahead, he shaded his eyes against the afternoon sun and scanned the forest and ledges.

How in the name of Illior were they supposed to find one stone, white or otherwise, in this wilderness? For all they knew they'd passed it somewhere yesterday. Yet Nysander insisted on pressing forward, the light of hope growing brighter daily in his eyes as they moved southward. Micum said little, but Seregil suspected he was as daunted by the unlikely nature of their quest as he was.

What if Nysander is wrong?

Seregil fought a daily battle against that question, and others. What if by losing the battle at the Orëska, Nysander had failed in his Guardianship? What if the wounds he'd received in that fight had addled his brain and he was leading them a fool's errand while Alec was carried off to some other part of Plenimar?

Yet each night the comet blazed ever closer in the night sky and the mark on Seregil's breast grew clearer as the skin healed, so he could not voice his doubts. Rational or not, in his heart he believed that Nysander was right. Clinging to this, he pressed on each day, scanning the coastline along the forest's edge until his eyes burned and his head ached, feeling his heart leap into his throat every time a patch of sunlight or the reflection of a tide pool tricked his eye.

Nysander and Micum had almost caught up. Sitting down on a slab of red granite, Seregil watched a flock of sea ducks bobbing on the waves beyond the breakers. Gradually his gaze wandered to the greenish-brown beards of bladder wrack clinging to the damp rocks below. Scattered patches of it marked the high tide line. Farther down, where the tide was nearly out, it blanketed the wet rocks in thick, slippery beds. He'd noted the difference the day before and the fact had been nagging at the back of his mind ever since, though he wasn't quite certain why.

Micum and Nysander climbed slowly up to where he stood. The wizard sank down on an outcropping, wiping his brow on his sleeve.

"My goodness," he panted, "I believe I must sit for a moment."

Seregil uncorked his water skin and handed it to him. "We only have a few hours of daylight left," he said, suddenly restless. "I'll go on ahead. If I'm not back by dusk, light a fire and I'll backtrack to it."

Micum frowned and held up a hand. "Hold on, now. I don't like the idea of us getting split up again."

"Not to worry," Nysander assured him. "I shall only need a short rest, and then we can follow. I agree with Seregil; there is no time to lose."

"It's settled," Seregil said, setting off again before Micum could protest.

A quarter of a mile farther on a broad cove cut into the shoreline like a bite from a slice of bread. An expanse of smooth ledge several hundred feet wide sloped gently up to the base of steeper layers of sea-weathered granite that embraced the cove like ruined battlements. Gulls picked their way through the rock pools and seaweed near the water's edge, spying out a meal left behind by the tide. It was a rather pretty place, Seregil thought, climbing up the rocks to stay near the edge of the forest.

Looking through the trees, he saw that the disused road curved to follow the upper ledges. He was just wondering if he should follow it for a while when something white caught his eye in the edge of the undergrowth across the cove.

Clambering over rocks and fallen trees, he braced for another disappointment; an equally promising flash earlier that morning had turned out to be the shoulder blade of an elk. Another had been nothing more than sunlight striking a spring-fed pool. As he came closer, however, he saw that it was a boulder of milky white stone nearly four feet high.

Dropping his pack, he pushed his way through the thicket of leafless bushes and dead fern that partially obscured it.

It was real—a great chunk of white quartz that had no business being in this type of country. He circled it, looking for carvings or marks, then reached down through the dry bracken until his fingers found a small, smooth stone. Pulling it out, he saw that it was a piece of polished black basalt the size and shape of a goose egg. Digging in farther, he found more of the black stones, as well as a tiny clay figure of a woman and an ornament of carved shell.

Clutching his finds, Seregil bounded back the way he'd come until he saw Micum and Nysander heading his way.

"I found it!" he shouted. "I found your white rock, Nysander. It's real!"

Micum let out a happy whoop and Seregil answered with one of his own.

"What do you say for Illioran mysticism now, Micum?" Seregil demanded breathlessly as he reached them.

Micum shook his head, grinning. "I'll never understand it, but it's surely led us well so far."

"There were black stones around the base of it, and I found

these, too," Seregil told Nysander excitedly, showing him the clay figure and the carved bit of shell.

"Illior's Light!" the wizard murmured, examining them. "Come along," he urged, grasping them both by the arm. "Carry me if you have to, but get me to that stone before the sun goes down."

But they didn't have to carry him. Swinging his staff ahead of him, Nysander strode over the ledges with much of his old energy. It was as if his news had revitalized the wizard, Seregil thought. Perhaps Nysander had needed this solid affirmation of his visions as much as the rest of them.

"Oh, yes, this is the one," Nysander said as they reached the stone. Placing both hands on it, he closed his eyes.

"It is old, so old," he said almost reverently. "It was placed here long before the first Hierophant landed on Plenimaran soil, but the echo of ancient worship is still so strong in it."

"You mean this is some ancient shrine?" asked Micum, examining it more closely.

"Something of the sort. Those objects Seregil found have been here for over a thousand years. They should be put back."

Seregil replaced the figure and shell ornament as he'd found them. "I looked the big stone over, but I didn't see any markings. Still, if this was a shrine, maybe it's the temple the prophecy meant."

Nysander shook his head. "No, this is only a marker. Of that I am certain. Before the forest grew up it would have been visible from the sea. From the trail, too, if it existed whenever this was placed here."

"Then the temple must be back up in these woods somewhere," said Micum. "You rest here, Nysander. Seregil and I'll take a look."

The forest here was old virgin growth, Micum saw with a certain degree of relief. The huge, wind-twisted pines were widely spaced, with little undergrowth beneath them. Despite the good visibility, however, after an hour's searching neither he nor Seregil had found anything remotely resembling a temple or any other structure.

Returning to the shore, they found Nysander down on the ledges. It was late afternoon by now, and the tide was nearing its lowest ebb.

"Nothing, eh? That is very puzzling." Leaning on his staff, Nysander frowned out at the sea. "Then again, if we are not finding what we seek, then perhaps we are not looking for the right thing."

Micum sank down on a rock with a discouraged groan. "Then what should we be looking for? We've only got three more days before this eclipse of yours."

Seregil scanned the cove pensively, then set off toward the waterline. "All it means is that it isn't a building."

"I know that look," Micum said, watching him cast back and forth along the ledges like a hound seeking a scent.

The wizard nodded in bemusement. "So do I."

"What are you looking for?" called Micum.

"Don't know yet," Seregil replied absently, poking through the seaweed floating in one of the larger tide pools.

"See how the formation of the stone forms a natural amphitheater?" Nysander pointed out. "You try those higher ledges. I shall take the right."

Micum scrambled diligently up and down the rocks, but found nothing but bleached shells and bird droppings. He was just wondering if Nysander ought to spare a bit of magic after all when Seregil let out a triumphant cackle below.

"What is it?" Micum demanded.

Seregil lay sprawled on his belly, his arms plunged nearly to the shoulder into one of the long, narrow fissures that ran down the lower ledges to the sea.

"Come see for yourself."

Climbing down, Micum and Nysander knelt and peered into the cleft in the stone.

"Look here," said Seregil, pushing aside a clump of rock weed. Beneath it, they saw rows of crudely carved symbols cut into the rock six inches below the top of the crack. Moving along on hands and knees, they found that the symbols formed a continuous band spanning both sides of the fissure all the way down to the sea. A second crevice near the other side of the cove was filled with the same sort of carvings.

"What are they?" asked Micum.

Nysander's pale face lit up with excitement as he studied the whorls, circles, and cross-hatching that formed the patterns. "Such carvings have been found all round the inner seas, but no one has ever deciphered them. Like that stone up there, they were placed here before our kind arrived."

"Another sacred spot," Seregil said, sitting up. "I found the crown in a cave the Dravnians called a spirit chamber. I felt their spirit after I'd gotten the crown. Micum, you remember that underground chamber you found in the Fens?"

"Of course." Micum grimaced, recalling the scene of slaughter.

"You said there was an altar stone of some sort there," Nysander said, exchanging an excited glance with Seregil. "That chamber could have been some sort of holy place, too, before the wooden disks were hidden there." He waved a hand at the carvings they'd found. "And now this place, this ancient temple site. All this suggests that the necromancers use the power of such places to enhance their own magic. Assuming that this is the case, then there must be some significance in Mardus' choice of this rather obscure location."

"I was just thinking the same thing," Seregil said, sighting down the right-hand fissure. Waves surged up the cleft with the gentle heave of the tide, churning up white foam as they lifted the seaweed. After a moment he began pulling off his boots.

"Fetch a rope, would you, Micum?" he asked, stripping off his tunic and shirt as well.

"What are you up to?"

"I just want a look at where these cracks in the rock lead."

Seregil tied one end of the rope around his waist and handed the rest to Micum, then waded into the icy water.

He was thigh deep when the undertow knocked him off his feet. Micum tightened his grip on the rope, but Seregil surfaced and motioned for him to slack up again. Struggling against the waves, he swam farther out and dove beneath the surface.

"What is it he's after?" Micum muttered nervously, paying out more line.

"I cannot imagine," Nysander replied, shaking his head.

Seregil dove twice more before shouting for Micum to haul him in.

Pale and blue-lipped with cold, Seregil staggered up the rock and flattened himself against its sun-warmed surface. Nysander unfastened his cloak and laid it over him.

Micum squatted down beside him. "Find anything?"

"Nothing. I had thought maybe, with the gift tide coming—" Seregil broke off. Sitting up, he smacked a hand across his forehead. "Illior's Fingers, I've had it all backward!"

"Ah, I think I see!" For the first time in days a little color stole into Nysander's bleached cheeks. "How could I have overlooked such an obvious factor?"

"A gift tide?" Micum asked, wondering if he'd heard right.

Seregil's teeth clattered like bakshi stones in a leather cup as he exclaimed, "It's the last piece of the puzzle. Now the rest falls into place."

"What in the hell are you—"

"Twice each month, the moon causes the tide to rise and fall to unusual extremes," Nysander explained. "The fishermen call it a gift tide. On the day of the eclipse there will be such a tide."

"It was the seaweed," Seregil went on, as if that explained everything. "It grows thickest around the low tide line. Last night I noticed that an unusually thick band of it was laid bare at low tide."

"But you just said there was nothing out there," said Micum.

"That's right." Seregil jumped to his feet and headed up the ledges. "And I might have saved myself a swim just now. Leiteus said the eclipse would occur at midday, which is when the tide will be unusually *high*! That's the other half of the cycle!" Water dripped from the tip of his nose as he scrutinized the fissure again, following it up toward the high ground. Suddenly he stooped over a collection of stones jumbled together near one of the parallel fissures, then began tossing them aside.

"Look, a hole," he said, showing them a round hole a hand's span wide bored deep into the stone. Scrabbling along on his knees he soon found another, and then a third.

With the help of the others, he uncovered a total of fourteen of the holes, spaced evenly to form a half circle around a broad, shallow depression in the stone just above the high tide mark. It was an unremarkable looking spot, littered with driftwood, shells, dried seaweed, and other debris, but both of the mysterious crevices in the rock ran through it.

"Here's your temple," Seregil announced.

"I think you may be correct," Nysander said, looking around in amazement.

"It's above the normal tide line now, but from the looks of the debris, the highest tides reach it. It's a sort of natural basin."

"It must have been used by the people who left the writing we found carved there," Nysander speculated. "I wonder what the holes represent?"

"So the eclipse and the high tide that fills this thing will happen at the same time," observed Micum, helping Seregil cover the holes as they had found them.

"The highest point of the tide will lag some minutes behind the completion of the eclipse," the wizard replied. "Which means Mardus will have only a few moments in which to complete whatever ritual he plans before the sun returns. It is generally believed that the more rare the conjunction, the more powerful its effect. With the added factor of the comet, I should say this conjunction will be an extraordinarily potent and dangerous one. That it is so focused on a specific locale makes it all the more so."

"By the Flame!" Micum muttered. "And the three of us are supposed to take on that, with however many Plenimarans thrown in?"

"Four," Seregil amended darkly, shooting Nysander a pointed look. "When the time comes, there are supposed to be *four* of us."

Time passed like a slow nightmare for Alec. By day the cart bumped and jolted over the rough coastal track the column followed. His mounted escort ignored him for the most part, talking among themselves in their own language. With only Thero for company, Alec spent the daylight hours dozing and watching the mountainous countryside go by.

And dreading nightfall.

At night the bear cart was stationed somewhat apart from the camp. Alec quickly learned to fear the moment when his guards faded away into the shadows; this was the signal for Vargûl Ashnazai's festival of nightmares to begin. Later, when the final horror was over and Alec had been reduced to terrified fury, the guards would reappear and whatever was left of the night would pass in relative peace.

The second night Diomis and his mother materialized in the cage, heads clutched beneath their arms as they cursed and accused him. Alec knew they were only illusions, but their accusations stabbed at enough of his own doubts to bring real pain. Turning his back on them, he stuffed his fingers in his ears and tried to ignore the prodding and buffeting of their cold, ghostly hands. It was pointless to fight back—they had no more substance than air.

Curling tighter in his misery, he waited for Ashnazai to tire of the game.

When it was over, Alec lay listening to the small sounds of the night—an owl's hunting call, the distant nickering of horses, the low murmur of the guards, who'd come back as soon as Ashnazai had gone.

Where did they go? he wondered, letting his mind wander where it would.

A better question: why do they go?

His eyes widened as he stared up into the night sky. Every time Ashnazai had tormented him, on the ship and now, he did it without witnesses. This seemed to verify something Alec already suspected. Vargûl Ashnazai did not want anyone, especially Mardus, to know what he was up to.

The following night there was no sign of Ashnazai. Huddled close to Thero's sleeping form, Alec stared out into the shadows, bracing for whatever new horror was to come.

The moon rose. The stars wheeled slowly past the branches, but nothing disturbed the surrounding stillness. A sweet spring breeze swept through the boughs, carrying to him the scents of resin, damp mosses, and tender green herbs sprouting from the forest loam. Closing his eyes, he imagined himself walking through those wooded hills with his bow as he had with his father. In spite of his fear, he drifted off and dreamed of hunting and forest trails and freedom.

He was awakened by someone whispering his name. A dark figure stood next to the cart, beckoning him to the bars.

Alec crouched warily. "What do you want?"

"Alec, it's me," the man replied softly. He pushed his hood back and the moonlight struck his face.

"Seregil!" Alec managed a choked whisper. Scrambling over, he thrust his hand out to his friend. Seregil clasped it and pressed it to his lips. He was real, solid, warm. Alec clung to him, heedless of the tears of relief rolling down his own cheeks. "I never thought— How did you find us?"

Reaching through the bars, Seregil cupped Alec's face in his hands. "No time to explain, *talí.* I've got to get you out of there." Releasing Alec reluctantly, he went to the back of the cart to examine the lock.

"Be careful. Vargûl Ashnazai put some kind of magic on it."

Seregil glanced up. "Who?"

"The necromancer who was with Mardus in Wolde. And he's not the only one around, either. They've got a dyrmagnos with them."

"Bilairy's Balls! But there's got to be some way. I'm not leaving you here!"

Alec's heart hammered in his chest as he watched Seregil inspect the lock. It was torture, being this close but still separated.

"Ah, here's something—" Seregil began, but just then torch-light flared behind him.

"Seregil, look out!"

Turning, they found Vargûl Ashnazai leering up at them, flanked by a half-dozen armed soldiers.

"How clever of you to have found us," the necromancer gloated. "I much appreciate your effort. And your boy played his part very convincingly, no?"

Seregil shot Alec a startled look.

It was the cruelest blow yet, that accusing look. It froze Alec's throat, so that he could only shake his head imploringly.

Seregil drew his sword and sprang from the wagon, away from Ashnazai's men. But others were waiting for him in the shadows.

Flinging himself against the bars, Alec watched with horror as Seregil fought for his life. He ran a guard through and slashed another across the neck before the others leapt at him from behind, knocking him to the ground and pinning him.

The necromancer barked an order and they yanked Seregil to his feet. His face was bloody, but he held his head high and spat at the necromancer, eyes blazing with hate.

Ashnazai gave another order. This time Seregil was dragged up into the bear cart and lashed hand and foot to the bars facing Alec.

"I didn't help him, I swear," Alec whispered hoarsely. "Oh, Seregil, I—"

"It doesn't matter much—now," Seregil growled, turning his face away.

"Not in the least," Ashnazai agreed, climbing into the cart behind him with Seregil's sword in his hand. "It's a pity you were cut, but then I'd hardly dare chance putting the two of you together again." He grabbed Seregil by the hair, pulling his head back. "Who knows what mischief you'd make, eh?"

Stepping back, he placed the point of the sword against the small of Seregil's back and pushed slowly, twisting the blade.

Seregil let out a strangled cry and grasped the bars. Alec reached through, grappling for the sword, but one of Ashnazai's men pulled him away, holding him back as the necromancer drove the blade out through Seregil's belly and then yanked it free.

Seregil let out a harsh scream and sank to his knees. Struggling free, Alec caught at him, trying to hold him through the bars. He felt hot blood under his hands. More ran from the corner of Seregil's mouth.

Alec wanted to speak, but no words would come. Seregil looked at him, his wide grey eyes full of sorrow and recrimination.

Pulling the dying man's head back again, Ashnazai drew the blade across Seregil's throat. More blood pumped from the severed arteries, spattering Alec's face and chest.

Seregil struggled weakly for a moment, his last breath gurgling horribly through the gaping wound. With a final spasm, he went limp, eyes open and vacant.

Sobbing, Alec clung to his friend's body until the soldiers cut it loose from the bars and dragged it from his grasp.

Ashnazai looked down at him with disdain. "That was most enjoyable. Your turn comes soon, but not so mercifully. But then, you know that, I think."

It had been an illusion, just another of Ashnazai's tricks.

Alec repeated this over and over to himself as the cart rumbled north the next day.

But the dried blood on his hands and clothing was real enough. So were the stains on the canvas ticking of the mattress and the wood at the back of the cart where Seregil had fallen.

Seregil is dead.
It was an illusion.
Seregil is dead.
It was—

His grief was too deep for tears. It was so vast that it blotted out everything else. He couldn't eat or sleep or take in his surroundings. Hunched in a corner of the cage, he clasped his hands around his knees and rested his head on them, shutting out the world.

Seregil is dead.

• • •

As the flat, empty day wore on, Alec often felt Ashnazai's gloating gaze on him, sipping at his anguish like wine. He kept his eyes averted, unable to bear the sight of that smug, satisfied smile. The necromancer bided his time, keeping his distance until the afternoon.

"The guards tell me you eat and drink nothing all day," he said, riding beside him.

Alec ignored him.

"Too bad not to keep up your strength," Ashnazai went on airily. "Perhaps a diversion will cheer you. The scouts found a cave where we will make camp. After so many days of this cage— so drafty, so many eyes looking—a snug cave will be nice for you, eh? It will be most, how do you say—?" He paused. "Most cozy."

His parting laugh left no doubt that something particularly unpleasant was in the offing. Alec shivered, partly out of dread, partly from a sudden burst of excitement. This could be his final chance for escape.

He gazed out over the ocean, trying to imagine how many miles lay between him and Rhíminee.

Nysander was dead.

Seregil was dead.

Cilla. Diomis. Thryis. Rhiri.

The names fell like stones against his heart. If he couldn't get away tonight, then he'd just as soon die trying.

Sometimes total despair was the best substitute for hope.

The column halted for the night at the base of a small cliff surrounded by forest. Below the road, the ground fell way sharply to sea-washed ledges.

By this point, Alec had taken stock of his limited options. Somewhere to the north lay the Mycenian border. If he did manage to get free tonight, it was the only direction worth going. If he followed the coast, it improved his chances of meeting friendly forces. It meant fleeing with Thero in tow and Mardus close behind, but if he could elude him, stay concealed and some distance ahead, then maybe they had a chance. If not, he'd put up a fight.

When the column showed signs of stopping for the night he

quickly transferred the precious nail from the seam of his tunic into his mouth and stood at the bars, watching. The wagoneer drove the bear cart some way apart from the main camp as usual, trundling to a halt at the ledges on the seaward side of the trail. Their position, Alec noted with growing hope, had the added advantage of being to the north of the main camp, which meant fewer pickets between him and freedom.

Ashnazai was taking no chances. Half a dozen armed guards came to escort the prisoners to their new quarters. The cave was a rough, deep fissure beneath a shelf of ledge overlooking the sea. It was damp, but large enough for a man to stand up in. A stout iron staple had been driven into a crack in the back wall and two lengths of heavy chain hung from it.

One of the guards asked something in Plenimaran. The necromancer answered at some length and his men laughed, then looped the end of a chain around Alec's neck and secured it with a padlock.

"He asked if I wished you shackled by the leg," Ashnazai told Alec. "I told him, 'An animal will chew off a limb to escape a trap but I think even this clever young thief cannot chew off his own head.' "

Still chuckling darkly at the *voron*'s little joke, the guards chained Thero in the same fashion while Vargûl Ashnazai looked on with obvious satisfaction.

"That should hold you nicely," he said, giving the staple a final tug. "I suggest you waste no effort in trying to free yourself from these bonds. Even if you did somehow manage to do so, you would find your way blocked by things more dangerous than chains or guards. Rest now, while you can." Favoring Alec with another sly, repulsive smile, he added, "Our time together grows short. I look forward to making this a memorable evening for us all."

Hatred welled up in Alec's throat like bile. Ashnazai was only a few feet away, well within the reach of the chain—Alec clenched his fists at his sides and mumbled, "I won't forget you anytime soon."

Ashnazai followed the guards out through the low opening, then turned and wove a series of symbols in the air in front of it. He walked away out of sight, but Alec could see at least two guards stationed outside. They spoke among themselves in low, bantering voices, their shadows passing across the entrance as they kindled a watch fire and settled down to the night's vigil.

With one eye on the entrance, Alec spat the nail out into his hand and set to work. First he examined the lock they'd used on Thero's chain. It was large and sturdy, but he recognized the design as one of only moderate complexity.

With the proper tool, he amended mentally. The nail was not a particularly delicate instrument for such work, but it did fit inside the keyhole. Closing his eyes, he gently worked it in against the wards until he felt them give way. There were four in all; it took several tense minutes to jigger them, but at last the lock fell open in his hand. He left the curved link holding Thero's chain in place. Anyone coming in for a quick look would be none the wiser so long as it was turned around to the back of his neck. He did the same with his own, then turned his attention to Thero's other restraints.

The lock at the back of the branks was too small for his crude pick. Shifting Thero into the faint light from the watch fire, he inspected the iron wristbands.

They were seamless, presumably put on by magic. Though too snug to slip off over Thero's hands, they turned easily on his bony wrists. Alec could easily slip a finger into the space between arm and band.

Perhaps, he smiled darkly to himself, the bands had been tighter before two weeks of abuse and scant rations had taken their toll. Apparently no one, not even Mardus, had taken that into account.

Looking up, he found Thero staring at him. It sent a chill over his heart. Irtuk Beshar had made a speaking puppet of the wizard before; who was it now, looking at him out of those foggy eyes?

"Thero," he whispered, taking one of the man's cold hands in his own. "Do you know me? Can you understand what I say?"

Thero gave no sign of understanding, but his gaze did not waver.

Alec shook his head, hardening his resolve. They had nothing to lose and everything to gain. If the dyrmagnos was spying on him through Thero's eyes and alerted Mardus, then he'd just shed a little of his own blood and force their hand tonight.

"I've had enough, Thero. I'm done going along like a sheep to slaughter," he went on softly, tearing a strip from his tunic and tucking it around the mouth plate of the branks. Thero offered no resistance as Alec moved the crude gag into place.

"You need to keep quiet no matter what happens next, all right? You hear? No matter what, don't make a sound."

Alec stood up and grasped Thero's thumbs firmly. Placing his foot against the young wizard's chest, he took a deep breath and yanked the thumbs with all his strength, twisting sharply as he pulled. He'd seen Seregil do this trick, but had never had the nerve or opportunity to try it himself.

To his mingled relief and amazement, both joints dislocated cleanly on the first attempt. Thero's thin hands folded in on themselves with sickening ease, allowing Alec to work the bands off. There was no time for gentleness; fortunately whatever magicks kept Thero dazed held until the second band was off. As it slipped free, he gave a soft, strangled groan and curled forward against Alec's knees, holding his limp hands to his chest.

Resetting the joints proved less easy. Alec could feel the bones skating around under the skin as he pulled and strained, trying to seat the bones back in their sockets. He could hear Thero's breath whistling harshly around the gag as he fought not to cry out. Both of them were drenched with sweat by the time the job was done.

"Damnation!" Thero whimpered, still biting down on the mouth plate.

"Not so loud," Alec pleaded, holding Thero's head against his chest to muffle any cries. His own stomach was doing a slow lurch of its own. "I'm sorry, it was the only way. Are you free of it?"

Thero nodded. "Saw, 'eard everythin'. Couldn't move— Saw every—"

"So did I," Alec told him, patting his shoulder. "We've got to forget that for now, while we figure out how to get away from here. What about these, though?" He pointed to the wristbands, unwilling to touch them again. "Can the necromancers tell you're not wearing them?"

Thero sat up. "Don' know. 'magos work."

"What about your magic?"

Before Thero could answer, they heard the warning sounds of the guards moving around outside. Alec's heart sank as he listened to their footsteps fading away.

Thero hid the wristbands in the shadows behind him. Alec moved a few feet away, out of the light.

This is it, he thought coldly, rising to his feet. *Whatever happens, this is it.*

A moment later Ashnazai entered carrying a small lantern. The sudden light stung Alec's eyes and he looked away, noting as he did that Thero sat half-turned to the wall, wrists out of sight in his lap.

Ignoring the young wizard, Vargûl Ashnazai closed in on Alec. "I trust you're prepared for the evening's entertainment?"

There was a mad possessiveness in his manner; not even the fear of Mardus was going to get in the way of whatever obscene pleasures he intended to grant himself tonight. The man's raw hatred was a palpable force in the confines of the cave. Trapped in the gaze of those hungry black eyes, Alec suddenly felt his plans of escape turning to dust in his hands.

"What about the guards?" Alec managed, his voice a hollow whisper. He was grasping at straws and they both knew it.

Ashnazai set the lantern on the floor beside him and pulled off his gloves. "They're of no concern. No sound will be heard beyond these walls until I choose to allow it. And even if it did, who would rush to your aid? Duke Mardus, perhaps? How fond he is of you! Almost as fond as I, but distracted just now by practical concerns. Fortunately, I have no task at the moment except you.

"Ah, I have been patient," he crooned, raising one pale hand to stitch a spell pattern on the air. "How I have waited for such a moment as this."

"So have I, necromancer!"

Alec scarcely had time to realize that the harsh, ragged voice was Thero's before he was blinded by a brilliant explosion of light. A screech of rage or pain rang out, but Alec couldn't tell which of them it came from.

Blinking away the black spots dancing across his eyes, Alec saw the twisted remains of the branks lying on the ground at Thero's feet. He also saw with alarm that whatever spell Thero had cast, it had only wounded Ashnazai, and not nearly enough. Bloodied but still standing, the necromancer rounded on Thero, hands raised for another attack.

Tearing the open lock off, Alec pulled chain from around his neck. Grasping a length of it in both hands, he sprang at Ashnazai, got the chain around the necromancer's throat, and yanked it tight.

Vargûl Ashnazai writhed like a huge serpent, tearing at the chain. Alec pulled it tighter and dragged him to the ground. He'd never strangled anything before, but rage proved a willing teacher. Nothing existed except the feeling of power coursing through his body as he braced a knee against the necromancer's back and hauled the chain tighter until it cut into the flesh of his hands and the necromancer's throat.

"This is for Seregil, you son of a bitch!" he snarled. "For what you did to Cilla and Thryis and Rhiri and Diomis and Luthas and Thero. And *me*!"

He yanked the chain back and heard bones snap. Ashnazai went limp under him, head lolling.

Alec pushed him onto his back and stared into the hated face. Ashnazai's tongue protruded from his foam-flecked lips. His bulging eyes were wide with agony and surprise.

Satisfied, Alec pulled the ivory vial from the necromancer's neck and hung it around his own. Whatever this was, no one was going to use it against him again.

"We've got to get out of here now," Thero warned, still weak and breathless. "That spell, the attack— We've got to go before the guards come back!"

"What about the warding spells he cast on the entrance?" Alec asked, helping the wizard to his feet.

Thero was shaky, but determined. "They were dispelled when you killed him."

"Good." Vargûl Ashnazai was nothing more to him than forgotten carrion now. Turning his back on the body, he extinguished the lantern, then crept to the mouth of the cave.

The guards were still off minding their own business somewhere, leaving their master to his pastimes, but the fire they'd built was still bright. The minute he and Thero stepped out, they'd be visible to anyone lingering nearby.

"Can't you translocate us or something?" Alec whispered, surveying the scene.

"I'd have done that already if I could!" Thero replied with a welcome hint of his customary brusqueness. "Get me away from here and I may be able to do something else, though."

"You'd better be praying for Illior's luck, then." Alec pointed north into the darkness. "We're going that way, understand? We'll have to keep low and follow the ledge below the road until we get away from the main camp."

Alec left unsaid the fact that any number of guards could be within fifty feet of them and they wouldn't know it until it was too late; he was trying hard not to think of that himself. With Thero at his side he sent up one last silent prayer and hurried past the fire into the darkness beyond.

There didn't seem to be anyone around, but peering up over the ledges they could see men hunkered around a campfire less than a hundred feet way.

Their bare feet made no sound as they stole along the rocky shore to the edge of the forest just north of the camp. The open ground between the stunted trees was treacherously laced with exposed roots jutting out of the thin soil. Alec clutched Thero by the arm, pulling him along as he stumbled.

They soon spotted several men on picket duty ahead of them. The guards were watching for trouble coming from outside the camp, however, and Alec skirted around their position with no trouble. Gauging their direction by the moon, he led the way north.

They'd been going for less than half an hour when Thero suddenly pulled Alec to a halt in a small, moon-washed gully.

"Look, I'm tired, too, but we can't afford to rest," Alec urged.

"It's not that," Thero whispered. "They know we're gone. I just felt something, a searching, I think. It won't take Irtuk Beshar any time to find us."

"Oh, gods!" Alec gasped, looking back the way they'd come. "We can't get taken, Thero. They'll sacrifice you and now that I've been bloodied there's nothing to stop Mardus from—!"

"Shut up," Thero interrupted, giving him an abrupt shake. "Kneel down."

"You've got your magic back!" Alec breathed, relief washing over him. "Can you translocate us now?"

"No, I don't have the power." Thero's lean, bearded face was lost in shadow as he laid cold hands on Alec's shoulders. "Clear your mind and relax. This spell will only last until sunrise; remember that if you can. Sunrise. You'll have to run hard, go as far as you can before—"

They both froze as a weird, preternatural howl burst out from the direction of the camp. It rose to a mad, sobbing cackle, fell away, only to erupt again, closer this time.

"Too late!" hissed Alec, then winced as Thero grabbed him by both arms and forced him back to his knees.

"No it's not!" Thero held him down, speaking urgently. "Clear your mind, Alec, relax. This takes only a moment."

Another gibbering howl floated to them through the night. Alec bowed his head, wondering what it was that Thero intended, and why it suddenly seemed so familiar.

"That's good, very good," whispered Thero. "Alec í Amasa Kerry, *untir maligista*—"

It was the unaccustomed sound of his full name that triggered Alec's memory. He opened his mouth to protest, but the magic had already taken hold.

"Untir maligista kewat, Alec í Amasa Kerry." Thero continued, pouring out all his remaining power as he pressed down hard on Alec's shoulders. Whatever horror Irtuk Beshar had unleashed was crashing through the trees toward them, bellowing its lunatic hunting call.

Throwing back his head, Thero cried out, "Let thy inner symbol be revealed!"

The change was nearly instantaneous. One moment Alec was kneeling before him, the next a young stag was shaking the remains of the tattered tunic from its antlers. Nostrils flaring, it leapt away from Thero, then looked back in confusion. A ghostly residue of magic still glimmered faintly around it, but that would soon fade.

Thero took a tentative step toward it, though he knew Alec was probably past understanding human speech.

"I didn't intentionally betray the Orëska," he told him. "Let this be the atonement for my blindness. Go on. Run!"

The stag lowered its head, lashing its antlers from side to side as if refusing to leave him.

"No, Alec, go."

A greedy snarl from the shadows settled the issue; the stag turned and bolted.

The last thing Thero saw was the white flash of its tail.

They'd had time now to learn the pattern of the Plenimaran camp. Pickets were stationed along the landward perimeter a quarter mile out, with a second line closer in. It made a tight net but, like any net, it was also a pattern of holes.

Silent and deadly as true *urgazhi*, Beka and her raiders quietly killed four pickets, stripped them of their tunics and weapons, then worked their way toward the mass of sleeping prisoners.

The clearness of the night was against them. The moon was nearing full and by its light they could make out the details of each other's faces as they gathered for the raid. By that same betraying light, they also saw that Gilly and Mirn had again managed to keep themselves as close as possible to the outside edge of the group. Stripped to the waist, they lay on their backs, heads resting on the plank.

Just then, angry shouts burst out somewhere on the far side of the camp. Whatever was going on, it was attracting the attention of the whole camp. Several of the sentries stationed among the prisoners moved off in the direction of the noise. From somewhere nearby came the snort and bellow of a bull.

"By Sakor, we'll never have a better chance than this!" Beka whispered.

Her plan was simple, direct, and fraught with the possibility for complete disaster. The others understood this, but had been unanimously in favor of the rescue.

Bows at the ready, Beka and the others watched from the cover of the trees while Steb, Rhylin, Nikides, and Kallas pulled on the stolen enemy tunics and strode casually out in the direction of the prisoners.

Still focused on the outcry, none of the sentries challenged the four raiders as they quickly lifted the planked prisoners and rushed them into the shelter of the trees. The whole act was accomplished in a moment's time.

The raiding party ghosted back the way they'd come until they reached Jareel and Ariani, who'd been left behind to guard the horses well outside the Plenimaran perimeter.

"Knew you'd come," Gilly said faintly as Kallas and Nikides lowered him gently to the ground on his back beside Mirn.

Their hands were swollen and purple where the long spikes pierced their palms. Their shoulders had rubbed raw against the rough planks. Looking more closely at them now, Beka saw from the numerous other bruises and abrasions that covered both men that they must have often stumbled and fallen beneath their awkward burdens.

"Rest easy, riders," she said, kneeling next to them. At her nod, several of the others held their legs and shoulders. Nikides bent to cut the ropes lashing their arms to the wood, but Sergeant Braknil stopped him.

"Best leave those on 'til we're done," he cautioned. "Give them both a belt to bite down on and let's get this over with."

Using a pair of farrier's pliers, he set his foot against the plank and wrenched the first spike from Gilly's hand.

It was an excruciating process. The flesh had swollen and festered badly around the spikes and Braknil had to dig into the skin to get a proper grip.

Gilly fainted as the first spike pulled free. Mirn gnawed doggedly at the belt between his teeth while tears of pain streamed down into his ears.

"Easy now," Beka murmured, trying not to let the rage and revulsion she felt show in her voice as she pressed her hands down on his shoulders. "It'll be over soon."

When it was over, Braknil bathed their wounds with seawater and bandaged them with strips of sweat-stained linen and wool each rider had cut from their clothing.

"Neither of them is in any condition to ride," said Beka. "Rhylin, you and Kallas are the strongest riders so you'll take them. Nikides, see that those planks come with us, and the spikes. Don't leave the bastards any more sign than we can help."

As the rest of the turma mounted for the retreat, a new cry came from the direction of the camp, one that brought gooseflesh up on every arm.

The mad, unnatural howl rose and fell, then burst out again, quavering as if some monstrous throat was about to burst with the effort. The horses tossed their heads, nervously scenting the wind.

"Bilairy's Balls! What was that, Lieutenant?" gasped Tealah.

"Let's hope we don't find out," Beka muttered. The awful cry came again. "No, it's headed away from us. Let's move on before it changes its mind."

"Which way?" Rhylin asked, shifting his hold around Mirn, who'd finally fainted.

"Inland, out of their path," Beka replied as another faint howl floated back to them through the trees.

"And away from whatever *that* is!" someone muttered as they spurred away.

Alec?

Nysander's brow creased as he stared unseeingly into the darkness. It had been Thero's essence he felt first; now there was only Alec's, glimmering in his mind like a distant beacon.

It took no expenditure of power to sense it—the energy was clear, perhaps due to the strong magic fused with it. Nysander recognized the familiar imprint of the spell.

Well done, Thero! But why had the young wizard's own essence disappeared so suddenly?

Feeling Alec's fleeting tremor again, he focused the slightest burst of magic on it, silently mouthing, *Come to us, Alec. We need you.*

They'd taken shelter beneath an old salt pine in the forest above the temple site. The tips of the tree's lower limbs swept nearly to the ground, forming a low, tentlike space inside.

Stretched out on the thick fragrant bed of fallen needles,

Micum snored softly. Beside him, Seregil tossed restlessly, muttering in Aurënfaie.

The wizard had felt little need for sleep since his arrival in Plenimar. The quiet hours of the night were too precious to waste. Instead, he kept watch and wove his meditations, nurturing his returning strength. He only hoped it would be enough when the time came.

Seregil shifted again, uttering a low moan. Nysander considered waking him, sharing this first sign of hope, but it was too soon; if Seregil believed Alec was nearby, then he would strike off on his own after him. Alec was still too far away.

Leaning back against the pine's knobby trunk, he resumed his lonely vigil.

The Four was whole again; they would find each other.

Beka's raiders pushed due east until the moon set. At dawn they found themselves on a rocky highland overlooking the misty blue sea in the distance.

Mirn's and Gilly's hands looked like bloated gloves, mottled with angry shades of purple, red, and yellow. When Braknil had finished with the new dressings, Beka drew him a little apart from the others.

"You've seen this before. What do you think?" she asked, keeping her voice low.

"I'd give a year's bounty for a drysian." The sergeant was careful to keep his back to the others. "Even then I don't know if the hands could be saved. As it is here, field dressing's the best I can do and I've got no simples to work with but brine. That might be enough to draw the pus off, but if they take the blood poisoning—" He gave a small, expressive shrug. "Well, it'd be kinder to speed them on."

Looking back to the others, Beka watched Tare coaxing the wounded men to drink.

"Thirty-four of us rode out of Rhíminee together, a green lieutenant and green troops, except for you," Beka said grimly. "Now look at us."

"It was that attack on the regiment that cleaned us out," Braknil reminded her. "You led us well there. What happened wasn't your fault. Every one of us that fell went down with honor. We've fared damn well with all the raiding we've done since and that *is* your doing. All that counts now is getting back to our own lines with what we've learned."

Beka gave her sergeant a weary half smile. "So you keep telling me. Let's see if Mirn and Gilly have anything to add."

"Some of the other prisoners spoke some Skalan," Mirn told them weakly, his head resting on Steb's leg. "One of them said the general's name is Mardus, a lord of some degree. He's got necromancers with him, too."

"Necromancers," snorted Gilly, staring down at his useless hands. "One of them looked more demon than wizard. Black as something raked out of the fire, but alive as you or me! No one knew where we were headed, but everyone knew what was going on at night and it was her doing it!"

"It was some kind of sacrifice," explained Mirn. "The guards came every night at sundown and you could see everyone trying to shrink down out of sight any way they could, hoping they wouldn't be the ones chosen. We were on the other side of camp from the ceremony most nights, but we could hear well enough to know that they were cutting up the poor buggers alive—" He broke off, shuddering. "Afterward the other wizard, the man, would conjure up a black fetch to take away the bodies. The next day we'd march right over the spot where it happened and I swear to you, there wouldn't be so much as a drop of blood anywhere."

"A black fetch?" several riders murmured uneasily.

"By the Flame! You suppose that's what we heard howling in the woods last night?" Tare asked.

"Go on," Beka urged, ignoring the others.

"What I'll never figure is why they didn't do us," Gilly groaned, his voice suddenly unsteady. "By the Flame, Lieutenant, we were enemy captives. They planked us, all right, but nothing more. All the rest of the lot were plain folk: sailors taken by press gangs, Skalans, Mycenians. Women and children, too. But most of them were Plenimarans. Their own people!"

Both men fell silent, then Mirn sighed. "Sorry, Lieutenant, that's about all there is to tell."

Beka shook her head. "Don't apologize. You rest easy now."

Getting to her feet, she looked around at the others. "I figure we can't be more than four or five days ride from Mycena. If we're lucky, our side's made some headway south by now. Ariani, I'm sending you back to the regiment with a verbal dispatch. Take the

two best horses, ride as hard as you can, and get word back to
Commander Klia about what we've seen."

Ariani snapped a proud salute. "I will, Lieutenant."

"Corporal Nikides, you're in charge of taking back the
wounded. We'll rig up drag litters for Mirn and Gilly here. Steb,
you'll go with them. The rest of us will dog the column for a few
more days."

Steb looked down at Mirn, clearly torn in his loyalties. "With
all due respect, Lieutenant, that only leaves twelve of you. I can
shoot and fight as well with one eye as ever I did with two."

"That's why I need you to protect the wounded," she told him,
and saw his look of relief. "That goes for you, too, Nikides," she
added, seeing that the corporal was about to object. "Head north as
fast as you can. You're my secondary couriers in case Ariani
doesn't make it. The rest of us are staying to spy, not fight."

Leaving Braknil in charge, Beka made a wide circuit of the
camp, coming to a halt at last on a west-facing outcrop downhill
from the others. She could hear them grumbling among themselves. Those being sent away were none too happy about leaving
the others behind; those staying wondered what more there was to
be learned.

Beka sighed heavily. She'd already wrestled with the decision
to further fragment what was left of the turma. None of her supe-
riors would fault her for turning back now.

But what would they say about her reasons for staying? As her
eye wandered north up the coastline she again felt the strange
impression of familiarity and rightness that had come over her the
night they'd first seen the comet.

Whoever this Lord Mardus was, whatever he was up to with
his necromancers and pointless marches to nowhere, newly honed
instincts told Beka that she was too close to learning his secrets to
leave off now.

47

JUST A STAG IN THE DARK

Cries rang out behind him as Alec fled the little clearing. The voices of the Man and the Other mingled for a moment, then were silent. An inchoate sense of confusion stirred again, but his animal consciousness drove him on, deeper into the forest and away from the carrion reek. He scented other Men in the forest around him but they were easy enough to evade.

The first time Nysander had cast the spell of intrinsic nature on him, all those months ago in the safety of the Orëska garden, Alec's conscious identity had been so totally overwhelmed by that of his beast form that Nysander had hastily changed him back before he could harm himself or anyone else in the resulting confusion.

It was the same this time, and it had been his overpowering animal flight instinct that had undoubtedly saved his life.

The wind was alive with scent as he dashed headlong through the darkness. Heeding the warnings that came to his nose, he avoided the Plenimaran pickets, bounding through thickets and over gullies and deadfalls with unthinking ease. As he fled, his mind slowly recovered from the shock of the change, blending with that of the stag into a state of heightened awareness that was neither animal nor human.

Emerging from the trees onto a rocky sea cliff, he stopped for a moment, muzzle dark with foam. Below him the tide crashed against the rocks, sending up great fans of spray.

The comet was burning across the sky and sight of it sent a fresh wave of panic through him. Every muscle trembled and twitched, every instinct screamed flight. But he remained still, long sensitive ears sharply forward, nostrils wide. As his strange blood slowly cooled, something new caught at his senses. Pawing the rock with one cloven hoof, he uttered a plaintive bellow, then stood motionless, listening.

The answering call was nothing more than the faintest of whispers in the silence of his mind. There was no voice or scent or image, only the summoning of instinct.

North, still north. Follow and trust.

Like a bird that suddenly recalls the route south after the first frost, Alec gave himself up to the pull of that faint glimmer, his mind still too clouded by the stag's to question or doubt.

With another deep-throated cry he set his face to the wind and bounded onward.

Moon shadow patterns slid across his broad back as he ran and his human mind gradually began to marvel at the sensation of this startling new body. He could feel the strain and bunch of the stag's muscles as he sprang, the pumping of its great heart, the weight of the heavy rack that it bore with no more thought than he'd ever given to a hat.

The familiar scents of sea and forest took on a new richness beyond human perception. Pausing to drink at a flowing spring, he couldn't resist the aroma of young mallow shoots growing around it. The wet green taste of them filled his mouth like honeycomb. A little grey owl winged across his path with a soft rush of feathers as he set off again.

The coastline grew more desolate as he moved north, and in the distance he could see a solitary peak jutting up against the stars. The ledges were broader here, extending out into the sea and cleft with crevasses and bands of darker stone. Farther up, where rock met grassland, mats of crowberry and lichen sent up a sweet aroma as he trampled across.

The sea slowly retreated down the rocks toward the low mark, leaving behind glistening tide pools that shone like black mirrors in the darkness. The moon sank into the sea and the stars danced toward home. As the wind shifted and night scents began to fade he smelled horses and men. Picking his way down into a gully, he stood motionless, sniffing the breeze, until they'd passed him and disappeared to the north.

Alec sensed the coming dawn long before the first tinge of it appeared in the sky. The pellucid light of the false dawn welled up behind the mountains, waking flotillas of gulls and ducks that had ridden the waves out beyond the pull of the breakers. Something in the change of light tugged at his memory, but consumed by the irresistible pull of instinct and the summons, he could not recall what it was.

The first ray of true dawn touched him as he sprang across a foaming cleft in the rocks. The stag form blurred in midair, leaving in its place a thin, naked youth.

Sheer momentum carried Alec across. He landed awkwardly, skinning his knees and elbows. Still reeling from the transformation, he sprawled on his back and blinked up at the marbled gold sky, wondering dully where he was and how he'd come to be there.

Waves surged up the cleft he'd just jumped, flinging glittering white spray across his bare skin. As Alec struggled to his knees, he realized he was still wearing the ivory vial he'd taken from Vargûl Ashnazai. Prying it open, he emptied the contents into his palm, a few dark slivers of wood.

A blinding flash of memory rocked him—Ashnazai toying with the vial as he wove his tortures aboard the *Kormados*, the look of satisfaction on his face when he cut Seregil's throat, Thero's last despairing cry as it mingled with the howl of whatever had been unleashed against them after their escape. With a choked sob, he flung the pieces into the sea and screamed his sorrow after them.

But even as he mourned, the summons was still there, fainter somehow but still clear enough.

North.

The first Plenimaran scouts reached the temple site just after dawn. Micum was on watch and heard their horses in time to hide in the underbrush next to the track. He waited until they passed him, heading toward the white stone, then hurried back to the pine shelter to warn the others.

"They're on their way," he whispered, crawling under the screen of branches. "Two Plenimaran scouts just went by on the road, headed north."

"It is fortunate that they keep to the road," Nysander murmured, stroking his chin absently.

"Why is that?" asked Seregil.

Nysander sighed heavily, then looked up at his two companions. "Alec is on his way to us. He is keeping to the shoreline, so it is fortunate that the Plenimarans take the road."

"He's on his way?" Micum gasped, incredulous. "How do you know? *When* did you know?"

Seregil said nothing, but Micum saw the sudden tension in him, and the hectic spots of color that leapt into his sunken cheeks.

"I sensed him just after midnight last night," replied Nysander.

"You *knew* he was out there and you didn't tell us?" Seregil hissed. "Illior's Light, Nysander, why not?"

"You would only have charged off in the darkness with very little hope of accomplishing anything but damage to yourselves. He was too far away for you to reach on foot. Thero seems to have had a hand in his escape—"

"That traitorous bastard?" Seregil's eyes narrowed dangerously.

"Stop it, Seregil!" Nysander ordered, finally giving rein to his own anger. It flashed across his face, startling as lightning from a clear sky. "Whatever Thero's past actions may have been, it would appear that he used his own magic to aid Alec's escape, quite possibly at the expense of his own life. Alec is alone. This has brought him closer to us than losing either of you would have. If Mardus' scouts have reached us already, then the man himself cannot be far behind."

Seregil opened his mouth to protest but Micum spoke first.

"I don't like it either, but he's right and we both know it," he said grudgingly.

"Well, what about now, then?" demanded Seregil, still boiling. "We can't just sit here hoping he finds us by sheer luck! Bilairy's Balls, Nysander, if you're so certain of where he is, magick him in!"

"You know I cannot expend that kind of power now. However, I was able to send a summoning and place some protections around him, as well. Mardus will not find him by magic."

Seregil reached for his boots and sword belt.

"But you knew about him last night," Micum said, frowning. "How did you do that, if not with magic?"

"I did nothing. The knowledge simply came to me."

"Then why don't Micum and I sense him?" Seregil demanded.

"Who knows? Go to him now; help him He is coming from the south."

"Ah, that's one of my titles, isn't it? The Guide?" Seregil growled, grabbing up a water skin and pushing out through the branches.

Micum moved to follow, but Nysander laid a hand on his arm. "Let him go."

Seregil's anger quickly gave way to cautious joy as he loped along over the rocks. During the long days on the *Lady*, hope had dwindled to a stubborn refusal to imagine the worst. Now it seemed Nysander's faith in the prophecy had been proven. Against all odds, the four of them were being brought together again on this hostile shore.

The tide had just turned past low, leaving tide pools and treacherous masses of bladder wrack gleaming in the morning sun. Great green swells rolled in from the open sea, wave upon wave smashing to geysers of glistening spume against the rocks. A freshening wind off the water carried the spray up the shore; Seregil turned his face to it as he stalked along, tasted salt on his lips.

Nothing else mattered. Alec was alive.

He kept one eye on the trees as he went. One patrol had shown up already; there would be others. Within the hour he spied the glint of sunlight off metal.

Taking cover in a rocky cleft, he listened as a group of riders passed at a gallop. From the sound of it, there were at least a dozen of them. Waiting until the last sound of their horses had faded away to the north, he continued on his way.

Another hour passed and he began to worry that they'd somehow missed each other. Alec could have taken refuge, as he had, under an outcropping or in the forest. Or had an accident or been recaptured. Reining in these dark thoughts, Seregil sat down on a damp block of stone to catch his breath.

His arrival dislodged a small nation of striped periwinkles,

which clattered and rolled away like a cascade of marbles into
the tide pool at his feet. A gull circled down to drink on the opposite side.

"I'll find him," Seregil sighed aloud, resting his head in his
hands. "He's here and I'll find him."

The gull regarded him with one skeptical yellow eye, then
flapped off with a derisive jeer. Turning his head to watch it,
Seregil froze in disbelief. A wan, battered spector stood looking
down at him from a shelf of rock not twenty feet away.

"Alec!"

Thin, bruised, and naked, Alec swayed visibly as the wind buffeted him. Despite his obvious exhaustion, however, he was
poised for flight.

"Alec, it's me," Seregil said more gently, watching hope and
fear warring in those dark, narrowed eyes. What had put such deep
distrust there? "What's wrong, *tali*?"

"What are you doing here?" Alec croaked, and the wariness in
his voice went through Seregil like a knife.

"Looking for you. Nysander's here, too, and Micum. They're
back that way."

"Nysander's dead," Alec said, taking a step backward.

"No, he almost died, but he's alive, I promise you. We know
what Mardus is up to now. We were right, Alec. We are the
Four—you, me, Nysander, and Micum. We're all here to stop
him."

Alec shivered miserably as the wind whipped his hair across
his pale face. "How do I know it's you?" he mumbled faintly.

"What are you talking about?" Seregil asked in growing confusion. "What did they do to you, *tali*? It's me! I'm coming up to
you now, all right? Don't be afraid."

To his amazement, Alec turned and fled.

Scrambling up the rocks, Seregil dashed after him and caught
him in his arms, holding Alec tightly as he struggled.

"Easy, now! What's wrong?" He could feel Alec's heart hammering beneath his ribs.

Panting, Alec twisted around and gripped the side of Seregil's
face in one hand. Fighting back his own sudden fear, Seregil loosened his hold.

Alec gingerly touched his hair, shoulders, and arms, his expression almost feral in its intensity and distrust. After a moment,

however, the look disappeared, replaced by the most wondrous look of relief Seregil had ever seen.

"O Illior, it *is* you. You're alive," Alec gasped, tears welling in his eyes. "That bastard! I should have guessed, but the blood, your voice, everything— But you're alive!" Shuddering, he grabbed Seregil in a fierce embrace.

"Last time I looked," Seregil rasped, his throat tight with emotion as he hugged Alec to him. The boy was trembling badly now. Releasing him just long enough to get his cloak off and swing it around Alec's bare shoulders, Seregil helped him down in the lee of a large rock and held him close as the boy trembled and wept.

"I thought you were dead," Alec exclaimed hoarsely, still clinging to Seregil as if terrified that he'd disappear. "It was Vargûl Ashnazai. He made me think you'd come to rescue me, and he killed—" Alec let out a harsh sound between a sob and a laugh. "But I killed the son of a whore!"

The story that spilled from him was broken and confused, but Seregil was able to piece enough together to begin to guess what kind of torture Alec had been subjected to. Tears of helpless rage stung behind his own eyes as he stroked Alec's hair, murmuring softly to him in Aurënfaie.

Coming to the end of his tale, Alec rested his head wearily on Seregil's shoulder and drew another shuddering breath. "The worst of it— When Ashnazai killed you, tricked me into thinking he had—he said things—" Alec squeezed his eyes shut. "I thought you died believing I'd betrayed you."

Seregil stroked a strand of hair back from Alec's forehead and kissed him there. "It's all right, *tali*. If it had really been me, I wouldn't have believed him. I know you too well for that."

"And I never told you—" Alec's pale face flushed crimson. "I don't understand it, but I—"

He faltered and Seregil pulled him closer. "I know, *tali*. I know."

It was Alec who brought their lips together.

Seregil's first reaction was disbelief. But Alec was insistent, clumsy but determined. It lasted an instant, an eternity, that one awkward kiss, and it spoke silent volumes of bewildered honesty.

The moment that followed was too fragile for words.

He's exhausted, confused. He's been tortured past the point of endurance, Seregil warned himself, but for once, the doubts refused to take root.

Father, brother, friend.
Lover.

He closed his eyes, knowing that whatever grew up between them, it would be enough.

Alec was the first to break the silence. Wiping his face on the corner of the cloak, he said, "We'd better keep going. If I fall asleep now I don't think you'd be able to wake me again. Mardus is on his way."

"You'd better get some clothes on." Seregil stood to pull off his tunic and felt the weight of the black dagger he'd carried inside it.

"I almost forgot, I've been saving this for you."

Taking the knife out, Seregil unwrapped the scarf he'd wound around it. He held it a moment, his symbol of both defeat and hope through the long days of their separation. At last he tugged the knotted hank of hair loose from the hilt and let the wind snatch the golden strands from his fingers, scattering them over the rocks and into the sea.

48

A Narrowing of Proximities

I rtuk Beshar rode to the front of the column and fell in beside Mardus. Captain Denarii, leader of the land force that had met them upon landing, gave place with a barely concealed shudder.

Mardus greeted her with a gracious nod. "Good morning, Honored One."

"And to you, Lord Mardus. Have your scouts returned?"

"Yes. They report no interference. We'll make camp by late afternoon today and be well in place for the final ceremony tomorrow."

"The will of Seriamaius is with you, as always, my lord." Irtuk studied the dark man's comely profile. "I must say, you seem remarkably sanguine, given the death of Vargûl Ashnazai and the escapes last night."

Mardus shrugged eloquently. "Ashnazai brought his death on himself, despite all my warnings. Losing Alec was regrettable, though. What a remarkable young man."

"But the prisoners?"

"My trackers say the Skalan raiding party numbered less than a dozen riders and that they fled east. No, the Helm will be restored and I shall serve Seriamaius as the *Vatharna*." Mardus' cold smile broadened perceptibly.

"Not a shabby attainment for an Overlord's unacknowledged bastard, eh?"

"I have foreseen this day since you were a child at my knee," the dyrmagnos said fondly. "Even now the young Overlord suspects nothing. When the time comes he will be forced to give place to you, his trusted half brother. With the Helm on your brow and the hand of Seriamaius over you, no one can contest your claim to the throne."

"And how is young Thero this morning?"

Irtuk Beshar gave a dry, whispery laugh. "Subdued. Most subdued."

The second scouting patrol was larger. Watching from the shelter of several large boulders, Micum counted a dozen Plenimaran riders moving up the track toward the temple site.

Stealing back to the salt pine, he found Nysander listening calmly to the scouts calling back and forth to one another as they spread out through the trees behind the site.

"What are they saying?" whispered Micum.

"From the sound of it, they are looking for a place for an encampment."

Before long the Plenimarans backtracked to a sloping meadow a quarter of a mile back the way they'd come. Micum and the wizard followed cautiously.

"Looks like they're settling in," Micum said, watching as several soldiers set to work felling trees at the edge of the clearing. "And right in Seregil's path, too. You can see the ledges from there."

"He must have seen them earlier," Nysander replied, heading back to the pine shelter.

"Let's hope so," Micum muttered. "I didn't like the way he stormed out of here. You know, there's nothing to do here just now. Maybe I should head out looking for him. Will you be safe?"

Nysander smiled. "From that lot? Oh, yes. You go on."

Keeping behind the underbrush along the road, Micum passed the Plenimaran camp without being seen. From the cover of a fallen tree, he counted ten soldiers in the clearing. That left two unaccounted for.

When he was well away from the camp he moved out onto the ledges and looked south for some sign of movement. Nysander had not been specific on how far away Alec was. Checking the sun, he guessed Seregil had been gone a little better than an hour.

The incoming tide boomed against the rocks as he continued south. Another hour passed before he finally caught sight of two figures moving toward him in the distance. Though too far away still to make out details, he could see that Seregil was supporting Alec as they made their way unsteadily over a rocky stretch of shore.

Seregil drew his sword at the sight of him, then sheathed it again as he recognized Micum.

"By the Flame, we found you after all!" Micum exclaimed joyously as he reached them. Throwing an arm around Alec, Micum gave him a welcoming hug and helped him to a seat on a driftwood log. The boy was hollow-eyed with exhaustion, and dressed in Seregil' boots, tunic, and cloak. "Are you all right? Where's Thero?"

"Dead or captured," Alec told him, and Micum heard the strain in his voice.

Seregil gave Micum a quick warning look. "Thero helped him escape. He's had a rough time of it these last few weeks. We've still got a ways to go, Alec. Do you want to rest before we go on?"

"No, let's just keep going," Alec replied. "Where's Nysander?"

"Don't you worry about him. He's safe. And by the Flame, so are you!" Micum said warmly, clasping Alec's shoulder. "Bilairy's Balls, Alec, I was afraid we'd lost you."

"Have the second group of scouts reached the place yet?" asked Seregil.

"Two hours ago, I'd say. They staked out a camp just below the temple. I didn't want the two of you running into them by accident, so I came out to meet you."

"Thanks. I'll need you to get him the rest of the way." Seregil glanced down at Alec with concern. "He doesn't have much left in him. I'm surprised we made it as far as we did."

"I'll be all right," Alec insisted, swaying as he got to his feet again.

"We'd better stick to the woods," Micum said, slipping an arm under Alec's. "It's too exposed out here and I don't know where they've posted guards. How far behind would you say Mardus is?"

"I lost all track of distance last night," Alec confessed. "If the scouts have reached you, he can't be much more than half a day behind."

"What kind of force does he have with him?"

"I'm not certain, but I think he has at least forty soldiers, plus a gang of prisoners—maybe a hundred. And there's the necromancer and a dyrmagnos."

Micum's eyes widened in alarm. "Damnation! He's got one of those things with him? And prisoners?"

"I imagine it takes a lot of blood to make this Helm of theirs," Seregil said bitterly. "Alec claims there were sacrificial murders on the ship as they came over, and more since they landed and met up with another force. That's where this bunch of prisoners came from."

"And the four of us are here to stop them?" Micum shook his head as they climbed up to the forest and started back.

With the help of Micum and Seregil, Alec managed to make it to the salt pine.

"Here you are at last, dear boy!" Nysander whispered, embracing Alec as he collapsed onto the carpet of dried needles. "I knew you would come back to us. And only just in time."

"Seregil told me about the eclipse tomorrow," said Alec, yawning as he settled with his back to the trunk.

"I know how weary you must be, but you must tell me all that you've learned. Then I promise, you shall rest. And you must eat!"

Seregil passed him some biscuit, cheese, and a skin of fresh water. Alec took a long gulp before he began.

"You were right, both of you," he said, looking ruefully at Mieum and Seregil. "I should've stayed at Watermead that night, but I was worried about Seregil. When I got back to the Cockerel—"

He paused, blinking back fresh tears.

"They know," Seregil told him, moving closer beside him. "I got there at dawn and saw everything. What happened after that?"

"They jumped me as soon as I came in, Ashnazai and his men. I managed to wound a couple of them before they took me down."

"Vargûl Ashnazai?" asked Nysander. "Ah, yes, I have heard of him."

Alec smiled bitterly. "You won't anymore. I killed the bastard last night. That's how Thero and I got away. At least I did."

He looked around at the others earnestly. "He saved my life. Whatever else he did, he saved my life and he's probably dead now because of it. He used his magic to help us escape, then he changed me into a stag the way you did, Nysander." Alec's chin trembled but he didn't stop. "I—I ran away. He chased me off and I ran. I can still hear—"

The wizard clasped Alec's hands between his. "I won't tell you not to grieve, dear boy, but you mustn't blame yourself. Please, continue with your story. You were speaking of the inn."

Alec wiped at his nose with a dirt-streaked forearm. "I don't remember much after that, until I woke up aboard the ship. Mardus was there, and Ashnazai, another necromancer I didn't see much of, and a dyrmagnos woman called Irtuk Beshar." Steeling himself, he related his treatment aboard the *Kormados*.

Nysander listened in silence until he reached the nightmarish dinner with Mardus. "Mardus himself told you that the Helm must be given lives to build its power? You are certain of this?"

Alec nodded grimly. "He said the younger the victim, the more power the death gives. It was Mardus' idea of revenge to have Thero and me be the last sacrifices at the final ceremony."

Seregil looked up sharply at this. "That's the key! If we strike quickly, before they complete the sacrifices, maybe we have a chance against this thing."

"Perhaps, but we must not underestimate its initial capabilities," warned Nysander. "It may well have some degree of power from the moment of completion. Very well. Go on, Alec."

Too tired to be anything but matter-of-fact about the nightly horrors Vargûl Ashnazai had visited on them, Alec quickly outlined the details of the overland journey.

Seregil went pale as he described the visitation by Cilla and the invectives she'd hurled at him.

"Phantasms, nothing but illusions conjured up by this terrible man," Nysander assured him. "Such spells turn your own fears and imaginings against you."

"But what about when I saw Seregil?" Alec asked. "That was real. I touched him, felt him bleeding. There was blood on my hands the next day."

"More illusion," said Nysander. "He created Seregil's image using some poor victim so that the death would be convincing. Someone certainly died in front of you that night. I imagine Ashnazai meant to break your spirit once and for all."

Alec glanced guiltily in Micum's direction. "I enjoyed killing him. I know that's wrong, but I did."

"Don't fret over it," Micum said with a grim smile. "I'd have felt the same in your place. There's no dishonor in killing a mad creature like that."

Seregil chuckled blackly. "I plan to enjoy killing Mardus just as much."

"Vengeance is not our purpose," Nysander reminded them firmly. "Never allow yourselves to forget that their god can use our own emotions and weakness against us. Now allow Alec to finish his account so he can rest."

"There's not much to tell. After we got away from the camp Thero used the same spell you showed me the day you turned us into animals. I didn't know what he was doing until it was too late to stop him. Once he'd turned me into a stag, I ran. If he'd just given me a chance maybe I could have helped him, but something happened to my mind, just like the last time."

"There was nothing you could have done against anything conjured up by the likes of Irtuk Beshar," Nysander said. "Thero's decision was wise and honorable."

"As I see it, the real question is how to get at the Helm in the first place," Micum interjected. "Alec says Mardus has at least two score soldiers with him. They're not just going to stand flat-footed while we waltz in."

"We'll have to see how they distribute themselves at the temple tomorrow," Seregil said, going to his pack. "Assuming Mardus wasn't lying to Alec, then the prisoners will have to be close at hand during the ceremony. If we could get them loose, they could provide a diversion." Turning, he handed Alec his bow case and sword.

"You brought them!" Alec exclaimed, pulling the limbs of the Radly from the case and fitting it together.

"And your quiver," Seregil told him. "If Nysander's right about this prophecy of his, then you'll be needing these."

"There's plenty of high ground overlooking the temple site," Micum noted. "Alec could pick off some of the guards around the prisoners, start a panic. If the prisoners have any spirit left in them at all, they'll fight or run. Either way, it would give the rest of us a chance to make a dash for it in the confusion."

"There are only a score of arrows here," Alec said, opening the quiver to check his fletching. "Even if I made every shot, that still leaves a lot of armed men to deal with. These are Plenimaran marines we're talking about."

"We'll have our hands full, all right, but I doubt we'll have to take them all on at once," said Micum. "My guess is Mardus will post sentries and leave some others on guard at their encampment. It's the dyrmagnos I'm most worried about. Tell me more about her."

"She's pure evil," Alec answered bitterly. "What she did to me, and to Thero—I don't even know how to tell you. By the time she was finished with me, I'd told her every damn thing she wanted to know. Nysander was right not to tell us very much. Once she started in on me, there was nothing I could do to stop her."

"I feared as much," murmured the wizard.

"When we finally did escape, she sent something after us. I didn't see it, but just the sound of it was enough to freeze your blood!"

"This is all excellent news," Nysander exclaimed, rubbing his white hands together in satisfaction. "The sacrifices, the spells she used on Alec and Thero, the creature. From the sound of things, she has allowed herself little respite since her attack against me at the Orëska House. No one, not even a dyrmagnos, can expend so much power over such a short period of time without it exacting a toll. Once she has finished with the Helm, she should be at least somewhat weakened. If we attack her then, perhaps we can disable her long enough to carry out our mission. And now, Alec, you should get what sleep you can. The greatest trial of all still lies before us."

"That's for certain," Micum muttered. "Four against forty. I'm going back down the road to keep an eye out for Mardus."

But Alec felt no dread as he stretched out under Seregil's cloak. No matter what happened, it couldn't be worse than what he'd already been through.

Micum found an outcropping that overlooked the coastal track and settled down to wait.

The weather had held fair; the sun felt warm against his back as he lay in his hiding place, listening to the sound of the birds in the woods around him. Looking out through the trees on the west side of the road, he could see the green waves rolling across the Inner Sea and the flocks of sea ducks that rode them.

What little he'd seen of Plenimar didn't look all that different from Skala. In fact, it appeared to be a pretty fine place overall—except for the Plenimarans.

It was midafternoon before he heard the first horses approaching. A vanguard of riders passed at a gallop. Soon after he saw more riders coming on at a walk at the head of a column of marines.

Micum had seen enough of Mardus up in Wolde the previous autumn to recognize him now, riding at the head of it. He wore military dress and the way he sat his mount told Micum this man was accustomed to command.

A woman in rich riding apparel rode at his side, her presence puzzling until Micum caught sight of her face and realized what she was. Flattening lower, he lay scarcely breathing, until the dyrmagnos had ridden past.

Behind them came more riders and marines. Micum spotted a few familiar faces among them, Captain Tildus and several of the soldiers who'd been with him in Wolde. The dispassionate calm that had kept him alive through so many battles settled over Micum as he silently marked men for death.

A line of wagons followed, including the bear cart Alec had described. As it came abreast of Micum's hiding spot, he saw a thin, half-naked man sprawled face down in the bottom of it. He couldn't make out the face, but from the build he guessed it was Thero. Another wagon was loaded with small wooden cages, and a black bull was tethered to this one.

Next came a long procession of prisoners stumbling along in chains. Women, men, and children, some hardly older than Illia, marched in dispirited silence beneath the watchful eye of their mounted guards. Behind them came wagons, servants, and livestock.

Micum's heart sank as he watched the last of the column pass. Alec had missed his guess; there were closer to a hundred soldiers.

By the Flame, he thought. *We've got our work cut out for us this time.*

While Micum was gone, Seregil spent some time spying on the Plenimaran camp, then went back to check on Alec.

He was still asleep, curled on his side beneath the cloak. A pained frown furrowed his brow, and his fingers twitched restlessly as he fought his way through whatever dreams still haunted him. Sitting down next to him, Seregil gently stroked Alec's tangled hair until the shadow left his face.

Nysander sat with several arrows across his lap. He'd produced a small dish of paint from somewhere and was painting symbols on one of the shafts with a fine brush.

Watching Alec sleep, Seregil shook his head with concern. "Do you really think he'll be up to fighting tomorrow?"

"He is young, and not badly hurt," the wizard assured him, not looking up from his work. "All he needs is rest."

Seregil rubbed absently at his chest. The last of the scab was peeling away and it itched. As his fingers brushed across the scar, he felt the tiny raised whorls of the disk's imprint.

It felt different.

Reaching for Micum's pack, he dug out the shaving mirror and held it out to see the scar. The round shape of the disk and the small square mark left by the hole at its center were still outlined in shiny new skin, but the imprint of the design had changed. What had originally been a cryptic pattern of lines and whorls had somehow transformed into a circular device of stylized knives, eyes, and necromantic runes.

"Nysander, look at this!" He pulled the neck of his tunic wider.

Nysander's bushy white brows shot up in surprise. "Do you recall me telling you that the design on the wooden disk concealed another? This is one of the siglas of the Empty God."

Seregil inspected it again. "I can read them. The runes, I mean. They're right way around in the mirror. I hadn't thought of it before, but since this is a brand, the whole design is backward."

Nysander tugged thoughtfully at his beard. "If this sigla is intrinsically magical rather than merely symbolic, such a reversal would have a significant effect on its power. It may even have helped protect you from the effects of the crown." He smiled ruefully. "I should have guessed it sooner, I suppose, but I had been putting your survival down to your magical dysfunction. This may well have been an ameliorating factor."

Seregil, hoping to get a little sleep stretched out beside Alec. "I'd call that left-handed luck, but I guess I'll take any kind I can get. I just hope it works for us tomorrow."

Nysander took up his brush again. "As do I, dear boy."

49

Under the Black Sun

Alec slept on through the night while Nysander and the others listened to the Plenimarans at work preparing the temple site. They also heard the chanting, and later the screams and moans that drifted to them on the wind from the encampment. Micum wanted to investigate, but the wizard forbade it.

"We know well enough what they are doing. The dyrmagnos is more dangerous than ever during such ceremonies. If not for the protective magic I have placed around us, she would have sensed us already. We are safe enough for now, but we must wait for morning before we move. You should rest while you can. I fear there will be little opportunity to do so tomorrow."

Scratching a circle around the base of the pine, he seated himself against the opposite side of the trunk and closed his eyes.

Alec woke just before sunrise the next morning and was surprised at how rested he felt. He had a few scrapes and aches from the previous day's journey, but he scarcely noticed them.

Seregil was asleep close beside him, one

arm under his head, the other stretched out toward Alec. His face was wind-burned and there were pine needles tangled in his long dark hair, but that only seemed to enhance his strange beauty.

I kissed him! Alec thought in a sudden agony of embarrassment. In the midst of all the horror they had faced, and all they'd face today, he had kissed Seregil. His teacher. His friend. His— what? Worse yet, if Nysander hadn't been sitting a few feet away, he might have been tempted to do it again.

I can't think about that now, he groaned inwardly, cheeks flaming. It wasn't that he regretted it. He just didn't know yet what it meant, or what he wanted it to mean.

Sitting up, he saw that Micum had gone out already. Nysander was sitting on the other side of the tree and didn't stir or look around when Alec went over to the pile of packs. He found a spare set of breeches and some low boots in Seregil's, then turned his attention to his bow.

Stringing it, he ran careful fingers up and down the braided string, looking for any frays or weak spots. After so many weeks of disuse, it needed waxing.

There was a tack pouch in his quiver, but he didn't see it with the rest of the gear. Looking around, he spied it lying on the ground next to Nysander. In with his red-fletched arrows were four newly fletched with white swan feathers. Taking up the quiver, he touched one of the crisp white vanes and felt a sharp tingle of magic against his finger. He jerked his hand away, then gingerly pulled the arrow from the quiver for a closer look. The shaft was covered from point to nock with tiny, intricate symbols painted in blue ink.

"No spell can improve on the skill of your hand and eye," Nysander murmured, eyes still closed, "but those four arrows carry magic that will pierce the skin of the dyrmagnos. She must be your first target once the Helm is complete. See no one else, aim for nothing else until one of these has struck her. Even my magic cannot kill her, but it will weaken her while we attack. Strike her in the heart if you can manage it."

"You can depend on it," Alec replied stonily. The boy who'd wavered taking first aim at a man was long gone. He touched the nock, imagining the feel of it on the string just before he let it fly.

I hope I see her face when it hits her.

Seregil sat up and brushed pine needles from his hair. "Any sound from our neighbors?"

"Not for some time now," Nysander told him, opening his eyes and stretching. "Micum went out a short while ago to check their camp."

Seregil peered out through the pine boughs. "I think I'd like a look at the temple again before too many people are stirring. What do you say, Alec. Fancy a walk before breakfast?"

They kept a sharp eye out for sentries as they made their way down to the north side of the cove.

"So that's what those holes were for," Seregil muttered, looking across to the temple site through the underbrush.

Sturdy wooden posts had been set upright in the mysterious holes surrounding the dry basin at the head of the ledges. A few men were still at work clearing debris from the area.

"There are plenty of good vantage points up on those rocks, but I bet they'll have men up there," Alec whispered.

"We'll manage something. Beshar will most likely be up there, behind those posts. Look for a place that will give you the best shot at her."

"Don't worry, I'll hit the bitch."

Seregil glanced at Alec in surprise and saw a hardness in his expression that had never been there before.

Soon more men began to wander up from the camp. Hurrying back to the pine, they found Micum there ahead of them. He held a finger to his lips as they entered, then pointed to Nysander kneeling in the center of a dancing circle of white sparks. Inside the circle he'd scraped back the pine needles and scratched a complex pattern of symbols into the packed earth beneath.

Eyes half-lidded, Nysander was calmly weaving shining figures in the air. He had stripped to his breeches and covered his arms, chest, and face with designs drawn in blue ink. A horizontal band of black paint across his eyes gave him an uncharacteristically barbaric appearance. In front of him, Alec's bow and quiver lay amid a clutter of bowls, wands, and parchments.

Alec and Seregil hesitated at the edge of the light circle, but Nysander motioned for them all to enter. Once inside, they smelled the scent of magic mingling with the aroma of the pine like the faint, rich odor left behind in a cupboard where spices had once been stored.

"The eclipse will begin soon," said Nysander, taking up a brush and a bowl of black paint. "This band across your eyes will ward off the blinding effects of it, even at the full. Unless the Plenimarans take similar precautions, it may work to our advantage."

Nysander painted a heavy band across each of their faces, then set the bowl aside. "Now, if you would hand me your weapons."

Using several colors of pigment, Nysander painted a few small sigils on each blade. He took the longest over Seregil's sword, covering it from hilt to tip with a line of tiny figures that flickered and disappeared as soon as they were completed.

"What's all this?" Micum asked.

"Just some necessary magicking. The dyrmagnos is not the only one with protective magic. Kneel with me here, close together, and hold out your hands."

Gathering them in a small circle, Nysander painted their palms with concentric circles of black, red, brown, and blue, then instructed them to press their raised palms to those of the person on either side of them. Seregil was on the wizard's right, Alec to his left, with Micum closing the chain.

The moment the circle of hands was complete they were enveloped in a sudden sensation of tingling warmth that raised the hairs on their arms and made their eyes water. A collective shudder ran through them as the feeling swelled and faded away.

Nysander was the first to lower his hands. "It is done."

The paint was gone. In its place each of them bore a complex pattern of red and gold on each palm.

"The great sigla of Aura," Seregil murmured, touching his left palm.

"What is it, some kind of protection?" asked Alec.

"It will not keep you from being wounded. It is to protect your soul," Nysander explained. "If any of us are killed today, the Eater of Death will not have us. The design will fade from sight in time, but the protection is permanent."

Seregil regarded his hands with a humorless, lopsided grin. "Well, that's one less thing for us to worry about."

At that moment, less than two miles to the north, Beka Cavish shivered suddenly when a sharp tingle passed through her as she tethered her horse with the others.

"You all right, Lieutenant?" asked Rhylin, who'd been out scouting the Plenimaran camp with her.

"Guess a snake must've crawled across my shadow." The strange sensation passed as quickly as it had come, except for a slight tingling in her gloved hands. Flexing them, she walked over to where Braknil and the others sat waiting in the shadow of a gully.

They had preparations to make.

An hour before noon a tiny, curved paring disappeared from the lower edge of the sun.

"There it goes," Seregil whispered as he and Micum lay in a brush thicket overlooking the temple.

The dry pool near the head of the cove had been cleared of all debris and painted with white symbols neither he nor Micum had ever seen before. More symbols had been outlined between each of the fourteen posts set into the rock and a large square had been painted to contain the entire site.

The sacrificial victims huddled under close guard on the rocks above the pool. Slightly apart from these, Thero stood between two of Tildus' men. He was dressed in wizard's robes, but below its full sleeves Seregil caught a glimpse of metal on Thero's wrists.

"Well, he's alive but they've got him under control again."

"Too bad," muttered Micum. "My guess is we could use his help before this is over."

Twenty soldiers stood formed up in ranks before the captives, unlit torches piled at their feet. A brazier stood nearby, filling the air with fragrant smoke.

Mardus sat on the white marker stone, studying a parchment. He was dressed in ceremonial splendor for the occasion; beneath his sweeping black cloak, his burnished cuirass and gorget glinted with gold chasing.

As Seregil and Micum watched, the dyrmagnos stepped from the trees and the failing sunlight glinted from the jewel work on her veil and gown.

"Don't they just make a handsome pair." Micum glanced up at the sun again. "Nysander said the eclipse would take about an hour. Looks like you were right about it matching the tide. It's already as high as it was yesterday and still coming in."

"Come on then, time to get started."

• • •

Irtuk Beshar laid a wizened hand on Mardus' sleeve. "The conjunction has begun, my lord."

Mardus glanced up from the document he'd been studying. "Ah, yes. Tildus!"

"Yes, my lord?" Never far from his master, the bearded captain stepped forward.

"Pass the word, Tildus; the eclipse has begun. Remind the men to avoid looking at it, particularly once it's complete."

Tildus snapped a quick salute and strode off.

The tide was climbing steadily toward the pool and with it came a warm breeze smelling of rock weed and salt.

Soon enough it would smell of blood, Mardus thought with satisfaction.

When all his men were in position, he strode down into the temple, his black war cloak sweeping out behind him. The waves were surging close to the dry basin now, and lines of foam ran ahead up the two narrow fissures that contained the carvings. He paced a slow circuit around the declivity, then moved to stand on the landward side of it and raised a hand. Trumpeters at the head of the ledges blew a blaring fanfare.

Irtuk Beshar stepped from the trees above at the head of a small procession. First came silent Harid Yordun bearing the carved chest containing the elements of the Helm. Behind him, soldiers led four unblemished white heifers with the symbol of Dalna painted on their brows and four young black bulls bearing the sign of Sakor. These were followed by large wicker cages containing four gulls and four large brown owls, symbolic of Astellus and Illior.

Harid placed the chest reverently at the landward edge of the dry pool and the animals were divided, one of each sort at the four corners of the great square.

Irtuk Beshar moved slowly from one group to another, laying hands on the beasts. They sank dead beneath her touch and were immediately gutted and piled in reeking heaps.

Lifting her arms to the sky, she threw back her head and shouted in the ancient necromantic tongue, *"Agrosh marg venu Kui gri bara kon Seriami. Y'ka Vatharna prak'ot!"*

Tongues of shimmering, unnatural fire flared up from the piles of carrion. The assembled soldiers cheered at the sight of it.

The sun was a thin, inverted crescent now against the leaden

purple sky. Beneath it, the long tail of the comet hung like an evil,
slitted eye. Shadows blurred and faded in the uncertain light,
lending a strange flatness to the landscape. Birds that had been
singing noisily since dawn gradually faltered to silence except for
the occasional puzzled hooting of doves and the rasping croak of a
lone raven.

Water surged up the fissures and spilled into the rock basin.
Mardus signaled to the guards standing over the prisoners. Ten
frightened men were dragged forward, stripped, and tied to the
posts. With Irtuk Beshar chanting tonelessly behind him, Mardus
drew his dagger and slit their throats in quick succession. They
died quickly, these first ones, their blood flowing down to stain the
swirling waters of the salt pool.

As the last sliver of sun narrowed to an edge, a raucous clatter
suddenly came from all sides. An immense flock of ravens
appeared out of the surrounding gloom, croaking and sawing in a
cloud of black wings as they settled on tree and ledge and post top.
At the same moment, crabs of every size and color came boiling
up out of the water. Sidling up the rocks, they swarmed over the
piles of dead animals and the corpses, feeding greedily.

Cries of terror burst out among the remaining prisoners. Tildus
barked orders and the torchbearers lit their brands at the brazier.
The whole ghastly scene leapt into sharper relief.

No one, not even the dyrmagnos, noticed when the three guards
stationed on the northern promontory were jerked back out of
sight. Any sound they may have made was lost in the general
outcry below.

Carrion eaters. Eaters of the dead, thought Seregil as he, Alec,
and Micum shoved the men they'd just killed into the undergrowth behind them. The black stripes across their faces gave
them all a deadly, feral look as they belly-crawled back to the edge
of the overlook where Nysander was keeping watch.

The moon overtook the last curve of the sun and a hazy corona
burst out around it. The black disk hung framed in light, like a
baleful, glaring eye. The burning arc of the plague star, visible
now in the darkened sky, glowed just below it.

With every surge of the surf, water foamed into the stone
hollow at Irtuk Beshar's feet.

The dead men were cut from the posts and thrown onto the

offal pile. Ten women took their places and Mardus' knife flashed again, severing their cries.

Seregil winced. It was agonizing to watch and not act. Beside him, Alec clenched his hands around his bow, eyes wide with horror.

"How can we just lay here and watch them die?" he hissed.

Nysander was on Alec's other side and Seregil saw him close a hand over Alec's. "Think of how many will die if we fail," the wizard reminded him. "Be strong, my boy. Let nothing distract you."

Raising her hands toward the sky, Irtuk Beshur began to chant again, her cracked, dry voice loud above the rush of the sea. More victims were dragged forward to the edge of the pool and beheaded by swordsmen, who then held the bodies so that the blood still pumping from the severed necks fell into the water.

Mardus opened the chest and lifted out the crystal crown. Taking it from him, Beshar held it up to the sky a moment, then cast it into the surging waters of the pool. Next came a plain iron hoop, then the crude clay bowl.

"It is almost time," whispered Nysander.

Seregil gripped Alec's arm. "Shoot true, *tali.*"

Alec pressed a white-fletched arrow to his lips. "I will, *tali,*" he whispered back, blue eyes glinting fiercely under the black paint.

Holding that image in his heart, Seregil hurried away after the others.

Alec gripped the arrow in his fist, feeling the power in it. The sound of the sea now was the sound from his nightmares, but this time the arrow had a head.

Looking down, he saw the dyrmagnos scatter the handful of wooden disks into the water. As the last one sank from sight the face of the pool went still and glassy. The tide still surged and thundered to its edge, but the power of the dyrmagnos kept any more water from flowing into the pool, which was now full. Like a dark mirror, it reflected the black eye of the sun.

The dyrmagnos raised her hands above it and began a new chant. A man was brought forward and thrown down on his back at her feet. Soldiers held him by the hands and feet and Harid Yordun came forward with the black ax.

Alec wanted desperately not to watch as he hacked the man's chest open, but he knew he must not look away for an instant.

Harid cut out the heart and threw it into the water. Quick, skirling ripples appeared and faded on its glassy surface as if a flock of swallows had darted past. Another heart was thrown in, and the ripples reappeared, more numerous this time.

Alec felt a silent tremor roll through the stone he was lying on. It came again as the ax rose and fell, growing to a steady rhythm like the pounding of a labored heart.

The pool went black and dull as tar. Tendrils of mist rose from it, and with them came disembodied moans that echoed softly on all sides.

Seregil recognized those ghostly voices, remembered standing over the crown as his blood fell into ice and crystal while they whispered around him. Crouched with the others now behind a fallen tree near the waterline, he saw shifting, half-formed shapes gathering out of the gloom beyond the torches, mingling restlessly with the vaporous exhalations of the pool. The black water began to swirl as if stirred with a dyer's paddle. The spirit voices grew louder, sighing and shrieking. Wraiths buffeted them, plucking at their clothing and weapons, twitching strands of hair. The air thickened perceptibly, muting what little light remained. Nysander sketched a quick sigil on the air and the wraiths retreated.

Working their way into the woods without being seen by the sentries, they followed the road to the head of the cove.

"Be ready," the wizard whispered. "It is nearly time."

Something slipped coldly across Alec's back beneath his tunic. The weird disturbances in the air were worse now, tenuous but too insistent to be denied. Spectral forms, half-seen from the corner of the eye, brushed light as cobweb against his face, only to flit out of sight when he tried to look at them directly.

The soldiers' torches flared green and spit off fragments of flame that skittered like rats around the edge of the pool before being sucked up into the column of ghostly mist that was forming over the roiling pool. Up and up it rose, thrusting a twisting grey pillar flecked with tongues of fire into the burnt sky. It stood over the pool for a long moment, spirit forms darting around and through it, then a single blue-white bolt of lightning forked down through its center with an apocalyptic roar, blasting the pool into an explosion of steam and rock fragments.

Soldiers fell to their knees, covering their faces in terror. The ravens rose in a screaming cloud, adding their raw voices to the din. From the direction of the road came the frenzied screams of the horses tethered there, and the clatter of carts being dragged off as the panicked beasts bolted. The mist slowly rolled back, revealing a shattered, steaming hole where the pool had been.

With a shout of triumph, Irtuk Beshar climbed down into it and retrieved something from the water and rubble. Straightening again, she raised a helmet in both hands with a screech of sheer triumph.

The bulging, peaked top and nasal of the helm were fashioned of dull iron but it was circled at the brow with a wide circlet of ruddy gold. This band was set around with eight dull blue stones and surmounted by a bristling crown formed from eight twisted black horns. A curtain of black mail hung down from the back of the Helm and skeletal, long-taloned hands served as the cheek guards.

Climbing out, she held it up before Mardus and launched into an invocation of some kind. Although Alec did not understand her language, he recognized two words: "Seriamaius" and "Vatharna."

Alec drew the bowstring to his ear.

Before he could loose the shaft, however, shouting broke out in the forest to the south. All eyes turned to see the bright glow of fire above the tops of the trees in the direction of the camp.

Mardus drew his sword and shouted an order, sending half the guards off in the direction of the disturbance. Still clutching the helm, Irtuk Beshar gabbled urgently at him.

Time slowed to dreamlike unreality as Alec rose to his feet and took aim again at the dyrmagnos. Ghostly forms imposed themselves between him and his target, swirling around him to buffet and natter but he ignored them, concentrating on his shot.

Shoot true, tali.

"Aura Elustri málreil," he whispered.

The black bow quivered like a live thing under his hand as he drew it, calling on every ounce of power the Radly possessed. When the nock was level with his ear he released it. The fletching nicked his cheek as it flew, carrying a drop of his blood away with it.

The arrow sped straight and true as any shaft he'd ever loosed, and made a sound like a sudden crack of summer thunder when it struck Irtuk Beshar in the chest just below her throat. The impact spun her like a broken doll. The Helm fell from her hands, tumbling back into the blasted pool.

"And now you, you bastard!" Alec yelled, taking aim at the startled Mardus.

But an arrow buzzed by his head, spoiling the shot. Another whined past and he dropped for cover as pandemonium broke out below. Still clutching his bow, he scrambled to the edge of the outcropping to see what was going on.

Arrows flew from all directions, but most found targets among the Plenimarans. By the wavering light of the fallen torches Alec could just make out a small group of archers on the high ground opposite where he lay. They were shooting down at the exposed men below. In the melee, he saw Seregil and Micum dashing down over the rocks with their swords drawn, closing in on the wounded dyrmagnos.

Mardus was nowhere to be seen, so Alec turned his attention to the soldiers, shooting two in rapid succession before he was momentarily blinded by a brilliant flash of light that flared among the prisoners.

As his vision cleared, he saw Thero standing over the smoking bodies of several dead soldiers, but apparently unaware of the armed man coming at his back.

The wounding of the dyrmagnos must have weakened her hold on the wizard, Alec thought. "Look out," he whispered, sending a red-fletched shaft at the guard. The man fell and Thero was lost from sight as the other prisoners surged forward in rebellion or panic.

"Got her on the first try!" Seregil exclaimed under his breath, watching from the ledges above as Irtuk Beshar whirled suddenly, clutching at the shaft protruding from her chest. The Helm fell from her hands, tumbling back into the hole it came from. Mardus dove after it.

Ignoring the sudden arrow storm that erupted around them, he and Micum left Nysander in the shelter of the rocks and charged down. Irtuk Beshar's spells on the pool were already unraveling. Water surged back into the basin, washing corpses and entrails down into the hole, and sweeping the Helm out of reach as Mardus bent to grab it.

Praying to Sakor that Nysander was right about her powers being exhausted, Micum charged the wounded dyrmagnos. She saw him and raised one gnarled hand. He swung, severing the arm, then struck again, taking her between the neck and shoulder. Her body split under his blade like a dry gourd. She screamed curses at him as her head and remaining arm tumbled away from her torso.

Despite the warnings of Seregil and Nysander, Micum hesitated for an instant, transfixed with horror as the severed parts writhed on the ground at his feet. Then a hint of motion caught his eye and he turned in time to deflect Tildus' sword.

Sakor's smiling today, he told himself as he sidestepped another blow and caught the Plenimaran captain a solid blow to the neck.

Other marines leapt forward to avenge their captain's death. Micum crippled two and killed a third. A fourth pressed in on his left side but fell before Micum could strike at him, an arrow through his back. Micum scarcely had time to register that the fletching color was not Alec's before more Plenimarans rushed at him. He doggedly stood his ground, aware of the clash of swords behind him but too closely pressed to look.

As hoped, the revolt of the prisoners, together with the mysterious fire at the encampment, had drawn off many of the soldiers. Micum made short work of the few who remained.

He was just looking around for Seregil when a searing bolt of pain shot through the back of his right thigh. Staggering, he twisted around to find Irtuk Beshar clinging to him, eyes shining like a wildcat's as she tore at his leg with nails and teeth. Too late he realized his mistake; she was whole again.

The lower portion of her gown had fallen away and Micum could see both the livid, uneven line of the joining and the splintered end of the arrow shaft still protruding between her shriveled dus. Her legs, black and withered as those of a burned corpse, kicked spasmodically as she tightened her grip and sank her teeth into his flesh. A deadly coldness spread slowly out from the wounds.

Micum hacked awkwardly at her. One withered leg flew off, then he managed the cleave her in half at the waist. Determined not to make the same error twice, he grabbed the lower torso by its remaining leg and flung it with all his strength into the sea, then kicked the other limb into the shadows beyond the torches.

But Irtuk Beshar was still horribly alive and clung on to him like a curse. The coldness of her bite spread up through Micum's vitals, stopping his ears, darkening his vision, numbing his fingers. His sword fell from his hand and he tore clumsily at her. Dried bone collapsed beneath his fists, strips of dusty scalp pulled away like rotten cloth, but still Irtuk Beshar hung on, plunging her poison into his veins with the last of her strength.

Micum's deadened leg folded under him and he felt her grip change as she slowly pulled herself up his body. He could hear Seregil shouting nearby. Micum's throat worked soundlessly, choked with the vengeful hate of the dyrmagnos.

Alec was down to the three white arrows when he saw Micum thrashing on the ground just above the pool. His belly went cold as he realized what the monstrous thing clinging to him must be. It was pointless to shoot from here; there was no way to hit the dyrmagnos without killing Micum at the same time. Gripping the arrow like a dagger, Alec bounded down over the rocks, praying he wasn't already too late.

Looking back over her shoulder, Beka saw that Braknil's decuria had succeeded in setting fire to the Plenimaran camp. At this signal, she and Rhylin's decuria opened fire on the Plenimaran soldiers massed in the natural amphitheater below. From where they stood on the ledges, it was like shooting pigs in a sty.

They were not the first to fire, however. Even as she loosed arrow after arrow, Beka wondered how Braknil had gotten back here so quickly and what his group was doing on the opposite side of the cove. One of them had managed to hit the sorceress before Beka could give the order for her group to fire. Whatever the case, the prisoners were breaking free below, just as she'd hoped.

"That's got them moving," she growled, turning to the others. "Come on, *urgazhi,* let's leave them to it."

"Hold on, Lieutenant," whispered Rhylin. "It looks to me like we're not the only ones who were after them!"

The frantic prisoners were pushing their captors back toward the cliffs, but a smaller knot of fighting was concentrated near the water's edge. Torchlight glanced off steel in the shadows of the natural basin that lay in the embrace of the two ridges of high ground. General Mardus was nowhere in sight, but the Plenimaran's sorceress was still alive and wrestling with a large swordsman.

Beka's heart skipped a beat.

"It can't be!" she gasped. Then Alec bolted into view from behind a jumble of rocks, splashing wildly through the shallow water toward the struggling pair with nothing but an arrow in his hand.

Dropping her bow, Beka began scrambling down the steep rock face.

"What are you doing?" Rhylin cried, catching her by the wrist.

Beka pulled free so violently that she nearly dragged the startled man over the edge.

"My father's down there!" she snapped over her shoulder as she plunged on.

"Riders," barked Rhylin behind her, "follow the lieutenant's lead! Attack!"

Micum was still struggling weakly beneath the dyrmagnos when Alec reached him. Grasping Beshar by what was left of her hair, Alec plunged the arrow into her neck. The resulting blast knocked him over onto his back, ears ringing.

Releasing Micum with a wild screech, Irtuk Beshar dragged what remained of herself at Alec and locked a hand around his ankle.

"I'll have you after all," she rasped, pulling herself along his leg with both hands like some nightmare lizard.

Alec saw his own death in her eyes. In his haste to aid Micum, he'd left the last two white arrows behind with his bow.

"*Aura Elustri!*" he panted, struggling to wrest his sword from the scabbard pinned beneath his leg. Before he could shift it, another blade flashed down, sending the dyrmagnos' head spinning into the surf.

Shaking off the clinging hands, Alec lurched to his feet and stared in disbelief as Beka Cavish hacked furiously at the flailing arms and trunk.

"Get away from it," he warned. "You can't kill it."

"What are you doing here?" she demanded, backing away from the twitching remains.

"No time for that. Where's Micum? Go see to him."

Beka found her father lying motionless where he'd fallen, eyes shut as he fought for breath. Sweat ran down his face in rivulets, carving trails in the black strip painted across his eyes.

"Father, it *is* you!" Beka exclaimed, kneeling to inspect the terrible wound in his leg. The dyrmagnos had torn away skin and muscle in her frenzy, and the raw flesh was already going dangerously dark.

"Beka?" he gasped, opening his eyes. "Scatter the parts, scatter—it won't die."

"Alec's doing that," she assured him. She pulled off her gloves to take his hand and saw for the first time the strange designs that had somehow appeared on her palms. Her father's hands bore the same device.

"First I find you here and now this," she said, bewildered. "What in Sakor's name is going on?"

Micum held his hand next to hers. "So you're a Vanguard, too. Things have come together in a strange way, Beka. You don't know the half of it." He closed his eyes and drew a wheezing breath.

She pulled open his tunic and laid an ear to his chest. His heart was pounding too hard and his skin was too cold. Looking around for help, she saw Alec and Rhylin hurrying toward her, supporting another man between them. This thin one with his matted black hair and young beard looked vaguely familiar. He'd been wounded, too; the side of his face was bloody and he had a sword cut across his ribs. Nonetheless, his pale green eyes were sharp and alert as he sank down beside Micum.

"Help him, Thero. There must be something you can do," Alec pleaded. "I've got to find Seregil! Has anyone seen him? Or Nysander?"

"I am here, dear boy," a hollow voice replied from the shadowed rocks above them.

Mardus crouched opposite Seregil in the uneven basin, the surge of the tide rushing around their ankles. They sloshed through icy water as they circled, vying for possession of the Helm that lay partially submerged between them, the newly awakened glow of the blue eye stones casting a pale phosphorescence up through the water. The blast that had formed it had deepened the shallow basin into a broad pit deeper in places than the height of the two men who fought there. Strewn with bodies, lit only by the dead glow of the eclipse that still stood overhead, it was like a place from a fever dream.

"I should have killed that whelp of yours when I had the chance," snarled Mardus.

"Yes, you should have," Seregil retorted through gritted teeth, sizing up his opponent. Mardus was not a brawny opponent, but he did have the protection of his cuirass. "You missed Nysander, too, you know. He's alive and the Four remains unbroken."

"Yet you failed all the same," Mardus gloated, pointing to the Helm with the dagger clutched in his left hand. "I am the *Vatharna*, the Chosen of Seriamaius. Do you think you can stand against me now?"

"I was chosen, too, you fatherless son of a

whore." Seregil tugged open the neck of his tunic with one hand to show him the reversed symbol pulsing there. "But it's my people at the Cockerel that I'll kill you for, and for what you did to Alec. For the runners and keeks you used and betrayed, the innocents who've died at your order. Hell, I'll kill you for the sheer fun of it. Come on, Lord Eater of Shit. Let's get this over with."

He lunged at Mardus and their swords locked in a resounding parry that sent a shock up both their arms. Seregil ducked Mardus' guard and tried for a stab below his cuirass. He missed his footing and the tip of his blade glanced off metal, but the point cut the man's left arm and fresh blood spotted the already stained waters of the pool; neither of the combatants had time to notice how the bleary light of the Helm brightened as it rolled in the wash of the tide.

Fighting for purchase on the broken stone underfoot, Seregil quickly realized that he was overmatched. On better ground his speed would have evened the odds, but trapped here in this watery pit he could only stand firm and fend off the taller man's bone-jarring swings. Mardus slapped his blade back and nicked Seregil's left shoulder. Seregil got his guard back up, made a lucky sidestep, and repaid him with a slash across the right forearm.

For the first time it occurred to Seregil that his role in the prophecy had been fulfilled, that he was expendable now. That he might lose.

Sensing his doubt, Mardus pressed the advantage and scored a shallow cut across Seregil's thigh. More blood spotted the water and the Helm, brighter now with this and every death that occurred in the fight that was still raging above them, shone more brightly still.

It was Mardus who finally noticed the light, understood its significance. Redoubling his attack, he beat Seregil back against the rocks. Pinned off balance in an indefensible position, Seregil decided to take a desperate chance. Springing past Mardus, he dove for the Helm. He hadn't gotten two steps when his foot lodged in a hidden crevice and he stumbled painfully.

Mardus struck at his back, slashing him across the ribs. Just as he drew back for the killing stab, however, a wave surged in over the shelf of rock, knocking them both off their feet with a blinding wall of spray that slammed them against the rocks.

• • •

Mardus was the first to recover when it subsided. Still gripping his sword, he looked around to find Seregil sprawled stunned and unarmed against the seaward rocks. Blood trickled down over one closed eye from a cut on his forehead.

A look of dark triumph spread across Mardus' face as he stalked toward him through the knee-deep water. Long experience had taught him where to strike to cripple and give a lingering death.

It was the glow of the Eyes that distracted him. As the foaming surge of waves cleared for an instant, Mardus found the Helm shining up through the water at his feet.

"It seems I'll have the pleasure of offering you to the Beautiful One after all," he gloated. "Wounded or not, you're still an admirable sacrifice."

Gripping the Helm by one of the twisted black horns, he raised it over his head. *"Adrat Vatharna, thromuth—"*

Seregil chose his moment. Opening his eyes, he reached underwater, yanked the poniard from his boot, and threw it.

Mardus froze, the Helm still poised over his head as he stared down in amazement at the knife buried between his ribs where the edge of the cuirass left his side exposed.

"You should've killed *me* when you had the chance," Seregil snarled, trailing blood as he waded unarmed toward his adversary. "You played a brilliant game until now, but you should always finish your enemy off before you reach for the spoils. Arrogance, my lord. It's a deadly vice. It makes you predictable."

Mardus' lips stretched in the parody of a smile. "Tricks. Always your tricks," he whispered. Clutching the Helm in one hand, his sword in the other, he turned woodenly and began to stumble toward the edge of the pool.

Seregil followed and blocked his way. Mardus was dying, but still he looked down at Seregil with searing disdain.

"The Eater of Death—" he began thickly, gouts of blood spilling down over his chin from his mouth.

"—will eat *your* heart today, not mine," Seregil finished, glaring up into his enemy's dark eyes.

He grasped the hilt of the poniard and twisted it, tearing

through muscle and sinew until the long blade lodged fast in bone. A hot, bright freshet of blood poured out over his clenched fist.

Mardus dropped the Helm and toppled backward into the water. A ribbon of red bubbles streamed up from his nose and mouth, then ceased. His eyes, already vague with death, mirrored tiny dual reflections of the sun's first, bright edge as it emerged from the moon's dominance.

Seregil spat into the water. A smaller wave surged over the edge of the pool, hiding Mardus for a moment beneath a rushing sheet of foam. When it cleared again, the long reflection of another man had interposed itself across the surface of the water in front of him. Seregil looked up to find Nysander standing above him at the edge of the pool, the sound of scattered fighting still audible from beyond.

"Well done," the wizard said gravely. "Now the Helm must be destroyed once and for all. Give it to me, then find your sword."

Reaching down, Seregil grasped the glowing Helm by two of its black horns, just as he had grasped the crystal points of the crown months before. And as before, invisible voices and insubstantial spirits coalesced around him as he touched it, trying to stay his hand.

The blue eye stones set in the band had taken on the appearance of flesh now and swiveled accusingly in their lidless sockets as he passed the Helm up to Nysander.

The wizard drew a fold of his cloak around the Helm, screening it from view. "Your sword," he said again, his voice gentle but firm. "I must have your help in this, Seregil. You are the only one who can aid me."

Seregil scarcely felt his wounds as he splashed back across the pool to find his weapon.

"Here it is," he called. "But what about—?"

The words died in his throat. With the foam of a fresh wave boiling in around his legs, he looked up at the tall figure from his nightmares towering over him. But this time he knew the face beneath the spiked brim of the misshapen Helm.

It was Nysander's.

The skeletal hands that formed the cheek guards clenched inward against Nysander's face, sinking their talons into his cheeks until the flesh dimpled. The unnatural blue eyes blazed, sending out rays of light. Nysander stood unmoved, waiting.

"Nysander, why?" Seregil rasped. The skin around the brand on his chest crawled and tingled, the sensation growing as it crept down his right arm. Sparks flickered over the quillons of his sword and along the shining blade.

But Seregil was aware of nothing except the sorrowful determination he read in Nysander's eyes.

Nysander—oldest friend, wisest teacher, second father.

Some sane part of Seregil's mind screamed for him to throw the sword away into the sea, but he couldn't move or look away.

"Nysander, I can't!" he pleaded, echoing the forgotten words of his dreams.

"You must." Nysander's voice was already thin and strained. "I have accepted this burden freely. 'First shall be the Guardian, a vessel of light in the darkness. Then the Shaft and the Vanguard, who shall fail and yet not fail if the Guide, the Unseen One, goes forth. And at the last shall be again the Guardian, whose portion is bitter, as bitter as gall.'

"You must strike now, dear boy. Too much blood has been spilled and I cannot hold back its power for long. If you fail, I shall become their *Vatharna*, the anathema of my life's work. Strike now, I beg you. There is no other way, and never has been."

Seregil's body felt weightless as he climbed up the broken rock, sword naked in his hand.

Lock away grief, a voice whispered deep in his heart. *Lock away horror and fear and outrage and pity—*

I understand. Oh, yes!

The Eyes of the Helm rolled to focus on him as he took his place in front of Nysander; this was a blow that could not be struck from behind. Hideous moans split the air around them, blending with the cries from mortal throats nearby as he raised his arm to strike. Some part of him recognized Alec's voice among the others but he did not turn.

Nysander staggered, sank to his knees, arms extended on either side. Orbs of light burned in the hollow of each palm, illuminating the symbols that still showed on his skin.

—to protect your soul—

The orbs flared and began to fade as the Helm blazed brighter. Even then Seregil might have hesitated if Nysander hadn't raised his head and looked up at him with eyes that glowed already with the same horrible light as the Helm. Something broke inside Seregil at the sight of those alien eyes staring up at him from that familiar, beloved face.

Raising his sword in both hands, he brought it down with all his strength.

The symbols Nysander had painted on the blade flashed out like lightning as it cleaved through iron, horn, and gold, shattering the great Helm of Seriamaius into a thousand ragged fragments that dissolved into shreds of shadow in the milky light of the returning sun.

A sudden wind filled with a thousand tortured voices roared down out of nowhere, smashing the waves against the rocks. Flinging the twisted, blackened sword away, Seregil fell to his knees and lifted Nysander's ruined head onto his lap, cradling the dead man in his arms. Another wave crashed in against the ledges, foaming around his knees, tugging at the dead man's legs.

You knew, Seregil thought as he gazed down into Nysander's face, plain and kind again in death.

You knew.

All along you knew.

youknewyouknewyouknewyouknew—

"You knew!" he screamed against the raging wind, blind to the friends gathered in horrified realization around him.

Bowed over Nysander's limp body, Seregil waited for the next wave to drag them both from the rocks and down into the trackless depths beyond.

51

Seregil watched the smoke from Nysander's pyre rise against the brilliant red and gold of the sunset and wondered why he couldn't weep.

Alec was crying softly beside him and Micum, too, as he lay supported by Beka, one broad hand over his eyes. Thero stood a little apart, tears streaming down his pale cheeks as the flames crackled up through the carefully stacked tinder and driftwood.

Seregil longed to join them. His grief was a dry, sharp-edged stone lodged in his chest; he could scarcely draw breath around it.

Rhal's sailors and Beka's soldiers stood in respectful silence on the opposite side of the pyre. Patrolling loyally off the coast, Rhal had seen the fire at the camp and taken it as a signal. Braving the crashing surf, he'd come ashore with twenty of his men in time to help Beka's raiders clear out the last of the Plenimarans. As word spread of Mardus' death, however, most of the remaining soldiers simply scattered into the hills to fend for themselves.

Afterwards, Beka and Rhal had marshaled their people together, clearing away the dead and all trace of the ceremony. When the site was cleansed, they stacked a funeral pyre on the ledges below the basin, then stood aside as

Seregil and Thero placed Nysander on the bed of oil-soaked kindling and sweet herbs.

Standing here now, watching unflinchingly as the flames blackened Nysander's skin and clothing, Seregil forced himself to recall the old wizard kneeling calmly among his paints and symbols, speaking words of encouragement.

But still the tears would not come.

Stars appeared overhead in the darkening sky and with them the comet, robbed now of its dread significance. The pyre began to settle in on itself and Nysander's corpse sank out of sight in a whirling cloud of sparks. Several of Rhal's men came forward and added more wood and oil, stoking the blaze until the heat of it pressed the onlookers back into the surrounding shadows.

With the solemnity of the funeral circle broken, people began to drift away. The fire would burn long into the night, reducing skin, bone, and wood alike to a fine ash for the tide and winds to scatter.

Turning, Seregil limped slowly up to the white stone and sat there waiting for some release.

None came; the emptiness he'd been plunged into from the moment he'd accepted Nysander's final charge still enveloped him, leaving him isolated, deadened inside. He could see Alec and the others gathered around Micum, a knot of shared comfort against the oncoming night.

He should be with them, he knew, but somehow he couldn't move. Sinking his head into his hands, he remained where he was, alone in the shadows where Nysander had stood awaiting his moment just hours before.

Some time later, he heard the sound of someone climbing up the rocks toward him. Looking up, he was surprised to see that it was Thero.

Worn and battered, dressed in borrowed clothes, he bore little resemblance to the prim young wizard Seregil had sparred with for so many years. Thero stared down at the pyre below for a moment before speaking.

"I wasted too many years being jealous of you," he said at last, still not looking at Seregil. "It hurt him, and I'd take it back if I could."

Seregil nodded slowly, sensing that there was more to be said between them but not knowing how to begin. Instead, he asked, "Will Micum be all right?"

"I think I've stopped most of the poison," Thero replied, sounding relieved to speak of practical things. "Still, even if he doesn't lose the leg, I doubt it will ever be much use to him."

"He's lucky to be alive at all. And the dyrmagnos?"

"She's finished. Alec saw to that."

"Good."

Another uncomfortable pause raveled out and Thero turned to leave.

"Thank you," Seregil managed, his voice thin and strained. "For helping Alec and all."

With a curt nod, Thero moved off through the shadows along the road.

Micum saw Thero leave.

"You go up to him," he croaked, looking up at Alec with fever-bright eyes.

"He's right," Beka said, raising a cup of drugged wine to her father's lips. "It's not proper, him being alone now."

"I know. I've been thinking that all afternoon," Alec whispered miserably. "But I don't know what to do for him, what to say. We all loved Nysander, but not like he did. And then he had to be the one to—"

Reaching out, Micum closed a hot, dry hand over Alec's. "His heart is broken, Alec. Follow your own."

Alec let out a heavy sigh and nodded. Climbing the rocks, he walked over to where Seregil still sat on the rock, face lost in shadow.

"It's turning cold. I thought you might need this," Alec said, taking off his cloak and draping it over his friend's shoulders. Seregil mumbled a thank you, but didn't move.

Feeling desperately awkward, Alec rested a hand on Seregil's shoulder, then slid an arm around him. He'd half expected Seregil to shrug it off, or finally weep, but not the black waves of emptiness he felt, leaning there beside him. Something intrinsic in Seregil had fled or died; it was like touching a statue, a scarecrow.

A fresh trickle of tears inched down Alec's cheeks, but he didn't move, just stayed there, hoping Seregil would draw some comfort from his nearness. His tongue felt like a dead thing in his mouth. Words were dead leaves lodged in his throat. What was there to say?

A breeze stirred, sighing through the forest at their backs, mingling its sound with the rhythmic surge of the waves. An owl sailed by close enough for Alec to hear its wings cutting the air. Its hooting call drifted back to them through the darkness.

They remained like this for some time before Seregil finally spoke, his voice barely audible.

"I'm sorry, Alec. Sorry for everything."

"Nobody blames you. You did what you had to, just like the rest of us."

Seregil's short, angry laugh was startling after such silence. "What choice did I have?"

They sailed the following morning, heading north along the coast. Still running with stolen canvas, the *Green Lady* again raced unchallenged through enemy waters, though she caused something of a stir at Nanta until Rhal showed his commissioning papers.

They lay in port for two days while Rhal refitted the sails and took on fresh stores. Beka found a drysian to tend Micum's wounds and Seregil's, then set about making her own preparations for departure. She and her riders were duty-bound to find their regiment. By the second day Braknil and Rhylin had rounded up sufficient horses and supplies, as well as word that their regiment was stationed a few days ride to the north.

Rhal had given over his cabin to the survivors of Nysander's Four and Micum lay on the narrow bunk, his leg swathed in linen bandages. Sitting down beside him, Beka pushed her long braid back over her shoulder.

"Word around the city is that the Plenimarans have been pushed behind their own borders for the moment," she told him. "We'll ride northeast until we find Skalan troops, then start asking directions from there."

Micum clasped her hand. "You take care of yourself, my girl. This war is far from over."

Beka nodded, her throat tight. "By the Flame, Father. I don't like to leave you, but I have to get back. I sent some of my people on ahead before we met up with you and I've got to see if they made it."

Micum waved aside her concern with a smile. "I've been talking with your Sergeant Braknil and some of the others. From what they say, you're a good officer and a brave fighter. I'm proud of you."

Beka hugged him tight, feeling the familiar roughness of her father's cheek against her own. "I had the best teachers, didn't I? I just wish—"

"What?"

Beka sat back and wiped a hand across her eyes. "I always thought, once I had some experience on my own, that maybe Nysander would, you know, find use for me the way he did with you and Seregil."

"Don't you worry about that. There'll always be enough trouble in the world to keep our kind busy. None of that dies with Nysander. I'll tell you, though, it's Seregil I'm worried about."

Beka nodded. "And Alec, too. You can see what it's doing to him, having Seregil so silent and sad. What's happened with them?"

Micum lay back against the bolsters with a sigh. "Poor Alec. He cares so much for Seregil he doesn't know what to do about it, and now this. And Seregil's hurting so deep I don't know if any of us can help him."

"Perhaps he has to help himself." Beka rose reluctantly. "You get Valerius to see to that leg when you get back. I still don't like the look of it. And take my love to Mother and the girls. Send word of my new brother when he's born."

"You keep yourself in one piece, you hear?"

Beka kissed him a last time, then hurried above. Seregil was standing alone by the rail.

As they clasped hands, he turned her palms up to look at the faded traces of the symbols there.

"You've got your father's heart as well as his hair," he said with a ghost of the old smile. "Trust either one of you to show up when you're least expected and most needed. Luck in the shadows, Beka Cavish, and in the light."

"Luck to you, too, Seregil, and the Maker's healing," Beka returned warmly, relieved to see even this small break in his sorrow. He'd scarcely spoken since they'd set sail. "Bring Father safe home again."

Alec was waiting for her by the longboat. Putting her arms around him, Beka squeezed him tight and felt the embrace returned.

"Take them to Watermead, both of them," she whispered against

his cheek. "Stay there as long as you need to. Poor Nysander, I can't
believe he'd ever have wanted things to turn out like this."

"Me neither," Alec said, still holding her by the arms as he
stepped back.

He looks so much older, Beka thought, seeing the depths of
sadness in his eyes.

When Nanta had slipped away to the horizon Alec went below.
Seregil was sitting on the end of Micum's bunk.

"I found something for you in Nanta before we sailed," Alec
said, handing Seregil a cloth-wrapped parcel. Inside was a small
harp, like the one he'd carried in Wolde.

"It's nowhere near as good as yours, I know," Alec went on
quickly as Seregil folded the wrappings back and touched the
strings. "But I thought it might— Well, Micum is still in pain and I
thought maybe if you played for him it might give him some ease."

A white lie, perhaps, but it did the trick. Micum gave Alec a
knowing wink as Seregil propped the instrument on his knee and
plucked out a few tentative notes.

"It's a fine instrument. Thank you," Seregil said, not looking
up. He plucked out a few searching chords, then swept the strings,
releasing a glissando of plaintive notes.

Thero came in to tend Micum's leg and stayed awhile to listen.
Seregil didn't sing, but plucked out tune after tune, the music
mournful and soothing.

Micum slipped into a peaceful doze and Alec sat quietly in the
corner, watching Seregil's face as he played on through the afternoon. His expression betrayed little. The mantle of silence
remained in place.

Seregil's spirits seemed to rally somewhat during the voyage
back to Rhíminee. He spoke more freely, though not of Nysander or
the Helm. Never of those. He walked the deck with Alec and Thero,
ate sparingly with neither relish nor complaint, and played the harp
by the hour, covering his own pain a little by easing Micum's.

Micum and Thero took heart at these small changes but Alec,
who shared a pallet with Seregil on the floor of Rhal's cabin, knew
how he trembled and groaned in his sleep each night. An intuition
uncomfortably like the one that had dragged him back to the

Cockerel that fateful night kept him by Seregil's side as much as possible. The man he'd known for so long was gone, leaving in his stead a quiet stranger with distance behind his eyes.

Alec sat alone with Micum the afternoon of their fifth day out from Nanta. Micum was dozing, his face pale and haggard against the bolsters. The harp lay at his feet where Seregil had left it after soothing him to sleep. Thero's continued ministrations had kept rot from setting into Micum's leg, but the little cabin was stifling with the flat, heavy odor of unhealthy flesh.

Moving quietly so as not to disturb Micum, Alec opened the cabin window and propped the door open with a pack. Just as he was about to steal out again, however, Micum opened his eyes.

"That's a long face you've got on," he rasped, motioning for Alec to sit by him. "Out with it. What's wrong?"

Alec shrugged unhappily. "It's Seregil. He's like a shadow. He doesn't talk, he doesn't smile. It's like he's not really here at all. I don't know what to do for him."

"I think you're doing right by just standing by him for now, just as you did when he ran afoul with that wooden coin. It made all the difference to him then. He's told me so himself."

"That was magic and he was fighting it, too. But killing Nysander—" Alec fiddled with the edge of the blanket, searching for words. "It's like he killed part of himself."

"He did. We have to give him time to sort out what's left."

"Maybe." But in his heart Alec feared that the longer they waited for Seregil to come around, the farther away he drifted.

Magyana was waiting for them on the quay the day they sailed into Rhíminee harbor. Alone and unattended, she wore a dark mourning veil over her silvery hair.

Seregil placed a little bundle containing Nysander's few belongings in her arms, his voice failing him when he tried to speak.

"I know, my dear," she murmured, embracing him. "Nysander and I said our farewells the day I sent him across to find you. He suspected that he would not return, and asked me to tell all of you not to grieve for him, but to forgive him if you can."

"Forgive him?" gasped Thero, standing rigidly beside Micum's litter. "What could there be to forgive?"

Magyana did not answer, but her gaze stole briefly back to Seregil, who'd turned away. Alec's eyes locked briefly with hers and in that instant the mutual understanding ran deep.

"It was also Nysander's wish, Thero, that you should complete your training with me," she continued.

The color fled from the young wizard's thin cheeks as he sank to his knees before her. "I can't go back to the Orëska, not after what happened that night. The attack, the Plenimarans getting in, it was my fault. If I hadn't told Ylinestra about Nysander's walks, his studies— Looking back now, I see what all her questions were leading to, but at the time—I just didn't know! But the Council would never allow me back."

Magyana laid a hand on his bowed head. "You forget that I, too, am a member of the High Council, as was Nysander. He spoke with them one last time before he left. There is no impediment to your return. His last words to me on the matter were that he hoped I would see to it that you completed what you have begun so well."

Cupping his chin, she gently raised his anguished face. "I would be honored if you would accept me as your teacher, Thero. In truth, it would be a great comfort to have you with me, and to see the education of my friend's last pupil completed. It would be the greatest honor to his memory."

Thero rose and bowed. "I'm yours to command."

Magyana smiled gently. "You will learn that, like Nysander, I seldom command anything. I hope the rest of you will accept my hospitality tonight?"

"I thank you, Magyana, but I don't think—" Seregil broke off, unable to meet her gaze.

"I understand." She touched his cheek. "Later then. Tell me where you plan to stay and I'll send word for Valerius to see Micum."

"Wheel Street tonight, then out to Watermead."

"I will see that he comes to you at once. *Aura Elustri málreis, Seregil talí.*"

Clasping hands with Alec, she bid him farewell, then bent over Micum. "Shall I send word to Kari?"

Micum took her hand with a meaningful look and said softly, "Maybe we'd better wait until Valerius has had a look at me, eh?"

Magyana pressed his hand. "Very well. May Dalna speed health to you, Micum, and peaceful hearts to you all." With Thero at her side, she walked away through the dockside throng to a waiting carriage.

"If you've no further need of the ship, the men are anxious to put out again," said Rhal, coming over to take his leave of them. "We've made two crossings with an empty hold and there are enemy ships to be plucked."

"The ship is yours to command, Captain," Seregil told him. "And the luck of Astellus go with you. I expect the *Green Lady* will be the scourge of both seas."

Moving Micum into a hired cart, Alec and Seregil set off for Wheel Street. The house was just as they'd left it. Evidently Mardus had been well apprised enough of their movements not to waste time on unnecessary destruction.

Old Runcer greeted them with his usual lack of surprise, as if they'd been gone for a day or two instead of months. Seregil's white hounds, Zir and Mârag, showed equal equanimity toward their master, padding softly on ahead as Seregil and Alec helped Micum up the stairs to Seregil's chamber.

Valerius arrived soon after, dour as ever, but subdued. His scowl deepened as he inspected Micum's wound.

"You're lucky to be here," he exclaimed, wrinkling his nose. "Who's been looking after you?"

"Thero, mostly," Alec told him. "He was there when the dyrmagnos attacked him, and he tended him all the way home."

"He may have saved your leg, Micum. He certainly saved your life. There's still a great deal of healing to be done, though." He turned to Seregil and Alec. "Runcer can help me. I suggest you both go out for a while."

"I'm not leaving," Seregil protested with a flash of his old fire.

"You heard him, Seregil. You'd just be in the way. Get out," Micum said from the bed, making a passable job of sounding cheerful. "Come see me in the morning."

"Come on," said Alec, taking him by the arm. "I could do with a walk after all that time at sea."

Valerius closed the door firmly behind them. Seregil glared at it for a moment, tight-lipped and grim, then followed Alec downstairs without another word.

Seregil hadn't worn a sword since the day of Nysander's death, but Alec hastily buckled on his own as they headed out into the cool spring evening. Lithion had passed into Nythin since he'd been gone and flowering trees scented the air.

They both still wore their rough traveling clothes and, with his sword swinging against his leg with no cloak to cover it, Alec worried fleetingly that the Watch might stop them to ask why two such ill-dressed strangers were hurrying through the streets of the Noble Quarter.

But Seregil soon took the lead, heading into poorer courtyards and alleyways. He was still limping slightly, but seemed not to feel it as he strode silently along. Along the way they passed Lazarda's Black Feather brothel. The door stood open and, glancing in, Alec saw that the carved ship on the mantelpiece was facing west, signaling that a message had been left there for the Rhíminee Cat. If Seregil saw this, he ignored it and they wandered on like ghosts through the familiar shadows of their city.

A slender moon stood high over the rooftops before Seregil finally broke his silence. Stopping suddenly in a weed-choked courtyard, he turned to Alec as if they were in mid conversation.

"He thinks he might die, you know?" he said, his face half-lost in shadow. The part Alec could see was a mask of misery.

"Micum? I don't think he will," Alec replied, adding without much conviction, "Valerius wouldn't have made us leave if he thought he would."

"I don't think I could stand to lose him, too," Seregil said, betraying more emotion than he'd shown in days. But before Alec could respond he was off again, heading west.

They'd gone several blocks in silence before Alec realized where it was that they'd been headed all along.

One scorched brass cockerel remained to guard the courtyard gate, its upraised claw empty. Beyond the low wall lay nothing but a gaping foundation hole choked with charred timbers. Everything had burned—the inn, the stables, the wooden gate of the back court. The stink of rain-soaked ashes hung rank on the air.

"O Illior!" Alec whispered in stunned dismay. "I knew it was gone, but still—"

Seregil looked equally bereft. "It was just starting to burn when I left. Cilla was only two years old when I bought it."

Alec shuddered, hating Vargûl Ashnazai all the more for giving him such memories of her and the others. "Do you think their ghosts are here?"

Seregil kicked at a bit of cracked stone. "If they did linger, you gave them peace the moment you strangled that bastard."

"What about Luthas?"

"I suppose the drysians at the temple will foster him out or make a priest of him—"

Seregil broke off as a small form bounded up out of the cellar hole with a loud, familiar trill. Purring frantically, Ruetha went back and forth between them, twining herself around their ankles and arching to have her ears scratched.

They stared down at the cat for a moment in mutual amazement, then Seregil scooped her up with shaking hands. She butted him under the chin with her head.

"By all the gods! Thryis used to complain about the way she'd disappear until I came back." Burying his fingers in the sooty fur of her ruff, he muttered huskily, "Well, old girl, you'd better come with us this time. We're not coming back."

"Not ever." Alec rested a hand on Seregil's shoulder as he reached to stroke Ruetha. "Not ever."

When they returned to Wheel Street a few hours later, Seregil and Alec found Valerius just finishing a hearty late supper in the dining room.

"Cheer up, you two. Micum will be fine," the drysian told them, brushing crumbs from his beard.

"What about his leg?" asked Seregil.

"Go see for yourself."

Elsbet was at her father's side, holding his hand as he slept. Weariness made her look older than her fifteen years; with her smooth dark hair bound back in a thick braid over the shoulder of her simple blue gown, she was the image of Kari as Seregil had first known her.

"He's going to be all right," she whispered.

The room smelled of healing herbs and fresh air. Bending over Micum, Seregil saw with relief the faint flush of healthy color that tinged the sleeping man's cheeks. Fresh blood had soaked through the lines wrapped around his thigh, but the leg was still intact.

"Valerius says he'll be able to ride again in time," she told them. "I've already arranged for a carriage to take him home tomorrow. Mother's been so worried!"

"We'll come out with you," Seregil replied, wondering what sort of reception he'd have from her mother.

52
LAST WORDS

"Mother, Mother! A carriage is coming, and riders," cried Illia from the front gate. "It must be Father coming home!"

Shading her eyes against the slanting afternoon sun, Kari joined her at the gate and watched the covered carriage make its way slowly up the hill toward them. She recognized the riders as Seregil and Alec. Micum wasn't with them.

She unconsciously pressed a hand across her belly as she set off down the road to meet them. Catching her mother's mood, Illia hurried solemnly along behind her.

Seregil cantered on ahead to meet her and Kari's sense of dread deepened as he came near. She had never seen him so pale and worn. There was something in his face, a shadow.

"Where's Father, Uncle Seregil?" demanded Illia.

"In the carriage," he told her, reining in beside them and dismounting. "He's wounded but he'll be fine. Elsbet's with him, too, and Alec."

"Thank the Maker!" Kari exclaimed, embracing him. "Oh, Seregil, I know about the Cockerel. I'm so sorry. Those poor good people."

He returned the embrace stiffly and she

stepped back to look into his face again. "What is it? There's something else, isn't there?"

"You've had no news, then?"

"Magyana sent word at dawn that you'd returned, that's all."

Seregil turned away, his face disturbingly expressionless as he looked out over the new green of the meadow. "Nysander's dead."

Kari raised a hand to her mouth, too stunned to speak.

"That nice old man who did magic tricks for me on Sakor's Day?" asked Illia. She danced around them impatiently, her face puckering to cry. "Why is he dead? Did a bad man kill him?"

Seregil swallowed hard, his face still grim. "He did something very brave. Very difficult and very brave. And he died."

The others drew up and Seregil straightened, his face betraying nothing but a strained composure.

Too composed, it seemed to Kari as she hurried to the carriage door. But then all her thoughts turned to Micum.

Haggard as he was, he greeted her with a rakish grin as she flew into his outstretched arms.

"I may be home for good this time, love," he said ruefully, patting his bandaged leg propped before him on the carriage seat.

"Make me no idle promises, you wandering scoundrel!" Kari gasped, wiping away tears of relief. "Where's Alec?"

She leaned out the window and took his hand as he sat his horse. "Are you well, love?"

"Me? Hardly a scratch," Alec assured her, though he looked as drawn and careworn as the others. Kari held his hand a moment longer, seeing what Beka had seen; he was no longer the boy he'd been when he first came to Watermead. Whatever had happened to him through these past weeks, it had stripped the innocence from him, and who knew what else besides?

The household hounds leapt around the carriage and horses as they entered the courtyard. A loud answering hiss issued from somewhere near Kari's feet. She looked down to find a pair of green eyes shining out at her from a crack in a wicker hamper.

"What in the world—?"

"Seregil's cat," Micum told her. "I bet there'll be some slashed snouts among the dogs before she's through. Poor creature, she's the last survivor of the inn."

Kari smiled to herself, but held her peace until Alec and Seregil had helped Micum into the main hall. When he was settled comfortably in front of the fire, she drew Elsbet aside, then whispered to Illia. The little girl disappeared into the kitchen, returning a moment later with a plump, curly-headed baby in her arms.

"Father, look what Valerius brought us. Isn't he pretty?"

Alec was the first to react. Jumping to his feet again, he lifted the child from Illia's uncertain grip and held him up, looking him over with a mix of wonder and joy.

"Cilla's baby?" Micum asked.

Kari took his hand. "Valerius brought him to me a few days after you left and asked if I'd foster the child. I knew Cilla would want him here, rather than raised by strangers who knew nothing of his people. I didn't think you'd mind."

"Of course not," replied Micum, watching in bemusement as Luthas tugged at Alec's hair, crowing with delighted recognition. "But with the new one coming, do you think you're up to it?"

"Up to raising the orphaned child of a friend? I should think so!" Kari scoffed. "With the older girls gone, I've got far too much time on my hands. And Illia adores him."

She looked up at Seregil, standing alone by the hearth. "When he's old enough, I'll tell him how you saved his life," she added.

"It might be better if he didn't know," Seregil replied, watching Alec and Illia fussing over the child.

"I'll leave it to you, then," Kari said, catching another glimpse of the desperate unhappiness she'd sensed in him on the road.

Lying close to Micum that night, she listened in silence as he slowly explained the manner of Nysander's sacrifice and death.

"No wonder Seregil's so lost," she whispered, stroking her husband's strong, freckled arm. "How could Nysander have demanded such a thing of him?"

"I don't completely understand it all myself," Micum admitted sadly. "But I do believe Nysander was right in thinking that no one but Seregil would have the heart to strike him down when the time came. I couldn't have done it, and I don't think Alec could have, either."

"We forget sometimes how cruel the gods can be!" Kari said bitterly. "To turn love to murder like that."

"You'd have to have been there," Micum said, staring up into the shadows cast by the fire on the hearth. "If you could have seen Nysander's face— It wasn't murder. It was an act of mercy, and love."

• • •

During the weeks that followed mixed reports came of the war; for the time being the Plenimaran army was held back in eastern Mycena, but their black ships ruled the seas, raiding the eastern coast of Skala as far north as Cirna, though they hadn't yet won control of the Canal.

Except for the absence of the young men who'd gone off to war, life at Watermead continued on largely unchanged. Gorathin followed Nythin, and then Shemin, bringing with it the lushness of high summer. Gentle morning rains nourished the fields and strong spring lambs and colts bounded after their dams in the meadows.

Kari flourished with the land and her great belly swayed proudly before her as she went briskly about her daily work and the welcome tasks of summer. But she continued to worry about Seregil, though the only outward sign of trouble was his unusual quietness. She knew Micum and Alec felt the same concern, yet none of them could see a way to help him.

He sought no solace from any of them, to be sure, but kept himself busy around the estate. Micum had made it clear that he and Alec were welcome to live at Watermead for as long as they wished, and Seregil seemed content to do so. From Alec, Kari learned that he'd sworn never to set foot in Rhíminee again.

If he'd been morose or self-pitying, she might have tried to cajole him out of it, but he wasn't. When asked, he would tell tales and play the harp. He worked with the horses, helped build a new stable, and spent his evenings devising clever devices to help Micum cope with his crippled leg, including a specially designed stirrup that let him ride again. Of late he'd even been able to bring himself to hold Luthas again, but left to himself he sank again into that inner stillness.

Alec, who'd endured the most abuse of any of them, was the quickest to recover. Farm labor agreed with him and he quickly grew brown and cheerful again. Kari saw him watching Seregil, however, trying to gauge the inner turmoil that underlay his friend's long silences and distant eyes.

At night they shared the bed in the guest chamber, but Kari could tell that no comfort was being found there either.

• • •

One morning in mid-Shemin Kari awoke just before dawn, too uncomfortable to sleep. No matter how she turned, her back ached. Not wanting to wake Micum, she threw a shawl on over her shift, checked Luthas, who lay asleep in the cradle by their bed, then went off to the kitchen to make tea. To her surprise, the kettle was on the hook over the fire already. A moment later Alec came in carrying a basket of pears from the tree in the backyard.

"You're up early," he said, offering her the fruit.

"It's this wretched child." She frowned comically, kneading her lower back. "He kicks his mother and puts his knees and elbows in all the wrong places. What woke you so early?"

"Seregil was tossing around in his sleep again. I thought maybe I'd go hunting."

"Sit with me a moment, won't you? It's so peaceful this time of the day." Kari sat on the hearth bench to warm her back while Alec made the tea. "Seregil isn't getting any better, is he?"

"You and Micum both see it, too, don't you?" he said wearily, pulling up a stool beside her. He held out one tanned, callused hand. "He hasn't once told me to wear gloves. He was always after me about it. Before."

He looked up at her and Kari saw the depth of unhappiness in his young face. "Now he goes out at night or sits up writing. He hardly sleeps at all."

"Writing what?"

Alec shrugged. "He won't talk about it. I even thought of stealing a look at his papers, but he's got them hidden somewhere. It's like he's fading inside, Kari, leaving us behind without going away. And I keep thinking about something he told me once, about when he was exiled from Aurënen."

He spoke of that to you? thought Kari. Even Micum knew almost nothing of that part of Seregil's life.

"Another boy was sent away with him then, but he threw himself off the ship and drowned," Alec went on. "Seregil says most Aurënfaie exiles end up suicides because sooner or later they fall into despair living among the Tírfaie. He said it hadn't happened to him. But the way things are now, I think maybe it has."

Kari watched his hands tighten around the mug he was holding. There was something else going on behind those blue eyes, something too painful to share. She reached to stroke his cheek.

"Then keep good watch over him, Alec. You two share the same blood. Perhaps in his sadness he's forgotten that."

Alec sighed heavily. "He's forgotten more than that. The day he found me again in Plenimar, something happened, but now he won't—"

Kari flinched suddenly as a sharp stab of pain lanced down one leg.

"What it is?" he asked, concerned.

Kari gasped through her teeth again, then grasped his arm to raise herself. "It's only the eight-month pains. A walk in the meadow will ease them and we can keep talking." The pain passed and she gave him a reassuring smile. "Don't look so worried. It's just the Maker's way of preparing me for the birth. You know, I've got a craving for some of that new cheese. Run and fetch us a bit from the dairy, would you?"

"Are you sure? I don't like to leave you."

"Maker's Mercy, Alec, I was bearing children before you were even thought of. Go on, now." Pressing her fists into the small of her back, she went outside by the kitchen door so as not to waken the servants still sleeping in the hall.

Alec was halfway to the dairy before he realized he'd forgotten to bring a dish for the fresh curds. By the time he found one, Kari was already out of sight around the corner of the house. Going around to the courtyard, however, he saw that the postern was still barred.

A deep groan came from behind him, and he turned to find Kari sagging against the stone watering trough near the stable. Her face was white, and the front of her shift was wet to the hem.

"Oh, Dalna!" he gasped, dropping the cheese as he hurried to her. "Is it the baby? Is it coming now?"

"Too early and too fast! I should have realized—" Kari grabbed his arm, digging her fingers painfully into his wrist as another spasm took her.

She was a tall woman and too heavy with child for him to carry. Getting an arm around her waist, he supported her as best he could to the front door. It was still barred and he kicked at it, shouting for help.

The door opened at last. Elsbet and several servants helped bring her inside.

Beyond them, Micum limped from his bedchamber. "What is

it?" he demanded anxiously, catching sight of Kari in the midst of the commotion.

"It's the baby," Alec told him.

"I'll go for a midwife!" Seregil offered, halfway to the door already.

"No time," Kari gasped. "My women can help me. We've delivered a whole house full of babies between us. Stay with Micum, you and Alec both. I want you with him! Elsbet, Illia, come to me!"

Arna and the other woman helped their mistress into her chamber and closed the door firmly, leaving the men stranded in the hall.

"She's not so young as she was," Micum said, lowering himself shakily down into a chair by the fire. Kari let out a cry of pain in the next room and he went pale.

"She'll be all right," Seregil told him, although he was looking a bit green himself. "And it's not so early for the child. She was due in the next few weeks anyway."

They sat exchanging uneasy glances as her cries echoed through the house. Servants drifted in and out, listening nervously. Even the hounds refused to be put out and lay whining at their feet. At last Seregil fetched his harp and played to soothe them all.

A final straining groan rang out just before noon, followed by a thin wail and exclamations of delight from the women. Micum pushed himself up as old Arna emerged beaming from the birthing room.

"Oh, Master Micum!" she cried, wiping her hands on a towel. "He's the sweetest little redheaded mite you ever saw. And strong, too, for an early babe. He's sucking already, nice as you please. It was Dalna's own mercy she brought him out early or she'd have had a worse time of it than she did, poor lamb. Give us a moment to clear up the bed and then come in, all of you. She wants you all!"

"A son!" shouted Micum, wrapping his arms around his friends' shoulders. "A son, by the Four!"

"He's all wrinkled up and red and covered in muck!" squealed Illia, bounding out to hug him. "And he has red hair like you and Beka. Come and see. Mother's so happy!"

Kari lay tucked up in the wide bed with a tiny bundle laid to her breast. To Alec, the least experienced in such matters, she looked dreadful, as if she'd been ill, but the serene smile she greeted him with belied it.

Micum kissed her, then took the child in his arms.

"He's as lovely and strong as all the others," he whispered huskily, gazing down into the wizened little face beneath the damp shock of coppery hair. "Come on, you two, and greet my son."

"I'm so glad you were there this morning, Alec." Kari reached for his hand and laughed. "You should have seen your face, though."

Seregil peered over Micum's shoulder for a better look at the child, and Alec saw a smile of genuine pleasure soften his friend's drawn features for the first time in months.

"What will you call him?" Seregil asked.

"We'd thought to call him Bornil, after my father," Kari replied, "but looking at him now, it doesn't seem to fit. What do you think, Micum?"

He laughed and shook his head. "I'm too fuddled to think."

Kari looked up at Seregil, who was still smiling down at the child. "Then perhaps you can help us again, as you did with Illia. As the oldest and dearest friend of this family, help us name our son."

Micum handed the baby to Seregil. Gazing at him thoughtfully, he said, "Gherin, I think, if you'd have another Aurënfaie name in the family."

"Gherin?" Kari tried the sound of it. "I like that. What does it mean?"

" 'Early blessing,' " Seregil replied quietly.

Thank the Maker, Alec thought gratefully, watching Seregil with the child. *That's the most peaceful I've seen him since we got back. Maybe his spirit is finally healing after all.*

A warm night breeze sighed in through the open window. The sound of it seemed to echo Seregil's inner loneliness.

It was ironic, really. The first time he and Alec had stayed in this room, Alec had kept stiffly to his side of the bed; these past weeks Seregil often woke to find him lying close beside him, as he was now. Alec had thrown one arm across Seregil's chest, his breath soft against his bare shoulder.

Why can't I feel anything?

Lying there in the moonlight, Seregil stroked Alec's fair hair and summoned the memory of the kiss they'd shared that day in Plenimar.

Even that had been sucked pale and flat. Since Nysander's death all his emotions seemed to have fled to a distance, felt dimly, as if through a pane of thick glass.

It was too late now, too late for anything. He was too empty. Covering Alec's hand with his own, he watched the stars wheel toward morning, thinking of Gherin.

His mind had ranged far these last weeks, turning round and round on itself as he struggled to reach some decision that would bring him peace. Looking down into the face of Micum's tiny new son today, he'd suddenly felt that the sign he'd been waiting for had been given at last. With this last thread of the past tied off, he could go.

An hour before dawn, he slipped out of bed and pulled on his clothes. Throwing his old pack over one shoulder, he took a small bundle from its hiding place behind the wardrobe, then closed the shutters to keep out the morning light. Alec mustn't waken until he was well away from here.

Moving with his natural silence past the sleeping servants in the hall, he went to Micum's chamber. A night lamp still burned there, and by its light he watched his old companion sleeping so peacefully in his wife's arms. Micum was home.

Seregil laid a rolled parchment at the foot of the bed, along with small packets of jewels for each of the children. On his way out, he paused beside Gherin's cradle.

The infant lay on his back, arms flung over his head. Seregil ran a fingertip lightly over one tiny fist, marveling at the fragility of the silken skin. Gherin stirred, sucking contentedly in his sleep.

In twenty years you'll be the young man your father was when I met him, Seregil told him silently, touching the infant's fuzzy red hair. *What would it be like to see you then?*

Seregil pushed the thought away and stole hurriedly away. He wouldn't be back, not in twenty years, not ever. He owed them all that much.

Leaving Alec was even harder than he'd feared. Against all better judgment, he went back to the open doorway of the room they'd shared so chastely, knowing full well that if Alec so much as opened an eye, he was lost.

Alec lay curled on his side now, blond hair tumbled over the pillow. A dull ache gripped Sergil's heart; all the nights he'd been lulled by that soft breathing, all the things that might have been, seemed to come together at once in a tight knot at the base of his throat.

If only Nysander hadn't—

Seregil placed a thick roll of parchments on the doorsill: the letter, too painful to be anything but brief; documents making Alec of Ivywell heir to all Lord Seregil's holdings in the city; the lists of names and secrets and money holders. It was all there, carefully set down. When Alec sorted them out he'd discover that even minus what Seregil had deeded to Micum and a few others, he would be one of the wealthiest young men in Skala.

Good-bye, talí.

The stars were dying as he led Cynril down the road below Watermead. When he judged he was far enough away to ride without waking the house, he swung up into the saddle and nudged the horse into a brisk trot. It was a little easier now, riding along at first light, the air already warm and redolent with the scent of the wild roses blooming in the meadow.

A flight of wild geese rose from the river. He could almost see Alec on the bank below, trying to coax Patch out of the stream with a scrap of leather. The boy had been all innocence and good intentions then; why had he worked so hard to sully that?

He rode up onto the bridge and reined Cynril to a halt. Mist was rising from the stream's surface, coiling up to turn gold with the first touch of dawn. It looked, Seregil thought, like some magical pathway leading up to unexplored realms. Pulling the poniard from his boot, he tested the well-honed edge, then looked up the shining stream again.

It was as good a direction as any.

Something brushed Alec's hand and he opened one eye, expecting to see Illia or one of the dogs.

Nysander was standing beside the bed.

"Go after him," Nysander whispered, his voice faint as if it came from a great distance.

Alec lurched up, his heart pounding. Nysander had disappeared, if he'd ever been there at all. Worse yet, Seregil was gone. Alec slid his hand over the sheets where Seregil had slept. They were cold.

Whether dream or vision, the urgency of Nysander's warning grew stronger by the second.

Just like that other night, riding back to the inn—

Scrambling out of bed, Alec hauled on breeches and a shirt and headed for the door. His bare foot struck something as he crossed the threshold. It was a thick roll of parchments bound with plain string. Untying it, he quickly scanned the familiar flowing script covering the first page.

"Alec tali, *Remember me kindly and try—"*

"Damn!" Pages scattered in all directions as Alec ran for the stables.

Too much to hope that Seregil had gone on foot; Cynril was missing from her stall. Mounted bareback on Patch, Alec searched for and quickly found Cynril's tracks, the distinctive print of the slightly splayed right hind hoof plain in the dust of the road outside the courtyard gate.

Kicking Patch into a gallop, he rode down the hill and across the bridge, reining in where the two roads met to see which way Seregil had gone.

But there was no sign of Cynril here. Cursing softly to himself, Alec dismounted for a closer search, then walked back onto the bridge and scanned the hillside, looking for telltale lines across the dewy meadow. Nothing there either, or on the hill trail. He was about to ride back for Micum when a patch of freshly turned gravel on the stream bank above the bridge caught his eye.

You went up the streambed, you sneaky bastard! Alec thought with grudging admiration. The bridge was too low to ride under and there were no other signs downstream. Upstream lay Beka's otter pond, and the ill-fated pass that Alec had crossed to Warnik's valley.

And beyond that, the whole damn world.

Mounting again, Alec rode up the trail. The streambed grew steeper and he soon found where Seregil had been forced to come up onto the trail. Judging by the tracks, he'd traveled quickly from here.

Heedless of the branches that whipped at his face and shoulders, Alec kicked Patch into a gallop again. When the clearing around the pond came into view ahead, he was both relieved and surprised to see Seregil there, sitting motionless in the saddle as if admiring the morning.

Alec's first reaction to Seregil's letter had been only the des-

perate desire to find him. He realized now that there had also been
a generous leaven of anger mixed in. When Seregil raised his head
now, looking back at him with an expression of startled wariness,
the anger took over. It was the look you'd give an enemy.

Or a stranger.

"Wait—!" Seregil called, but Alec ignored him. Digging his
heels into Patch's sides, he charged Seregil, bearing down on him
before he could turn his own horse out of the way. The animals
collided and Cynril reared, throwing Seregil off into the water.
Alec leapt down and waded in after him. Grabbing Seregil by
the front of his tunic, he hauled him to his knees and shook the
crumpled note in his face.

"What's *this* supposed to be?" he yelled. " 'All I have in Rhíminee is yours now'? What is this?"

Seregil struggled to his feet and pulled free, not meeting Alec's
eye. "After everything that's happened—" He paused, took a deep
breath. "After all that, I decided it would be better for everyone if I
just went away."

"You decided. *You* decided?" Furious, Alec grabbed Seregil
with both hands and shook him. The wrinkled parchment drifted
across the pool, hung a moment against a stone, and spun away
unnoticed down the stream. "*I* followed you over half the earth to
Rhíminee for no other reason than you asked me to! *I* saved your
damn life *twice* before we even got there and how many times
since? *I* stood with you against Mardus and all the rest. But now,
after moping around all summer, *you* decide you're better off
without me?"

Color flared in Seregil's gaunt face. "I never meant for you to
take it that way. Bilairy's Balls, Alec, you saw what happened at
the Cockerel. That was my fault. Mine! And it was only thanks to
Ashnazai's twisted vanity that you didn't end up dead with them.
Micum's crippled for life, in case you didn't notice, lucky to be
alive. Do you have any idea how many times I've almost gotten
him killed before? And Nysander—let's not forget what I did for
him!"

"Nysander *sent* me!"

Seregil went ashen. "What did you say?"

"Nysander sent me after you," Alec told him. "I don't know if
it was a dream or a ghost or what, but he woke me and told me to
go after you. Illior's Hands, Seregil, when are you going to forgive
yourself for just doing what he asked you to?" He paused as

another thought dawned on him. "When are you going to forgive Nysander?"

Seregil glared at him wordlessly, then pushed Alec's hands away. Sloshing up to the bank, he sank down on a log overlooking the pond. Alec followed, settling on a rock beside him.

Seregil hung his head and let out an unsteady breath. After a moment he said, "He knew. He should have told me."

"You would have tried to stop him."

"Damn right I would have!" Seregil flared, clenching his fists on his knees. Angry tears spilled down his cheeks, the first Alec had ever seen him shed.

"If you'd done that, we'd have failed," Alec said, moving to sit beside him on the log. "Everything Nysander worked for would've been lost. The Helm would have taken him over and he'd have ended up as their *Vatharna*." For an instant Alec thought he felt the wizard's touch against his hand again. "I think he must be grateful to you."

Seregil covered his face, giving way at last to silent sobs. Alec wrapped an arm around him, holding him tightly. "You were the only one who loved him enough not to hesitate when the time came. He knew that. In the end you saved him the only way you could. Why can't you let yourself see that?"

"All these weeks—" Seregil shrugged helplessly. "You're right, right about everything. But why can't I feel it? I can't feel *anything* anymore! I'm floundering around in a black fog. I look at the rest of you, see you healing, going on. I want to, but I can't!"

"Just like I couldn't make myself jump that time at Kassarie's keep?"

Seregil let out a small, choked laugh. "I guess so."

"So let me help you, the way you helped me then," Alec persisted.

Seregil wiped his nose on his sodden sleeve. "As I recall, I threw you off the roof into a gorge."

"Fine, if that's what it takes to show you that I'm not about to let you slink away like some old dog going off to die."

The guilty look that crossed his friend's face told Alec his worst fears had been correct. "I'm not letting you go," he said again, gripping Seregil's sleeve for emphasis.

Seregil shook his head miserably. "I can't stay here."

"All right, but you're not leaving me."

"I thought you'd be happy at Watermead."

"I love everyone there like my own family, but not—" Alec broke off, feeling his face go warm.

"But not what?" Seregil turned and brushed a clump of damp hair back from Alec's face, studying his expression.

Alec forced himself to meet Seregil's questioning gaze squarely. "Not as much as I love you."

Seregil looked at him for a moment, grey eyes still sad. "I love you, too. More than I've loved anyone for a long time. But you're so young and—" He spread his hands and sighed. "It just didn't seem right."

"I'm not *that* young," Alec countered wryly, thinking of all they'd been through together. "But I am half 'faie, so I've got a lot of years ahead of me. Besides, I've only just begun to understand Aurënfaie, I still don't know one style of snail fork from another, and I can't jigger a Triple Crow lock. Who else is going to teach me all that?"

Seregil looked out over the pond again. " 'Father, brother, friend, and lover.' "

"What?" A coldness passed over Alec's heart; Mardus had spoken almost those same words when asking about his relationship to Seregil.

"Something else the Oracle of Illior said that night I asked about you," Seregil answered, watching an otter slip into the water. "I kept thinking I had it all sorted out and settled, but I don't. I've been the first three to you and swore that was enough, but if you stay on with me—"

"I know."

Catching Seregil off guard, Alec leaned forward and pressed his lips to Seregil's with the same mix of awkwardness and determination he'd felt the first time. But when he felt Seregil's arms slip around him in a welcoming embrace, the confusion that had haunted him through the winter cleared like fog before a changing wind. *Take what the gods send,* Seregil had told him more than once.

He would, and thankfully.

Seregil drew back a little, and there was something like wonder in his grey eyes as he touched Alec's cheek. "Anything we do, *tali,* we do with honor. Before all else, I'm your friend and always will be, even if you take a hundred wives or lovers later on."

Alec started to protest but Seregil smiled and pressed a finger across his lips. "As long as I have a place in your heart, I'm satisfied."

"You always have to have the last word, don't you?" Alec growled, then kissed him again. The feel of Seregil's lean body pressing against his own suddenly felt as natural and easy as one stream flowing into another. His last remaining worry was that he had very little idea about how to proceed from here.

The sound of a horse coming up the trail at a gallop forestalled the issue for the moment.

"I can guess who that is," Seregil groaned, standing up.

Micum burst into the clearing. "So here you are!" he exclaimed, glowering down at Seregil. "By the Flame, the whole house is in an uproar because of you!"

He pulled a rolled letter from his coat and held it up angrily. "You gave us a scare with this, you idiot. I don't know whether to kiss you or kick your ass from here to Cirna!"

For the first time in months, Seregil summoned a cocky, crooked grin. "Don't strain your leg on my account. Alec's already done both."

Micum took a second look at the two of them and returned the grin knowingly. "Well, it's about time!"

Two days later Micum and his family gathered in the courtyard to wish Alec and Seregil a proper farewell.

"Will you be heading to Mycena from here?" asked Micum as they made a final check of their horses and gear. "I imagine the queen will have some use for a couple of trustworthy spies."

Seregil shrugged noncommittally. "Winter's not that far off. Idrilain is supposed to be somewhere above Keston now. There won't be much to do once the snow flies. Maybe in the spring."

Kari shifted Gherin in her arms and embraced him tightly, then Alec. Blinking back tears, she whispered, "Take care, both of you."

Micum rested a hand on Seregil's shoulder, looking at him as if he didn't expect to see him again. "By the Flame, it's hard not riding out with you. I wish you'd take my sword."

Seregil shook his head. "That blade belongs with you. I'll find another if I ever feel the need of one again. In the meantime, Alec'll keep an eye on me."

"You see that you do, Alec, or you'll answer to us," Micum

said with gruff affection, exchanging a quick look with Kari. They'd both noted the new light in Seregil's eyes whenever he looked at Alec, and how that same warmth was returned.

After all their farewells had been said, Seregil and Alec swung up on their Aurënfaie mounts and rode out the gate.

"What if the Queen doesn't want us for spies in the spring?" Alec asked as they cantered down toward the bridge.

Seregil shrugged again. "Well then, we're still some of the best damned thieves I know of. Never any shortage of work there."

Kicking their mounts into a gallop, they raced down the hill side by side, and swung north to the open road beyond.

About the Author

Lynn Flewelling grew up in Presque Isle, Maine. Since receiving a degree in English from the University of Maine in 1981, she has studied veterinary medicine at Oregon State, classical Greek at Georgetown University, and worked as a personnel generalist, landlord, teacher, necropsy technician, advertising copywriter, and freelance journalist, more or less in that order. She currently lives in western New York with her husband, two sons, and other assorted mammals.